D1585851

RUN FOR FREEDOM

KICK UP THE SECTARIAN DIRT

RUN FOR FREEDOM

KICK UP THE SECTARIAN DIRT

Kevin Muir

JANUS PUBLISHING COMPANY LTD
Cambridge, England

First published in Great Britain 2001
by Janus Publishing Company Limited
The Studio
High Green
Great Shelford
Cambridge CB22 5EG

www.januspublishing.co.uk

Re-printed: 2007

A CIP catalogue record for this book
is available from the British Library.

ISBN: 978-1-85756-464-8

Typeset in 10pt New Baskerville

Cover design Hamish Cooper

Printed and bound by PublishPoint at
KnowledgePoint Limited, Reading, UK

This book is dedicated to the people of Ireland, North and South, each and every one.

Contents

Prologue

1984 – The death toll: 36 civilians, 9 soldiers and 19 members of the Royal Ulster Constabulary and Ulster Defence Regiment.

Why?

1985 – The death toll: 25 civilians, 2 soldiers and 27 members of the RUC and UDR.

Why?

1986 – The death toll: 37 civilians, 4 soldiers and 20 members of the RUC and UDR.

Why?

1987 – The death toll: 66 civilians, 3 soldiers and 24 members of the RUC and UDR.

Why?

And all in God's country.

This is the statistical nightmare from which there may never be an awakening for the inhabitants of this magical, mystical and mythical isle, where only death brings lasting peace.

If God truly created this planet then an enchanting garden must have been his illusion and intention, but Ireland was to be no eugenic fairy-tale kingdom, instead a land engulfed in the tragedy of religious hatred and bigotry. Perhaps if he had known the mouldered harvest his seeds would reap, then maybe he would have scattered them far from this planet and today's generation would be living in the Utopia he had contemplated. But that was long ago.

Chapter 1

Subterranean Homesick Blues

It hadn't been much of a leaving party. Still, what had come up to Paul O'Donnell's expectations since his arrival six months earlier? Not a lot. Stirring from his slumber, he was met by an icy cold December morning descending from the placid twilight. Sitting up, he stared at the window pane with his sleepy blue eyes and he felt a deep nausea escalating from within. No, it wasn't the excessive amounts of sticky whisky he had consumed the night before, as he had led the chorus of the 'Irish Rover,' it was the apprehension of what lay before him, now that he had decided to call time on his exile.

Watching the sun come up for the last time for him in the British capital, he reminisced on his failed voyage of self-discovery. London hadn't fulfilled his aspirations, or was it just that he hadn't met the criteria? A bit of both, he'd conceded. His decision to return home hadn't been one he had taken lightly, unlike the spur of the moment determination in the spring, when he had given up his job, packed a few belongings and left his girlfriend behind in war-torn Belfast, convinced the neon metropolis would be his oyster as he set out to put his name in bright lights. Recruited by a West End hotel deep in the heart of theatreland, he had taken the first step on the ladder to success. However, after the novelty of an unexplored city and its sightseeing attractions had passed, his life had soon become a mundane treadmill of routine. Rise, eat two slices of toast, drink the foul coffee, work while your mind went to sleep, eat again, sleep again; sheer boredom, only his sedulous nature had postponed the inevitable.

1

The haunting words of his angry father echoed around his head, forcing him up from the cosy bed to clash with the frosty chill which had numbed his nose.

'You're a damn fool, jacking in a bloody good job. London's a shithole, full of arseholes, and all to be a ten-bob-an-hour porter, you need your head looking at and you needn't bother coming back here when it all goes to cock like I warned you.'

Paul screwed up his eyes, sighed and remembered his defence speech. 'Yeh, well maybe it is a lowly position, but I have to start somewhere. I'll make it to the top, just you wait and see.'

'Well, I'll not be holding my breath,' his father had caustically returned.

Paul had tried everything, but to no avail. On every occasion that a junior management position had arisen, he had always been overlooked. It seemed his biggest handicap in life was his broad Irish accent, closely followed by his Catholic upbringing. What had always surprised him was the amount of people who had inquired of his creed on discovery of his Belfast roots.

'Why?' he would always reply. He had quickly found that such an immense three-letter word could shatter any conversation. People couldn't cope with that response for they didn't understand the complications involved, and there were plenty. Paul looked on religion not only as a catalyst for war, but mainly as a pretext for anarchy. He'd watched how his friends, countrymen and, most saddening of all, his own brother Michael, had been sucked into the vacuum of hypocrisy fashioned by the propaganda demagogues, who preyed on the people with ancient history and failing economic statistics.

Belfast's main industry was two-sided terrorism and the end product was hatred, measured by the grief of the death toll in square inches of cemetery. Paul just wanted to live in peace and he was not in the minority, but you wouldn't dare publicise those beliefs, not for fear of ridicule, but for dread of a bloody good hiding, so you learnt to live with the status. Some who couldn't beat it joined it, others just headed for pastures new and more often than not found the grass was no greener.

Paul was no quitter, never had been, nor ever would be. Strangely enough, it was his love of Belfast that was magnetising him home. Even all the intricacies that laid the foundations on which the Northern Irish capital was built upon couldn't stop him loving the majestic city. Home is where the heart is, and his heart was most definitely there, especially since it was only two days to Christmas, the annual event where sentimentality unquestionably stirs the greatest upheaval among human life on the planet. The people he loved were there and he wanted to be with them and that even included his father, who had nothing but contempt to offer his second son, for reasons which had always been a mystery to Paul. It was an enigma he had given up trying to get to the bottom of a long time ago. Perhaps one day all would be revealed, until then he would just have to live with the situation and make the best of it.

As the watery winter sun climbed through the cloud-free, azure sky, Paul sat on the edge of the bed and watched the spray of dust particles which skipped and floated like butterflies and a vision of his stern father appeared with finger pointed. The silent words from the apparition pierced his skull, sending a violent shudder through his body, turning his stomach to jelly. 'Yer too bloody soft.'

A twinge shooting through his left ear reminded him of how his father had shown him affection. His mind was confused now as he glanced at the bus ticket perched on top of the wardrobe. Perhaps going home wasn't going to be any better than this hellhole he had built his hopes upon. No, he had to. Yes, his old man was probably right; he was too shy, weak, naïve and vulnerable, but he did know how to graft. Unfortunately, he now knew even that wasn't good enough. He'd watched in disbelief as the lazy work-dodgers, who were afraid of getting their hands dirty, had always got the breaks and how they'd command the utmost respect, only a centipede could count on its limbs the amount of times he had been privy to that. It was the mutual appreciation society and he was not a member of the clique.

Moving from the bed, he quickly dressed himself, covering the field of goose-pimples that had germinated on his muscled work-hardened body. He had a bus to catch and enough pride to swallow to feed an army. Glancing at his wristwatch, he read it was 6.13 a.m. just enough time for a hot drink before embarking on the fourteen-hour homeward journey. Washed and hair combed, he stood with a stained porcelain cup in hand and took one last look around the small square room which had been his castle for the last half year, with its one wardrobe, sink, bed and a wastepaper bin

Suddenly the sticky nights of late July seemed an eternity ago, time flies when you're having fun, and he hadn't been. As he sipped at the coffee, he smiled at the thought of his mother's kitchen in Ireland, where the aroma of coffee beans would centrally heat the house. That was the first thing he was looking forward to experiencing when he got home; a decent cup of caffeine made with sweet pure Irish water, not like the scummy, tasteless, been-through-seven-human-bodies, poor excuse for liquid he'd been made to suffer for the duration of his sentence. Ostracising the bitter liquid to the sink, he rinsed the cup and swilled the dark splashes from the basin. He picked up the holdall, which was no heavier now than it had been on the day he arrived, slung it over his shoulder and took his ticket of destiny. Taking one last look around, to make sure he hadn't forgotten anything that he would suddenly remember half way across the Irish Sea, he noticed the once white kettle, now jaded and out of steam like its owner. The contrivance had been the only thing he'd bought during his term of residence, not through luxury, but necessity. About turning, he left the room heading for his fate, leaving the electrical appliance behind for the next individual who was seeking fame and fortune, or a place to hide from whatever situation forced them into the exploitation of the London hotel business.

Paul had seen the hotel staff annexe for what it really was, a sanctuary of escapism. He'd worked with all sorts over the period, plenty of fellow Irish, fleeing from the fear of the troubles, a Scots girl from Dundee, whose father was sexually abusing her, a battered wife from Swansea, many who simply couldn't find employment in their home towns and cities, but mostly people who were running from families who no longer made them feel welcome and even some who had no traceable kin to speak of. Paul did have a family, and he hadn't absconded from the past. He wasn't part of this congregation of lost souls and he had to check out before he became entangled in the net of pity.

Heading to nearby Piccadilly Circus underground station, he glanced at the statue of Eros and thought of Bernadette - she was another problem he would have to tackle sooner or later. She was fiery tempered at the best of times, with a mean streak as long and curvaceous as the Nile. She had gone to the same school as Paul from day one, although the classes were never mixed. Having caught her eye in the playground one lunch time, she knew at eight years of age what she wanted and would never stop until she had succeeded, which had been two minutes after the school bell had tolled emancipation. Dragging him behind the bike sheds she'd marked her territory with a passionate kiss that had almost suffocated him off his feet.

All those years later, and their frangible relationship was hanging by a thread of sympathy on his part. He didn't love her, she'd never been able to put him off his food and his stomach never churned at the thought of her. Somehow, he'd managed to evade the noose of marriage for five cunning years, when throughout she had hinted, nagged, gnawed, clawed and even utilised the leap year of 1984 to propose. And, to make matters worse, his parents thought the sun shone from her arse. She'd been the only girlfriend he'd ever had and even though many opportunities for amour had arisen during his London stint, he'd declined the invitations. Thinking it best to leave without letting her know, he had gone in the knowledge that if he were to return one day then there would be hell to pay, and not just a verbal lambasting.

That day had now dawned. He remembered two previous incidents, when a girl had made a play for him in the last year of school and how the red-headed Bernie had defended her property, administering a barbarous attack leaving the pretty blonde with shredded hair, two black eyes and a broken jaw. Then there was the time when Paul himself had got into a fight and how she had come to his rescue, kicking his opponent full force in the face, knocking him unconscious.

At first he had written and phoned and she'd been wild, demanding to know his whereabouts so she could join him immediately.

'I'll send for you when I'm on my feet,' he'd promised.

Abruptly, after three months, their correspondence through wire and paper ceased completely, yet still he had remained faithful to the last, principally because no one had stolen his heart. He wasn't sure what the symptoms were, but was positive that he'd be the first to know when and if they came to call. Having assumed, or more so hoped, that she might have found someone else to fill his shoes, ironically it was he who dwelt on their presumed breakup, to such a magnitude that he was often tempted to demand a explanation for her silence, before his senses always talked through the situation with his bruised male ego.

She's probably playing games to entice me into an early return, he'd thought, knowing that she was scheming and devious. Former experiences had taught him he should put nothing past her. No doubt news of his yule-tide arrival would bring them on to a collision course and he was ready, he'd been through his speech a million times, so often he could even say it backwards when he was drunk.

'We're finished, I don't love you, it's as simple as that, go and find someone who does.'

5

He knew that short, sharp, concise sentence would pack more punch than a thousand fists; it would hurt her below the belt, but it had to be said. He was a man on a mission, if London hadn't turned out to be his prospective gold-mine, it had certainly made him wealthier, not in the four hundred pounds it had taken him twenty-six weeks to accrue, but in strength and purpose. The shy boy with the baby-face good looks and dimpled chin, who had sympathised with his country to world champion extremes, would do it no more.

Holding his breath through the pungent air of the underground concourse, he bought a one-way ticket to Victoria station. The sweet, sickly stench of sweat, urine, perfume and carbon residue from the train's braking system blended to stun his senses and turn his stomach to produce a squeamish effect, which this time was down to his alcoholic antics the night before. That seedy smell would always bring a vision of London to his mind were it ever to grace his nasal passages again. Swaying in the humidity of the platform, he waited patiently. A gust of warm air flickering through his golden fair hair, and the sight of the station vermin clambering across the oily tracks for tiny cracks of safety, denoted that the first leg of his transport was nearing fast. Alighting one stop later, he drifted along with the deluge of commuters, as all races, religions, diplomats and down and outs walked side by side in an ocean of unity. It was a unique scenario, one which he felt he could quite happily drown in. Changing from the Piccadilly to the Victoria line, he was one stage away from the point of no return.

Looking around as the train careered and snaked its way through the bowels of the Earth, he began to suffer the Subterranean Homesick Blues. Spotting a redhead with glossy painted fingernails and ruby-red lipstick, he pictured Bernie. Isn't it funny that when you begin to feel contempt towards an individual, as he did for her, that the slightest idiosyncrasies in their make up snowball into planetary issues. She had a litany of faults which he had grown to despise, like the way she teased her thumb around her mouth, pretending to chew her nails and the way she couldn't form a sentence without the inclusion of the word 'pacifically,' when she really meant 'specifically.' The list was long, and each and every one made him cringe just as much as the previous one. The screech of the brakes and the shunt of the carriage jolted him from his nit-picking. Checking his watch, he noted it was now 7 a.m. His bus was due in half an hour. Crossing the last two streets of London, he arrived at the bus station, carefully stepping over tourists and the exodus returning home for Christmas, he found his check-in booth. Joining the queue, he scanned around the pin-drop silent departure lounge, where the faces were longer than the wait. Misery bred a deafening silence when clock watching became a natural pastime.

Unbelievable, he thought, spotting a silhouette from the past. Was Victoria coach station the centre of the universe? For, on arrival, he'd met someone he hadn't seen for years, on this chancing the somebody was a nobody. It was the school idiot from five years ago and, to his incredulity, he was still dressed in exactly the same navy-blue coat, with matted fur growing around the hood, that he had been famed for wearing way back then. Like an Eskimo, he'd been frozen out from the playground social circle, the games and pranks, he was the Craic.

His name was Tommy, always the centre of attention, mocked, ridiculed, pushed, shoved and spat at every day of his sad school life. He was the kid whose bag of sweets couldn't even buy him friendship. Dyslexic and slow on the uptake, the cogs of his brain had seized up early in life, leaving him with a mental age of around twelve, but he meant no harm. The black-sheep of the Falls Road couldn't hurt a fly, yet he was the one that took the beatings and abuse, perhaps he frightened the children because he was so different. A child can be excused, society, however, cannot, and sadly it had followed the precedent in expelling him from the pack.

Throughout the pedantic dark days of erudition, Paul hadn't been one of his arm-long list of tormentors, he'd just watched from afar, knowing that one day Tommy would have the last laugh. Life brings pain to all in one form or another, especially in a city as hate-filled as Belfast. When all around were suffering, whether it be deprivation, divorce, destitution, death, dementia or demarcation, Tommy would take his plateau. Paul had dreamt on numerous occasions after that religious education class which foretold, 'the meek shall inherit the earth,' that the symbol in the blue parka would stand, alive, laughing wickedly and incessantly, as he looked over the carnage of dead in the burning aftermath of Ireland's final conflict.

As he did not relish the prospect of sharing his company on such a marathon fourteen-hour voyage, were it to be that the simpleton was heading homeward also, Paul focused his attentions on the

7

television screens relaying the departure information, in a bid to avoid recognition. He didn't know it, but, if nothing else, the ten years of taunting had indoctrinated Tommy to never look anyone in the eye; suffice to say his head was bowed to his superiors, trained to the ground as always.

Standing with his back to the wall and his right hand dug deep into his jean's pocket comforting his money, Paul spent the last ten minutes to boarding time observing the suspicious characters, who could pick your pockets or steal your bag while asking for directions. Then there was the nouveau trend of station thief, a real smart bastard if ever there was. Sharp suit, gold tie pin, Rolex timepiece and a crocodile skin briefcase, looking like an Eton scholar who had made it on to the back bench, that was him. He'd come and sit next to you, all airs and graces, give you some fodder about being on the opposition side and could he rely on your vote? Having gained your trust, he'd ask if you would mind his briefcase while he took a leak. In a flash he'd return to the scene of his crime and his gullible prey would ask if he'd reciprocate the favour. As soon as you'd unzipped your fly he'd be half way to Paddington or King's Cross, but what was really clever about this trickster's technique, was how he spotted the punters who were in need of relief – most certainly a specialist conman.

Eventually the clock ground its way around to boarding time. Ticket inspected and torn, Paul found a window seat over the front wheels of the bus and gazed out below at the oil stains which merged to form a slimy skin on the tarmac. Among the chewing gum and cigarette ends, he spied a white feather which had become fossilised in the slick; always a deep thinker, he looked upon it as a sign. Maybe an ornithologist would've seen it in a different light, Greenpeace in yet another, but for him it was divergent in its meaning, for just by sitting on the coach he was proving that he was no coward.

The shudder of the double seat told him he had company. Stealing a glance, it was the apparel he distinguished, blue parka with hood still drawn over the head concealing the thin ashen-grey features of Tommy's old face. It's gonna be one of those days, thought Paul. There were plenty of other free seats, yet it had to be Paul whom he'd chosen to sit beside.

Eventually, ten minutes late, the long haul to the Emerald Isle commenced. As the huge vehicle crawled its way north, Paul fixed his sights on the scenery, avoiding eye contact with the passenger from yesteryear, though his sixth sense sent a burning sensation through his neck telling him Tommy was also sightseeing. When Marble Arch was but a memory in his mind, the never-ending belt of English countryside combined with the relentless heating system, diluting the oxygen, began to hypnotise him to sleep. Giving himself a shake he checked the time. Although it had seemed like a lifetime since he had first sat down on the lumpy, hard upholstery, it was only 8.45 a.m. Only another five hours to Carlisle. The next forty-five minutes brought irritation, agitation and lethargy, as his blood began to rise, simmering in the cauldron of his head as the heat demanded an escape route from his aching body. The delayed hangover had arrived. All of a sudden, the tasteless, gritty coffee, which he had denied his kidneys the pleasure of, would have been nectar to his system were it now available. Dehydrating and head pounding as the blood vessels swelled and throbbed, he fidgeted in discomfort. Turning his head from the cold window which was inciting his migraine, he focused on the torn headrest in front and moved his right hand to massage the swollen glands in his throat, which the previous night's whisky had burned red raw. As he began to smack his lips to produce saliva to lubricate his scorched tonsils, the cry for help provoked the good Samaritan to break from his cloak of silence.

'Are you thirsty?' whispered Tommy timidly, refusing to turn his head.

'Aye, I sure am.'

'Are you gonna Belfast?' probed the shy young man, on hearing Paul's stiff Irish accent.

'Aye,' he replied, still stroking his throat.

'Well . . . do you mind if I sit here beside you? I've a drink here if you'd like some?' Tommy offered, unzipping his bag to reveal a litre of Irish whiskey and the exact same maroon school jersey from all those terms ago.

'I don't mind,' Paul replied, taking his offer of friendship and unscrewing the cap with stressed urgency.

Ducking to drink, so as not to be spotted by some old woman passenger, whose envy at not being able to drink from the bottle would no doubt prompt her into informing the driver, with the attitude 'if I can't drink, he can't drink,' Paul slugged at the 'hair of the dog' remedy then coughed as the ardent liquid anaestheilsed his throat; soon it would be his brain.

'So, have you been to England? My name's Gerry, though everybody calls me Tommy, it's 'cause of the soldiers, that's why I got my nickname, 'cause I'm not too bright. Are you bright? What's your name?' he rattled, firing a salvo of questions in the excitement of having someone who was talking to him as if he was a human being.

'I know,' Paul revealed lamely, taking another long swig from the bottle in the knowledge that he was going to need it to get through the next twelve hours.

'How do you know about me?' came the confused reply.

'I went to the same school as you.'

Stopping dead in his tracks, Tommy turned his head and stared at Paul. 'But I can't remember you.'

Even though his brain was stunted, his mind was etched with a gallery of every boy and girl who had victimised him, stills in his head that would never fade over the years. Yet this stranger's face had no place in his hall of infamy. Again, he searched the album without success. 'Why weren't you like the others?' he enquired, bemused.

'I don't know,' Paul replied, softly. 'But I know I was no better than the rest.'

'Why?'

'Because if I had been, I would have attempted to stop it, but I couldn't, I just turned a blind eye. Anyway, my name's Paul, here – have a slug.'

It was as if his speech of humanity had gone right through Tommy's head without touching the sides, as he swerved on to a backward tangent.

'Paul, that's a good name, I'm Gerry but you can call me Tommy, like a soldier taratatatatatat, I like soldiers.'

Although the wavelength of communication was unparalleled, the firewater helped bring the conversation into perspective and kill the time. At 1.50 p.m. the coach somnolently crept into Carlisle bus depot, where they had just over an hour to stretch their weary legs and recuperate before the next leg of their trek. More than merry, the boozing pals assisted one another down the aisle and off the cosy bus into the nippy air, which quickly brought them back to sobriety.

'I'm gonna get something to eat, are you coming?' said Paul, knowing that if he didn't see to his hunger soon, then the lining of his stomach would come looking for nourishment of its own accord.

Noticing his newly acquired friend had come to an abrupt standstill, he stopped and turned to face him. 'What's wrong?'

'I've no money. I spent the last of my money on a present for me mother,' he revealed, placing his hand into his coat pocket to produce a bar of chocolate that squelched like clay in his heavy hand.

Paul laughed at the sight before him while Tommy burst into tears.

'What the hell's up with you now?' Paul moaned, now wishing he had refused that seductive first mouthful of the evil spirit.

'It was a Christmas present for me mother,' sobbed Tommy.

'And you forgot to give it to her?'

'No,' he sniffed, rubbing his limp left wrist over his runny nose. 'I couldn't find her. I walked around all day and all night, but there are no housing estates in England. I looked in every window, but she wasn't there.'

Suddenly, Paul felt as if the roles were reversing and he was the fool as he searched through the bewilderment of the last statement. 'Didn't you have her address?'

'No,' he replied, wiping the salty tears which were freezing around the crusts on his spotty face.

'So, let me get this straight. You came all the way from Belfast to London without an address?'

'No!' snapped Tommy. 'England, I went to England. My mum left a long time ago, she said in a letter that she'd gone to England.'

Realising that Tommy thought England was a housing complex like the Falls estate, in which he had led such a sheltered life back home, Paul walked back towards him and put his arm around his shoulders to dispense some comfort. Against all the odds, the glue of male bonding had begun to coagulate.

'Come on, let's get some fish and chips and some more whisky, we can find your mother later.'

Bellies satisfied and stocked up with beer and spirits they reboarded their transport and resumed their libation. By the time they had boarded the ferry at Stranraer three hours later, Paul had learnt that Tommy's mother had left his father, who worked constant nightshifts at a fertiliser factory. Wading through the quagmire of Tommy's darting and sometimes confusing oration, Paul had interpreted that both his parents were alcoholics. Conceivably, their descendant had been so intoxicated in the womb that brain damage was the consequence, if this was indeed the case then Tommy was certainly living evidence. Whatever the cause, their son had certainly followed in their footsteps – he too loved a drink. Throughout the tempestuous channel crossing they sat at the bar, where they drank until they were thirsty again and Paul listened. Sometimes he thought about sharing his own plight, but he always refrained; after all, what gave him the right to shower his trivial problems on this son of God, whom the world had turned its back on. Storm beaten, the ship cruised up Belfast Lough towards its final port of call. Through blurred vision, Paul caught a glimpse of the winking lights in the distance guiding them home and a distinct intuition swept over him – a feeling that he had made a mistake in coming back.

'Paul.'

'What?' he moaned, swaying in time with the boat's curdling movements.

'You are my friend, really, aren't you?'

'Aye, course I am,' he slurred, screwing up his eyes, fighting against the moving kaleidoscope of the pattern in the carpet, which was swimming before him, mesmerising his brain cells into elevating acid from his stomach to his mouth and making sickness as proximate as the shores of Ireland. Holding his left hand over his mouth he raced on to the deck and returned the cod that he had earlier gorged to the sea. When he had vomited until he could no more, he looked through streaming eyes at the stars twinkling over the misnomer of Holywood on the horizon. He could see two giant yellow superstructures towering into the night sky; they were the cranes of the Harland and Wolf shipyard, affectionately known as 'Samson' and 'Goliath.' In a city steeped in religious history, it was biblical irony that the metal giants had been baptised so, for they helped in the fabricating of the most famous ship of them all, the Titanic. To the right he would have been able to see Napoleon's nose in the rockface of the Cavehill, were it not for the darkness which engulfed it. With a sarcastic laugh, Paul wondered whether this was to be his 'Waterloo.' Attempting to regain entry to the bar against the sobering cold wind which made his face tingle as if a thousand pins were enacting a voodoo ritual upon his fair skin, he found himself taking one step backward for every two forward. Eventually, with face as white as virgin snow, he slumped back on to the barstool just in time for docking.

'So will you always be my friend?' posed Tommy, whose handling of the alcohol was showing a reverse effect. Suddenly, under the influence, his sentences became clear and concise to Paul's ears, even eloquent and articulate, he was most certainly taking command of the situation.

'Yes,' panted Paul, hyperventilating in a desperate bid to bring himself around.

'Really? And you'll let me hang around with you and you won't treat me like the others?'

His words were exciting the nausea again as they bombarded his premier concentration, which was keeping the lining of his stomach where it belonged.

'Yes, yes, anything, just get me off this bloody ship, I need land.'

Rising to meet the challenge of his new-found camaraderie, Tommy helped Paul from the bar and down the labyrinth of metal rungs to the bus below deck. Safely onboard, Paul fell fast asleep on his saviour's shoulder. Half an hour later, and the long haul trip was all but over.

'Paul, Paul, come on – wake up, we're here.'

Neck brittle and stiff, he came to and checked his watch through oblique eyes. It was 9 p.m. Still feeling terrible, he inhaled deeply at the sweet Belfast night and smiled wryly. He was home, maybe the city was ploughed to hell, but his roots were firm. During the five-minute taxi ride from the Europa bus depot to the Falls Road, he looked out for the metropolis hidden behind the masquerade of Christmas decorations and lighting and the adrenaline and nerves gained momentum in his bloodstream, dampening the alcohol which had temporarily taken his fears away.

The brightly tattooed brickwork glaring awesome under the street lights up ahead brought the taxi to a halt outside the Royal Victoria Hospital on Grosvenor Road; it was the end of the road - the Falls Road. Only the black hackney cabs, owned and driven by Catholics, would dare enter this road and negotiate the estates of snipers, flying bottles and concrete slabs. They had been driven by a city taxi, most likely by a Protestant firm in a normal saloon car, therefore the driver had not taken the usual route to the Falls by way of Divis Street. Although the city cabs would enter during the daylight hours, things were tense, it had been a bad year for the communities. Ten weeks earlier the ugly atrocities of the Poppy Day Massacre at Enniskillen had stunned the Island, and only yesterday, the UDA's second in command had bit the bullet at the hands of the IRA. The threat of reprisal was very real, and the streets were no safe place, especially after dark.

Fare paid and driver tipped, they gingerly entered the estate, neither man uttering a word. They prudently walked around smashed glass and over strewn boulders quiet as mice with eyes peeled, as a hundred

Christmas trees watched them every step of the way. They stayed calm and composed, always aware that they were under constant surveillance from human owls lurking in the rooftops, until finally they came to Paul's house.

'Well here I am Tommy, I'll be seeing you around then.'

'Do ya promise?'

'Aye, no doubt down the job centre on Monday when she opens. Anyway, I'll be going, it's time to eat humble pie.'

'I've had apple pie and cherry pie, but never humble pie, what does that taste like?'

'It's just a saying. Listen I'll see you Monday, eh?'

Heading to the next street, Tommy muttered over and over, 'Job centre Monday, jog centre Monday, dob shenter Monday,' and then he was consumed by the night.

Paul snorted the needle sharp air through his nostrils, as he turned to face the battered green door, then marched up to the entrance and knocked on the bruised, warped wood. An era of seconds passed before his mother appeared. Although she was in the prime of her life, she appeared to have one foot in the grave. Her hair had turned platinum too soon and her eyes were dark, as was her life. In her bony, fragile, weathered hand she held a string of rosary beads; they were merely a substitute for Valium or gin. Confined to the annals of her kitchen, with the exception of her once-a-week shopping expedition, she was a prisoner of her marriage. In a union that had been dead for twenty-two years there could be no resurrection. She had sworn her vows of allegiance – she had made her bed and she would have to lie in it. Sinking in her wretched existence, it was only the love of her two boys that kept her afloat. She knew that one day they'd both fly the nest, but she never dwelt on that near certainty, besides, she'd had a good innings thus far in that respect. A quarter of a century later and they were still her babies.

'Paul, Paul, what a surprise, let me look at you,' she vociferated in her excitement.

Wrapping her arms around his limp body, she hugged him and the tears flowed down her face of a thousand anxieties.

'Come away in out of the cold and let's get a hot meal inside you.'

As she ushered him past the living room towards the kitchen, he sensed a figure which disrupted his progress towards the alluring pot of Irish stew simmering at the end of the aromatic rainbow. Breaking through the silence, he could hear the smacking of jaws torturing a piece of chewing gum. Oh Fuck, he thought - Bernadette.

Turning his head he saw the moist cherry lips and the rusty iron hair. It was time for his deliverance speech, but even after all the disciplined trial runs, he could not action it through his astonishment. Moving his eyes downward from her frightening stare, he caught sight of a sparkling chip glimmering from her left hand. He hadn't bought her it, and why would she be in his family home if she'd found new love? For a split second it made no sense. With the art of ready reckoning he smiled broadly as he raised his eyes to meet hers.

Michael, poor bastard, he thought. His elder brother was twenty-five years old, their relationship had been good. Being four years older than Paul, he had always looked out for him, though he had a malignant streak like his new fiancé, but what else did they have in common? Paul's prayers and problems had now been answered, yet it didn't stop him hurting internally. Betrayed by his own flesh and blood, would their relationship be able to stand this strain? They'd fallen out in the past, fought and argued, but this was oh so different, and it would test their nexus to the limit.

'Well, what did you expect me to do, running off like that? You didn't expect me to wait for ever, did you?' she detonated in defence.

'No, no you're right and I'm genuinely pleased for you and I wish the pair of you all the best,' he replied, before making his way to the kitchen where his mother awaited, her face displaying deep sadness for her long-lost son.

'Did you really mean that?'

'Aye I did, Mom. I wish them all the luck.'

Smiling at his forgiveness, she began to serve him a hot meal. 'You must be starving son. So tell me all about London and why didn't you phone and tell me you were coming home for Christmas?'

'I'm not home for Christmas, I'm home for good, me daddy was right. I held no aces, I was the joker in the pack. Where is he anyway?'

'He's down the pub with your brother. Michael's doing well, he's got a job now, you know, at the docks, he's only labouring but the money's good.'

Things have changed in my absence, he thought. Paul had always speculated that the chances of his brother working for a living and becoming a husband were as remote as an outbreak of peace in the Province. The only passion he had shown, when growing up, was for the

15

Cause. He'd messed around at school and any wisdom he'd acquired had been ascertained on the mean streets. However, he was no fool. He simply resented the presence of the British soldiers who supervised the civil feud. Having taken to the fight like a duck to water, he didn't care who knew it. His heart was a burning torch, fuelled by abhorrence for the Protestants, who in his eyes had settled like vermin on his sacred land. Adopting the role of a pest controller, he had been arrested more times than a blind man in a nudist colony and had been beaten in RUC custody more often than a stubborn egg. Despite this, they were to have no softening effect but the utmost opposite as they strengthened his hatred towards his Orange landlords.

'You haven't eaten your stew. Come on son, you're all skin and bone and so pale.'

'I'm not too hungry,' he replied, feeling the worse for the drink. 'I think I'll pop down the pub and announce my homecoming. I'd rather face the preacher in his chapel than bring the trouble home here.'

'Oh, be careful Paul, he's been out drinking all day. Come away, why don't you just go to your bed, we can confront him in the morning.'

'No, I need to do this. Is my lodgings still twenty pounds a week?'

His mother nodded. There was no way she wanted to take his money, but she knew she'd have to, his father would demand it. After counting out ten twenty pound notes he handed them to her.

'That'll give me a roof for ten weeks, I should've sorted myself out by then.'

With a long face she accepted the money as he headed for the pub. She didn't envy his task one iota for she knew he would be given no red-carpet welcome home, only a hostile reception and she knew why. She was the only one who possessed the truth, that is, with the exception of her husband Joe. It was a secret that she'd pledged never to tell her boys, for she knew that it would sever her already tattered family. Not even the priest at confession could know the painful truth, it was her crucifix and she would have to bear it.

The moon above shone wickedly, catching the film of frost which bit hard into the concrete pavement, mischievously they married, ready to break the limbs of anyone unfortunate enough to slip into their trap. Approaching Paddy's Bar, which was proudly flying the tricolour ensign, defiantly stating it was a last outpost in a Protestant-majority city, Paul's apprehensive heart began to race. Sensing that someone was trailing

16

in his shadow, he spun around to see that it was only an old page of newspaper chasing up the kerb in the freezing breeze. He followed the growing crescendo of music, laughter and wild banter welling from the inn of happiness and arrived at their source. Every drop of Dutch courage that he had pumped incessantly into his bloodstream throughout the long day had now vanished, leaving him high and dry, nervous and scared. Looking above the small chunky window panes he studied the sign. It should have read, Paddy's Bar, Publican - Patrick McCleary, but some genius of the English language had respectfully added their own tribute changing it to RePublican - Patrick McCleary, and it was no lie. He glanced across the road at the imposing Clonard monastery and sucked in the winter air to freeze his mind before bulldozing through the door past the two lookouts who constantly scanned the street for the RUC and army, who frequently encroached to exercise their mandatory jurisdiction to search the pub. He stopped in the centre of the heaving bar, the boisterous noise clashing against his head, numbing his ears momentarily as he lost his hearing. Eyes bulging from his head, he scanned around the bar for his relations. With all eyes transfixed on him, he had to make a composed move. Almost tripping head first over an old greyhound which had found its ideal retirement home, he found his way to the dark teak counter to be met by the rapturous guffaws of mockery which he had brought upon himself. And with his face burning fire-engine red, from a melding of the drunken heat generating within the establishment and his great embarrassment, he landed next to his father, who stood stony-faced watching his every movement through the mirror behind the row of optics.

'Can I get you a drink, Da?'

For a ten-second decade his father stared at him through the shiny glass in an if-looks-could-kill-you're-dead manner and then he spoke in a tone of hate and embrute: 'I won't take a drink from you.'

Humbled and belittled, as the barmaid was ready to take his order, Paul bit on his lip so hard that the blood squirted between the whites of his teeth.

'What can I get ye?' she enquired. 'I've not got all night.'

'I'll be havin' a pint o' Guinness and a whiskey chaser and wee one for me daddy there.'

'I said I didn't want your drink,' growled his father, refusing to turn and look at him.

17

'What's your problem, won't you even look me in the eye?' snapped Paul, sinking the amber liquid before thundering the glass onto the bar. Inside his belly the warmth of the shot had fired his anger. 'Come on then, give it to me, I'm waiting. Tell me how much of an eejit I am and how you warned me, come on, come on, come on.'

Like a stuck record, he roared over and over so loud that the lively congregation all stood silent. Even the jukebox, which had perpetually pumped out the Pet Shop Boys rendition of 'Always On My Mind', had other things on its mind as it stopped to allow him the centre stage.

Denying him the argument, his stubborn father took the verbal blows which sent the blood racing into his hand to produce a clenched fist. Delivering twenty-one years of pent-up anger, the rushing adrenaline clouded Paul's senses so that he could not hear the loud silence he'd created in the bar. It was at this point of lost control that he overstepped the mark with a stray verbal attack which landed way below the belt.

'You've always been a bastard to me.'

In a flash Paul's vision had been robbed, although his eyes were still wide open. The return of the jukebox blasting out 'The Fairytale of New York' and the raucous laughter had a smelling-salts effect on the recumbent young man's consciousness. Lights on again, he picked himself off the floor and teased his hand over his swollen jaw. He staggered to the opposite end of the bar and ordered another drink to ease the pain.

From the cellar door behind, a man in a faded denim jacket, matching jeans and heavy leather safety boots entered and made his way to join his father. The steel toe-caps protruding through the tufts of torn leather were daubed with dark crimson speckles. Although he had only recently acquired his first real position of employment, they had always been his workwear and his trusted allies. His shiny black hair which draped on to his spine was styled in a centre parting. He was wiry in build yet powerful and athletic and a terrifying prowess oozed from his person. This was aided by baleful dark eyes which always appeared to look half shut and his always raised, rigid upper lip. A vision of rancour that could strike fear into the heart of the devil himself, he was Michael, Paul's elder brother.

While all the action had taken place he had been passing on information to his Intelligence Officer in the pub's hidden vault, a dark room where secrecy was paramount and plotting was tantamount. Michael's revulsion for the Protestants was of such magnitude that he

18

was in the throes of joining the covert organisation of the IRA. But his hunger was not based on researching the history books, nor was it justified by personal tragedy; well, not much anyway. It was like it is for every baby born into the world of Belfast, it was learnt from the womb. It all boils down to what side of the fence the stork drops you off at. It is an inbred maternal instinct. No matter the species, a newborn ascertains the code of survival from its mother and it's no different in Belfast. By the time you learn how to walk, it's not so much look out for the traffic or don't accept lifts of strangers, it's don't go near the Catholics or vice versa, dependent on your parents' religion, that's how it's tutored and that's how you'll teach your own. It's sad but it's fact, it's a necessity if you are to inhabit this mean city.

Then it's off to school, where sectarianism is taught in the playground. A child's mind is easier to infiltrate. Remember after watching your first horror movie how you pulled the covers over your head to black out the dark, convinced the monsters would come and get you? Well, that's exactly the vision for the children of Belfast. They imagine the adversary as axe-wielding ogres, though at that tender age they haven't seen any. They're taken into the city centre shopping or for whatever reason, where they have no concept that the people they must beware of are walking all around them, but no one tells them in those early childhood years between five and eight that the enemy is just like you. No, they don't let them know that, do they?

As puberty arrives life becomes worse, you now realise the devil is human and the media stir it up, it's in the tabloids and on the television, everywhere you look it's in your face. Bombarded by 'tit for tat' killings on your own doorstep, you have to resent; why wouldn't you? 'An eye for an eye', isn't that what the Bible instructs? Humanity is lost, and like a threatened animal you stick to the safety of your pack. The graffiti of hatred etches into your mind, so that even when you close your eyes it can be seen as clear as day. Finally, and most hurtfully, you spot a member of the opposite sex who stops your heart as you melt, but they're not of your tribe so love cannot blossom; it's socially and morally incorrect. You're forced to look elsewhere, even love hurts in Northern Ireland.

The hard core are those who cannot merely despise from afar, they have to take the fight on to the streets. Some are incited by loss of near or distant relatives, many believe that the land and air are rightfully theirs, a few are simply fanatical extremists who thrive on anarchy. Lastly, there are those who exploit the scenario to provide an income and purpose to their sorry lives. Michael fell head first into the first three categories. His grandfather had been lost, not to a Protestant bullet but in the squalor and depravity of poor housing conditions, bronchial pneumonia was the prognosis, death the outcome.

At ten years of age, Michael took his first step on to the ranking ladder of the Irish Republican Army; for thirteen years he had taken his own beloved terrain in his hands and thrown it with verve and venom at the invaders from Britain who policed the streets in a bid to deter terrorism.

As the boy turned into a man, the bricks turned to glass and petrol bombs, now he wanted lead. Many of the young soldiers caught up in the hostilities were actually Catholic, some of these recruits even held the Cause in their hearts, but stringent discipline and a weekly wage was enough to instil Judas Escariot ethics. They should have learnt from America's ass kicking in Vietnam, yet although they changed their routes on a daily basis they were always sitting ducks. They didn't mind the constant verbal abuse or the dogs trained to attack their uniforms, they could even live with being spat at and dodging the fresh-filled shit nappies which were hurled from the high rise Divis Flats, which they nicknamed Zanussi City because of the occasional flying washing machine dropped on them from a great height. No, these were the minor hardships of the task at hand. It was the unsurpassable anxiety that comes when you can't see the enemy - living under a threat that a sniper could end your life at any given second or that you could walk nonchalantly into a booby trap and you'd never see your wife again and the children that you were here to feed. It was life on a knife edge, and yet they still came to prevent the unstoppable.

Fervent in his beliefs, Michael continued to charter progress towards his boyhood dreams of serving the IRA in an Active Service Unit, the killing machine, but before he could achieve his aim, trust beyond fanaticism had to be gained. At twenty-three years of age, the outstanding commitment he had shown during rioting was rewarded and promotion followed. He had become a reconnaissance man, termed by the British army as a 'dicker.' Reporting to his Intelligence Officer, his duties were to raise funds by the distribution of the Republican newspaper An Phoblacht, stir up the gangs of youths to wreak as much havoc as possible in order to divert the RUC and army away from the real targets, and, lastly, constant surveillance of the enemy. This was done mainly by hanging around the street corners, watching and listening.

20

His position even meant him temporarily burying the hatchet, as he'd offer cigarettes and talk about the weather to the soldiers in an attempt to gain their trust and lead them into a false sense of security, hoping for a scrap of classified information that might be crucial enough to catapult him up the ranks. Associating with the enemy was a policy he detested, but the job demanded it. Already he'd spent two long, hard years snatching at the threads of advancement and his patience was growing thinner by the day.

Resting his right boot on the dulled brass foot rail, he noticed that his father's face was ashen white with fury and his white-knuckled fist was shaking.

'Are you all right, Da? You look like you've just seen a ghost.'

'Worse than that, son, your brother's at the other end of the bar, like a bad penny he's come rolling back. You'll have to put him straight, he'll still be thinking that Bernadette's his property.'

Although the brothers were like chalk and cheese, with Paul gifted with all the attributes that his brother was not, like being a good scholar, feeling compassion towards his fellow man and finding employment, Michael had never before felt any resentment through envy for Paul, as he simply had no care to be blessed with any of those traits, but now that there was a woman involved, things would be different.

The seeds of doubt his father had just planted sprouted like weeds, spreading a penitent guilt through his conscience. For the first time that he could remember in his life, he felt frightened, threatened and vulnerable. Fundamentally, the thought of his own brother despising him was too hot to handle. Paranoid and cornered, he'd have to take the only route out he knew, by letting his fists do his bargaining. After ordering a pint of ice-cool Guinness, he headed for a showdown with his young brother at the end of the bar.

'Home for Christmas?' he enquired, gulping at acerbic black liquid in a vain effort to quell his temper, which was brewing out of shame.

'No, I'm home for good,' informed Paul.

'Well, things have changed since you ran away.'

'Aye, I heard.'

'And?' prodded Michael, starting to lose his brittle temper.

'And I think you make a fine couple and I wish you all the luck in the world,' congratulated Paul, swivelling around on the stool to look his brother in the eye.

21

'Don't patronise me you little bastard or I'll wipe that silly grin off yer face.'

Stunned by the reply, having never seen his brother behave like that towards him, Paul stuttered his offering. 'N-no Michael, I'm serious. I didn't come back for Bernadette. I just had to come home, me and her were history a long time before I went to London.'

'I don't believe you and I don't want you around here no more. You're the one that turned your back on your family and country, you're a coward. You're not my brother with yer fancy morals.'

Endeavouring to diffuse the amber situation, Paul placed his hand on his brother's shoulder to convince him of his words. 'What's happened to you, Michael?'

'Get yer fuckin' hand off me now,' he snapped, 'or I'll break it.'

Once again the volume in the pub died and all eyes focused on the impending entertainment.

'Christ, I'm your own brother and you treat me no better than you would a Protestant. I can't believe it.'

'Well, believe this.'

In a mad rush of blood to the brain, Michael released the anger of humiliation with a fierce right hook which sent Paul spiralling from his perch. Before he could pick himself up from the sticky floor, the tools of Michael's trade were raining down upon him as he put the boot in without remorse. Attempting to curl up into a human football to weather the storm, he felt the cold steel of the toe-caps crack against his head. On the verge of blackout, it was only the putrid cocktail of stale beer, whiskey and vomit which filled his snorting nostrils that sustained his consciousness throughout the frenzied onslaught. The sight of blood spraying on to the nicotine walls constituted the throwing in of the towel and resulted in a retreat.

At the other end of the bar, the man with the silver stubble masking the shoal of ruptured blood vessels which swam around his face like eels feeding off the alcohol, smiled with satisfaction. Turning to face the mirror, he rolled his tongue over his eye tooth as he waited on the victor's presence to share a celebration drink.

Nose bleeding heavily, mind stupefied and ribs aching, Paul required assistance to find his feet and it was at hand in the form of the two doorman he'd passed on the way in. Having failed to intervene during the entirety of the fracas, they were quick enough to expel the troublemaker now. Taking an arm each, they dragged his flaccid corpus through the pub, into the street and dropped his heavy bulk into the frosty gutter, they washed their hands of him.

'Don't come back here until you can handle yer drink,' shouted one of the men as he kicked Paul in the ribs for good measure before returning to the frivolity inside.

For five tediously prolonged minutes Paul lay in his own intoxication, his eyes rolling whilst the moon above watched over him and the spiteful elements tackled his sores, gnawing like scavengers on a defenceless carcass. Even the thick salty blood and saliva trickling from his mouth was congealing in the polar temperatures. He knew he needed to find some inner reserve of strength to find his feet or even crawl to the warmth of his home, before hypothermia consumed his crippled body. He pushed his blue hands onto the gritty roadside and with the might of strong will forced himself up onto his knees. Bringing his head, lethargically, to the level he saw another pair of boots standing before him ominously. Another beating and I'll surely die, he thought, as fear and panic surged through him, reducing him to a sobbing wreck.

'Paul, it's me, I'll help you home,' said the dark figure.

Putting Paul's arms around his shoulders, Tommy supported him home. At the front door and out of breath, he placed his only friend on the doorstep.

'You said you'd be my friend, did you really mean it?'

Coughing phlegm and blood to clear his throat, Paul replied, 'Who needs friends when you have family like mine?'

Hearing no reply, he raised his head to see his only ally had vanished into the night. He threw his head back onto the door in an effort to gain attention. When his mother opened the door his head fell on to the welcome mat which sarcastically read 'Home Sweet Home.'

'What in God's name has happened to you?' she shouted.

There was to be no reply, for his consciousness had drifted away into a sea of sleep.

Chapter 2

And This Is My Four-Leaf Clover

An intense altercation of heated words rising from below penetrated Paul's sleep. Lying lifeless on his back, the incidents of last night flashed through his mind to induce a shiver as he relived the steel toe-cap bludgeoning into his face. With his eyelids still closed, he wasn't sure if it had all been a dream, but he was soon about to find out. Attempting to open his eyes, he knew in an instant that it had been no alcohol-induced hallucination. His right eye opened while his left remained airtight shut. It was so bruised and puffed with internal bleeding, that it enveloped the bottom lid to rest on his cheekbone, welded there by the solid crusts of yellow puss which had been discharging throughout the night.

Through Cyclop's vision he saw a wooden crucifix nailed to the wall directly above him, but he wasn't ready to forgive his father and brother for the persecution they had shown him, for they had known what they had done. Licking his dry lips, he could taste the vile salty blood which had dried into the creases. Thirst raging, he turned in search of liquid. The furry water he'd encountered in London had taught him to, invariably, leave a can of juice by the side of the bed, particularly if he'd been on a drinking bout the night before. This Christmas Eve the only fresh orange to greet his eyes was the tangerine in the Irish Republican ensign draping the bedroom wall. And if he still held any lingering doubts about his whereabouts, the message emblazoned to the flag definitely quashed them. In bold black lettering it read:

We are the Cliftonville, the Pride of the North,
We hate Glentoran and Linfield of course,

24

We drink all the cider and sing till we're hoarse,
We are the Cliftonville boys.

Paul was home on the Falls estate all right, for nowhere else in the universe could he imagine reading the immortal words of the Cliftonville Football Club supporters' song. The only reason he knew the words off by heart was because he'd hoped, upon the off-chance, that it may have won him the jackpot in the London pub quizzes he enjoyed participating in. Like everything else in London, it hadn't happened for him.

As he coughed, sharp pains below announced the probability of broken ribs and it was only his father's argumentative tongue, directly underneath, which gave him all the strength he required to rise from the magnetic mattress. Luckily enough he was still dressed, albeit that his clothes were covered in the stains of combat, but they'd have to do for now. Mastering the aches, he hobbled stealthily downstairs, unheard by the warring factions in the living room. Nearing the door he caught sight of Michael and Bernadette sitting around the kitchen table laughing, unaware of his presence. Placing his hand on the doorknob he could hear his father's indignant voice:

'If he's no job he can damn well sling his hook, he's not living under my roof free gratis, I want him out.'

'He's paid me ten weeks' lodgings. In the name of God, Joe, it's Christmas, have you no heart?' vindicated his mother.

'Ten weeks and he's out and I mean it, no job – no reprieve. Why didn't he just stay in London? I'll tell you why, because he's as soft as shite.'

Having heard enough, Paul forced open the door and entered and, as if a gunshot had gone off in the wild-west saloon of the front room, the squabbling was arrested.

'How do you feel son?' inquired his mother, showing deep concern for his injuries. 'And, more to the point, who did that to you?'

'He fell over, can't handle his beer,' intervened his father.

'What really happened? I want to know.'

'He's right mom, I fell over.'

'Come on, I'll get you some breakfast and clean you up,' she sighed, realising she was wasting her breath in trying to unlock the conspiracy afoot.

Before turning to follow his mother he glanced at his father who blatantly looked away, denying him any eye contact. Arriving in the kitchen, he was met by the same reception as the joviality between the happy couple inverted to the serious talk of last-minute shopping.

'So, what are your plans for today Paul?' asked his mother, cracking an egg into the sizzling frying pan which spat at her in defiance of having to work on the eve of Christmas.

'I've a few odds and ends to get myself, but I'd like to force a bath first, if that's all right.'

'Of course it is, but I think you should pay the hospital a visit.'

'I'll see how I feel after a good soak,' he replied, making no promises he could not fulfil.

Throughout the silence of Paul's two egg sandwiches and mug of coffee, Michael watched Bernadette like a hawk for any gesticulations of undying love toward her ex-boyfriend. One of her main attributes had to be her spontaneous ability to interpret the eyes and minds of others and she could read her fiancé like a book. She'd have made a superb psychologist; as it was she had to make do with selling shoes. A pulled face from her now and again secured her lover's insecurities. She was undoubtedly a master in the art of pulling the wool over one's eyes.

Breakfast dispatched, Paul was chaperoned by his mother upstairs to the bathroom, where he retired for a well-earned dip to soothe away his aches and pains, while she headed for the resumption of the confrontation. Turning the taps on full to drown the argument, he then painfully began to undress himself. Forty minutes later he emerged from the cotton wool of the bath to discover that only half the pain had returned. When he had dressed himself in clean clothes from the wardrobe he'd sorely missed over the last six months, he crept downstairs and sneaked out into the open world so as not to disturb the perfervid discussion that persisted on his behalf.

Having perspired heavily in the tub, the bitter cold air made straight for his open pores, freeze drying the beads of sweat aggregating on his brow. For a few minutes he stood motionless. As if trying to find his bearings, he scanned up and down the street with its painted kerbstones and bright streamers cascading across the road suspended from the lampposts. These were no festive decorations, these were the all year-round constant reminder of the location, for they were the green, white and gold trimmings of the Republican colours, which the habitants of this community were willing to accept as their standard. Attached to the concrete necks of the street lighting were wooden adornments which contemptuously read IRA. Paul's evaluation, based on almost twenty-two years knowledge of this area, was that nothing had changed in his short absence. Many of the redbrick façades had their windows boarded up and there were no visual signs of home improvements to be seen. The artistic murals impressed upon the sides of every end house were the Irish equivalent of the Bayeux Tapestry and told it the way it was, frightening. The Falls was, as everyone who lived there tried to convince themselves, merely a stepping stone to a better life. Sadly, however, the reality was very different. For the majority, there was no way out, they'd been born into this ghetto and they'd die in it. Looking to the skies for some divine inspiration, he saw that they were grey and overcast as they always seemed to be around these parts. Even in the height of summer when the sky was blue and the sun shone brightly, it appeared to be cloudy overhead.

As he headed to the bus stop, Paul watched as an army of young children enacted a thematic doorstop battle between the Brits and IRA. Using sticks for guns and stones for grenades, yet only uniformed in short-sleeved T-shirts, their runny noses manifested that they were ill equipped to combat the winter chills. Nearing his goal, he had that nagging feeling that someone was dogging his movements, and turning impetuously his instincts were confirmed. It was Tommy, attired as ever.

'I've waited all morning for you to come out, I was worried about you after last night.'

'Was you now?' returned Paul.

'Why did that happen to you? Was it because you had been with me?'

'No, not at all, it was the inevitable,' he explained, keeping an eye out for his bus.

'I don't understand.'

'No, neither do I. Anyway, I've got to go into town to get a couple of presents, I'll be seeing you around.'

About turning, he walked the last few yards to the shelter, knowing that Tommy was in hot pursuit. Arriving at the stop he checked his watch, it was almost midday.

'Is it okay if I come with you? I haven't been into town since my mother left, she'd always take me to the town at Christmas time, I love Christmas don't you? Did you know that it's Jesus's birthday? God, he must be over a hundred now.'

Exhaling deeply, Paul swivelled to face him.

'Don't take offence, but I'd rather go on my own, I need some time alone to think.'

'You don't want to be my friend any more, do you?' Tommy returned dejectedly.

Once again the sympathy began to race through Paul's veins, heading for his brain as he realised the harm his words had inflicted.

'No, I do, aye by all means you can join me. Do you have bus fares?'

Judging by Tommy's thrilled response, it was as if he'd just been bequeathed a million pounds. 'Aye, I have. I don't get a Giro until next year, so I stole ten pounds from my dad's wallet. He's always drunk so he'll never miss it.'

'Aye, you're not as daft as you make out to be, are you?' congratulated Paul.

Again they shared a double seat. However, on this occasion the trip would only last fourteen minutes.

'So who are you buying presents for?' inquired Tommy, whose shyness had dissolved into effervescent chatter.

'Me mom, dad, brother and, I suppose, his fiancé,' he replied grudgingly, still bitter about the way she had dumped him.

'I miss my mom you know, she'd buy me presents because I know Santa Claus doesn't really exist. Well, I know he does for young children, but I'm too old now. He stopped coming to visit me when I was about ten, that's why my mom would buy me some gifts, but now she's gone it's just another day to me.'

Although Paul listened to every word of the unpretentious philosopher, his mind was far away, he did have his own problems after all. At last they entered the city centre, and with just a solitary stop to go, PTS reared its ugly head, Public Transport Syndrome, that is. As if by magic, Paul's clairvoyant mind conjured up an erection; that no matter how hard he tried to quell it, it simply wouldn't lie down. Approaching their get-off point, he glanced around the upper deck to see what had set off the rocket in his trousers, but there were no naked woman or high testosterone enhanced perfumes arousing his passions. What he did notice, though, was that a high percentage of the male contingent were in possession of newspapers, and now he knew why - it was a front, they were the 'stiffy' brigade. Sticking close behind Tommy to conceal his embarrassment, but not that close, he made it off the bus slightly flushed and instantaneously his hard-on was no more. He immediately

28

made for a street vendor and purchased a copy of The Belfast Telegraph for the return journey.

Surfing their way through the tidal wave of last-minute shoppers who had deluged the high-street shops, they were swept into a large department store. It was as if the world's end was nigh, as what seemed like the population of Red China panic-bargained against the clock, as like famished piranhas they feverishly stripped the shelves to the bone. The old age pensioners were the worst, showing no courtesy or remorse as they took your ground, barged into your side, prodded you in the back with their shopping baskets and stood on your feet. Then they'd have the audacity to glare at you awaiting an apology; it was hell on earth. These old farts had all day, everyday to organise their shopping expeditions, but no, scared that perhaps they might miss a discount, they came to wreak havoc and some of them just came to gloat on earlier purchases that may have gone up in price due to seasonal inflation. Standing motionless while the stampede ensued all around, an executive decision had to be made. A glance at the cash registers helped to make up Paul's mind. The queues were meandering throughout the entire length of the shop, those who thought they had a place in the line didn't, they were merely impeding the shoppers and displays. And those who thought they weren't waiting to be served were causing spurious rows. It was mass confusion and, to top it all, those who had solved the riddle were all paying with plastic. Life's always about finding out the hard way and gaining knowledge from your mistakes. Never ever take to the high streets on Christmas Eve was today's example.

Mission aborted, Paul led the way into the first pub that appeared for some stress relief. Entering The Crown, closely tailed by Tommy, he headed straight for the elixir of life. Successfully served, they took their glasses and without spilling a drop carved a passage through the madding crowd to find a secluded niche in the corner, where they could rethink their strategies.

'What about the shopping?' inquired Tommy, puzzled by the prompt retreat.

'Balls to the shopping, getting an umbrella up your arse isn't my idea of a fun day out.'

'So how are you gonna buy presents?'

'I'll just find an off-licence and get a bottle of whiskey each for the menfolk, they're bound to sell chocolates there as well, so problem solved. There again, if I give Bernie chocolates it'll probably be misconstrued, so three bottles of whiskey and one box of chocolates, why make life difficult? Besides, she can drink most blokes under the table.'

'Who can? Your mother,' quizzed Tommy, losing his way in the philosophy.

'No, Bernie, my ex-girlfriend.'

Staring in admiration as Paul lifted the glass to his lips, Tommy wished he could be like him.

'I think we'll have another, then find that off-licence.'

Taking the hint, Tommy headed for the next round while Paul decided to read the newspaper in his usual procedure. First, he found his horoscope to map out his day. Under Capricorn it stated that the unattached 'goat' might encounter romance at a public event or party. Bullshit, I like the way they always cover their arses with the inclusion of the word 'might', he thought. Still, reading his stars was the most religious activity in his life. Wrestling with the paper which had a mind of its own, he turned to the rear and looked through the sports columns and spotted the greyhound card for Dunmore.

If there were no other traces of Ireland to be found running through his veins, at least this was one. He loved dog racing. He realised just how much he had missed it, even forgotten it. Watching the elegant canines kicking up the sand in all weathers as they chased the elusive hare had been his favourite pastime, in fact, if truth be known, it had been his only hobby. He'd adored it so much that he had even taken a 'dregs of the world' job to be near it. At fourteen, he'd been a glass collector at the local track; it had had its perks though, free admittance to the stadium every night, not that he didn't know how to gain illegal entry through every hole in the circumference fence, hell no, he'd made at least four of them. Then there were the unfinished pints which he'd save from the sewer to pour down his sink. Thinking back, that exercise in 'waste not want not,' had been pretty unhygienic and stupid, then again AIDS hadn't been discovered yet and if it had, the northern hemisphere was ignorant to its birth. At sixteen promotion followed; moving up in the world he became a handler, parading the dogs before putting them into the starting traps. It was a dream job that turned out to be a nightmare for he was allergic to animal hair. Each night he'd return home sneezing and wheezing with his eyes streaming, but he would not be denied. Two years later he was forced to quit when his full-time position as a lathe operator demanded shift work and overtime. Becoming a legitimate punter, he'd rarely missed a meeting.

There had been good nights and bad nights, these were always gauged by how much money you had in your pocket at the end of the last race. He could clearly remember the evening he had barely enough collateral to attend, yet he'd backed seven out of eight winners, turning a mere two pounds in shrapnel into two hundred and forty pounds in crisp notes, and what a feeling when he'd walked into the front room that Saturday night and threw the bundle into the air, watching with pride as the currency had fallen like autumn leaves on to the carpet. He'd always given his mother a few pounds to treat herself and his brother, enough for a few pints, but his father's policy was never to accept a bribe.

Then there was the night when he'd put his money where his mouth was. So convinced that he had a sure thing, he'd invested a whole week's hard-earned wages on trap six in the last race, at meagre offerings of even money. Knocked over at the first bend, he'd discovered that the only certainty was that the bookies satchel was always loaded at the end of play and that the odds were stacked high in their favour.

After that heartbreaking incident he became as good a gambler as one could be, only staking what he could afford to lose; that way the enjoyment remained. There were stories of some owners who had taken out bank loans or put their mortgage repayments on their beloved animals, to find that thirty seconds of hope had netted a lifetime of debt. Some would release their frustrations by shooting the animals, while others simply unleashed them on to the streets, these placid creatures were never ready for society. The end result was nearly always death at the hands of a poor motorist, the fortunate ones would be caught and handed to the police, where they'd live on death row in squalor, ignorant of their impending fate, which was everlasting sleep through lethal injection. These were no fabled rumours, this is the sadistic truth. Is it any wonder that the noble greyhound evolved into the most timid canine on the earth? Who said it was a dog's life? And whoever coined the phrase 'a dog is a man's best friend' was obviously drunk at the time and spoke words of effluence not affluence.

Returning with the second course, Tommy sat in his depression as he watched Paul reading the tabloid. He couldn't read, for as hard as he tried throughout life it just hadn't happened for him. Petrified his friend would discover this and fragment their partnership, he sat speechless, tabling his excuses.

'Have you ever been dog racing?' inquired Paul, closing the paper.

31

'No, what's that?'

'It's when six dogs race each other around a track trying to catch a hare and you can put money on them,' he explained, attempting to keep it as simple as his friend.

'Won't it fall off when they run?' researched Tommy in all sobriety.

Almost choking on his pint, Paul burst into a fit of laughter before noting by the scowling expression written across Tommy's face that he had upset his drinking partner.

'Sorry,' he apologised, raising his hands into the air in surrender. 'Anyway, would you like to come with me tonight? I think you'd enjoy it.'

The hurt of being twitted soon vanished in the excitement of the offer. 'Aye, I can't wait, can we go now?'

'No, it doesn't start until 7.30 p.m. We'll finish this drink then I'll get my presents organised. If you come to my house at 6.30 tonight, we'll have a night to remember.'

Christmas Eve was always a good time to go dog racing as there were always a few runners who had been given outstanding chances to strike gold. It was as if the handicapper and bookmakers were saying 'thank you' to the patrons for their annual support. Unfortunately, it was a one off gesture and the only night of the year when they'd give an inch. So it was a case of be there or be square.

After departing the pub, they found a quiet off-licence where Paul purchased his festive offerings. Ten stops later and they were home.

'6.30 then, don't be late.'

'I won't,' Tommy assured, heading for the next street and home.

As Paul entered his house it was deadly silent. 'Mom, Mom, are you in?'

'Aye, I'm in here baking.'

Entering the kitchen he found her all alone, up to the elbows in flour, trying to rub her nose on her shoulder.

'Can I make you a coffee?' he offered.

'I'd love one son, but first, could you scratch my nose? I've a terrible itch.'

Baker's itch dealt with, she continued. 'So tell me, who did that to you last night and what did they say at the hospital?'

With back turned to her he spooned the granules into the mugs then forwarded his reply. 'I didn't go to the hospital. I feel all right now, besides, if my ribs are broken there's nothing they can do anyway.'

'That doesn't tell me who done it though.'

He'd never been able to tell a lie to his mother while looking her in the eye, for she knew him too well, so he remained with his back turned to her.

'I spilt someone's pint and they were none too happy.'

'And where were yer father and brother when this supposed event took place?'

'I think they must have been in the toilet. So tell me, where is everybody?' he inquired, quickly changing the subject.

She knew he was lying, but she decided to probe no further.

'Yer daddy's where he usually is and Michael and Bernadette are in the city shopping,' she revealed.

'She doesn't half spend a lotta time here, doesn't she.'

'Well, I would have thought so seeing as she's moved in here now.'

Turning to face her with steaming mugs in hand, it was if he'd been struck by lightning. 'Did I hear you right, she lives here?'

'Aye son, her mother passed away late October, so she had nowhere to stay.'

'Why didn't she go and live with one of her four sisters?'

'She said they wouldn't take her, no room or something along those lines.'

'Aye, well, you know why that is don't you? They were probably scared they'd come home and find her in bed with their husband.'

'Wash your mouth out, Paul. How dare you say that about your brother's intended wife.'

'I was being facetious,' he defended.

'Well, I don't think you're very funny at all,' she replied, shocked at his quip, for it wasn't what she'd come to expect from her youngest son.

'So, where's she sleeping?'

'Your father cleared all the junk out of the box room and she brought her own bed.'

Shaking his head and sighing out loud as he sat at the table, his mother couldn't help but notice that something was eating away at him.

'What's up son?' she asked, as she stopped kneading the pastry to give him her full attention, realising that he was the one who needed help.

'Well, under the past circumstances, it's not the most ideal of living arrangements, is it?'

'Don't worry, it won't be for ever, they're saving hard for a place of their own. They'll be moving out after the wedding in October. That's the anniversary of when they first started courting.'

33

'Well, that's convenient isn't it?' he snarled caustically, feeling the pain of the salt being rubbed into his wound.

'I thought you said you were happy for them. Do I detect a hint of jealousy?'

'Me, jealous? Never in a month of Sundays,' he lied.

Maybe he hadn't loved her, but after thirteen years of courtship he felt betrayed and what made it worse was that she could now flaunt it in his face anytime she wanted.

'Bernie's a good girl, she's turned your brother's life around, she's put him on the straight and narrow.'

Digesting her words he had to agree, but why the hell did it have to be her who had achieved the unthinkable. In time the hurt would fade and eventually disappear, he wasn't aware of that now, though he would be soon enough. Glancing at the clock above the cooker almost made her jump from her skin.

'For goodness sake, it's a quarter to four. Your father will be home for his supper in an hour, I'll have to get my skates on. Can you wash the dishes for me? You know what he's like if there's no food on the table.'

Answering in actions, he headed to the sink to save his mother's bacon, while she fell back onto the contingency plan of the slap-up meal.

'So, are you going to midnight mass tonight?' he inquired, beavering amongst the soapy water.

Preparing vegetables against the clock, she resumed the conversation. 'Well, after all the trouble with the drunks appearing last year, I had second thoughts initially, but Michael and Bernadette have agreed to accompany me. After all, Father O' Reilly will be uniting them in holy matrimony. Why don't you come too?'

'No, I'll give it a wide berth. I think it's for the best, don't you?' he abnegated.

'Not at all. If we're all going to live under the same roof, we can get the practice in at God's house.'

'Thanks, but I've got other plans for this evening.'

'Oh, and what might they be?' she angled.

'I'm going to Dunmore tonight with a friend. By the time I get home it'll be past midnight anyway.'

Stopping in her potato-peeling tracks she turned on him. 'Now you listen to me and listen good. I don't think you're in any position to be gambling, do you? You're gonna need all your money to see you through until you find a job.'

34

'But . . .'

'No, you listen, you've been back a mere five minutes, you've been in a fight and there hasn't been a moment when I've not been able to smell drink on your breath. What's happened to you? If you don't buck your ideas up fast you're gonna lose everything.'

'How can I lose what I haven't got? I'm so low I may as well have a good blow out, get rock bottom then the only way is up. It's something I've got to do,' he argued, methodically.

'Then why don't you talk to Father O'Reilly? He might be able to help you.'

'Oh, come on mother, for God's sake, how can I get help from a man who won't condemn the murders of Protestants.'

It was a verbal slap in the face which was to bring only one consequence, retaliation with the physical equivalent. 'Don't you ever, ever take the Lord's name in vain again in my presence, do you hear?' she stressed.

Nursing his ripe cheek, he headed for the door.

'Where are you going?' she called.

'Out.'

'What about your supper?'

'Put it in the dog.'

'You know we don't have a dog.'

'Then put it in Saint Bernadette.'

After slamming the door in temper he turned to view his brother and his fiancé walking hand in hand up the path towards him, giggling like schoolchildren who had just robbed an orchard.

'Not stopping for supper?' taunted Michael.

'No, I've lost my appetite,' he snapped.

'And why might that be wee brother?'

Pushing past them he gave his reason.

'Because you pair make me sick.'

Turning left into the street he knew he'd shown his hand now and, worse than that, he'd given Michael what he'd wanted, justification to continue the feud. Once again a religious dispute had led to a declaration of war. Storming towards the fuel depot of Paddy's Bar with his head held low, he cursed and muttered to himself as the indignation gained momentum inside him. Reaching the corner of the street he almost died of fright, when a voice from the left flank thundered down his one track mind: 'Where are you going, Paul?'

Turning to face the question he spied the enigmatic Tommy.

35

'For Christ's sake, have you been waiting on this corner all afternoon for me to make an appearance? Have you no fucking presents you could be wrapping like any normal fucker?'

Cowering like a scared animal and shaking like a leaf, Tommy stammered a reply: 'I . . I . . I thought you said we were going to the dog track?'

Still enraged, Paul continued with the scything offensive. 'Aye, well you thought wrong. I've enough problems of my own without breast-feeding you through life, now go on, piss off.'

Deeply hurt, more than he had ever been before in his marred life, Tommy slumped to the ground wounded by the remarks, while Paul restarted towards the pub, cussing as he went. The glimmer of hope and warmth at the end of the tunnel provided by Paul's humanity, which had burnt a deep affection into Tommy's dark life had now been extinguished, leaving only another scar to remind him of his purpose in this world, a human punchbag. For one day in his life he'd actually believed he could be normal. He'd feasted on the confidence of having companionship, convincing himself that one day soon everybody would treat him as a member of the community. At the end of the day they'd been right after all, he was a fool.

Marching onward to the watering hole, Paul lifted his head to observe four 'bricks' of gun-toting soldiers surrounding an RUC Hotspur vehicle approaching the pub from the opposite end of the street. It was a sight that brought him to an abrupt halt. It wasn't their awesome presence, for he had got used to that over the years. It was the khaki green uniforms holding the charcoal-black rifles which derailed his train of thought, as he flashed back to the bus ride home from England and how Tommy had spoken of the soldiers. Placing his fingertips on to his head, he began to massage his pulsing temples as he sucked in the frosty air through his teeth. What the hell's happening to me? he cogitated. In less than twenty-four hours, he'd changed. He'd experienced jealousy over something he didn't even want. He'd felt hatred towards his own flesh and blood and had now picked on a defenceless simpleton who could offer no argument.

It was so uncharacteristic that he knew he had to make amends, and fast. He raced back to the street corner.

'Tommy, it's me, I'm sorry.'

Sitting sobbing on the pavement with head buried into knees, Tommy could force no reply through the heartache.

'Look at me, Tommy – I'm genuinely sorry. We have more in common than I thought. You're not alone. I've problems too, perhaps we can help each other from now on, what do you say?'

Through the tears Tommy strained the words: 'Does that mean you still want to be my friend and I can come to the track with you?'

'Aye, dead on, now come on, look over there, the soldiers are patrolling the street.'

Assisting Tommy to his feet, he watched as the sixteen strong mini-battalion jockeyed down the street, continually pirouetting around each other in ever-decreasing circles, looking for snipers in a manoeuvre termed 'ballooning'.

'They must be clever, you know,' said Tommy.

'Why is that then?'

'Well, when I try to spin around like that I get dizzy and fall over,' he returned, before commencing to rotate on the spot.

'They can't be that clever,' stated Paul. 'Most of them end up as pound-an-hour security guards when they return home, not much of an incentive to enlist for your country, is it?'

Mulling over his words, Tommy could only submit one reply to vindicate his heroes.

'Well, I'd love to work for a pound an hour, but no one will give me a job.'

'Aye, well – I'm going to help you find a real job in the new year, but first I need something to eat before we go to the dogs, aren't you hungry?'

'Aye, how would you like to come to my house for supper?' offered Tommy, pointing down Odessa Street. 'It's only a few houses from here.'

'Won't your daddy mind?'

'No, he won't be in, the pubs aren't closed yet, are they?'

Having already instigated enough upset for one day, Paul reluctantly accepted the offer of hospitality. Unified again, they walked the short distance through the twilight to Tommy's home.

From the outside, it was no different to any other house in this scheme. The tiny plot of garden at the front was out of control, only the harsh winter stunted the vegetation's growth to keep the path clear and bring an air of respectability to the façade. Like so many others, one of the front window orifices was boarded over, no doubt a casualty of a stray stone missing the intended target of the security forces.

37

Insurance policies ran at extortionately high premiums around the Falls and not many people could afford one, they had better things to spend their money on - the main vice being alcohol to ease their depressions, albeit that it was only an interim escape from the tragedies at hand. Another reason why nobody worried too much about house contents insurance was that crime was at an all time low. This had a dual explanation, firstly no one had anything worth stealing, so why bother, but the biggest deterrent in this enclave was the fear of getting caught in the act.

Not for the dread of being sent to prison, no, the law around here was the IRA inquisition. Anyone who dared to screw society without their consent would have to answer to them. Their punishments were brutal, not like spending a few months in the Butlins of the Crumlin Road jail. Their code of sentence ranged from a mere thrashing or having concrete slabs smashed on to your limbs for trivial offences, to getting a bullet through your kneecap or elbow for middle-of-the-road iniquities. If you really pissed them off then it was death by the odd bullet or a hundred. Bearing those preventatives in mind, sales of burglar alarms were less than thriving in this community.

Reaching under the sodden ton weight of bristly doormat, Tommy produced his means of entry. If the external aspects of his home had been par for the course, the internal decor was definitely not. The shell was dark and it was as cold inside as it was outside. The coarse smell of stale dampness hung in the air, stripping the moist wallpaper which draped on to the wooden staircase. Looking up the stairs, Paul noticed sprouts of wool growing around the raised carpet tacks, which was the only evidence to support a theory that a carpet may have once graced the warped steps. As Tommy led him to the kitchen, he glanced above to see that the once white ceiling was losing its fight against leukaemia, as the dark stains of mold were now in ascendancy. Entering the kitchen, his jaw sagged at the sight which lay before his eyes, for on the table stood the biggest slab of Danish Blue he had ever seen. Closer inspection revealed that it was, in actual fact, a decomposed loaf of bread.

God, there's enough penicillin there to start a pharmacy, thought Paul. And enough to cure every sufferer of venereal disease in the entire world. Scanning around the pigsty surroundings his stomach began to turn in the squalor. The sink was overflowing with every single utensil in the house and the jaws of the pedal-bin were no longer visible, as a mountain of chip papers formed an albatross's nest in the corner. Everywhere he looked, he could envisage germs breeding, while under his feet he could feel a stir-fry swimming on the greasy tiled floor. Wading through the refuse, Tommy opened a cupboard door which revealed two tins of soup and a packet of cereal. A twitching motion on the floor brought a state of apoplexy over Paul as his eyes dilated at the sight, for there in the middle of the room, unmoved by the human presence, was the biggest rat he'd ever seen, happily munching on a cornflake.

'It'll have to be soup.'

Hearing no reply, Tommy turned to face him. 'Paul, it'll have to be soup.'

'I'm not hungry,' Paul replied.

His appetite had deserted him and it had no intention of returning while he was in this propagation colony for vermin and germ warfare.

'But you said you were starving a minute ago.'

'I was, but I'm not now,' replied Paul, as he continued to keep his eye on the rodent, worried it might decide to run up his trouser leg.

'Oh please, I'm really good at cooking,' Tommy begged.

Taking the diplomatic exit, Paul agreed. Reaching into the sink, Tommy produced a pan which was encrusted with what looked like mushy peas, there again no, it was more fungus.

'Stop,' shouted Paul. 'I'm not eating until those dishes are clean, I think we need to talk. This place is a bloody disgrace.'

'It wasn't before me mom left,' interrupted Tommy.

'Doesn't your father eat in here?'

'No, he eats from the chip shop, he says it's my responsibility to clean the house.'

'Well, what do you think your mother would say if she walked back to this. We will have soup, but we'll have it in a civilised manner. If you want to be treated as a human being you're gonna have to start behaving and living like one, do you understand?'

Looking around the carnage, Tommy nodded in agreement. Together they performed mass genocide on the bacteria, washing and scrubbing until the kitchen was fit for a king. Eight bin bags later, and they were finished. At opposite ends of the table they devoured a tin of mushroom soup each, yet every time Paul felt a tiny piece of fungi enter his mouth he cringed at the thought of how the kitchen had once been.

'So where's the rest of the food hid?' inquired the guest.

'That's all there is, unless there's any in the fridge.'

'Haven't you been shopping this week?'

'Aye, me da gives me twenty pounds a week, but I only buy a tenner's worth of soup and cereal and I spend the rest on sweets.'

Opening the refrigerator Paul discovered a bottle of milk that had turned to butter and a solitary egg.

'Okay, we're going shopping the day after Boxing Day and you're gonna start eating properly before it's too late. Do you have a pen and paper?'

When Tommy left the room in search of his request, Paul realised that perhaps his predicament was paltry after all. Returning with pen and paper, Tommy also brought a picture frame which he handed over for Paul's perusal.

'That's me mom,' he revealed with pride. 'She was like you, she looked after me. I miss her.'

'She's very pretty,' acknowledged Paul. 'Now come on, help me make this shopping list up. We'll devise a weekly menu first, that'll make it easier to make our list. So what do you fancy to eat on Monday, then?'

'Soup.'

'Followed by what?'

'Just soup. I like soup. Me mom said if I ate it, it'd put hairs on my chest.'

Paul checked his watch in the knowledge that this exercise in home economics was going to take an era, and discovered it was 6.55 p.m.

'Shit,' he exclaimed, 'we're gonna miss the first race, come on – if we're quick there's a bus at seven o'clock.'

Racing from the house, they spotted the headlights of a single-decker at the junction. Sprinting as if their very existence depended on it, they forged towards the winning post of the bus shelter, fuelled by the hope that someone was already waiting to sanction the transport to stop. Again, Paul felt the sharp pains tear across his sides from yesterday's arguments, but still he maintained the gallop, refusing to succumb to the agony. For once their luck was in. The bus pulled in and enough people fumbled with their fares, giving them the precious seconds required to reach the doors.

The bumpy twenty-minute ride to Dunmore Greyhound Stadium on the outskirts of Belfast served as a recuperation period, enabling them to catch their breaths and wallow in the exuberance of their achievement. Joining the circle of latecomers making for the turnstiles, Paul suddenly pulled Tommy away to the right.

'Where are we going?' Tommy inquired.

'We're using another means of entry,' revealed Paul.

'What do you mean?'

'Well, let's just say, we're not paying in.'

'Won't they put us in prison if they catch us?' panicked Tommy.

'No, don't be daft, they'll just throw us out if we're caught then we'd have to pay in. Come on.'

Creeping through the darkness, following the loud barks coming from the kennels, they arrived at a six-foot brick wall with a six-foot corrugated iron fence mounted on top of it.

'Listen,' whispered Paul. 'I need you to be as quiet as a mouse. Just do as I do, and when we get in, walk casually. If we're approached by a security guard and he asks to see our programmes, we'll explain we've been to see our dog and our girlfriends have them, got it?'

'But we don't have girlfriends.'

'Aye, I know, it's hypothetical. The guard wouldn't know that, would he? Just forget it, I'll do the talking if we're caught.'

After scaling the wall successfully, Paul stood on his tiptoes and scanned over the metal partition for any signs of enemy activity, but there was none.

'Okay, quick, let's get over, the coast is clear.'

Placing his hands on to the sharp sheeting to haul himself over inspired an articulation. 'Bastard.'

'What's wrong?' whispered Tommy, who was climbing the wall below.

'The sneaky fuckers have coated the fence in black tar or something.'

Having cleared the impediment, he jumped down on to the embankment and took cover behind a large poplar to await his partner in crime.

'Come on, what's keeping you?' Paul growled.

Tommy's heart was pumping with the trepidation of getting caught as he hesitated on the wall, yet he knew this was a big test if their alliance was to hold firm. Confronting his worst fears, he hauled himself over and fell on to the grass verge beside Paul.

'Okay, stand up and act normal,' instructed Paul.

Chatting about the state of the River Lagan they walked collectedly down the path and into the terracing of the track.

'Well played, Tom, you are now a qualified member of the most elite organisation in Ireland known as the DSS.'

'Really, what's that?'

41

'Dog Stadium Skivers,' grinned Paul.

'So what does that mean?'

'Well in financial terms, it means your first bet's on the house.'

Tommy wasn't exactly sure what Paul meant, but he laughed along anyway.

'So, what happens now?'

'Well, if you look over there, you can see the dogs are going into the traps for the first race. We'll watch that, it'll give us a good indication to whether the track is suiting the inside or the wide runners. After that, we'll go to the toilets and see if we can remove this shit off our hands, then we'll have a pint and study the form. Oh, by the way, keep your eyes peeled to the ground for a race card, we'll need one of those. Someone always drops one,' explained Paul.

Greyhounds all boxed and lights dimmed, the loud ringing of a bell combined with a public announcement that 'the hare was on the move' signalled mass panic amongst the punters. Fiercely, the terrace emptied, as everyone converged along the barrier, jostling for the best vantage point to view the action. Through Tommy's eyes and ears it was just a high-pitched mishmash of blur. When the thirty seconds of thrills and spills had elapsed, some of the faces were grinning from ear to ear while others were long and dejected. Dispersing to the warmth of the bar the debate would begin, when the 'ifs and buts' of the race would be analysed in depth by the patrons from both sides of the religious fence. Dunmore Stadium was perhaps the only retreat in Belfast where Catholics and Protestants could socialise under the same roof. Maybe the politicians should have built a dog track on every street corner.

Finding the Gents toilets, they scrubbed and scrubbed at the oily black tar to no avail, as it smeared, repelling the water. Reverting to paper towels they did their best, but still the traces of bitumen tarried to remind them of their skulduggery. As they headed to the bar, Tommy spotted a stray race card cowering at the bottom of the wooden steps of the terracing, picked it up and handed it to the expert.

'Well done, that deserves a pint,' congratulated Paul.

After ordering two pints of beer, he attempted to explain the interpretation of the programme to his friend, which was no mean feat. Eventually Tommy decided the easiest way to pick winners was by name or number and Paul wasn't willing to dispute that, seeing that the night was running away from him fast. During their third pint, race six had come around and still they hadn't had a gamble. Paul fancied the chances of the trap one runner. She was a bitch in form who had won last time out from a middle slot and, in addition to being faster away than traps two and three, she had three lengths on the clock over the remainder of the field. Having missed two winners already, he wasn't going to miss this one.

'Look after the drinks, I'm going to have a bet in this race.'

'Will you put a bet on for me too?' inquired Tommy.

'Aye, but you'll have to hurry, what do you fancy?'

'I can't make my mind up between traps five and six.'

'Okay, give me a pound and I'll do you a reverse forecast.'

Taking the money, he kept to his word and placed Tommy's bet, although being the authority, he didn't give his selections much hope of making the frame. Scouring the bookmaker's plinths for the best price on his fancy, he spotted a lone book that was offering odds of 9/4 instead of the general 2/1 about his choice. He placed his twenty pound wager at odds of 9/4 before the accountant was engulfed and scrubbed his price to 7/4 in the mêlée. Returning to Tommy in the bar, they had a grandstand view to watch the events unfold. As the lids sprung open, trap one had missed the kick, whilst on the wide outside the striped jacket of trap six had gone two lengths clear as the bend approached. With trap one failing to gain its anticipated flyer, all the inside runners collided at the first turn allowing trap six to poach a five length lead. Looking further afield, Paul saw that trap five had ridden the pileup best and was hot in pursuit, going clear of the 'also rans.' Ubelievable, thought Paul, as the dogs crossed the winning line in Tommy's favour. Perhaps it was a numbers game after all.

'Well done,' he conceded, patting Tommy on the back.

'Have I won?'

'You sure have.'

'How much?'

He glanced at the electronic totalisator board, and relayed the information.

'You've won half of £48.12, so I guess it's your round.'

While Tommy headed to refill the glasses, Paul had one last look at the card and decided to put all his eggs in one basket with the red jacket in the last race. Returning with the refreshments, Tommy was shaking with the excitement.

'So what now?'

43

'How do you fancy going outside for a while? It's a bit too hot and smoky for me in here, how about some fresh air?'

'Aye, I'm sweating buckets too,' agreed Tommy.

Walking into the cold evening, Paul smiled, as the smell of hot Bovril and newspaper print amalgamated into that greyhound racing aroma he'd grown to love. He sat on the haemorrhoid-inducing steps, looked across at the tractor smoothing the sand of the running surface and brooded over yesteryear, when he hadn't a care in the world.

'I'm glad you brought me here,' said Tommy. 'I really like this place, I feel so safe and no one has stared at me all night. I've even been confident enough to go to the bar on my own, thanks.'

'That's okay,' replied Paul.

'Will you really get me a job?'

'I'll try. Listen, Tommy, if you want people to start to take you serious your gonna have to take a bath and change your clothes. You've got to disassociate yourself with your past and strive for the future. Your appearance is your stigma.'

'But I don't have any other clothes.'

'I have some old ones. I'll give you them tomorrow. If you come to the back door at 4 p.m. I'll have them ready and I'll have some Christmas dinner waiting. I'd ask my mam if you could come for your dinner, but in light of today's events, it's best if I don't.'

'Paul?'

'What?'

'You've had a girlfriend, haven't you?'

'Yes, why?'

'So what's it like then?'

'Well, you can't live with them and you can't live without them, I think that best sums it up.'

'Do you think I'll ever get a girlfriend?'

'Aye, if you clean yourself up and change those clothes, why not?'

'Really?'

'Yes, really,' stressed Paul, tiring of the conversation.

'What, like her over there?'

Turning to look over his left shoulder Paul saw a vision of beauty if ever there was. Slim with long dark hair, she was drop-dead gorgeous and suddenly he now knew what that elusive feeling felt like as he melted at the sight of her.

44

'Well, Paul, like her?'

'Similar, Tom, similar, she's mine though,' he returned slowly.

'So, what you gonna do?'

'I'm thinking. I need to talk to her. Did you notice if she was with anyone?'

'No, she's been on her own all night. I've been watching her for the last fifteen minutes. So are you gonna talk to her?'

'Aye, I'll give it a go.'

Twisting his neck to owl extremes, he stared as she moved gracefully down the stairs to the barrier to watch the dogs parading for the penultimate race. He'd never had to chat up a girl before, so he didn't really know what the procedure involved. Were it not for her stunning visage, he would probably never have mustered up the courage to approach her.

'I thought you were gonna talk to her?' prodded Tommy.

'Oh, be patient will you, in me own in time.'

Deciding it was now or never he stood up and made his move.

'So, do you come here often?'

'Well, that's a new one,' she returned, sarcastically, taking a photographic glance at him before returning her attentions to the track. 'Can't say I've heard that one before.'

'I'm sorry,' apologised Paul, leaning over the barrier to stare into her captivating green eyes which were like shimmering emeralds set into chunks of sparkling icebergs, on which he would have been more than happy to be shipwrecked. Noticing from the corner of her eye that he was still there stalling for something to say, she turned her head in the opposite direction.

'Can I get you a drink?' he offered, refusing to be beaten.

'No,' she replied stubbornly, 'I'm not thirsty.'

'Well, what's your name then?' he persisted.

'Nan,' she snapped, still declining to look at him.

'That's nice, is that short for Nancy then?'

'No, it's short for nan of your business.'

'I'm sorry, I was just trying to be friendly.'

On this occasion she turned to face him, bidding to extinguish his burning insistence once and for all.

'Have you had a look at yourself in the mirror lately?'

'No, why?' he replied spellbound, as he fantasised about holding her close to him.

45

'You look as if you've just gone ten rounds with Barry McGuigan.'

In all the excitement of meeting his dream girl, the battering of last night had totally eclipsed his mind. Pride dented again, his speech froze and he felt as if he was two inches tall, although at nearly six foot he towered above her petite frame of five foot two inches. He wished the ground would open up and swallow him whole but she took him out of his misery, for when realising that she'd really hurt him, she made for the exit and home. After all, if every book could be judged by its cover then she would have had him down as a murderer or a rapist, even if he wasn't. At the very least she saw him as trouble and that was the last thing she needed in her life. She was already carrying the weight of world upon her shoulders.

Hailing a saloon-car cab she directed the driver to Riga Street in the Shankill estate. As the taxi drove her homeward, she mulled over the events of the preceding five minutes and they brought a transitory smile to her cheeky face to wipe away some of the unhappiness from her life. Maybe he hadn't been Belfast's answer to Marti Pellow with his black eye and fat lip, but nevertheless he'd made her laugh, if only for his prehistoric chat-up routine. Although she didn't find him attractive in the slightest, not even through sympathy, he had given her a sorely needed ego trip.

Angela Hamilton was the double of how her mother had once been, inch-perfect curves, silky hair, entrancing bone structure. She had it all, yet no one ever asked her out; well, not in the last two years anyway. Prior to that she had had no end of offers, hundreds of males had tried unavailingly to sweep her off her feet. Eventually, the proposals dried up, many thought she was a lesbian, she was simply a walking no entry sign.

It was her lifestyle that permitted her no time for the opposite sex. Almost every minute of her hectic schedule was devoted to her terminally ill mother. At the age of twenty-two, as Angela was now, her mother had been gifted with the world at her feet. She had just won Miss Belfast 1965 and the modelling agencies were queuing up for her signature; then disaster struck. One month later she was pregnant and with that her aspirations of escaping the backstreets of Belfast were fading fast. Being a Protestant, her options were open from day one, but the thought of a baby of her own closed those doors.

Marriage followed immediately to her boyfriend of two years, William, who had followed in his family tradition when joining the Royal Ulster Constabulary. After Angela's birth Liz attempted to resurrect her modelling career, hoping to fulfil her illusion of abandoning the Shankill estate, however the contracts were too few and far between. At twenty-seven her big chance had gone and her bubble had burst. Having missed her one golden opportunity, the depressions ensued as she'd often dwell on what might have been.

It was thirteen years later, when they say life begins, that cancer came and took her breasts and her marriage. Unable to come to terms with the loss of her vanity, she cried herself to sleep and shunned her husband's outstretched arms. Six months after the trauma of her double mastectomy, she found a niggling lump under her arm and a CAT scan revealed the unthinkable. Although the troublesome lump was benign her remission proved to be short-lived when secondary cancer of the bone was diagnosed. Understanding that her predicament was incurable, she refused chemotherapy in favour of retaining the little narcissism she had left. Her hair had been silky black and she knew the loss of it would only catalyse the end for her. In her case, the wonders of modern medicine could have no prolonging effect.

For the first year she chose to ignore her affliction by working herself to the bone within the confines of her home. It was a self-administered medication which resulted in initial success. Unable to accept the imminent outcome, her husband had searched for his answers at the bottom of the glass, as he drowned in his own sorrows. During the second year of the malignant disease, the pain arrived and her strength began to depart. Perceiving her mother dying incensed Angela to enrol as a nurse. Throughout her three years of training, she watched helplessly as her mother's pain and suffering grew stronger in parallel to the drugs. She'd gone through the medicine chest from coproxamol to co-dydramol, now she had advanced to morphine slow release. Currently, the distilled heroin of MST was doing the trick, but no one was kidding themselves - it was a treatment, not a cure. She was a drug addict now, dependent on her daily fix, not for pleasure, but for her very existence. It was the next phase of the morphine pump that Angela dreaded, for then she knew that the end was just around the corner.

Angela had never had a proper boyfriend, when she wasn't on the wards tending to the sick of Belfast, she was looking after her mother.

47

Receiving no help from her alcoholic father, she had to clean, cook, wash, iron and do all the shopping for the household. And being an only child, all the burdensome responsibility of running the house fell heavily on to her. Thanks to her fevered itinerary, the troubles of the city seemed a million miles away, though they were part of her work on a daily basis. The Shankill was the Protestant equivalent of the Catholic Falls district, a well of lost souls and an open prison from which few escaped. For Angela it was home as it always had been, her wings clipped by circumstance, but she had no will or want to fly, for it was all she knew. Having never been able to meet the social demands, she had no friends outside of her work.

Her only escape was Dunmore Greyhound Track on the sporadic Saturday evening, when her mother insisted that she take a break from her mundane commitments. Angela's love for greyhound racing was born when her father had taken her to the track as a young girl. It was the first and last time he had taken her anywhere with him. Fascinated by the elegant stature and cuddly, cute faces of the canine Rolls-Royces, she had become infatuated by their swift grace. Dunmore was the only place in the world that had any meaning to her, it was a serene location where she could gather her thoughts and recollect when her mother was fit and well and the family was strong. Dunmore was her 'somewhere over the rainbow'.

Arriving outside her home, she paid the driver and rushed through the front door to her mother's side.

'Did you have a nice evening-sweetheart?'

'Aye, not too bad,' she replied, heading to the kitchen to make some tea.

'Did you meet any boys?'

'Not really.'

'What does that mean, exactly?'

'Well, I met one.'

'Was he handsome?'

'The very opposite, he looked as if he'd been dragged through a hedge backwards,' she revealed, bringing two mugs of piping hot sweet tea into the room.

'Then why have you got a twinkle in your eye?'

'I have not,' she defended, her face turning lobster red. 'It must be the fairy lights catching my eyes.'

'So, do you have a date?'

'Oh will you behave yourself, Mother, he was really horrible, I'd rather become a nun than have gone out with him.'

'That bad, eh?'

'Worse.'

Still standing facing where the pretty girl had been, a million thoughts were sailing through Paul's mind at a rate of knots, as he became submerged in an identity crisis. Was he really unattractive to the opposite sex? Had all the years of clinging to the false security of Bernadette made him lapse in his appearance? Suddenly he found himself a very lonely young man, no wiser than his naïve comrade. Putting his arm around his distant friend, Tommy revived him from the analysis of his detriments.

'So how did it go, are you gonna see her again?'

'No, she's out of my league,' he confessed.

Having reached his objective of sub rock-bottom and feeling gutted to the core, he decided tomorrow would be the first day of the rest of his life, but before he instigated his early New Year's resolution, he had one last thing to do. Racing to the nearest turf accountant, he slapped fifty pounds on the dog he fancied at 4/1. Watching as the dogs were loaded up for the last race, he thought to himself, if this dog wins I'll marry that girl. It was the last of his money, and it was a bet that he could ill afford to lose. It was a gamble made out of frustration.

As the mechanical lure made its final journey of the night, he cringed at the thought of what he'd done, was any woman worth such a hasty act? Especially when he didn't even know her. Usually, during the thirty seconds of a race, his adrenaline would soar through the roof, irrelevant of his stake, but on this occasion it could not rise above his lament. Watching without a care, he saw his charge flash first past the winning post unchallenged, yet still he could not bring himself to smile at his change of fortune. After collecting his £250 winnings, all he wanted to do was curl up and sleep off the humiliation. Throughout the silent bus ride back to the Falls, her hostile words continued to eat into him as they reverberated around in his brain. 'HAVE YOU HAD A LOOK AT YOURSELF IN THE MIRROR LATELY?'

Having lost every battle since returning to home territory, he told himself he would have to fight harder, after all there was still a war to be won. Bidding Tommy farewell, he marched into the house and headed straight for his bedroom, in no mood for further confrontation.

Unbuttoning his trousers, he removed his winnings from the pocket and placed the bundle on the bedside cabinet. Staring at the thick wad of notes, he now understood for the first time in his life what they meant when they had said that money doesn't buy you happiness.

Chapter 3

Should Auld Aquaintance Be Forgot and Never Brought To Mind

Christmas Day arrived as the traditional anticlimax it always is, but this year it was more dispiriting than ever. Although Paul was surrounded by his family, he felt more isolated than Robinson Crusoe must have done on his desert island. Reneging to join the hypocritical celebrations below, he pulled the duvet over his head seeking to black out last night's adversities, which were still playing heavily on his mind. Safe and warm in the cocoon of his bed, he wondered what lay in store for him in the coming year and how he could combat the depression that was growing like a cancer within.

If he'd been in London, he'd have been working now, carrying the bags for the 'made it' set, who, he always felt, looked down at him with contempt as they grudgingly parted with their gratuities of commiseration. That was no longer an option, there was no way he was willing to go back to that. Paul was not only well educated, he was also a time-served machinist and they were always crying out for engineers in that discipline, but that was just a means to an end as far as he was concerned. A new challenge and a new Paul were high on the agenda. They say it's all about job satisfaction, and he had hated every dull minute of those long boring shifts. He'd find something that he actually enjoyed doing and then he'd go all out for it, that was the only way forward. The next year couldn't come quickly enough; having always preached that life was too short, he found himself wishing his life away in the hibernation of his bed.

At two o'clock his mother was finalising the painstaking preparation of the turkey and trimmings. Assured that the situation was contained,

51

she left the array of labour-saving devices to complete her culinary composition. Entering the living room she could have mistaken it for Paddy's Bar, seeing as Top of the Pops was clamouring over the conversation and the beer was fluent.

'Where's Paul?' she addressed the room.

A simultaneous trio of shrugged shoulders told her he had failed to rise as of yet and that nobody cared anyway. About turning, she made her way up the stairs to the lost world of the boy's bedroom, where she sat on the edge of Paul's bed.

'Are you gonna surface and make an appearance today? It's gone two o'clock, you know.'

'I'm better out of the way,' came the muffled reply from under the bedding.

'Don't be silly, son, you can't just lock yourself away from world like this, especially not on this great day.'

Popping his head out from under the quilt to reveal his exploding mattress hairstyle, he looked at his mother. 'I'm sorry about yesterday. I was out of line, I won't make any excuses for my behaviour but I've a lot on my mind at the moment. I just don't feel very welcome in this house at the moment with this and that.'

'I know you didn't mean it, son. Things will get better you know, I guarantee it, but running and hiding from the situation will only prolong the animosity, can't you see that?'

'Aye, you're right,' he concurred. 'I'll get washed and dressed then come down for dinner.'

'Good, I'm glad to hear it. There are a few presents under the tree for you to open and you know if you want to share your problems with anyone, I'm always here to listen.'

'Okay, thanks, I'll be down in a minute.'

'Come on son, chin up, I hate to see you like this.'

Mother gone, he eased himself out of bed and began to dress. Fully clothed, he began to sift through his wardrobe and drawers for clothes he felt were no longer fitting for the new image he was resolute to portray. Placing at least three full outfits into his holdall and a bottle of vintage aftershave, which was also celebrating its birthday today, he headed downstairs and into the kitchen. All alone, he expeditiously threw a few tins of soup and a packet of cereal into the bag before placing it outside the back door.

'What were you doing out there?' interrogated his mother, almost catching the cunning larcenist in the act.

'Eh, eh, I was just checking the weather. I had a sneaking suspicion it might snow today.'

'It's too cold for snow,' she said in her wisdom. 'Now go on, get yourself into the living room and open your presents while I start to serve dinner.'

Lethargically, he obeyed her request. Upon entering the room, Michael spoke and it was soon apparent that a one day cease-fire of hostilities had been called.

'Merry Christmas Paul, thanks for the whiskey. Can I get you a beer?'

Knowing it would be foolish to reject such an offer, even if it was a truce of insincerity, he accepted. 'Aye, go on then.'

Taking the aluminium can, he snapped the ring pull which cracked like a pistol shot startling his father who had begun to nod off. Holding it into the air he declared his toast. 'Well, Merry Christmas everybody.'

In unison all the tins in the room were raised into the air with the exception of one. Glancing to the left, he saw that his father would not capitulate to the terms of the amnesty.

'There are some presents under the tree for you,' informed Bernadette.

Turning to the rusting evergreen, he removed three parcels from under its wilting feathers. The gift tag attached to the first package read, 'From Michael and Bernadette, Merry Xmas' and he knew exactly what it contained before he opened it. It was, as it always had been for the last decade from his brother, Old Spice aftershave and talcum powder. If only he could have bet on his beloved greyhounds with such predictability, then he would have surely been a very rich young man by now. Moving to the others, he read the labels, 'Merry Xmas son, love mum and dad,' both in his mother's rickety handwriting as always. Removing the wrapping paper he uncovered a water resistant wristwatch and a cream, Arran jumper whose oily wool would no doubt irritate his sensitive fair skin. Not wishing to look a gift horse in the mouth, he thanked all parties concerned then found a chair away from the curled-up lovers on the sofa.

On the stroke of three o'clock, a fine mouth-watering meaty aroma, combined with the television set being switched off, meant dinner was served. Sitting adjacent to Bernadette and facing his mother, he looked at the eyeball-massaging feast before him and he thought about what

Tommy might be doing now, oblivious that he was outside on the street corner counting down the seconds until 4 p.m. Grace said, all began tucking into the sacrificial bird, stabbing at it until the juices flowed. Midway through the banquet, Paul felt Bernadette's foot touch his before teasingly and suggestively running up his leg. Almost choking on the dry white meat, he moved his limb away and glimpsed over at his brother, anxious to see if he had noticed the foul play. Too busy racing to clear his plate first, he was none the wiser to his fiancé's flirtatious demeanour.

In the kitchen of 22 Riga Street, Angela was soaked to the skin with perspiration as she sought to suppress the mutinous festive dinner, which was threatening to wipe the deck with her.

Straining the boiled potatoes, a gust of steam attacked her pores, forcing her away from the sink. As she glanced at the cooker, she could see that the pan boiling the carrots had overflowed and thick blue smoke was belching from the oven. Releasing the red-hot-pan into the sink, she bolted to the mischievous contrivance and opened the door, allowing a back draft of sweltering smog to escape, then evanesce into her new red dress. Fit for a nervous breakdown as the tension mounted, she stepped back and took a deep breath and bit upon her bottom lip to hold back the tears that were fermenting within.

'Angela, Angela, come and turn the sound up for me, the Queen's speech is on,' bawled her mother, who sat upright wrapped in a blanket, ageing by the minute in a posture of contabescence.

Angela bent down to adjust the volume.

'For God's sake, you're in the way, I can't see,' her mother whined like a spoilt child. 'What were you doing through there anyway?'

'I was trying to serve the dinner.'

'Well, I'm not hungry,' she spat venomously. 'And you look like a little harlot in that dress.'

The morphine was perhaps making her dwindling life span more comfortable, but there was a price to be paid in the side effects. There were mediocre days and there were soul-destroying days, but there were few normal ones to be found. On the particularly bad days her mother would snap and snarl, scream and cry, vomit and wet herself and even become violent and paranoid as she climbed the walls in desperation. Then she'd simply drift in and out of consciousness.

Admirably, Angela had learnt to cope with all the dilemmas thrown at her by her mother's wait on death row, though at times she felt like slashing her own wrists. What she couldn't handle were the poisonous words that constantly rolled of her mother's tongue. She was hurting now, yet she knew it would be when her mother's pain had gone that hers would really begin.

She glanced at her watch. It was 3.15 p.m. and still no sign of her father. For a split second, she wished he'd walk through the door and give her a hand, then again she knew he'd be in no fit state when that moment arrived. Living with an alcoholic and a drug addict, her sanity was teetering on the brink. Picking up the oven gloves she proceeded to remove the bird from its cage. With so much plaguing her mind, she forgot that the heat resisters had a hole burnt through the right mitt. As the cold pain flashed through her finger like an Excocet missile targeting her nerve endings, she threw the tilted roasting tin back at the oven, but missed. Clattering on to the slate floor, the red hot fat spewed like molten lava as it headed for the contours in a capillary action. She slumped to the floor with her back to the wall and began sucking her blistered finger, rocking herself back and forth until she cried so loud that it drowned her mother's shouts in the next room.

After dinner, the usual format in the O'Donnell household on December the 25th, was that the men would retire to the living room for more drink before a well-deserved nap, whilst the women would clean up the aftermath of the dishes. Checking his new watch, which read 3.50 p.m., Paul decided it was time for a change to that antediluvian custom, knowing that Tommy would be punctual in his arrival.

'Mom, I'll do the dishes this year, go and get yourself sat down, there's bound to be a good film on.'

'No, you're all right son.'

'No, I insist, away and get yourself parked in front of the telly for a change.'

'Are you sure you don't mind?'

'I'm positive,' he emphasised.

'I don't mind giving you a hand, if that's all right with you, Michael?' offered Bernadette, turning to smile at her fiancé.

'Well I was hoping we could snuggle up and watch the film together, but if it makes you happy,' returned Michael, giving her some slack.

'No, there's no need,' stressed Paul. 'Away and watch the movie.'

'No, I'll help, I wouldn't feel right if I hadn't done my fair share.'

Commencing on the tidying-up operation, Paul reasoned it best to ignore her as he cleared the plates and cutlery from the dining table. Reaching into an overhead cupboard, he removed a couple of Tupperware containers then began to prepare Tommy's meal from the abundant leftovers.

'What are you gonna do with that?' nosed Bernadette.

'Let's just say it's for the less fortunate amongst us.' he replied.

Nipping out into the backyard he found that Tommy was already waiting on his handout.

'Here Tom, take this holdall. There's clothes and some after shave in there and here's yer dinner. Remember to clean the containers and have a bath will you? Oh, I almost forgot, there's a few wee surprises in there to keep you going. If you come back at 5 p.m. tomorrow, I'll get you some more food, and we'll go shopping the next day. Now go on, on yer way.'

Taking his Red Cross parcel, Tommy scurried away at a pace. About-turning to re-enter the kitchen, Paul almost clashed heads with Bernadette who had come to spy on whom he was feeding.

'Was that Tommy O'Brien, the school eejit?' she inquired.

'What if it was?' he replied, manoeuvring around her to the sink.

'What are you doing hanging around with a fool like him?'

'He's not a fool, he's just quiet and shy, that's all,' he defended.

'Ohh,' she purred. 'That's why I fell for you, still have a heart of gold haven't you, what a big softie.'

'Aye, maybe, but I'm getting tougher by the day, now come on, get drying those dishes or Michael will be getting the wrong idea with the time we're taking in here.'

'So you enjoyed me stroking your leg then did you?'

'How are you getting on in here?' interrupted Michael, appearing at the door.

'We're nearly finished darlin',' she returned, skilfully calming his insecurities.

'Well hurry then, the film's about to start, I'll go and pour you a wee dram.'

'Okay sweetie, and keep my seat warm won't you?' she charmed.

Her betrothed safely gone, she returned her attentions to Paul. 'Now, where were we?'

Grabbing the dish towel from its hook, he dried his hands then thrust the cloth upon her.

'Well, that's my bit done, I'll be off to watch the film now, bye.'

At 8 p.m. when he was so bloated with the gases of the beer and he could nibble no more, Paul decided to retire for an early night's rest. Lying on his back, he stared out of the window at the flickering stars dotted in the clear black sky and he thought about the girl from the track. Soon he was acting out a scene with her, where they were walking hand in hand along a placid blue lagoon, toasting their feet on the baking beach as the sun yawned overhead. Turning to his bronzed goddess, he pulled her close and wiped the white powdery sand from the sides of her glazed lips. Closing his eyes he placed his mouth to hers. The sudden thud of Michael's heavy boots falling on to the wooden floorboards as he clumsily prepared for bed soured his taste of heaven. He squinted at the luminous green hands of his new timepiece; it was 11.45 p.m. Turning over, he desperately attempted to regain the plot, but it had vanished into the night for ever. When he had almost nodded off again, he heard the floorboards creak and the faint pattering of tiptoes enter the room. It was a sound he knew only too well, though on this night it was not music to his ears.

Straddling on top of her fiancé, she began to rock to and fro, twanging the excited bedsprings which echoed off the walls, the acoustics enhanced by the crisp still of the night. Then she began to moan and groan in rhythm with her gesticulating gyrations as she sought to reach her climax.

'Ssshh,' whispered Michael, trying to calm her down. 'You'll wake the whole house.'

Fully awake, Paul gazed into the darkness and felt seasick. What was playing on his mind more than anything was the volume of her ecstasy, for she'd never hit those highs when she'd been between the sheets with him. Now feeling inadequate in other departments, he squeezed his eyes shut and began to wonder exactly where he fitted into the equation of human existence.

Boxing Day was much the same as the previous twenty-four hours, a typical Sunday as Sundays go. The only visible difference was when Tommy arrived on the stroke of five for his food ration. His hair was actually brown now that he had washed it. His once anaemic complexion had been replaced by a rosy pink glow, a combination of a reaction to soap and water and the impurities, which had laid dormant for years beneath his pores, rising to find out what the hell he was playing at. Dress wise, the clothes he had been handed down, if slightly long on the leg and wide at the chest, were bright and tailor-made for what he needed, and brought incandescence into his dark life. And the smell, well, that was unquestionably the most obvious transposition to his person. Having once smelled like a sewage plant in high summer, he now gave off the aroma of a whore's handbag.

Taking the holdall, Paul scrutinised the plastic dishes and observed that they were spotless. Tommy's appearance and etiquette well on the road to recovery, all that was needed now was to jump start his brain. After nipping into the kitchen, Paul returned with another meal that would have only ended up in the bin anyway.

'There you go, Tom, Irish stew made with tender lamb and half a loaf of bread to dip in it. I want you to start that shopping list tonight, write down as many things as you can think of then bring it here tomorrow morning at ten o'clock and we'll fill your cupboards. Oh, and don't forget to get twenty pounds off your da.'

Trudging home pensively, Tommy was beginning to understand that holding down a friendship was not like cooking soup, but more like pulling hen's teeth. It was indeed a stressful business, for less than twenty-four hours ago he'd almost killed himself attempting to obey Paul's commands. After allowing the bath to fill, he had stripped naked to discover there was no hot water. All he knew was that the water was heated by gas. Unable to start the heating system in the hall, whose pilot light had gone out weeks ago, he ventured to the kitchen to investigate whether there actually was any gas being supplied to the house. Turning all the oven knobs to full, he waited for a good fifteen minutes before his olfactory sense picked up the sickly sweet scent of gas above the pungent odour of his own person. Satisfied there was an incoming supply, he returned to the boiler without a Corgi certificate, to re-examine the apparatus. As luck would have it, his father made a rare appearance and managed to diffuse the situation before it was blown out of all proportion.

Tonight he had to devise a list, and he had no hope whatsoever because he could not read and write. Surely it would now be the end of their companionship. Throughout the night he tossed and turned in the torment of being a failure, as he worried himself to sleep over how Paul would react to his ignorance.

* * *

58

The pomp and revelry of the yuletide over for another year, Paul woke bright and early. Stretching the cobwebs away, he garbed himself with silent precision, not wishing to disturb the snoring giant in the next bed. Peeking through the drapes, he could see that it was quite a fine morning in the making. The sky was white and the streets had benefited from a passing shower during the night. That signified it would be milder than it had been of late and that was most welcome for him, as the cold had been postponing the mending of his broken ribs.

Moving to the bathroom he gave himself a 'cat's lick' wash so as not to disturb the healing process in his eye. In the mirror, he perceived that the purple-black bruising had faded to a jaundiced yellow with a strawberry patch dotted along the sac, under his eyelashes. Slowly but surely, the real Paul was returning. After brushing the furry plaque and acid stains of last night's sleep from his teeth, he made his way to the kitchen to find his mother and Bernadette chatting over a pot of tea.

'Good morning, Paul, you're looking better today, can I get you some breakfast?' offered his mother.

Seeing that Bernadette was present called for tact.

'No, I'll just have a quick cup of tea, if there's any left in that pot. I'm late as it is.'

'So, where are you off to today?' pried his mother.

'I'm helping a friend to stock his cupboards and then I'm going into Belfast to have a look in the job centre .'

'Well, I wish you luck with the job hunting,' she returned.

Pouring himself a mug of well-stewed tea, he couldn't help but eavesdrop on the conversation that he wasn't aware was for his benefit only. In the past, he may have read it as a suspicious innuendo for his behalf, but after last night's live sex show, he dismissed it as motiveless chatter.

'I'm really gonna miss Michael over New Year. Do you know, Mrs O'Donnell, it'll be the first time we've been apart since our engagement.'

'Oh you'll be fine, besides it's only for a few days and they do say absence makes the heart grow fonder,' his mother assured her daughter-in-law to be.

Taking a huge mouthful of charred liquid, Paul poured the remainder down the sink then rinsed the cup and said his farewell: 'Right, I'm on me way then, I'll see you later, Mam.'

Having been coerced into making an early exit by Bernadette's presence, he had left the house at 9 a.m. Looking up the road to the corner of Tommy's street, he quite expected to see him waiting there, but he was not. Thinking of how well Tommy had adapted to the culture shock he had been subjected to for his own good, Paul thought it only fair to nurture him along, showing that friendship was a two-way commitment. Just by calling at his house for a change would probably give him a well-merited moral boost. When he knocked at the front door, Tommy was sitting deep in vexatious embarrassment. It was a riddle that only his discretion could solve. Scanning around the now antiseptically clean kitchen, then down at his new fashion accessories, he knew he had to make a resolution. Did he want the metamorphosis to progress, or was it all too much too soon for him? Entangled in a web of confusion, he malfunctioned to hear the first knock. Again the visitor rapped his knuckles on the wood, then half turned to witness a false start, as half a dozen net curtains returned to their starting positions.

Hearing the tap purged Tommy's fears, as the excitement of someone at his door imbued his psyche. And as this was an occurrence that didn't happen on a regular basis, he always presumed that it might be his mother returning. On the two previous occasions that he could recall, it had been the kids on bonfire night and the gas man wishing to read the meter. Jumping from the starting blocks of his chair, he bolted to the door, hoping it was to be third time lucky. Eagerly removing the chain, he opened the door to view Paul's healing face.

'I thought you said ten o'clock,' he panicked, tapping his watch and straining his eyesight through the condensation bubbling on the glass, from the one and only time he had participated in the joy of bathing.

'No, your watch is correct, I just had to get out of the house. I thought we'd make an early start, did you manage to make the list?'

'Yes, well no, well I've lost it,' he stammered at being caught unawares.

'Okay, never mind,' accepted Paul. 'Get your coat and we'll fill the basket as we go.'

Stress relieved, he reverted to the kitchen to retrieve his trusted parka. Nearing the supermarket, Tommy was miles away; although he had got away with it again, even he knew it was only a matter of time before Paul discovered that he was illiterate.

'Did you bring the money?' asked Paul, on entering the store.

'What?' said Tommy, still thinking about revealing his handicap.

60

'The money for the groceries. Have you woken up yet, you've nearly stumbled over a dozen times in as many steps. Well, do you have it?'

'Aye,' he replied, handing over the cash.

Having noticed that something was haunting his friend, Paul decided he wanted to get to the bottom of it.

'Okay, Tom, what's up with you. Have you been arguing with your father?'

'No.'

'Well, what is it then? I can see that you are in turmoil with yourself. Come on, you can tell me, I'll understand. I might even be able to help you,' he coaxed.

Unable to live with his deceit any longer, he began to spill the beans. 'You won't go mad, will ye?'

'Why, what have you done?' inquired Paul, worried that he may have mugged an old lady to gain the money at such short notice.

Not able to look him in the eyes and snivelling like a guilty schoolboy, he parted with the truth and the tears. 'I couldn't do the shopping list because I can't read and write properly.'

'Don't worry about it,' replied Paul, softly. 'It's no big deal. Did you know that Einstein was dyslexic as a child and he became a genius overnight.'

'But no one will ever give me a job, will they?' he disputed, refusing to accept Paul's condescension.

'They will if I teach you.'

'Would you really?' he replied hungrily, raising his head to nibble at the bait on offer.

'Only if you promise me one thing.'

'Anything,' he begged.

'Just try, that's all. I'll help you as best I can, but you've got to input twice as much, no temper tantrums when the going gets tough, just total commitment on your part. The first time you spit your dummy and the deals off, it's all up to you.'

'Aye, aye, I promise,' he seized at the opportunity.

Paul knew there would be a mountain to climb, but it was something he, too, wanted to do. If he could succeed where all the specialist education gurus had failed, then he, too, would be on the road to recovery.

'So when can we start?' quizzed Tommy.

'This afternoon, after I've been to the job centre in Belfast.'

When every last penny had been judiciously spent, they returned to Tommy's home and began to nourish the ravenous cupboards. Then, after a whistle stop coffee break, they headed in search of employment.

With Christmas barely out of sight, they arrived at the job centre and found it deserted, a bit like a pub without a licence on St Patrick's Day. Having the full run of the displays, Paul studied the boards conscientiously and then read them back to Tommy one by one, all except the engineering section. He feared that if he applied for a turner's position, he might get it, then history would repeat itself and he'd be trapped in an eternal rut. His new-found determination to win would not allow him to become typecast. He was no fool, he recognised that a change of direction could initially set him back financially, but he kept drumming it into himself that at the moment he had no income, so any earnings were welcome.

Having read more than a hundred situations vacant, he opted to apply for a scant two. The first was with Aer Lingus, who were advertising for cabin crew; the thought of jetting off to Europe on a daily basis enticed him into this choice and the money was good too. The second was along the same lines, it was as a steward on the ferries which sailed to the United Kingdom mainland. With both posts, he realised that the role would be none better than that of a glorified skivvy, but the perks were there, he loved to travel and he liked to meet different people.

Removing the job description cards, he walked up to a desk occupied by a pretty little blonde who had her head buried in one of those offensive woman's weeklies, proving for once that the old cliche was indeed justified. She was dumb. Heavily engrossed in the serial feature, which was in-depth analysis of different sexual positions taken from The Kama Sutra, she didn't heed his approach. This week's speciality was the art of cunnilingus. Clearing his throat, he politely announced his need for assistance. Dropping the magazine in alarm, she raised her eyebrows above her gold trimmed designer spectacles and gave her robotic introduction.

'Next.'

Taking a seat, he handed the cards which sparked a mutual love to hate relationship.

'Can't you read?' she snapped.

'Why?' he inquired, taken aback at her elitist attitude.

'It clearly says above the boards, that you are not to remove the cards from the display.'

62

'Well, I am sorry,' he replied caustically.

Shaking her head at his incompetence, she began to read out loud the first card.

'It says here that the job is with Aer Lingus.'

Pausing for a split second, she looked at him, then down at the magazine which she had been previously absorbed in. Satisfied by the momentous look on his face that his intentions were honourable, she continued. 'The minimum requirement is three O Levels, English a must, do you have three?'

'No.'

'Then why are you wasting my time?'

'I have eight,' he replied, unwilling to be tamed by her female instincts.

'Listen, I've no time for games, both of these positions require written application. I take it you can write?'

Not impressed with her behaviour, he gave no reply. Taking a pen, she jotted down the addresses and reference numbers then handed him the piece of paper.

'Thank you very much for your oral assistance,' he sneered, winking towards the magazine as he rose from the chair and gave her the Nazi salute.

'Did you get the job then?' inquired Tommy as they left the building.

'No, it doesn't work like that, I have to apply in writing. It'll take a few weeks before they decide whether they want to interview me. They don't give you jobs in there, just sarcasm'. he educated.

'So, can we go home now and learn me how to read and write?'

'No, not yet, I have to go to the Unemployment Benefit Office and stake my claim, then we can go.'

It was as busy and as daunting as a dentist's waiting room, as everyone who had told their bosses what they thought of them with their fists at the Christmas parties, waited to become statistics on a government chart. After an hour and a half's mind-blowing stay, it was over in a matter of seconds.

'You should have made an appointment,' he was told, being handed an equatorial rain-forest of paperwork to cover with ink. 'Complete the forms. Come back on Wednesday at 11 a.m. It'll take about two weeks to process your claim, goodbye.'

Any conceptions of arguing had been snuffed out in the preceding ninety minutes of consummate boredom. Questionnaires in hand, he morosely walked over and nudged Tommy, who had dozed off in all the excitement.

'Come on Tom, let's go home and start your tuition.'

After half an hour of careful preparation, Paul was ready to teach his pupil. The paper and pen were at hand, the teapot was full and a packet of paracetamol was within reach in case of emergency. On a plain sheet of paper, Paul scribed four lines, leaving a blank line directly underneath each sentence for Tommy to copy his writing. The lines read:

My name is Tommy.

Tommy lives in a scary old house.

Tommy is learning to read and write.

Tommy likes soldiers.

Handing the paper over to the scholar, Paul transmitted his instructions.

'Okay, I want you to copy exactly what I've written down, then we'll take it from there.'

While Tommy tried to remaster the hieroglyphics, Paul began to wade through the quagmire of his claims form which was, beyond any doubt, a farce on a titanic scale. Too many irrelevant personal questions and, if they'd cut back on paper and print, they could have increased the miserable handout of £32.75 a week, was Paul's evaluation. It would always remain one of life's great mysteries – how all the clever bastards have no common sense. Then again, you could always avoid the hardship of the humiliating paperwork exercise and remain incommunicado, by taking a YTS and working a forty-hour week for an insulting pittance of £25, with the negligible hope of a full time job at the end of twelve months. Paul opted for the extra £7.75.

'I've finished,' revealed Tommy.

'Okay, pass it over and I'll have a look,' ordered Paul, who was in desperate need of a break from trying to fathom out how many times he went for a shit each day.

The writing was messy, what you'd come to expect from a six-year-old, but it was readable and it was correct, which pleased Paul. Learning is all about wanting to do so and opening your mind; if it's not open then how can the information enter. Tommy's was ajar, all it needed now was to be prised wider.

'Okay, do you know the letters of the alphabet?' inquired Paul.

'Yes,' replied Tommy.

'Good, then read that letter to me,' he said, pointing to the first character on the top line he he'd written.

'Mmi,' offered Tommy.

'Good, and the next.'

'Yi.'

'Excellent,' he encouraged, his student. 'Now I want you to put them together really fast and think of a word that you speak which sounds like what your reading.'

'Miya, miya, miya myie, my.'

'Well done,' exclaimed Paul, delighted that his tuition was coming to fruition. 'Now let's try the next word.'

'Ni, ahh, mmi, ee. Niame, nyame name.'

'Brilliant,' shouted Paul, even more excited than his friend, who was now moving at his own pace, unassisted.

Within minutes he could read 'My name is Tommy.' Pouring a well-earned cup of tea, Paul quipped. 'You don't fancy filling in these forms for me, do you?'

While Tommy read his letters over and over, Paul wrote his for the vacancies. Over the next three days leading up to New Year's Eve, the pair spent ten hours a day grafting at the basics of the English language and it was actually working. Paul estimated that if Tommy sustained his gradual progression at his existing rate, then it would only be a matter of months before he was ready to tackle The Lord Of The Rings.

The shuffling sound of Michael packing his holdall in conjunction with his mental awareness that it was New Year's Eve, roused Paul from his light sleep. Throughout the night he had racked his mind over a million speeches that might win his dream girl's heart. Inspired at the prospect of making her acquaintance again, he threw off the quilt and made for his wardrobe to select his optimum attire, with a view that it just might make him attractive enough to warrant a second glance.

'I'm borrowing your holdall,' stated Michael.

65

'Why, where are you off to?' he investigated.

'I'm going to Glasgow for New Year. I won't be home until the early hours of Sunday morning,' informed his brother.

'What are you going there for?'

'The Celtic – Rangers game on Saturday the 2nd,' he revealed. 'I'm selling An Phoblact to raise money for the Cause. Oh, and by the way, if I find out that you've even looked at Bernadette, so help me God you'll wish you'd never been born when I return.'

As Michael departed, Paul swithered over his best dress prospects for the big night. Slimming it down to two possible outfits, he tried each on four times before opting for a pair of dapper, shiny black dress trousers and a jade silk shirt. By the time he had left the bedroom, Michael was on his way to Scotland. Carrying a black pair of brogue shoes, he entered the kitchen whistling and smiling to himself as he pictured her dainty face in everything he saw. Ignoring his mother and Bernadette, who were having their habitual morning meeting, he found the boot polish and brushes in the cupboard under the sink, then began to shine his shoes to military criterion.

'My, we do look pretty today,' remarked his mother. 'Going anywhere special, or with someone special perhaps?' she fished.

'No, I just thought I'd make an effort seeing as it is New Year's Eve, that's all,' he replied.

Eyeing him up and down, Bernadette focused on his perfect, masculine rump, as it wiggled and shimmied in time with his impassioned polishing actions and her lust boiled from within, whetting her from the inside out. Knowing her future mother-in-law had been invited to a neighbour's house to ring in the New, she combed her conniving head for an excuse to be at home when Paul finally rolled in from his secret whereabouts. Excusing herself, she ran up the stairs to his bedroom and began to rummage through the pockets of the jeans he had hung on the floor the night before. When she had found what she had been searching for, she detoured to the toilet and pulled the flush to wash away any suspicion below. When she returned to the conference table, Paul had already left for his day with destiny.

'Has Paul gone?'

'Aye, sweetheart,' confirmed his mother. 'I'm pleased he's finally perked himself up. I hope he finds himself a nice girl soon, don't you?'

'Mmm,' mumbled Bernadette methodically, desperately hoping that he wouldn't.

66

It was more like the midsummer solstice than the death of another year, as the day inconsiderately dragged on. Tommy remained rooted to his studies while Paul's nerves jangled to new extremes with every passing hour. By five o'clock, when Tommy served his speciality of mushroom soup and bread, Paul's appetite had faded with amour.

Finally, and not before time, the clock pointed out that it was 6.45 p.m., time to head in pursuit of romance. When Paul had made his way to the classroom of Tommy's kitchen all those hours ago, it had been a rather nippy morning, now that school was over for another year, the chill had been replaced by a severe but tepid gale, which buffeted them, chasing them with a thousand hairdryers, as it set out to restyle their hair to that of the Sex Pistols. On a night when first impressions could count for so much, it was a blow job he could have done without. Joining the queue of hogmanay revellers they waited patiently, each of them craftily utilising the individual in front as cover from the carnivorous wind. For a minute, Paul's mind was swept away, as he thought about the file of party animals before him. I wonder how many will end up in hospital or in the cells or laid face down in the gutter in their own vomit, or even on a slab in the mortuary come the morning. It was his hypothesis that people high on alcohol became nuisances and frightened others and even themselves, so tonight he would celebrate the wake in moderation, as always. Saying farewell to the blustery gusts, they boarded the bus and were on their way again. On this night of such dimensional expectation, Paul was in no mood to risk not paying into the stadium. It had been a considerable achievement keeping himself as preened as he possibly could throughout the long day, and he wasn't willing to get his hands dirty at this late stage for a mere £1.50. By using the turnstiles, they were unknowingly feeding the meter to keep the track's life support machine supplied with electricity. On the whole, greyhound racing was in demise, dwindling attendances and lack of sponsorship affiliated to cripple the once democratic sport. Financially, Dunmore was on its last legs

Throughout the eight-race meeting the lights flickered ominously, as the spoilsport wind turned the track into a sandstorm which blew on to the terraces, coercing the patrons to seek asylum in the warmth of the bar. It was an unpleasant evening, where Paul spent more time scanning the passers-by than studying the card. The distractions were to pay heavy consequences on his pocket; by the last race the bar was deserted, he was £50 poorer and to crown it all, the girl hadn't shown. Dejected and demoralised, he turned to Tommy.

67

'Come on let's go home.'

At 10.30 p.m. they arrived at Paul's front door.

'Well, Tommy, I won't be calling round tomorrow, seeing as it's New Year's Day. I'll have to show face for dinner, but there's a dog card on Saturday night, if you fancy it?'

'I'll be there,' said Tommy, supportively.

'Great, I'll see you sometime Saturday, then. With a little luck the pretty girl may make an appearance.'

'I'm sure she will, perhaps she was at a party or something, I'm sure she'll come again,' soothed Tommy, noting that his best friend was really down in the doldrums.

'Okay,' smiled Paul, realising that Tommy was feeling for him too. 'I'd better shake your hand now for New Year.'

Hands clasped together, their relationship was setting rock solid. Paul felt that he could tell Tommy anything, without becoming embarrassed or for the fear of being ridiculed. Having a slightly touched companion definitely had its rewards, not that he would ever take him for granted, he was now more than an ally, he was a confidant.

'Oh, and Tom.'

'What?'

'Keep reading and writing, next week I'm gonna give you a special book to read.'

'I can't wait,' Tommy shouted back from the corner.

Even though he had no drink with which to welcome in the New Year, it was the best New Year's Eve that Tommy could ever remember.

On the doorstep, things were going from bad to worse. Digging into his empty pockets, he could not find his key, but noticing that the living room light was illuminating the inadequate excuse for a garden, he knocked on the door.

'It's open,' shouted Bernadette.

Entering the hall, he saw her standing there holding a glass of whisky, clad only in a skimpy silk dressing gown which clung to her voluptuous curves like paint to a wall.

'You look like you could do with a drink,' she offered.

'It wouldn't go amiss,' he replied.

'Well, come away in and I'll fix you a glass.'

'Where is everyone?' he inquired, nervous at the way she was clothed.

'They've gone to bring in the New Year at a neighbours,' she revealed.

68

'Then how come you're still here?'

'To let you in, of course, forgot your key didn't you? I must admit I didn't really expect you back so early,' she purred.

'I can see that,' he commented, taking the glass then looking away from her bulging cleavage, which was tactically on exhibition for his perusal. 'Well, I'm home now so you can get yourself dressed and be on your way.'

'I thought we might bring in the New Year like old times,' she winked with a smile.

'Should auld acquaintance be forgot and never brought to mind, that's my motto,' he enunciated, sinking the firewater before handing her back the glass.

'Another?' she posed.

'Goodnight,' he replied, turning towards the staircase.

Lying in bed with head resting on hands, he couldn't help but mull over what a disastrous beginning to the New Year it had been. Hearing the pitter-patter of Bernadette's footsteps, he turned over and closed his eyes hoping that she might go away. Coming around to the side of the bed where he was, the fortifying scent of her perfume told him she was within millimetres of his face. Opening his eyes, all he could perceive through the bleary darkness were her smooth naked legs swaying before him and the thin tie of her gown, hung perpendicularly from both sides of her devious hips. Raising his eyes past her glistening mound and beyond her erect nipples which stood to attention awaiting inspection, their eyes finally met.

'Make love to me Paul. I love you, always have and I always will.'

'You're drunk,' he snarled. 'Cover yourself up will you, and go to bed.'

'Well, let me in then,' she laughed.

'Bernie, what are you doing?'

Kneeling down, she placed her hand under the snug duvet and found his manhood. Stroking gently she sought to incite an arousal. Giving her just enough time to conceive that he no longer functioned to her touch, he removed her hand firmly.

'For God's sake, you're to wed my brother.'

'I don't love him, let's elope in the morning, no one will ever find us,' she pleaded.

'You can't love me, you got engaged to Michael.'

'I needed someone when my mother died and he was the first who asked me out. It could have been anyone, I was vulnerable, but it's

69

you I've never stopped thinking about. I love you. I couldn't believe it when you came home, it was like a million Christmases wrapped up into one.'

For a minute he listened to her intently, but he didn't believe her, although on this occasion her words were genuine.

'Well, I don't love you. Why do you think I up and left without informing you. You were weighing me down like an anchor with your constant demands for marriage. I was drowning in my own pity. It was so claustrophobic with you that I couldn't breathe, it was sink or swim and I chose to stay afloat,' he lambasted.

'I can change, if we leave, we don't have to get married as long as I can be near you and it's me you come home to on a night, then I'll give you as much space as you need, I swear,' she begged, unconditionally.

'No, Bernie. Get it through your thick head, marry Michael and use your powers to steer him clear of the IRA or you'll be a widow to the Maze Prison, because that's where he's headed.'

Realising she was getting nowhere, she changed her tune.

'Okay, so don't love me then, but at least sleep with me tonight for old time's sake.'

'No, and come to think of it, I don't think I could satisfy your needs judging by your vocals the other night. You were never like that with me.'

'I put it on to make you jealous,' she revealed, as she began to bite her nails aware that her sexual shenanigans had dented her hopes of a reconciliation.

'Well I wasn't, hurt maybe, but never jealous. I've new things in my life now so just go away and let me live it.'

Tying up her gown in concession, she headed to the door then turned to him before leaving.

'I'll never give up until I've won you back; trust me, I'll make you love me again if it's the last thing I do.'

During the night, her zealous words, which had impacted upon his mind, haunted him, denying him sleep, for he knew it was a promise which she would strive to keep, no matter what consequences resulted.

Her rota having fallen sweetly for Christmas, Angela found herself drafted into the Accident and Emergency department of the Royal Victoria Hospital for the last nightshift of the year. New Year's Eve was one shift where the NHS got more than its pound of flesh from its already worked-to-the-bone staff. On a night when every big city throws its inhibitions to the wind, it was accountably the worst twelve hours of the year, not only were they forbidden to drink, although rules are made to be broken, but they also found themselves on the wrong end of drunken irascibility. Scuffles would even break out in the waiting room, which meant a police presence was a necessity if they were to perform their life saving duties.

The painstaking preparation for such a phenomenon had started early, yet at two minutes to the new year, the night had been relatively quiet. It was, however, between the hours of 1 a.m. and 4 a.m. that the fireworks started and the boat would begin to rock, as waves of drunks would flood into casualty. It was then a case of all hands to the pump and a fire-fighting exercise would launch amidst the mayhem.

For Angela, the only perk of the job tonight was that when the rush hour traffic began, she would have no time to dwell on her sad homelife. In the morning, she would be off for three days and she'd need them to recover both mentally and physically from the incidents of the next six hours.

The Irish people are renowned for their love of a gamble and it was no different in this institution. The New Year's sweepstakes had been placed, one for the amount of gastric lavages performed and one for the fatality count. This was the night when envious medics took pleasure in the art of stomach pumping, showing no mercy as they'd force down the rubber pipe with malice, if they couldn't have a belly full of alcohol then why should you? If you were unfortunate enough to experience this healing method, their crude unsympathetic treatment would make you think twice before drinking inordinately again.

Nursing, on this dawning of a new year, was a slimmer's paradise – you were guaranteed to sweat off at least seven pounds in all the rush. At 6 a.m. it was all over and she'd seen it all, blood, vomit, guts, violence, urine, excrement, a knife attack inside the hospital and an eye gouged from its socket by an empty glass that no one would fill.

New Year's Day was a non-event for Paul, who decided to steer well clear of Bernadette. He only appeared for his meals, ignoring her insinuating glances in favour of the walls or ceilings. When Saturday came, he enacted the same routine as he'd done on hogmanay. Bathed and dressed immaculately, he headed to Tommy's. In a single day, the advancement in his literary skills had come on leaps and bounds and

71

warranted a bonus. Handing Tommy the thickest text he had ever seen was in itself a compliment to his achievements.

'What is it?' Tommy inquired, his eyes almost popping from his head.

'That is the Encyclopaedia Britannica. It's not a story as such, but a compilation of facts. As well as helping your reading, it will educate you. I want you to read it ten times, yes I know it'll take months, but when you know it like the back of your hand you'll be the wisest man in all Ireland.'

'Will I really?'

'I swear,' promised Paul.

When they arrived at the dog track, Bernadette was busy sifting through Paul's belongings for clues to his whereabouts. With Michael due home in the early hours of Sunday, she knew it would be one of her last opportunities in the foreseeable future to persuade him of her undying love. If only she knew where he went when he got dressed up, smelling as if he'd just showered in aftershave. Having been through every pocket and drawer she was no further forward in learning the facts. Turning to leave the room, beaten in her quest, a small white pamphlet on his bedside cabinet caught her intuitive eye. Picking it up she read '. . . Dunmore Greyhound Stadium, racing every Thursday and Saturday evening. . . Having the evidence, she smiled at her powers of investigation, then left the scene of the crime to prepare for a surprise visit to the dogs.

Tonight the weather was kinder to Paul, the high winds had been replaced by a nippy frost which made straight for the perforations in his footwear, tingling his toes. Treading on the spot, he roared home the first winner and had that sanguine feeling that it might just turn out to be his night in more ways than one. Starting towards the same bookmaker who had relieved him of his £50, forty-eight hours earlier, he saw her arrive from the corner of his eye. Zeroing in on his target, he continued to advance for his money, losing all idea of the surroundings. As often happens when the mind drifts to a greater prize, an unknown force sneaks up from behind to wreak catastrophe. Totally transfixed to her catwalk movements, he barged straight into a collecting punter who was counting his blessings. The collision attracted undue attention from all around, including Angela. Apologising profusely to Hindu amounts, he glanced over to see that she was smiling at his misfortune. Telephone numbers and insurance policies exchanged he trudged back to Tommy with all the confidence knocked out of him.

72

'So how much did we get?' inquired Tommy rubbing his hands together.
'£25 for me and £5 for you.'
'That pretty girl's over there.'
'I know,' replied Paul.
'So, gonna talk to her again?'
'What's the point,' sighed Paul, all conviction lost in his embarrassment.
'Well, she just looked over this way.'
'Honestly?' he raised, clutching at straws. 'Is she still looking?'
'No, she's reading the programme, so go on, talk to her. I'll be all right here. I'm quite enjoying reading this card, but there are a few words I'm struggling with.'
'Which ones?' inquired Paul, biting his lower lip as he stalled for time.
'Blkd, and Hmp,' he spelled out.
'They're simply abbreviations,' enlightened Paul.
'What does that mean?'
'It means they're shortened words, squeezed up if you like, to save space. Blkd is condensed for baulked and Hmp is for hampered, Fa, fast away and so on. Are you catching on?'
'Aye, that's really clever, so this one here Impd, is that short for impudent?'
'No,' laughed Paul. 'That was a good guess though; it's for impeded, means the dog got into traffic problems during the race.'
'Oh I see,' he whispered, engrossed in attempting to work out ShHd.
'Right, I'm boldly going where no man in the history of the universe has ever dared go.'
'Where's that?' inquired Tommy, wide-eyed and enthralled.
'I'm going to see if I can melt the ice queen's heart.'
Leaving Tommy to have fun with the compressed wording, he approached her from another angle.
'Hi there, I just wanted to apologise for the other night. I must have given the impression of being trouble, but I'm not. I'm just a normal guy, can I have a second chance?'
'Have as many as you want but I'm not interested in you,' she told him.
'Can I get you a drink then?'
'I don't drink.'
'Then perhaps you could pick me a winner, you obviously know your stuff. Do you own a dog?' he persevered.
'No, I don't, and I don't gamble either.'

73

'So let me guess, you don't drink, smoke, gamble or like men, that means you're a nun who's escaped from the convent for the evening, am I right?'

'No, I'm a nurse actually. I just come here to get some peace and quiet, which at the moment you're doing your utmost to deny me.'

'I'm ill, I'm running a temperature.'

'Not funny.'

'How about a coffee then? It's a cold night, you need to keep warm,' he persisted.

'When I want a drink I'll get my own.'

'All right you win Nan, I give up,' he surrendered, holding his hands into the air.

'It's Angela actually,' she revealed.

For the first time since setting eyes upon her, he felt as if he had at last made a pioneering inroad and therefore decided to hang around just a little longer.

'Well, angelic Angela, my name's Paul, but you can call me Paul.'

'Yer not funny.'

'It would appear not,' he agreed.

'Ah there you are,' said Bernadette, coming between them from out of the blue. 'So this is where, and why, you sneak off twice a week.'

Having stared at the track throughout the duration of Paul's speech, Angela turned slightly to weigh up the competition and noticed an engagement ring winking at her. Turning away in fright, she headed for the exit, not wishing to be misconstrued as the guilty party for the lover's tiff that she was sure was about to ensue.

'What the hell are you doing here?' Paul snapped irately.

'I told you I won't give up. So you've got your eye on another woman or has it gone further than that? You never got smartened up like this for me. What's she got that I haven't? Not beauty that's for sure, she reminds me of a little pixie,' she raged, her bitchiness coming to the fore.

'You're just jealous,' he replied.

Brushing past her he raced from the stadium to explain his predicament to Angela. When he approached her she was busy scanning up and down the street for a cab.

'Angela, that wasn't what you thought.'

'What do I care?' she returned.

'I just wanted to put the record straight, that wasn't my girlfriend.'

'I worked that one out from her fingers, she was your fiancé.'

74

'No, she's my brother's fiancé, I swear on my mother's life.'

'As I said, I'm not in the least bit interested, besides you're just a charmer.'

'Ha,' he laughed. 'Chance would be a fine thing.'

Finally she flagged down a taxi.

'Can I take you out sometime?' he asked, as she was about to leave his life once again.

'You're joking, aren't you, why can't you get it through your thick skull, I don't like you.'

As the taxi crawled off towards Belfast, he solemnly walked back into the stadium to collect Tommy, his heart broken by her wounding words.

'Tom, I'm going home now, it's up to you if you want to stay.'

'I'll come with you,' he replied fearfully, moving directly in front of Paul to obstruct the oncoming apparition.

Noticing that something had petrified Tommy back into his shell, he probed for a explanation. 'What's wrong?'

'That girl with the red hair, she was one of the people who hit me and called me names at school and she's coming here now.'

'It's okay, you're with me now,' he assured him.

As Paul swung around to confront her, Tommy concealed his person, clinging tightly to his back like a newborn to its mother's breast.

'What do you want now?' he barked.

'I've a proposition for you,' she offered.

'I don't want to hear it, come on Tom, let's go home.'

'What are you doing hanging around with that imbecile?' she sneered spitefully. 'He'll bring you down to his level.'

Feeling the anger boil within, he mentally counted to ten, permitting his temper to simmer. He was so outraged, that if she had been a male he would have had no qualms in planting his fist into her face. Turning away from her evil tongue, they made for the exits and she stalked, biding her time to pounce with her proposal.

'I hope the bus comes soon, 'cause I'm freezing,' expressed Tommy, his teeth chattering as they neared the shelter, where he stood beguiled in front of a poster emblazoned to a billboard. It enticingly advertised, 'Come To Sunny Turkey'.

'Looking at that won't get you warm,' stated Paul. 'Come on, there'll be a bus along in a minute.'

'Wouldn't you like to go there? It looks so warm and beautiful.'

'Go where?' queried Paul, watching Bernadette approach.

75

'Turkey.'

'If I don't find a job soon I'll not be able to afford to buy a turkey never mind visit the country.'

All the way home Bernadette was never more than a few seats or steps behind them, yet no words were ever exchanged. Having bought himself a bottle of vodka from one of the multitudinous corner shops dotted off the Falls Road open at nine o'clock on a Saturday evening, he found himself tucked up in bed with the meagre solace of his bottle. Attempting to numb the mental pain, he began to drink himself into oblivion as his heart languished for Angela. Two hours after the ceiling had spun him to sleep, he was woken by a soft female hand stroking his thigh and the tickling of her sweet hair as she nuzzled into his neck.

'Angela,' he moaned, smiling, still half asleep.

'Try Bernadette,' she whispered.

Eyes opening impetuously as if a thousand volts were running through him, he jumped up and turned to face her, breathing a distillery over her as he whispered with ferocity. 'Get out of here this instant.'

Glancing at his digital clock radio, he saw that it was 1.30 a.m.

'For God's sake, Michael will be home any minute.'

'He won't be in until around 4 a.m.,' she allayed his fears. 'So that gives us plenty of time to get reacquainted.'

'Get lost will ye, I want nothing to do with you, you're just a tart.'

'Only for you Paul.'

'I mean it, get out.'

'Come on Paul, make love to me.'

'Not if you were the last woman on God's earth.'

'If you don't sleep with me, I'll tell Michael you tried to seduce me in his absence,' she grinned wickedly.

'You wouldn't dare.'

'Don't tempt me, I mean it, I will.'

A naked women in bed begging to be made love to versus another battering, it was a choice that most men would have found no difficulty in making, but Paul was adamant he would not succumb to her needs. He knew that it would only escalate to more blackmail demands in the long run.

'I don't care, I'll tell him how it really was,' he returned her serve.

'Now who's he gonna believe, you or me?' she stated smugly.

'Not even you could be that stupid.'

'Oh I will, you know I will.'

'Then do it then, go on, get out you conniving bitch, I don't care because I'll never want you again.'

Departing without a tail between her legs, she left him to another sleepless night of anxiety.

Chapter 4

No, I Won't Be Told There's a Crock of Gold at the End of the Rainbow

Unable to capture any sleeping pattern, Paul was still ruminating over whether Bernadette would keep to her word, when he heard Michael staggering about below, crashing into everything. Supported by the walls, he shuffled up stairs and crash-landed, nose down on his bed, no black box recorder requisite in this instance – pilot error, high on alcohol the verdict. After finally drifting into a light sleep, an amalgam of activity in the bathroom and his brother's seismic snoring in the next berth penetrated his snooze. Rising swiftly, he was met by shooting pains galloping around his head; lowering his sights to the floor in search of his attire, he spotted the quarter-full bottle of vodka and his stomach began to convulse in remembrance of last night's binge.

Grabbing his clothes and with his right hand cupped over his mouth, Paul rushed to the bathroom which had just been vacated. Lifting the toilet seat, he kneeled down to pray for absolution from his sins. Had it not been for the preceding occupant, he may have been granted a respite. As it was, his mother's potent perfume seduced his will to retain the distilled Soviet potatoes that his body was so determined to expel. Narcotised like a melliferous bee as he inhaled the polliniferous odour, there could only be one harvest. Retching down the pan, he spat clear the strings of membranous mucus which dangled from his mouth like spaghetti. He dried his wet eyes and gazed into the mirror to view an achromatic complexion; then widening his eyes as he moved in closer, he saw the thin red lines of ruptured blood vessels darting across his glazed sclera. Realising he was not the fairest of them all, he turned his back on the reflection of veracity and staggered to dress himself, before wavering downstairs in search of medicinal relief, in the form of black coffee and aspirins.

Sunday morning was his mother's weekly pilgrimage and it allowed her to have her chit stamped, so that when the time came for her to stand before St Peter at the pearly gates, she would be able to produce her entry pass. All said and done, it was a bit like collecting Green Shield stamps, a long haul for little reward, yet it was an equivocal covenant that she had no wish to question. Even if the other side turned out to be weak fiction, while on this planet, it ministered to give her all the strength she sorely needed to live from one week to the next.

Still light-headed, Paul jolted into the kitchen, his face looking as white as if it had been through a boil-wash.

'Did you have a good night, son?' his mother inquired, turning to meet his presence. 'You look like you've overdone it though, can I fix you a black coffee before I go to chapel?'

'If it comes with a side salad of painkillers,' he stammered.

Slumping into a chair, he sat with his head buried into his arm as he awaited remedial service.

The sounds of the seven seas swishing earlier and the rumbling of the cold pipes filling the cistern had disturbed Michael. Opening his eyes, he knew by the meandering crack along the ceiling that somehow he had found his way home. Rising from his bed on the impulse of seeing his beloved, he crept through to her room knowing full well that being Sunday, his mother would be at Holy Communion and his father would be dead to the world until opening time. Arriving at her bedside, he found her fast asleep sporting a Cheshire cat grin on her face. Removing his brewery-scented clothes, he joined her under the quilt and snuggled into her warm back. Too tired himself for action, he floated off to sleep, drugged by her lingering hypnotic perfume. An hour later when they stirred in unison, downstairs, Paul had dozed off again, finding that the seating arrangements in the kitchen made as good a bed as any.

'Have you missed me then?' asked Michael.

'You know I have,' she replied, still so in love with Paul that the thought of Michael lying beside her brought a state of revulsion sweeping over her.

'I bought you a present in Glasgow.'

'What is it?' she inquired, slightly raising her spirits at the expectation of a gift.

'A Celtic scarf,' he revealed. 'It'll keep your neck warm when you go to work.'

How bloody romantic, she deemed, not at all surprised by his concept in woman's beneficence.

'Thanks,' she replied, finding it difficult to conceal her disappointment that he'd made it home, having prayed the night before that some tragic accident might have befallen him, or he'd found a nice Scots lass. 'So how was the football match?' she probed, desperate to disguise the fact that things had turned in his short absence.

'Brilliant, we stuffed those orange bastards good and proper, two-nil, then we chased the fuckers down London Road and gave some a good hiding, but what about you?'

'What about me?'

'Well, what did you get up to on New Year's Eve?'

'I had a few drinks and an early night.'

'What about him, didn't try anything on did he?'

'No, he knows where I stand,' she said with conviction.

'That's good.'

As he rose from the bed his eye caught sight of her handbag and the dead give-away of the protruding white racecard. Ominously she watched and cringed as he removed it. Scrutinising the evidence his top lip curled to reveal his nicotine stained teeth.

'What the hell's this?' he demanded, knowing that Paul was an avid greyhound patron.

Dumb-struck at her own incompetence to eradicate the evidence, she swallowed stale air and her face turned sallow with panic.

'He . . . he asked me to go to the dogs with him last night,' she stuttered, like a scratched recording.

'And you couldn't say no, I should've known better,' he scathed.

'It wasn't like that,' she argued in defence.

'Then how was is it exactly?' he growled, dressing for combat with some urgency.

'He'd been pestering me since you left. I didn't tell you because I knew he'd stop when you returned and I didn't want any trouble to come of it. Your parents don't need it and I'd only get the blame.'

'The bastard,' he shouted. 'I'll knock his fucking head off.'

80

Suddenly his anger made him deaf to her appeals for calm. Sizzling downstairs like a lit fuse, he exploded into the kitchen to find his target curled up motionless, innocent to what was about to transpire. Dragged by the scruff of his best shirt, Paul awoke startled into a nightmare. Legs and arms riddled with pins and needles there was nothing he could do to protect himself from the raging bull. Opening the back door with his free hand, the aggressor then continued to drag his prey, who was still attached to the kitchen chair which he had become ensnared upon. Making for the concrete lawn of the backyard with a vengeance, the chair became jammed in the recess of the door, blocking any hopes of intervention from Bernadette who was on her way down to ringside.

By the time she had freed the obstacle the champion had regained his title and was circling his defeated opponent, lecturing him profoundly to alarm-clock volumes as he woke the sleepy neighbourhood. Lying battered with his hands protecting his head, Paul remained as static as a stone, fearing any slight movement might excite a second wave of the dreaded boots. Sucking her thumb at the door, Bernadette was also experiencing the misery the man she loved had been exposed to. Had Paul surrendered to her charms the previous night, then she would now be telling Michael the way it really was and he too could suffer the distress but, as of yet having no guarantee that she could win Paul back, she had to suffer the guilt. She had nowhere to go, after all. If she explained her true feelings to Michael then she would lose her dwelling and her hopes of a life with Paul, it was Catch 22 on the highest scale.

Disturbed by the emissions of violence below, their father opened his bedroom window and poked his head out into the bitter ambience to observe the aftermath. Satisfied that all was well, he returned to the stale, sweat-stained mattress.

In the back alley behind the redbrick wall, with the smashed glass cemented to the top to repel intruders, Tommy stood shaking, his fingers inserted to his eardrums, his eyes squeezed shut and his teeth biting hard on to a notional piece of cloth. Oh, how he wanted to scale the partition and help his friend, but he just didn't know how to. The boil lanced and the anger drained, Michael brushed past his shaking fiancé and into the kitchen where he began to fill the kettle with schizophrenic nonchalance. Once Paul was aware that his brother had finished dealing out the punishment, he forced himself up off the cold damp paving slabs as Bernadette looked on despairingly, wishing she could help.

81

'Why don't you go and help him?' sneered Michael. 'Because I know you're longing to.'

'It's you I love,' she retorted.

'You're a liar,' he roared, banging the kettle onto the worktop. 'You could have refused his advances but no, you ran after him, you're as bad as he is.'

'No, Michael, I swear, he said if I didn't go out with him, he'd lie to you that I had attempted to seduce him.'

In his twisted reasoning, it was an explanation that made total sense to him and it was a pacifying alibi that he had no alternative but to condone, only because he loved her, although he was sure, deep down, that he was her second choice. Even when Paul had been away in England, Michael had always tormented himself over her past. The thought of his future wife having been sampled by his brother ate at him like arthritic pain and it always would, as long as the cold draught of his brother was creeping around the scene. Liberating his frustration through violent conduct every now and again served only as temporary mitigation from his inferiority complex.

Having been half asleep had helped to act as suit of armour for Paul, cushioning the cascading blows which had rained on to his torso during the fierce assault. As he limped through the back gate, the only visual damage he appeared to have sustained was to his favourite shirt, which unlike the slight grazes and bruising on his limbs, was irreparable. Turning to the right, he noticed Tommy, his face fit to burst.

'I was just coming to see you, thought you might lend me a shirt,' Paul joked, looking on the bright side.

'Why did your father do that to you?'

'That wasn't my father, it was my brother, Michael. I think he's a little insecure now that I'm back in town. He's gonna marry my ex-girlfriend and he thinks I'm still holding a torch for her, but I'm not,' revealed Paul.

'Well, you could always come and stay with me if you want,' offered Tommy.

'Thanks for the offer, but I'll hang in here for a while longer. If I could only get a job I'd seriously consider getting a little place of my own.'

For the remainder of that day, while Tommy showed off the melioration in his studies, Paul deliberated, introspectively, over his future. By the time the dust had settled, he had come to a conclusion that he knew would please the majority. His decision was to wait and see if he could secure employment over the next few weeks. Failure to achieve this goal would result in his return to London, a runaway with motive on this occasion. For the next eleven days, as the severe winter frosts took hold, he kept out of Bernadette's and Michael's paths and suffered in the monotony of life without an income. As each tediously dark day inched by, he grew to despise the postman, as day after day he failed to bring any news of an interview. To cap it all, Angela had never returned to the racetrack since that fateful Saturday.

Rising as usual on the assumption that 'the early bird catches the worm,' Paul stood at the window with coffee in hand and waited on his newly found antagonist, the postman. It was Thursday, 14th January, no ordinary day. It was his twenty-second birthday, yet so far he had nothing to celebrate. Observing the overgrown paper boy a few doors away injected a momentary high as it had done every other morning, until he'd gone and left nothing, contravening in Paul's case that no news wasn't good news. Alerted by the thud and shuffle in the hall he sighed in pessimism, even though he knew at least his Giro would be there. Habitually first to the mail, he checked to discover no birthday cards but two far greater correspondences. The first was stamped with an Aer Lingus seal. Impetuously he tore the envelope and read excitedly. He had been selected for an interview on Monday 18th January at 11.30 a.m. at their city centre headquarters on Castle Street. Opening the second letter, it read that he had also been selected for an interview with the ferry company on Thursday 21st January at 1 p.m. at the Donegall Quay Ferry Terminal. Now he knew that within seven days his future in Belfast would be resolved for better or worse. Bursting into the kitchen to convey the good news to his mother, his father and brother were sitting around the breakfast table charging their batteries in preparation for work.

'Mom, I've two interviews to attend next week.'

'Oh, that's marvellous son and on your birthday of all days,' she congratulated. 'There's a few cards for you to open on the table.'

'Thanks,' he acknowledged.

From behind the Belfast Telegraph, his father voiced his deliberation: 'About bloody time you got off your backside, and if you don't get either then you can just head back to London.'

He left the scene with the wind blown from his sails and headed for Tommy's. He found him finger pressed hard down on to the text of the encyclopaedia.

'Take the day off, Tom, we've something to celebrate.'

'What's that then?' he asked, lifting his head to see two envelopes being flaunted in his face.

'I've two interviews to attend next week and it's my birthday today.'

'Happy Birthday,' Tommy said coolly before returning to the book. It wasn't envy, it was just that Paul appeared to be making no effort to find him a job as he'd pledged.

'What's up with you today?' queried Paul, noticing Tommy's couldn't-care-less attitude.

'It's just that you said you'd help find me a job and you haven't tried once yet,' he moaned dejectedly.

'I will Tom, but you need to learn more before we can throw you into the lion's den of an interview. Let's just get our preparation right and we can establish a pedigree, okay?'

'Paul.'

'What?'

'Do you honestly think I can turn out to be a normal person?'

'You are normal, there's nothing wrong with you, we just need to build your confidence high enough for you to realise it. If you doubt yourself then we may as well call it a day now. When you go out into the world, I want you to hold your head up high and look people in the eye and always remember that you are an equal. It's gonna happen for both of us, I can feel it in my bones,' he lectured.

Having never missed a meeting at Dunmore this year in the hope that Angela might make a reappearance, tonight would see no deviation from this routine. On the last three occasions he'd managed to convince himself that there was a plausible excuse. She'd be working early shifts, or afternoons, and was too tired to attend was always his prognosis.

Little did he know, but she was deliberately boycotting the track because she feared being dragged into a domestic wrangle that was none of her business. Having been gifted the best birthday messages he could have ever wished for, she was to give him no extra surprise by making an appearance.

The last few days leading up to his first interview dragged by in the now accustomed grind. Early rise to avoid his family, then all daylight hours spent laboriously feeding Tommy's hungry brain. The only highlights were the racing on Saturday evening and the forlorn hope of seeing her again. Once again, she did not arrive to treat his eyes and his money had evaporated in the heat of the gambling. Dehydrated of her

84

presence, his mind began to blur and trick him as he saw mirages of her almost everywhere he walked, yet when they turned round it was never her and the cherry-red lipstick that had sealed his fate.

In front of the bathroom mirror, he shaved away the weekend's disappointments and understood that today could be the pivot on which his stay in Northern Ireland hinged. Removing his one and only suit in life from the depths of his wardrobe, he couldn't believe his bad luck. Having laid dormant for almost a year the damp winter had taken its toll, attacking with venom, to leave the cloth diseased with patches of white mildew and an offensive deathly odour. Existing on a weekly state handout, he had no means of finance to purchase a replacement, so it would have to suffice.

Having preached to Tommy about the rigorous preparation required for the Grand National course of an interview, he had fallen at the first fence. Cradling the contaminated article, he headed for the quarantine of his mother's kitchen to see if she could resuscitate its fitness for purpose. Using a wet flannel and fresh air spray for antibiotics, the operation was an initial success but, like any patch-up job, the symptoms would reoccur without the correct treatment. In its prime, it had been a suit for all occasions, profound flexibility at its utmost, for it had fitted for a capacious range of events, such as weddings, christenings, funerals, functions, interviews and even nightclubs. Dressed in the grey jacket and matching trousers, which had been designed with objective rather than style in mind, and with hair gelled to thwart the wind, as well as giving him that 'just walked from the shower' clean look, he headed to collect his lucky mascot in the shape of Tommy.

The butterflies were stirring in his stomach to produce nerves as he arrived at his friend's, just like the ones he experienced every time he saw Angela. Entering the house, his rebellious kidneys forced him to make straight for the bathroom. He refused a coffee as he decided it best to take no chances in arriving late for his interview. Living in the Falls and being dependent on public transport was a dangerous pursuit if you were restricted to a timetable. Nine out of ten destinations had to be attained via the city centre, like their twice-weekly adventure to the greyhound track. However, today, a solitary bus from outside his house would take him the short journey to his assignation. Although Paul held a driving licence, he had never been able to afford to run a car.

Bernadette's embezzling had meant that as fast as he'd earned it, she'd always been able to find a cash register hungry enough to consume all his wage; like a leech she'd bled him dry. Looking back on it, he'd bought the smile on her face and carried the argument that marriage, or even courtship for that matter, was but an institution for legalised prostitution.

Reaching Castle Street, deep in the heart of the beating city, he checked his watch to note that he had an hour to kill before his grilling. Deciding to waste the time window shopping amongst the plethora of brightly adorned eye-catching emporiums at hand, only added to his despondency. So much within arm's-length reach, yet all untouchable to his empty hands - still, he had the chance at his fingertips to change all that. If he could only sell himself to the airline then he would possess the lifeline of an income. Never had he worshipped or idolised it, but to a certain degree money was his god, for when he had prosperity, it was heaven and when he was destitute, it was hell.

Stopping outside a jeweller's outlet, he stared at the most magnificent diamond-encrusted engagement ring he had ever seen, and the vision of an angel flew across his mind. Turning to the crowds of passers-by, he searched in vain for her, then smiled, convinced that they would cross paths again. Looking at his watch, it was now 11.10 a.m., time to make himself known to his prospective employer.

'Okay, Tom, I'll have to go now, cross your fingers and wish me luck.'

'I will, how long do you think you'll be?' inquired Tommy, already feeling the chill bite at his nose.

'I honestly couldn't say. Why don't you find a café to get you out of the cold and have a hot drink. I would have thought that I'll be out between twelve and twelve-thirty.'

Bidding Tommy farewell, he straightened his tie and marched towards the poignant edifice of Aer Lingus's head office. He entered the architecturally ostentatious interior, with its lavish putting-green carpet, trickled up to the flag and introduced himself to the artificial image of the Miss World contender dressed as an air hostess. Told to take a seat and wait, he reclined into a plush leather-upholstered chair then scanned the opulent surroundings, wondering if the grounded stewardess found it painful to smile constantly for eight hours a day. He picked up the company sales pitch from the bullet-proof-thick glass table, and flicked through the pages anxiously as his mind began to freeze with the protocol.

At 11.35 a.m. after a five-minute delay, a tall gent with silvery-white hair offered his gold-ornamented hand. Carrying a Filofax for flamboyance, he taxied Paul down the corridor and into a spacious office, where already waiting were a young yuppie bimbo, most probably the Silver Fox's personal secretary, and a senior female flight attendant, who had obviously passed her sell-by date, judging by the thick coats of warpaint which failed to mask the wrinkles of age. After offering Paul a seat, the pristine effigy of a tailor's mannequin took his place in the centre of the jury before making the preludes. After a brief perusal of Paul's letter of application, he began. 'So, Paul, what was the attraction to apply for this position?'

'Well, to be honest I love to travel and the thought of seeing Europe was the real temptation and I love to meet people,' he rifled nervously, feeling the blood rush to his head.

'What do you think the appointment actually entails?' he inquired.

'Seeing that our passengers needs are catered for and putting their minds at ease, as well as providing a friendly comforting service that'll keep them coming back to use the airline again and again.'

Pointing his gold pen on to Paul's application, he continued to investigate. 'It says here you enjoy flying. So how many times have you actually flown?'

Clearing the bile settling in his dry thorax before swallowing it, he lied, 'About a dozen times.'

Paul had never graced the skies in his life, but he knew the truth would reduce his odds of securing the position. Having soared through the first twenty minutes of the interview after overcoming the initial turbulence of nerves, he had aired himself as the prime candidate, yet engine trouble was just over the horizon, when the sly fox paused the nib of the pen on the interviewees address and thought cunningly. 'Clonard Street, isn't that in the Falls?'

'Yes,' replied Paul softly, knowing that the question propelled impended overall disaster.

'Okay, that's about it for us. Is there anything you'd like to ask?'

'No thanks, I think you were very thorough,' said Paul, opting for the parachute, rather than the kamikaze exodus.

'Okay,' he said rising. 'Obviously we have more applicants to interview, but you can expect a decision from us either way within the next week.'

Leaving the building empty, Paul had made his own executive judgement. Outside Tommy was waiting, itching for the news.

'Well did you get the job?'

'No, they shot me down in flames,' he revealed.

87

'Why?'

'I guess my geography wasn't up to scratch. I've decided, I'm going back to London, Tom. There's nothing for me here.'

'But what about the girl?' reminded Tommy vehemently, not wishing to lose his one and only friend.

'The girl was just a dream and as for you, well, you're doing fine now. Just keep at it and you'll find a job in due course.'

'But you promised you'd always be my friend,' he implored, lip curling close to tears.

'And I will. I'll keep in touch through the post, besides it'll help your reading and writing.'

Head bowed, Tommy trudged behind as they made for the bus stop.

'So when are you going?'

'First thing in the morning. I'll phone the hotel where I worked before; they said they'd have me back anytime,' revealed Paul, realising that the quicker he made the break, the less chance there was of him being press-ganged into staying by his sympathetic traits.

'Why don't you wait until your second interview on Thursday, then go?' urged Tommy.

'No, it'll just be the same come Thursday.'

'Oh please, we can go to the library now and get some books to practise your geography, you said it's never too late to learn.'

'I'm sorry, but I've confused you again. When I said geography I actually meant where we live, the Falls,' explained Paul. 'When they found out you could see it written all over their faces. Bomb alert. I could have been Sigmund Freud for all they knew, but when they found out where I lived then they'd still have overlooked me.'

'I know that Freud bloke,' said Tommy.

'Good,' returned Paul, pleased that his gift of the encyclopaedia was already paying handsome dividends.

'Aye, he's the one who looks like his dog on those meaty-morsel adverts on the telly.'

'No, I meant . . . oh, never mind,' said Paul, losing his patience in the melancholy of his failure.

'So are you gonna stay, at least until the next interview?'

'No, I don't think so. I'm not being a pessimist but a realist, nothing's gonna happen for me around here.'

'Well at least toss a coin, please,' badgered Tommy, unwilling to be disowned. 'I'm sure you'll get the other job.'

88

As if by an act of god, a uniform joining the queue imbued his sights and helped him to focus his mind on procrastination. A young nurse, no doubt on her way to the RVH, watched as he spun the coin into the air.

'Heads I stay, tails I go. Heads it is,' Paul revealed to his friend, who could not bear to watch. 'Guess we have a stay of execution.'

As Paul straightened his tie, he glanced out from the bedroom window and saw the sky was a clear, cadaverous blue and the streets were arid, even the hardy perennials were shooting to life, tricked by the uncharacteristic clement spell. In Paul's eyes, it was no doubt the lull before the storm.

Journeying to Donegall Quay, Paul couldn't help but think that he'd forgotten something - it was his holdall. If no employment was to be offered, as he'd predicted, then tomorrow he would be making the same trek to the ferry terminal. Heading for this interview, the tension and fears were no longer a part of him, it was Tommy's nails that were bitten to the quick. For the last four weeks, he had found something to believe in, an escape tunnel from his prison, and now it was on the brink of collapse. Alighting as near to the terminal as the double-decker would sanction, their nasal passages were met head on by a pungent fishy odour, which blended with the mordacious salty breeze to manufacture a nauseous wallpaper stripper.

In an attempt to escape the rancid mélange, they walked briskly along the quayside, where below the majestic River Lagan embraced the Irish Sea and Paul was reminded of a Hitchcock movie that had petrified him as a child. Hunching for safety from the shrills and shrieks of the squabbling scavenger seabirds which flapped uncontrollably over rotting morsels, he realised that the intermittent drops of rain descending from the cumulus-free sky, were in fact the seagulls' method of letting them know that they had infringed their territory. Producing an emergency handkerchief from his pocket, Paul spat onto the cloth before wiping away the ruinous carnage of the bombing raid.

'Isn't that supposed to be lucky?' asked Tommy.

'So they say, but I'm not banking on it,' confirmed Paul, in defeatist tone.

'You don't want this job' do you?'

'Of course I do, I'm just not pinning my hopes upon it this time. I've resigned myself to the fact that people from the Falls aren't allowed to broaden their horizons, so it'll spare me the disappointment. Anyway Tom, this is it, the end of the road,' he stated as they arrived at the offices of the terminal. 'Wish me luck.'

'I always do, but my mommy used to say that sometimes you've got to make your own.'

Taking Tommy's food-for-thought, he entered the building, announced his arrival and was instructed to have a seat and wait. Sitting with elbows on knees and his hands supporting his heavy head, he looked beyond the huge glass panes out on to the peaceful channel and for the first time in his life, he really knew where he wanted to be. He rose to meet the outstretched hand, smiled and a surge of confidence flashed through his body to form static electricity. As their hands met they fused with a crisp crack which both men felt.

'Must be the carpet,' laughed the short rotund individual, who had no suit jacket but sweaty palms. 'I'm Martin South, onboard services manager.'

'Paul O'Donnell, pleased to meet you,' he returned.

Following the stout asthmatic to his office, the conversation was light and jovial as they immediately hit it off, sharing the same common vernacular. Entering the compact berth with its tarnished walls and well trodden carpet he took a seat and was offered a coffee.

'No thanks, I never drink while I'm interviewing,' joked Paul, feeling totally at ease in the pragmatic surroundings.

'Ha,' laughed the decision maker. 'A joker.'

'Well, you've got to be, living in this city,' added Paul.

'Aye, I suppose you're right. So, do you smoke, Paul?'

'Only when I'm on fire,' he returned.

'Very charismatic aren't you and that's exactly what we intend to portray in our business. Anyway, I do, so if you have no objections I'd like to smoke.'

'Not at all, fire away,' said Paul, animated with his witticisms.

Reading his application as he lit his cigarette the man began. 'So eight 'O' Levels, engineering background, before you jumped ship to London, any reason?'

'Just needed a change from the humdrum of factory life, felt as if I wanted to get out and meet people,' half-lied Paul.

'Well, you'll certainly meet people as a steward on one of our vessels, but it's hard work, not plain sailing, if you'll pardon the pun.'

90

'I don't mind hard work, it makes the day sail by, if you'll pardon mine,' he answered positively.

'Excellent, so Paul, seasickness, do you suffer?'

'Not that I'm aware, but I've only made two ferry trips,' he replied truthfully.

'And you're not on any drugs or medication and have no long term ailments?'

'None whatsoever.'

'Great, well, if you're offered the position it will be subject to a medical and a survival course. Nothing too heavy, we just have to make you aware of safety regulations and first aid procedures; the law is becoming more stringent every day and safety is paramount, our number one policy. So, you live in Clonard Street.'

Having sailed on the crest of a wave, Paul was suddenly dumbstruck and felt as if he had just been torpedoed from the water.

'Yes, is that a problem?' he reciprocated.

'No, not at all, I was brought up a few streets from there in Lucknow Street. Do you know it?'

'Aye, it's just up the road,' replied Paul, feeling that perhaps the tide was turning in his favour.

'Well, I started out as a steward and made me way up, got out of the Falls and here I am, large as life to tell the tale, but it was hard work. So when can you start?'

'What, I've got the job?' quizzed Paul, not sure that he was interpreting the question correctly.

'As I said, subject to medical and survival course.'

'As soon as you want,' said Paul excitedly.

'Great, I'll get my secretary to book you on the survival course for Monday, she'll give you all the details of your contract etceteras; the pay's not bad and there's always overtime for sickness cover when required.'

Rising from his chair, he offered his hand again, which Paul gratefully accepted.

'Well Paul, welcome aboard.'

After collecting his itinerary and contract of employment, he walked exuberantly out to meet Tommy. With fist clenched and a new strain of adrenaline pumping through his body, he wrapped his arms around his waist and lifted him off the ground.

91

'I got it, Tom, you genius, we're gonna celebrate tonight.'

Strolling back towards the city centre they breathed in the now sweet aroma of yeast, fish and salt and jumped high into the air, grabbing at the seagulls, letting them know that the worm had turned.

A few miles away, in the casualty department of the RVH, Angela was nearing the end of her beleaguering shift. Following the doctor into a cubicle with drawn curtains, she saw that her last patient of the day was an old dishevelled man attached at the wrist to an RUC officer. He was obviously drunk to hell, judging by the prominent waft of spirit emitting from his person, so the policeman acted in the role of ventriloquist for the outcast of society.

'We picked him up outside a bar in the city centre. He's been drinking all morning, then got into a fight. As far as I can ascertain it's only the cut above his eye that's in need of repair.'

Going on the officer's statement, the doctor used his healing hands to touch around the wound, feeling for any tell tale signs of fracture. Satisfied that a few butterfly stitches and an anti-tetanus jab would remedy the injury, he passed the buck to Angela then left the scene for his next patient. Uncomfortably aware that the constable was eyeing her up, she began to clean around the wound with cotton wool soaked in antiseptic lotion and urgency.

'So, I bet you see some sights in this line of work,' he activated the conversation.

'You get used to it after a while,' she replied, concentrating on her work.

'So when do you finish work today?' he inquired.

Glancing at his face for the first time, she captured a picture on which to make her decision, knowing exactly what his next move was going to be. Tall, well built, clean shaven with dark hair was all she saw, a typical, off-the-production-line policeman, she thought. Then again, his hazel eyes did appear to have a gentle side to them.

'In about five minutes,' she said, placing the mock sutures into place.

'Any plans for tonight?' he probed, looking away, afraid to face the answer.

'Yes, I'm going to the greyhound racing at Dunmore,' she revealed, removing a syringe from the toolbox of her kidney bowl, which made the swaying vagabond's eyes dilate with apprehension.

'With anyone in particular?' he angled.

'No, as always, on my own,' she dangled a carrot.

'I've never been to the dogs,' he revealed. 'What's it like?'

'Not everyone's cup of tea I imagine, but I enjoy it.'

'So, do you think I could perhaps accompany you there tonight?'

Preparing the tetanus injection, to save her client's jaw from locking, so that he would no doubt drink himself further into trouble, she thought it through Well, I don't fancy him that's for sure, but what harm can it do. Besides, the bitchy redhead might be there, waiting for a fight, convinced that I've been seeing her fiancé. The concept of police protection certainly had its attraction even if his appearance was less than arresting.

'You're welcome to join me if you want.'

'Great, shall I pick you up from your house?' he asked.

'No, I'll make my own way there and I'll make my own way home and I'll be honest with you now, I'm not looking for a boyfriend, but I could use the company. If you can't handle that, then forget it,' she stated her independence with verve.

Having been smitten by her beauty, he wasn't willing to surrender his hard-fought gain that easily. 'So what time do I meet you there?'

'About 8 p.m. That's what time the bus gets me in, but I always get a taxi home. I don't trust the city centre late at night,' she said, instructing the down-and-out to drop his trousers.

'So, what's your name then?' he questioned, moving with the tramp.

'Angela.'

'I'm Alan.'

'So what happens to him now?' she asked, removing the needle from the drunk's bleached flesh.

'I'll take him back to the cells to dry out for a bit. We couldn't let him loose into society in that state. He'll be cautioned, then he'll re-offend next Thursday. It's the old classic isn't it, what's green and gets you pissed?'

'I have no idea,' she returned shaking her head in confusion.

'A Giro cheque,' he laughed.

Not that impressed by his humour, she checked the watch invertedly pinned to her uniform. 'He's all yours, take him away,' she chastised in matronly fashion.

Arriving outside his front door, Paul was bursting to convey the proud tidings to his mother.

93

'So, Tom, where shall we celebrate tonight?'

'I'd like to go to Dunmore,' he replied.'I like it there.'

'Well, I was thinking more of banishing the bad memories of the dole with a good skinful of drink in one of those trendy pubs in the city,' said Paul.

'You can have a good drink at the track,' returned Tommy, intimidated at the thought of leaping from the serene pond of Dunmore into the tumultuous shark-infested ocean of the Belfast night-life scene.

'Why don't you come in and meet my mother and we can discuss it over the finest coffee in Belfast?'

'Are you sure?' he asked, eyes lighting up at the invite and honour.

'I'll just pop in and clear it with her, back in a tick.'

Entering her kitchen, his beaming countenance expressed the news without reports.

'You got it, didn't you?' she asked, excitedly.

'Aye, I start a survival course on Monday. I can't believe it, my ship's come in at last.'

'Oh son, I'm so pleased for you,' she congratulated, throwing her arms around him and squeezing him tightly.

'Mom, my friend Tommy is outside, is it all right if he comes in for a coffee?'

'Of course it is, son, bring him away in.'

Racing to the front door, he called him forward. Entering the hall, Tommy's wide eyes darted over the pretty floral wallpaper and looked down in amazement as his feet sank into the lush green fairway of the carpet. At this moment, if someone had told him this was Buckingham Palace, he would have had no cause to doubt the validity of such a statement. Struck by the spic and span cleanliness, his heart yearned for his mother.

'Mom, this is Tommy, Tommy, my mom,' introduced Paul.

'Pleased to meet you son, would you like a cup of coffee?'

Nervously, he accepted. As his friend's mother made the drinks, he stood rigid, overawed by the ceremony, while Paul gave her a scrupulously technical commentary of his successful interview. Noticing that Tommy was sticking out like a blind cobbler's thumb, his mother offered him a seat. Accepting her compassion, he sat at the table and sipped his drink, fighting the urge to put his elbows on the tabletop. When Paul had elaborated every last technicality of his occupational gain for the fourth consecutive time, it had now become a fisherman's tale.

94

'So you'll be hitting the town tonight to celebrate,' his mother presumed.

'Aye,' he replied, turning his attentions to Tommy, who had sat engrossed in the lecture of how Paul had fought off a navy of applicants to become the Poseidon of the Irish Sea.

'Tom wants to go to Dunmore, don't you?'

'Aye, I like that place and I feel so safe there,' he returned.

'Well, why don't you pair stop here for your supper before you go?' invited his mother.

Checking his watch, Paul saw that it was now 4 p.m; within an hour the workers would all be home demanding sustenance. Knowing that Tommy would be uncomfortable, he refused the offer for him.

'No thanks, Mom, Tommy's already prepared his meal for this evening, haven't you?'

'Aye, Mrs O'Donnell, maybe another time,' he said politely.

'Well, Tom, I'll call for you at a quarter to seven,' said Paul, rising to show him the door.

After being ushered from Paul's warm entrancing home, Tom walked solemnly through the dismal twilight to his derelict, cold and lonely abode.

Their government handouts having fallen nicely, the funds were available for a merry night. Standing at the bar inside the stadium, they were already on their third pint as the clock edged towards eight o'clock and still Paul was replaying his successful afternoon.

Alighting the bus, Angela headed to the turnstiles where Alan had waited patiently for the last fifteen minutes, wondering if she would really show. Almost swooning as she neared, he couldn't believe the transition in her appearance. If he had thought of her as an attraction a few hours ago, she had now become an infatuation. Her long black hair, having been tied in a pony-tail and veiled in a paper hat, now flowed like spun silk on a summer's breeze in its emancipation. The one piece, dowdy uniform which she had to conform to had been replaced by stylish black trousers, a lemon lambs' wool sweater and a camel coat. Oozing natural class, she needed only a thin film of blood-red lipstick and a pair of petite golden earrings, to become a modern day Cinderella and strike Cupid's arrow into the heart of any Prince Charming.

'I didn't think you were coming,' he said.

'Neither did I,' she admitted.

Earlier that afternoon her mother had thrown one of her perfidious tantrums and had accused Angela of attempting to poison her. At the height of her alienation, she had threatened to call in the police, but by teatime the drugs had tranquillised her on a magic carpet ride through clouds of cotton wool.

Doing the chivalrous honours, Alan paid her into the stadium which met with instant disapproval.

'Here,' she attempted to hand him her entrance fee.

Refusing to accept her money signified the beginning of the end. 'Take the money or I'll go home,' she insisted. 'This isn't a date, I thought I made that crystal clear.'

'What's the matter with you?' he probed, taken aback at her severe stance.

'If you pay for everything you're gonna be pretty miffed at the end of the evening. I'm not available and I won't be bought.'

Leaving him in her wake, she headed to the terraces to view the action. Numbed by her cold words, he realised that she was out of his jurisdiction, but she was so beautiful, even if nothing was to develop, what harm could be done by having a second bite at the cherry. Adopting a never-say-die attitude, he followed her into the track then offered to buy her a drink.

'No, I'll get you one to make up for paying me in, so what will it be?' she asked, reinstating the position.

'Just a coffee,' he replied, subdued by her intense will to have the final say.

Up above in the gods of the bar, Paul was drinking as if it was going out of fashion as his high appeared to have no limits. Returning from the bar with a fourth round of drinks, he glanced at the race card and spotted that the trap two runner was named 'Night Nurse'. Having come with the noble intentions of a gamble free evening, he now decided that a small flutter was in order. Looking across the track to the starting traps he saw that the dogs were making their final approach to the lids.

'I'll be back in a minute,' he told Tommy. 'I'm just gonna stick a few quid on this two dog.'

Dancing down the worn wooden steps to the bookmaker's plinth, he placed a £5 wager at odds of 4/1. Receiving his docket he kissed it and turned to look at the spot where she always stood. His jubilant smile turned to one of melancholy, and he froze as he watched her hand her male companion a steaming polystyrene cup. Turned to stone, he remained transfixed to the spot, back turned to the evolving race. As the dogs thundered past behind him, her bewitching eyes engaged his. For a split second they stared at each other before synchronously their gaze was deflected in opposite directions.

Trudging back to Tommy, he was in a state of deep trauma. Shaking with devastation, he slumped into a chair and focused on the ashtray centrally positioned on the tabletop.

'That was a bit unlucky, wasn't it,' comforted Tommy.

'What?' inquired Paul, sluggishly.

'Your dog finishing second.'

Hearing no reply, he pushed further. 'Paul, is everything all right, you don't look well.'

'I need a cigarette,' he stammered.

'But you don't smoke,' reminded Tommy.

'Well, it's time I started then, isn't it.'

Staggering in a daze to the cigarette machine, he fed the slot and brought the packet back to the table. He felt completely torn apart by the vision, which had rocked his foundations to almost collapse. He began to unwrap the cellophane with about as much finesse as a child opening a Christmas present. Removing a cigarette, he placed it between his thin pouting lips.

'Matches, get me some matches from the bar,' he ordered Tommy.

Acting as if it was a dying soldier's last request, Tommy surged to the bar and purchased the sulphur-coated splints. Hands quivering, he struck the tool of arson and held it to the end of Paul's stupidity. Sucking hard the clouds of toxic combustibles raced towards his lungs to stem the flow of his adrenaline pump. At first his respiratory system defended valiantly, sending the smoke back with a violent cough and splutter but, on the sixth rapid fire draw, they were able to fight no more, as the poisonous fumes engulfed their resistance. Having now been captured by the enemy, like a prisoner of war they would now become dependent on the foe for sustenance. As he stubbed out his first cigarette, he now felt physically as well as mentally nauseous.

For half an hour solid, Alan had chipped away at her invisible shield to no effect. Exhausted by his haranguing advances and conceiving that they could never share a platonic relationship, she decided it was time to read him his rights.

'I have to go home now,' she said. 'I have another early start tomorrow, be seeing you around.'

Starting towards the exit, he followed her. 'Wait, I'll drive you home.'

'No, I told you I'm very capable,' she stressed, wishing she had never agreed to meet him in the first place.

'Well do you think I could take you out on a proper date, say Saturday night?'

'No, I'm not ready for any relationship,' she replied, blunting his sharp unremitting tongue.

'Well, if you change your mind then perhaps you could give me a ring?'

Realising that if she conceded a little ground, she'd quickly win the battle of escaping his persistency, she agreed. She removed a pen from the Swiss army knife of her handbag and jotted down his telephone number. Writing him off, she headed from the track to hail a cab, filing his number in the street. Feeling egotistically confident that she would make his phone ring, he returned to the stadium to watch the last few races.

Paul took a second cigarette in as many minutes, lit it and coughed again.

'What's it like?' inquired Tommy, passively inhaling the fumes, excited at the chance of reliving the childhood he was denied.

Lifting the carton he tossed it gently to his friend. 'Go ahead,' urged Paul. 'You can't knock it until you've tried it.'

Taking a cancer stick from the packet, he placed it between his lips and struck the match. His face turned red as he choked and spluttered on the foul blue smoke. Catching his breath and his colouring now green, he grimaced and decided to kick the habit before it kicked in.

'I don't like them,' he revealed, stubbing the health offender into the graveyard of ends.

Head spinning with the introduction to the nicotine, Paul decided he needed fresh air and wanted to abandon the meeting now that his night had been ruined by his own misconstructions. As he left the bar, the frosty night amalgamated with the alcohol and cigarette toxins to turn his head into a honeycomb. He headed for the exit, passing the spot where Angela and her escort had been standing, to find that she was not in view, yet he was. Walking past her choice, Paul looked him up and down and dispelled the myth that it's only women who are bitchy.

What a deg, he thought, not impressed by her poor taste in the opposite sex.

At the bus shelter, he doubled over and vomited, exorcising the demonic cigarettes and alcohol from his system to form a putrid pool of liquid from which the smoke arose.

In the back room of Paddy's Bar, Michael sat awaiting the weekly debriefing with his Intelligence Officer, who had not yet arrived. Of late, the meetings had started to become an irrelevant chore in Michael's dark eyes. Every Thursday he'd arrive with the high hopes that his superiors would give him the green light to declare war, but on every occasion thus far, he'd leave with a stalemate. Guerrilla warfare was a slow and calculated business, where the targets were painstakingly and ethically selected, with the maximum damage intended with least repercussion in mind; like any modern business venture the cost outweighed the motive. Certain targets could incite a civil war and the price of that consequence was too high to pay. In the land where the soldiers came from to instil the peace, they were ignorant of the facts that for every Protestant murdered, the retaliation was threefold and that was a media concealed truth that would always bring an advantage to the ruling government. Michael's train of thought was that if his country was to regain its rightful territory, then it could only be achieved by a mass national uprising and, if need be, a fight where the last man standing in all Ireland would win the day. Many who also subscribed to his point of view had splintered and formed their own paramilitary factions. If the amber light stuck much longer, he would have to review his allegiances.

Tonight as he waited patiently, things were different, although his mind was tuned into war, it concerned his love life. Bernadette had captured his heart and turned his world upside down, yet part of his mind was convinced that her feelings towards him were no longer there, now that his pretty-boy, young brother had returned from his failed crusade. Suddenly, the creaking of the door startled him from his festering worries.

'Sorry I'm late, but I was held up with one thing and another,' apologised the regnant voice, attached to the metabolically thin man, with a face riddled with the scars of a youthful defeat against chickenpox.

99

Limping to the other end of the room he opened the meeting. 'I've good news, we have a mission for you.'

'Aye?' said Michael, rising his head to the occasion.

'This one's nice and easy for you, no travelling involved. Saturday night at 7 p.m. as regular as clockwork, yer man will be leaving his house in Argyle Street via the back alley, as always, and he'll head south. At the north end of the alley three doors from his house, there's a streetlight, it'll be painted with a black X to mark the spot, so you can't miss it. Here's the key to open the lamppost, inside you'll find a 9 mm Browning automatic pistol. It will already be loaded with one up the spout, so just cock and fire. You're not to eliminate him though, just make sure he doesn't walk again. Once you have the gun, position yourself down the alley so that there's no mistaking yer man. Order him to face down and blow his kneecap out from behind, if you push the gun into the cup of his leg it'll act as a silencer. When it's done head south and drop the gun over the wall of the last house on the right, someone will be waiting there to conceal the evidence. Finally, make your way back here, to confirm your alibi. It's as easy as that. Oh, and one more thing, he'll be armed, probably a knife, so be careful.'

'So who's the target?' quizzed Michael, slightly confused as why his initiation should be in the Falls district.

'No names, just remember this face.'

Reaching into the inside pocket of his raincoat he removed a brown paper envelope. Tearing it open he hobbled over and placed it in front of Michael's anticipating eyes.

'This guy went to the same school as me,' revealed Michael, confused by the mark.

'It'll be dark, mask your face and there'll be no need for communication, the gun'll do all your talking for you.'

Retrieving the print from the table, the lame man produced a Zippo lighter, then set the evidence alight.

'But he's a Catholic,' contended Michael. 'I didn't think I'd be killing my own people.'

'I told you, don't you fucking listen,' he stormed, banging his fist on the table to show the rookie he meant business. 'It's just a punishment for being a naughty boy, he's had his verbal and written warnings and now we must take disciplinary measures.'

'But why? Surely we need every Catholic available to fight, for when the time comes?'

'This guy's bleeding us dry, he's dealing in hard drugs. How would you like it if he sold your girlfriend some lethal concoction and she ended up in a coffin?'

'She doesn't do drugs,' argued Michael.

'Okay son, let me put it another way. Yer man has no authorisation to vend, we're losing money hand over fist and what do you think pays for the weapons to fight this fucking war? Bastards like him mean that we won't be able to arm everyone for this grand civil uprising that you've got your heart so intent on,' explained his superior, informing him of the facts of life.

'Think about it, son, you don't think we're gonna give you a licence to start shooting up every Protestant in this city, that has to be earned. Now, if you do well here, this will stand you in good stead for future advancement. Who knows, this time next year you could be planting Semtex. The choice is yours, don't fuck it up, don't let history repeat itself. I think that concludes our business, so if you've no more questions, I'll be on my way.'

'What if there's a patrol in the vicinity?' inquired Michael.

Smiling wryly, his Intelligence Officer mitigated his fears on that score. 'Don't you worry about that. I can guarantee there'll be no soldiers within a mile radius, they'll be too busy engaged at Ballymurphy.'

As he headed for the door, he noticed that Michael was still showing signs of uncertainty about the task. Reaching the exit he turned and made the position clear once and for all:

'Oh son, if you decide that you don't have the stomach for this, don't ever acknowledge me again and if I ever hear that you've spoken of my existence, expect an unfriendly visit.'

He left the room. Michael had more than he had bargained for. Staring into the vacuum of the single light bulb suspended from the ceiling, he knew this aberration was going to be the biggest decision he would ever have to make. He headed home to gather his thoughts. Walking through the bar, he looked at the permanent fixture of his father holding the bar up, and his superior's words flashed through his head: 'Don't let history repeat itself.' Watching him leave in despondency through the mirror, his father shared his torment as his mind revisited a summer's day a quarter of a century ago.

As he neared his home, he looked up to see his brother and the local half-wit approaching. Coming face to face at the path leading to the front door, they looked into each other's sad eyes. On a day when both men had been gifted the realisation of their aspirations, this night neither had anything to smile about. Saying nothing, Tommy kept grinding his teeth as he went, cringing at the thought of what might occur. Reaching the corner, he turned his head to view the two silhouettes still standing like gunfighters outside a saloon at high noon. Trembling with the fear for the worst, he continued onwards to his home.

Chapter 5

Against All Odds

That Thursday night had ended in a stand-off. With both brothers having had more than enough on their minds, they had entered the house united for the first time since Paul's return.

It was the next day when Bernadette, having initially dismissed Michael's reticent behaviour as the habitual Saturday morning hangover, received the first real indication that something was agitating her fiancé in the unusual form of his presence in the house at midday. Every Saturday since their relationship had begun, come lunchtime, whether it be rain, hail or shine, he'd be on his way, home or away, to watch his beloved Cliftonville FC. Nervously, she poured herself a cup of tea, convinced that he had read her game plan for the day. Having called in sick with the certainty that he would be miles away at the football match, it was her intention to have another attempt at winning back her ex-boyfriend.

'Not going to the match today?' she asked, feigning a cold with a subtle cough.

'No, I think I've caught your flu,' he returned, morosely.

Sucking hard on his cigarette, he gazed at her across the table and craved to confide in her with regard to the task in hand. Somehow, he felt certain that she'd know what to do and yet he dared not subsume her in his predicament. Like Delilah was to Samson, she had the power at her fingertips to cut away his strength at any given moment.

'Shall I make us some lunch?' she offered.

'No, I'm not hungry,' he replied, lighting another cigarette to steady his consternation.

Having managed to raise his chin off the floor, Paul sat and gaped at the scuffed and stained wood-chip wallpaper in Tommy's kitchen, which appeared to have contracted Dutch Elm disease. It promoted a notion he wasn't willing to share, just in case something better came along and he'd made another impetuous promise that he'd have to keep. He needed something to occupy his life, and he'd been pondering over decorating the ill-clad interior of Tommy's abode, but he was sure he'd live to regret such an offer. Anyhow, Monday would bring a new dawning with the challenge of employment, surely he could suffer the monotony for a few days more?

Looking at Tommy, who was at this moment keeping to his side of the bargain, Paul had the feeling that the new job was bound to bring new friends and an innovative social circle. He also knew that, even if he'd been granted the love he desired from Angela, his protégé would take it hard now that he had become dependent on his fidelity; perhaps he'd even lapse to his old ways. It was an acute riddle from all angles, but one that had to be solved if he was to move on with his life.

'So what are you gonna do with yourself now that I'm gonna be away for a week at a time?' he asked.

'I'll keep learning, so that I'm ready for a job when you find one for me,' stated Tommy, categorically.

Paul was also aware that if he was to start afresh, he would have to gradually phase out his love of greyhound racing. Seeing Angela, and now worse, with another man, was having dire effects on his health; not only had he started to smoke, but he had become abstemious, losing a full stone in weight, plummeting to a bantam nine and a half stone since he'd set his hungry eyes upon her.

'Tom, I think we should frequent the track a lot less now,' he eased in his bold statement gently.

'Why?' returned Tommy.

'You're closer than you think to being ready for applying for a job, the racing will only distract you, besides if I don't break away I'll never get her out of my system,' he finally revealed the real reason behind his reckoning.

Although he looked depressed by the facts, Tommy agreed. If Paul said that was the way it should be, then so be it. Tommy truly believed that under Paul's guidance, one day soon he would find a job and forge his link in the chain of life.

'Can we not just go tonight?' said Tommy.

'I don't think so, I've not a lot of money left. I'll need to keep every penny I have for bus fares next week and no doubt I'll have to work a week in hand, so I'm gonna be scraping at the bottom of the barrel before I get my first wage.'

'We can skive in and I'll buy you a couple of pints, oh please Paul,' he offered.

'Okay,' smiled Paul, out of guilt, having previously cogitated over how he didn't really need Tommy now that he was back in the big league.

At 5.30 p.m. Michael, with only the street light's timid glow for company, was sat on his bed glaring at the bright orange tinctures of nicotine running up his fingers, which eight hours earlier had been a mere sickly yellow. An abundance of over forty cigarettes had brought no calming respite, as his nerves had accrued in time with the fading daylight, which had now disappeared. Twiddling with the hexagonal-headed butterfly key, he knew he held his own future in his hand. The flicking of the light switch sparked him from his anxieties, as his eyes retracted to defend themselves from the intense illumination. Turning his head to view who had come to intrude on his private solemnity, his eyes were drawn to the second of the Tricolour ensigns embellishing the walls and the message was there for him at long last, in the Gaelic writings of his forefathers. Tiocfaidh ar la, – 'our day will come', and his most certainly had. As he contemplated the venerable scripture that would outlive every generation Ireland had to offer, his vision was pervaded by Bernadette, who was on a mission of remonstration.

'What are your plans for this evening? Because if you're out drinking, then I'm off into town with a girlfriend. I'm sick and tired of living my life around your needs, I feel like a bloody prisoner in this house. You never take me out, if this is how marriage is gonna be then I don't want it,' she scowled.

Too entangled in his own deceitful plight, she was shocked by his docile response. 'Just do what you want, will ye.'

Having spent the afternoon mustering up the courage, frightened that he would blow his top, she had come to the decision that if a blazing row had ignited, then she would have no option but to extinguish it by informing him of her true feelings. Paul being around was tearing her apart and she was astute enough to realise that if she gave up the chase, then sooner or later another would win the race for his affections. The consequence of that happening had to be countered at all costs, even if it meant being expelled on to the streets; that was the amplitude of her profanity. She despised Michael: he was evil, possessed no romantic attributes, held negligible compassion and had no remorse. She knew that life with him would be a life sentence of hell.

Earlier that afternoon, when she had ventured to the corner shop to purchase her weekly magazines, she had discovered in her purse an old photograph of herself and Paul taken a few years back, and it made her weep with joy and pain as she relived better times. Yes, she knew she'd been selfish and pugnacious during their vernal relationship, but he'd needed a second mother in those early days. Now that he was exposing another side to his personality, she idolised him more than ever. Staring at the photo, she had watched as a salty tear had fallen on to the tarnished memorabilia, then she made her vows with malice shining through the windows of her scornful eyes. Never again would she sleep with Michael, she would adopt a fresh approach to show Paul that she too had another aspect to her character, one of understanding. Her final pledge was to do everything possible to prevent him falling into the arms of another.

Not hanging around for Michael to come to his senses, she grabbed at the aperture to escape his hard-line reforms with both hands, leaving him to his pestilent speculation. Heading to the confines of her tiny boxroom, which was measured in the ability to swing a feline, she began to dress to kill while, in the next room, her estranged fiancé began attiring to maim. Rummaging through his drawers in search of the darkest clothes available, he found a navy-blue jersey and decided to go with the blue jeans he was already wearing. Removing the existing cream pullover, he felt under his armpits – they were saturated with the perspiration of apprehension, although the central heating system had yet to spark to life. Hyperventilating to such severity that a vomiting session was just around the corner, he surged to the bedroom door knowing it was now or never. Almost blacking out under the tension, he stopped at the door and gave himself a stern mental talking to.

Come on, Michael, stop worrying, it can't be any easier, just shoot the bastard if he pulls a knife. Come on, let's do it, just make sure he doesn't see yer face. About turning on his words, he headed back for the prerequisite of the job, suitable head camouflage, knowing full well that if his identity was breached by his victim, then he would become the subsequent target and the retaliatory punishment might not be so

Run For Freedom

lenient. Retrieving his black woollen ski hat, he put it on his head and pulled it down over his face, stretching the material until it rested in line with his neck – he had made himself a wolf in sheep's clothing. Then he removed the headgear, lit another cigarette and used it to burn two eye holes before trying it on for size. Satisfied with his tailoring skills, he checked his watch, it was now 6.10 p.m. – time to see if he was cut out for the job. He picked up a pair of woollen gloves and was ready. Walking past his fiancé's room, all his senses had abandoned him as he failed to smell the rich, sweet scent of perfume which she had dowsed herself in.

As he negotiated the short ten-minute walk to the hunting ground of Argyle Street in the north of the Falls, his whole body was so numb that he couldn't even feel the bitter wind burning his face. Arriving at the south end of the entry, he paused under the amber streetlight and lit another cigarette. Taking deep inhalations to dilute his adrenaline, he continued walking towards the opposite end and the stash, circumspectly mapping out the terrain for any defects or impediments that might trip him on his escape route. Slightly past half way the light faded and, looking to the heavens, Michael could see that the streetlight had been vandalised by some kid's boredom. It was a perfect venue for an ambush and he decided he would exploit the poor light to his advantage. Moving further up the acrid smelling, penurious alley-cum-open-air-public-convenience, he manoeuvred around the obstacles of beer tins, smashed glass and dog excrement, before arriving outside the wooden gate of his victim's backyard. He placed some pieces of a broken bottle and a few aluminium cans in front of the gate, to let him know when he had company. By the time he had reached the end of the treasure trail, where the X marked the spot, his fears had been supplanted by the passion of expectancy. Suddenly, he was enjoying himself, proud to be a part of the game.

Looking round for any witnesses, he removed the key from his pocket, and saw the area was chillingly deserted, which was strange for a Saturday evening. Opening the cover which housed the electrics, he reached into the lamppost and removed the hefty pistol. For a moment he stared at the deadly mechanism and he knew he had the power in his hand to take away a life, then he thought to a contrary comment his brother had once made: 'It's hard to be a man when there's a gun in your hand.'

107

'Arsehole,' he muttered under his steaming breath.

About turning, the predator headed back into the desolate entry to his waylay position, where he lurked in the shadows, stalking his prey. At 6.50 p.m. when the suspense and anxiety had quenched his optimism, he was startled by the resonant echo of an explosion way off in the distance. Looking up to the dark sky, he saw a cloud flickering as the teasing orange reflection of a fire below danced upon the water carrier. Concentrating hard to re-establish his senses, he listened to hear faint sirens in the distance, like a referee's whistle they signified that the game was underway for, as promised, the mêlée a few miles away at Ballymurphy was his decoy. Pulling on his home-made balaclava, he began to tremble violently, a combination of the bitter elements assaulting his body and the thought of the knife. He took the gun from his pocket, cocked it as instructed to counteract his fears, but there was nothing he could do about the strain on his bladder demanding that he urinate. Pondering whether he had enough time to relieve the pain, his head jerked as he heard a tin can being kicked about twenty yards up ahead in the darkness. Eyes piercing through the dim light to see if it was his man, he felt the cold shiver of someone walking over his grave run up his spine, as his target was confirmed. As he leapt from the gloom with gun pointed, a flood of hot sweat secreted from every pore in his head, blurring his vision with the intense heat of the situation. Through his stinging eyes, he could make out that the stocky, bulldog of a man, clad in the denim jacket and matching jeans was reaching into his back pocket for assistance.

'Put yer fucking hands up or I'll shoot,' Michael blasted, to be clearly understood above his panic.

'Fuck you,' roared the dealer in dissent, indignantly guarding his territory.

Pulling out his weapon, he flicked it ready for combat and for a second they were suspended in deadlock, as they stared into each other's fearsome eyes.

'Drop the knife or I'll shoot,' said Michael calmly.

In a moment of madness rather than bravado, the defiant drugs baron surged forward, provoked by the knowledge that his assailant had been sent to inflict harm and would not be susceptible to bargaining. Hesitating until the glinting blade was merely inches away, Michael clenched his teeth and somehow found the wealth of strength required to squeeze the trigger. As the scorching bullet left the barrel, he felt it recoil through his entire body and it was a sensation that brought prodigious relief. He looked up at the windows of the surrounding houses like a frightened rabbit, but could see no interested parties.

Returning his considerations to the enemy, he could see that he was on his knees and in such deep trauma from the bullet that had entered and left the top half of his arm, that all he could do was pant like a sweating dog. With the bit between his teeth now, Michael raced around behind him and used his cumbrous boot to flatten him to the floor; then crouching beside his shaking target he forced the gun into the cup of his leg behind the kneecap. On this occasion it was effortless. As the bullet removed the kneecap, a ferocious spray of blood splattered over Michael's mask and neck. One scream of hysterical pain and it was all over, as the dealer lost all consciousness in the depth of the shock. Standing upright, Michael yanked of his guise and gulped at the refreshing polar air; then he began to laugh, it was his first taste of blood and he liked it.

Racing down the alley as if he had just scored the winning goal in the cup final, his own speed almost tripped him up as the chemicals inside his brain acted to enhance his performance. At reaching the drop off point, he didn't stop, tossing the gun over the wall, he ran for his liberty, making all out for the sanctuary of Paddy's Bar. Five minutes later he arrived at 7.15 p.m. with black rings around his eyes and legs of rubber. The only evidence of colouring on his face was the speckles of another man's blood, dotted like measles around his chin and neck.

Spotting his father perched in his usual spot, he joined him immediately and lit a cigarette, which on this occasion had the desired calming effect, comparable to an after-sex smoke; it stabilised his excessive heartbeat.

'Go and clean yourself up and I'll get you a drink, go on,' urged his father.

Standing in front of the mirror in the gents' toilets, he scrubbed and rubbed for ten minutes solid at his neck and head, until he was red raw with sores and the pigmentation had returned to his face; then he smiled at his accomplishment.

Having breached the stadium's security measures again without getting their hands dirty, thanks to the advance planning of wearing gloves, Paul and Tommy stood in the bar out of the lashing rain, nursing their drinks Once again the precondition for life as we know it had intervened, in the form of Murphy's Law. When Paul had been determined to get drunk, he couldn't stomach it; but tonight, having come with the intention of having a few quiet pints, he now had the taste for greater quantities, yet the funds were unavailable to meet his demands.

'Do you think you could do something for me?' inquired Tommy.

'As long as it doesn't cost money,' he replied.

'You know how you'll be going to England every day with your job, well, do you think you could try to find my mother?'

'But how, she could be anywhere, besides it's Scotland I'll be landing in. I wouldn't know where to begin. Do you have no clues whatsoever to her whereabouts?' soughed Paul.

Taking it as a refusal to co-operate, Tommy's head dropped and his eyes began to fill up, which didn't go unnoticed.

'Aye, all right, but we'll – I mean, you'll have to devise a plan of strategy. I'll need all sorts of details like recent photos, age, height, weight etcetera. Perhaps we can report her to the police as a missing person.'

'Oh Paul, do you really mean it? It would be my only wish in life apart from getting a job. Just to see me mom again would be fantastic. What about you, if you could wish for anything what would it be?'

Gazing across the track at the torrential rain sweeping over the terraces, Paul replied in all honesty. 'I don't really think I've ever thought of that. I suppose I'd like two things if I were to chance upon a leprechaun. I'd love to have Angela as a girlfriend and I'd love to experience the feeling of my own greyhound crossing the winning line. Yeh, that would be something.'

'Why don't you get a dog then?' Turning to face his nihilistic friend, he paused and gave him a mellow smile founded on pensive admiration. Having swung fruitlessly for a pastime, Tommy had just hit the nail on the head, but was it that simple?

'Hey Tom, what a great idea, then again, it's not as easy as it sounds.'

'Why?' came the puzzled answer.

'Well, commitment for starters,' stated Paul, talking through the experiences of working as a handler.

'What does that mean?' probed Tommy.

'A greyhound is a professional sportsman with four legs, a living racing car. It requires a lot of attention and fine tuning, plenty of exercise, a strict diet and routine; to sum it all up, dedication. I'll be working away for a week at a time, so I couldn't give it one hundred per cent.'

'But I could do everything in the weeks when you're away, so it wouldn't be a problem.'

'We'd need a kennel and, of course, transport to ferry it to the track; can't expect a top athlete to travel by bus.'

'So that's it then,' said Tommy downheartedly. Now that his incipience was waning, he was beginning to understand that rainbows couldn't be ascended.

Taking a mouthful of beer, Paul swilled the ferment around in his mouth and chewed it over. Swallowing the bitter sweet liquid, he allowed impulse to drown his scepticism.

'You help me to build a kennel fit for a champion and I'll get a bank loan for two thousand pounds. I'll buy a car for a grand, that'll leave us a thousand to buy a decent pup.'

'Really?' said Tommy, excited by the proposed involvement.

Raising his glass to Tommy's, Paul called the toast: 'To greyhound ownership, next stop Shelbourne Park.'

Clashing glasses to cement their partnership, Paul put his arm around Tommy and put the icing on his cake. 'You're a real mate, Tom, so how about you promise me that you'll always be my friend?'

'You'll know I'll always be that,' he confirmed, proudly. 'But where's Shelbourne Park?'

'It's a theatre of dreams, it's in Dublin, where they run the Irish Greyhound Derby; it's the biggest forum for dog racing in the entire world. Win that and you've won the moon,' explained Paul.

Flicking through the race card to see if any dogs were for sale, he had a gut feeling that Tommy's concept was kismet. At the rear of the programme there was an advertisement for a forthcoming greyhound sale and it was only three weeks away, on Valentine's day. That has to be an omen, he thought, as his mind drifted again to Angela.

'Okay Tom, we're gonna have to move on this one. I'll organise the loan midweek. We'll have to build the kennel over next weekend, because there's a sale of pups three weeks tomorrow. We can go car hunting the week after I come back from my first trip offshore.'

In all the effervescent discussion of their ambition, neither noticed nor smelled the third party who stood behind, eavesdropping upon their blueprint.

'Paul, I have to talk to you,' interrupted Bernadette, adorned for seduction and caked in make-up, which Paul looked upon as war paint rather than a compliment to her beauty.

111

'What are you doing here?' he retorted, turning to face her.

'I haven't come to fight with you and I'm truly sorry that Michael got to find out that I was here with you a few weeks back, that was never my intention. I swear I never meant to threaten you into anything. I've come to clear the air between us and as to your friend, I apologise to you,' she said focusing her sights to Tommy, whose colouring had absconded.

'I don't like this,' stated Paul. 'Does Michael know you're here?'

'I don't care about him, I despise him, it's like living with Sherlock Holmes the way he demands to know my every move. I want you back, I'll make any concessions you request of me. It won't be like before, we don't need to rush things,' she implored.

'I can't, my life has changed so much. I could never give you something that I haven't got,' he returned composedly.

'But I don't want anything material, just you.'

'That's exactly it, you see, I don't love you. There's no spark there for me, no chemistry, if you like. Even if you don't want my brother, then there are plenty other blokes in Belfast who would jump at the chance to partner you, I'm dead wood that could never rekindle for you. I'm sorry, but that's the way it is.'

Holding back the tears, she sniffed, inwardly tensing the muscles in her pain-ridden face. Carefully constructing her next sentence, to keep him on the line, she used her simulant powers of guile to good effect.

'Okay, I understand, no more flaunting myself in front of you. I'll behave myself from now on and as soon as I can get on my feet I'll be out from under yours.'

'What are you saying?' he quizzed.

'I can't marry Michael, just the same as you can't love me. It wouldn't be fair on him, but don't tell him until I find new lodgings, besides it's something that I have to do myself. Can I buy you a drink to celebrate our friendship. We can still be friends, can't we?'

Shifting his eyes to watch the rain streaming down the condensation on the stained windows of the bar, he felt her heartache and thought that maybe he had misjudged her all along.

'Of course we can still be friends and, as to the drink, we may as well get wet inside too,' he accepted. 'But I won't get paid for a fortnight and I'm a little short right now, so I won't be able to afford to buy you one in return.'

'No problem, you were good to me all along, it's the least I can do, pay back time if you like,' she smiled at his integrity.

Watching as she headed to the bar, he shook his head, more so at the abandonment of her frugality, then he turned to Tommy.

'Guess I got her all wrong, too.'

'I don't know, she still frightens me,' contended Tommy, as he remembered the past.

'No, she's a poor soul searching blindly for love. She didn't know her father, he ran off to America with another woman when she was a bairn, brought up in a household of five women - must have been difficult. I bet there was a lot of bitchiness and jealousy, and no doubt hatred towards the father. Maybe I took his place and she used me to release her frustrations. I know it sounds absurd, but that's my philosophy anyway.'

She returned with two pints of beer and a large brandy and Babycham, Paul relieved her of the tray and parted with a smile.

'So when did you start smoking?' she asked as he lit up a cigarette.

'Last week,' he revealed, blushing, slightly ashamed.

'Well, I never thought I'd see the day. Do you know Tommy, it is Tommy, isn't it?'

He nodded in reply.

'Paul was very asthmatic as a child, his heart even stopped once during the panic of an attack, didn't it?'

'Yes,' replied Paul.

'They had to give him an injection straight through the heart to bring him back to life,' she continued to reminisce.

'So you died, then came back to life again?' said Tommy, totally intrigued by the story.

'Well I suppose I did really, aye.'

'What was it like?' pushed Tommy.

'I can't remember, I think I saw an angel pushing me back into the world and one day I'd like to thank her.'

Tilting her glass, Bernadette guzzled her double measure and slammed it on to the table in true drinking competition fashion. She then opened her handbag and produced her purse.

'Well, I'm up for another, any takers?' she offered.

'Not yet,' replied Paul, who was savouring the taste.

At the bar, she unbuttoned her purse and saw the photo of them kissing under the mistletoe from all those years ago, and she began to fill up again.

113

'What'll it be?' served the barmaid, shaking her from her withdrawal symptoms.

'Two double brandies,' she ordered.

If the only way she could be in his arms tonight was with having to be carried home through intoxication, then so be it. Returning to the table, she rejoined the conversation in a bid to extract the intelligence she deeply longed for.

'So you boys are gonna buy a greyhound then?'

'Aye,' admitted Paul. 'And a car to transport the beast.'

'What about your allergy?' she inquired.

'No pain, no gain,' he conceded.

'So where's your girlfriend tonight?' she asked confidently, appearing nonchalant over the situation.

'Oh, she's not my girlfriend, she kicked me into touch. I asked her out once and she said I ought to go look in the mirror, Michael had just beaten me up after all, black eyes and . . .'

Abruptly he stopped his sentence in full flight, his joviality brought to earth by gravity in the knowledge that he had let something slip.

'So it was Michael who gave you that beating the day you came home,' she growled.

'Aye, but that's water under the bridge now,' returned Paul.

'Bastard,' she snapped, throwing another two shots down her neck.

No wonder he wouldn't have anything to do with me, she thought.

'Just forget it Bernie, it's all done and dusted now,' stressed Paul, seeing she was seething.

Catalysed by the fuel of the alcohol consumption, her brain slipped into overdrive as, suddenly, she realised that perhaps the Grand Prix was not out of her reach after all, and maybe the last few weeks had been but a pit stop and the chequered flag of reconciliation was there for the taking. Maybe he went to the pub to confront Michael, to tell him he still loved me and the severe hiding put him off, she thought, clutching at any straw available. I'll kill him, the evil bastard, she continued to cogitate.

Watching her eyes squint as she stared at the glass on the table, for a moment Paul actually thought that the glass might explode under the intense volume of hatred she was subjecting it to. Finishing his drink, he slammed it on to the table to break her spell.

'I'll have that other drink now, if the offer's still open.'

114

Staggering to the bar on six brandies of gravitational pull, she ordered another two pints and two large brandies while the bar began to rock like a boat on the high seas before her.

'Tom, go and help her with the drinks, after this we'll put her in a taxi, she's well pissed. I may have to sleep on your couch tonight, I can smell trouble brewing.'

As Tommy obeyed his commands, Paul embraced his hands together in prayer mode and sighed deeply into them, as he looked over in the direction of where Angela had stood on all of her rare appearances. Closing his eyes, he sent her a mental greeting. God, Angela I wish I was Uri Geller right now, if by some weird chance I have the ability, then come back into my life and mend my heartache, that's it. Opening his eyes, he glared through the misty windows to find he did not possess the gift of telepathy. Tommy arrived back at the table first with the tray of beverages as Bernadette wavered zigzagging towards the table, then slumped on to the chair and let out a hiccup from her beetroot face.

'Perhaps you shouldn't have that drink,' suggested Paul, concerned for her welfare.

'Jusht thish one and home,' she slurred. 'I really mished you when you ran out on me you know.'

'There were times when I missed you too, mainly when everything in my favour was against me, when one door was closing and another shutting, if you know what I'm trying to say, but hell we've both got new lives now. Right?'

'Whatever you say,' she replied almost falling off the chair.

'All right, that's enough, I think we'd better get you a taxi home.'

Guzzling at their pints in a race against time, both men felt their lungs cry out for oxygen as they decked their glasses synchronously. Taking an arm each they escorted her from the bar in search of transport to the fraternity of unimpressed shaking heads. As the brick wall of the cold air smacked her in the face, she temporarily perked up and realised that Paul had his arm around her waist which provoked her to fake, just like a woman.

Closing her eyes, she went with the current and began to sleepwalk, dreaming of the last time Paul had wrapped his arms around her at the reception of her second eldest sister's wedding. That night they had danced an eternity until they were soaked to the skin and, as she remembered, it was the only occasion when there was a suggestion that one day soon it would be their turn to become the centre of attraction and take their vows. It could be said, paradoxically, that through drink, everything becomes a haze of transparency. If only she could have seen that it was the mood of the festivities that had aroused him into providing her with such false parameters to work her dreams within. Hailing a taxi, Paul opened the door and assisted her on to the cold imitation leather upholstery. Lightly slapping her face, he sought to revive her.

'Come on, Bernie, wake up. Will you be okay when you get home?'

'Aye,' she replied, her eyes rolling and her head bobbing like a jelly. 'I just want my bed.'

Opening her handbag, he wisely removed the evidence of her evening's whereabouts, in the form of her race card, before instructing the driver of her destination.

An hour later, at 10.45 p.m., Paul and Tommy arrived outside the O'Donnell residence.

'Okay Tom, if you come around here tomorrow, we can measure up for the kennel and work out exactly what materials we require.'

'I thought you wanted to sleep on my couch?' reminded Tommy.

'No, it's okay, I'll face the music if there's any. Chances are she's tucked up in bed sleeping it off and me brother's still down the pub.'

Paul's prognosis was spot on. When Michael eventually rolled in, both Paul and Bernadette were in their respective beds, dreaming about loves that neither could have, his insomnia finally laid to rest in the confidence that their liaison would remain clandestine.

Sex, sex, sex rang the alarm clock in Michael's head, as it always did, come Sunday morning. Sneaking into his fiancé's bed, he cuddled into her warm flesh and let his hands do the whispering. Stirring with an almighty hangover, last night's vague events began to filter through her mind.

'Leave me alone, Michael, I have a headache and your breath smells terrible.'

'That's never stopped you before.'

In the coming months, migraines, period pains and sciatica would become her allies, as she set out to keep his advances at bay and frustrate him into breaking up their now frangible relationship. Turning on to his back with a deep sigh of disapproval that brought a corrupt smile to her face, he searched for answers.

116

'So where did you go last night?'

'I went into Belfast with a work colleague for a drink,' she prevaricated.

'Who?' he probed, enviously.

'Just a girl I get on well with, you don't know her. I got home early, a lot earlier than you. Do you have any more questions or can I get back to sleep now?'

Leaving the bed with plenty on his mind, he returned to his own bedroom where he began to dress himself.

Catching his mother on the best day of her week and with the kind of vivacious sweet talk that could sell sand to the Arabs, Paul successfully persuaded his mother to waive her right of veto on planning permission for the six by four foot kennel that he intended to build at the bottom of the backyard. A bill of materials formulated, all that was needed now was to raise the cash.

After good preparation and an early night, Paul was ready to start earning a living again. He took a seat alongside the other fortunates of the epoch at the breakfast table and nibbled gingerly at the slices of toast his mother had laid before him. Putting the newspaper down to reveal his infelicitous expression, his father turned on him again.

'So, a steward eh, once again you cease to amaze me. Like cleaning out toilets and bowing to all and sundries needs, do you? You're just a loser and you always will be.'

Refraining to be drawn into a Monday morning mêlée with his bombastic father, Paul excused himself and made straight for the bus stop. With only his swimming trunks for company, it was a lonely journey into Belfast, soured by his father's bitter tongue which bit deep into his ego, sapping the taste of confidence he had hoped to savour. Slowly, but surely, he was fast running out of pretexts to respect his father, even love him.

Connecting to a smaller blue Ulsterbus, he was driven north, through the pretty suburbs which merged with the munificent countryside, where money dangling from the naked branches was but a figment of his philosophical imagination. After twenty minutes of observing how the other half lived, he arrived at his destination, Jordanstown College. Enlisting with another five new recruits from rival ferry companies, he began his one-day Basic Sea Survival course, which was no great hardship.

Press-ganged back into the classroom, the morning session was spent listening to a longwinded awareness seminar. An idiot's guide to the logical do's and don'ts of maritime safety, simplicities and statistics, like, 'always tie your shoelaces or they're as sure as damn to trip you up when you're in full flight', only to be contradicted by, 'never run around the ship', and, 'did you know that the mean temperature in the Irish Sea will bring hallucinations within fifteen minutes, induce a moribund coma around twenty and climax in death from acute hypothermia around the half hour mark, dependent on an individual's fat ratio and will to survive'.

Now who the hell in their right mind would have volunteered for that logistical experiment, thought Paul. Living in a day and age where statisticians rule the world, if we were to obey their monitored findings, then we'd all die from starvation, dehydration and asphyxiation and that's a fact. Calling an hour's adjournment for lunch gave a languid Paul all the time he needed to shake off the sleep inducing jargon and, more importantly, visit the bank manager during the interim.

Having caught a bus immediately, he alighted fifteen minutes later and began sprinting as fast as his legs would carry him towards Royal Avenue, where a few banks nestled pretentiously amongst the vaunting contemporary architecture of financial institutions, such as insurance brokers and assurance companies. It was no different from any other money-to-burn clique in the first world, inwardly, it was a pinstripe regime, desperate to screw every penny they could get out of you; outwardly, the profits of legal racketeering were on display for all to see, projected in the bold white Portland stone façades which looked down upon you and laughed in your face.

Reduced to a jog, Paul had no time to pick and choose the best interest deal on offer, no doubt they were all alike anyway, with variant wording to entice the mass public into believing that they could beat the indomitable system; besides, he already had a dormant account with one of the leading high street banks and that would save him time in unessential administration. Entering the bank, he formed a queue behind a frail, hoary lady who was making a foolish deposit. Surely she can't have long to live, he thought. And I bet she's got at least twenty grand in there. Silly cow, she'll pop her clogs and her beneficiary will no doubt piss it up against the wall, I hope. If people truly save on the assumption of a rainy day, then as in her illustration, in the winter of her life, it was surely monsoon time.

'Can I help you sir?' asked the pretty teller, whose accent had been through a refinery.

'Aye, I've already an account with you and my wages shall be getting paid in on a weekly basis, so, can I borrow two thousand pounds?'

'You'll need to fill in a few forms and make an appointment with the manager,' she replied.

'But, will I get the money for Friday? It's really important. I have a deal and if I don't get the cash, I'll lose out,' he cajoled.

'Subject to terms and conditions, I don't see why not. If you've no outstanding arrears against your name, then it shouldn't be a problem. What time is convenient for you to see the manager?'

'Anytime this week after 4.30 p.m.,' he replied.

'How about a quarter to five on Wednesday?'

After agreeing, he took the forms then headed for an afternoon in the swimming pool.

After the monotony of the morning, the after-dinner session proved to be an invigorating shock to the system. Dramatising a simulation of abandoning ship, all participants had to jump off an eighteen foot platform into a manmade, swirling cold current. When they had found their bearings and swallowed their testicles, they then had to inflate a life raft, before climbing in and battening down the hatches to repel the lashing rain and wind, only to find out that a lifeless plastic corpse was in need of rescuing. Volunteering for the mission, Paul had to swim the full length of the swimming pool against the tide, then husband the effigy back to safety. Although at times there seemed to be an immense lack of communication, as loud screams drowned any structured procedure, the end result, achieved by synergy amidst the confusion, was the intention of the exercise, survival.

Tuesday brought the dreaded medical. The night before, he had been apprehensively shitting himself yet, when he was asked to provide a stool sample, constipation reared its head. The afternoon was spent in the classroom at the Donegall Quay ferry terminal, where induction presentations taught him in the virtues of customer service, retail, hygiene and merchandising. At the end of the day, Paul learnt that tomorrow he would make his first two trips on the ferry that would become his second home, so that he could be type-rated and become familiar with the layout and muster stations. He was also informed that he was not suffering from food poisoning and come Monday, he would be thrown in at the deep end to make his first seven day trip offshore.

119

Entering the bank on Wednesday with five minutes to spare, he clutched at the forms he had toiled to complete. At 4.50 p.m. he was summoned into the manager's office.

'So Mr O'Donnell, you want to borrow some money, two thousand pounds to be precise, over a period of twenty-four months,' stated the obese pinstripe banker, whose appearance gave good argument for the benefits of keeping your cholesterol down.

'Aye, and I must have the money for Friday,' he returned quickly, in case the fat man suffered a coronary before he had authorised the loan.

'Well, it's not quite as simple as that,' said the lender, continuing to scrutinise the application. 'So you want to buy a car?'

'Aye, if I don't pay cash on Saturday the deals off.'

'I can't see your last three payslips.'

'That's because I've just started work this week and if I don't get this car I'm gonna find it difficult to get there on time, then I'll lose my job,' said Paul.

'Well, I'm really sorry Mr O'Donnell, but it'll take at least a week to process this application.'

'Listen to me,' underlined Paul raising his voice acrimoniously. 'You check your computer out will you? I've had an account with this bank for six years and it's always been in credit, I can easily take my savings elsewhere, yes, close my account this instant.'

'Now come, there's no need to be so hasty, I'm sure we can speed this up for you,' he conceded without checking the validity of his statement.

Yes, Paul had an existing account, but if the balance had been investigated then the administrator would have discovered the life savings to be a petty one pound and seven pence. Shaking hands before they parted ways, the deal was struck.

Being dismissed at 2 p.m. on Friday, for good behaviour, Paul headed to the bank to sign away the next two years of his life. Eyes almost popping from their sockets, as the teller counted out a century of twenty-pound notes, the thought of the repayments seemed insignificant in the euphoria of the moment.

Up with the larks on Saturday morning, the partners invested £70 all told with a timber merchant on the outskirts of the city, then returned home to await their delivery. At just after 2 p.m., when tedium had began to take root under dark cloudy skies, the ingredients of wood, nails, screws, hinges, perspex and felt arrived. After assisting in the unloading operation, they stood soaked in sweat, looking at the pieces, knowing that the backbreaking task of the jigsaw puzzle was yet to begin. After four hours of constant bickering through a lack of cohesion and the screams of tired hammer blows, they stood together in the darkness and looked upon their creation, limbs aching and hands callused.

'All we need now is a greyhound,' remarked Paul.

One by one they stooped to enter the sweet-smelling kennel then sat to bask in their accomplishment. Lighting a cigarette Paul turned to Tommy. 'It's really cosy isn't it, at least if I get any grief in the house, I'll be able to sleep out here.'

For two hours solid, they dwelt in their sanctuary and watched the stars spangling in the banner of the clear night sky, each wishing they could pluck a few for different reasons.

When Monday arrived, Paul was still stiff and lethargic from Saturday's exertions. With holdall slung over his shoulder and the anticipation of a million voyages of discovery in hand, he presented himself for his primal stint at sea. Although he was fostered through the initial twelve-hour shift by a namesake from Glasgow, when the immense floating football pitch sat moored like the Mary Celeste, now that the nigh on two thousand passengers and two hundred and fifty plus vehicles had disembarked at the Scottish port of Stranraer, Paul was absolutely drained of all energy. Too shattered to explore the first class buoyant hotel, he made his way to the main deck for an open air smoke. Savouring the taste in the placid, idyllic surroundings, where even the timeless subtle tinkling of a bell onshore could not infringe upon the tranquillity, he looked down at the lapping sea caressing the ship's hull and watched as the moon danced upon the surf. If only Angela was here to share this peaceful seascape, he thought, then this would have to be the most complete moment of my life.

By the time Saturday night had come around, his appetite had grown in demand with the amount of kilojoules his body was sweating out during the tiresome shifts, and although every second night had been spent at Donegall Quay, he had become quite nostalgic. Paul enjoyed the job, though at times he gasped for energy. Some of the chores, like cleaning up the seasickness left behind by the passengers who had lost their sea-legs and cleaning the urinals which were often missed as the boat rocked in the winter weather, didn't really bother him. It was when he was stowed away in the annals of the ship's galley that he hurt. For an arduous third of his shift he tolled non-stop in a sauna-like atmosphere washing the dishes, cutlery and titanic cauldrons that served as pots.

121

Even the industrial dishwasher that partnered him whinged and wheezed at the obscene workload.

On Sunday evening at 5 p.m. Tommy closed the book he had just finished reading and glanced at his watch. He thought; I wonder what Paul is doing now? I can't wait to tell him I've read a whole book on greyhounds.

Paul stood on deck with his Scottish lookout enjoying a smoke as the ferry made its final approach towards the conspicuous shores of Ireland and the ice-cool head wind tore at their rosy faces.

'So, what are you getting up to on your week off?' asked the Scot.

'Sleep, I think,' replied Paul, his fingers clamped-knuckle white to the rail for fear of being swept into the sea. 'No seriously, I'm gonna buy a car and go to the greyhound sales next Sunday, how about you?'

'Drink from breakfast to breakfast if she lets me.'

'Your wife?' probed Paul.

'No, you're joking aren't you, do I look stupid? My girlfriend and that's all she'll ever be. I was married once before and I'm still paying for it. The girlfriend's a hard bugger, like all your lot.'

'She's Irish then,' replied Paul.

'Aye, lives in Rathcool; I've been shacked up there for a few years now. I met her when I was pissed onshore one night, never looked back, I moved in with her that night, well and truly left the past behind.'

'So what's Scotland like then?'

'Much the same as Ireland, when you're sober, you learn to retaliate first. So what about you, have you got a bird?'

'No, not at the moment, there is a girl I have my eye on but I think she's seeing someone,' admitted Paul.

'So what part of the Bronx are you from?' said the head steward with the illustrated arms of iron.

'The Falls,' returned Paul

'Fuck me,' he exclaimed. 'So you're a Taig then.'

'Aye, I certainly am, and you, Rathcool, you must be a Prod,' inferred Paul.

'Nope, but it doesn't bother me, my bird's staunch though; if she found out I was a pape, she'd fuckin' knife me. I like Prods though, less chance of getting them up the duff,' he quipped in thick Glaswegian.

Laughing together they returned to the work of ensuring customer satisfaction.

At 7.45 p.m. safely harboured, the last dish was dry and the back-to-back crew had arrived to relieve the relieved. Still sweating, the two Pauls chatted merrily as they headed in search of taxi cabs. Refusing the temptation of a liquid supper, Paul opted for a quiet evening in Clonard Street. All washed out, he arrived home to be greeted by his mother, who wanted to know all the details of his week on the high seas.

'Well, son, did you enjoy it?' she asked, producing his overcooked meal from the oven.

'Aye, I love it, the food out there is amazing,' he replied, as he stared at the rubbery chicken and tough vegetables swimming in the thick-skinned gravy. 'But it's no picnic out there, twelve hours solid and I don't care if I see another dish in my life.'

'So have you made any new friends?'

'Aye, a Scots lad who shares my name. He lives in Belfast now though,' he replied, struggling to stay awake through the effort of his meal.

'Oh that reminds me son, Tommy called at the back door an hour ago, he said he would see you in the morning and he left you a letter.'

'A letter?' quizzed Paul, interestedly. 'Where is it then?'

'Here,' revealed his mother, lifting the article from off the pine bread-bin.

Taking the letter, intrigued, he smiled as he read the composition. 'Hi Pall no yew will be tyred so ile see yew tommorrow'.

'He can't spell, but he can write,' he exclaimed.

'What?' inquired his mother, looking to the ceiling as loud music began to pour from the bedroom above.

'Tommy couldn't read or write a few weeks ago, now he's Oscar Wilde,' explained Paul, thrilled for his friend.

'I wish she'd stop playing the same record over and over,' moaned his mother.

Listening to the distorted lyrics, Paul knew it was the first record he had bought Bernadette six years ago and that was ominous to him.

'So where's Michael tonight?' he asked.

'The pub, he's getting more like his father with every passing day. If he doesn't give himself a good shake, he's gonna lose that girl. She's not happy you know, I can tell.'

'Well, I'm shattered,' Paul yawned. 'Think I'll have an early night.'

Creeping up the stairs on tiptoes so as not to disturb Bernadette's melancholy, as he turned into his room his holdall brushed against his mother's treasured jardiniere vase.

123

'Oh fuck,' he whispered, watching inertly as it rocked in slow motion before crashing onto the landing. Picking it off the cushioning carpet, he surveyed the damage to find that lady luck was smiling upon him. After breathing a sigh of relief, he replaced the artefact then turned to observe Bernadette at the door, swaying in time to Chicago's 'If You Leave Me Now' with glass in hand.

'Do you remember when you bought me this?

'Aye, how could I forget,' he replied.

'Well, you've taken away the biggest part of me and I want it back.'

'Come on, you've been drinking,' said Paul.

'I haven't slept with him again and I never will. Come on Paul, you know I still love you and I'm pretty sure you feel it too, of course I understand you're hurting because I slept with that evil bastard, but it was a just a mistake. Isn't everyone allowed one?'

'Aye, course they are, but can't you see it? I don't love you,' he said tersely. Leaving her to suffer in her own delusion, he retired for the evening.

By Thursday afternoon, Paul and Tommy had trudged around every cowboy used-car sales dealership and over a dozen private vendors. Entering Waterloo Gardens in the leafy suburban area of Fort William, North Belfast, both men were captivated by the contemporary country ambience portraying wealth in every physiognomy. From the clean streets devoid of strays, to the non-existent graffiti and the intact street lighting, it was a world light years away from their own. Even the grass was greener and smelled sweeter and the sun was battling with the rain clouds to shine in this part of the Lebanon of the west. The only sign of Belfast to lower the tone of such a serene painting was the mail box, with its thin slotted metal plate bolted to the interior to thwart the posting of letter bombs.

Glancing at the newspaper, Paul found the ringed advertisement for the T Reg. Ford Escort retailing at £1,095 o.n.o. Walking up the oil-free, block-paved driveway, which meandered parallel to the perfectly pruned privet enclosing the gnome-ridden garden, they arrived at a bold lion's-head brass knocker. They struck twice and were startled as the curtains behind the lattice lead windows shimmied in time to the high-pitched excuse for a guard dog, which was a ball of fur on springs known as a Yorkshire terrier.

As the seller opened the door, the young men glanced at each other in the shock of seeing the burlesque proprietor. Studded ears, ring through nose and a shocking pink Mohican hairdo was the sight which imbued their vision.

'I've come about the Escort,' Paul announced.

'I'll just get the remote control for the garage,' said the throwback from the late seventies.

Following him around the side of the house to the garage, they waited with bated breath as the mechanical door stammered and groaned open. Like Angela, the moment Paul cast his eyes upon the vehicle, he knew it was the one for him. The red paintwork was unblemished and as pristine as the day it had rolled off the production line. The dark interior was also in mint condition, no cigarette burns in sight upon the suede upholstery, even the dashboard was scratchless. To the rear, the very haughty owner had fabricated a sporty mien with the jack-up kit and spoiler he had installed. To the front a double set of spotlights gave it that flashy rally look. Lifting the bonnet for the prospective buyer's inspection, the young punk revealed that there was more than met the eye.

'The engine's actually a 1.6 litre for speed, but the documents state 1.3 for insurance purposes. So what do you think?'

Knowing that if he showed he was smitten with the car, he would lose his right of negotiation, he tried his hand at amateur dramatics.

'Well, I won't deny it's nice, but it's a little out of my price range. I've only £950 and no chance of raising any any more,' Paul bartered, composedly.

'Okay, I'll tell you what, £1,000 and it's yours,' came the response.

Producing the thick wad of twenty pound notes from his pocket to entice a further discount, Paul began to count out the money.

'No, I'm sorry. I've only £950. Wait, I've another tenner stashed in my back pocket.'

'All right, you win, £960 it is,' agreed the seller, persuaded by the pound signs flashing in his eyes.

'Oh no, I can't,' said Paul, 'I need to keep a fiver back for petrol.'

'Okay, £955 it is,' came the concession.

Shaking hands, the deal was done.

For the remainder of the day before and after the greyhound racing, Paul managed to find the longest route for a shortcut and the new love in his life meant that his thoughts refused to refract to the absent Angela.

125

Parked outside Tommy's on Sunday morning, they waxed away the last twenty-four hours' grime, until their muscles weighed as heavy as the great optimism and pessimism which filled them. Looking forward to the midday sales seemed to be outshone by the fact that Monday would see Paul vanish from the land for a full week.

'Do you think you could teach me to drive one day?' asked Tommy.

'I don't see why not, but first we have more important challenges to confront. If we get a dog today it's gonna need some careful handling when I'm away, there's a lot you need to know. Greyhounds are extremely alert animals and need your utmost attention, the snapping of a twig or sight of a cat and they're off. They can wrench the lead and be gone before you know it.'

'That strong?' asked Tommy.

'Stronger, trust me - you'll have to be tuned in at all times.'

'Will I manage?' queried Tommy worriedly.

'Aye, you'll be fine. If we get one today then I'll have to go through everything with a fine toothcomb; you'll have to be dedicated Tom. If you sleep in and miss feeding time, it'll cry like a baby and do itself an injury in the kennel; they're very temperamental with built-in alarm clocks. They keep better time than a Rolex, no shit.'

Relieving the stress through a sigh, Tommy was wishing that Paul had a few days to nurse him through the requirements.

Having watched twenty-three dog trials, Paul's valuation was to bid for a mere two greyhounds from the sixty strong pack on offer, both dogs by sex. The first was a lively brindle named Waterford Crystal, having missed the break, the two-year-old whelp had shown a sparkling turn of foot to whittle down the eventual winners margin to a scant head, after the line and the youngster had sprinted clear leaving the other two in its wake. The second choice was a huge black September dog which had displayed electric pace from the starting traps, only to run out of steam close home, its name was Irrelevant.

Watching carefully with admiration as the auctioneer dredged the best prices out of the patrons with ambiguous promises of glory days, Paul was beginning to understand that £1,000 might not be enough to procure the commodity he had set his heart upon. Failing by £300 to become the registered owner of Waterford Crystal, lot seventeen finally arrived, importing the last chance. Having led the bidding from the outset of £400, just like the lot's performance in the trial, it was his tribulation to be outbid on the line by a derisory £25.

126

Having been tantalised, they departed the stadium, heads bowed in disconsolation, their moon waning. Refusing to take the scenic route home, Paul tested the authenticity of the car's braking system; screeching to a halt outside Tommy's door, he turned off the engine then slumped himself over the tiny steering wheel.

'So, how we gonna get a dog now?' asked Tommy in defeatist attitude.

'Don't worry, that second beast was nothing special anyway. When I come home next weekend we'll have a good scout around, there's always good dogs for sale in Eire. We may have to travel but, when it's meant to be, the right one will come along I'm sure,' consoled Paul.

For a whole week at sea the pagan winter returned with a vengeance. Having worked through seven days of force seven gales, Paul arrived back in the Falls feeling the worse for the weather.

In the warmth of her single bed at 22 Riga Street, Angela had decided on an early night now that her household chores were complete and her mother's tantrums had faded to tranquillity. Catching up with the events outside her shallow world, she read the print of the Belfast Telegraph with such deep desire, she even spotted the typing errors. Scanning over the articles-for-sale-section she was attracted to the pets column. Jumping out at her from the tabloid was a unique advert headed, 'Free To a Good Home'. Stealing her interest, curiosity impelled her to read on to discover a retired greyhound was in desperate need of a loving home. Sorely missing the track, the concept of a transfusion of company in the form of her greatest love acted as an instant booster to her flagging morale. She picked up her handbag and impulsively jotted the telephone number into her diary. Being on early shift tomorrow, she could arrange a viewing time after work at 2 p.m. which would not conflict with her mother's feeding times. Throughout the night the dreams of owning her very own greyhound afforded her minimal sleep.

After a visit to the newsagent where he bought a copy of The Sporting Life, Paul arrived at Tommy's backdoor and in the operations room of the kitchen, Paul revealed the plan of action for the week.

'Right, here's what we're gonna do. We'll scan the papers daily for greyhounds for sale, then we'll go buy one, so stop worrying, by Wednesday you'll be a trainer.' But Monday's edition of the Greyhound Life was extinct in the sales department.

'So what now?' whinged Tommy.

127

'Have you a copy of Saturday's Telegraph?' asked Paul.

'Aye, me dad buys that, I'll just go and find it.'

After ten minutes of hunting high and low, Tommy returned empty handed.

'No, I'm sorry, I can't find it, what now?'

'I suppose we could always go raking through the bins,' chaffed Paul.

Pouncing on the pedal bin, Tommy dug deep and produced the archaeological scripture. After five minutes of browsing around the denigrating smudges of potato peel, Paul revealed more bad news.

'No, not a thing Tom, just flea-bitten mongrels and a retired greyhound that's free to a good home. We'll just have to try again tomorrow.'

'So what's wrong with a retired greyhound, won't that do?' asked Tommy.

'No, the ad said retired due to injury, so it won't race and it'll probably be ancient.'

'Oh, can't we just take it to practise until the right dog comes along?' Tommy pleaded.

'No, you'll only get attached to the beast and won't want to part with it when the time comes, there's no sentiment in business.'

For an hour solid Tommy nagged like a wife and fought his case like a judicious barrister. The more Paul mulled it over, he realised that it might not be such a bad idea after all, with so much to learn and teething problems inevitable in the weeks when Tommy would have to take the reigns of the training mantle single handed.

'All right, all right, you win, do you have a phone?'

'No, me da had it taken out when me mom left.'

'That's no problem, come on, we'll call from my house.'

'Well?' said Tommy, itching to hear the verdict as Paul replaced the receiver.

'It was a woman, anytime after 4 p.m. It's at a farm west of Mossley.'

At 3.30 p.m. they set off, the back seats covered in a blanket borrowed from Paul's mother without her knowledge. After a gallon of wrong turnings and dead-end streets they found a sinuous dirt track which led them to a picturesque, whitewashed rural farmhouse nestling in a clearing surrounded by huge conifers. Alighting the car at 4.20 p.m. into a quagmire of adhesive mud, a middle-aged woman in knee-high Wellington boots came to meet them half way.

'I'm really sorry boys, but I think you're too late,' she said.

128

'What do you mean?' quizzed Paul, cringing at the splatters of mud clinging to the body work of his prestigious car.

'The dog's around the back, but a young girl arrived fifteen minutes ago and I think she's gonna have Toby. You're quite welcome to come and see him though.'

Having come this far, they decided to take her up on the offer. Whining in unison, they followed her around to rear of the black thatched-roof property. Turning the corner, Tommy spotted the imposing internee raised on hind legs, supported by the wire mesh enclosure, while Paul noticed the flowing dark hair and breathtaking figure which filled his dreams night after night. Half turning to spy the new arrivals, her face slowly returned to the attention seeking dog as Paul shook his head warily in disbelief at her presence.

'I think you're too late,' said the farmer.

'Aye,' moaned Paul, 'and it's not the first thing she's stole from me either.'

'As I was saying, the dog's only two years old, my friend who's a trainer sent him up to me from Shelbourne Park in Dublin. The dog has the pedigree to be a champion, but he slipped his handler and was hit by a car. He's still very fast but can't negotiate the bends, so we tried to give him a life on the farm. However, he's killed a few chickens lately so I have to let him go.'

'Aye, and I was here first,' interrupted Angela, besotted by the awesome white dog with the fawn patches.

'My wife and I named him Toby, but his real name is History Maker. We'll be sad to see him go but captivity was never our intention. He's a liability to the wildlife around here, so as I said lads, hard lines.' He handed Angela Toby's Irish Coursing Club papers and the ownership had changed hands.

'Do you mind if I have a look?' asked Paul, interested to view the dog's credentials.

'Not at all,' she smirked, rubbing salt into the wound.

As Paul read the pedigree and form lines, he understood that the farmer's words were genuine, the whelp was indeed a dormant racing machine, unbeaten in three trials and three races in 'hare'-raising times at both Dublin tracks, Shelbourne Park and Harolds Cross. Handing her back the book, he used his expertise to win a share in the animal.

'You never told me you had kennels,' he said.

'I don't,' she replied.

129

'Then where are you gonna keep the dog?' he probed.

'In the house, dippo, where do you think?' she replied sarcastically.

'Ha,' he sneered. 'It'll eat your furniture, you do realise that, don't you?'

'Really?' she asked.

'Aye, and I thought you were a nurse, don't you work shifts?'

'Aye.'

'So who's gonna feed and walk it when you're working afternoons? You'll come home to a mess and the neighbours will hate you. These dogs aren't pets, they're born to run, shit and eat. They don't know any better,' he told her, bluntly.

Just like the first moment Paul had cast his eyes over her, she too was now experiencing love at first sight with the large canine.

'I'll get by somehow.'

'What about if we all own it?' suggested Tommy, who was allowing the dog to lick his salty fingers.

'So, your monkey speaks,' slandered Angela.

'There was no need for that,' Paul defended, incited by her wit. 'Tom's getting wiser every day and you go and scythe his confidence with your sharp tongue.'

'What do you mean?' she said nervously, understanding that she had aroused his passions.

Taking her aside he explained Tommy's predicament. 'My friend's an orphan of society, you know the kid they all bullied at school, backward, toils to read and write, his mother up and left, do I need to paint the picture any further?'

'No, I'm sorry,' she replied humbly.

'Don't apologise to me, it's him you want to convince, seeing as he's gonna be the third member of our racing syndicate.'

'What?' she quizzed, confused.

'A three-way partnership. I have the kennel and transport, you can supply the food and as I work away from home every second week, Tom can keep up the training programme. What do you say?'

Against all the odds, they shared their first smile.

'What about your fiancé though?' asked Angela, throwing a spanner in the works.

'Contrary to your belief, she is not my fiancé, she's my inimical brother's. She was my girlfriend many moons ago, but the sun's come out in my life now.'

130

'Are you sure?' she returned.

'Aye, do you think I'd expect you to partner me if Bernadette and I were still an item?'

'No, I suppose not,' she conceded. 'Okay, we have a deal, as long as I can come and see the dog anytime I want.'

'Of course you can,' assured Paul, shaking with the excitement of knowing that she had now become his partner, even if it was only on a business scale.

'Come on then, we'll have to get some food supplies for Toby and get him settled into his new home,' said Paul.

'We'll have to be quick then, I have to get home to look after my mother,' said Angela.

As they drove back to Belfast, she opened her heart to him about her mother's terminal condition, while in the back Tommy cuddled the dog who wagged his tail in appreciation. Finding an open supermarket on the fringe of the city, Paul and Angela headed into the shop leaving Tommy and Toby to continue their male bonding. Paul's nose was already beginning to weep and his eyes were becoming irritatingly sensitive; sneezing as they marched up the aisle, he hoped it would be the first step to a another aisle one day in the future.

'I think you're coming down with flu,' she forwarded.

'No, I'm allergic to dogs.'

'Get away,' she smiled.

'No seriously, pollen or animal fur and I'm in a bad way.'

'Have you got antihistamine tablets at home?' she asked.

'No,' he replied. 'I haven't been near a dog for years.'

'Well, get some soon, they'll help you no end. So what do we need to feed this dog?'

'We'll need brown bread, eggs, cereal, pasta, some bones to clean its teeth, as well as a toothbrush and a high protein mixer; a fifteen kilogramme sack should last us a while. We'll need three and a half pounds of mince and a chicken; oh and, of course, plenty of green vegetables. I'll make a cauldron of broth once a week from the chicken and veggies to supplement the mixer and mince. About £10 a week should cover the food costs. We'll need grooming mitts, a wire racing muzzle, as well as a plastic muzzle for walking the streets, cod liver oil tablets and eventually a set of racing jackets, but I'll pay for all those extras.'

'How do you know all this?' she asked, impressed by his wisdom.

131

'I used to work as a handler at Dunmore five years ago, so you pick up these little things. There are other things we'll need, but they're all at hand within the home, these animals are GDUs.'

'What do you mean?'

'Garbage disposal units, they'll eat any leftovers. So if you ever have any, make up a doggie bag and bring it when you come to visit. Oh and before we go any further, no sweets or treats behind my back, is that clear?'

'Now just wait a minute, the dog's retired, is there any need for such an oppressive regime?' she argued.

'Didn't you read the pedigree? Toby's only two and a bit years old, he was undefeated until his accident. We already have the engine, if we can put the body work back together, we have a formula one racing car in that there dog.'

'Do you really think so?'

'I know so,' he emphasised.

Shopping wrapped, they returned to the car.

'Can you take me home now?' she urged, checking her watch.

'Aye, no problem, I'd better give you my address for tomorrow, you will come tomorrow?' he researched.

'I finish at two, so I'll come straight from work,' she said, putting a smile on his face.

'Well, do you have a pen and paper, so I can give you the address?' asked Paul.

'Aye, but can you start driving, my mother will be climbing the walls for her medication.'

Starting the engine, he asked her for a destination as she fished in her handbag for pen and paper.

'Do you know Riga Street?' she asked.

'No, where's that?'

'Well, do you know the Shankill?'

Turning off the engine, he turned to face her, devastated by her geography. 'I've a feeling our business partnership has just gone into liquidation,' he said.

'Why, what's wrong?' she demanded.

'I'll give you three guesses where I live, and it's not a million miles away from you.'

'Oh come on, I've no time for games, I'm running late as it is.' she pressed.

132

'The Falls, I'm from the Falls.'

For the first time since she had known him, she looked at him closely in a different light, up and down throughout the tense silence.

Chapter 6

In Like a Lamb, Out Like a Lion

After a minute's deliberation, Angela issued her statement. 'So you're a Catholic?'

'Well that's what it says on my birth certificate,' Paul replied, dejectedly.

'I suppose that's it then,' she said. 'There's no way you'd want me round your house.'

'Of course I would, but I know you wouldn't come.'

'So it doesn't bother you that I'm a Protestant?'

'No, not in the slightest. I've no time for religion.'

'Then give me your address and I'll be around after my shift tomorrow.'

'What? It doesn't bother you that I'm a Catholic?'

'No, now if we've cleared the air, will you please drive me home?'

'I can't take you to the Shankill,' he apologised.

'Why, have you no balls?'

'Oh, I have those, but I was intending to be a father one day so if it's all the same I'll steer clear.'

'Well, can you drop me off at the bus stop on Waterloo Place then?'

Driving into the illuminated city centre, the conversation turned to the dog and the times to come. Pulling the car over outside City Hall, Paul leaned over on to the warm seat where she had just been parked.

'So you're definitely coming tomorrow?'

'Of course I am, the Falls doesn't scare me, my father's in the RUC anyway,' she revealed the mother of all show-stoppers.

'You're pulling my leg?' Paul whispered, turning a whiter shade of pale with her undertone.

134

'I don't joke,' she replied, turning to see if there was a bus ready to transport her home.

'For God's sake, don't tell him you're coming to the Falls and that your co-owners are Catholics. He'll come hunting us down,' Paul stressed with conviction through his anxiety.

'My dad's not like that,' she said, shaking her head.

'They're all like that, RUC, Rapacious Usurpers of Corruption, they make La Cosa Nostra look like amateurs, villains with jurisdiction,' Paul savaged.

'I think you read too many comics.'

'There are none so blind as those who don't want to see, and in the land of the blind the one-eyed man is king,' Paul riddled.

'What are you trying to say?' she demanded, becoming flustered by his innuendoes.

'I'm saying don't tell you're father you're coming to the Falls.'

'Okay, I rarely see him anyway. Look here's my bus, I'll have to go, see you tomorrow.'

If it had all ended in a first kiss, for Paul it would have been the perfect ending to an amazing turnaround in fortunes. As it was, he was more than satisfied with the outcome to date, even if their divergent birth rites would only add to the mountain of difficulties he already had to surmount.

At 10 p.m. Paul finally persuaded Tommy, who was reluctant to leave, that Toby would still be there in the morning. Spending a restless night, Paul cringed at every whine and pine as the animal struggled to settle in, for he knew that too much noise would bring disapproval from the neighbours, as well as his own family, and that Toby's probation period would come under severe scrutiny come first light.

Rising at 6 a.m. with blocked nasal passages, Paul staggered downstairs into the kitchen, where he began to organise the dog's breakfast. Although the kennel was the full fifty foot length of the backyard away, and he had sagaciously refrained from switching on the light in the kitchen, the dog's extra sensory perception saw through his motive. Barking loudly and using his powerful frame as a battering ram against the wooden prison, Toby demanded room service. With the slops in hand, Paul rushed towards the padlocked kennel.

'Shut up,' he whispered aggressively. 'I'm doing my best.'

As the lock sprung the intolerant animal leapt out, almost knocking him over. Looking to the icy sky as Toby gulped zealously, with head

135

arcuated into the mash of cereal, eggs and brown bread, Paul knew that keeping a greyhound on a compact housing estate was going to be an immense burden, but the girl was worth the weight. As he collared the dog, whilst it tongued the sides of the stainless steel bowl clean to save him a job, his nasal orifices began to clear in the nippy morning air.

'Oh shit,' grimaced Paul. Following the wicked smell, he poked his head into the kennel, to discover that he'd forgotten to tell Toby his new home wasn't equipped with the facility of an en-suite bathroom.

Meandering along the dark alley to avoid the detrimental broken glass and sharp ring-pulls, Paul was being sent to sleep by Toby's timidly lethargic progress, as he sniffed out the other furry residents of his new neighbourhood. Then, in an unprovoked flash, the dog bounded forward almost dislocating Paul's arm from its socket, as it took the slack like a rabid Marlin hooked at the jaw. As the tension dispersed, Paul looked up to see that the dog was standing on its off fores, licking Tommy's face.

'I think you've a friend for life there,' Paul commented, swallowing his heart which had leapt into his mouth.

'I've hardly slept a wink, it's so exciting,' Tommy revealed. 'When can we race him?'

'I've had no sleep either, but only because he whined and barked all night and he's shit in the kennel. We can trial him on Sunday, that's if we still have him then.'

'What do you mean?' Tommy inquired, nervously.

'If he doesn't lower his tone and start behaving, I'll be forced to get rid of him.'

'Can't you leave the kennel door open at night so he can roam the yard?' proposed Tommy.

'I suppose it's worth a try,' agreed Paul. 'We could fix some rubber flaps over the entrance to keep the draught out, that way he can come and go as he pleases. Here, you can take the lead, just keep your eyes peeled for glass, a splinter in his paw and his racing days are over before they've even begun.'

'Why don't you go back to bed, I'll walk him for a few hours.'

'Are you sure?'

'Aye,' replied Tommy, enthusiastically.

'Well, just remember what I said, watch the glass and stay attentive.'

When Paul resurfaced at 10 a.m., he rushed into the kitchen and looked out of the window to see if Tommy had returned with the dog.

136

'He's been there since nine o'clock son, making snow,' said his mother.

'Snow? What do you mean?' Paul investigated.

'He's been massaging that dog so hard, the fur's been coming away like a blizzard. I took him out a cup of tea and asked him whether I should wake you, but he told me to let you sleep. It's a fine beast, son, but you do realise it'll have to go unless the noise stops.'

'Aye, I know, we have an idea that should combat that,' Paul persuaded a stay of execution.

'Okay, but one more night like last night and he's gone,' expressed his mother animatedly.

Joining Tommy half an hour later, Paul couldn't believe the difference. Already the animal's muscles were growing, it was more sprightly than ever and its shabby coat shone immaculately.

'Well, what do you think?' asked Tommy.

'Magnificent on the outer, but what about inside. Shall we find out?'

Returning to the house, Paul pilfered a cup of his mother's washing powder then returned.

'What's that for?' probed Tommy.

'Right, we need to worm him. We'll give him a course of tablets with his food tonight. When you walk him and he does his business, always keep an eye out for tapeworm amongst his stools, we can't afford those parasites. The best way to avoid contracting those is by not allowing him to eat rubbish off the ground, like chip papers, half-eaten sweets, other dog's excrement. Be strict with him. As to this washing powder, well sometimes they eat grass, that's not permitted either as their stomachs can't digest it, so we have to remove it by force. When I hold his jaws open you pour in the powder, he'll cough, convulse, then vomit, but don't worry, it'll do him good.'

As Paul prised Toby's jaws apart, Tommy fed the vomit-inducing soap into the dog's huge mouth to begin the cycle. Not amused the dog retreated from its enemies, then began to spit clear the foul mixture, but it was too late. Within seconds Toby arched his back like a branch at breaking point and began to cough violently, before emptying the contents of his stomach, which included a foam saturated, slimy ball of yellow grass just as Paul had forecast.

'What did I tell you,' said Paul winking.

'Wasn't that cruel?' asked Tommy.

'You've gotta be cruel to be kind, he would have had a sore belly for weeks with that blocking his intestines. Now we'll move on to his teeth, they'll have to be brushed everyday and I want him to have three bones a week,' stipulated Paul.

After a demonstration, he passed the brush to Tommy, who repeated the procedure.

'Is that all I need to know then?' asked Tommy.

'No, just the beginning, grooming and massage next.'

Straddling the dog, Paul bent over and placed his hands on to Toby's legs.

'Always massage upwards, nice and firm towards the heart, never away, it'll get the blood circulating, which contains a lot of oxygen to stimulate his performance. A good hour a day will suffice, if you want to win races. As to grooming, we need to get mitts today, they're easier than a brush. Keep your eyes open for fleas and dandruff, find the latter and the dog's deficient in his diet. Check his paws twice a day for cuts, and toenails shall be no longer than five millimetres in protrusion. If they're torn out during a race, it's curtains, they're okay for now though,' concluded Paul after giving them a thorough inspection. 'Do you think you'll remember all that?'

'I think so,' Tommy replied, nervously.

'Oh, and make sure he always has a plentiful supply of water, in fact we'll get some six inch nails for his water bowl.'

'What for?' quizzed Tommy confounded.

'Nails rust and give off iron, a great source for building strong muscles. We'll also pick nettles once a week and feed him those, they are also abundant in iron, but then again you should know all this if you read a book on greyhounds.'

'I read nothing about nails and nettles, won't they sting?'

'No, we boil them first then liquidise them into a soup, anyway, finally we must extend the forelegs prior to a run or gallop to loosen the tendons, they are very important, also known as leaders. Give me your hand, can you feel that?' asked Paul, locating the elastic gristle underneath Toby's muscle-bound leg.

'Aye, it feels like a long string of rubber.'

'And that's the way it has to stay. If you ever find a pea there, his racing days are over, it's as simple as that. We'll massage those with olive oil prior to racing to keep them nice and supple, that'll reduce the risk of injury. Come on, let's take a trip to the pet shop, we need to get a few things.'

As they drove towards the city centre, Paul rubbed at the itch in his left eye and its irksome associate on his right nostril. Within minutes, his eyelid had become tumefied and violent sneezing fits had begun with such force, that he might have had justification in claiming whiplash damages. After purchasing a course of worming tablets, a wire racing muzzle and the plastic equivalent for training purposes, they headed to a DIY store, where they bought a sheet of heavy duty rubber to replace the kennel door.

Upon returning home Paul took a bath and three paracetamol, in an effort to clear his sinuses and spruce himself up for the visit of his beloved Angela, despite wondering whether she would actually materialise.

At just after 2 p.m. Angela left the nearby Royal Victoria Hospital and embarked on the five minute walk to Clonard Street. Strolling down the Falls Road audaciously, she began to observe subtle tell-tale signs that began to creep up her spine, chill her blood within and question her nerve. On passing a set of traffic lights, she couldn't help but notice they were chastised with wire mesh grills for their own protection. Carrying onwards, she passed a shop whose sign read 'Gruaigare'. Intrigued, she glanced into the window to grasp by the adult high chairs, that it was a barbers, then rotating her head further afield she could see that most of the shop fronts had bilingual signs. Walking onwards she had a thought, God, it's like a country inside a city, then again the Catholics have another don't they, the Vatican inside Rome.

Regaining her poise she blended into the surroundings and went on her merry way, accruing confidence with every step. Suddenly, as she crossed another of the side street entrances to the Catholic ghetto, she stopped in her serendipity, flabbergasted, gasping, she stood jaw almost touching the pavement, as she observed the most awesome and formidable mural she had ever seen. It was an artist's impression of the Republican hunger-striking martyr and member of parliament, the late Bobby Sands. Standing menacingly in a red and black jersey, the haunting image stared at her with finger pointed and he had a message for her, which amplified through her mind louder than any megaphone could:

EVERYONE
REPUBLICAN OR OTHERWISE
HAS HIS OR HER OWN PART TO PLAY

Heart pounding so intensely that she could hear it above the cars whishing by in the drizzly rain, she quickened her stride as the autonomous, surrealistic graffiti seemed to close in around her, subsisting to her panic. Scanning around the ugly houses, pragmatised, she moved onwards, back and forth struggling to find his street. Eventually having successfully located Paul's home, she hammered her trepidation upon his door.

'Can I help you dear?' asked Paul's mother, opening the door to the petite cold caller, whose distress didn't go unnoticed.

'Paul, is Paul home?' spluttered the twitchy nurse.

'Aye, come away in,' she said, glancing up and down the street to see what had caused the trauma. 'He's in the backyard, I'll just go and call him. Paul, you have a visitor.'

'I can't believe it, Tom, she's actually come,' Paul declared excitedly.

Skipping to the house to greet her, he noticed by her gothic appearance that she was disturbed. 'Are you all right?'

'Aye, I've just seen a ghost, that's all, the graffiti is frightening.'

'Well, one man's graffiti is another man's gospel, can I get you a cup of tea?' he offered.

'Aye, that would be nice.'

'Can I get you one, Mom?'

'No, I'm fine, I'll go clean the bath shall I?'

'I've brought you a present,' Angela divulged, as she took the mug of tea, her hands still quivering.

'A present for me?' he asked, stunned, 'what is it?'

'Open it and see,' she replied, handing him a polythene carrier bag.

Searching the bag, he removed a cardboard box full of medical face masks. 'What are these for?'

'Why, they're for your allergy of course. If you wear these when you're working with the dog and you religiously wash your hands after every contact, you'll reduce the odds of the nasty symptoms. I've also got you some antihistamines, by the look of your eye you'd better take some now.'

'Thanks,' he said sincerely, absolutely delighted. 'I'll treasure those for ever,' he continued, allowing infatuation to put the words into his mouth for him.

'What?' she probed.

'No, I really appreciate the thought. Are you sure you're okay?'

'Aye, I'm fine now. I understand why you wouldn't come in to the Shankill now. Does your mother know I'm a Protestant?'

140

'No, and no one in this family must find out either. My daddy and brother are staunch believers in a Catholic Ireland; they despise Protestantism, they're of the old school and will never bow to the Orange order. I wouldn't trust Bernadette either; I could be wrong but she's easily led. As long as you're with me no one will ever suspect you.'

Watching as Angela and Tommy fussed over the playful dog, Paul felt as if they were all one big happy family, united by a common denominator, Toby. At a quarter to five Angela announced that visiting time was almost over.

'Can I drive you into Belfast?' offered Paul.

'Are you sure you don't mind?' she replied.

'It would be my pleasure,' he insisted, with a smile.

As they sat in the car, Bernadette, who was walking home, spotted the pair engrossed in conversation and she was less than impressed. Having driven against the rush-hour traffic and beaten every amber light, Paul pulled the car into the bus station in record time.

'So will you be around tomorrow?' he ventured.

'No,' she replied, 'I'm on afternoons until Friday, then I have the weekend off, so I'll come Saturday morning if you have no objections.'

'I thought that perhaps we could all take Toby for his exercise up the Cavehill; there's some good undulating ground that'll help to strengthen his legs ahead of his trial on Sunday,' suggested Paul.

'Aye, I'd like that,' she returned.

'Great, so how about 10 a.m.?'

'Aye, all right. Oh God, here's my bus, I'll have to go.'

Watching her run for her bus, he felt physically sick as his stomach churned at her departure.

When Paul arrived back at his house, a double confrontation awaited. First, his mother pulled him aside. 'What do you think you're playing at? Bringing a Protestant into this house. If your father gets wind of this, he'll have a heart attack, it can only spell trouble.'

'How do you know she's a Prod?'

'Her brogue sticks out a mile; twenty years ago I could have told you the street she lives on. You're playing with fire and you'll be burnt.'

'Only if you let on.'

'You know I'll say nothing, but if your father hears her accent, I won't be able to defend you, just be careful will ye?'

Taking Toby his supper and with Tommy gone, it was the first time that day that Paul had managed to gain the dog's undivided attention,

141

and that was only because it smelt the food. From the kitchen window Bernadette watched, full of ire, riled at how Paul could have carved out a relationship behind her back, having sworn blind that there was nothing between him and the pixie. Surely he had lied to her. Either way, she was determined to find out exactly what was going down.

Turning to Michael, who had just sat down to his meal, she caustically decreed her intentions. 'I'm going to see Paul's greyhound. Do you have any qualms with that, or should I say is it likely to result in him being rewarded with yet another beating?'

'What's your problem?' he replied.

'Your callous jealousy. Anyway, he has a new girlfriend now, so you can keep off his and my back.'

Saying nothing, he allowed her to leave without a fight, knowing that all his efforts would have to be channelled into winning her back, now that his constant mistrust had put a divide between them.

'I thought you said that you and her weren't an item, that she'd having nothing to do with you,' she addressed him, her arms folded in disgust.

'We aren't, she's just the co-owner of Toby. What do you think of him?' asked Paul.

'Well, you seemed all lovey-dovey to me,' she continued to peck at him.

'Unfortunately, you saw wrong.'

'So you don't deny it then, you do love her?'

'Hardly,' he laughed, turning to face her seething visage. 'I do fancy her rotten though, but business is business and that's all it is for now. I take it you don't approve of my taste?' he said, with a smug smile plastered over his face.

Accepting she was on the ropes, she took it on the chin and pulled herself from the edge of the precipice, shrewd enough to see that any further setback might just turn a molehill into Mount Everest.

Tommy's innovation in allowing the dog to have the freedom of the backyard was an instantaneous winner. Settling in without a whimper, Toby swung the vote and secured his future term of office. Over the next three days as they walked the dog through its fitness paces, Paul made sure that around 2 p.m. they were always in the vicinity of the RVH, where he hoped to catch a glimpse of his elusive soul-mate, but not once did she appear to mollify his soaring blood pressure.

Having prophesied snow for Thursday and Friday, the meteorologists had once again shown their incompetence, as a severe cold snap forbade the clouds to defrost and redecorate the landscape with their havoc paint. Come Friday night and the satellite pictures told the weathermen to forecast clear skies and a significant rise in temperature.

Rising at dawn on Saturday to satisfy Toby's appetite, Paul crept downstairs to find the kitchen showered in a soft orange incandescence, which could only connote one thing. Opening the back door, the blizzard whistled at and around him, desperate to gain entry. Squeezing his eyes for protection from the raging elements, he lumbered down the yard to supply breakfast in bed to the astute dog who had no wish to become a part of the new colour code.

Battling through a three inch carpet of squeaky clean weather, Paul returned to the kitchen and made himself a cup of coffee, then stood in awe, watching the graceful infestation of white locusts swarm on to the land. As they spiralled and danced to conquer the earth, he remained transfixed, mesmerised by the wondrous spectacle and the glimmering purity it exemplified. Suddenly his wide-eyed gaze inverted to a grimace, as he wondered whether the snow might postpone his love match.

At 9.30 a.m. Tommy returned from a ninety-minute lap of the dilapidated community which had been transformed into a scene from a Christmas card. Cheeks rosy and hands numb, he was welcomed by Paul and a much needed hot cup of sweet tea. Allowing him to burn his lips on the thermal liquid, Paul then asked for his head kennel lad's advice.

'So, do you think he'll run tomorrow? I mean chase the hare.'

'Aye, he saw a cat this morning and tried to jump off, I thought I was on water skis,' laughed Tommy.

'Do you think Angela will come, with all this weather?' asked Paul, seeking assurance.

'Aye, it's stopped snowing now, course she'll come.'

'I'm not sure,' Paul replied cynically, depressed by the snow which was showing no signs of an early thaw. 'If you give Toby a good going over with the mitts, I'll go and keep an eye out for her.'

At the living room window with his sceptical thoughts, he cursed the weather again and wished he'd had the sense to have given her his phone number, then again, phone books were in circulation. Curiously, he parted the aged, grey net curtain and stuck his nose to the brittle cold glass and, to his incredulity, saw her walking towards the house like a pair of scales, carrying two carrier bags, which were supplying her with inadmissible traction. Rushing to the door on a thrust of relief, he relieved her of her burden.

'I didn't think you'd come,' he gasped, overjoyed.

'Why?' she said, confused.

'The weather.'

'Aye, it's beautiful, isn't it. Anyway, how's our dog?'

'Great, Tom reckons he'll run his socks off tomorrow. Can I get you a cup of tea before we head up the Cavehill? You still want to go don't you?' he researched.

'Of course I do and the tea would be nice.'

'How's your mother?' he asked, leading her through to the kitchen.

'Not too good, I think this is maybe the last snow she'll see.'

'I'm sorry,' he whispered.

'Don't be, and thanks for asking. I've brought next week's food. Now then, what's the plan for next week, you're away aren't you?'

'Aye, but if you tie in with Tom, he'll make sure he's here for you, he could even meet you after work.'

Taking her tea, she smiled as she watched Toby chase Tommy around the yard, as he teased him with a succulent marrowbone.

'He loves that dog, doesn't he?' she commented.

Not as much as I love you, reflected Paul, who was staring at her, as his heart pounded like it had never pounded before.

'I'll go and get Tom and Toby and we can be on our way. Are you ready?' he shouted to Tommy from the back door.

'Aye,' came the acknowledgement.

'Then collar him up and bring the plastic muzzle,' Paul instructed. 'No doubt half of Belfast will be out walking their dogs.'

Having cleared the snow from his windscreen, it took three attempts to start the car.

'You should have your mask on,' mothered Angela.

'Don't be daft, people will think I'm not wise or we'll be stopped as terrorists, I think I'll suffer for a bit.'

When they arrived at the estate of Belfast Castle, Paul's nose had held out, too numb to be bothered into plaguing him with a sneezing fit. Looking from the window, he could see that the once rugged, rolling hills had been transformed into a smooth alpine ski resort, as religion and class unified to enjoy the slopes.

'Damn, we should have brought some bin-liners, we could have sledded down the hill,' whined Paul.

144

'I had a real sledge, shiny wood and metal runners and my mother brought me here one day and I played with the other children, but only because they didn't know me,' said Tommy.

Finding a secluded plateau, where the vibrant children's screams of joy were but a distant echo, they looked over the pretty city and watched the smoke billowing from the rooftops to pollute the serenity.

'It looks so peaceful,' sighed Angela.

'Aye, but looks are deceiving and beauty is only skin deep,' marred Paul.

With March just a few weeks over the hill, it had, thus far, been a relatively quiet start to the year with respect to the ongoing troubles. The only exchanges had been the verbal ammunition supplied by the politicians, to be fired by the media, who portrayed themselves as peacemakers. In all reality, they were no more than instigators, full of hot air that would keep sectarianism buoyant through the storm of calm and all for the sake of newspaper sales. It could only be a matter of time before talk degenerated to violence as it always did.

'Can we let him off the lead?' begged Tommy.

Scanning around to note that there were no other canines in the vicinity, Paul issued his verdict: 'We shouldn't really, but seeing as there are no other dogs around and we have a muzzle, we'll give him one chance. If he does a runner then it'll be the last time he gets off the lead.'

As Tommy unfastened the collar and lead, Toby was too engrossed in trying to rid himself of the plastic headgear to notice that his shackles had been removed. Racing across the deer park towards the ancient castle, Tommy shouted Toby to follow. Upon hearing his master's voice, the dog whipped into action like a lasso and started tearing towards the call. Turning to face the oncoming charge, the last thing that Tommy saw was two patches of brown hurtling at him, before he was lying flat on his back, mowed down by Toby's excitement. Noticing by the raucous laughter that his party trick had gone down a treat with the audience, the athletic animal about turned and focused on Angela's camel coat. Freezing in her shoes, as he thundered towards her, she grimaced before she became the next victim of the raging bull. Two down and one to go, Toby turned to Paul who was almost doubled over with the joviality, but like a crafty matador he swerved at the last moment. Cupping her hands to make a snowball, Angela outlined her intentions.

'You don't think you're getting away with it that easily do you?' she screamed, before launching her missile which struck its target with incisive precision, exploding on the side of Paul's head.

And so it escalated and war had been declared; for ten minutes solid they burnt their calories in a triangular snowball fight, while Toby ran around improvising, using his muzzled head instead of the compacted spheres of snow.

Concentrating on a dual-pronged attack from Tommy and Toby, Paul turned to become the bull's-eye, as a ball of frozen ice shattered over his face. Rubbing his eyes to regain his vision, he heard Angela in raptures of laughter which incited him into a new furore. Racing across as if he were Toby, he tackled her to the ground in Gaelic football fashion, then began to force snow down her sweating back. Wriggling for her life as the sharp tingle of snow touched her warm flesh, she found a hidden energy reserve and managed to force him on to the soft white blanket to repay the favour.

For a few slushy moments they convoluted, entwined like lovers on the saponaceous ground, while Tommy and Toby refereed in the distance, then they were spent. Resting on their knees they stared into each other's sparkling eyes, fighting over the air to nourish their screaming lungs. Breathing stabilised, they continued to gaze earnestly at one another and slowly their heads began to inch closer simultaneously. As Paul relaxed his mouth, within millimetres of a first kiss, Angela heard the alarm clock in her head and snatched her head away at the last second. Closing his eyes and mouth, Paul felt the cold for the first time that morning.

'I think we'd better go home,' she announced.

'Aye, I suppose we had better make tracks,' agreed Paul despondently.

As they drove back to the Falls, silence reigned, and although the heaters were on full blast they could not thaw the mood. After a sombre cup of acclimatising tea, Angela decided she wanted to go home.

'I'll run you into Belfast,' he offered.

'No. It's okay, I'll get the bus.'

'No, I insist, besides I have to get a few things in the city,' he lied.

When they arrived at the bus station, he turned to her. 'Are you still coming to trial the dog tomorrow?'

'Of course.'

'I'll pick you up here at ten then.'

'Fine,' she replied, opening the door to alight into the slush.

146

'Oh, Angela,' he said, prolonging her departure.

'What?'

'I'm sorry about earlier,' he said, seeking a reaction.

'No, I'm sorry I gave you the wrong impression, this partnership has to stay platonic,' she emphasised.

'But why?' he disputed through his frustration, having felt his chances were growing after the earlier incident.

'It wouldn't work,' she chided, almost sad herself. 'There's far too much against us, more than before. Anyway Paul, you're not my type.'

Deeply afflicted by her snub, he retaliated. 'Then what is your type, you're not a . . .'

'No, I'm not a lesbian,' she interrupted, having heard that inference so many times before.

'So what's your type then?' he demanded, raising his voice.

'I'm not sure, but when I meet him, I'll know. Goodbye Paul, see you tomorrow at ten.'

As she waited for her bus, she watched as he wheel-spun the car away, then drove through a red light before his red Escort disappeared. Nipping the flesh at the side of her mouth between her teeth, she began to wonder exactly whether their business partnership would stand the strain at this early stage.

After steering his upset through the treacherous conditions, the rally drive terminated safely outside his front door. Banging his fists on to the wheel, he translated the pain of rejection from his heart to his hands. As Paul calmed his nerves with a cool cigarette, he couldn't help but reflect on how his attempts at courtship had made him look like a clown. For the remainder of that day, no matter how hard he attempted to find seclusion, or tried to banish the earlier happenings to the annals of his subconscious, like Ebeneezer Scrooge the ghosts of past, present and future would not depart him until the light of morning.

After a restless night and a million action replays in his mind, he arose, revived, with confidence. He had managed to persuade himself that he was only human and that if she would not have him, then it was her loss. No more would he be the scapegoat for her infinite pre-menstrual tension. No more would he play the role of the deluded greyhound chasing the elusive spoof hare, no way, he wouldn't do it. Well, at least, not until she was in his sights again.

Halving the dog's ration in order to give him that little extra hunger, that just might give him the impetus to shave a tenth of a second off

147

the clock, which might just turn out to be the difference between qualification and rejection, Paul fed the disgruntled animal whose bowed head, large sad eyes and skeletal protrusions communicated a classic line from the Dickens novel; 'Please sir, can I have some more?'

Paul's urgency to get the dog back into racing was undoubtedly the motive which outweighed the general rule on this occasion, which was that when you began to trial your greyhound on to a track, you wanted to give away as little as possible to the handicapper, so that when the conditions were right and the handicap was in your favour, then you would have saved your dog's best runs for when your money was down. 'Stopping' a dog was like a dabble on the stocks and shares, it was not without risk. One almighty crash and your investment was lost. A sluggish dog could result in sustaining a bad injury, which could abbreviate a greyhound's already limited racing life of an average three years, although some dogs defied age to win at seven years' old. Then again, patience, planning and having the stomach to hammer your savings on could profit in kissing your mortgage goodbye.

Putting a dog away for a rainy day could be achieved in a number of ways, the most favoured being the old 'pie' scenario; a hefty feed prior to racing, which would blunt the animal's appetite to chase the feast, a dozen eggs would do the trick nicely. Other methods included smearing petroleum jelly over the dog's eye, which would catch sight of the lure first; dependent on inside or outside hare, the dog would 'miss the break' and lose valuable 'spots' on the clock. Some owners even wound an elastic band around a dog's testicles to subdue the excitement to chase the bunny; obviously if the greyhound was a bitch then the latter method was void. Performance-enhancing drugs worked both ways, although random chromatography testing prior to racing could detect most illegal substances, making this practice extremely difficult to employ. If found guilty both owner and dog would be sine died from the track. As it was, all the aforementioned chicanery was only damaging the health of the already flagging sport, as disgruntled patrons showed their disgust at backing 'non-tryers' by boycotting the meetings. As far as Paul was concerned, he wanted to compete to win every time, his love was the taking part in the game. Of course, he wanted to win vast amounts of money, but he knew intense gambling would only spoil the fun.

By the time his master arrived at 9 a.m., Toby was friskier than ever, infuriated at his paltry morning measure. Throughout the ten-minute drive to the bus station, Tommy fought tooth and nail to control the beast as it saw food in the car's gear stick and sought to become a front-seat passenger. As he waited for Angela, Paul's nose was exploding, showering the windscreen with transparent mucus and his neck had sprouted a crop of white blotches upon the red acreage, where Toby had licked at him. Checking his watch to see that it was 10.05 a.m. as yet another bus pulled in from the Shankill without her on board, Paul began to wonder if yesterday's embarrassments had indeed quenched their fiery partnership. He was about to restart the engine at 10.15 a.m., when a spark flashed across the carburettor of his heart to re-ignite his smouldering love as she alighted the last chance bus. She spiritedly forwarded her apologies, as the dog bayed for her attention.

'Good morning Toby, have you missed me? I'm sorry I'm late but I had to clear the snow from the pavement outside my front door; there's a lot of pensioners on my street.'

Driving towards the track a resumption of normal service returned as they chatted freely, neither mentioning yesterday's prelude to a kiss.

Paul and Tommy left Angela by the win-line and led Toby round the snow-covered circumference of the track, noting the pools of water which had flouted the draining system and were now only a few inches of thaw away from forming a river. Arriving at the starting traps with another two handlers and their dogs, the cock and bull stories began to flow ('. . .my dogs been off the track for sixteen weeks with a damaged tendon . . .' and ' . . he's only a pup, hasn't chased the hare before, might not even come out of the boxes . . .') to which Paul added his own, but his was no untruth.

'Well, this animal here was hit by a car and hasn't seen a track for six months, in fact he's actually retired, but I'll give him a chance, you never know.'

While the others argued over trap allocation, Paul took the leftovers and gave Toby the widest berth available, remembering the farmer's words, '. . . he won't go around the bend.' Paul straddled the dog and loosened the collar as Tommy watched, attentive to every detail, knowing that one day it would be his turn. Opening the trap door, Paul dropped the lead and persuaded the heavy hound into the cramped starting blocks with a little duress. Carefully making sure Toby's tail was free from impediment, he bolted the trap door, picked up the sodden lead and made for the pick-up point hurdling the puddles.

The whizzing and whining of the mechanical apparatus signified that the hare was on the move and the moment of truth was only seconds away. Skittering ever closer in jerky movements along the inside of the track, the heavy-duty luminous green polythene bag attached to a protruding metal rod accelerated the excitement within each of the owners' hearts until finally the lids sprung open. To Paul's shock, Toby was first away and, as the first bend approached, he had established a four-length lead but, when the initial arc arrived, having no rudder to pull himself hard to the left and heading straight for a brick wall, he slammed on the anchors; skidding across the slippery surface, he cartwheeled over before stopping fractionally shy of the redbrick partition. As the other two runners curved successfully, Paul and Tommy raced to Toby's rescue. Disorientated by the crash, Toby was dazedly bounding back and forth. Upon seeing Tommy, he galloped towards him, seeking the kind of comfort a child requires from its mother, having just suffered a trip out of the wide blue yonder of fun. Collaring the dog, Paul gave him a quick once over, checking for visible signs of damage, to find all appeared to be sound. Refusing to comment, his pride having suffered the same fate as Toby's first bend knockdown, Paul walked briskly off the track and into the kennelling enclosure to wash the gritty sand from the dog's paws. As he employed the hose pipe provided to extricate the harmful residue, Angela appeared from over his shoulder.

'What happened? Is he okay?'

'Aye, he's fine, but I can't see him ever running a race for us,' he replied, despondently.

'Why? He was winning until he slipped,' she returned.

'No, he couldn't take the bend, as the farmer said, the injury must be too great. I'm sorry but our aspiration just died, he's finished.'

Eavesdropping on Paul's post-race analysis, the owner of the sprightly young pup who had gone onto to turn the trial into a procession pitched in some friendly advice through his jubilation.

'Have you tried James Haddow at Holywood?'

'What about him and who is he?' inquired Paul, rising to greet the elderly gent dressed in the Donegal tweed jacket and matching cap, built to last any retirement campaign and all weathers the outdoor conquest of greyhound racing could throw at the resilient cloth.

'Why, he's the finest vet in all Ireland. He'll sort your dog if it can be sorted.'

'Do you have an address where we can find him?' asked Paul.

'Aye, if you follow me to my car I'll give it to ye, but you'll need to take him a bottle of whisky and it has to be Scottish, Glenmorangie at that.'

Slowly driving back to Belfast, Paul could hardly conceal his disappointment at the decline of both his dreams over the last twenty-four hours. Only having opened his mouth for the occasional sneeze in between pouts, he pulled the car into the bus station.

'God, your face paints a thousand pictures,' Angela stated, attempting to break his lament, 'and why have you stopped here? I thought I could spend some time with my third of Toby. It's not the winning that counts, it's the taking part.'

'Jesus wept, the dog's a rag. He'll never run, I'll tell you that now. You don't honestly think a top trainer from Shelbourne Park would have parted with such a pedigree if he hadn't already been down every avenue to put him right. Christ, you're so naïve at times,' lashed out Paul.

'No, Paul, you're forgetting to remember. I wanted the dog as a pet. Of course it would be great to see Toby race, but if it's not meant to be, then tough,' she reminded him.

'Aye, she's right, you did know the dog was retired,' ganged up Tommy.

Nodding his head in agreement, with a wry smile, Paul accepted the criticism knowing he was wrong. 'Aye, you're right, but do we attempt this guru vet or not?'

'If you think it's in our interests, then why not,' conceded Angela, starting to feel for his plight.

'Well, I say we give it a bash. When I get back onshore next week, me and Tommy will take a drive over to Holywood on Monday and see what yer man has to say,' decided Paul.

'So I'm not involved any more?' she asked light-heartedly.

'I'm sorry, but I thought. . . .'

'You thought I'd be working,' she interrupted. 'Well, I'm not next Monday, and you presume too much. So come on, back to the Falls, I want to spend some time with my dog.'

For the first time since they had been spending time together, Toby's disastrous performance overshadowed Paul's obsession for Angela and it allowed her to begin to learn his true character. And it was one she quite liked, one of strength and determination to succeed. With Paul acting himself, that afternoon brought them closer than ever and on a few occasions she even stole long interrupted gazes, while he drummed the tasks required for the coming week into Tommy.

'So, do you fancy giving him a massage?' asked Paul, turning to catch her staring. 'I'm sure a woman's touch would inspire him to run.'

'I don't know how to do it,' she replied.

Assisting her, Paul took her by the waist, which for once she had no objection to, and helped her straddle the dog. He took her hands, placed them on to Toby's bulging muscles, then began to move them up and over the fur in circling motions.

'It's as simple as that,' he whispered into her neck, sending shivers down her spine with his warm breath, 'once you have the rhythm, just add a little pressure.'

Up above, from her bedroom window, Bernadette was watching, her face as bitter as the invisible lemon she appeared to be sucking.

It wasn't until Paul lay in his bunk on Thursday night that his thoughts sailed to Angela. Having earlier nipped into Stranraer to file a missing person's report on Tommy's mother, he'd been told in no uncertain terms that he was wasting police time. On the way back to the ship, he'd gone for a few pints with Scots Paul to cool off and re-evaluate his next move in that direction. Moving on to his fourth pint, it appeared to him that all the couples in the bar were playing to his misfortunes, laughing at him, showing him what he was missing. Staring at the bulkhead from his top bunk as his Scots counterpart's snoring forbade him sleep, his heart ached for a woman, but the only girl he could think of was Angela. On the ferry there were around thirty stewardesses, no doubt some single and looking for Mr Perfect, but so far none had managed to give him a love transfusion.

During his last trip across the Irish Sea on the afternoon of Sunday March 6th, the grim news broke via the radio that three IRA volunteers had been shot dead in Gibraltar, one of whom was a woman and worse, early rumours suggested they may have been unarmed. Paul knew that Republican anger would spill on to the streets were the security forces to enter the Falls that night, so he hoped, prayed and took the precaution of leaving his car at the ferry terminal, as well as the gamble of trying to get home. Taking a black cab, which was only willing to take him half way up the Falls Road, he sprinted like a petrified gazelle being pursued by a ravenous cheetah through the last half mile of desolate streets. Arriving home safely in a lather, he laughed until he cried at his fortuity to have made it unscathed.

Once fully composed, he went to check Toby, only to find that Tommy had hung around to await his return. Although the first thing he should have done was inspect Toby and praise Tommy's efforts, his heart was a thousand beats elsewhere.

'So has Angela been around much?' he asked unperturbed.

'Twice, no. . . three times,' replied Tommy, who just wanted recognition for his handling of the dog.

'The dog looks fine, any trouble?'

'No,' Tommy smiled, with pride. 'He's been as good as gold, but your mom says he pines for me when I go home at night.'

'Has Angela asked any questions about me?' delved Paul, searching for a mere five loaves and two fishes to feed the five thousand.

'Aye, she did actually. Mind you, every night she's been here, Bernadette has been down asking her all sorts,' Tommy let slip.

'Like what?' asked Paul, his eyes squinting in anxious thought.

'Lots of things, like where she lived and whether yous were going out together.'

'And what did she say?' demanded Paul, distressed.

'She said she lived at Ballymurphy and that she had a boyfriend already. Then Angela was asking me some stuff, but I didn't know the answers.'

'What sort of stuff?' pressed Paul, his hopes rising.

'Silly ones like, how long we had been best friends and if you still felt anything for Bernadette, that's all I can remember.'

'Okay Tommy, you'd better go home now; if the soldiers come the streets will be dangerous. I'll see you tomorrow, now go on,' he urged, deeply concerned for his friend's safety. 'Oh, just one thing more, I'm really sorry but I have bad news. The Scottish police won't look into your mother's whereabouts. They say she's not a missing person.'

'Then what can we do?' whimpered Tommy.

'I don't know. She could be anywhere, not necessarily the British Isles.'

'But she is,' contested Tommy, stamping his foot in frustration, 'she sent me a letter once, said she was in England.'

'If you have the letter it'll have an address or at least a postmark, that'll narrow down the scope of search. Do you still have it?' inquired Paul, showing he hadn't given up just yet.

'I'll look but I'm not sure where I put it, I know I kept it though.'

'Go on then, go home and find it and we'll take it from there in the morning.'

Entering the house, there was a chilling air of death and ominous expectancy. And although it was only 9.30 p.m. the whole household had retired to bed, all except the irascible Michael. Making himself a hot drink, Paul decided he would catch up with the events at Gibraltar on the television. When you lived in the core of the bad apple city, no matter how opposed you felt towards the troubles and how hard you tried to turn a blind eye, it was on your doorstep. It was your inheritance and there was no escaping it.

In the living room Paul found Michael fuelling his courage with a bottle of whisky; beside him he had two primed Molotov Cocktails keeping him company. Spotting his brother's homemade arsenal, Paul turned to leave, but Michael was in the mood to talk.

'The murdering bastards have shot three volunteers in Gibraltar, they were unarmed. I knew them all personally, did you?'

'I'm sorry,' whispered Paul, and he literally was, for he knew the implications.

Over the next few days lynch mobs would take to the streets to vent their anger at the British soldiers. The Falls would become a battle zone. The taken-for-granted normality of civilian life would be replaced by organised chaos and no one would be immune to the hatred deluging through the arteries of the streets to poison the community. It could only be likened to the worst snowdrift one could ever imagine engulfing a rural village, confining the habitants to their homes. Electricity could be lost at any moment and simple trips to the supermarket would become a life endangering expedition. It was a period which would see people rush to the loft in search of all the old tried and tested board games and a time when a new generation would be made out of frustration.

When the signal came, both men raised their heads simultaneously, one with a smile, one with a deep grimace. It was the clattering of dustbin lids, announcing that the Army was in the neighbourhood. A call to arm yourself and take to the street for the Cause. Picking his petrol bombs off the floor, Michael brushed passed Paul, then turned to face him.

'Are you coming brother? It's time to make a stand.'

'It's not my fight,' replied Paul.

For as much as he wanted to persuade Michael to rethink his fidelity, he knew it would be a waste of breath. As Michael headed into battle with his anger between his teeth, Paul picked up the whisky bottle to numb the pain and wondered if whoever had named the country had done so with some malicious preconception of how history would unfold. Ireland, land of anger and keen resentment. Now why the fuck hadn't they named it Peaceland, thought Paul. In bed, his insomnia returned as he worried for Michael and he attempted to find the answers to why Angela had asked Tommy those two questions.

Paul rose nice and early and set out to collect his car so he could meet Monday's itinerary. Taking a bus he noted that Clonard Street had been fortunate to have missed last night's blitz. Most of the skirmishes had been concentrated on the Falls Road, with the security forces reluctant to be lured into the depths of the ghetto, to be met by a hornet's nest of insidious Republican sympathisers. As the bus crawled around the clearing up-operation, Paul observed a couple of torched vehicles among the strewn debris, which consisted of anything that was not bolted down. He even spotted an old kitchen sink which had been utilised as a weapon against the alien forces. With the battle having fizzled out in the early hours, Paul desperately hoped that all the anger had been vented and some kind of normality would now return to the streets, because the last thing he needed now was to explain to Angela that she could not visit for her own safety.

Having picked up Angela at the bus station as arranged, the drive over to Holywood was arduous enough trying to fight his allergy, without the added hindrance of driving against the fiercely glowing icy sun, which unmercifully attacked his pupils to bring flash headaches and blinding green spots in the road to impair his vision. Although she must have heard the news of the IRA murders, not once did she comment upon the tragedy.

Finding the address, the posse knocked upon the warped wooden door of an old grey cottage sprawling with creeping ivy and which gave the impression that the last visitor had been a tidal wave. On the third attempt, their prayers were answered by an old man with white tufts of silk-thin hair and matching razor-sharp stubble, growing on a rotund beetroot. Breathing sickly, wallpaper stripping fumes, he spoke in a cantankerous manner.

'Yer dug's a cripple, it'll never run. Forget it laddie,' he rebuked in broad Scots, before turning to close the door in their faces.

'Wait,' shouted Paul, 'I've brought you some medicine.'

Hurrying to the car, he produced advance payment, a bottle of Glenmorangie as he'd been prescribed to do. Grabbing the bottle with trembling hands, the old Scot impetuously unscrewed the cap and took a long swig before agreeing to help.

'Well, bring the beast around the back, I've not all day.'

They scrambled over each other as they obeyed his strict orders with headlong speed.

'So what's exactly the problem?' snapped the old medicine man.

After a deadly silence, Paul decided to speak on behalf of the cause, 'Well, we got the dog from . . .'

'Oh Jesus Christ, I don't want a life story, laddie. Sharp, concise facts if you will.'

Gulping hard, Paul composed himself before nervously answering. 'He won't go around the bends, since he was hit by a car six months ago.'

Employing brute force the chiropractor yanked at Toby's legs and crunched his vertebrae with his heavy-handed thumb.

'Good and bad news, I'm afraid. Well laddie, which first?'

'Good news,' dithered Paul.

'He has no injuries and now to the bad news children. It's psychological, yer dug has a mental block. He may never race again, the trauma of being hit by the car has scarred his mind. Tak his fear awa and he'll run. However, don't be holding your breath, they're stubborn bastards. There's nothing I can prescribe. All you can do noo is pray, be on yer way then.'

Taking his words of wisdom, three brains rattled in unison throughout the homeward journey. By the end of the day a democratic decision had been reached, being as it was the only plan they had been able to come up with. They'd give Toby another two trials, one a hand-slip on Thursday before the racing began, and subsequently a three dog trial on Sunday morning.

In just spending time with Angela, as he had done over the last few days, Paul was now growing to love her for real reasons, seeing her true stature as she showed tremendous patience and benevolence. At times as he watched her spend more time with Tommy, he became slightly jealous, but the introverted Tommy needed that special attention. Little did she know it, but she had filled the void left by his mother's departure. For Paul, what had been an infatuation based on a pretty face had now progressed to the realisation that he wanted to spend the rest of his life with her. Now that she had relaxed her guard to expose a beautiful nature, Paul knew that a cautious overture was needed if he was to channel her emotions in his direction, yet he knew that was easier said than done. Especially now that time was not being kind, as another week at sea loomed.

Standing on the putty sand just shy of the first bend at Dunmore, Paul held Toby and waited for the mechanical lure to pass. As the sacrificial hare neared, he could feel Toby's heart pump faster as he attempted to emancipate himself from his captor. Allowing the dog its liberty to hunt, Paul watched in disgrace as Toby jogged towards the bend, then walked around the arc before about turning cunningly, in the knowledge that the foolish rabbit would reappear and he'd be waiting to pounce. Shoes soaked and humiliated, Paul walked off the track in need of some sympathy and he was not to be disappointed.

'Cheer up, it's not the end of the world, Toby will run when he's good and ready. I'm certain of that,' she consoled. 'Besides, you have me and Tommy.'

Aye, she's right, he thought to himself. Had it not been for the insurance policy the dog had brought, he would now be placing an advertisement in the tabloids exactly like the one they'd followed up. While he had the dog, he had her in his sights and at last his patient approach had paid its first premium. She had shown him in her last statement that there was an ember in her heart for him, all he had to do now was ignite it into an inferno.

With Toby and Tommy settled for the evening, Paul then drove Angela to the bus station, which favoured him all the intimacy he required to begin engineering upon the foundation she had earlier presented him.

'So what are you up to on Saturday night?'

'Oh, the usual I suppose; have a bath, watch Casualty, dull,' she replied.

'Well, eh, how do you fancy a night at the dogs, with me?' he coughed out the last two words.

'Aye, that sounds good, and Tommy too?'

'Aye and Tommy too,' he returned.

'All right, pick me up at seven on Saturday. Look, I'll have to go, here's my bus,' she said.

As she opened the door he called her back.

'What is it?' she asked, keeping one eye on her bus.

Hesitating, the words he wanted to say wouldn't roll off his tongue, 'Nothing, go on, you'll miss the bus.'

157

Driving home to his side of the peace-line, his mind ran with the gear changes, as doubts reversed to smiles then sanguinity to frowns.

Having managed to shake Tommy loose for the evening, Paul arrived at the bus station on Saturday a sharp ten minutes early to find that Angela was already there, walking on the spot to keep warm from the chilly wind. Drawing her attention with a blast of his horn, she jogged across the road then entered the vehicle smelling like the garden of Eden. God, you look tasty, edible in fact, he thought, wished I could get to find out what flavour you are.

'Where's Tommy?' she asked, suspiciously.

'He's not well,' he schemed, 'he has a tummy bug, I knew you wouldn't come, but as I didn't have your phone number, I had to turn up to inform you. I suppose it's a night in front of television after all, what time's your next bus?'

'Why? Don't you want to go to the dogs now?' she replied, falling into his snare.

'Aye, course I do. I just didn't think you'd believe me about Tommy. I thought that you'd think I'd planned all this to get you alone,' said Paul with an air of nonchalance.

'And did you?'

'No, besides, I have my eye on someone at work. She may not be as pretty as you, but she makes up for it in personality,' he said, dying to smirk.

'What's wrong with my personality?' she asked, screwing her face up to shun the hurt.

'Well, let's be honest about it, you don't actually give off heat, do you, and I've seen more supple corpses.'

'Drive me to the dogs,' she commanded.

Driving with a cheeky smile across the right side of his face, he knew his game plan was going to perfection.

'Where are you going?' she asked, as he headed for the illicit entrance.

'Oh, I'm not paying in, I'm skiving in. I'd ask you to join me, but you couldn't handle scaling the wall, so I'll meet you in there,' he said cockily.

Glancing at the wall and fence, she spoke bravely. 'I can get over that fence.'

'Na, you pay and have a coffee ready for me.'

'Get lost,' she bickered, 'I'm going over the fence, I'll show ye.'

158

Ascending the wall with ease, Paul watched as she struggled to pull her delicate frame on to the wall.

'There ye go, easy,' she jibed.

Removing gloves from his pockets, he put them on.

'Do you have any?' he asked.

'No, why?'

'The fence is sharp and what's more, it's covered in tar. Since I'm a gentleman I'll nip over first then let you borrow mine.'

Having sprung with kangaroo effortlessness over the corrugated sheeting, his head popped up from the other side before he passed her the gloves. Unable to watch her attempt to keep parity, as the iron rattled and buckled in tune with her squeals and pants, he checked his watch. I'll give her another minute then I'll offer assistance, he resolved. Within seconds of an intervention, she landed at his feet with an almighty thud. Bowing to look at her, he smiled. 'I always knew you'd fall for me one night.'

'Oh shut up, will ye, look at the state of my clothes,' she whinged, brushing down her mud-stained attire.

Joining him on the terraces ten minutes later with wet patches on her knees, she wasn't aware of it, but Paul's fun at her expense was just beginning.

'So do you still think I'm as stiff as a board with no personality?' she chirped.

'Aye,' he replied.

'What do you mean,' she demanded, incensed.

'Bet you couldn't drink a pint down in a oner. No, you don't drink do you?' he taunted, insinuatingly.

'Bet I could,' she snapped, accepting his challenge.

'A fiver then?' he teased.

'No, you drive me home at the end of the night,' she said, pausing for a split second with a wry grin, 'to my front door in the Shankill.'

Confident his pint-sized partner had no chance of downing the measure, he grabbed at the gamble. 'You're on.'

Leading her to the bar, he ordered her a pint of ice-cold beer and a bucket, adding insult to the injury.

'What's that for?' she asked.

'Oh, that's for when you throw up at the half-way mark,' he told her facetiously. 'In your own time, then.'

Taking a deep breath she tilted the glass to her moist lips and began to guzzle at the bitter nectar, her face growing redder in time with the emptying of the tumbler. As she reached the three-quarter mark, her eyes were almost popping from her head, but her childbearing feminine grit and determination maintained the gallop through the final furlong until, in disbelief, Paul's eyes matched hers. Fighting the urge to vomit as the hot acid swam like molten metal in her mouth, she coughed with her lips sealed tight. Thumping the glass on to the bar merited a round of applause from a small crowd who'd chanced upon the show, but there was never going to be an encore.

'Well, I think I've won,' she laughed, 'what's the matter, cat got your tongue?'

Over the next two hours as the minutes motored past, the effect of the solitary pint of beer lubricated her mood, as she relaxed, allowing her communication to flow, while the burgeoning consternation of a drive into the Shankill rendered him speechless.

Entering the Protestant stronghold, his heart was jumping so high it felt as if it was in his mouth and his legs were so numb that he could not feel the pedals, only his darting eyes appeared to be working, overtime at that. He stopped the vehicle on her instruction and his hand spontaneously shifted to his neck to feel whether his gold crucifix had jumped over his round-neck sweater, as his eyes zeroed in on a gang of pub crawlers approaching.

'Would you like to come in for a coffee?' she offered, 'I'll introduce you to my mother, but I'll warn you she can be highly strung, it's all down to her condition.'

Staring into his rear-view mirror, he exhaled his relief in the breath he had held for an age, as he watched the menacing youths turn the corner.

'Okay,' he replied bashfully.

Entering the small cosy living-room was comparable to alighting an aircraft on to the tarmac of an equatorial holiday destination. And as the heat surged at Paul's face, it almost turned him into a tornado as he threatened to spin out into unconsciousness.

'It's very humid in here. Can't you open a window or something?' he asked, pulling at the collar of his jersey as he acknowledged her mother with a shy nod.

'Mom, how are you? This is Paul, Paul my mother,' Angela made the introductions, before returning to her guest. 'And as to the warmth, it has to be like a greenhouse, if my mom catches cold it'll lead to pneumonia and then . . . well, anyway. Mom, Paul and I are partners in a greyhound.'

'You didn't tell me you had a dog, never mind a boyfriend,' said her mother, glancing him up and down.

'No, it's strictly a business venture,' stressed Angela, 'I'll just go and make some coffee.'

'Take a seat, son. So you like my daughter?' stated her mother, who had noticed the disappointment written all over his face in light of Angela's last remark.

'Aye, she's very beautiful,' he replied.

'So haven't you asked her out properly?' she snooped.

'I can't, she's made it crystal clear, she's not interested. I've tried all sorts, even lies,' he admitted.

'Aye, she's a tough nut, but if you want to crack her you'll have to try harder, a faint heart never won a fair maiden. Have you tried flowers and chocolates? They always worked on me when I was younger,' she reminisced with a half smile, which revealed her crumpled tinfoil skin. 'Well, take it from me, she must feel something, you're the first boy she's ever brought into this house, so if you want her, go all out for it.'

'Hope you're not talking about me,' intervened Angela, returning with three mugs of steaming coffee.

'Oh, I was just asking Paul where he lived,' said her mother winking at him.

'Rathcool,' she snapped.

As if his throat was blessed with an asbestos lining, Paul gulped down the coffee then stood up, 'Well, I really have to make tracks.'

'You don't have to go so soon, do you?' her mother said disappointedly, for it was a rare privilege to talk with someone from the outside world.

'Aye, I'm sorry, but the dog will need a walk. It was a pleasure meeting you though.'

'You will come again won't you?' she said, shimmying her eyebrows at him.

'Aye, I'll pop in sometime,' he replied.

In the car he rolled down the window.

'Why do you have to go so soon?' asked Angela, suspiciously.

'The pubs will be out soon, it's best for a Catholic not to be driving around these parts at this hour of night. Thanks for allowing me to meet your mother. I really have to go. Are you coming to mine before the trial

161

or should I pick you up at the bus station?' he asked, with edge in his voice, as his heart began to pick up speed again.

'I'll come to your house at ten, oh and Paul, I'll give you my telephone number in case you ever need to contact me.'

Finding a pen in his glove compartment, he tattooed her number on to his arm, then warily drove out of the Shankill without attracting any attention.

When Angela arrived munching from a bag of crisps, Paul and Tommy were busy finalising the preparations for Toby's next attempt at the track, while Bernadette was spying from her usual vantage point above. Turning to see Angela with mouth full, Paul walked over and put his hand into her crisp packet and removed one without her consent.

'Oi,' she uttered in dispute.

Holding the crisp in his hand, he looked at her with a serious expression. 'Is it grudged?'

'No,' she replied, blushing.

'Well, in that case, I don't want it,' he remarked, placing it back into the bag, 'they don't taste the same if they're not grudged. Anyway, I need your say, what's our next move if Toby won't go around the bend today?'

'I say we keep trying like that Scotsman Robert the Bruce, you know, the guy with the spider.'

As she turned her attentions to Tommy, the cat was only moments away from escaping the bag. 'So how are you feeling today? You look a lot better.'

'Eh?' quizzed Tommy, 'what do ye mean?'

'Your upset tummy, is it all better now?'

'I don't know what you're blethering about. I've never had a sore tummy.'

Cringing on Tommy's revelation, Paul began to tiptoe towards the house.

'Stop right there this minute!' she shouted. 'So you did lie to me last night.'

Paul turned to face her, shrugged his shoulders, smiled and came clean.

'Aye, all right, but what else could I do, I'm besotted with you. I'm in love with you. I'm sorry if you don't like that word, but I can't help my feelings. Let me take you out on a proper date,' he pleaded.

162

'No chance,' she scowled irately, 'I can't stand deceivers and I feel nothing for you, I'm only here for the dog. I was beginning to think that we could be friends, but I guess I was wrong.'

'So last night meant nothing to you?' he probed.

'Nothing happened last night. If you thought I was trying to impress you, you've obviously misread the plot, have you been at the dog's rusty water? I knew this was all a mistake. I'll have a kennel built and I'll have my dog back.'

'It's my dog now,' shouted Paul, rising to the custodial tug of war, waving his arms in the way she'd previously expressed her outrage, 'possession is nine tenths of the law.'

Watching bemused, as they locked horns, Bernadette's stomach churned with her interpretation of the wrangle. They are an item, she thought, they have to be, only husband and wife fight like cat and dog. I can't believe it, the bastard lied to me. Throwing herself on to the bed, she pulled a pillow over her head to smother her grief and began to sob.

Together Tommy and Toby watched speechless and barkless, their heads shifting from side to side as the tennis rally of words reached breakpoint at love all.

'It's no wonder you haven't brought a guy home to meet your mother before, no one would put up with your petty mindedness. Do you know if you were a bar of chocolate you'd eat yourself, I love me, who do you love?' he ridiculed, mimicking a girlie voice.

'Quite finished?' she snapped.

Staying silent and shaking his head in disgust was the only reply she was to get.

'All this boils down to is the hard truth that I don't fancy you. If you can live with that then we can still be partners in Toby, if not, then you give me no option but to take the dog with me. I still have the documents, remember?' she stated composedly.

Pouting like a child who had just been informed that it would have to finish all its main course before being allowed a pudding, he muttered in agreement for the sake of Tommy.

After a frosty drive to the dog track, Paul entered Toby for another inevitable horror show run. Again the dog shot out first and again he threw the anchors overboard at the bend, skidding across the slippery sand like a duck on a frozen lake. Handing the dog to Angela, he insisted she get her hands dirty for a change as he washed his of the animal.

'You wash his feet for once, perhaps you can anoint them with yer healing hands while yer at it. I'll be waiting in the car,' he said mordantly.

While Tommy held the lead, Angela hosed the track from the panting dog's legs and feet then, using her thumb, she removed the deposits of wet sand which had formed like sleep around his sorry eyes.

'Why won't he go around the bend?' asked Tommy.

'I don't know, if Paul's wisdom says it's impossible then maybe we are wasting our time. Are you that bothered?'

'No, I love Toby anyway, but Paul wants a racer almost as much as he wants you. He's a good guy you know, I'm sure he didn't mean all those things he said earlier.'

Standing up she smiled at him. 'I do like him, but not in a loving way; things may change but at the moment I need him as a friend the same as you do.'

Having parted on a sulk, Paul spent the remainder of Sunday afternoon ruminating, as he watched Toby from the kitchen window, strutting in circles, counting down the seconds to his next meal.

'What's the matter, son?' asked his mother. 'You've been stood there for nigh on three hours.'

'What's right, you mean. The dog can't run and I've made a complete and utter fool of myself with Angela,' he revealed.

'Maybe it's for the best, having a relationship with one of her kind will bring nothing but trouble.'

'God,' snapped Paul, 'you're just like the rest around here. Why do you go to church? I'll tell you why, because you know no better. If God's such a smart bastard, then how come Angela's mother's dying of cancer?'

'Mind your blasphemous language in the house. If her mother believes in God then she'll have nothing to fear, he'll welcome her with open arms.'

'Shite,' disagreed Paul, 'the only reason people go to worship fresh air is because they're all scared to die. You all want to believe there's something else. Well, God pity you if you're wrong. Show me proof and I'll become a disciple, until then don't ever preach to me about an invisible dream, my dreams are for today.'

Seeing Tommy enter the back gate, he left the kitchen and his shell-shocked mother.

164

'Do me a favour will you,' he addressed Tommy, 'take this money, buy a dozen red roses and have them sent to this address. Just write sorry on the card. Can you manage that for me?'

'Aye,' replied Tommy, taking the money and slip of paper. 'She does like you, you know.'

'Who, Angela?' asked Paul.

'Aye, she told me this morning after the trial.'

'Honestly, what did she say?' pressed Paul.

'Just that she liked you and needed you as a friend, and perhaps a boyfriend one day.'

'She really said that?'

'Aye,' confirmed Tommy.

'Christ, this is killing me, I feel as if I've been walking across the Sahara for a week without water, I'm so thirsty and I'm gonna die then I chance upon a pool of liquid, it looks so sweet and enticing that I just want to dive in and quench my raging thirst, refresh myself and live, yet it's acid, do you know what I'm saying?'

'No,' replied Tommy turning to the gate to walk his dog, 'but I'll make sure she gets the roses.'

'Tom,' he called him back, 'did I tell you about the time I broke one of my eyelashes in four places?'

'No, was it sore?'

'Not as irritating as the itchy teeth I'm experiencing now.'

'Well, do as the Romanians do,' advised Tommy.

'What's that then?'

'When in Rome, scratch them.'

Leaving the bewilderment behind, Paul entered the kitchen to be met by a sobbing wreck.

'You lied to me,' sniffed Bernadette.

Looking beyond her into the hall for eavesdroppers, he then replied, 'Have you been peeling onions?'

'Bastard,' she roared, throwing her fists at him.

Catching her temper in mid-flight, he tried to calm her down. 'What's the matter with ye now?'

'You said that you and that slut weren't an item. Well, it doesn't look that way from where I'm standing.'

'Well, you need a visit to the opticians then. She needs me about as much as a moth needs bonfire night,' he said. 'And so much for all that

165

crap you spouted at Dunmore, just leave me alone, I've had a bad day all round.'

Another lost episode in Paul's sorry life began on March 14th, the only highlight would be a week of calm seas, while on shore the turbulence would return with a vengeance.

At 11 a.m. Angela was having a coffee break at the RVH, while Paul was hard at work in the ship's galley half way across the Irish Sea; both were listening to the radio, their minds a million miles apart. Angela was looking forward to spending the afternoon with Toby and Tommy, while Paul was concentrating on banishing her from his mind so he could do his work. Having a radio for company seemed to help the hours pass more quickly when he had to work in the anus of the world, as he saw it. But it had its downside, for when they played the slow songs his thoughts would drift to her. On the radio the disc jockey announced his weekly feature, which was a blast to the past. 'This morning we're going back in time to this very week in March 1985, here's REO Speedwagon with Can't Fight This Feeling.'

As the words bit deep into their hearts, they stood motionless and reflected to each other for different reasons. An hour later on the midday news it was revealed that a Ulster Defence Association press conference had given a statement from the allying faction the Ulster Freedom Fighters, the UFF claiming that 'innocent Catholics' had nothing to fear from the organisation. Having remembered a similar ostensible story in history class at school, of Chamberlain's triumphant return from his meeting with Adolf Hitler in 1939, it was no surprise to Paul that, when he sat down at the end of his shift on Tuesday night to read the Telegraph, the UFF had claimed responsibility for shooting dead a Catholic trade union official that day.

Confined to the ship, all he could do was hope and pray for Angela's safety. Following his nightly routine of reading the paper before bunking down for the night, Wednesday's despicable tidings impelled him to make a long distance phone call from the ship. Using the numbers he had memorised instantly off his arm all those nights ago, he punched in the digits and waited anxiously for a reply.

'Is that you, Angela? It's Paul.'

'Aye, what is it?'

'Have you seen the news?' he asked with panic in his voice.

'Aye, I have it on now.'

166

'For God's sake, stay away until I get home. It's far too dangerous, there'll be hell on, people will take to the streets to show their condemnation, expressing it with violence, promise me you'll stay away,' he begged.

'But I have to take Toby's food down on Friday.'

'No,' he snapped. 'I'll phone my mother and get her to tell Tommy to buy the food, just promise me you won't go near the Falls.'

Before she could reply, his money disappeared into the ravenous pay phone. Earlier that day a lone Loyalist gunman had attacked the funerals of the Gibraltar Three, taking another three innocent, unarmed lives. For the next two nights Paul phoned home to inquire whether Angela had made an appearance, and each call stabilised his heartbeat.

Saturday May 19th brought the climax to the killing spate and the first Catholic retaliation. Laying the Milltown murdered three to rest, two plain-clothed British soldiers unaccountably drove into the path of the funeral procession. Having learnt their lesson three days earlier, the cortège, protectively flanked by black taxis, took fright and asked no questions. Cordoned off by the black taxi brigade, the out-of-uniform soldiers were set upon by the vindictive mob, badly beaten, shot, then dropped on to their heads from a great height and, just like Humpty Dumpty, all the king's horses and all the king's men would never put them back together again.

That fateful Saturday night the residents of the Falls relived the 1940s as blackout status returned to the enclave as a necessity. British soldiers menacingly aborted their designated routes to cascade on to the IRA nerve centre. Guns traded for baseball bats and bedpost batons wrapped in electrical tape for handle-grips, the venal hunted became the vigilante hunters, bringing with them paint to deface the Republican murals were it to be that no poor bastard stumbled into their path.

Known IRA members' homes were pinpointed and ransacked, but they were nowhere to be seen. They'd learnt that lesson in the mid-seventies, when the RUC backed by the British Army had gone through a phase of so called tip-off searches, terrorising, wrecking and burning people's homes in a wave of oppression, like the Norse beserkers who had came to Ireland's placid shores all those centuries ago. Nine out of ten tip-offs and the subsequent arrests had revealed nothing. Later that night, some of the hard-core Republicans, including Michael, had taken to the streets to meet the confrontation head on and defend their territory. Most would have to wait until their wounds healed before being presented to the courts for sentencing; Michael had been lucky to escape that night.

When Paul drove into Clonard Street on Sunday evening, he thanked his lucky stars he'd been elsewhere the night before as he steered around the carnage of uprooted paving stones and burnt-out vehicles. Parking his car, he scanned up and down the street and wondered where it would all end and, moreover, how long before his vehicle became the next victim if not himself. Peering from the kitchen window towards the dog kennel, he could see that there was no sign of life.

'Tommy has just taken the dog for its first walk since Wednesday. Angela left a message, you're to phone her as soon as you get home,' said his mother with deep sorrow etched across her worn face. 'You know son, I couldn't even get to church this morning, perhaps your theories may have some foundation. I fear for Michael, I've saw the hatred burn in his face like his father, like never before.'

Paul left her to her deliberations and made the telephone call.

'Angela, I meant to ask you, did you get the roses?'

'Aye, but you shouldn't have bothered, a verbal apology would have sufficed. I gave them to my mother, I'm not too fond of flowers, they remind me too much of work and sympathetic condolences.'

'Can I take you out one night this week? I need to talk to you. How about a meal or something?'

'No, Paul it wouldn't work. Listen, there was a reason I asked you to call. It's not working out, I haven't seen the dog all week. I want Toby here with me in a proper environment, you wouldn't believe the sights I've seen at work this week because of your barbaric people.'

'That's a joke,' he butted in. 'Your lot started it, are we supposed to sit like ducks waiting to be picked off, so your people can get their sick kicks. Don't they say a cornered rat will come out fighting?'

'I knew you were no different,' she snapped.

'Hey now, hold on, I don't give a shit about past chronologies, all I know is I love you and I can't stop thinking about you so, aye, you're probably right, perhaps we shouldn't see each other again, 'cause it's tearing me to pieces. I can only take so much, come and take the dog whenever it suits ye.'

Slamming down the phone he sought comfort from the only thing that couldn't argue or advise him - alcohol. After taking a lonely stroll to the corner shop where he bought a bottle of vodka and a crate of beer, he returned to find that he'd missed Tommy. Sitting in his solitude on the stone floor of the backyard under the watchful eye of Toby, he began his binge.

'Get off, you stupid mutt, why won't you run or are you just like her, stubborn as a mule,' he argued with the dog who had come to lick his face.

Despite knocking back the drink as if it was prohibition day tomorrow, he was so low that he couldn't get high. Dropping his head between his knees, he saw a tiny spider through the darkness, crawling across the weathered cracks in the stone and he saw a vision of her before him, lecturing him about the Robert-the-Bruce determination needed to succeed. Then he heard her say, 'Don't worry, you still have me and Tommy.' Shaking his head, he dismissed them as innuendoes which he had misinterpreted through the mist of love. A week spent in the doldrums of drink did nothing to cure his mind as he tried in vain to pickle her from his mind for, like any depression blunter, as soon as the effect wore off the pain was worse than ever.

Ignoring society and even Tommy, Paul imprisoned himself in his room, only venturing out with an inebriated stagger to replenish his supplies. On the sixth day of his hunger strike, he stumbled into the bathroom. Breathing heavily, he stood transfixed at the reflection of a young old man in the mirror and ran his yellow, quivering fingers over the sharp beard which had propagated like raspberry seeds over his chin, to conceal his main feature which was once a dimple. Neck swollen, he opened his mouth and saw a field of white ulcers marauding his angry crimson tonsils.

Suddenly, he had no time for poor literature as he made some snap decisions, which he immediately set out to put into action. He'd had the rest and it had borne no fruit; now it was time for change. At one time his patient attitude had shown her he couldn't care more, now in the height of his cerebral anguish, he was about to show her he couldn't care less. Marching downstairs into the backyard clad only in a T-shirt starched with a week's perspiration, and a pair of shorts, he found Tommy and Toby.

'Has Florence Nightingale been around?' he barked.

'Who?' asked Tommy.

'Angela, god damn it, Angela,' he roared with such ferocity that Toby bolted for the sanctuary of his kennel with fright.

169

'N-n-no,' replied Tommy, shaking like a washing machine on fast spin.

'Okay, I want you to take the day off tomorrow, don't come round here tomorrow, understand?'

'But what about his trial tomorrow?' questioned Tommy.

'No trials tomorrow, just come as usual on Monday suppertime, I'll even walk him before I go offshore. Have you got that?'

'But why?' moaned Tommy.

'Just do it, it's like a surprise,' said Paul.

Angela had tossed and turned that week and came to her own conclusions. She knew that she'd hit him below the waistline in the frustration of not seeing her beloved Toby and she also knew that she couldn't keep the dog, so it was time to let bygones be bygones and give Paul an apology. There were other words in his telephone conversation that she felt the time was now right to act upon. Words that had filled her heart with warmth, words of affection that were soothing and gentle, words that had put her on stilts.

As he turned to the house she was standing there looking more beautiful then ever.

'Paul, I wanted to . . .'

'Stop,' he barked truculently, 'just stop, you tell him your plan to take away the dog, he's the one you're hurting now, not me, no my days of bowing to you are long gone,' he blasted, spraying his saliva within millimetres of her frozen face.

'But Paul, all I wanted to say was . . .'

'No,' he interrupted again, 'I've heard it all, I know where I stand, so leave me alone. This barbarian has to go shave and clean up.'

'Are you taking Toby away?' asked Tommy, gently.

'No, not at all, come on, how about you, me and Toby all go for a walk? I think Paul's mad at me for a few things I said last week.'

'Well, I know he's mad about you, he loves you, don't you feel anything for him?' asked Tommy.

'I'm not sure and even if I did it could never work,' she sighed.

'Why?' asked Tommy.

'Well he's a, a . . .'

'A Catholic,' helped Tommy.

'Well, aye.'

'And don't you like Catholics?' probed Tommy.

170

'No, it's just that Catholic and Protestant relationships are frowned upon and can bring the sort of trouble we've all witnessed in the last week.'

'Then move away.'

'As I said, I don't think I feel the same way and I'd always have to put my mother first, I don't think any man would understand that.'

'Well, I think Paul would die for you if you asked him to,' said Tommy.

At 6.45 a.m. on Sunday morning, Paul was impolitely awoke by Michael's outstretched foot from the next berth.

'For Christ's sake, that fucking dog's going wild out there.'

'The dog went yesterday,' replied Paul, turning over again.

'Get up, you lazy bastard, it's your responsibility,' growled Michael.

Hearing Toby's wails and barks, Paul fell out of bed in a daze and began to dress himself, underpants inside out and jersey back to front, it didn't really matter. Hands trembling from the withdrawal symptoms, he stuttered against time to make Toby's last meal, as the hungry beast gave no relent in its noise emissions. As Toby lapped away at the sodden broth, Paul knew that he had no option but to go with his original plan.

At midday, when he was sure that Tommy had remembered to take a day's holiday, he marched Toby to the RUC station on Springfield Road.

'Can I help you?' asked the stout constable.

'Aye, I found this dog running loose, so I thought I'd better hand it in,' lied Paul.

'Aye, all right, do you want to leave your name and address in case there's a reward? Occasionally when these dogs are retrieved the owners can be quite generous.'

'No, no that won't be necessary,' replied Paul.

'Fair enough,' came the reply.

Paul knew that Angela would never forgive him or speak to him again and that was the intention of his malice.

'So, what'll happen to him?' asked Paul, trying to exonerate himself already.

'He'll go to the USPCA kennels, if he's claimed then everybody lives happily ever after, if not he'll be destroyed. I think they get around seven days on death row.'

Biting his lip, he left hurriedly before his guilt persuaded him otherwise. That afternoon, as his actions plagued him, he wrote two

171

letters which he placed inside the kennel, one for Tommy and one for Angela. Back at sea on Monday, he washed away the memories along with the dishes in the galley.

Chapter 7

The Resurrection

That Monday afternoon, Tommy knew that something was wrong long before he arrived at Paul's back gate. Not only did the cold tingle that accompanied the ill-omened premonition of doom he was experiencing foretell of some iniquitous act, there was further foundation for his incertitude when he turned the corner into the back alley. Toby's sense of smell, especially towards his master, had always resulted in a friendly greeting acknowledged by the acoustics of a long howl. Entering the gate there was to be no frenzied licking session today, only an eerie pin-drop silence.

Heart in mouth, Tommy parted the rubber flaps and spotted two white envelopes. Picking them up with trembling hands, he ferociously ripped open his post. Staring until the words leapfrogged each other and swarmed until they were a colony of ants on the paper, he found that he'd lost the deftness to read Paul's hand written epilogue. Even if it had been composed in clarifying print, the panic that was surging through his mind would still have reinstated him to his dyslexic days of yore.

Bolting up the backyard, he chapped hard at the back door in search of an interpreter.

'Mrs O'Donnell, can you read this letter for me? What's happened to Toby?'

'Aye, I thought it was awfully quiet around here latcly,' she returned.

Fetching her reading glasses she began to read the note of vindication

'Tom, I'm really sorry, but Toby wasn't working out. We need to find a dog that will run at the track. I promise that next week we'll have a concerted effort to buy a new dog, remember I still have £1,000. For that kind of investment, we should get a Derby entry. Toby is in the hands of the USPCA, they'll find him a new family, most likely with children who'll cherish him. No tears Tom, it's for the best. Keep reading and writing and I'll see you Sunday night. Your friend, Paul.'

Handing Tommy back the letter, Paul's mother didn't know what to say. Tears trickled down Tommy's face as he walked towards the kennel to gather his thoughts. I won't practise my reading and writing, what's the point? He rebelled in his bereavement. I've been lied to so many times. So much for, 'I'll get you a job, Tom,' and 'I'll find your mother.'

Feeling betrayed and exploited, he sat with head in hands torturing himself in his sorrow. At around 2.30 p.m. Angela arrived to find him breaking his heart.

'What's wrong?' she inquired, bending down to his level.

'Paul's got rid of Toby, said he was no good, he would've run, you know. I miss Toby so much, he left you a letter too,' he said sobbing.

Taking the letter, she began to read the efficient 'dear Jane' of attrition.

'Angela, I'm really sorry that there was no spark for you. I know this sounds stupid, but the way I feel/felt for you was one which I know only comes once in a lifetime. Don't blame me for trying on numerous occasions to ignite your passion, I'm only human after all. I'm not saying that you despised me because you could never love me. Just being in your presence hurt me more every day, that's why I had to cleanse you from my mind, give you something to hate me for, hence the dog. Toby was the last and only link in our paper-chain and that's why I had to cut him loose, so I could move on with my life and stop playing the cricket ball. You have to understand that when I saw you or heard your voice, I was hit for six and you were the bat. I've lost weight, tried to find the answers at the bottom of the glass. I would have given you the world if you'd let me in, but I've grown to accept that you couldn't. I truly hope that when

174

the 'big' feeling knocks your senses to pot, that your choice
feels the same for you as I did. Paul.'

For a moment her thoughts were with him on the Irish Sea, then she
turned to Tommy.

'So what could he have done with the dog that would make me hate
him? His spite couldn't have been so great as to have ended Toby's life,
could it?'

'No,' Tommy assuaged her worst fears. 'He said Toby would find a
new home with children.'

'So, where could that be?' she asked herself out loud.

'I don't know, but he wrote about some place with loads of initials,
one of those abbreviation things,' he replied.

'Where's your letter?'

Taking Tommy's piece of the jigsaw, she completed the overall picture.

'Ulster Society for the Prevention of Cruelty to Animals. If we get
there in time we could get Toby back, but then again, where could we
keep him?' she sighed.

'We'll keep him at my house,' indicated Tommy excitedly. 'Paul will
never know, we could train him and make him win races, couldn't we?'

Smiling at his 'get up and go' she agreed. 'Aye Tom, let's show him.'
Automatically, she glanced at her watch. 'Come on, we'll have to get
our skates on.'

Asking politely to borrow the O'Donnell's household Yellow Pages
and phone, she found the address and made a phone call to see if Toby
was still available.

'Well?' urged Tommy, anxiously.

'The man said they have a race card of greyhounds, all colours and
sizes, so he may still be there.'

When they arrived at the dog pound an intense symphony of canines
each barked their case for love and ownership, but the offensive odour
which overpowered all the attempts of disinfectant and clung to their
clothing as if it were chewing gum in their hair, made the strays easy
to be sniffed at. They were met by a lanky young man with greasy hair
and cross eyes which Angela did her best to ignore out of courtesy,
but Tommy's fascination magnetised him to stare rudely, captivated
by the keeper's handicap. So intrigued by what he saw, Tommy looked
towards his own nose and twisted his eyes to find that everything had

become duplicated, then wondered if the man thought that the world was full of twins.

Following their escort into the concentration camp they began to understand the system employed. The more immediate a dog came to the light at the entrance, the nearer it was to its expiry date and the long sleep. The precise rotation of stock meant that every canine's shelf life was no greater than the sell-by-date products on offer at the local supermarket. Continuing on past the pick and mix cages of sad eyes, they eventually found the reason for their search. Lying, fur matted in his own filth, Toby was a mere skeleton of his former self. Feeling as sick as the liberating allies must have felt at Belsen or Auschwitz, Angela's mind was scarred, for this was no refuge for the rational. Head resting on his paw, Toby's silence and expressionless face denoted that he had resigned himself to the inevitable. Raising his sleepless eyes to see what had blackened the already dim shadow, not even the sight of Tommy could hide his resentment towards the betrayal he'd been made to suffer.

'That's him,' confirmed Angela.

Not even the shattering noise of the sliding lock yelling freedom could stir the dog. Collaring him, the camp commandant began to tug at his neck in a bid to induce movement.

'Stop that,' intervened Tommy taking the lead, affected by the heavy-handed persuasion he was witnessing.

'Come on, Toby, you're coming to live with me now,' he assured the petrified animal.

When Angela arrived at Tommy's house on Tuesday afternoon, the skills that Paul had taught Tommy were there on show for all to see. Already his summer coat was shiny and his shape had returned.

'God, you've been busy,' Angela commented.

'Aye, he's coming round,' beamed Tommy.

'Shall we take him for a walk?' she proposed.

'Aye, but I've had an idea, it was in the book I read about greyhounds. I didn't really read all the book 'cause it was too hard, but I seen some pictures of how they train puppies to run in circles. Should we give it a try?' he asked.

'Why not,' she agreed. 'Perhaps he will go round a bend after all and Paul will be forced to eat his words.'

'But we'll need a rabbit,' he said, pessimistically.

'I have an old teddy bear, that'll do, won't it? I'll bring it tomorrow.'

'No, I have a pyjama case rabbit, but it reminds me of my mother 'cause she bought me it,' said Tommy, staring vacantly into the past.

'Never mind, I'll bring an old teddy tomorrow.'

'No, I'll get the rabbit. Toby's worth it,' he concluded.

Taking the tools of coursing in the form of a ball of string and cuddly toy they set out for the expanse of nearby Dunville park. After rigging up the apparatus, Tommy gave Toby a good, long hard look at the pyjama case which was met by a transparent reaction. As he hurled the pseudo hare in an anticlockwise direction, it soon became apparent that Toby was in no mood for futile games. After fifteen minutes of obstinate perseverance, it was time to call it quits.

Later that afternoon in the grimy kitchen of Tommy's house, as Angela sipped lethargically at a cup of tea, Tommy began to prepare his evening meal. Tilting the kettle, he poured the boiling water on to a few crushed Oxo cubes to flavour his mince which brought a double reaction. From the corner of the room, by the concealed hot water pipes where Toby had adroitly made his bed, Toby jumped into action impelled by the rich aroma of the meaty juices. Still having the mind of a pubescent youth, Tommy's brain tended to flash dramatically as the crow flies to the root of the problem, whereas adult problem-solving inclined to build bridges and roads to reach the same destination.

'What if we soak the rabbit in gravy?' shouted Tommy, as if he was Archimedes jumping from his bath.

'Do you think that'll work?' she inquired, her excitement rising.

Once they had tanned the white rabbit brown with their fortuitous ray of hope, they returned to the park to initiate Tommy's conception. This time the game was more to the dog's taste. At first he chased in agitated square movements. Then, after ten minutes of dour insistence by all parties, Toby's psychological injuries soon began to heal as his hunger and frustration accrued. Infuriated as if he was Elmer Fudd, Toby was about to rewrite the script. This Bugs Bunny was about to meet his match as the coarse stop-start movements bent to fluent, smooth circular arcs of supreme grace. Gathering confidence and speed, Toby snapped viciously within inches of a kill, forcing Tommy to turn around faster, faster and faster until he spun off his feet. In a heap on the grass, he watched through blurred vision as Toby pounced on the out-of-puff hare. Helping Tommy off the ground, Angela hugged him, their elation incommensurable.

'We did it, we did it,' they screamed, dancing together.

177

During Wednesday, Tommy would not allow the dog to relapse, running the legs off Toby with the aid of the medicinal stock cube. Thursday being trials night at Dunmore, Tommy introduced Toby to the public transport system, which the dog had no objection to as he became a menace to society. If he wasn't attacking the female passengers' shopping bags, he was sniffing crotches. Never fully in control, Tommy experienced stress for the first time in his happy-go-lucky life. Mitigated to alight at the bus terminus, he was even gladder to see Angela awaiting. And the added pair of hands placated the dog, making the second half of the bumpy ride to Dunmore lighter work.

Having arrived at the track on numerous occasions before, with jangling nerves from the excitement of the unknown, tonight was different. Calmly and composedly, they strolled into the stadium knowing it was just a matter of time. Confidence and expectation were running so high that Angela had even taken the counting chicken measures of bringing History Maker's registration card for when he qualified. She carried out the administrative duties of entering Toby for his three dog trial, while Tommy set out to use his brawn to put the dog into the starting traps. Following Paul's earlier decision to seed the dog out wide, Tommy battled to dress Toby with the striped jacket. Grateful for a helping hand from the starter, Toby then decided he would walk into the trap of his own accord. When the other two owners headed to the pickup point for the post-race collection, Tommy instinctively made for the first bend in remembrance of all the dog's past efforts, before his brain turned the corner, as he was sure his charge would do this evening. As his legs carried him north, his head watched southward to see the lids flash open and Toby's inauguration of the 435-yard trip.

Toby missed his accustomed electric break and swerved across to the rails to his favoured position, and it was in this hungry manoeuvre that he made hefty contact with the white-jacketed runner of trap three. Skirmishing for the inner supremacy at the first turn allowed the red jacket of trap one unhindered passage, which that animal quickly worked to good advantage stealing a march of three to four lengths. Using his heavy frame to good effect throughout the mêlée, Toby won the dual for the bend and curved, not gracefully or sweeping as he tickled the brake pads, but nevertheless he made it around. Motoring up the back straight, he showed his frightening pace and began to mow down the leader. When the third and fourth bends approached, Toby was challenging and within a whisker of pole position. And taking the

178

shortest route, he forged a full head in front as he negotiated the third curve, but once again he checked the bend allowing the 'red' to poach a two-length lead off the last. Straightening up again for the run in, the valiant animal showed he had the staying power as he whittled away at the advantage with every stride. When the line came fast and furious, only the camera could judge the outcome of the split decision. After the line and Toby set sail, blasting clear to the pickup point. Filled with emotion, Tommy successfully collared the panting athlete, before walking off the track to meet Angela with his head in the clouds. Angela hugged Toby as if he was a long-lost brother.

'Well done, Tommy, you've just trained your first winner, how does it feel?' she asked jubilantly, sending him into orbit.

'Did he win?' he gasped, not sure of the tight result.

'I think so, does it matter? He can only get better.'

'Oh God, I wished Paul was here to see this.'

'Aye,' she replied. 'So do I,' with an acidic turn in her voice.

When the final placings were called, their initial response was one of slight dejection. History Maker had been touched off by a slender short head in a winning time of 24.77 seconds; however, it was the tail end of the public announcement which had them jumping for joy. 'Can the owners of the traps one and six greyhounds please present their dogs to the judges' box for marking up.' Toby's finishing time of 24.78 had fallen into the net of qualification by a slender two-hundredths of a second, and that was more than enough.

Taking History Maker's identity card, the dapper racing manager set about confirming the dog's validity. First, it was an ear inspection to see if the letters and numbers tattooed inside matched. Satisfied the codes corresponded, he moved on to the birthmark patches of fawn on the dog's head and sides. All well, he flicked through to see History Maker's previous form and his eyes almost popped with respect.

'So,' he coughed. 'So when would you like him on the card, Saturday or Thursday?'

'Thursday,' intervened Angela, knowing that Paul would be home and available to rue his mistake. Now it would be his turn to loathe her for spiting him.

During that week at sea, slowly but surely Paul regained his self-esteem. Invigorated by the daylight hours he emitted a fresh air wherever he went on board. Throwing his tame personality to the wind, his newly

179

acquired prodigal charisma was not to go unnoticed. It was only the hours of darkness that brought lapses to his work-hardened state of mind, as Angela would visit him in his fevered dreams to drive a stake into his heart.

Departing Scottish shores for the last time late Easter Sunday afternoon, Paul found a last second wind in his work rate to blow him home, as he attacked the dishes in the knowledge that every clean plate and glass was one nearer to Belfast. Taking a well-deserved smoke break, Scots Paul was to reveal some news in his usual manneristic flair.

'You jammy fucker.'

'What do you mean?' asked Paul, bemused.

'You've only got the babe of the boat screaming over you and wetting her nappy,' he grouched.

'Who?' asked Paul.

'Mairead from the souvenir shop, just about every guy on board has tried to jump ship with her and all to no avail. Yet she wants you.'

'How do you know and what's she like?' probed Paul, spirits rising that someone with such a beautiful reputation could be smitten with him.

'Well, here's her phone number,' said the Scot, handing him a slip of paper before continuing with the story. 'I know one of the other girls she works with. She told me that Mairead has had her eye on you for a wee while.'

Racking his brains to put a face to the name, Paul was suddenly unmoved by it all, for he'd drawn a blank. Therefore, if he had passed her and failed to take a blind bit of notice, that meant, in his eyes, she was nothing special.

'I can't picture her,' he admitted.

'Small, shoulder-length dark hair, green eyes, deep, absolutely gorgeous,' described the envious Glaswegian.

Now a picture was starting to develop, but it was an image he'd perspired all week long to erase from his mind. Intrigued by the depiction, he decided it best to take a look.

'No, I still can't think of her. I'll have to go and sneak a glance. So when do I have to phone her and are you sure it's me she likes?' questioned Paul, wanting assurance.

'Aye, it's you all right and all I know is that if you're interested you've to give her a bell any time,' replied his senior. 'If you don't go out with her, you must be queer, that's all I know.'

180

As the floating emporium crawled up Belfast Lough for the last time that trip, and the galley was spotlessly clean awaiting handover to the returning crew, Paul resolved to take a casual saunter past the souvenir shop. Combing his hair with his left hand and straightening the white shirt of his uniform was the best he could do at such short notice. Then again, he thought, if she finds me attractive in my work clothes looking as though I've just been dragged through a hedge via a sauna, what will she think when I have the cosmetics of some decent gear, a razor, a bath and some aftershave? Stopping shy of the entrance to the gift shop, he stole a celeritous glance, to observe a dark-haired female settling the till, innocent of his presence. Taking a second, long, undiluted gaze, he saw that she was indeed as narrated, petite and exceptionally tempting, almost as he'd framed her in his mind, frighteningly like Angela. Hypnotised momentarily, he had to shake himself from the incubus as she lifted her head with the human perception that eyes were burning into her laser deep. Giving her a demure smile, she returned the compliment before he disappeared.

Earlier that morning as Bernadette had slept, Michael had sneaked into her bed. Having not consummated their relationship or even shared a fragment of intimacy for over a month now, Michael's frustration was overflowing as was his passion. Stroking her warm thigh, he sought a reaction and was granted only half his wish, he got the slap but not the tickle.

'Get off, will ye,' she snapped in umbrage, jumping out of the bed.'

'What the hell's wrong now? We haven't made love for weeks,' he reminded her.

'I'm on my period,' she spat.

'Again? You were on last week and the week before. You're the only woman I know who has one good week a month,' he blasted, riled at her rejection.

'Do you want to check?' she invited, commencing to lift her nightshirt.

'Don't be so fucking stupid,' he retorted, turning away convinced, by her bluff.

'Then get out, if that's all you wanted,' she pointed to the door belittling him. 'And take this with ye.'

Removing her engagement ring, she threw it at him with all the vehemence of a woman's scorn. Glancing his head to the side to protect his eyes, he flinched, feeling a hot sting as the diamond chips nicked his face like a blunt razor. Employing his index finger as a swab, he wiped away the trickle from just below his dark protruding cheekbone, then examined the crimson blood.

Like a red rag to a bull his weak temperamental yield point gave way. In a flash, his temper detonated and he leapt over the bed yelling at her as if she was no more than an animal. Unable to control his perverse desire to inflict harm, he lashed out, smacking the side of her face with the back of his heavy hand. Shock-still, virgin-white with disbelief and hatred towards his failure to take the moral high ground in their acrimonious dispute, her piercing eyes did her communicating. Eyes glazing over, she ground her teeth to combat the tears. She would not give him the requital of seeing her weep. Hand still suspended high in the air from the follow through, Michael wilted his arm and closed his eyes recognising that the damage had been done. Deep down he already knew that her love for him was on a life-support machine, and now his mindless behaviour had effectively switched it off. And to iron out the creases his ruffled temper had just made, he would now need a steam roller.

Having laboured harder than ever that week to take his mind off Angela and his spiteful actions through his inability to rationalise what was happening in his life, as well as the lost hour from the change to British Summer Time, Paul should have been fit to drop with the conjunction of mental and physical exhaustion. As it was, he was home and raring to go. With the coming of spring with its long days, light nights and warmth, he too was blooming with a new lease of life. He had a pretty girl's phone number and £1,000 to buy a greyhound. Having removed the winter cold and darkness of Angela from his mind, he'd concluded that at the crossroads, the only road was forward and he was eager to start upon life's new highway.

Entering the house, he hugged his mother dynamically.

'Happy Easter, son. What was that for?'

'Just felt like it,' he replied. 'Any messages from Tommy?'

'No, I haven't set eyes on him since last Monday.'

Strange, thought Paul before dismissing it. Tommy would be around tomorrow and they could begin their quest for a practical dog. Becoming weighed down by the banal church gossip, Paul finished his coffee and decided that perhaps an early night was in his best interests after all. In ascending the stairs two steps at a time, the creaking of the floorboards alerted Bernadette that Paul was home. Upon reaching the half-landing, he paused, touched by what he witnessed. Bernadette was at her bedroom door, her left eye was swollen and bruised so badly that it was almost closed.

'What happened to you?' he inquired, genuinely disturbed, noticing that she was still white and trembling.

'Michael did this,' she sniffed, before breaking down, then about turning and scampering on to her bed to conceal her misery.

Following her in, concerned for her plight, he closed the door behind him and sat on the edge of the bed to lend his support.

'Do you want to talk about it?' he probed with kid gloves.

Sitting up she removed a tissue from the box resting on her bedside cabinet, then blew her nose and wiped her eyes.

'I turned him down again, so I got the brunt of his anger and shame,' she explained.

'What do you mean?' asked Paul.

'I wouldn't let him sleep with me, like I promised you, and I threw his ring back at him. I really hate him, Paul. God, look what he's done to my face.' Again she burst into tears. 'I don't know what to do, I've nowhere to go,' she continued to sob. 'I'm trapped. I don't earn enough money to get a place of my own. Why did my mother have to die? I need her more than ever.'

Affected by her anguish, he opened his arms to her and offered his strong shoulders. As she used him as a sponge to soak up her lament, it all became clear to Paul how much of an insensitive cad he'd been. He'd always been under the impression that she'd thought that she was mothering him and he couldn't fly without her. It was her constant pecking in the end that had forced him to flee the nest from under the shadow of her wing, but that wasn't really how it was. She, in fact, needed him to protect her and be there for her always to hold her hand throughout life. On the outside she was hard and strong, but inwardly she was emotionally soft and vulnerably weak.

Standing at the bar a few hundred yards away, Michael was arriving at his own conclusions and he, too, was filled with deep regret. Gazing at the pint glass as he twiddled nervously with it, he differentiated that the ale could not cure his ills and that he had no chance of exhuming their relationship from this position. The only way was to leave the pub behind, and the IRA if need be. The bottom line and he knew it, was that he had to change his ways. Leaving almost half a pint, he exited the bar and headed home for peace talks and, optimistically, an agreement.

Having rocked her tears for fears away, Paul attempted to remove her from his person ever so gently, yet the more he intimated with his broad shoulders, the more she clung to him. Raising her head she looked into his eyes with unfeigned ambiguity.

'What am I gonna do Paul? I'm so scared.'

'So am I,' he returned, for he knew this would be the fulcrum on which his fate hinged.

Paul knew he had the power to save her right there and then. Things might be different, he thought. But I don't love her. I could learn to love her, I suppose; no, I'd only be cheating myself. Sighing aloud he began the argument for. If I don't take her back, she'll be out on the streets or have to live life under his tyranny for ever. What the hell do I do? Lost deep in the labyrinth of righteousness, the swinging open of the bedroom door saved him from a regretful decision. For once Michael was lost for words, overcome by the sight of his fiancé in the arms of his brother, it was all too much for him. Heart impaled, he shook his head as his body twitched to shake off the cold sweat nipping at his skin.

'This isn't what you think,' Paul pleaded his innocence to the charges. 'She was crying, you've made a mess of her face. How could you?'

About turning, Michael left to return to the goldfish bowl of the drink tank to drown his ignominy. Pulling himself away, Paul headed towards his room.

'Come back, it's over now, we can be together again,' she said.

Turning to face her one last time, he spoke his true mind. 'Bernie, I don't want a relationship with you, it wouldn't be right. I couldn't love you properly. You're obsessed with me, but I'm not with you, I never was. I was possessed by Angela, then one day I woke up from my dreams and realised I couldn't have her. Even if I could, she'd have never felt the same, I'd have smothered her and she'd have left. She was the first girl I've really ever loved; I think it has to be a two-way infatuation or nothing. I'm not convinced there's actually a lot of people out there who have been blessed with that gift. I know I've got to look elsewhere and so must you. I don't want to sever our friendship, we go back a long way, but if you can't understand that I'm talking sense then I'll have no choice but to do so, goodnight.'

184

Mulling over his words, her brain agreed with his declamation, but her heart was not willing to conform. It was now her turn to make a decision pertaining to her future. Leave tomorrow or live and die this way with Michael. After all, he was obsessed with her.

After a lie-in, Paul made a telephone call to the racing manager at Shelbourne Park in Dublin to seek some information and received a boost. Every second Tuesday, there were greyhound sales and, by good fortune, they fell in with his shift pattern. As the morning marched into early afternoon, Paul was becoming unsettled regarding Tommy's absence. By 2.30 p.m. his torment had no limits as he began to wonder if Tommy's new loss had actually sent him over the edge. Earlier that morning by no stretch of the imagination could he have conceived of such an outcome, but by lunch time it was niggling away at him as a slight possibility; now, in the midst of the afternoon it had become a feasibility.

Tearing from the house driven by guilt, he motored the short distance to his 'sold down the river' friend, desperately hoping that he hadn't opted to throw himself into the Lagan. Upon receiving no reply from the front ingress, Paul raced around to the back alley, his wits on a sword's edge. Entering the backyard, he must have thought he was gate-crashing a party. Suddenly the conversation ceased to be replaced by an eerie, deafening silence as Angela, Tommy and even Toby glared at him, as if he was an infectious leper. It was the look of sheer disgust and the dentigerous growl of the dog that struck a chord and rendered him humble.

Unable to look them in the eye, he bowed his head like a shamed samurai warrior awaiting decapitation. Having been dishonourable, a degrading sentence was imminent. After all, he'd been the one who'd brought it all upon himself, with a moment's madness effected by his inability to rationalise his behaviour. Once more it would be up to him to make the first move.

'I see you found the dog then.'

'Aye,' replied Angela, coldly. 'And no thanks to you. I must say, you really went down in my estimations, lower than a snake's belly. Aye, I could understand why you could've carried out such a petty childlike act to get back at me, but Tommy, your supposed best friend. You ought to be ashamed of yourself, he idolised Toby.'

'I am sorry, but the dog's no good. I'm going to Dublin tomorrow,' he said, now addressing his distant friend, who would no longer look at him. 'We can buy a real dog.'

'We have a real dog,' whispered Tommy.

'Aye, I know that, but I mean a racing dog,' replied Paul.

'We have that, too,' added Tommy.

'No, I mean a racing dog that will run races at Dunmore.'

'But we have that,' insisted Tommy.

'Don't be daft, he's a crock,' sighed Paul, feeling as if he was fighting a losing battle against Tommy's torpid pigheadedness.

'What he's trying to tell you is that Toby has already qualified, he's entered on Thursday and all thanks to Tommy's patience and expertise,' Angela divulged.

'But how?' Paul quizzed, taken aback.

'Tommy coursed him as if he was a puppy, all his idea. You do know about coursing greyhounds?' she jibed.

'Aye,' he returned, raising his eyebrows at her defamatory remark.

'So we took him for a trial on Thursday and he qualified at the first attempt,' she continued to rub his face in the dirt.

'Brilliant,' congratulated Paul. 'Well, we have a lot of preparation to organise before then.'

'No, not we, us,' she emphasised. 'Myself and Tommy that is, you're no longer a part owner, you gave up that right when you betrayed us all.'

'But I have the transport and the kennel,' he contended.

'The dog lives here now, happily may I add, and we'll take buses,' she stated the position.

'You can't take buses,' laughed Paul.

'We'll manage, won't we Tom?' she called for backup.

Detecting by his non-response that he might not be totally out of Tommy's calculations, Paul turned his charms in that direction.

'Come on Tom, tell her I've got to be part of this team. I'm your best mate, remember?'

Aware that it had taken him all his life too find a friend, the last thing Tommy wanted to do was give it all up over a woman's brittle spleen. Besides, Paul was his only hope of being reunited with his mother.

'Have you found my mom yet?'

'I'll be honest with you, I. . . I . . . I haven't been looking since you mentioned the letter,' he stumbled across an excuse, before milking it

186

for its worth. 'You never got back to me on that score, so there's not a lot I could do.'

'But you promised me and you said you'd find me a job and you won't, will you?' Tommy chided from the driving seat.

'I'm trying, Tom,' Paul replied softly, for impact. 'I'm trying, I'll mention it to my boss next week, but you'll have to be patient and wait for an opening, and as for your mother, if you find the letter we have greater odds of success. Britain's a big place, so what do you say Tom, still friends? Owners?'

'No,' intervened Angela. 'You prove to us with hard evidence that you're looking for his mother then we'll re-evaluate the situation. Now go on, go home, we have to train a dog for a race.'

Turned on by her power and verve, Paul found himself falling for her all over again, but in the light of what he'd preached to Bernadette the night before, he knew it would only result in a return to the state of borderline sanity his infatuation kept pushing him towards.

Deciding it best to leave them to their own devices and perhaps let the mountain come to him, if that's how it was meant to be through life's strange twists, Paul spent Tuesday and Wednesday contemplating Mairead's telephone number, as he tried to compass exactly where his life was destined. Suddenly, all the tables had turned on him, for he had no friends to confide in and really needed someone to talk to before he returned to the drink for an interest. Walking a tightrope at home when Michael and Bernadette arrived from work each day, he found himself driven away from the Falls to the solitude of the coast, where he'd introspectively watch the shimmering sunsets over Belfast Lough.

In a blustery yet tepid gale, he watched his ship depart for Scotland and it bestowed him with the brainstorm he required. He wasn't on it, for if he was he'd now be working hard, no doubt jaded and grumpy. Here he was with a week of heaven and all he could do was make it hell. Turning to look at his parked car, he spotted a telephone booth and resolved to give Mairead a go. It was a man who answered, and a familiar voice at that, yet one that he could not put a face to. When she eventually came to the phone, Paul detected that she was even more nervous than him.

'It's Paul from the ferry. I work in the galley. I was given your number so I was wondering if I could take you out sometime?'

187

'Aye, if you want?' she replied, gaining in confidence immediately.

'Well, when are you free?' he inquired.

'Tomorrow,' she replied excitedly. 'Friday I'm out with the girls and Saturday night I babysit my brother's kids.'

'Oh, well it'll have to be later on then,' said Paul. 'I used to have a share in a greyhound and it's running tomorrow night, so I'd like to go see it race first then I could pick you up. The only snag is, I don't know what time it's running yet.'

'I'd quite enjoy seeing the dog run if that's okay with you, then perhaps we could go for a drink or maybe to the pictures if you fancy,' she suggested.

'Are you sure? The dogs isn't that exciting, you know.'

'Aye, I'd really love to watch it run,' she enthused.

'Okay then,' Paul agreed, won over by her dulcet tones. 'If you give me your address, I'll pick you up at seven.'

He memorised her address as they bade each other farewell for the time being.

Even though Paul was no longer part of the racing consortium, when he awoke on the morning of Toby's debut, he was just as excited. After rushing to the newsagent, he was almost run over as he paid all his attention to the dog card for History Maker instead of the deadly road. Cringing at the draw of the coffin box of trap four, Paul immediately wrote off the dog's chances, then smiled to himself. A bad run and he might just be able to weasel his way back in to the syndicate.

At 6 p.m., as Paul was manicuring the final touches of his first-date appearance, he glanced from his bedroom window to see his estranged partners heading to the bus stop with Toby in tow. Fighting the urge to run out and demand to taxi them to the track, he managed to put a restraining order on his desires. Waiting until their transport had collected them, he then set off for the suburban district of Glengormley in North Belfast.

With the inauguration of the light nights, Paul knew that the car would now be worth its weight in gold. Although the Falls was an impoverished eyesore, a ten-minute drive from that subtopia could transmigrate you to another world, one of breathtaking countryside where mature oak trees shaded running streams and rugged hills climbed and dipped like a petrified ocean of serenity. It was a green belt of fertile sanity stretching to the shores of the Atlantic. As Paul had ripened from boy to man, the dark winters had always brought a depressive cloud to envelop his existence, but the lazy long summer days cultivated his lust and generated effulgence to his life. The only thing missing was someone to share those wonderful warm times and anticipated adventures with.

Driving into Cherryvale Avenue, he reflected upon how he'd made the right choice in coming. It wasn't the upmarket detached houses with their huge runways for drives, nor the bright eye-pleasing collage of daffodils and tulips radiating happiness, not even the skipping lambs cavorting naïvely to their impending Sunday dinner fate. No, it was the overall picture, it was spring and he was in that season of his life and bouncing with exuberance. A time for exploration and amour.

Alighting his car outside Mairead's door, he took a deep breath through his nose, not for composure, but to inhale the sickly sweet, musky odour of the vegetation gifting its essence of life. Raising his head into the descending twilight to observe an aircraft on its final approach, he could hear the chirping and chattering of nature's flying wonders growing louder to be heard above the droning engines of their man made analogy, and they would not be denied. For Paul, the birds' singing was the sign that always struck home most, the worm had turned and the winter was dead and buried. Walking up to the front door of the house which portrayed the epitome of success, Paul cleared his throat and knocked. When the door opened, the voice at the end of the telephone had finally met its match.

'Hi son, come away in, Mairead will be down in a minute. Can I get you a drink or something?'

'Eh, no – I'm driving,' Paul declined nervously.

Mairead's father was none other than Martin South, the man who had given Paul his big break in life. Two months later and he was about to take out his daughter but, although the omens for success were there, Paul felt largely intimidated by her ancestral heritage.

'Aye, very wise son,' agreed her father, impressed by Paul's responsible outlook.

Upon entering the luxurious and splendid living room with its fine crystal ornaments and stone-featured interior, Paul couldn't help but ogle at its refinement and wonder what Mairead would think if she ever came to meet his parents at their unpretentious abode in the rundown Falls.

'So, how are you enjoying life at sea?' inquired his employer, making small talk.

189

'Very much so. You were right though, it's no pleasure cruise – but it's a good life,' Paul replied.

'Work, work, work,' she said, making her appearance. 'Is that all you men can talk about.' As Paul turned to acknowledge his date for the evening, he noted that if every one of God's creations had its own method of showing that spring was here, then the human female's fashion was to express this via a short skirt and skimpy see-through blouse. With Mairead dressed for the maximum impact, Paul could feel himself being blown away by her sultry appearance.

A few minutes into the journey to Dunmore, Paul attempted to break the ice. 'You could have told me your father was our boss.'

'Then you wouldn't have called me, would you?' she smiled, brimming with confidence, a confidence that he knew only too well.

'Just answer me one thing in truth,' asked Paul.

'Anything?' she agreed.

'I was under the impression that loads of guys were asking you out, but you were rather selective. Yet why do I get the distinct feeling that I've been set up and nobody has asked you out because of your dad.'

'No, you're totally wrong,' she told him. 'Plenty have asked me out from the ship, you're just paranoid. I just felt that if I'd waited on you asking me out, I'd be old and grey before you got around to it.'

Although she was very beautiful, had good character and was even a Catholic, she wasn't Angela and there were no headless chickens bombarding his stomach. Reaching the terraces by way of the gentlemen's entrance, Paul scanned them for Angela and Tommy, but they were busy in the dressing room of the kennelling enclosure giving History Maker a last-minute team talk. Studying the race card, Paul noted that Toby's qualification time was less than impressive, then again, he had been badly baulked at the first bend; still, the form logistics seemed to add up to the hard fact that Toby would need to sprout wings to win. Finally, the scent of Mairead's perfume reminded him of his courtship duties.

'Can I get you a drink?'

'Aye, that would be nice, half a lager if you don't mind,' she accepted.

Leaving her in the maze of her race card, he made his way to the bar where he bought her drink and a pint of lager shandy to quench his dry throat. Upon leaving the bar, he met Angela on the stairs, as she was making her way in search of the tote to place a genial bet on Toby.

'Might've guessed you'd make an appearance. Who's the half lager for?' she asked, almost breaking into a sulk.

'I met this girl called Mairead through work,' he said.

'Aye, I was right all along, you're just a charmer,' she rebuked.

'I resent that outrageous accusation. What am I supposed to do? Give up on the female sex, because I can't have you, because you're scared of the day you never saw,' he blasted in defence of his reputation.

'So where is this Mairead then?'

'Just down there,' he pointed.

Turning to take a look, she had a strange feeling pass through her. Mairead was exceptionally attractive and Angela was green with envy.

'Listen, I'll have to go, can't keep a pretty girl waiting,' said Paul, having detected the tinge of jealousy in Angela's blush. 'I wish the dog well.'

Leaving her to analyse her new experience, he rejoined his date. He handed Mairead the half pint, and quickly returned to the race card in favour of her. Trying to make conversation, she asked which dog he had once held a share in.

'Trap four, History Maker, but his pet name's Toby. Look, here he comes now,' said Paul, avoiding eye contact at all times.

When Tommy walked past, his face was beaming with pride, this was his moment. All his determined efforts were on show and he was lapping up every second of it. As the handlers began to put the greyhounds into the starting traps, Mairead turned to Paul. 'Aren't you going to put a bet on him?'

'No, he has no hope tonight. If he wins I'll strip naked and dance on the track. There's no point in sympathy-betting, you know, throwing good money away for the sake of it.'

Within seconds the hare was on the move. Four days had passed since Easter Sunday and Toby's racing career was, coincidentally, resurrected.

Missing the break again, a concerted effort to gain pole position as the bend approached put paid to Toby's slender chances, as he became the meat filling in the ham sandwich at the first turn. Trailing the field by a distance, by the time he had navigated safe passage to his preferred rails slot, victory was forlorn. Finishing last, beaten nine and a half lengths in total, Paul had seen enough to suggest to him that it would be sooner than later before History Maker was living up to his name.

'Well, you were right,' said Mairead, pouting. 'Guess there's gonna be no male stripper show after all.'

191

'Just,' he replied. 'If he'd made that first bend unscathed, he'd probably have won. I'm just nipping to see my friend Tommy then we can head into town for a drink or whatever you want to do.'

When he reached the kennels, Angela was helping Tommy, wash the dog and supply it with a cool refreshing drink.

'Come to gloat have ye?' she started on the offensive. 'With an, "I told you so"?'

'No, not at all, I thought the run was more than creditable. I've actually come to give you some advice, that's if you're interested?' offered Paul.

'Go on then, let's hear the wisdom,' she replied, sarcastically

'I think you should enter the dog for Saturday night, he needs a few races under his belt. Practice makes perfect. It's up to you,' he said before about turning and leaving.

Finding a nice quiet and secluded country pub near Mairead's home, on her recommendation, Paul learnt a lot about her during the few hours they spent together. It seemed the more he discovered only furthered his belief that they were incongruous with one another. Unable to get a word in edgeways, he found himself listening but not hearing for long periods, as his thoughts returned to Angela and schemes to manipulate his way back into her life.

Paul declined the offer of a coffee as he stopped the car outside Mairead's house.

'Maybe another time. I feel a little off colour,' he fibbed.

'Would you like to take me out again?' she asked, not backward at going forward.

'Eh, I'm busy on Sunday, I have to take my mother down to Dublin,' he fabricated with the first thing that came into his mind.

'Okay, we can discuss it at work next week,' she replied, turning to face him.

Lunging at him, she planted a robust kiss on his mouth which caught him off guard, before leaving him gobsmacked to retire for the evening. Driving back home, he tasted her lipstick around his lips and he knew by the negative reaction spawned by their embrace, that she was not who he wanted.

When Paul arrived at Tommy's on Friday afternoon, he was delighted to see that Angela was there, grooming the dog.

'I want to make a deal,' he addressed the pair.

'And what might that be?' Angela inquired, commandeering the stance of spokeswoman.

'Did you enter the dog for Saturday?' he queried.

'Aye,' she replied.

'Good, let me train Toby for that race. If he wins, I get my third share back and he comes back to my kennel to live. However, if he loses, then I lose my share, what do you think?'

'I agree,' intervened Tommy, who had never wanted Paul to drift out of his life in the first instance.

Angela had been Tommy's ventriloquist of late, making all his decisions as he'd been frightened to apply his shareholder's vote, that was, until now. Pausing for a second, it didn't take her long to give Paul another bite of the cherry. When she'd arrived home the previous evening, after the racing, she'd hardly slept a wink. And when she'd finally nodded off, she'd dreamt about Mairead, laughing perversely in her face as she marched Paul up the aisle.

Earlier that morning, she had witnessed a death at work. A young girl had been playing outside her house and had run across the road to protect her pet cat from the traffic. Death is what happens to you while you're busy making other plans; she never saw the car or heard it coming. Angela had concluded that life was for living today, yet she remained worried by Paul's religion, although he did not subscribe to it. If only she was a Catholic or he was a Protestant, then perhaps they could board the love train without fear of derailment.

'I agree,' she smiled, then added, 'but if you ever do anything so stupid and malicious again, you'll live to regret it.'

'Is that a threat?' joked Paul.

'No, it's a bloody promise,' she replied.

Differences put behind them, they all took the dog to the park for some intense coursing. As Tommy teased Toby with the utility pyjama case, Paul watched the animal's sweeping movements closely to monitor any improvement, while Angela wanted to research in other directions.

'So, eh, did you go anywhere nice with your new girlfriend last night?'

'Not really, we went to a little intimate pub in the countryside near her home. I don't know if I'll see her again,' he let on.

'Oh, and why's that?' she quizzed. 'I thought that you looked quite a couple,' she probed further, all ears, wanting to hear the words spill from his mouth, that she was still the one he craved, but on this occasion she wasn't going to get them.

'Aye, she's nice and bubbly, but I'm a bit worried. We don't seem to have a lot, if anything, in common, and to make things worse, her father's only my boss.'

With Tommy tiring fast of the spinning frenzy, Toby caught his tormentor and began ripping at the succulent meat-flavoured fabric. See-sawing with the dog, Tommy attempted to recover the pyjama case, but the dog was too hungry to be denied at least a share of the spoils. As Toby's reborn passion for the game ripped the lure in two halves, Tommy fell back on to the grass, to hear the derisive laughter of his friends.

Then Paul stopped abruptly as something caught his eye. In the bust up something had been uncovered from the innards of the cuddly toy. It was the missing letter that Tommy's mother had sent him.

'Look, Tom, is that the letter you've been searching for?' Paul asked.

'Aye,' he replied, jumping off the grass to thank Toby with an almighty hug. 'Read it, Paul, read it, it might tell us of her whereabouts.'

Reading the letter as requested, imported an abstruse thought provoking ambience to the initially joyous climate. His mother had explained to her son that it had been the most difficult decision of her life to leave him behind, as she strove for a new beginning in England. She blamed his father for her drink problem before contradicting herself, by wanting Tommy to understand, that although she would always love him dearly, he had always been the onus upon her. His learning difficulties and inability to mould into society had prolonged her departure and the writing of this letter merely signified that she could wait no more for him to adapt. He had been her shackles in a defunct marriage and she'd had to smash them and break free. Even Tommy could fathom out that she held him culpable for half of her misfortune.

'I don't want to find her no more,' stated Tommy, fighting off the tears.

'Why?' asked Paul. 'You can read and write now, you've friends. Your life is evolving every day, you're achieving more with every minute. Surely you want to show your mother how far you've come. Besides, the way I see it, reading between the lines, that garbage was her way of acquitting herself of any blame for what she did.'

'I don't understand what you mean?' sobbed Tommy.

'She probably thought you'd never forgive her for running out on you, so she retaliated first, she's hurting for what's she's done. This letter was written through anger and confusion, people don't really mean what they say in those circumstances, trust me, I've been there. Think about what I did to Toby when I couldn't think straight. I didn't mean it, I was simply fighting back because I'd been hurt,' Paul explained, with the assistance of some reverse psychology.

'So it wasn't my fault then?' Tommy asked, requiring reassurance.

'No, I promise,' comforted Paul.

'So can you find her then?'

'Well, she hasn't divulged her whereabouts, but if we can do some forensics on this postmark, we have a good start.'

The envelope was tattered and stained, but there remained a faint imprint of where the postmark had been franked.

'I'll ask my dad if he will give it to the forensic scientists at his work, they'll have no problem in tracing it,' offered Angela.

While Tommy resumed his training exploits with new-found enthusiasm, Angela gave Paul an injection of hope.

'You were really good there, you should have been a psychologist, more money to be earned than stewarding as well.'

'I can't be that good,' he retorted sullenly. 'After all, I misread everything about you.'

'Did you?' was all she replied, questioningly.

Having had a good hour's coursing, Paul instructed Tommy not to exercise Toby any more. Twenty-four hours rest prior to the race was the only preparation his expertise preconditioned. After returning to the old custom of giving Angela a lift into the city centre, Paul detoured on the way home at a newsagents to buy an evening paper. Scanning the next day's advance card he had convinced himself that if Toby was to blessed with the auspicious red jacket then all his problems would pale into insignificance. Squeezing the paper he looked to the heavens when he read: History Maker, trap one, in the 8 p.m. race. His prayers had been answered. All he had to do now was make sure the dog came out running . . .

Saturday was judgement day. Up with the larks, Paul arrived at Tommy's house bright eyed and bushy tailed. Halving Toby's breakfast quota following a brief five-minute stroll to stretch his legs, were the only ingredients that Paul felt were needed to stir the dog into winning mode. Playing cards to defeat the tedium, the hours dragged by.

At 5 p.m. Paul initiated his master plan in the covert laboratory of his own kitchen. Cracking an egg into a bowl, he added a slice of toast then poured in the final secret constituent of the magic potion: three capfuls of whiskey. The slice of toast merely acted as the incentive for the animal to consume the vile mixture, otherwise, the dog would undoubtedly turn its nose up at the strong pre-race offering. Returning to Tommy's, they stood and watched over Toby as he came of age. A rigorous half-hour session of physiotherapy and stretching of the limbs and their charge was ready to take on the field. Removing his surgical face mask and scrubbing the dog from his hands, Paul felt sure the operation would turn out to be a pioneering success.

When Angela appeared on the scene at just after 6 p.m. she was to be the bearer of good tidings. The enigma of the flagging postmark had been successfully unfurled.

'Your mother lives in Cleveland,' she revealed.

'Where's that?' asked Tommy.

'Guess you were way off the mark, Tom, she's not in England, she's in America,' sighed Paul.

'What, with the Queen's head on the stamp,' sneered Angela. 'There's a Cleveland in England, it's a county and the really good news is, it's one of the smallest. The main town is Middlesbrough, it's in the north-east.'

'So, can you find her now?' fizzed Tommy.

'I'll do my best. I'll find out the local newspapers and take out a personal ad. Leave it with me, but give me time, we'll not strike gold overnight.'

High spirited and emotionally revitalised, they set off to Dunmore. Arriving with forty-five minutes to spare, they presented the pacified canine at the weigh-in. Tipping the balance at 35.5 kilos, Paul's mathematical brain thought that Toby was a touch on the heavy side, having perused the documentation of his early career history. All his six wins had come when he was a kilo lighter, still it was too late now - that would have to be addressed at a later stage.

'Do you want to parade the dog?' Paul inquired of Tommy.

'I'd love to,' he accepted with a warm smile.

'Okay, here's the tactic I want you to employ for tonight,' whispered Paul. 'When all the other handlers are placing their dogs in the starting traps, I want you to hang back for a bit, try to make sure he goes in last. I don't like a dog having to wait an eternity before the hare arrives, it gets into a lather which often leads to a missed break.'

'Okay, I'll try my best,' agreed Tommy.

196

Leaving him to his handling duties, Paul and Angela began to make their way around to the winning line in front of the main grandstand.

'So, do you really think he can win?' she asked.

Scrutinising the race card, Paul outlined his prognosis of how the race would unfold.

'Well, we have the precious red jacket, so that's a plus for starters. If he can hold trap two off to the first bend, who according to this form is an erratic trapper, then we have a solo run; that only leaves one question. Is he fast enough, this is a poor race, a 24.40 time will be more than good enough to secure victory. That means we have to improve six lengths on his trial time to figure in the outcome. I think I found those earlier.'

'What do you mean?' she quizzed, intrigued by the glint of expectancy in his eye.

'Well, I've rested him all day so he should be fresh. I halved his food ration, so he'll be hungry and irate and I gave him a secret potion.'

'Like what?' she inquired.

'As I said, it's a secret, if he wins I'll tell you then. So how's your mother anyway?' he veered off course.

'Hanging in there. I'm gonna miss her,' she said reflectively. 'She's been asking about you.'

'And I suppose you told her how much of a cad I've been,' he sighed presumptuously.

'No, actually I didn't, I just tell her you're working all the time when she harangues me to ask you to come visit.'

'Perhaps we could take her out to the countryside one day, or along the shores of the Lough,' offered Paul.

'Would you really do that?'

'Well, I wouldn't have suggested it otherwise,' he confirmed.

'I'll ask her, then. Look, here's Toby,' she pointed out.

Savouring the ceremony again, Tommy paraded the merry hound past the stands, as its bloodshot eyes darted around, eagle-eyed for a morsel of sustenance to nourish its demanding appetite. Opening at odds of 4/1 against, Paul punted a pony before returning to watch the contest with Angela.

'Aren't you having a bet?' asked Paul, walking on the spot with nerves as the moment of truth neared.

'No, I think I jinxed him the other night. I just want to see him finish one better than the last run, that'll be sufficient for me.'

197

Struggling to put the dog into its starting trap, Tommy found himself carrying out Paul's tactical instructions to perfection without even having to try.

As the hare made its first spin of the evening, Paul muttered the dog's pseudonym under his breath. 'Come on Toby, just hit the lids and the rest's history.'

Flashing from the lids like a fork of lightning, Toby streaked past the win line for the first time with a sweet two-length lead. Turning the curve as if it wasn't there, he blew out the cobwebs down the back straight, forging six to eight lengths clear of the also-rans and, refusing to brake, he swept around the final two bends devoid of company on his pre-emptive, superfluous run, roaring home to win unchallenged by a rhetorical half the track. Screaming their lungs out, all hope had turned to hysteria in less than half a minute. Cavorting on the spot, Angela flung her arms around Paul. Lifting her off her feet, he spun her around and when her feet eventually touched the ground she stared at him with kiss me eyes, but in the light of past differences and misconstrued signals, Paul had no faculty to see through them at this precise moment.

'Ssh, ssh,' said Paul, toning his ears for the public announcement of the order of placings.

'And here is the complete order of finish for the first race. First, trap one, History Maker.'

With bated breath, Paul awaited for the winning time and eventual margin of victory, for he knew it had to be fast.

'The winner's time was 23.68, the winning distance twelve lengths.'

Placing his hands through his hair before dragging them down over his face to his neck, he shook his head in disbelief.

'What's wrong?' she asked, worried by his animations.

'What's right, you mean,' he returned. 'There's gallons more improvement in his tank, all we have to do is siphon it out and we have an open racer, a champion.'

'Really?' she gasped.

'Aye, a world-beater, an emulator, a living machine, a rabbit catcher,' he rambled in the excitement of his discovery.

In the races that would follow, the authenticity of Toby's marvel run was rubber-stamped by the fact that the fastest win time outside his was a 23.86. That winner had walked off with £500 and a trophy, yet for Toby's efforts, an insulting £20 in prize money was all they would

198

collect. After collecting his £125 winnings from the sore bookmaker, Paul rejoined Angela.

'Come on, we'd better go see Tommy and Toby, then it's celebration time.'

Inside the kennels, Tommy was the hero of the hour, as he was bombarded with the other owners' questions. Twitching nervously with all the attention, he was relieved to see his co-owners appear for some support. Shepherding Tommy and his dog from the limelight, they left the madness of the stadium to bask in the solitude of Paul's car.

'So what's our next move?' asked Angela.

'Lose weight,' replied Paul.

'I beg your pardon,' she retorted, remembering how he had lifted her earlier in their elation.

'The dog, that is,' he recovered the situation. 'According to his past form, he's a kilo overweight, but that might not be an actuality. So what we must do now is experiment, cover every angle to determine what brings out the best in him. It's all trial and error from here on in. When we find the correct formula then we'll stick with it, but first we stay with tonight's conditions. We have to prove tonight's exhibition was no flash in the pan.'

'So when do we run him again?' asked Tommy.

'Realistically, the sooner the better. I'd say next Saturday, but I'll be away, so no transport,' grimaced Paul.

'We can manage,' said Tommy with great conviction.

'Aye,' agreed Angela. 'We can take taxis; we can use some of the prize money, if that's all right with you?'

'It's cool with me if yous can manage,' accorded Paul.

Taking from his pocket his £100 profit, he handed his partners £30 a piece.

'What's this for?' she inquired.

'I want both of you to celebrate on me. I had a nice touch off Toby. It's just a little bonus for all your efforts and a thank you for giving me a second chance and I'll be really offended if you refuse.'

'Are you really sure?' asked Angela.

'I'm positive, and I'm not trying to buy your friendship, now can you earn your corn by going back in and entering Toby for a run next Saturday and another for the following Thursday, for when I'm home. I want to get moving, I can feel my nose starting to play up,' he sniffed.

199

Smiling, she accepted his token of appreciation then made her way back into the stadium to action his request. Watching her as she headed off, Paul was deep in thought as he reflected on the dog's run and suddenly things began to jump into perspective. Being no fool, his brain finally grasped the implications of yesterday at the park and now tonight, when she had done everything but beg him to kiss her. Mind enmeshed with her enigmatic behaviour, the thought of another denial that might stunt the growth of their budding friendship, which had sprouted to new heights in the last twenty-four hours, deferred him from any irrational moves. She was different after all, strange at times, deep and shallow all at once, that's why he loved her. A sneezing fit and the sight of her return brought him to his senses for the lively drive home.

Earlier that evening, after a week's in-depth analysis weighing up the pros and cons of her predicament, Bernadette had reached a conclusion. Having drawn up a list of ultimatums, she convened Michael for peace talks in conciliatory mood, where she would emphasise that it was not an unconditional surrender. An afternoon phone call to her closest sister, who would not give her a temporary roof over her head, affiliated with the reminiscence of how things had been with her fiancé prior to Paul's homecoming, brought gravity to her up-in-the-air plight.

'So what do you want?' Michael inquired, catching sight of the engagement ring he had bought her, back where it belonged on her third finger, left hand.

'I want to clear the air between us and give it another go, but not without reforms. I can never marry you while you're engaged to Paddy's Bar. You haven't taken me out since I moved in here. I feel hemmed in, as if I'm just a possession that you can pick up and throw back into the corner when I've served my purpose which, let's be frank about it, is to satisfy your sexual appetite. Here's what I want. A little space for starters; I need you to take me out at least once a week, I don't mind you going to the pub sometimes, but not all the time and, finally, if you ever raise your hand to me again, I swear I'll have no hesitation, or regret, in having you charged,' she stressed, setting out her stall.

'What about Paul?' he probed, watching her eyes carefully to see if they would lie.

'What about him?' she returned.

'I come in and you're in his arms, what am I to believe?' huffed Michael, still hurting at the thought of it.

'My supposed husband-to-be had just struck me across the face, it was only a comforting gesture on his part. There's nothing between us, I swear.'

Michael loved her immensely, and he knew he'd let it slip of late. The lack of aplomb brought about by Paul's return had accelerated his jealousy with such speed, that when he needed to apply the brakes to his temper, they'd seized in his time of need. Although she had felt the pain instantly, it was he who was suffering the long-term effects of the hurt that had lingered all week, dogging him akin to a viral infection, sapping his vitality and purpose. She was the only manna he required to remedy his malady.

For an hour solid they amicably aired their gripes and thrashed out a deal to reach a common equilibrium. Michael had agreed to concede to all her demands, in return they would start saving for their own home and, as far as Michael was concerned, the further away from Paul the better. After a night tucked away in an intimate corner of the local pub, where they promulgated their reconciliation and discussed their wedding plans, they returned home to passionately reconsummate their exhumed relationship.

It was the bubbly emissions of laughter that woke Bernadette on the late Sunday morning of Toby's emphatic homecoming. Turning over to banish the drumstick from the pigskin of her head, she smelt the pillow where Michael's head had rested the night before and it turned her stomach as her thoughts relived last night's lie. Rising from the bed, she was drawn to the sunlight flooding into her room and the frolicking uproar welling from the backyard. Spying below she watched Paul joking with Angela and she knew that the honeymoon of last night was already over. She stared into space distraught and agreed that Michael had indeed told the truth. If they were to survive as a couple then they had to find their own place; just the mere sight of Paul and her world was turned upside down.

When Bernadette arrived home from work on Monday evening Angela was still there. Now that Toby was more than just a pastime pet, extra time would have to be devoted to honing his talent. Paul had left detailed instructions regarding the training criteria to be met in his absence, and Tommy and Angela were following it to the letter, desperate to emulate Saturday's success. Although Bernadette had been a popular character at school, under Michael's autocracy she had gradually lost contact with her clique, which left her with no one to trust

201

and confide in. Now that Angela was back on the scene there appeared to be a perfect opportunity just begging to be taken. Joining the spit and polish brigade near the kennel, she forwarded her hand in friendship and Angela, still overjoyed at Toby's turnaround in form, was only too willing to accept. Bernadette learnt that the dog was now an earner and much more. Over the next few nights she listened attentively for most of the time, while at other times she simply stared at Angela from a distance, wondering exactly what is was that Paul saw in her.

On the seas, Paul had managed, through over exerted efforts, to put distance between himself and Mairead, and by Wednesday evening their paths had yet to cross. Settling down with the Telegraph for his third consecutive early night, he heard a faint knock upon his cabin door.

'Come in, it's open,' he yelled to be heard above the relentless drone of the ship's gas turbines and generators, which even rang in his ears for several days after he'd returned to shore.

Entering his quarters, Mairead came and sat beside him on the edge of the bunk.

'Now then, why do I get the distinct feeling that you're trying to avoid me. I suppose it could be something to do with all the messages I've been passing through your friend, that you've refrained from answering,' she said with a question mark written all over her face.

'I'm sorry, it's just that I'm a bit wary of your father being who he is.'

'But why?'

'Well, say we split up under a bad cloud, then he'll make my life a misery, I might even lose my job. There's a recession on out there, you know.'

'Don't be stupid, is that all that's putting you off me?'

'Well no, I'm really not ready for anything heavy. I'd like us to be friends though, if that's all right, then we can see what develops with time, can you handle that?' he asked, borrowing the idiom that Angela had once appeased him with.

'So you don't want to go out with me?' she sighed.

'I'm not saying that, it's all too soon, can't we just slow things down a little, *que sera sera.*'

'What?' she inquired.

'You know, whatever will be will be.'

202

Once again his inability to master his compassion had let him down. Having been unable to deliver his true verdict, he had left the case wide open and he knew that at a later date Mairead would change her plea and appeal.

'Okay, I understand, but I wasn't asking you to marry me. You have my phone number, if you change your mind. I'm going nowhere,' she said, putting the ball in his court.

Earlier that evening Bernadette had brought a tray of tea and biscuits for her new friends. In all honesty, she didn't know what she was doing. Half of her despised Angela for owning the rights to Paul's heart, but as she was led to believe the feeling was not reciprocal, her better side needed some female company of her own generation. Loosening her tongue, she let her grievances towards Angela leave her for the meantime. For a good hour they chatted as though they'd known each other since nursery school, covering a wide expanse of female topics from cosmetics to cooking, yet not once did they embark upon the opposite sex. With everything simmering along nicely, impetuously the temperature was about to rise in the heat of a bad joke.

'Oh, I heard a few jokes at work today,' voiced Bernadette.

'Go on then, I could do with a laugh,' permitted Angela.

'Okay, what's the odd one out, an intelligent man, an intelligent woman or a leprechaun?'

'No idea,' replied Angela, turning from her grooming duties to face the punchline.

'An intelligent woman, 'cause the other two don't exist.' Laughing in unison their friendship was taking hold.

'Okay, this one's better,' began Bernadette. 'A Mother Superior is canvassing for new blood at the local school, aiding the girls in making their career choices. So she asks the first girl, "What do you want to be when you leave school?" The girl answers "I want to be a nurse." "Well we have a sickbay at the convent, so you could become a nun and it would not conflict with your nursing ambitions" informs Mother Superior. The girl therefore agrees and signs her life away. Anyway, she then persuades another girl who wants to be a librarian in the same way, finally the last girl comes in and reveals she wants to be a prostitute. "What did you say?" shouts the Superior, turning white with shock. "A prostitute," replies the girl. Crossing herself in relief the Mother Superior says, "Oh, thank God, I thought you said a Protestant".'

Although Angela faked a smile and applauded with a negligible chuckle, she didn't laugh loud enough and it didn't go unnoticed by the now suspicious Bernadette.

Mulling over the implications that night, Bernadette was convinced that Paul's sweet little Angela, in whose mouth butter would not melt, was a Protestant as she'd thought all along. All she needed now was a little proof. Smiling wickedly at her ingenuity, she arrived at her decision. She would follow Angela at the next available opportunity, to find out exactly where she lived.

Chapter 8

The Show Must Go On

Totally obsessed with her suspicions, Bernadette was not willing to manifest the same patience she had afforded Paul. Rising early on her new-found vendetta, she interrogated Tommy at dawn and gained the intelligence she required. Ascertaining that Angela was expected at 11 a.m. prior to her afternoon shift at the RVH, Bernadette set off to work at the usual time with no intention whatsoever of selling shoes. Arriving in the city centre, she bought a newspaper, then took cover in a small café with panoramic vistas of the bus shelters. After ordering a coffee to cover her charade, she sat by the window giving herself the optimum vantage point to initiate her personal stakeout. Taking no chances just in case Angela decided to make an early appearance, she scanned like an ornithologist through the rush-hour flocks centering on the city.

At 10 a.m., when the deluge of commuters had evaporated to a trickle of sleepyheads and shoppers, Bernadette knew she had to make herself more inconspicuous. A redhead seated in a front window was about as obscure as a mountain of coal in the Arctic Circle. Taking a pair of sunglasses from her handbag and utilising yesterday's headlines, she successfully camouflaged her mien. At 10.20 a.m. having tarried through the suspense of three coffees and a sore bladder, she spotted Angela alight her bus. Dressed in work uniform, she stuck out from the crowd akin to the Pied Piper in a stream of verminous rats. Allowing Angela to vanish from view, as she made her way to another bus stop to catch a bus to the Falls, Bernadette then fixed her sights to the vehicle that had originally transported Angela into the city centre.

Waiting anxiously through a change of driver, it was planetary reward to discover that her deviated morning had not been a waste of time to add her loss of earnings. This bus never went anywhere near Ballymurphy as she'd been led to believe, its round-trip destination was no other than Woodvale via the Shankill and that was a bonus. Although there were many predominantly Protestant hard-core areas like Rathcool and Taughmonagh, the Shankill was the most publicised of them all. It was the icing on the cake, the lion of the animal kingdom, the one suburb that the Republican contingency most feared and loved to hate and no other than the past haven for the legendary infamous Shankill Butchers, a ruthless loyalist gang responsible for nineteen murders during the late seventies before their capture, conviction and incarceration in February 1979.

Bernadette smiled perniciously at her ingenuity for she was fully aware that it would take very little to persuade the right people that corrective action was warranted. With Paul due home on Sunday evening, she'd have to work fast. Catching the next bus after Angela's departure, she headed back to the Falls to call on an old friend by the name of Siobhan Daly. A tomboy of a girl if ever there was, as hard as nails but not easily hammered. At school she'd constantly thrown her weight around the playground, running the usual juvenile protection rackets to keep her in cigarettes and sweets. Being one of her accomplices, Bernadette had shared in the spoils of war, serving her as a debt collector. When school was over she inveigled most of her menials to accompany her in the natural progression of enrolling into the IRA. If, in the end, Bernie's relationship with Paul had left her with nothing, at least he had managed to dissuade her with an ultimatum that she had no future with such an organisation. Unable to dismiss her new-found hatred towards Angela, Bernadette knocked at Siobhan's door.

'Bernadette,' she laughed. 'It's good to see you, but what brings you here?'

'I have some gossip that may interest you,' she revealed.

'Well, come away in then,' urged Siobhan.

Following Siobhan into the kitchen, Bernadette accepted the offer of a cup of tea. For a good hour they ran through the formalities of catching up on their past histories, before getting down to the serious business which Bernadette had come to put her old friend's way.

'What would you say if I told you that a Protestant girl from the Shankill came into the Falls on a daily basis to see a lad?' probed Bernadette.

206

'I'd say I don't believe you. No one could be that stupid,' came the reply.
'Well, I'm telling you, it's gospel.'
'So, who's the lad she comes to see?' asked Siobhan.
'No, leave him out of it, I'm sure he's in the dark about her true background,' insisted Bernadette before pressing on. 'So what would you do?'
'I think we'll have to meet her in a dark alley and give her a stern talking to and I'll let you do the honours with her hair,' grinned Siobhan.
'No, I can't do that, she knows me. She'd be able to recognise me then we'd all be at risk,' revealed Bernadette, edgily.
'Okay then, if you point her out to me and the girls, we'll make sure she won't have the audacity to show her face around here no more.'
'Great, but it'll have to be tonight,' Bernie urged, with a staunch smile.
'I guess you have a plan then for such short notice?' raised Siobhan.
'Aye, sort of. She's a nurse at the RVH, so when her shift's finished she has to catch the bus into town for her connection, between nine and ten I think. So if I signal her out, you and your crew can get ahead and catch her in the city centre. It should be quiet enough at that time. I presume there will be transport available?'
'Aye, dead on,' confirmed the butch Siobhan.

At 8.45 p.m. a small black Mini sat strategically in the entrance of Sorella Street just across from the bus stop outside the RVH. Siobhan, not anticipating much resistance, had hand picked a light team of only three, inclusive of the driver who would act in the dual role of lookout. At 9.30 p.m. the off-duty nurses began to emerge in small huddles from the huge hospital.
'Oh shit,' exclaimed Bernadette, upon seeing Angela. 'That's her there getting into that white Capri, she must be getting a lift home,' she sighed, banging her fist in frustration upon the headrest of the front passenger seat where the ringleader sat.
'Not necessarily,' said the driver. 'We'll head into town just in case she's only getting a ride into the city to catch her bus.'
'Aye, good idea,' agreed Siobhan before continuing. 'Go on, get out, you can leave this with us, we know her face now.'
Alighting the car as ordered, Bernadette watched as the Mini screeched off towards town, before shifting her observations to the Capri as it began to manoeuvre its way out of the immense car park.

* * *

207

In the back room of Paddy's Bar, Michael was learning of his next mission. Now that his love life seemed to be heading in the right direction again and although he had curbed his excessive drinking, he had never had any intention of deviating from the road to a United Ireland, that was still a romantic dream that held par with Bernadette. Having accomplished his first real task with true professionalism, Michael was confident promotion into the Active Service Unit he laboured to be a part of was now within his grasp. Expecting a crack at the security forces or an influential loyalist with a gun or bomb, he was dismayed to learn the tools for his next sortie were to be merely a cigarette and a dozen or so matches.

Having been subdued for a while, the IRA had decided to have a foot-stomping, insurrectional weekend to remind everyone that they were simply a sleeping giant biding their time, with a Fe Fi Fo Fum, we smell the blood of an Orangeman. A terror campaign of bombings and a spate of destruction through Molotov Cocktails and incendiary devices, aimed mainly at businesses and the usual hotels which the RUC and army used for their weekend soirées would do the trick. Evacuation warnings would be emanated in a bid to prevent civilian casualties. The intention was not to take human lives but to maim society. Such an onslaught upon the city would keep the heat in the cauldron of hatred simmering within the communities as well as procreating other benefits for the IRA.

In addition to the antipathetic publicity which was good for Republican morale, the disorder would be used as a training programme for the up and coming volunteers. During these defiant outbursts of anarchy, the untried and untested new blood would be thrown into a baptism of fire like cannon fodder, where they'd have their chance to shine, while the established big guns would be kept under wraps for another day. The only part they'd be asked to play would be to make hoax phone calls to catalyse the mayhem, as the services would find themselves stretched to their limits to cope with the hue and cry. On days like these, Belfast would be turned into a Beirut with Guinness.

A successful dare meant that you inflicted the maximum damage, then evaded capture to fight another day. Michael's part to play in this derailment of community harmony was reflected in the light of his earlier commitment. His task was relatively simple and one which, unlike planting a bomb at a luxury hotel, would carry less penalty were he to be tracked down on the evidence of video footage. Like every other recruit employed in the fracas, he would learn specifically only of his own objective for obvious safeguarding reasons, one loud mouth could ruin months of prudent planning for the paramilitary faction.

A leading high street store of British descent was to be his target on Saturday afternoon at 1p.m. to coincide with the height of the shopping week. A single cigarette, with matches taped around the circumference about half an inch from the end was the unsophisticated incendiary device to be employed, yet it had the firepower to result in thousands of pound's worth of fire damage and loss of sales. And all he had to do was light the cigarette, then simply pop it into a jacket pocket snuggled in a packed rail of garments. The half-inch of tobacco leading to the matches would act as a fuse, presenting him with a good five minutes' burn time with which to make his escape, before the kindled matches caused a mini explosion to ignite then spread through the fabric like wildfire.

In his bunk aboard the ferry, Paul was drafting his 'Desperately Seeking Mrs O'Brien' personal ad. Earlier in the week, directory inquiries had supplied him with the telephone number for the Middlesbrough tourist information board, who had in turn provided him with the numbers of the two most popular local tabloids which were the Evening Gazette and the Northern Echo. After discussing terms of payment, all Paul could do now was place his supplication and wait. Struggling to word the prose with a mind to keeping the expense at a minimum, he chewed at the end of the pen to help focus his ideas, but even that brought no brainstorming outcome. Glancing at his wristwatch he thought it best to attempt the composition in the morning, seeing as his head wanted to join the rest of his body which had long since gone to sleep. Yet, as soon as his head touched the pillow the lost thoughts began to appear in his mind's eye, obliging him to write the few lines that just might reunite Tommy with his mother. The way Paul defined it was, if she'd been able to turn her back so easily on her son, then the more difficult it was going to be to lure her from her new life, wherever that might be. The best prospect of success might, therefore, be to use deception through artifice. The bait he used was subtle to say the least. After a distant relative's sudden and regretful demise, she had become the sole heir to a substantial unnamed sum of money. And all the rightful benefactor had to do to claim their inheritance was come forward and validate their true identity. Licking the envelopes to seal the fictitious work, he felt a cold shiver pass through his body – that unexplained phenomenon that usually prognosticates a death in the family.

* * *

209

Parking the Mini up a side street, Siobhan ordered the engine and lights to be cut then expeditiously discussed the objective to be executed if the white Capri was to drop off the target. Her blueprint was simple yet ingenious, in relation to Angela's line of work. For the operation to come together without a hitch the malicious posse needed a cardinal player with medical experience; Angela would therefore play the main role in her own downfall if she was to make an appearance. After a few minutes' wait the Capri arrived and Angela alighted to join a middle-aged gent at the bus stop. Siobhan realised that the streets would never be devoid of passers-by hopping from pub to pub, so there was never going to be an ideal time to strike; however, she did have two significant advantages with which to work with. The city centre public houses were trendy night spots and therefore their clientele was generally the young spendthrift set, who in this day and age found it easier to turn a blind eye than involve themselves in rushing to an underdog's assistance. Secondly, and more salutary, there was only one other individual keeping Angela company at the stop. With a bus imminent, Siobhan gave the thumbs up for the offensive to begin.

Racing to the bus shelter, Siobhan feigned panic and hyperventilation.

'Can you help me?' she panted. 'My daddy's just collapsed around the corner, I think it's his heart.'

'Just calm down and lead the way,' exhorted Angela.

'Is there anything I can do to help?' offered the third party.

'Aye, you can phone an ambulance while I survey his condition,' instructed Angela composedly, taking command of the situation.

Angela's words were music to Siobhan's ears. Leading her into the trap, the second girl was curled up on the pavement as the decoy, while the third waited at the wheel to provide the quick getaway needed. As Angela bent over in the dark to loosen the collar and check for a pulse, before she had time to realise the casualty was not male, she had swapped places with the postulated coronary victim on the hard cold pavement. A thundering karate chop to the base of her neck had momentarily robbed her of her senses. Dazed and stunned from the mighty blow and the impact on the concrete flagstones, her legs were so numb that her assailants had to haul her off the ground and prop her up to attention against a wall, for the verbal attack that was to ensue.

'Don't you ever show your face around the Falls again, you Orange bastard,' spat Siobhan. 'This is just a friendly warning of things to come, stick to your own kind or you're dead.'

Head bobbing and struggling to breath from the slight concussion she had sustained, Angela quickly came to. Eyes dilating instantaneously, she caught sight of the sparkling metal of a blade glinting in the moonlight and with a blinding flash of fear her brain tripped out sending her spinning into unconsciousness. Neck as limp as a festive turkey's, her chin fell sweetly on to her breastbone making it more effortless for Siobhan to create a new genre in hair styling. It was the final primitive act of repugnance in the form of a vicious boot to the ribcage that stirred Angela. Kick-started to life, as if receiving electric shock cardiac resuscitation, she winced as the sharp pains surged through her side. Vision still blurred, she desperately endeavoured to focus in an effort to make out the screeching Mini's registration number but, by the time her sights were fixed, the getaway was clean away. Picking herself up, she staggered towards the stentorian crescendo of the ambulance siren nearing fast.

Driven back to work in the company vehicle, she was x-rayed for fractures and given the strong medication of a cup of hot, sweet tea. After submitting a sketchy report to the police, she was informed by the doctor there was no substantial damage, only to her vanity. Finally, arriving home by taxi, she rushed to the bathroom to survey the aftermath. Looking into the mirror, she saw that her shoulder-length silky strands had now been replaced by intermittent tufts of petrified hair rising from her grazed and nicked, livid scalp. Bursting into tears at the catastrophic sight, she wished there was someone strong and caring to hold her. Suddenly, Angela was no longer immune to emotional pain and yearned for security and, although she wasn't yet aware of it, a time of vulnerability was about to encroach upon her traumatised existence. Leaving the taunting mirror behind, she retired to bed, where she sat, mind activated, staring into the darkness, as she searched for the answers which would shed light upon the earlier events of her terrifying night. When the dawn of the new day arrived she was no further forward in that direction; however, she had made a few decisions, one of which would be later revoked in defiance. Taking her mother a light breakfast along with her prescribed cocktail of painkillers and antidepressants, she had forgotten to bring an infallible explanation.

'Oh my God, Angie, what happened?'

'I was mugged in the city centre last night,' she replied.

'What for?' inquired her mother, as flashes of anxiety passed through her, transcending the pain of her cancer.

'What do you think, for money, of course,' retorted Angela, turning her face away to mask the lie.

'Come on Angie, this is your mother you're talking to now. They don't cut your hair off during a mugging. Paul's a Catholic, isn't he?'

'No, he isn't,' she snapped becoming flustered with all the deceit, 'and even if he was, what difference would it make?'

'To me none,' comforted her mother softly. 'Unfortunately there are a lot of people in the Shankill who disapprove, your father for starters. I think that's because he lives under the threat of the Provos every time he puts on his uniform but, as it's a subject we've never discussed, I couldn't really say how he feels towards the Catholic people in general. So I think it would be best to keep Paul away from him just in case he has a hidden resentment that he's never shared with me.'

As Angela listened carefully, she felt so sickened by everything that was happening in her life that it catalysed another outburst of tears. Falling into her mother's arms, she sobbed out her vexation.

'Oh Mommy, why did they do this to me? What am I gonna do?'

'Come on Angie, it's not the end of the world, your hair will grow back before you know it. You can wear a wig in the meantime. As for Paul, you and him are gonna have to do some serious talking, you'll have to make plans if you love him. Nobody, but nobody, can come between your love. If that's what the two of you really want then love will find a way, they say it conquers all and I'm sure they're right. I just want to leave this world in the knowledge that you were happy and settled.'

'But I'm not sure if I really love him,' said Angela.

'Then what do you feel when you're with him?' her mother angled.

'This won't make sense but I feel happy and sad, secure yet insecure, safe but frightened all at once. What does that indicate?'

Although her mother knew exactly what it meant, she also realised that her daughter had to find her own interpretation of the consternation she was experiencing.

'It means you're suffering from fatigue and that you need time to gather yourself. Why don't you take a few days off work and relax for a while, maybe spend some time with Paul away from here?'

Taking the hit-squad's advice, Angela decided to avoid the Falls. She phoned Paul's mother, and asked her to convey a message to Tommy, that something had come up to sidetrack her, but for him to take a taxi and collect her outside City Hall at 7 p.m. on Saturday night. If she was to be wrung through the mangle of circumstance then Toby had to keep to his diary of race engagements, after all it was her love of the sport that had kept her coming back for more. Well, that's what she kept trying to persuade herself, anyway.

Wearing a headscarf to veil her embarrassment, she spent the remainder of the morning 'chasing the hair' as an acute priority, desperate to acquire a wig for more than one reason. Not only would her new style attract attention to her at work and within her community, but questions would be asked and accusations made. Colleagues and passers-by would whisper behind her back and many weak in the art of subtle restraint would insinuate to her face. She would quickly become the spiteful subject of conversation on everyone's lips. To Angela these were only trifling issues, her biggest worry was what Paul would think of her now if he saw her like this. Like any woman on a shopping expedition, she knew exactly what she wanted, yet never seemed to be satisfied before turning full circle to make the purchase at her first port of call.

Gauging the response of everyone she met, would either raise her confidence or send her current state of paranoia into a disintegrating demise. Her mother had thought it best not to comment. Her father – well, when they crossed paths on the landing outside the toilet, he adopted his usual stance of taking no notice of her. On the early shift on Saturday morning it didn't go unnoticed, though. Angela simply said she was experimenting and they all accepted her words for now.

On the stroke of midday, the terror campaign returned. For four hours, Belfast city centre was relentlessly thrown into anarchic turmoil, as bomb warnings were issued right, left and centre. The heroes of the afternoon were without question the fearless bomb disposal units who worked against the clock, racing from one diffusion to the next, somehow maintaining calm when all around were losing their heads in the hysterical stampede. Coping admirably, the fire department played its huge part, quickly controlling the incendiary blazes which often threatened to overrun the very city, one of which was started by Michael. And on one occasion only did the Crown forces miss their target. At 3.15 p.m. two simultaneous phone calls forewarned of two bombs primed to go off at 3.30 p.m. Undermanned and overstretched, they managed to evacuate both areas, but had only enough time and resources to carry out a controlled detonation on one of the suspect packages. They chose the hoax, still no one's exemplary, and everyone is allowed a mistake once in a while. The second device ripped apart an engineering firm which practised sectarianism in its selection of employees. The only casualties that day were the insurance companies. By early evening it was over and, as if it had never happened, people returned to the city centre, seemingly undeterred and unaffected by the earlier pandemonium.

When Tommy pulled up in his chauffeur-driven black cab, Angela had no idea how he would view her artificial hair, if at all.

'I've followed Paul's instructions all the way – I gave him his three capfuls right on the button of five o'clock.'

'Oh God, I smell it,' declared Angela, trying to shield her complexion from Toby's amorous tongue.

'What have you done to your hair?' he inquired noticing, where others had failed, that it had in fact grown a full two inches.

'I had an accident with it, why?' She blushed at his perception.

'I think it really suits you. I liked it before, but this is better, wait 'til Paul sees it, he'll be knocked off his feet.'

'That's what worries me,' she muttered under her breath.

Reaching Dunmore at 7.20 p.m., the anticipation of Toby's progression would linger longer tonight. Under the grading system, the early races were for the slower greyhounds. A8 class was the bottom of the heap, then as the night proceeded the dog's became faster and the A number dropped, finally climaxing at A1 category. These canines were not quite the cream of the crop, but animals that were verging on the deep-end jump into 'open racing'. These were invitation races that attracted both punters and owners, as the quickest and cleverest canines in the land battled it out for inflated prize money, trophies and prestige. Most of the greyhounds making this supererogatory grade would end up at stud after retirement, so the incentive was large scale, although they didn't know it. Tonight Toby had been promoted an astounding four grades, so in theory his chances were less than appealing to the experts. Nevertheless, a repeat run and time would be more than adequate to double up his tally of wins. Having been drawn from the 'red' again would certainly go a long way in helping to bridge the gulf in class, but A4 dogs were faster all round. If he couldn't hold the rails at the first turn, then it would be an uphill struggle to thread a passage through the field later. At 9.15 p.m. History Maker was sent off at ambiguous yet perspicacious odds of 3/1 which reverberated to his last clock-bashing spin.

Breaking level, he offloaded bags of early to slip the field at the first bend. Again, the further he went, the farther he won. Having lost two-tenths of a kilo in racing weight thanks to a minor adjustment to his diet, he had improved a length in time, clocking a 23.62 in his six-length demolition job of the more than half-decent field.

It wasn't until midmorning on the ship's first dock of the day in Belfast that Paul learnt of the result. The euphoria of success and the thought of seeing his friends and the dog again eased him through the last two crossings, not to mention the added sweetener that once again History Maker had run the fastest time of the night. Already the dog was gaining supporters and was earning the title of the punter's friend and the bookmaker's enemy.

When he arrived home late on Sunday night, Tommy had hung back as he had a verbal message to deliver.

'I see he did it again,' shouted Paul from the back door.

'Aye, he oble. . . oblit. . . oble. . .'

'Obliterated,' helped Paul.

'Aye, he did that to the field all right,' said Tommy.

'So, how's Angela?' asked Paul.

'Oh, she's fine and she asked me to pass a message on to you.'

'Go on then,' urged Paul, as he inspected Toby's legs and paws for cuts and grazes as a matter of routine.

'She wants you to ring her as soon as you get home, so I guess that's now.'

'Okay, I'll go and call her now.'

'Oh, Paul,' Tommy called him back. 'Have you found my mommy?'

'I've placed an ad in the local papers, all we can do is sit and wait. It won't be long now.'

'Hope not,' smiled Tommy.

Paul didn't even hear the rings before Angela had answered.

'Were you sitting by the phone?' he teased.

'No, it rang twice this end, besides it's late and my mom has just nodded off. I don't want her to waken, she's suffered a lot today.'

'Oh, I'm sorry,' replied Paul, detecting a return to hostilities in her voice. 'So the dog won again and faster too.'

'Aye, he did well. Paul I've something to tell you,' she said sounding nervy.

'I'm all ears,' he replied.

215

'I was jumped by a gang of girls in the city centre on Thursday night.'

'What?' he exclaimed. 'How are you? Who were they? Why? What did they do to you?' he blurted out an overabundance of questions in his anger and panic.

'Calm down, I'm okay now, it was only superficial, but they did cut my hair off and warn me not to show my face around the Falls again. Paul, are you still there?' she quizzed as speechlessness reigned at the other end.

Immediately his speculations pointed to Bernadette. 'Aye, I'm still here, did you see their faces. Was one Bernadette?'

'No, it had nothing to do with her, we've been having a great laugh together all week. I think she needs a confidante. Something's not right in her life, she seems unhappy. I feel sorry for her,' defended Angela.

'Well, if it wasn't her, who else could it have been?' he demanded irately.

'She thinks I'm a Catholic, doesn't she? Someone must have spotted me going home and then caught sight of me in the Falls. So I won't be able to come over any more. I'll just have to see the dog on race nights. Perhaps you could bring Toby to meet me in town and we could take him out into the country now and again. Will you?' she asked.

'You know I will. Listen when are you off work?'

'Tomorrow.'

'How about me, you and your mom go out for a drive somewhere?' proposed Paul.

'I'm sure she'd appreciate that, weather permitting. I'll phone you in the morning to let you know if it's a date.'

'Hey, Angela,' he said softly. 'I'm really sorry about what happened. I somehow feel I'm to blame.'

'Don't be silly, I come to yours for the dog remember.'

'Aye, silly me,' he derided dejectedly, disappointed at her revelation.

Lying in bed he looked to the skies and thanked his lucky stars that he hadn't bowled in head first the week before, when he'd conjectured that perhaps she was beginning to succumb to his aloof demeanour.

Leaving Tommy in charge of the training programme for the day, Paul sat and waited beside the phone, tempted to pick it up and call her. At 10 a.m. he decided he could wait no longer. Reaching for the receiver, he jumped as it began to ring.

'Hi Paul, it's me, I've spoken with my mom and it's not raining. She'd love to go out for the day, if you've nothing better planned.'

216

'So when shall I pick you up?'

'Whenever you're ready, you don't mind coming to my house?'

'No, I'll be safe won't I? I mean you haven't told anyone that I'm a Catholic?'

'I think my mother is aware of it, but she doesn't mind.'

'Okay, I'll be over in about half an hour.'

On his journey over to Angela's, Paul perceived none of the anxieties that he had suffered on his first visit to the Shankill on that dark February night all those weeks ago. In the daylight he felt ten foot tall and capable of any feat. That was until he actually entered the area. It was even more minacious and mind-blowing than the Falls must have appeared to her and suddenly he felt insignificant. Vaguely remembering the street parties being broadcast from London for the Queen's Silver Jubilee just over a decade ago, he wondered if he'd slipped back in time. The kerbstones were painted red, white and blue, the colour of the union ensign. Streamers and rosettes hung from the lampposts to portray that general election campaign ambience. And, of course, there were murals too, even more imposing than their Catholic counterparts. Persuading himself that no one could tell his religion by the look of his face or the colour of his clothes, he drove onward as if he'd been cruising around these parts all his life. The best way to remain inconspicuous was, of course, not to ogle at the embellishments or the impoverished architecture. Then again, there was even a more unquestionable camouflage, her father was a member of the RUC, people must have been aware of this, so there would be no justification for them to suspect Paul was a quisling to their beliefs. Almost thrilled to be disobeying the tribal rule book, he acknowledged a few passers-by, then knocked at her door.

'Can you help me with my mommy?' she asked. 'She's too weak to walk, so we'll have to take her wheelchair. Will it fit in your boot?'

'Well, if it doesn't, I've a towrope, so we can pretend we're doing a breakdown recovery,' he jested.

'Hey, I heard that,' shouted her mother from inside the house.

'Oh, I'm really sorry,' Paul apologised, blushing.

'Don't be, I thought it was quite humorous,' she pardoned him.

Acting as crutches, Paul and Angela lifted her emaciated mother's fragile body outside and into the sunlight before resting her on to the back seat of the car. Squinting her eyes from the ultraviolet glare that she had been denied so long, she felt a deep resentment grow for her

217

husband. She knew Paul was a Catholic, it was a mother's intuition to recognise those things and yet here he was bringing some vividness into her gloomy life, when all her husband could do, the man she had given up everything for, was turn his back upon her in her time of privation. Leaving her in her senescence while he drank himself into oblivion. Had someone forgot to tell him that it was her who was dying?

'Well, Mrs Hamilton, the day is yours, anywhere you choose to go and I'm yer man,' announced Paul.

'I'd like to sit and watch the ferries sail up and down the Lough at Whiteabbey. I used to spend hours there dreaming of far-off lands as a child – take me to my aspirations of yesteryear.'

Sanctioning her request, he drove six miles east towards Carrickfergus where there was a lengthy promenade they could walk along at their leisure, since Belfast had not been blessed with planate golden beaches, but a smuggler's paradise of jagged coves which embraced the Irish Sea. Pulling the car into a beauty spot layby juxtaposed to the shoreside, Paul glanced into his rearview mirror to see that Angela's mother's face was sparkling. It was as if ten years had been washed away at the sight of the ablatitious Lough. Subsequent to fastening her into her conveyance and wrapping her up in a fleecy tartan rug to combat the nippy sea breeze, they embarked on their deliberate stroll in the direction of the sky-piercing chimney at Ballylumford power station. After some ten minutes, Mrs Hamilton decided she wanted to pause for a while, giving Paul and Angela a respite and a chance to talk. Scanning over the lough, absorbed in her memories from the comfort of her wheelchair, she watched the anchored yachts bobbing up and down on the choppy surf and began to reflect on her childhood, when she loved to come here and watch the ferries come and go, dreaming that one day she would make that voyage into the deep blue yonder of the unknown. Sadly, there were no ferries on show that morning, only an ugly dredger coughing out its heavy catarrh of thick black smoke.

'Do you still want to come and see the dog?' asked Paul.

'Of course I do, but I can't. It was no idle threat, believe me,' Angela replied.

'What if I collect you from the city centre and when it's time to go home, drive you back again and wait until you're safely on your bus. When you're with me no one will harm you. I could even pick you up outside the RVH. Could you go for that?'

218

'I couldn't impose upon you that much,' she said shaking her head.

'You wouldn't be, I think I owe you at least that,' he pleaded.

'What do you mean?'

'It was coming to the Falls that brought all the trouble wasn't it? So I feel somewhat responsible,' explained Paul still seething over the attack.

'It was my choice, wasn't it?' she absolved him.

'So, will you go with my idea then?'

'Aye, all right, I must be a glutton for punishment though,' she smiled weakly, still apprehensive following her visitation. 'Do you want to move on now, Mom?'

'No not yet, just let me be for a while longer. You could get me an ice-cream though.'

Heading into the wind towards a mobile kiosk positioned on the grass verge by the main road, Angela began to hug herself to keep warm.

'It is cold isn't it,' remarked Paul.

'It wouldn't be so bad if you put your arm around me, body heat is supposedly one of the best insulators known to man,' she offered from her medical knowledge.

Rigidly, still scared that conceivably he was misunderstanding her gesture again, he gingerly put his arm around her shoulders. Heart pumping intensely, Paul was less than comfortable with the scenario. Had he thought, or even better known, that she was falling in love with him then it would have been so different, supple and natural. As it was he was more uptight and confounded than ever. Judging by his weak grasp, Angela was herself now unclear as to whether she had pushed him so far away that he had become distant, or worse, he'd actually gone off her. Whatever it might be, she was determined to find out. Initially Paul was relieved to break bodily contact when they arrived at the kiosk, but within seconds he felt as cold without her warmth as the three ice-creams he purchased. As they started back to her mother his impulse took over and without asking, he put his arm around her again then squeezed her tight as he pulled her in close. Smiling to himself internally, he wished that the world would grind to a standstill right there and then, so they could be suspended in this rapport for ever. When they returned with her mother's dripping cone, Angela was enjoying the comfort and security of his shoulder so much that she forgot to wriggle free from his clutches, further adding to her mother's blissful day.

219

'How do you fancy a walk round Carrickfergus?' suggested Paul.

After a unanimous nodding of heads they set off for the cobble streets of the stunningly picturesque medieval town. Stopping for a pub lunch when some seasonal cloudbursts threatened to mar their day, Angela joined Paul at the bar.

'I just want to thank you,' she said sincerely, echoing how she felt.

'For what?' he asked.

'I really appreciate this, giving my mother the chance of a day out. It's too difficult for me to get her on buses.'

'Don't mention it, I'm enjoying it as much as you. Perhaps we could do it more often?'

'Aye, I'd like that,' she smiled.

Having scoured the gift and charity shops, as well as burning some rubber off the wheels of her mother's mobile chair, they decided it was time to call it a day. As they journeyed back along the esplanade, Miss Belfast 1965 spotted a ferry crawling up the inviting estuary.

'I've only ever had one selfish yearning in life,' she disclosed.

'What's that, Mommy?'

'To sail away on one of those grand ships, if only for a day, it would be a dream come true.'

'Granted,' interrupted Paul, as if he was the little green man at the end of the very rainbow that was painting the indigo sky overhead, now that the April showers had expired. 'I'll organise a daytrip, for when it's convenient for you,' he continued, now addressing Angela.

'I won't have time off until next week and you'll be at sea, then I'll probably be working all that week when you're home,' she explained, always seeming to have the knack of making life more difficult for Paul than it was already.

'Okay, a fortnight today. If you're working then we'll just go ourselves, won't we?' he asserted, winking at her mother.

'Aye son, I can't wait,' she accepted, ironically wishing her life away.

After chauffeuring them home and arranging to meet Angela from work the next day, Paul headed home to the Falls, passing the welcoming mural of Our Lady, who pointed to the light shining through the fissured heavens near the Divis Flats. To many, she symbolised this was the road to heaven, but for Paul, his firmament was in the Shankill. During that splendid day, although he had wanted to talk about her ordeal, not once did he raise the issue or comment on her artificial hair, and that had impressed Angela immensely.

220

When he collected Angela from outside the hospital on Tuesday, he drove the short distance back to 6 Clonard Street, where it was business as usual with regard to emulating Toby's last run and notching up an amazing hatrick. Juggling with the dog's diet, supplanting the carbohydrate levels with added proteins in the form of nettle stews, chicken and fish was Paul's latest experiment, as well as attempting to walk off the half kilo he surmised Toby was carrying as burden during his races.

At 5.30 p.m. when Bernadette arrived home and looked down the back yard from the kitchen window, she could hardly believe her eyes. Feeling as if she'd just been slapped in the face, she watched as Angela groomed the dog, all smiles. Being a woman herself she began to wonder if in fact her bullying tactics had produced a reverse effect. Maybe Angela had now become more determined to see Paul; she might even fall in love with him to spite society. Realising a failure to make an emergence would most likely cast a shadow of guilt over her, she marched into the yard with an air of flamboyance, that on the other hand had its own culpability written all over it.

'So, how's the dog coming on?' she addressed Angela, with a hypocritically friendly smile.

'Well enough,' intervened Paul in an iceberg tone, letting her know he was not fooled by her audacity in making an appearance.

'You'll have to tell me when he's going to win next, so I can put some money on him,' she said, trying to keep the conversation afloat, pretending that she hadn't heard Paul's bitter attitude distil through his voice.

Turning to Angela, Paul began to stir the trouble that had been stewing inside him for days. 'Did you tell Bernie that you had a wee visit from a gang of thugs?'

'No,' replied Angela, glaring at him, annoyed that he couldn't hold his water.

'What do you mean?' asked Bernadette, showing bogus solicitude.

'Well go on then, tell her,' he urged.

'A few girls lured me into a side street and told me never to show my face in the Falls again, they thought that Paul and I were an item, then they cut my hair off,' she said, almost reduced to tears as she thought of the wig she was forced to wear.

'But why would they do that?' inquired Bernadette, acting puzzled.

221

'Because she's a Protestant,' said Paul. 'And how did they know, I can hear you ask. Well, how did they, Bernie?'

'I guess they must have followed you home one night or something,' she replied, shaking with the impact of his mood.

'Oh aye, come on, don't insult my intelligence,' he mocked, temper rising. 'We'll just follow this nurse, she looks like a Prod. Oh fuck me, we're in luck, she is. Don't think I can't read the script.'

'Are you accusing me?' she laughed, 'because if you are, you're wrong, besides I was led to believe that Angie was a Catholic and we've been getting on famously, haven't we?' she demanded sanctimoniously, seeking an ally in an enemy.

'Aye, Paul,' agreed Angela, turning against him. 'We've been having a laugh every night.'

'You've been taken for a ride,' he reprimanded Angela, before turning to face Bernadette. 'I know you were behind this and God help you when I have the proof.'

'Are you threatening me?' she returned fire with fire. 'Because if you are, I don't think Michael would be too pleased to hear about it, seeing as he's already given you a good hiding for trying to seduce me at New Year.'

'You fucking lying bitch,' he roared.

Turning to face Angela, he measured her reaction and noted it was not in his favour.

'You don't believe her do you?' he queried, deflated.

'I don't know what's happening here, I think I'd better leave,' Angela returned.

Still enraged by Bernadette's lies, he swung to her again. 'You tell Michael what the hell you want, and if he comes looking for me I'll give him the biggest shock he's ever known.'

For a fleeting moment there was a peculiar silence, even the drone of the police helicopter, which seemed to hover indefinitely over the Falls, scanning for terrorist activity, was frozen out in the cold atmosphere. The arrival of Tommy signified the departure of the wrathful Bernadette who, as she headed to her room, was met by Michael who had just got home from work. Stopping her at the foot of the stairs, he wanted his 'welcome home, had a good day at the office honey?' cuddle and peck on the cheek.

'Get yer hands off me,' she stressed, tensing the muscles on her burning face, before thundering up the stairs.

222

More hungry for food than he was to resolve the current crisis in his love life, he decided it in his best interests to give her time to calm down before he tackled her latest mood swing.

While Tommy took Toby for his accustomed walk, Paul drove Angela into the city.

'What the hell was that all about back there?' she demanded an explanation.

'I'm really sorry, but she's as guilty as sin,' he replied.

'And what was all that about New Year?'

'Michael was in Scotland, she told me that if I didn't sleep with her then she'd turn the story and tell Michael. I didn't, so she did. I swear. You do believe me don't you?'

Angela never replied. For half an hour as she missed bus after bus, she listened to the entire side of his story. Then she eventually made a statement.

'Oh God, Paul all this madness is driving me crazy. I think we'll leave it until Thursday night. I need time to think about all you've told me. Pick me up here at 7 p.m. and don't let me down, if I can't see the car I won't get off the bus.'

Nodding his head in agreement, he could not disguise his sadness. Walking her to the bus stop, he made sure she was safely onboard before he headed home, more than ready for any conflict that might come his way.

When Michael opened the bedroom door holding a mug of sweet tea to sedate his fiancé's nerves, Bernadette was staring into space, tuned to the moon.

'I've brought you some tea, are you ready to tell me what's wrong with you?'

'Paul's tart is a Prod,' she said with psychotic sang froid.

'How do you know that?' he said, disbelievingly.

'An old friend told me she spotted her boarding a bus to the Shankill.'

'What the hell's up with him? He'll not bring her here again, that's for sure, I'll see to that.'

'What will you do?'

'I'll have a word in his ear, that's all it should take,' he replied confidently. Hearing the door slam downstairs, Michael turned to leave the room. 'That'll be the stupid fucker now.'

Lighting a cigarette, Paul looked from the kitchen window to see that Tommy had yet to return, abruptly he turned to face the heavy boot steps that his induration through circumstance was supplying him the sinew to walk over.

'I want a word with you outside in private, so Mom doesn't get on her high horse,' demanded Michael.

'Fine with me,' snapped Paul, still enraged.

Standing head to head, Paul waited for the first verbal blow to land.

'I'm told this Angela of yours is a Prod. Have you fucking lost it all together? First, you bring home the village idiot as your best mate, now a fucking Prod.'

'I suppose your precious Bernie declined to tell you the whole story as usual, like how she had a gang beat up Angela and cut her hair off,' exposed Paul, staring into Michael's eyes with vengeance.

'Only what she had coming.'

'So you condone that shit do you, well, do you?' he repeated, plotting to light Michael's short fuse. Hearing no reply, Paul continued to incite the riot he longed for. 'And while I'm at it. It's about time you learnt some home truths, like when you fucked off to Scotland for New Year, it was Bernie who tried to get me into bed not the other way around.'

'I don't believe you,' replied Michael, cut to the quick.

'That's 'cause you don't want to.'

'If I was you I'd shut your mouth before . . .'

'Before what?' interrupted Paul, with insurgent insolence.

'You know what I can do to you.'

'Aye Michael you're right, but I'm still standing here coming back for more. If you touch Angela, you'll see what I can do. I'll do time for you brother, and that's not an intimidation, trust me.'

Rocked by his demeanour, Michael backed down from what looked imminent, then he laughed out loud.

'You've really fucked up this time. You'd better have eyes in the back of your head. If the UVF get wind that you're screwing one of theirs they'll blow your head off.'

Suddenly Michael's words paralysed his temper, as the thought of the recrimination of UVF gunmen ending his life brought a deep sense of nausea from inside. Parting right there and then, Paul knew that he no longer had a brother and would never have again.

When Tommy returned from his exercise duties, Paul was attempting to put the pieces back together following his explosive conduct.

Run For Freedom

'How's it going, Tom?' he asked, impassively.

'He just gets stronger every day, one of these days he's gonna rip my arm out. I met this man walking two greyhounds in the park,' said Tommy. 'He knew Toby and said he was brilliant. He asked me how I trained him. I told him we just fed, exercised and massaged him. He said I was lying, but I managed to convince him. So he told me if we wanted to get the best out of him we should give him a jar and a cosy at least 36 hours before his next race and he'll come on leaps and bounds.'

'A what?'

'I meant a jar and a cosy, or was it a jar of cosy,' said Tommy, scratching his chin.

'Well, let's just say we knew what the hell it was, where would we get it and is it legal?' quizzed Paul, becoming agitated by Tommy's inability to explain.

'No, he gave me this card and told me to phone the man who has a jar of cosy, he'll let us use his. It only costs a quid, he said.'

Taking the business card, Paul shook his head and read the mini-statement: 'Horse and Greyhound hydrotherapy, reasonable rates, tel 741440.'

'Well?' probed Tommy.

'It's a jacuzzi; jets of pressured water which pummel the muscles to relieve aches and pains as well as tone them. I've heard it works, but never really thought of applying it to a greyhound. We'll phone this guy in the morning,' Paul concluded.

Having earlier booked an appointment, they arrived outside a panel beater's unit in the Cliftonville estate. Entering the converted spray shop, they observed a circular swimming pool with an island in the middle. On the central platform, a short old man, who looked like a trawler skipper, was gently walking a thrashing greyhound around the moat.

'Is that a jar of cosy?' asked Tommy.

'No, that's a swimming pool designed to get the animals fit much quicker. It's like having a race without the bumps and scrapes. That's a jacuzzi over there,' said Paul, pointing over to the left at a huge rectangular water tank positioned by the wall.

Waiting patiently until the hydrotherapist had seen off his current tryst, it then became their turn.

'Will one of you boys put on these oilskins,' he said, throwing a pair of water repellents before them.

225

Doing the honours, Paul dressed himself in the fisherman's attire then lifted the initially acquiescent dog into the overgrown septic tank.

'Okay, you'll have to hold on tight - this will ennervate him,' forewarned the captain of the ship, with a dirty cackle that almost turned into an asthma attack. 'When I turn on the power it'll scare the shit out of him and he'll try to break out.'

Pressing the button, Toby shivered as the jets bombarded his muscles. As the hound wriggled to free himself off the bone-shaker, Paul could feel his heart pounding fit to rupture in the struggle to put this newfangled experience behind him. Co-operation lost in the trauma of uncertainty, Toby raised his paws on to the sides and began to scratch out his SOS, compromising the worth of the exercise.

'Tom, I need a hand, get his paws under the water or he's gonna rip a bloody claw out,' shouted Paul, losing control.

Holding him into the healing streams, they battened down the hatches and rode the storm, as the tropical water splashed and swept over them for a seemingly never-ending five minutes. Then it was over with the touch of a finger when, as if he was Moses parting the Red Sea, the old man, who could've passed for 120 years of age, cut the power to the relief of Paul, Tommy, and moreso, Toby.

'Let's see how fit he really was then,' vented the old man.

'How will you know that?'

'If he stands up easily he was super-fit, if not then he soon will be,' he revealed, in his wisdom.

Lifting Toby from the calm jacuzzi, Paul placed him on to the concrete floor and for a split second the dog's legs buckled under his own weight before his brain caught them from collapse in the nick of time. Straightening his posture, Toby gave himself an almighty shake and everyone an unwelcome shower.

'Not bad,' confessed the old healer, 'not bad at all.' And like every good salesman he had a little extra advice to pitch into the proceedings. 'Have you tried using Falamino racing supplement?'

'No, what is it?'

Producing a small bottle of treacle-like liquid, he handed it to Paul. 'Sprinkle a capful over his meal the night before racing, then the same dose three hours prior to the actual race. He'll hit the lids like you've never seen him. It sharpens their alertness.'

'Is it kosher?' asked Paul, not in favour of pumping the dog full of drugs or cheating, for that matter.

'Certainly is, it's an amino acid, bodybuilders use it. It has slight traces of caffeine, but nothing that a chromatography test would question. It's all above board, ask the racing manager if you doubt me. Only use it, though, when you want him to win, overuse and like anything he'll become immune to the stuff and sluggish without it, so use sparingly.'

Paying four pounds in total, they left with more in the bank than they could have ever imagined. Paul's allergy took a turn for the worse on the drive home. Gasping for breath his windpipe began to close, yet he needed a cigarette to marshal the adrenaline into the battle. Coughing and spluttering, he felt his face burning. Glancing into the rearview mirror, he noticed large white lumps swarming over his neck, then glimpsing down at the steering wheel, he saw the blotches had also taken root on his hands and arms. Resisting the temptation to scratch the demanding itches he made it home, where after a cold bath, he dabbed them with soothing calamine lotion before retiring to bed for the remainder of the day, allowing the allergy to run its course.

At 5 p.m. on Thursday all efforts towards Toby's next run had been fully implemented, so Paul decided he would pop out to the newsagents to buy the evening paper. Shutting the front door behind him, he turned and felt so sick that he almost retched right there and then. Daubed across the glossy red paintwork of his pride and joy was the huge white lettering that spelled out trouble in the words, PROD LOVER. Rushing back indoors, he found half a bottle of turpentine and some old rags in the cubby-hole under the stair and seizing them he quickly returned to the scene of the crime. Scrubbing with intensity and purpose until his fingers were numb, his head slumped on to the car-door in defeat – the paint was stubborn and the damage was irreparable. Close to tears, he opened his eyes and saw that his front tyre had been slashed. Racing around the car, his worse fears were allayed, seeing as it was the sole casualty in that department. Glancing towards the Falls Road, he spotted Bernadette and Michael walking home joined at the hip as thick as thieves. And the sight of them signified that his old enemy was back in town to add to his current crisis, which was lack of time.

It was now 5.35 p.m. and he had to be there early and waiting for Angela, or she would simply stay on the bus, forget about them and put the blame on him. Rushing back into the house, he ransacked the same cupboard in search of cover-up paint. With no rooms in the house furnished red, Paul knew he would have to strike a compromise as there were only two tins lurking in the dark arachnid sanctuary, and oddly enough, neither of them were white. The first was blue. Can't use that, he thought, it'll be misinterpreted as a unionist attribute. The second tin was sunny yellow and would have to do. He fumbled around in the darkness and found a tacky brush, then brought it into the light for inspection to observe that the streaks of paint clinging to it were in fact white. As he faced a tight schedule, he had no choice but to destroy his own evidence. So he returned to his car with the decorating utilities, glaring at his brother and his fiancé with piercing revulsion. After wrestling with the airtight tin, he levered wildly with a screwdriver, almost stabbing himself as the sweat dripped from his forehead. Finally, the obstinate tin gave up the struggle to bare a thick custard skin. Punching through the layer to find the liquid and soften the brush with the same stone, the thick film intermingled with the gloss to form a lumpy consistency. Paul soon realised he required quantity not quality to disguise the graffiti. After splashing on the first coat, he then left it to take hold, as he set out to change the punctured wheel. It was ten past six when the pit stop was complete. Turning to review his aesthetic skills, he distinguished that the faint outline of the penetrating message was still pouting, visible. Using every last lick of paint, he plastered the passenger side and could now only pray that his loyal feelings would not come through again.

He summoned Tommy, and left in a mad rush, bidding to meet Angela's deadline. Motoring to beat every red light, Paul whined all the way into town, putting down Toby's chances with all the pessimism of what had gone before and that all things come in threes. The truth was that Toby had been catapulted to the top of the tree. Having emulated his first illustrious winning time, the handicapper had no option but to throw the dog into the deep end of the A1 grade. To make matters worse, Toby had been drawn from the middle slot of trap three, indicating that the chances of a clear run were slight.

Paul slouched deep into his seat, seeking a low profile to conceal his embarrassment, while he waited for Angela to arrive. Feeling that all eyes were on his artistic impression, he wondered what the girl he so wanted to impress would make of it all. Jumping from her bus, she galloped over to the car waving the evening paper, her face beaming with excitement, not like the way he remembered it on their last parting.

'Mind yer hands on the paint, it's not dry yet,' he shouted as she went to open the door.

'Oh God, what happened?' she inquired.

'Somebody decided they wanted mobile graffiti.'

'Kids no doubt, I blame the parents you know. Anyway, have you seen this?' She changed the subject, waving the newspaper in his face.

'No, why?'

'There's a write-up about Toby, the sports' correspondent is napping him to win as his bet of the meeting, shall I read it to you?'

'Aye, go on then,' replied Paul, more interested in the traffic.

'Okay. "Tonight's banker bet is History Maker in the 9.30, who is making only his fourth start at Dunmore since joining the Belfast track last month. Having clocked sensational win times of 23.68 then a follow up run of 23.62, the fawn and white January 86 whelp has rocketed his way into the top flight, defying the grader with an arrogant turn of foot. Although tonight is undoubtedly the acid test, a decent break and a clear run should see him come home alone to chalk up a sweet hatrick." The rest is all about who'll be second. Can you believe it?'

'Not until I see it with my own eyes,' dismissed Paul, before revealing his doubts. 'He'll be found out at this level, even if he is good enough to live with these dogs it'll take time for him to adjust. Most of these pundits don't know their arse from their elbow.'

'Well, I want £10 on his nose,' said Angela

'Aye, and I'll have £2 on,' supported Tommy from the rear.

'Well, don't say I didn't warn you when he falls flat on his face,' lectured Paul.

As the hours dragged by and the evening crept into darkness, the supporting races on the card had suddenly lost their attraction, becoming unexciting and monotonous. Then at 9.20 p.m. Tommy appeared from the shadows with the dynamic History Maker, who gave himself a healthy shake to acclimatise to the chilly night air that welcomed his appearance. Suddenly all the punters who had been scattered around the terraces, snack outlets and bars, began to flock towards the once deserted barrier to weigh up the six contenders to the throne. People were talking amongst themselves, then occasionally they pointed over to Paul and Angela in the knowledge that they were the owners. For a few moments they became the centre of attention, then, from the crowd, a teenager walked over to them and asked them what chances the dog had. With the youth having set the precedent, for the next couple of minutes the owners were hounded by the general

229

public's demand to know whether they expected Toby to take the upgrade in his stride. Being diplomatic, Paul reminded both his juniors and seniors that there was no such thing as a certainty in dog racing.

When Toby opened up at odds of 2/1 favourite, Paul laughed out loud.

'What's so funny?' queried Angela.

'He's favourite, that has to be a joke.'

'Well, put mine and Tommy's money on will you?' she urged, handing him the wager.

Taking odds of 2/1 against, he placed their bet, then watched in amazement as all hell broke loose. Like a pack of scavengers having waited until the lion had taken its fair share, the gamblers swamped the bookmakers. When the crowd had dispersed, Paul observed that the odds had been slashed. Toby had been backed off the boards to an odds on 4/5.

When the lids opened he was not to let his growing fan club down. Flashing out first, Paul cringed as the roar of victory went up and one certain punter screamed in his right ear 'How far the History Maker.' Showing a blistering turn of early, he scorched around the first two bends as if the very devil himself was snapping at his tail. Screaming down the back straight, he began to pull right away, five to six lengths clear in time to the united chants of, 'easy, easy, easy', which Paul and Angela joined in with the chorus. As Toby crossed the winning line, they hugged each other again as they were reigned upon with pats of congratulations from the jubilant punters. Then came the announcement: 'First, trap three History Maker; second, trap six Coolbeg Ceri. The winner won by seven and a half lengths in a new track record time of 23.07 seconds.'

As Paul rubbed his eyes to hold back the river of emotion, Angela reached into her handbag and offered him a tissue. 'What's wrong? Are you all right?'

'Aye, I just can't believe it,' he sniffed.

'Well, you'd better. You're a genius, the best trainer ever,' she complimented.

'No,' he refused her commendation. 'All the credit must go to the real trainer. Tommy did all the work for this, not me. Go on, get the prize money and I'll collect your winnings.'

Shaking his head as he collected Tommy and Angela's winning ticket, the bookmaker spoke to him. 'You didn't fancy him, did you?'

'No, not at all,' admitted Paul, 'two weeks ago and he couldn't beat eggs.'

Turning to go and meet Angela she almost walked into him in her trance.

'What's up with you?' asked Paul.

'The racing manager would like to see both of us together,' she replied.

'Why?' quizzed Paul, wondering if their charge was to be the subject of a post-race inquiry into his record-breaking run.

'He wants Toby to represent Dunmore on May 7th in an open race for £500 and a trophy in Dublin. He also reckons he may be considerable enough to have a crack at the Derby in September.'

Although there was no discussion, together they ran towards the racing manager's office, neither with any intention of declining such an offer.

'Congratulations,' acknowledged the well-groomed manager, offering his hand to Paul. 'That's some dog you have there. So has your girlfriend explained about representing the track at Shelbourne?'

'Well, a little,' confirmed Paul, 'when is it exactly?' He was worried that the date might conflict with his work schedule.

'Two weeks on Saturday, May 7th, and there'll be a few English raiders over getting a feel of the track for the Derby later on in the year. There's only really one problem I can envisage, the distance is 550 yards, but by the look of him he should get every yard of the trip. Just to be on the safe side I suggest that you give him a trial over that distance a week on Saturday, do you agree?'

'Aye you're right, that would appear to be in our best interest,' consented Paul.

And so it had been carved in stone, Toby's next competitive race would be at none other than the stadium of dreams itself, Shelbourne Park, Dublin.

Driving home, Angela and Tommy replayed the race a hundred times in between hugs for Toby, while Paul simply drove, quietly gathering negative thoughts.

Turning her attention to Paul, Angela tapped him on the arm. 'Well, are you gonna stop so we can buy some cans of lager to celebrate?'

'And whose gonna drive you home then?' he reminded her that their partnership was still under curfew.

'I'll get a taxi,' she returned.

'Well, whatever,' he replied in a tone of dejection.

Stopping at an off-licence in the city, they bought a case of lager to wet the dog's head. Having arrived back in Clonard Street at 10.15 p.m.

231

they began to celebrate the star turn with a victory toast. For the next hour Angela and Tommy partied with Toby, yet Paul sat sipping at his drink, miles away in deep deliberation. At 11.30 p.m. when the alcohol had drowned the volume, Bernadette, who had been sitting up in bed reading, switched off her light then peeped through her curtains to see Angela approaching Paul whilst Tommy headed out the back gate with the dog. Still livid that they were continuing to see each other, she watched them through the dim illumination the streetlight was generating.

'What's wrong Paul?' Angela explored, kneeling down in front of him. 'Do you want to talk about it?'

Sighing out loud, he gave her a weak smile. 'I just wonder about when all this is over.'

'What do you mean?'

'Toby. Will I still have you in my life when his racing days are over?'

'Come on, the dog has years in him, hasn't he?'

'Aye, I suppose you're right. I just wished that . . .'

'Wished what?' she urged him to continue.

'Oh nothing,' he jammed up.

Gazing into his sad blue eyes, she felt sure she knew exactly what he was wishing because she was wishing it too. 'Hold me Paul, I'm cold,' she said, reaching out her arms to him.

As he took her into his arms, she put her lips to his and they began a slow, long tender kiss. Breaking off their engagement momentarily, he squeezed her tight then returned his mouth to hers. Up above Bernadette turned away from the window, she had seen more than enough. Holding Angela close, Paul almost ran his quivering fingers through her hair before his brain engaged to keep his moment of heaven alive. Stroking her face, she nuzzled into his protective chest and purred. As her warmth tingled and surged through him, Paul knew that his emotions towards her had not been deceiving him all along. She was the one, the only one for him in the whole wide world, this was love and now that he had it in his hands he was not willing to let it squirm from his grasp. Placing his finger under her chin, he raised her lips to meet his again. For five beautiful minutes they savoured each other and Utopia before Tommy returned with Toby to part them.

'Can you get me a taxi now?' she asked.

'No, I'll drive you home, I've only had one can.'

Opening the door for her, he was no longer suffering the niggling pain of the scarring to his car. Outside her front door, Paul leaned over to give her a goodnight kiss, but on this occasion she was no longer willing to participate.

'So what happens now?' inquired Paul, detecting a retrogress in her feelings towards him.

'It won't work, Paul, I'm sorry. Let's be realistic, you're from the Falls and I'm from the Shankill. I know it's only half a mile away, but the distance between us is too far, if you know what I mean.'

Interpreting her earlier kisses as a heady mixture of alcohol and the euphoria of Toby's success, as opposed to her true feelings for him, Paul turned away and closed his eyes. If for one minute in the spur of this moment he'd thought otherwise, he'd have argued his case to the last to assure her that their relationship could beat the odds.

'So when will I see you again?' He tried to hide his distress.

'Sunday will be best, I want to see the dog again before you go offshore and I'll have to make arrangements with Tommy for next Saturday's trial. Can you pick me up in the city at 10 a.m.?'

'You know I can,' he affirmed.

Waiting until she had entered her house, he reminisced the indelible kiss and thought about knocking on her door, to find out once and for all if there was an iota of love in her heart for him to build upon. Whilst driving home to the Falls, he cursed the hidden force that kept holding him back as he now felt sure there was more to her earlier conduct than met the eye.

Friday brought a return to the loss of Paul's appetite, as he sat lethargically in the back yard smoking heavily. Only venturing indoors to make the occasional cup of coffee for himself and Tommy, it seemed the less he did the more tired he became as Angela ran amok in his mind. If only he could persuade her to leave Irish shores with him then he was sure there would be no looking back.

After buying the evening newspaper, Bernadette slumped into the window seat of her bus home and began to read the quotidian headlines. Her eye was caught to the left in the contents index by the words History Maker. Aware that Paul's dog's fundamental name was this, her annoyance drew her to the article, although not for an instant did

233

she presume that it had anything whatsoever to do with the greyhound lodging at 6 Clonard Street. 'Track record smashed at Dunmore last night, see page 32 for details', was what she read. Turning impetuously, she registered that indeed it was Toby who had made the penultimate page and that local bookmaker Eastwoods had given History Maker a 150/1 ante-post quote for the Respond Irish Derby. Incensed at the way Paul's life seemed to be filled with success, love and excitement, while hers was in the doldrums of failure, bitterness and boredom, she began to scheme again, scratching for a plan that would punish the star-crossed lovers for mocking her.

On Sunday, Paul picked Angela up as usual and all day she was nice to him, acting as if she wanted more than just a platonic friendship at times. Whilst walking the dog she encouraged Paul to wrap his arm around her waist which left him totally bamboozled again. Having organised next week's trial with Tommy, Paul drove her back to the city centre.

'Phone me next Sunday when you get home, better still call me on Saturday night and I'll let you know how Toby faired in his trial. Are you still gonna take my mother out next Monday?' she asked.

'Aye, I'll organise something. I've seen it advertised, where they do day trips to Edinburgh and Glasgow. I'll let you know on Saturday night.'

'Okay, in that case I'll try to get the day off. I've always fancied a trip to Edinburgh. I've seen it on the television a few times, it looks so pretty and peaceful.' Kissing him on the cheek to say thank you, she left him feeling that if love was a circus, then he was the clown.

As he packed his holdall for another long week at sea, Paul realised that he had to let her know exactly how he felt and somehow drag down her barrier to learn precisely what was going on inside her capricious mind.

As Bernadette lay in bed reading the piece on History Maker's history-making run over and over again, a notion suddenly flashed through her duplicitous mind. Having picked the bones out of a thousand devious plots and then discarded them as folly or too dangerous to implement, there it was, in the palm of her hand. If the paparazzi were to get wind that the record-breaking greyhound was owned by lovers from the belligerent Falls and Shankill neighbourhoods, who collaborated to defy the troubles and race the animal, she was sure they would be falling over themselves to print the story. After all, they loved to write about that sort of unfaithful imperilment, which was classed as outlawed inter-community harmony. The spotlight would then fall on to them and, once out in the open, they would be condemned and they'd have no choice but to discontinue their clandestine liaisons. Bernadette was on a winner all the way and she knew it, at the same time, however, she was aware that she would probably be making Paul a target of the UVF or another loyalist cell. Bearing that in mind, she decided she would sleep on it.

Taking her lunch break on Monday, Bernadette bought a copy of the Telegraph. Standing outside a telephone kiosk she glanced at the telephone number on the tabloid then to the booth and back again. Finally, unnerved by the vision of them kissing passionately on that Thursday night, she walked into the phone box, fed the slot then picked up the receiver and dialled. Entranced by the mellow timbre, she broke from the spell when an urbane voice answered at the other end. For a moment she paused, dithering as to whether this was the orthodox route to take, or not.

Chapter 9

A Tale of Two Cities, Fading Like a Flower

'Hello, hello, is anyone there?' demanded the voice.

'Aye, I'm here,' replied Bernadette, biting her lip to control her nerves.

'Which department would you like?'

'I have a good story,' she said, becoming tangled up in her actions.

'Regarding what?' moaned the voice, becoming impatient at her lack of professionalism.

'Well, have you read about the record breaking greyhound at Dunmore?'

'I think I'd better put you through to the sports' desk.'

'No, this has no bearing on the racing side, it's more like a current affairs story and it's big. If you don't want it, I can easily pass it on to a rival newspaper,' she stated, rising in confidence.

'Okay, calm down, we have a reporter in the office now. I'll transfer you, I'm only security covering for the receptionist's dinner hour.'

'Hi, I'm Matt Williamson, how can I be of assistance?'

'You know this greyhound that smashed the track record? Well, the owners come from the Falls and Shankill respectively, lovers may I add. Can you use this story or not?' she asked with conviction.

Having been rocking on his chair with his feet upon the desk, he jumped up as if he'd sat on a pincushion. 'So where and when can I discuss this with you, can I come to your house?'

'No,' snapped Bernadette, 'I have to remain anonymous at all costs.'

'Well, discretion is my middle name, so how about I meet you somewhere. We could go for a drive into the country and discuss this over a drink.'

236

'Aye, that sounds best,' she agreed.

'So, give me a convenient place and time and I'll be there,' he said.

Picking her up as arranged, the young, smart-suited reporter watched in his rearview mirror as the fiery redhead scanned around the street prudently before entering his plush vehicle.

'Had a busy day?' he asked from behind his designer sunglasses and fake tan, endeavouring to calm her fears, having noticed that she was on edge.

'No more than usual. How long will this take?' she asked, keeping her head low at all times.

'You just tell me the story and then I'll ask a few questions. Half an hour perhaps.'

Pulling into the gravel car park of a small country pub on the road to Bangor, which he obviously frequented on a regular basis for its way-off-the-beaten-track location, the tall dark and handsome playboy journalist then led her into the lounge.

'What can I get you?' he inquired.

'Half a lager, no better, make it a large whiskey,' she replied, surveying the other three patrons, just in case by some outlandish coincidence she knew someone. Satisfied she was safe, Bernadette began to unwind a little.

'Do you mind if I tape this conversation?' he probed gently, as he brought over her whiskey and his pint of Guinness. 'It'll save me jotting down notes.'

'Whatever, but can we cut the formalities and get this over with as soon as possible,' she urged.

'Please do, the stage is all yours,' he said activating his dictaphone, then taking a modish sip from his pint.

Twenty minutes later and the story had been blown out of all proportion into a sordid fantasy that the gutter press couldn't have edited any better. As luck would have it, Matt saw it as an opportunity to start the ball rolling for peace in the province. If both communities took the story to their hearts, as he was sure they would, then perhaps a domino effect could take place to underpin a thrust for harmony. With this in mind, he decided to write the piece omitting the exaggerated lust aspect.

'Can you drive me home then?' Bernadette asked.

'No problem, there's just one thing though, the main characters in this story, where can I find them?'

'You can't talk to them.' She was definite.

'Oh well, if I can't have a chat with them then how do I know this isn't just a fantasy story to stir up bad feeling within the community? I won't be able to get this published if I can't validate their identities,' he stated his position.

'They own the dog don't they? I thought you people were renowned for your research abilities,' coaxed Bernadette.

'Come on then I'll take you home,' he replied, impressed by her attitude.

As he dropped her off in the Falls Road, she turned to him. 'Will this make the papers then?'

'I would have thought so,' he replied.

By Thursday afternoon the article had been written, but Matt wanted to hear it from another angle before submitting his work to the editor at the Telegraph. Telephoning the sports' desk, he was dismayed to hear that History Maker was not one of that night's runners. Totally committed to his career and having never written a front page story, Matt decided he would get a feel for the atmosphere of the local track, hoping that he might just bump into the dog's owners who might have come to spy on the competition.

With pint in hand Matt mingled with the patrons looking for the most likely candidate to interview, who, perchance, knew the dog's owners. Opting for what he saw as the portrayal of the sport, he approached an old gent wearing a matching tweed jacket and cap, then asked him if he could point him in the right direction.

'A pair of teenagers as far as I'm aware, but they won't be here tonight 'cause their dog's not on the card, but if you go and see the racing manager he'll be able to tell you when the animal's running next.'

Thanking him for his help, the roving reporter set off in search of the racing manager. At the judge's box high in the grandstand, he forwarded his hand and press card to his suavely attired clone.

'I'm Matt Williamson from the Telegraph. I'm writing a public relations feature on the owners of History Maker but no one can tell me where I can find them. Do you have their address?' he inquired.

'I'm sorry, but I'm not privy to that information and even if I was, it would have to remain confidential. I do have a telephone number, though, in case of emergency, for example if I needed to contact them were the meeting to be cancelled at the last minute, but once again I'm not permitted to divulge such personal data,' the manager explained, before throwing a lifeline. 'However, the dog is due here on Saturday night for a trial before racing, so you could catch up with them then.'

'What time will that be?' quizzed Matt.

'Between 6 and 6.30 p.m..'

'Well thanks for your time,' said Matt about turning to leave, before the prerequisite of his job stopped him in his tracks, as his nose incited his inquisitiveness. 'Oh, one more thing, why's the dog having a trial as opposed to a race?'

'He's headed for an invitation race at Shelbourne Park in Dublin the following Saturday over a longer distance, so they need to give him a solo to establish whether he stays the trip.'

Having a strong intuition that he had been dealt a winning hand with this story, Matt smiled.

By the time the last edition of Saturday's Telegraph had hit the streets, Bernadette was fuming that the news hadn't broken and that her plan seemed to be in tatters.

Earlier that same afternoon, Paul had fixed it for Angela's mother to fulfil her lifelong ambition. Not always guaranteed to cross the Irish Sea with a full cargo of passengers, his ferry company, like their competitors, thought it wise to cut their losses by providing a subsidised day trip. Merging with Ulsterbus in a joint promotion, their offering of a cheap day out to either Glasgow or Edinburgh enticed the public to fill both boats and buses. The theory was that the customer would come back again and again; better to give a bargain and make a profit than to keep the tariffs inflated and sustain a loss. Always up for a gamble, Paul employed the perk of his job and bought three discounted day trips to the Scottish capital on the offchance that Angela would make the effort to attend.

Being at sea for those 'month-long' weeks, served to provide, if nothing else, unhindered time for the reassessment of his current situation. During the week, Paul had quarrelled with himself over how close he had really come to achieving his prime objective in life. A thousand relived kisses had inspired him to give it another shot and his best at that. In hindsight, he now knew that he should have argued the case for their relationship. Yes, she was veracious when saying they

239

would face asperity around every corner, but where there's a will there's a way and Paul's volition was big enough for both of them. The coming seven days would see them in two new environments. If he could just relax her then she might just become so laid back, that she'd fall over at his feet.

As arranged, Tommy readied the dog for its trial. The pre-race embrocating and limbering up exercises were integral to the routine, but through Paul's sagacity, Toby was denied his wee dram of Dutch courage, instead he was given his main meal prior to the solo run. Although Paul wasn't in favour of slowing down greyhounds as a means to an end, he had now witnessed Toby's raw potential and as always Paul's sights seemed to be set firmly on the future, September to be precise. Being superstitious, if History Maker was to have a crack at the illustrious Derby, then he didn't want the dog to carry the added burden of ante-post favourite into the competition. Highly fancied greyhounds at the outset had an appalling record over the years. With everything to play for in the early autumn, Paul wondered if Toby had peaked too early and whether he would be able to sustain his incredible form. Always a realist, Paul looked to the downside and decided it might be best to strike while the iron was hot. There were trophies and substantial prizes within reach now, so it would do no harm in collecting a few along the route to the ultimate plunder. For that reason, and with nothing at stake in the trial, he resolved to blunt Toby's race sharpness, preserving his best form for another day. Paul already knew that Toby would get every yard of the extended trip, but he didn't want the whole of Ireland to know just yet.

Matt Williamson glanced at his watch and yawned with the tedium of the wait. Rubbing the wetness from his eye, he spotted a young couple enter the stand with a large white and fawn greyhound. Already at the win-line beside a few keen race fanatics, who'd even come equipped with their own stopwatches to vindicate the win time announcements which were sometimes dubious, to say the least, Matt decided to let them get their business dealt with before he began his own out-of-hours extra for his employer. When Angela joined him at the winning post, pretty confident that she was a co-owner, he knew that the public address system would clarify everything for him, so he needed to probe no further for the time being.

As Tommy arrived at the starting traps the tannoy revealed, 'There will now be a solo trial over 550 yards for History Maker.' Watching as the hare flashed past and the lids cracked open, Angela banged her fists on the handrail and yelled, 'Come on Toby,' before realising everyone had turned to look at her as if she was from another dimension. Having nothing to beat except the handicap of his swollen belly, Toby sailed around in a time of 30.40 seconds, which was only half a dozen lengths outside Carter's Lad's 30.05 track record. Not really clued up as to how good, bad or indifferent the run had been, Angela eavesdropped to hear the stopwatch anoraks agree that indeed it was a fine effort, considering it was Toby's first attempt at the distance.

As she headed to meet Tommy, the sleuth reporter followed her at safe braking distance. Allowing them to wash down the exhausted dog and see to its raging thirst, he was patient until they turned to leave the stadium.

'Excuse me, my name's Matt Williamson from the Telegraph. I was wondering if I could have a five-minute interview with the pair of you.'

'What about?' queried Angela, intrigued.

'I'm doing a piece about your dog breaking the track record last week,' he explained, leading her into a false sense of security. 'So where did you buy the dog and how much for?'

'Oh, we didn't buy the dog, he was retired due to injury. I guess we just had God smiling down on us,' she revealed, beaming with pride.

Fascinated by the fairy-tale slant, he pursued the conversation for a whole ten minutes before throwing a curve.

'So how did you pair meet?' he switched tact ever so adroitly.

'We all arrived at the same time for the dog, so we decided to have a joint venture,' she revealed, quite relishing the spotlight of attention.

'So do you live near each other?' he gently dug a little deeper.

'Eh, not quite,' she stuttered, becoming slightly nervous.

Picking up on her sudden loss of trust, he decided to terminate the conversation in a bid to garner the intelligence he desired.

'Okay, that's about all for now, but I may need to ask further questions later, so can I have your addresses and telephone numbers should I have to contact either of you.'

Although Angela divulged hers, she didn't give out Tommy's, not because she didn't actually know it, but for the perception that the reporter would use it to his advantage to sell papers at their cost.

Explaining that Tommy didn't possess a telephone, but lived just a few doors from her and that the third-part owner was really the dog expert amongst them, she thought she'd covered her tracks to perfection.

Having thought that Tommy was her lover from the Falls all along and not realising that this was a three-way consortium, Matt suddenly began to wonder whether this was all indeed a scam from a faction trying to stir up trouble. Worried that his story was now falling apart at the seams, he needed to find out more about this third party and whether or not he was her sleeping partner.

'So can I have his address?' he asked.

'Well no, I don't really know where it is exactly, but I have his phone number if you want to give him a call. You'll have to leave it until late Sunday night though as he's working offshore at the moment,' she explained, resurrecting his hope.

Thanking them for their time, he bade farewell and drove home.

Using the first two digits from the number she had kindly given him, he began to look up the telephone directory, praying that the 32 area code matched that of the Falls. 'Bingo,' he said out loud as his finger rested on the confirming print.

As he docked that evening in Stranraer for the final time, Paul's long wait to hear Angela's sweet voice again was all but over. Picking up the handful of loose change he had been setting aside all week, he headed onshore with his Scots workmate for a few pints and a telephone. At a lively pub on the shorefront, Paul ordered the drinks, almost shouting to be heard above the loud music pumping from the mobile disco. Replacing the fluid he had perspired through the labours of the day, he gulped and guzzled down his first beer without touching the sides. Gasping for air, he slammed the glass on to the bar then wiped his lips dry.

'For Christ's sake, I thought we Scots could knock back a pint, but that takes some beating,' remarked his drinking partner.

'Aye well, I needed that, it's from carrying you all week,' joked Paul, before continuing the banter. 'And I thought you Scots were supposed to be hard workers.'

'Ah well, you see, it's like this, you Paddies are not as clever as us Jocks. We breeze through and do twice as much while you lot make it look difficult in achieving half,' he returned.

'Well, show me the art then by getting the next round in,' replied Paul.

Glancing at his watch Paul saw that it was fast approaching ten and still he hadn't phoned Angela. He observed a phone at the end of the bar and, thinking it might be better to find somewhere more quiet so they could hear each other, he attempted to excuse himself from the company for a while.

'Paul,' he raised his voice above the clamour, 'I'm just nipping out to make a phone-call.'

'Why? There's one over there,' returned the Scot, pointing to the end of the bar.

'I know, but I'll not be heard,' he replied.

'Are you phoning that girl?'

'Aye, why?'

'Well, call her from here. I always phone my bird from here, lets her know I'm having a whale of a time, it really annoys them you know, gets them jealous.'

Pausing for a moment's thought, Paul agreed that it wasn't such an absurd tactic after all. Standing with a finger in his right ear and the phone clamped to his left, he awaited her response.

'Paul, is that you Paul?'

'Aye it's me,' he shouted back.

'Where are you, it sounds wild there?'

'I'm in some bar in Stranraer. It's heaving in here.'

'Sounds more like a nightclub.'

'Aye, well it does have a dance floor and flashing neon lights. Anyway how did Toby get on?'

'He did a time of 30.40. The people at the track seemed to be impressed.'

'What?' he shouted down the phone, struggling to hear her.

'I said people thought it was a good time,' she repeated.

'Aye, it was considering I had him put away. Listen, I've booked three day trips to Edinburgh for Monday. Tell your mother I'll pick her up at 6 a.m., the coach leaves at a quarter to seven.'

'So, who's the third ticket for?' she asked, her voice suddenly dropping a few octaves.

'You, if you can make it,' he offered.

'I haven't asked for time off yet.'

'Well, I really need to know now if you're coming, if not, I'm sure I'll find somebody who would jump at the chance,' he teased, setting the bait before acknowledging his Scots namesake at the other end of

243

the bar, who was shaking his head as he pointed at his watch. 'I'm just coming,' Paul shouted to him.

'Who was that you were talking to?' she inquired, anxiously.

'Oh, just a friend. So are you coming on Monday or not?'

'Aye, I'll be there,' she replied with conviction in her voice.

'Okay then, see you Monday, I have to go now, bye,' said Paul tactically, concealing any excitement in his speech.

Replacing the receiver, he put his thumbs up in acknowledgement of his mentor's sound advice.

At teatime on Sunday May 1st, news began to filter through that three British airmen had fallen prey to the IRA in Holland. Of late the Provisionals had been spreading their killing net over foreign lands, to show the British hierarchy at the Ministry of Defence that they meant business and were willing to carry the fight anywhere as they stepped up their demand for home rule. All of a sudden, anywhere that British servicemen were stationed had become the IRA's back yard as they'd earlier given warning when targeting Germany and Gibraltar. Now in Holland, ironically the birthplace of William III, the Prince of Orange, they had proven that there was no safe place to hide, not even the home of the luminary of Irish Protestantism.

Submitting his work to the editor quietly confident that he had the story of a lifetime, Matt was dismayed to hear of the events in the Netherlands for he knew that as ever, the IRA's flagrant levering tactics were almost certain to fill the front page, but this Sunday night the editor had his own ideas. Newspaper sales in Belfast were simply constant, rarely did they contain the kind of interesting good news that had the mass public flocking to the news-stands to boost the profit margin. The majority were sick and tired of the same repetitive black reports, so palled, that many even refused to allow the media to encroach upon their lives, on the assumption of what you don't know can't hurt you. Unexpectedly, the paparazzi now had a golden opportunity to rectify that situation, by giving the public hope for the future as well as lining their own pockets at the same time. Calling Matt into his office as the presses had began to roll for Monday's edition, the editor conveyed his resolution.

'Matt, this is a damn good story, I'm giving it top billing. Since you have no photographs I can give the Dutch incident a third of the front page, I think that'll strike a nice balance don't you?' said the obese cigar smoker, with the sweat-saturated striped shirt. A good advert for the benefits of keep fit if ever there was.

'Aye,' agreed Matt, astounded that he had knocked the IRA off the number one spot.

'Now, if I'm correct and this sells like hot cakes, we're gonna need a follow up, in fact I want this bled dry. We'll need photographs of the happy couple, the public's response on the street, the punter's view at Dunmore, the works. Do you have any ideas of your own?'

'Well, as a matter of fact, the dog will be representing Dunmore in Dublin this coming Saturday in a big race,' revealed Matt.

'Excellent, portray it as Northern Ireland's peace dog in Sinn Fein's back yard or something along those lines. Are these kids good looking? I need models, I want them to become celebrities overnight, a picture of health and beauty, a vision of peace.'

'Well, the girl's very pretty, but I haven't met the lad yet, he works away, offshore somewhere. What if they won't co-operate? This could put their lives in serious jeopardy,' asked Matt, aware of the religious hatred, having been brought up in Protestant Rathcool.

'I don't give a flying fuck, don't ask for their consent to take photos, just get them. Besides, with all this publicity the rival factions wouldn't want to make them martyrs now, would they?'

After arriving home, Paul had a light snack in his mother's company before taking a twilight stroll into the back yard where he found Tommy talking to Toby.

'How is he?' Paul inquired.

'Really well, aren't you Tobes?' Tommy replied, tickling the placid animal's chin. 'Is there any news of my mother yet?'

'No, not so far, but I'll keep the ad running for another fortnight, after that I'll do some research to see if there are any other papers. I'm really sorry, but I'm doing the best I can.'

'Paul,' shouted his mother from the back door, 'telephone call for you.'

'Do you think?' said Tommy, as their eyes widened in light of their past conversation.

'There's only one way to find out,' returned Paul, rushing towards the house.

'Hi, my name is Matt Williamson, I'm a reporter from the Telegraph, are you the co-owner of History Maker?

245

'Aye,' replied Paul, disheartened that it wasn't Tommy's mother. 'What can I do for you and how did you get my telephone number?'

'I've already spoke to your partners. It was your girlfriend who gave me the number,' revealed Matt, probing for a reaction.

'Oh right, but unfortunately she's not my girlfriend,' stated Paul, firmly.

Not too bothered with the Catholic boy's refusal to admit the affair, presuming that he would have denied courting a Protestant to the last anyhow, Matt dismissed the statement as protective endearment.

'Well, Paul, I'm doing a feature on the dog's rags to riches story and I've been told you're the expert in the camp. Can you tell me anything that may be relevant?'

'All I can say is, I'm no genius, it's been a team success since day one, that's all,' said Paul, not interested in the inadmissible puffery.

'Do you think I could have a photo shot with all of you with the dog?' proposed Matt.

'No, we're happy as we are,' he dismissed the idea, before giving him some slack , 'but I don't mind you taking some snaps of the dog.'

'But wouldn't you like to have your picture in the paper, most people jump at the chance.'

'No, it doesn't appeal to me in the least,' replied Paul coldly, tiring of the conversation.

'Fair enough, if that's what you want. So when can I get some photos of the dog?'

'Tomorrow would be best,' Paul returned thinking quickly, knowing that he and Angela would be safely out of the picture.

'So could you give me an address where I can find this dog and a convenient time, or should I contact the girl?' quizzed Matt flatly, despondent that Paul wasn't willing to play into his hands.

'Ten o'clock in the morning is best, 6 Clonard Street, the Falls, ask to see Tommy, I'll tell my mother you're coming.'

As Paul replaced the telephone, he had no inkling as to what imprint the media would have on his life in the following months. Returning to Tommy, he first revealed the bad news followed by the good, which made some amends to slightly re-inflate him.

'Sorry, Tom but it wasn't your mom, but hey, a journalist wants to take some photos of you and Toby for the newspaper, so you're gonna be famous.'

246

Having collected Angela and her mother as promised, Paul caught his first sight of Angela's father as he nosed from behind the bedroom curtains in his string vest. And from what Paul could ascertain, her father was very well built with jet-black hair and matching moustache. Driving away, Paul's impression of him was that he wouldn't particularly fancy getting on his wrong side. With all the organisation and work involved in getting her mother on and off the coach, it wasn't until the ferry had set sail that Paul and Angela had time for a chat, let alone find time to notice a newspaper. Walking together to buy some coffees, Paul turned to Angela.

'You never told me the press paid you a visit.'

'Aye, I didn't trust the guy, he appeared to be a right slime-ball, with his designer suit, I bet his socks were even Gucci's. He seemed to have something on his mind, always fishing all the time, you know, as if he knew we were from different neighbourhoods. That's why I didn't give him your address,' she rationalised.

'You didn't give him your address, did you?' he asked ominously.

'Aye, why?'

'Oh no, I gave him mine last night, he wanted to photograph the dog. He's bound to put two and two together, you know what these people are like, they can get blood from a stone,' moaned Paul.

'Oh come on, get real, he wouldn't jeopardise our lives for a two-bit article. You worry too much.'

'I'm still not convinced, I'll phone him when we get home tonight and explain the trouble it'll cause. With him not having any pictures until this morning we still have time to change the future. I'll just sweet talk him, I'll give him an in-depth interview or something to keep him happy,' said Paul.

Both content that their secret was still intact, they returned to her mother all smiles looking forward to their day out in Edinburgh.

'I'd like to sit out on the deck,' Mrs Hamilton said, for having led a parochial existence she wanted to miss nothing, not least the broad horizons.

'I don't think that's such a good idea, you might catch a cold out there,' said Angela, noting that the damp early morning mist had yet to evaporate.

'I don't care, you only live once and I want to live for today, so stop mothering me and take me outside or I'll wheel myself there,' her mother threatened.

247

After wrapping her up as well as they could, they all went out onto the deck into the eddying gusts and clinging sea-fret. Watching her mother as she sat mesmerised by the vertiginous sea, Paul reflected as to whether this would betide to be his dream day too.

When the coach departed Stranraer the sky was still overcast, although the light drizzle had been left behind at sea, but by the time they had arrived in the Festival City at lunchtime, the loitering clouds had dispersed propitiously, leaving pellucid blue skies which permitted glorious sunshine to shower on to the city. Alighting their transport at St Andrew's Square bus station, they followed the sweet sounds of the swirling bagpipes which conducted them on to Princes Street, with its serene gardens and playful squirrels tamed by generations of tourists. Transfixed by the magnificent august monuments, they just didn't know where to turn first so, like every foreigner in this city, they allowed their instincts to lead them towards the sublime castle perched on its scabrous extinct volcano. Ambling their way up the haggard, cobbled High Street, they marvelled at how the ancient architecture had stood the test of time to keep the city roots firmly in the past. Intermittently, they paused at the tartan and souvenir emporia which lined the rise to the Castle Esplanade and Paul sensed that the day was overtaking them.

Looking over the battlements to the thriving city below and the Firth of Forth estuary in the distance, Angela remarked on how pleasant and tranquil it all was. 'I love it here you know, it's so safe. I think I could stay here forever.'

'Really?' said Paul, who would have relocated to the moon, or even a cave, if it meant that he could be with her.

'Aye, the place is so alive, so enticing.'

Taking her arm, he half turned her and gazed deep into her eyes. Having planned this moment for an eternity, he wasn't willing to suppress his feelings any longer.

'Why don't we leave Belfast behind and make a new life here, together? I know we could be happy, I'm sure it's only the worry of other people's reactions back home that's putting you off. Tell me I'm wrong.'

Turning to look over the city again, she sighed. 'Paul, I don't know what I'm feeling. The only thing I am sure of is that you're a great guy and you could have your pick. I've already seen that, but me, well I've more faults than Silicone Valley.'

'Come on, I'm being serious. I love you, I don't want anyone else,' he pleaded sincerely, with a straight-faced expression that corroborated his words.

'Don't Paul, this is killing me, everything is against us. Besides, my mother's health, or lack of it, has to be my number one priority,' she stated her position.

From a few feet away, her mother who had been eavesdropping put in her twopenn'orth. 'Angie, don't let me get in the way of your happiness. I've had my shot at life, don't throw your chance away because of me. You'll only live to regret it when I'm gone. I'm quite capable of looking after myself.'

'Well, that's where you're wrong, mom. You're not fit to do that,' retorted Angela.

'Maybe not, but it's about time your father started to meet his responsibilities, anyway.'

Now that her mother had entered the conversation, Paul had become too embarrassed to resume bartering for her hand and so, for the time being, the subject would have to be put on the back burner, until the opportunity of another time, another city, arose.

Heading down Auld Reekie's Olde Worlde High Street, they passed the Heart of Midlothian outside St Giles Cathedral and watched as passers-by stopped to spit on the heart modelled in the paving stones. For a few minutes they stood enthralled, as even women paused to ostracise their phlegm onto the walkway. Paul asked a citizen of Edinburgh what the custom was all about and found it was the site of the gallows inside the old prison from centuries ago. Taking Tommy's advice about when in Rome, he carried out the ritual before explaining the habit to Angela and her mother. Reaching the end of the road, they spotted John Knox's house and read the placard outside. As Paul digested with interest, he felt a deep sense of déja-vu and apprehension emanate from the well of his soul. John Knox, a Roman Catholic priest, had converted to Protestantism and was then forced into exile in fear of being burned at the stake for heresy; in four hundred years nothing much had changed. They stopped for a bite to eat in the swank, newly opened Waverley Market shopping centre near the railway station, and Paul spotted a vendor selling flowers from a mobile stall. Excusing himself, he went to the florists and bought a bouquet for her mother and a single red rose for his distant beloved. When Paul returned, he watched as the ex-beauty queen enacted her winning role from over two

249

decades ago, as she wept with joy. Espying Angela from the corner of his eye, knowing that she was not too fussed for flowers, he held back his smile, now that he saw by her wide-eyed expression, that, once again, she had been hiding her real personality.

At 6 p.m. they left Europe's number one city (according to Prince Charles), and Paul knew that he'd given a right royal performance, and that the queen of his heart was not altogether out of his reach.

Cruising into Belfast Lough and reality, Angela's mother sat out for the count clinging to her bunch of flowers like a child to its teddy bear, as did her daughter, using his shoulder as a pillow. Gently relocating Angela so that she was comfortable, Paul decided he would take a walk around the ship. With it being his mother's birthday later in the week, he thought he'd surprise her by actually remembering on time this year. Being a typical male, Paul was prosaic when it came to buying gifts for the opposite sex, so he decided to take advantage of the tax-free savings on offer within the fragrance range. Selecting his mother's customary perfume, he stood in the queue waiting to be served when his eye caught sight of the magazine racks to the left. Rooted to the spot, he stared at the headlines in disbelief: 'HISTORY MAKING GREYHOUND RUNS FOR PEACE'.

'Sir, can I help you?' offered the shop assistant, breaking him from his stupor.

Handing her the perfume he nipped to the shelves of literature and picked up a copy of the Telegraph. Taking a seat outside the shop, he began to read, riveted. As usual, the media's ability to tell the truth was as rare as rocking-horse shit.

'The Telegraph can exclusively reveal that the co-owners of Dunmore's current track record holder, aptly named History Maker, are in fact lovers who boldly defy to conform to the sectarianism running through the arteries of this poisoned city. Paul O'Donnell and Angela Hamilton from the Falls and Shankill respectively have beaten the odds, to not only find it in their hearts to love one another, but their persistence in the face of bigotry has reflected in giving retired greyhound History Maker a new lease of life.'

Enough, thought Paul, who could not find it in himself to read any further, knowing that both their lives were teetering on the brink of disaster. Walking solemnly back to Angela, he realised he had to break the news and that it was going to be the hardest undertaking in his life.

Standing over her with the paper in his hand, he watched as she slept so peacefully, so beautifully. As he saw the twinkling lights outside and the turbines lulled to allow the ship to turn for docking, he realised it was time to wake her: 'Come on Angela, wake up, we're nearly home.' he whispered painfully, as he shook her lightly.

Coming to, she smiled at him. 'You better have a look at this,' he said, handing her the newspaper.

Still sleepy, it took her a few minutes to register the implications. 'Oh my God,' she uttered in shock, 'what's my father gonna say and everyone at work? No one will believe me, oh no.'

Putting his arm around her to console her misery, she shook him off. 'Don't Paul, if my life was a mess before, it can't get any worse now. What will they do to us?'

'I don't know. I guess we'll just have to hold on tight until the storm blows over, and it will,' he stressed, trying to assure her. 'I'll phone the paper and tell them to retract their suppositions. They can make a statement to say they've made a mistake and we can carry on as we were.' Although he was attempting to convince himself as much as he was her, he realised that their rendezvous would now become a thing of the past for a long time to come. Keeping the tabloid hidden from her mother when they awoke her to return to the coach, Paul suddenly wondered how he was going to get them home.

In his car at the Europa bus station, Paul swallowed hard at the thought of the drive into the Shankill. Glancing at her mother through the rearview mirror, he could only pray that with it being nearly midnight, the streets would be deserted. In the Shankill, Paul never moved his head from the road ahead as he fought off the tremors of anxiety that were resounding through his body to agitate his arms and legs. Having met no resistance, he stopped outside Angela's home then looked to the window to observe her father prying from behind the curtains. Alighting the car to help her mother out, the man of the house appeared at the front door then walked over to render his piece. Towering above Paul, he looked him straight in the eye.

'You've got some bloody nerve coming here,' he said in a methodical tone, before continuing in the same vein. 'Take some good advice. Get back into your car and don't stop driving until, when you look back, you can't see Ireland, now go on get moving.'

Saving his temper, his sheer presence was more than sufficient to have Paul quaking in his shoes. Looking behind the imposing figure,

251

Paul watched Angela's charade, which let him know she would phone him at a later date. As he drove away slowly, all his fears had dispersed and they would probably never return. At this moment in time, he simply didn't care whether or not a gang of loyalist youths sprung from the darkness to confront him. The way he felt, they would be doing him a favour now that he understood his days with Angela were numbered.

Having shown cool restraint towards Paul, her father closed the door to shut out the world's ears then began to vent his anger with a scorching attack. Grabbing his wife's bouquet, he threw them against the wall.

'I could expect this from you,' he roared at Angela then turned to address his wife, 'but you, how fucking stupid could you be. Have you any idea of the consequences? The windows will be stoned for starters. Jesus I wouldn't put it past some of the fanatics round here to put a petrol bomb through the letterbox, and fuck me what'll they say at work, I'll be laughed out of the fucking force.'

'I'm dying Bill and you've given me no support, you've just run and hid,' returned his wife before resuming her speech. 'What about our marriage vows, in sickness and in health, don't they mean anything to you? You've changed so much, I needed you and you weren't there. Paul's shown more compassion for this family than you ever have.'

Stalling on her words, he suddenly burst into tears. 'I can't cope with this any more, I love you Liz and I'm gonna lose you.'

As he collapsed at her feet, she opened her arms to him and held him close to her wasting body. Leaving them to reconcile their marriage, Angela headed upstairs to bed.

When Paul arrived home, he could see that the front room light was still burning bright and he construed why. Entering the living room, he was met by a crashing blow across the head in the form of a rolled up newspaper. Catching the follow-up swing in mid-flight, he squeezed his father's hand so tight that it turned white and yet the muscles on his face never flinched. After a few seconds, Paul released his grip as the tension mounted.

'You've gone too far this time,' yelled his father, backing away. 'I'm disowning you, I want your bags packed and you out first thing in the morning.'

'Over my dead body,' intervened his mother, appearing in the doorway attired in her dressing gown.

252

'Might've guessed you'd defend him,' sneered his father, brushing past her to leave the room.

Shaking her head, she looked straight at her son. 'Well, what did you expect? I warned you the trouble she'd bring.'

'I don't really care any more, they'll have to kill me to keep me from seeing her. There's no legislation that states I can't fall in love with a Protestant. Tell me, Mom, what would God say? Will I go to hell over this or will the priest absolve me?' he asked sarcastically.

Hearing no reply, Paul headed upstairs to bed.

As the enterprising editor at the Telegraph had anticipated, sales had rocketed. Phone lines were jammed by the public ringing in to add their support and salute the modern day Romeo and Juliet, even the radio stations had Paul and Angela as their topic of conversation, as they incessantly pumped out love songs from dawn till dusk. In general there was a new buzz of optimism on the streets of Belfast as people went about their daily business with a spring in their step.

Staying in bed until the house had cleared, Paul only came down for breakfast when he heard the door slam shut for a third time.

'You're the talk of the town,' informed his mother, handing him the morning paper.

'You're joking,' moaned Paul, who had hoped that the story would fade away to be replaced by something more appropriate, like a Third World famine or a football player's wild antics on the drink.

Looking at the front page, he saw Tommy's proud picture with Toby under the headline: 'UNDERDOG AIMING TO OVERCOME SECTARIANISM'.

Reading on with great interest, Paul was quite affected by how the public were rallying behind them. Over the next half hour the phone rang non-stop as the Telegraph, ITN and the BBC demanded interviews, all of which Paul denied, fearing that being in the public eye could only add to his troubles. Ready to refuse another offer of instant stardom, Paul was delighted to hear Angela's voice at the other end. 'Have you seen the papers?'

'Aye, I've had the media promising me the earth all morning.'

'Me too, but at least all this attention should keep us safe. My daddy has forbidden me to see you again, he really gave me a hard time this morning. Still at least my mommy and him are talking at long last.

253

It means I'll only be able to see the dog on race nights and, speaking of which, what time are we setting off for Dublin on Saturday?'

'I was thinking we could make a day of it, leave around 9 a.m. We can put Toby in the kennels at Shelbourne Park then do some sightseeing if you like? We could go see the Guinness brewery.'

'Aye, it's a date. I think I'll need a day away from it all come Saturday. Hey Paul, you watch yourself until then.'

'I'll be fine, so nine o'clock then at the Europa?'

For the next couple of days, Paul kept a low profile and now that the distraction of Angela's appearances had retrogressed, he occupied himself partaking in Toby's training programme, determined to scoop the prize.

At work Angela was shunned, as both Protestant and Catholic nurses whispered maliciously behind her back and even started false rumours of how she had slept with a whole Gaelic football team after a party. With every dragging hour all she had to look forward to was the dog race on Saturday and, strangely enough, Paul.

Although the media mined the story to rock-bottom depths, the leading lady and gentleman's intractability to collaborate spelled that the hype would inevitably dry up soon, exhausted. Never seen together, the press had nothing exciting to report and so it appeared the worst was over, that was, however, until Thursday.

Drawing the curtains to check what weather conditions the supreme being had delivered, Paul noticed that his car had been vandalised yet again. On this occasion the recreant attack had left his bonnet streaked with battery acid and his exhaust pipe jammed up with a potato, which seemed sardonic considering the great potato famine of 1845 which had every Catholic at the time forced to eat grass. Now they had forgotten to respect what they were fighting for. Walking outside to survey the extent of the damage, he noticed that the paving stones had a message for him also: 'TREASON IS PUNISHABLE BY DEATH'.

Over in the Shankill as Angela readied herself for an afternoon stint at the RVH, she instinctively blenched when she heard the smashing of glass accompanied by a tremendous thud below. Rushing downstairs, she observed that it was a brick which had trespassed into the living room. Picking the offender up, she removed the elastic band which held the junkmail to its clay pigeon before reading the scurrile threat with angst. 'BETTER TO BE RAPED BY A PROTESTANT THAN TO BE FUCKED BY A TAIG.'

Banishing the maundering intimidation to the bin, she carried on with life as best she could. There were to be no more deleterious incidents that week to hang over them and slowly the pain began to subside. Menacing words did more damage than sticks and stones in these parts. Looming over you, they made sleep impossible, as normality shifted to life on a knife edge. Perpetually on red alert, relaxation was not permitted for one minute, for that could be the time when they sprang from obscurity to inflict the bodily harm, now that they'd already carved up your mind.

'What are your thoughts on this?' demanded Michael's Intelligence Officer, thundering the last four editions of the Telegraph down on to the battered antique table. 'I'll tell you this now, this is not going down well higher up. It needs sorting and fast. So far your brother has been overlooked because of your family's tradition, but this will be tolerated no further. If you don't put him straight, then we'll have to. This constitutes as sheer defiance against the Cause and it's not doing you any favours either regarding your advancement. There's no way we can use you when there's infiltration in your camp, do you understand that?'

Michael simply nodded.

'Well, I'll make you understand it better shall I? The girl's father is a member of the RUC, how clear does that make it?'

'Crystal,' responded Michael, his eyes widening to the challenge.

'All this propaganda is turning the community soft and it's making us vulnerable,' his superior began to lecture, 'before you know it there'll be a queue of informers a mile long outside every RUC station this side of the border. We have to stamp out the orchestration of this revolt before it rises above us. This time next week I want this to be resolved once and for all. The only other alternative, and God help me it's the last thing I want to see, is an ASU sent to kill our own people to reinstate the hatred towards the rival faction. We've done it before, usually around election time to win a few votes here and there and we'll do it again. Fear causes gullibility and in the past neither side has minded sacrificing a few of its own pawns in the game, if it meant the opposition would be blamed.'

Although Michael was no genius, even he could ascertain that he'd been deceived by the allurement of his boyhood dreams, yet he was in too deeply to swim to safety. All he could do now was go with the flow and see it through to the bitter end. In his mind, it was appalling that the IRA could kill innocent Catholics in cold blood to keep their

255

war machine ticking over, but Paul, well he was different, he was a traitor through and through and that's why Michael had no intention whatsoever of having a quiet word of admonition in his ear. No, as far as he was concerned, the quicker the ASU was dispatched, the sooner he would be exorcised of the jealous demons of Bernadette's past which haunted him so. Even if the IRA didn't kill him, they'd leave him with no option but to flee Ireland when their calling card arrived.

Saturday, May 7th was D-Day anent to Toby's immediate future in the top flight. Waiting for Angela at the Europa bus station, Paul began to read what the newspaper had to say that day. Again, they filled the headlines, this time the press revealed that there had been a massive betting coup within both communities, as well as the whole of Belfast. It seemed as though every Tom, Dick and Harriet wanted a slice of the action as the bookmakers had been flooded with bets of support. Now that Toby was carrying the weight of public demand, Paul wondered if it would all be too much for him to shoulder. Reading a statement from Dunmore's racing manager, it was relayed that six extra coaches had been laid on to transport History Maker's amassing legion of followers to Dublin, so they could roar him home, and that serious consideration had been given to postponing tonight's race meeting, in view of the fact that most of the Dunmore race patrons would be out of town. When Angela arrived, Paul noticed that she looked very drawn, most noticeably her cheekbones which were protruding more than usual.

'So how have things been with you?' he asked.

'Not good,' she admitted. 'People have been really awkward and nasty to me at work, my father's had hassle at the station too. I also had a brick delivered through my front window and to aggravate matters I've had little sleep and have a poor appetite. What about you?'

'Much the same, but Toby's raring to go, isn't he, Tommy?'

'Aye,' he concurred, restraining the excited animal.

Leaving behind a dismal, wet Belfast morning, by the time they had reached the bandit country of the border, already the sun was niggling away the clouds. As they headed across the somniferous countryside, Angela gazed captivated in awe of the wondrous landscape which was the true Ireland, a country where, although she had lived within its coasts all her life, her provincial existence had never allowed her to see it for its true worth. This was the breathtaking scenery that people travelled from distant lands to admire, talk about over and over again then come back for a second helping. It seemed that the deeper south they travelled the more quintessentially Irish it became. For the duration of the drive, Paul kept his window open, allowing the natural air conditioning to keep his allergy at bay.

At just before midday, they entered the 'fair city' with its Georgian style houses and height-restricted buildings. It was everything that Belfast was not, truly Irish in everything from the lazy accents to the tranquil, still Liffey. The pace in general was subdued, this was the land that time had forgot, whereas the Northern Irish capital, with its monotonously drab buildings, was like any other city in England. Dublin, having only gained its independence in 1921, was not yet willing to surrender to the overpaid architects' arrogant vision of how we should approach the millennium. Instead, it was as if the Dubliners wanted to make up for the lost time of English rule, wallow in their independence and even though Eire's capital boasted the youngest population in Europe, put the city back to how it once might have been.

They made straight for the impoverished district of Ringsend and soon arrived at Shelbourne Park. Alighting the car, they simultaneously took a deep breath of the sweet humid air, then smiled at each other, telepathically communicating, 'who would have thought we'd come this far in such a short time.' Heading to book Toby into his new lodgings for the day, they all scanned over to the magnificent, eerie grandstand and could almost hear the buzzing atmosphere it would later breath. Making the acquaintance of the hospitable racing manager, who proudly showed them around the immaculately maintained kennelling facilities, they then left, satisfied that Toby was in good hands. With just over seven hours to kill before another star-studded gala evening of greyhound racing got underway, Paul thought he would use his initiative to get into Angela's good books.

Leaving the car behind in the track's car park, he hailed a taxi to take them to the shopper's paradise of Grafton Street. Meandering through the cultured pedestrian-friendly side streets, where a renaissance of artists and buskers plied their trade, motivated by the mouth-watering aroma of a mélange of culinary delights rising from the subterranean cafés, Angela suddenly felt her appetite return. Finding a reasonably priced eatery, by following the natives converging on its premises, they all ordered steak in a Guinness marinade and three pints of the local speciality, and biggest export, Guinness. As they watched from their table, they marvelled at the meticulous pouring routine. It's said that

257

there is no pint of stout to match the home brew available in this city and it's no untruth. Pouring three half measures, the barman then waited a full four minutes in a tantalising ritual that had them licking their lips in anticipation, before he filled their glasses to the rim. If ale was gauged by fuel grades then lager would be unleaded petrol, beer - four star and Guinness - diesel. As they savoured the creamy, velvet-textured nectar, they agreed that indeed the iron-abundant measure had no rival. Walking off the rich meal through a labyrinth of outlandish stalls and shops, where you could buy anything from Celtic jewellery to the anecdotes of Oscar Wilde, they ran out of the precinct and into the serene setting of St Stephen's Green, a municipal park situated smack bang in the middle of Dublin's equivalent to London's illustrious West End. As they entered the gate by the pacified duck pond, they watched with warm smiles as families unwound with their young children, feeding stale bread to the grateful amphibious birds.

Putting his arm around her again, Paul spoke. 'So what do you think of the Fair City?'

'It's beautiful, it reminds me of Edinburgh so much,' she replied, her mind easing after all the tension of the last week.

'I love you, Angela,' he said from nowhere but his heart, not caring that Tommy was just a few yards away in front of them.

'Don't Paul, don't love me. I can't love you back. Sometimes when we're in a different world like this, I feel as if I could but, oh I don't know what I'm saying,' she said before becoming flustered.

'So are you saying there's hope for us?'

'No, I'm sorry. If there was any possibility then last week's events killed it off.'

Feeling that if she did love him as much as he loved her, then she would've given up anything to be with him as he would have for her, Paul now realised that his long-shot dream was over. So numb inside that he couldn't expel the tears her onion words had forced upon him, he couldn't imagine where they went from here. Leaving by another gate where an artist had rearranged a pile of elongated rocks to form Ireland's answer to Stonehenge, Paul wondered whether he was to live life as a Druid priest. Throughout the remainder of the afternoon as they explored Dublin's quaint streets, the conversation was lost in the stalemate.

When they arrived back at Shelbourne Park, somewhat jaded by the sightseeing excursion, the grandstand was already filling up nicely. By eight o'clock, a crowd of approximately five thousand jam-packed the venue to make the order of the evening attempting to manoeuvre from A to B without having your clothes burnt in a close encounter with a cigarette. The sizeable contingency from Dunmore had now invaded and secured a corner of the stand, and it was they, the away supporters, who appeared to be making the most noise as the drink flowed relentlessly. Having procured a window seat overlooking the awesome galloping track with its sand bends and grass straights, both Angela and Paul agreed for once that the view was spectacular. Straight ahead the sleepy Wicklow Mountains rolled and dipped, filling the landscape with their misty enchanting beauty, only recessed by the centrepiece of the handsome Landsdowne Road rugby stadium, which simply had to be the tallest building in the whole of Dublin. To the right beyond the huge scoreboard towered the rusty frame of the old storage tank at the gasworks, which unpremeditatedly posed as a monumental landmark that no commissioned artisan could equal. It was a soothing portrait that massaged the eyeballs to sleep - sheer natural, unspoiled beauty that no modern-day arrangement could emulate.

Wading through the claustrophobic, chattering crush, Matt Williamson and a photographer stretched their necks scanning for the rebellious couple, desperate for pictures and a story to maintain the saga that was fast nearing the end of its run. Spying the couple sitting apart, engaged in nothing but solitude, Matt ordered his accomplice to stay out of the picture for the time being, fearing he may frighten off the camera-shy infidels. As he joined them, he wasn't really sure how they would receive him, but what did he care? Being a reporter doesn't reflect upon your literary skills; no, the prime attribute is being gifted with a congenital thick skin and he was bullet-proof.

'Could I have a few minutes of your time?' he appeared from behind them.

Turning to face him, Angela recognised him then spoke to Paul. 'He's the reporter from last Saturday.'

'Have you any idea of the trouble you've stirred up for us?' said Paul, without raising his voice.

Without knowing it, Paul's failure to take the fifth amendment had activated Matt's interview. 'Come on, the people are rallying behind you, we've been inundated with well-wishers and besides, we've kept the story clean. This dog and your relationship is doing more for the peace process than all the politicians put together. Believe it or not, it's within

259

your hands to reunite Northern Ireland, now isn't that worth fighting for?' romanticised the journalist.

Shaking his head, Paul gave a sarcastic half laugh. 'This so called relationship you think we're having is a figment of your vivid imagination. If it was anything other than platonic then, aye, I would fight society to the end, but it's not real. So print what you will, but just remember this: when you pick up your fat salary at the end of the month, your misinterpretations are putting our lives at risk for nothing.'

Burning up from all the sweltering heat being generated in the sardine tin of Shelbourne Park, Paul turned to Angela. 'I'm going to get some air before I black out, are you coming?'

Uniting for once, they left the sweating reporter to deliberate over Paul's sincere declaration. As he watched them at the win-line enjoying the welcoming breeze that had kicked up from nowhere, Matt decided to keep his distance and wait in the wings for the one-off photograph, that just might belie Paul's words, and yet he really did believe him.

At 9.20 p.m. Tommy entered the arena with the bouncing History Maker clad in the black jacket of trap four, which reflected the lucrative odds of 5/1 on offer. The Shelbourne congregation also had a star performer in a dog called Ardfert Sean and by more than luck it had been drawn from the plum red-jacket slot. To make matters even worse, plausibly the fastest-starting greyhound on the circuit, an English raider from Hove named O'Dell Schooner had been allotted the white jacket of trap three, making Toby's chances of a first bend lead less than slim. Having never run competitively over this distance before, the Dunmore track record holder should have been realistically priced at 14/1, but as it was, the travelling army from Belfast kept faith and gulped at the 5/1 against. With the race doubling as an early Derby trial, every animal on show would be tuned to advertise its claims; for many of the runners, this was the penultimate spin before embarking on the long, hard road to glory on August 29th.

Each co-owner investing a £10 wager, Paul placed a sum of £30 on Toby, just in case he was to defy the odds, the handicapper and the pride of Dublin and England. When the hare began its journey, the noise was deafening as the crowd attempted to spur on their favourite's chances.

When the lids cracked open, as anticipated the white jacket was first to show. Storming past the win-line for the initial time, Toby was within a half length of the Saxon leader and challenging for first-bend supremacy. Tussling at the curve, the traffic problems which ensued allowed the red jacket of Ardfert Sean to slip around clear, culminating in an eruption of ecstasy from the home crowd. Using all his preponderance, Toby robustly shook off O'Dell Schooner and then began to claw away at the three-length disadvantage. Opening the throttle down the back straight, the black jacket was closing the gap with every stride, and in seeing this, Paul and Angela spontaneously reached for each other's hands as the adrenaline pumped inside their bodies to start their mouths screaming. 'Come on Toby, come on Toby.'

Unwilling to be denied as the challenger drew level, the local champion used all his track craft to poach a valuable half-length lead by hugging the rails around the final turns, forcing Toby to take the long way around. Straightening up for the gruelling, long run in, still an also-ran, Toby began to dig deeper than he'd ever been asked to before. With pain etched all over his diehard face, his gutsy determination saw him draw level as the line beckoned. Sticking his neck out as if he were a giraffe, he scorched over the line to stun the home crowd into silence and impel the vast majority to begin ripping up their betting slips. Angela and Paul jumped into each other's arms as a shower of beaten dockets rained upon them reminiscent of the World Cup final of Argentina '78. Unbeknown to them, they were writing Monday's headlines. With Paul's jubilation carrying him away, he lifted Angela from the ground and swung her around, and, for a fleeting moment, he actually thought it was confetti in their hair. And, all the time blinded by exultation, they hadn't noticed that the photographer had snapped into action. They say the camera never lies and most of Belfast wouldn't want to argue against that come Monday morning. Up above, high in the stand, the three hundred strong Northern Irish bevy were about to drink the bar dry as they'd raise their glasses again and again to proclaim their idol.

In all the furore of winning, by the time Paul and Angela had caught their breaths, the press had sneaked off into the night satiated with a job well done. During the next five minutes as they awaited the cheque and trophy presentation they were mobbed by patrons offering to buy them a drink, both Northerners and Southerners. Gathering for a group photo, as Angela received the silverware and Paul the cheque, it was Tommy's wide grin as he held History Maker on the winner's podium that almost filled the lens alone. Having given the current track champion a solo run and come through a dogfight and severe turbulence, even the Dubliners were so swayed that they stood

261

and applauded the tenacious revelation. Wanting to make tracks immediately, with a two-and-a-half-hour journey still ahead of them, they worked for each other in the kennelling enclosure to beat the traffic. The dog fed, watered and bathed, they all headed for the car park where they were stopped by a middle-aged man offering his congratulations. 'So, will you enter him for the Derby?' he quizzed.

'Well, we'll have to see how it goes,' returned Paul, modestly.

'I see he's not frightened of cars now, how did you do it?'

Realising immediately that this was Toby's original owner, Paul offered his hand in friendship before introducing the remainder of the syndicate.

'We tried everything,' revealed Paul, 'top vets, handslips the works, then our resident genius Tommy here came up with the solution.'

'And?' the small, rotund greying man asked eagerly.

'He coursed him with the added incentive of OXO cubes, dipping a cuddly toy into gravy made him race again.'

'Unbelievable,' he said, astonished by the method in the madness. 'Well, I'm Johnny McKenna, my wife and I own a stud outside Wicklow. Having bred the animal we had real high hopes until his unfortunate accident. I realise you all have a long drive back to Belfast so I won't keep you any longer, I will however give you my card. Just call me if you need any assistance for the Derby, you may decide to relocate him for the event, if you do, then we would be willing to keep the dog on our farm and put you all up overnight, any night.'

Thanking him for the offer, they bade him farewell and set off on the long drive north. Absolutely drained from his run, Toby was the first to nod off, then Tommy and finally Angela.

As the orange lights of Belfast came up ahead in the distance, Paul glanced at Angela sleeping so peacefully, cradling Toby's achievement as if it was her child and he smiled before frowning at the city with abhorrence as he entered its outskirts. Stopping at their starting point of the Europa bus station, Paul gently stirred his dream girl and walked with her to find a taxi. 'So what now?' he said.

'What do you mean?'

'Toby, when will you see him again?'

'Well, I can't next week, can I? If he really has Derby credentials then perhaps we should only race him once a fortnight on the Saturday when you're home. Call me next Saturday night if you want and we can discuss it then. I really have to get home, thanks for the day out. I want you to give Tommy this, he deserves it,' she said, handing him the sparkling trophy.

Without even a peck on the cheek she was gone, leaving Paul empty. Ironically, the same lame dog that had brought them together, now a champion, was tearing them apart.

Heading back to work early Monday morning, Paul stopped off for a paper to see if his opinion had perturbed the journalist, knowing that it was his last chance if he was to keep on seeing Angela. Staring at the front-page picture of better times as he held Angela, he was pretty sure that this was the final nail in the coffin of any relationship that might have blossomed in another climate. Again, the officious media had fiddled the facts with temerity to keep their bandwagon rolling.

Paul joined the ferry, knowing that Angela had received nothing but revilement from her so called workmates, so he could only wonder with apprehension what lay in store for him. The initial response was surprisingly good: Scots Paul thought it was great, hailing him as a celebrity, and most of the other crew he bumped into were just as enthusiastic. Docking in Belfast after the second trip of the day, the ship's public announcement system called for Paul O'Donnell to report to the bridge. Eyes rising to meet his Scots adviser, he searched for an explanation.

'It's either a phonecall for you from shore or the boss wants a quiet word in your ear.'

Walking slowly, Paul's mind was racing, he hadn't done anything wrong to warrant a verbal warning, so it had to be a phonecall. Fearful that Angela had come to harm, he began to sprint towards his destination. Arriving on the bridge, he was relieved at first to discover there was no message from the mainland, but his joy defected to mass anxiety upon sighting his visitor. It was none other than Martin South, the Onboard Services Manager. Thinking that all the press coverage had made him a liability to the company, Paul tried to prepare himself for the golden handshake that always accompanied the DCB, don't come back.

'Still enjoying life at sea?' asked Martin, offering a cigarette to calm Paul's nerves.

'Aye,' he replied, refusing the smoke, 'I was even wondering if I could have an application form for a good friend of mine, should a vacancy arise.'

'Aye, I'll organise that for you,' he sanctioned abruptly, to show Paul that this wasn't a social call after all. 'Come on, let's go for a walk.'

Following his boss to a reserved cabin, Paul waited as Martin shut the door to gain the optimum privacy he required before commencing the sermon.

'Have you any idea why I've called you here?' he asked, pacing back and forth.

'Are you gonna sack me?' queried Paul.

'Hell, no,' he replied, removing another cigarette from his packet.

'Then why have you?' said Paul, now confused.

'I just felt that you needed to heed some friendly advice that's all. I've seen this story snowball in the newspaper all week and it worries me. I'm impressed that you've managed to keep the company out of it, and of course that's the way it has to remain, so keep it like that and you have a job for life. I know Mairead likes you, so that's why I feel it's my duty to administer you with some words of wisdom. I know that all this with the Protestant girl is merely a fabrication to promote sales, but I'm worried for your safety. You can't oppose these people. I should know,' he let it slip inadvertently.

Having been listening in a daydream, Paul abruptly stirred to life.

'What do you mean?'

'Come on Paul, think about it. How do you think I've made it from the Falls into this position? They made it happen. I turn a blind eye now and again, plead ignorant, what I don't see I don't know, work it out. In return, well – here I am, good job and a nice house. If I ever show dissent I'll be disciplined, everyone has a price, that's why I'm imploring you to watch yourself. Don't give the press any ammunition, it'll only end up being fired at you. Why don't you think about taking out Mairead again, it'll divert the attention from you, flaunt it in public, it might just save your life. That's all I have to say. I hope you've listened well, these people won't think twice about silencing you with a bullet.'

Leaving Paul with more than the reprimand he had expected, Martin left the room. As the week sailed on there was no let up from the media as they began to dig deeper, leaving no stone unturned in their quest for stories to send ripples through the pond of Angela and Paul's lives.

* * *

Come Thursday night and Michael was back for his weekly debriefing.

'I thought you were going to use your fraternal influence to put an end to this,' slammed his Intelligence Officer, obviously feeling the strain of the pressure being forced upon him from above.

'I warned him what would happen, but he just laughed in my face, he seems to think he's immune with all the media backing and the community support towards the dog. Do you want me to sort the animal?' suggested Michael.

'No, don't be stupid, the press would have a field day over this. We'll probably send someone to pay him a visit. I'm sorry but this has gone too far,' he expressed, watching Michael's face to see if it showed any sympathy for his own blood.

'I'd like to be a part of this,' offered Michael. 'He's really pissed me off lately,' he continued, to show his true fidelity.

'We'll see,' said the officer, concluding the meeting by leaving the room.

Paul was shaking with fear when he called Angela at 8 p.m. on Saturday evening. Not only had he dwelt all week on Martin South's warning, but the thought of her father answering the phone was just as daunting. Having stayed rooted by the telephone, it was her reassuring voice that renewed some confidence to his timid state.

'Had any hassle?' he asked immediately.

'Only ignorance, no one wants to talk to me at work, only about me, even my father glances at me in disgust since the Telegraph exposed that he was a policeman, and yet I've done nothing wrong. What about you?'

'Funnily enough, everyone has been supportive, so what are the plans for Toby?' he changed the subject quickly, to clip her growing temper in the bud.

'If you enter him next Saturday, I'll meet you at the track.'

'Don't you want to see him through the week?' said Paul, who wanted to see her again to keep the heat on his endeavour to win her over, not in favour of the absence makes the heart grow fonder approach.

'You know I do, but until the papers run out of words it's simply not worth the risk. Seeing us together will just prolong the hype, don't you agree?'

'Aye, I suppose you're right. I've missed you, Angela,' he sighed, still suffering the symptoms of love-sickness that the recurrence of her voice had brought.

'Okay,' she extinguished his fire, 'I have to go now, see you at Dunmore next Saturday.'

When he left the boat on Sunday evening, Paul felt a cold rush of trepidation pass through his body identical to the one he'd experienced on the night of Angela's attack. Having profited from at least some security at work, even if anxiety had spread through him like a terminal cancer with every passing day, he now felt really vulnerable, even paranoid. Walking over to his car, he scanned around, convinced that his every move was being monitored. Seeing no one, he checked under his car in case someone had planted him an explosive homecoming. Satisfied that there were no extra parts protruding, he entered the vehicle. Still twitchy, he clenched his teeth, held his breath, then cagily tickled the ignition. With a disgruntled cough and a splutter at having to return to work after a week's holiday, the engine started to stabilise the severe palpitations that had pounded his senses. He valued the drive home, and thought to himself how foolish he'd been; after all it was always other people who were killed or maimed, it could never happen to you, could it? There again, Paul did seem to spend much of his life worrying over everything and nothing all at once.

He joined his mother in the kitchen and she revealed that all had been quiet on the Western Front during his absence. Looking down the back yard, Paul could see no sign of Tommy nor Toby, only weeds beginning to sprout through the drainage cracks in the paving stones. Now that the summer was almost in sight, all the vegetation was growing at double pace, as if it was coming to meet the new season half way.

'Seen much of Tommy?' Paul asked.

'Aye, he's here regular as clockwork day in day out, you've just missed him, actually. I saw him take the dog for its walk only a few minutes ago.'

'Have there been any phone calls for me during the week?'

'Aye, now you come to mention it, there was a call for you on Friday night, some woman asking for you. I told her you wouldn't be back till today so she left her telephone number for you to call her back.'

'Probably a smooth-talking journalist, no doubt,' moaned Paul.

'Well, the number wasn't a Belfast one, although her accent was,' she said.

Taking the slip of paper his mother had safeguarded, Paul's eyes lit up realising that the area code was that of Cleveland, the last-known locale of Tommy's mother. Darting to the telephone to see if there was to be some reward for his persistency in keeping the personal ad

266

running when all seemed lost, Paul dialled the number then awaited a response.

'Hello, my name's Paul O'Donnell, I believe you replied to my advertisement in your local paper?'

'I certainly did, regarding a supposed inheritance,' confirmed the female voice from over the water.

'Aye, but you must appreciate, I have to be sure you're who you claim to be,' stated Paul.

'Oh, I can prove that no problem, but how much is the sum involved and who has bequeathed it to me?'

'We can get to that later,' Paul said. 'So tell me, do you have any children?'

'Aye,' she murmured, 'I've a son called Gerald.'

'What can you tell me about him?'

'He's twenty-one, a little backward,' she reeled off, becoming tired of the conversation that was digging up her past. 'Where's this all leading, am I entitled to a legacy or not?'

'Okay, calm down and don't hang up while I explain myself,' pleaded Paul. 'I'm your son's best friend, I promised him I'd find you. He's so desperate to see you again to show you how much he's changed. He did it all for you, all he wants is for you to be proud of him.'

'Wait a minute, did all what for me?' she asked, curious.

'Gerry taught himself to read and write, he now trains a champion greyhound, he was even on the front page of the Telegraph last week. He's also been offered a job with a ferry company,' he fabricated, straining to keep her on the line long enough to reel her in. 'He loves you immensely and he does realise that you have a new life, but if he could only see you again for one day then that would be a dream come true and more than enough. Will you meet him or can he meet you?'

For a long half-minute there was a missed-penalty silence before Paul spoke again. 'Are you still there?'

'Aye, I'm here,' she responded.

'Well, will you see him again?'

'I need some time to think, the past haunts me, oh I don't know, this is all so sudden. I still have your number, I'll contact you when I've got my head around all this,' she declared, flustered with the guilt of walking out on the son who had needed her then, as much as the air he breathed.

267

'Wait,' shouted Paul, but it was too late, she'd hung up on the shame.

Returning to the kitchen he looked out towards the kennel to see that Tommy was back, full of smiles, happy to be a part of the world and Paul wondered whether he should publicise his findings. Turning to face Paul's hesitant expression, Tommy just knew that it was to be an antithetical announcement.

'You've found my mother haven't you, and she doesn't want to see me?'

Astounded at Tommy's clairvoyant perception, Paul stood with his tongue temporarily frozen as he searched for the warm, cottonwool words to comfort his partner.

'No, it's not as bad as you think, she just needs time. I think she's a little worried about how you'll react over her deserting you, but the way she sounded on the phone I'm pretty certain you'll see her soon, whether it'll be on Irish soil, though, is a different matter,' explained Paul.

With Tommy maturing with every passing day, he shed no tears though, took it on the chin like the man he'd evolved into. 'I don't really care any more, as long as I have Toby I'm the happiest man alive,' revealed Tommy, convincing no one.

When Thursday arrived, things had got better for Paul, there had been no threats, detrimental deliveries or defacing of his property, even the papers were thin. Sensing that life was returning to normality, he called Angela to inform her that the dog would run as promised on Saturday night. Through an informal conversation made by the suppression of twin anxieties, Paul had learnt that her life too had turned for the better, now that the media had run out of words. Having once looked as though it would drag out like a storyline in a soap opera, like good plumbers, Paul and Angela had managed to seal the leaks. As usual Paul had terminated the call with his customary 'I've missed you' and for once she'd actually repaid the compliment. Skipping to the back yard on his lifeline, he caught Tommy heading out for his evening stroll with Toby.

'Wait up, I'll come with you,' he shouted, grabbing his shoes from the mat outside the backdoor. Walking up Clonard Street past the sandy-coloured, timeworn monastery, all the talk was of Toby's next outing, an open, over the extended 550-yards trip.

'If he wins, who'll get the trophy?' inquired Tommy.

'I think we'll worry about that when and if it happens,' replied Paul, never one to cash a cheque before it had cleared.

'Do you think we really have a chance of winning the Derby?' Tommy continued to look forward. 'I'd love him to win that so much.'

'Me too,' agreed Paul, 'but it's a while away, a lot can and will happen between now and then.'

As the sun slowly diminished under the horizon for the evening, they continued to ramble, reminiscing Toby's victories. Turning into Cupar Street, Paul suddenly stopped dead in his tracks, for up ahead in the distance he could see two men clad in khaki jackets and ski-masks approaching, each menacingly holding a crow bar. Shifting his head to the left, he witnessed another two intimidating figures armed with baseball bats, closing in fast. Heart pumping with panic, he glanced behind from where he and Tommy had just come.

Paul swallowed his Adam's apple so he could regain the gift of speech. 'Tom, I want you to get back as fast as you can with Toby then call the police. I'll see if I can make it past them,' he said, in the knowledge that the gang had been dispatched for his benefit alone.

Hurdling over the garden wall that was nearest him, Paul began to race in the direction of the two men carrying crow bars. Banging his fists on every front door in between clinically timed vaults from garden to garden, he soon found the rhythm which enabled him to reach topspeed. Having managed to deliver his message to half a dozen households, the men who had been slowly tracking him abruptly quickened up their attack now that they'd seen through his plan. Closing in on him with the urgency needed to snuff out his cries for help, Paul eventually ran out of safe haven. With his back to the wall as his heart raced on, he glanced both ways to see the whites of their eyes as they hurdled the final two partitions without making a sound. Ducking as one of the men took a wild swing at him with the bat to thwart his resistance, Paul began to scramble towards the street. Failing to clear the trajectory of the bat, the hot pain of the solid timber smashing against his shoulder blade was all the inspiration he needed to find an extra spurt of energy. He sprang over the gate, turned right with a half a second to spare and put his head down to run for his life. Scorching up the street like a fox on the run, he raised his head to see if he could keep the hounds at bay with cunning, but his luck had just run out, as had the road. Gulping at the oxygen, he saw that smack, bang in front of him was the huge honey-coloured brick-wall of the peace-line which separated the Falls from its neighbour from hell, the Shankill. Even if a pole had fallen from the heavens to allow him to vault from

269

one crisis to another, the sharp razor wire spiralling along the vertex would have lacerated him to pieces. Legs so tired that they refused to carry him any further, he idled down at the Belfast wall. With one hand on the Republican flag painted on the brickwork, he arched over and began to cough through his panting, within seconds the phlegm had turned to eruptions of vomit. When he could be sick no more, he turned, beleaguered, to see through streaming eyes that the light had been blotted out by the four masked partisans towering over him.

Chapter 10

The Stars Around Me Are Shining, But I Feel Thunder In My Heart

Cowering defencelessly, Paul used the only weapon he had as he invoked, high-pitched, from the bottom of his lungs.

'No fucker can help you now,' came a sharp voice, which penetrated him more than that of his father's when he was a child.

'Hold him down and I'll smash his kneecaps,' screamed another, revelling in his duties.

Upon hearing their intentions, Paul began to wriggle and struggle to avoid crutches, or worse a wheelchair for the foreseeable future, and this only infuriated the batsman as he waited for the perfect strike that wouldn't break one of his team-mates fingers. After putting up a game fight for a couple of minutes, Paul's energy was finally expended. Reduced to the occasional spasm, he closed his eyes with fortitude and waited for the pain to arrive. Raising the bat over his head for maximum vitality, the obvious leader's arm locked in mid-swing as he aimed to deliver the punishment. And as he moved his head to apprehend what was happening, he saw three men, two armed with garden forks, the other holding the end of the bat. Dumbfounded, he turned fully to observe that at least a dozen more locals were approaching with anything they had managed to lay their hands on that would compensate for a weapon at such short notice. Even a woman had come with a rolling pin to flatten the callous attack. Within minutes, an almost fifty-strong mob of fremescent vigilantes had besieged the IRA disciplinarians.

271

Still lying on the ground, Paul looked to the heavens with tears of joy in his eyes as he heard screaming sirens approaching from the distance. Defeated by public outcry, the ASU dropped their weapons and scampered off into the evening like rabbits from a farmer's gun. By the time the RUC Land Rovers and Armoured Personnel Vehicles rolled into Cupar Street, the crowd of good Samaritans had dispersed back to their homes, one individual heading straight for the telephone to inform the media of the humanitarian insurrection.

Stunned by the trauma of the incident, Paul was still in a state of profound shock, so elected to take up the RUC's offer of a courtesy drive home. Staring at the streets with a blank expression, his head bobbed in time with the potholes in the road, yet he saw nothing as his brain failed to function. Driven on autopilot, Paul wandered mechanically through to the kitchen, where he could make out Tommy seated at the table with his head buried in his arms, sobbing. Paul swayed as his mother surged over and hugged him, her tears dripping on to the side of his cheeks. Upon hearing all the commotion of relief from the woman of the house, Tommy raised his head to see that Paul was unharmed and safe.

The press were quick to react to their tip-off as they had to be, this was a huge moral victory in their crusade to inflict detrimental body blows to the terrorist movement. And now that they had the upper hand it was crucial to sustain the pressure, for earlier that afternoon an IRA bomb had detonated at the RUC stand at the Balmoral Show injuring 13, including some children buying ice-cream nearby. Friday morning's front pages were adorned to entice a reaction that would influence the floating voters and strengthen the existing turncoats. The main headline of 'The People's Revolution' told of how the public, sick to the back teeth of the nagging and niggling toothache of the IRA, were now demanding to rid themselves of the offensive plaque that had stained their lives, and how they had begun to do so with an unprecedented show of unified defiance.

With a state of schism and reviewed allegiance raging through the Republican stronghold that threatened to crumble the very foundation upon which the IRA's terror campaigns were built, Sinn Fein's countermeasure had to be swift and impacting. As ever, their heavy-handed tactics went before them. In a point-blank statement to the media, Sinn Fein once again managed to thwart the coup d'état before it gathered any more momentum. Taking the evening edition's front page they addressed their own creed with a despicable sentence:

'Interference will not be tolerated and in future anyone obstructing the work of IRA volunteers will be shot.' What the paper didn't print were the death threats that Matt Williamson and his editor received. By mutual consideration and compromise the IRA and media realised it was in their best interests to pursue the People's Champions no further, before they were washed away on the tidal wave of hysteria. So, for the time being, the press allowed the outside world to dictate the headlines, only printing snippets of the fabricated saga infrequently, to encourage their readers, while the IRA left Paul and Angela to run their dog as they attempted to win back their flagging support.

When Angela read of her associate's ordeal a cold shiver twanged at her heartstrings, impelling her to make a phonecall.

'Is that you, Paul?'

'Aye,' he replied, languidly.

'How are you, did they harm you?' she asked, concerned.

'Nope, at least I'm having some luck in one direction.'

'What's wrong with you? You sound so down in the dumps.'

'Well, I've not much to be cheerful about right now. Have you?'

'Not a lot, no, but I'm trying to keep my spirits up. I've been more hard done to by all this than you, I can't even see my dog.'

'Aye, right,' he retorted in disbelief. 'See you tomorrow at Dunmore.'

Hearing the line go dead at the other end, she was almost tempted to call him back right that second and demand an explanation for his ignorant conduct, before she put herself in his shoes. For an hour solid Paul just stood gazing from the window at Tommy, who was hard at work grooming Toby. Although not a drop of alcohol had crossed his lips, it was by far the worst hangover he'd ever experienced. Brain inebriated from an overindulgence of self-pity, he had to find a way out of the doldrums as well as the house. Trying to divorce himself from the thoughts of last night's terrifying crucible, he found he could not separate them from his mind as they perpetually returned to nag at him. He began to weigh up his options and realised that if the IRA wanted to get him, then four brick walls wouldn't perturb that big bad wolf. Not fooling himself that he could hide for ever, he decided it was time to face the world again and get down to the business of keeping Toby on track for a distinguished five-timer. Living on the sustenance of misery loves company; as long as he had an ally around him at all times, he felt confident enough to proceed with life. When he joined Tommy at the kennel, Paul had come to at least one decision, the time

273

had now come to show his protégé the last trick in the greyhound training manual, an act that he believed his partner's naïvety was now ready to accept.

'How's Toby today?'

'Raring to go as ever,' Tommy replied.

'Can you do me favour?' asked Paul. 'I want you to come with me into town, there's something I have to get.'

Stopping on double yellows outside a pet shop in the city, Paul told Tommy to stay inside the car while he nipped in to make his purchase. A few minutes later he returned with a jumping bean cardboard box, which he then placed on the back seat.

'What's in there?' pried Tommy, curious to where all the hush-hush secrecy was leading.

'I'll reveal all when we get home.'

Paul rested the box on the kitchen table and began to cryptically unveil his plan of action.

'Ever done any fishing, Tom?'

'No,' came the confused reply.

'Anyway, let's just say you went fishing eight hours a day for a whole week and caught nothing, you'd be a little disgruntled now, wouldn't you?'

'I suppose so,' agreed Tommy, wondering where all this nonsense was leading.

'You may then decide to jack it in for a while or perhaps just go once a week for a few hours, but if you caught a fish, well the appetite for the sport would return, wouldn't it?'

'Aye,' he returned, enthralled, pondering what all this had to do with a visit to the pet shop, if not for the fact that there was a goldfish in the box.

'Well it's the exact-same principal with Toby. He keeps chasing a hare that he's never gonna catch, and therefore he'll soon lose interest.'

'So let him catch the rabbit,' interrupted Tommy catching on fast.

'Exactly,' exclaimed Paul, opening the box then lifting out a real, live, cute and cuddly brown rabbit. 'We'll throw this into his kennel so he can savour the kill.'

'You can't,' voiced Tommy, shocked, 'it's alive.'

'I know it's alive, that's the whole point of the exercise,' Paul stressed.

'No, take it back. Can't we get a dead one from the butchers? It'll taste just as good,' pleaded Tommy. 'This is wrong, it's murder in fact.'

274

Looking at Tommy, whose face had turned ashen with the fear of perpetration, Paul deliberated that indeed his compatriot was correct.

'I suppose you're right, it's our ability to kill animals with such ease that leads the human race to commit the cardinal sin. We'll take this back to the shop and buy one from the butchers.'

An hour later they stood and watched as Toby pinned the limp carcass to the ground then tore away at the pink flesh, which stained his white whiskers to remind him of what he was pursuing every time he went to the track.

Saturday was like old times for Paul and Tommy as they played cards to scuttle away the hours leading up to Toby's next race, but there were noticeable differences. The sun was fulgent in the clear blue sky for starters, baking the concrete upon which they lay, and cooking Paul's brain, as he huffed and puffed to break the lethargic suffusion that had engulfed him. Even Tommy had the notion that something was not right with his best friend by the way he won hand after hand without a moan of complaint. This was definitely not the same Paul that he had come to respect and idolise over the last few months, for the go-getter of a role model characterised by his ambition to succeed and tolerate no failure had got up and gone.

Tommy was deeply concerned. 'Are you all right? You don't seem to be enjoying yourself.'

'I'm just tired that's all, the heat always saps my energy,' Paul returned, making excuses for his lacklustre mood.

'Shall we take a walk to the newsagent?'

'No, you go if you want though,' replied Paul.

'Aren't you curious to see what Toby's up against tonight and whether they're tipping him?'

'I'm not really that interested,' Paul replied, slipping further into his melancholy.

'But what about Angela?' reminded Tommy, attempting to raise his floundering spirits. 'Surely you must be looking forward to seeing her again?'

'To be totally honest, I'm not that bothered; besides seeing her just frustrates me, even annoys me, knowing that I've kidded myself all along. She'll never leave this shit-hole with me. I've been living on cloud nine for too long and I think it's time to jump off.'

'So what are you gonna do now?'

275

'I haven't a clue Tom, all I know is that I'm really scared, ill in fact. I think I've overdosed on an elusive dream. I haven't been able to think straight for a long time. Suddenly I realise the rules can't be bent in this city. I may have to return to Britain or just move anywhere where I can feel safe again. I don't think there's anything here that can save me from ruin.'

'They won't try to get you again, I'm sure,' comforted Tommy.

'They don't really have to, the damage is already done, I'm a nervous wreck. I just can't believe the mentality of those sad bastards,' Paul growled. 'Why can't they all live in peace, it has to be easier and if they can't manage that, then at least fight amongst themselves and let the innocent people live their lives. I'm beat Tom, they've won but I'll never join them.'

'I'm gonna get a paper,' Tommy said softly, leaving Paul in the quick-sands of his torment.

Paul never moved a muscle in Tommy's absence, because his pessimistic thoughts had sapped every last drop of motivation. When Tommy arrived back twenty minutes later he brought with him the nascence of good tidings. 'Paul, you'd better double-check this, but I can't see anything about you and Angela in here.'

Grabbing at the paper, Paul began to laugh like a madman as he grasped the implications.

'What is it?' urged Tommy.

'They've finally realised.'

'Realised what?'

'They've dropped the story, knowing if they hadn't backed off the IRA would have killed me,' Paul expounded, presumptuously.

'So what does it all mean?'

'Well, if the media leave me alone, then this will probably all fade out into obscurity within a week. People have short memories, they might just forget about me.'

Turning to the sports section, even the greyhound card had decreased in size with only a diminutive write up and no mention whatsoever of History Maker.

At 6.30 p.m. over in the Shankill, Angela squirted on a few extra drops of perfume as she prepared to head for Dunmore. It had been two weeks since she'd been in Paul's company and, to some degree, she'd actually forgotten to remember what he looked like. In the knowledge that he'd come home last Sunday, on several occasions during that week her thoughts had defected to him, especially when she'd sporadically glanced at the silent telephone each evening, but it was yesterday's headlines that had hit her for six. At first she'd put it down to feeling somewhat responsible, identical to the way he'd felt accountable for her mishap, but there was a lot more to it than just guilt. The distant phonecall for one, when she'd attempted to offer him sympathy and how he'd thrown it back in her face with phlegmatic effortlessness. Angela hadn't realised it until now, but she needed his love as much as he did hers. Having been nurtured from all his attention and advances, suddenly she felt starved. Whereas Paul had been living in the land of make believe and had now found his way over the border to reality, Angela now wanted to migrate from sensibility to mutiny.

When she arrived at the track, Paul and Tommy were already there, heads buried into the racecard, sweating over the 9.30 heat. Back on home soil, History Maker, Dunmore's ambassador, had been gifted with the perk of the red berth. And the only danger appeared to be Shelbourne's Ardfert Sean, drawn from the contiguous blue jacket, who was on a revenge mission having been humbled at home. With another £500 and a trophy up for grabs, Paul, inspired by the media's definitive release, was desperate to win.

Unannounced, Angela tapped them on the shoulders from behind. 'So what do you think his chances are?'

Having made a substantial effort with her appearance, she was stunned when Paul didn't even turn around to face her.

'He has a chance,' he said, stolidly. 'I'm not being funny, but don't you think it would be wise if you watched the racing from the owner's bar, away from me?'

'Can I have a word with you in private?' she demanded, angered by his blatant snub.

Strolling to find seclusion, not once did Paul's eyes divert to her as he kept them trained stringently elsewhere, fearing that one glance at his Medusa would turn his heart to rock and once again he'd be stone in love.

'So, you gonna tell me why you're being so cold to me and why you can't even look me in the eye?' she interrogated like a headmaster, manoeuvring in front of him.

Although Paul endeavoured to keep his head turned away, the mere sweet smell of her seductive perfume tempted him to steal a glance.

277

'I really think it would be better if we kept our distance,' he remarked, in a sad tone of voice. 'It's not fair on me. You know how I feel about you and I know you'll never feel the same, but that's not all. I thought they were going to kill me the other night, and now that I've had time to put it all into perspective, it wasn't worth it. I suppose I gave my mind a treat all along, clutched at straws, somehow convinced myself that you'd fall in love with me, but I grew up on Thursday night. I've a good memory Angela, and every word you've said to me over the last few months, well I've used them to build false hopes.'

She looked to the heavens and sighed, 'Okay, do you want to know exactly how I feel?'

'No, save your breath, you don't have to console me, as I said, I've done a lot of maturing lately.'

'Can I get a word in edgeways? I want you to look at me and listen to what I have to say for a change.'

Gazing into her hypnotic, cool green eyes, he lent her his ears.

'I do feel something for you, Paul. I don't know if it's love but I think about you lots, all the time lately, if you must know. If we didn't have the obstacle of religion, I would go out with you, no hesitation.'

'Stop, Angela, stop – you're just making matters worse. It's no solace to hear all this when nothing can ever transpire between us.'

'Well, I'm willing to give it a go if you are,' she stated, almost giving him an ultimatum.

'Wait a minute, am I hearing this right? Are you actually asking me out, or I am dreaming again?'

Slightly embarrassed, she turned away before resuming the conversation. 'Aye, if I must, I'm asking you out.'

Not sure whether to laugh or cry, jump for joy or fall flat on his face, Paul stumbled over his reply. 'I. . . I accept.'

Falling into each others arms, they immediately broke and scanned around for nosy onlookers before returning to their hug of alleviation. Parting again, they swiftly made plans. Now that they had consented to become an item, it was so much simpler. With a common goal, their close intimacy would enable them to act out with ease an overall performance of distance.

For the hour leading up to Toby's race they stood apart in the swelled crowd, who had turned out in their droves to pay homage to the track champion, snatching a casual glance now and then and sharing the odd smile here and there. And when Tommy walked past with Toby on his way to the starting traps, both found themselves engaged in new conversations with inquisitive, adulating punters attempting to cajole a guarantee from them. Politely excusing himself, Paul took the favourite's odds of 6/4 against History Maker with a £100 stake.

Maintaining their remoteness, Paul and Angela watched as Toby broke level with the Dublin dog. As both animals arrived at the first bend, neck and neck, Toby utilised the rails slot to gain a half length advantage off the second turn. Levelling up for the long back straight, the red and blue coats pulled clean away from the struggling field and turned the race into a match. When the two prime contenders reached the penultimate arc, Toby was a length in front but still had a lot of work to get through, as Ardfert Sean was showing no signs of an early surrender. As the dogs blasted off the final turn, churning up the sand like a sirocco, a shudder of doubt began to pass through the puritanical-sized crowd as they witnessed that the southern raider was staying on gamely and making substantial inroads into History Maker's slender superiority. Voices rendered speechless by the sight which pervaded their disbelieving eyes, the home crowd began to stamp their feet and bang their fists anxiously as they willed the line to arrive in the nick of time. And somehow it did! Flashing past to win by a neck, Toby was greeted not by a roar of elation, but an eruption of pandemic relief.

Refraining from the desire to jump into each other's arms again, Paul and Angela simultaneously turned to each other and exhaled all the stress of the last fifty yards. For a few minutes whispers of doubt blew around the stadium, as sharp tongues stabbed at how History Maker's bubble seemed as if it was about to burst. Whilst others were inclined to believe that last year's Derby finalist, Ardfert Sean, was back to his baneful best. The public announcement of the winner's time and distance brought the belated ovation and recognition that Toby had deservedly merited in running his socks off. 'First trap one History Maker . . . by a neck in a winning time and new track record of 30.02 seconds.' After posing on either side of Tommy, Toby and the podium, where they collected another sparkling memento and fat cheque, Paul and Angela went to discuss the future of History Maker with the racing manager, while Tommy returned to his post-race duties. Following some careful consultation and calculation, it was decided that Toby would only trial once a fortnight leading up to the Greyhound Derby, in a strategic effort to keep the edge on his race sharpness. Then it would be on to Shelbourne Park to pit his wits against the finest from Ireland

279

and the United Kingdom. With Toby having just cemented his place in Dunmore's history book again, the Derby couldn't come quickly enough, for although Paul knew that at present Toby was the fastest greyhound in Ireland, he was also very aware that there were other dogs out there somewhere, waiting in the wings to peak just in time for the paramount event.

Strolling around to the kennelling enclosure opposite the main stand to meet Tommy, Paul inspected the heavy token of success then began to speak. 'Did you really mean what you said earlier?'

'Aye, but I want to take it real steady. I'm still confused about my feelings towards you, all I know is that I miss you when you're away. Don't take this the wrong way, but it might just be that I need your friendship, then again it may be more. What I need from you is understanding and patience, and not to hate me if it doesn't work out. I'm willing to give it a try, but no more than that, no promises, okay?'

Having been in a dead-end situation for the last few months, Paul now found that he was on the sliproad to the motorway, now all he had to do was make sure that he kept an eye on his speed.

'How do you fancy going for a drive out into the country tomorrow, we could have a picnic if you like? It'll be the last chance for us to spend a few hours together before I go back to work,' suggested Paul.

'I'd like that,' she accepted.

The following morning Paul rose early, thanks to a sleepless night, induced by the conjugation of a humid night and the excitement and expectation of a day out with Angela by themselves and far away from their fears. He walked out of the house and into a crisp morning, and smiled at the lucid blue skies which were about to play their part in the meteorologist's prognostication – that a heat-wave would sweep over Northern Ireland for the next week. Heading to a supermarket which had no objection to violating the Sunday trading mandate, Paul set about selecting the ingredients for a banquet fit for his queen. Conscientiously, he sifted through the aisles for the choicest produce obtainable, determined to make the kind of impression that would linger in her mind for a long time to come. A tin of salmon, a jar of olives, the juiciest grapes, softest cheese and herb bread, shiniest apples, most succulent celery, tangiest garlic dip, richest cheese, crispiest crackers and, last but not least, the sweetest bottle of champagne – was Paul's conception of the aphrodisiac of love. Returning to his home, he entered the kitchen to concoct his culinary extravaganza and found that Michael and Bernadette were busy breakfasting. Ignoring their inquisitive stares he began to prepare his picnic.

'I see your dog broke another track record,' said Michael begrudgingly.

'How do you know that?' Paul inquired.

'Your mugshot's in the back of the paper.'

Worried that renewed publicity from the media could jeopardise his breakthrough with Angela, Paul turned to the kitchen table and picked up the tabloid apprehensively, to find that the annotation was in the sports supplement and the modicum of an article kept in line with its position at the rear in the results section, with no mention whatsoever of the owners' relationship. Satisfied that things were still turning in his favour, he returned to composing the packed lunches.

'I take it that's for your Proddie girlfriend,' sneered Michael.

'No, I'm seeing a Catholic girl if you must know,' Paul lied, not wishing to be dragged into another round of verbal combat with his estranged brother.

Hearing this, Bernadette was none too pleased. Having successfully split Paul and Angela, she was now being led to believe that he had a new girlfriend and that infuriated her. Paul completed his task then started towards the front door.

'Well, I'm off then,' he said, overflowing with self-confidence, 'have a nice day.'

'Paul,' shouted Bernadette, 'can I have a lift over to the Cliftonville? I'm going to see my sister.'

Glancing at Michael, who never raised his head from the tabloid, Paul submitted his response. 'Aye, no problem, but you'll have to come now. I'm running late.'

Picking her handbag up from under the table, Bernadette immediately left the kitchen without so much as a peck on the cheek for her fiancé, sending his jealous mind into overdrive: he said a Catholic girl, but never gave a name and Christ, she was all set to go on the spur of the moment, and she didn't even give me a kiss goodbye, the bastard. Rushing to the front room window, he witnessed them heavily engrossed in conversation as the car pulled away.

'So who's this new girlfriend you've made all the effort for?' probed Bernadette.

'Oh just someone I met at work. It's quite amusing actually.'

'Why's that then?'

'Well she's drop-dead gorgeous and I would never have contemplated asking her out for the fear of rejection, then, would you believe it, she only asked me out,' he divulged, revelling in every second, still holding her responsible for the problems with Angela.

Returning to the kitchen seething with his surmising, Michael looked down the back yard to see Toby all alone, taking a drink from his waterbowl, and a wicked idea flashed across his mind.

Feeling even better for gaining at least some kind of last laugh over Bernadette, Paul pulled into Donegall Square and spotted Angela waiting, wearing an unadorned but stylish summer dress, holding a lemon cardigan, and looking as mouth-watering as ever. Making sure they were not being watched, he drove the car over to pick her up. As they headed in the general direction of Bangor, Paul had just one thing on his mind, something that needed addressing earlier, rather than later in the day, when he'd have given his all only to find out that once more she'd had second thoughts.

'Can you remember all you said last night?' he asked, nervously.

'Aye, course I can,' she replied, bubbling with certainty.

'And did you really mean it?'

'I meant every word, but no pressure, okay? Let's just see what happens,' she returned, then attempted to convince him by placing her hand on his thigh, which sent a nice tingle flowing through his body.

Having planted the seeds, it was now time for Paul to enjoy the harvest of his perseverance.

'So where are we going?' she inquired.

'Either Bangor, or there's a beautiful, secluded lake I know of near Marino train station at Holywood.'

'Oh aye, taken many girls there for a picnic?' she delved in jest.

'No, Michael took me fishing there when I was younger and, you guessed it, all I caught was a cold.'

Parking the car in the small shingled car park at Marino station, they took a ten minute saunter through the dense woodland trail, before arriving at a clearing where long, ungoverned grass and reeds led to the shore of the lapping lake. All alone, they found a sunspot in the wanton rushes near a forest of fresh-smelling fir trees. Spreading the travel rug from the car, they lay down then stared at the few wisps of thin cloud overhead, laughing at what each other could see in them from griffins to greyhounds. At around 1 p.m. Angela remarked that she was a little peckish, inspiring Paul to unveil his masterpiece. Feeding her celery sticks dipped in garlic sauce, she returned the favour by teasing him with a bunch of grapes while he lay on his back, like the emperor Caesar basking in his empire. Neck sore from overstretching for the fruit that she kept dangling, he was willing to suffer no more and pouncing, he rolled her over to swap places in one fell swoop. Placing their lips together, they shared all the passion they'd denied each other for so long. Gently kissing her cheeks, he inhaled her womanly scent before moving down to her neck then breasts, as she smiled with inherent pleasure.

Having bided his time, allowing his temper to ferment while Tommy had maintained his training routine, Michael was pleased to see the freak of the Falls head homeward at 3 p.m. With a wicked glint in his dark eyes, Michael headed into the back yard with his evil supplement in hand and was half way to his objective when Bernadette entered the front door. Pouring a decent measure of blue weed-killing crystals in to Toby's drinking vessel, he quickly returned to the house, grinning in the knowledge that a dog's eyes are always bigger than its belly. As he penetrated the kitchen, he was startled to see Bernadette approaching from the hall. Face turning incarnadine with the insuppressible guilt of being caught red-handed, he quickly turned his back to her and scrunched up the deleterious packet before exiling it to the bottom of the pedalbin.

'What are you up to?' she queried, puzzled by his blameworthy countenance.

'Nothing, I was just catching some sun outside and eating a packet of crisps,' he supplied his alibi. 'So how did Sunday lunch turn out at your sisters?'

'Well, she still manages to burn the roast, but fine thanks. Anyway, I thought that you'd be down the pub with your daddy?' Sunday afternoon at the local was as religious for the male contingent, as going to mass was for the female of the species.

'I didn't really feel up to it earlier, but I think I'll nip down there later for a few jars. Do you fancy it?'

'No, I want to see the third part of the Sidney Sheldon bestseller that your mommy and I have been watching for the last fortnight,' she replied.

When Tommy arrived to take Toby for his late-afternoon exercise and feed him, he noticed that the dog was very tired and sluggish.

Though feeling hot and listless himself in the Mediterranean climate, he disregarded Toby's bizarre, contrasting demeanour as heat-induced lethargy. As he collared the canine, Toby made it quite clear he was going nowhere.

'Come on Tobes,' Tommy coaxed, tugging at the insubordinate animal.

The animal was behaving out of nature and Tommy began to verge on the edge of panic mode, fearing that the radical change spelled something more drastic than he'd originally presumed. Battling against the irrational impulse to fall to pieces under pressure, as Paul had taught him, he assessed the situation and reached a premeditated plan of action. Fixing Toby his meal and a fresh drink, Tommy knew that if the 'gannet' dog turned his nose up at the food then there was indisputably something seriously wrong. Feeding times were unremittingly part of the rigorous training syllabus. And when the meal arrived, Tommy would always keep the bowl lofted high into the air which incited the dog to stand on his hindlegs, strengthening them in his eagerness to eat, but this evening, Toby wouldn't even make the exertion to stand on four. As Tommy placed the food and water by Toby's twitching head, he saw that there was no attempt to eat and that propelled him into seeking alternative means of diagnosis. It was now 5.30 p.m. and there was still no sign of Paul, so Tommy headed home for the tattered greyhound manual, which he hoped might just be worth its weight in the two months of library fines it had accrued, if it held the solution and antidote to Toby's ailment.

By six o'clock the stifling heat had been replaced by a lukewarm zephyr which skimmed across the inviting lake, and the brilliant yellow sun had faded to a smouldering orange that allowed the human eye to marvel at its beauty. Running his gentle fingers through her short dark hair, Paul watched as goosepimples germinated on Angela's bronzed skin.

'I'm gonna miss you more than ever next week,' he said with a deep sigh, understanding that the sands of time were running out on him again.

'Me too, I've had a wonderful day. You will phone me next week won't you?'

'Every night if that's all right with you?'

'Wednesday, Thursday and Friday will be okay. I'm on afternoons for the next two days.'

After packing up the leftovers from their stay they began to walk arm in arm back towards his car. Reaching the beginning of the trail, they looked back at the idyllic setting and mentally agreed that this was their place, their heaven on the hell of earth.

Parking outside his home, Paul saw his father and Michael up ahead in the distance strolling towards their second home. He glanced at his watch with a long yawn and massaged his sleepy eyes before entering the house. Passing the living room, he caught sight of his mother and Bernadette glued to the television set and smiled to himself, perhaps it was possible after all for so many divergent individuals to live unilaterally under the same roof. Pouring himself a glass of water, he looked down the yard to observe Tommy sitting head in hands with a thick tome at his feet. When Tommy heard the back door creak open, he jumped to his feet and surged towards Paul.

'Where have you been? Toby's dying, he won't stand up or eat. I don't know what to do. What's wrong with him?' he allowed the tears of stress and relief to spate.

Rushing to the animal's assistance, Paul noted that the food was untouched and the sprawled out canine's jaws were clamped shut. In observing that the sick dog didn't even possess the strength to move his eyes and look at the visitor, Paul conceived that this was indubitably much more than just a bout of off-coloured, kennel sickness that habitually raged in the summer months.

Looking over his shoulder to where the weeds had shot from the paving stones, Paul wondered if new ones had sprouted since he'd removed them midweek and that he hadn't noticed them, having had more important matters on his mind, like Angela. No authority on plantlife, Paul had thought them innocuous anyhow and it had only been precaution that had motivated him to tear them out. He did, however, know that ragwort and buttercup were poisonous and that they were extremely palatable to greyhounds, but what he had seen growing looked just like thistles.

'We'll have to get him to the vet immediately, he must have eaten some weeds.'

'But he couldn't have,' remonstrated Tommy. 'I never allow him to eat anything off the ground.'

'I'm not blaming you,' stated Paul, detecting that his friend felt culpable about the situation. 'I think it may be my fault, there were a few weeds starting to shoot through the concrete.'

285

'No, I've kept my eye on them all week since you pulled them out, I swear there's been no more.'

Having the tendency to believe Tommy, as his life revolved around Toby's health, Paul began to suspect that foul play had come into this equation. Still, there was no time to initiate a witchhunt at present. Flicking through the Yellow Pages in search of an emergency veterinary surgeon, Paul's cursing to his destination drew the attention of Bernadette, who came into the hall to see what all the commotion was about.

'I think my dog's dying, can you help me?' Paul begged of the vet.

'What are the symptoms?' investigated the unruffled voice at the other end.

'He won't eat or drink, he just lays there inert.'

'Has he eaten any plants?' probed the animal doctor, trying to get to the root of the problem.

'Not that I'm aware of, we're very strict about him trying to nibble anything, seeing as he's a champion greyhound.'

'Okay, you'd better bring him over to my surgery immediately. If you could retrace the last twenty-four hours, then perhaps you may remember something that might help us to treat the infirmity quicker.'

'I'll try,' Paul replied before replacing the receiver.

Having listened to Paul's side of the conversation, Bernadette's mind reverted to earlier that afternoon and Michael's perturbation.

'Paul, we need to check the bin. When I came home this afternoon, Michael had been out the back and he had something in his hands that he obviously didn't want me to see, by the flustered look on his face.'

'You have a look while I get Toby into the car,' he ordered, racing the clock.

Carrying the dead weight of Toby, who sagged like a wet sack of potatoes in his arms, Paul rushed him through the house and onto the backseat of his car. As he was just about to drive off, Bernadette came running out waving the evidence.

'Look Paul, it's weed-killer. Can I come with you?'

'Aye, quick, jump in.'

Screeching the car away, he mopped the sweat from his brow with the same hand that had helped to carry the sick animal, but there was no room for his allergy to encroach upon his irritable crisis, for his pumping adrenaline would see to that.

'It contains Paraquat and Diquat chemicals,' Bernadette divulged, reading the packet. 'Which are extremely harmful to animals.'

'The fucking bastard,' roared Paul, banging his fists on the steering wheel and stepping on the gas.

'He will live, won't he?' pleaded Tommy.

After violating two red lights, Paul brought the car to a halt outside the vet's surgery. Lugging Toby inside he laid him on to the workbench for repair.

'It was weed-killer, we have the offending packet here,' informed Bernadette, handing the surgeon the verification for him to examine.

'Good,' he mumbled, digesting the toxic constituents of the harmful cocktail.

'What's good about it?' demanded Paul.

'Well, at least we know what we're fighting,' he replied.

'So can you save him?'

'There's every chance now that you've got him here, yes.'

Within ten minutes, Toby was well on the road to recovery. After inducing vomiting the vet gave him a paregoric tonic and administered an intravenous saline drip to rehydrate and cleanse his blood of the toxins. Joining them in the waiting room, he told them all to go home as the dog would have to be kept in overnight for observation.

After dropping Tommy off at his home and giving him enough cash to cover the bill when he went to collect Toby next morning, Paul and Bernadette returned home to discover that Michael was still out. Sitting by the kennel cooling off with a cigarette, Paul's thoughts shifted to his heartless brother and to what action he should take, if any. Realising that this was a great opportunity to wheedle her way back into Paul's life, Bernadette joined the philosopher with two cups of coffee in hand.

'I've made you a cuppa. I hope you don't mind?' she treaded lightly.

'No, not at all, thanks,' he smiled, 'and thanks for enlightening me about the dog, you've probably saved his life.'

'Paul,' she said, hesitantly.

'What?'

'I want to clear the air between us and I feel this is as good a time as any. I know you hold me responsible for what happened to Angela, but I swear I had no idea whatsoever that she was a Protestant. In light of this afternoon's episode, couldn't it just be possible that Michael was behind that too? I mean, he has links with all the hoods in this area, but I don't,' she lied, straight-faced.

Pausing for a moment to analyse her words, he deliberated that what may never have seemed plausible, now might just be feasible, in fact more than probable.

'Aye, it must have been him all right. I'm sorry for going off at you back then, I guess I should have made certain of all the facts before jumping to conclusions.'

'There's no need to apologise. I'm just glad that you now realise I could never have done such a dastardly deed and I'm really sorry that things didn't work out with you and her. I thought she was a really nice girl when I got to know her.'

Feeling belittled, Paul thought it only right to reveal to her that he had lied about his and Angela's split, before he checked himself at the last second. The affair had to remain clandestine, and if Tommy wasn't privileged to know the secret, then there was no way he could tell Bernadette.

'So what are you going to say to Michael when he returns?' she asked.

'God only knows, what can I do or say? If I go looking for a fight, win or lose it'll achieve nothing and if I remain tightlipped he'll think he's got away with it. I'm in a no-win situation What would you do?'

'Tell him you contacted the police and they're investigating the incident. They know it was weed-killer and that they're making inquiries. The chances are he bought it earlier today, so that should strike some fear into him.'

With the way the perfect solution had just rolled off the tip of her tongue, Paul began to experience doubt about her once again, she was in all honesty, time-served in deviousness.

When Michael returned home, Paul and Bernadette were still sitting in the pleasant moonlight chatting away and that only served to fuel his jealousy as he stared from the kitchen window, their image stirring his resentment. He staggered down the yard to join the social gathering and stood over them tottering in the mild breeze.

'This is cosy isn't it?' he slurred scathingly. 'Just what I suspected.'

Unable to control his anger any longer, Paul jumped up to face the controversy. 'What the fuck are you rambling on about now?'

Coming between them, Bernadette attempted to referee the impending fracas. 'Calm down, Michael for God's sake, someone's gone and poisoned the dog.'

'Is he accusing me? 'Cause if he is I'll knock his head off,' spat Michael, moving his head around her to deliver his poignant threat.

288

'Oh fuck off, will ye. I know you tampered with the dog's water, maybe I can't prove it, but the police will,' informed Paul.

'What do you mean by that?' quizzed Michael, his temper quelling with awareness.

'They're making inquiries around the area to see if anyone bought weed-killer earlier today and if they find the culprit they're gonna prosecute,' said his fiancé.

'Aye, and then he can kiss my arse with an apology. I'm going to bed, so you pair can carry on with your little love reunion.'

'Don't be stupid, the dog's fighting for its life. Have you no heart?' she castigated.

Heading to the house less popular than a rattlesnake in a luckydip, Michael's petulant mind was not aided by his intemperate drinking and bordered on the outskirts of insanity. Now that she had prised an opening back into Paul's life through a show of cunning compassion, Bernadette retreated for the evening, invigorated with a new lease of hope in regard to her ultimate aspiration, which was making Paul her property again.

Back at sea, Paul struggled to get through each day as his mind constantly gallivanted to that wonderfully illicit, lazy Sunday afternoon by the lake. When he called Angela as promised on Wednesday evening, Paul was delighted to learn that her feelings for him hadn't lessened in any way. In fact it was Angela who was relishing the relationship even more than him now, for she was at ease, since in her mind there were no lingering doubts that he would break off the affair at any given moment. For the duration of their thirty-minute dialogue, Paul thought about every sentence carefully, making sure he never ruffled her feathers with some misconstrued comment that only distance can allow. Forbearing to enlighten her of the poisoning incident helped to keep the conversation sweet, before he ended the call with the pledge of another dose of the same in twenty-four hours. However, it was Angela's terminating words which really put the icing on the cake. Revealing she was missing him and that she couldn't wait to see him again, she smacked her lips to blow him a kiss down the wires and send him into orbit.

When the ship docked in Belfast last thing on Thursday night, things just avalanched to Paul's advantage. About to phone his sweetheart, he was mustered to the bridge. As ever it was Martin South, but on this occasion it was to show his fledgling some receptivity as they walked together alone on deck. Each lit a cigarette and looked towards the scintillating city through the sticky night.

'Paul, I'm really pleased that all the media coverage has died down. I really feared for you for a while back there. Have you had any more thoughts about Mairead?'

'To be honest with you,' perjured Paul, 'I'd rather wait until I'm totally convinced that all the dark clouds have passed overhead, I wouldn't feel too good about taking her out with you know who's dark shadow still looming over me.'

'Aye, I suppose you've a good case there, anyway,' said his boss removing an application form from the inside pocket of his jacket, 'if your friend's still looking for a job I'll need this on my desk no later than next Friday. There's a position about to arise on this ferry in the very near future. I'll be in touch during your next trip.'

Taking the questionnaire with an enormous smile, Paul almost shed a tear of joy for his best friend at the thought of how he'd react to the fantastic news.

Heading to phone Angela, slightly worried that calling her an hour later than planned might incite her temper, he was pleased to discover that once again there was no ostensible indication of an ebb in the tide of her commitment towards their courtship. Talking for approximately half an hour again, the main topic was Tommy's opportunity to shine at the interview, that he had in not so many words been guaranteed to land. Each determined to blow the last kiss, when Paul's money finally perished, he was so self-possessed, fired and inspired that he decided to remind Tommy's mother she'd pledged to return his call, an obligation that thus far she had failed to fulfil.

Having run to hide from her compunction, Tommy's mother hadn't had the slightest intention whatsoever of contacting Paul again, hoping he'd empower her to leave her afflictions behind once and for all.

'Hi, Mrs O'Brien, it's Gerry's friend again. I've waited patiently, but still no word from you.'

'Aye, well, I'm still mulling it over,' she replied, bothered by his persistency.

'What's there to think about? Either you want to see your son again or you don't.'

'Maybe, but it's not as simple as that. I can't just come over there at the drop of a hat, I have work commitments, I'd have to ask for some time off work etcetera,' she replied, making excuses.

'So you will come then?' Paul forced, demanding a decision.

'I didn't say that. I need more time.'

'Well how long are we talking here? Life's a short business.'

'Okay son, I promise I'll phone you next weekend. I'll have reached a decision by then. You don't expect to be welcomed with smiles and open arms when you've run out on someone, now do you?' she stated, finally revealing the reason for her hesitancy.

'I'm telling you, you're in for a pleasant surprise. Gerry doesn't care about the past, he even understands your motives. It's not a great deal to ask, a few days from a lifetime, now is it?'

'I'll call you next Friday,' were her parting words.

Putting the phone down, she looked to the ceiling, stricken in the awareness that this ghost from her past could not be exorcised until she found the courage to confront it head on.

Come Sunday, Paul punched the air of another humid Belfast evening. A full week off work and, for once, a light at the end of his tunnel; seven days where he intended to cram in as much activity as possible. Joining Tommy as soon as he arrived home, he learnt that the dog was making steady progress under his partner's instrumental fine tuning. Having come home very weak, Toby was now getting stronger with every day and the lost weight was gradually returning as his appetite went from nibbling to insatiable greed.

In their last communication, Paul had revealed to Angela that the dog had suffered the indisposition of kennel sickness and needed plenty of time to recuperate, so the midweek trial she had suggested was completely out of the question. However, barring any additional setbacks, a Sunday morning solo run on the last day of Paul's shoreleave was a date for the diary. When Tommy had finished bragging to him of last week's training itinerary, it was Paul's turn to impress his colleague. Reaching into his back pocket, he pulled out the folded application form with the red cross penned on to the top right-hand corner, which would draw Martin South's attention to it when it lay in the mind-boggling swarm upon his desk later in the week.

'My boss says there's a vacancy set to arise on my ferry in the next couple of weeks. We have to fill this in and return it as soon as possible, then you'll get an interview. He didn't actually confirm that you'd definitely get the job, but he gave me the impression that even a mediocre interview from you would be enough to secure the position.'

Almost expecting Tommy to do cartwheels up and down the yard, Paul was quite stunned to note little if any enthusiasm from his friend, perhaps he too was dumbfounded by the incredulity of the announcement.

'I thought you'd be over the moon,' Paul expressed.

'I am, but who will look after Toby?'

'To be honest, I've already given that a great deal of thought. I think the poisoning scare was just a warning of worse to come, don't you? The time may have come for Toby to go home to Dublin, he'll be safe and well looked after there. We can go and stay over at the weekends, do you think that makes sense?' prodded Paul, expecting the worst reaction.

'Aye, you're right, I'll miss him but it has to be for the best. He won't have to go before I start work though, will he?'

'Of course not,' replied Paul, putting his arm around him for comfort.

'So, do you really think I will get this job?' Tommy asked, his excitement now welling from the inner out, showing Paul that he'd really meant his last statement.

'I'm almost certain, and I'm convinced you'll be seeing your mother soon too. I spoke with her on Thursday night and she said she's gonna phone me this Friday, she has a lot to organise at her end so she can have time off work to come visit you for a few days.'

Overjoyed to learn the second part of the double-header of good news, Tommy hugged the bearer as if he'd just given him the gift of life, and now Paul could only hope that his own final declaration turned out to be genuine.

With Angela's continental work rota apportioning her time off on Wednesday and Thursday, they had resolved to spend her first day off by returning to their lake were the heatwave to continue, so Paul granted Tommy and Toby one hundred per cent of his time on the run up to his next date. On Tuesday, for the second consecutive evening, Bernadette brought Paul a coffee, bidding to lubricate his tongue into divulging what was happening in his social life. Watching them share a drink and a smile, Michael clenched his fists and gritted his teeth before heading off to the pub again.

Wednesday June 1st began where May had left off, as the hot spell akin to Angela showed no sign of letting up. Just kissing and cuddling in the long sheltering grass by the lake was the closest thing to heaven either of them had ever experienced. She'd asked him to take it slowly and being the perfect gentleman, he respected her wishes, fearing that putting one foot out of line might import disaster. Sitting in the car near Marino station on Thursday evening, they agreed that their next meeting would be when trialing the dog at Dunmore on Sunday morning. Having spent another splendid afternoon together, it seemed such a shame to put their love on hold until then, but that's the way both understood it had to be. In Paul's mind it would be harder for him to get through the next few days, but he didn't know how wrong he could be. About to embark on the twenty-minute journey back to Belfast, Paul turned on the radio. For three minutes as the car engine idled, they sat in silence moved by a beautiful ballad where every single word related to their insuppressible feelings for each other:

The song was 'Never Tear Us Apart' by INXS.

Taking her teabreak at 6 p.m. on Friday evening, Angela found that she'd been all at sea for the first half of her shift, becoming clumsy and forgetful in her work. Nibbling at a sandwich, she discovered that her appetite had no interest in food, only in Paul. Feeling that if she could just hear his voice once it would feed her addiction and get her through to Sunday, the temptation became too great to resist. So using a public payphone, she dialled his number to hear Bernadette on the other end of the line.

'Can I speak to Paul?' she inquired nervously.

'I'll just get him, who's calling?'

'It's Angela.'

As she made for the backdoor to inform Paul of his call, Bernadette's suspicions began to magnify again. Yelling him from the kitchen, she quickly disappeared into the living room so she could listen in on the conversation.

'Hi, I thought we'd agreed to keep this all secret,' stressed Paul.

'I know, I'm sorry, but I just needed to hear your voice, I'm having a nightmare at work. Anyway I thought you'd be glad that I called you, aren't you missing me?'

'You know I'm missing you and I am pleased you've called, I just don't want anyone to know we're seeing each other. Listen, how about I pick you up after work?' he suggested.

'I'd love that,' she replied, 'I'll be out at ten o'clock.'

They blew each other a kiss and their business was concluded. Walking back to tell Tommy that it wasn't his mother on this occasion, Paul felt light-headed at the way she'd broken their rules in her insistence to be near him and suddenly he sensed that their relationship could become more unadulterated now that she'd given him the sign to move forward.

'Sorry Tom, it wasn't her, but it's early yet. She said she'd call and I'm sure she will.'

'I think I'll take Toby for a walk, I can't stand the suspense,' Tommy said.

'Well, I'd better wait here in case she calls,' said Paul, looking to relish some free time in which he could funnel his thoughts into his next move with Angela.

After giving Tommy a good few minutes to clear the scene, Bernadette came marching out with her arms folded, unaware that Michael was just arriving home from work.

'You told me that you weren't seeing her any more,' she barked.

'I thought you were over that now?' questioned Paul. 'You won't say anything will you?'

'I'll never get you back, will I?' she asked, beginning to cry.

'Please stop that,' he begged. 'I love Angela and I always will, we've moved on, can't you find it within you to be as happy for me as I am for you and Michael, even after all the trouble he's caused me?'

'But I don't love him,' she sniffed through her deluge of tears.

'Come on, you have to rid me from your mind, I'll never be available again,' he emphasised.

Spying on them from the kitchen window, Michael himself felt a tear of bitterness squeeze itself from the corner of his eye. Turning away at the final straw of his brother holding his fiancé close to alleviate her heartache, he knew that this was the sight that had finally broken his back. Totally enraged, he left the house in a condition of apoplexy then began to wander around the neighbourhood searching for the ultimate retribution.

The unmistakable echo of the telephone parted Paul and Bernadette for the final time and racing for the phone, Paul was relieved to hear Tommy's mother at the other end.

'Okay, I've made my decision, I'll come over for a few days to see Gerry, I think I owe him at least that.'

'Brilliant,' exclaimed Paul. 'So when is that likely to be?'

'I have five day's holiday booked in for a week on Monday, that's June 13th, so I'll be over on the evening ferry from Stranraer on the Sunday.'

'That's excellent,' he gasped, 'I'll be working on that ferry, so I'll be able to give you star treatment. And it's my last trip of that week, so I can give you a lift into Belfast. Have you booked your ticket yet?'

'No, not yet,' she replied. 'I'm driving up to Stranraer and I'm going to leave my car at that end, so I'll buy my ticket when I get there.'

'Well, don't buy a ticket. I'll be able to get you a free ride over the sea. I'll call the night before to arrange where and when I can meet you.'

'Oh, thanks. Just before you go there's a few other things I have to tell you.'

'Go on,' urged Paul.

'I've got lodgings at Fortwilliam, and it's imperative my husband doesn't know I'm in Belfast, do you understand that?'

'Aye, completely, not a word will pass my lips,' he assured.

'That's part of the reason I don't want you to tell Gerry I'm coming just yet, besides, I want to surprise him there and then.'

'Aye, that'll be something,' beamed Paul.

'Okay until I hear from you next Saturday, keep an eye on him for me, will you?'

'Will do,' he confirmed.

Reverting to the backyard, Paul found that Bernadette had gone and Tommy had yet to return. He lit a cigarette to kill the time and smiled thankfully at the sky; things just couldn't get any more expedient. Reflecting back on that swig of whiskey on the coach ride home, where he'd first met Tommy, Paul, a self-confessed atheist, was now having his doubts about the existence of God. For it now seemed to him that it was more than just a coincidence of fate which had brought together those two down-and-outs from the brink of tragedy, to the pinnacle of success. When Tommy arrived back, the first thing he noticed was two crystal glasses of amber liquid winking at him from their perch on the roof of Toby's kennel. Gazing towards Paul, his smiles brought tears of joy as he saw his best friend casually nod.

'When's she coming?' he demanded, awash with emotion.

'Soon,' Paul replied. 'I've no exact date, but it'll be before the month's out. There is one thing she asked me to tell you. She doesn't want you to tell your father that she's coming over, will you be able to keep that secret?'

'Course I will.'

Raising their glasses for the toast, they both had a lot to smile about.

* * *

295

Having walked around in circles, bemused for a few hours, Michael found himself all alone on a park bench with only a bottle of whiskey for company. It seemed befitting that he should have ended up in this vagrant posture, considering he appeared to have lost everything from his girl, to his mind. Drinking beyond the argumentative state, he strained his eyes across to the RVH with its shimmering lights and he could've sworn blind that he saw Paul's car pull into the carpark. Staggering out of Dunville Park and across the busy road to the irate shouts and loud horns of motorists as they attempted to avoid running him over, he slumped on to the perimeter wall and squinted his eyes at the dancing number plate in the distance. Widening his eyelids and stretching his face to focus properly, he observed that indeed the registration number was T414 LBA, and that was the number of the satanical beast that was making his life hell. He wanted to go over, right that instant and crack Paul's head open with the bottle, but he tripped over his own legs and ended up slouching back over the small dyke. Raising his head for air, he watched as Angela ran to his brother's vehicle and got in. Not seeing straight as it was, Michael was now more confused than a dyslexic librarian, all he could discriminate, however, was that Paul was still seeing a Protestant. As Paul's car raced past the drunk underpinned by the wall, by the time the down-and-out had hoisted his flagging senses and managed to launch his missile, the target had zoomed off into the night.

Paul parked the car in the centre of Belfast and put his arm around her as they stared at the full moon suspended in the night sky, and it maddened them to think they were curtailed to this no-man's land of the city. Caressing with an intense, innocent passion, both parties were reluctant to part for the night, but all good things must come to an end. Watching her bus as it pulled away, Paul turned on the radio and he smiled in disbelief as the same sweet sonnet they'd heard at the lake soothed his heart.

They returned to the charade of platonic entrepreneurs on Sunday morning to watch Toby struggle around the circuit inuring himself in a time of 30.50, which wasn't as bad as it sounded when taking into account that only a fortnight ago he had been knocking on heaven's door. Paul explained to the racing manager that the below par trial was down to a viral infection, and he suggested a competitive run a fortnight on Saturday to sharpen Toby's race fitness. Deciding to spend their last afternoon together at their special haven near Holywood, Angela found herself back in the Falls en route while they dropped off Tommy and Toby. She was persuaded by the assured invincibility of being in Paul's secure presence to enter the premises of 6 Clonard Street. With Paul's mother still at mass, his father and brother down the pub, the sole confrontation was with Bernadette who acknowledged her with a long-lost hypocritical smile.

At the end of another momentous afternoon, as they sat in Paul's car the mood had decayed to slight depression in the knowledge that a week apart would test their resolve to the limit.

'What time do you start in the morning?' she asked.

'6.30 for the 7.30 crossing,' he sighed.

'I'm gonna miss you.'

'Me too, but I've bought you something to remind you of me. Open the glove compartment.'

Like any female, the thought of a gift brought a wide-eyed and excited response. Following his map to the treasure, she opened the storage chest then removed the plastic 45 r.p.m. disc that had become their tune. Smiling at one and other, they fell into each other's arms and kissed their final moments together goodbye.

The next morning he locked his car, then, swinging his holdall over his shoulder, Paul turned to face his penitentiary for the next seven days. Heading through the tranquil morning to the terminal, he felt bitter at having to return to work now that his freetime had turned so sweet. Passing through the automatic sliding doors, there she stood to confirm just how much love's pendulum had swung to his prosperity of late.

'I had to see you,' she said, excusing herself in case her presence was embarrassing him in front of his work colleagues who were steadily flowing into work.

Grinning from ear to ear, he picked her up, swung her around then placed his lips to hers. All smiles, they parted after a few minutes, but when Paul looked back he experienced a cold shiver of dread running through his body; it was a presage that he knew only to well, as if the world was about to collapse from under his feet. Loitering to blow her a kiss, he wondered whether to rush back into her arms or board the ship. Telling himself it was all in his love-dizzied mind, he crossed the gangway to begin his stint.

They communicated by wire around her shift patterns and the week dragged by, not ameliorated by the soaring heat, as for six sultry days there was not a cloud to be seen over the British Isles, allowing the nation to bask in an equatorial climate which had the weathermen chanting for rainfall as they cried 'drought'. Finishing his shift sticky with sweat, Paul headed straight for a cool shower to freshen up before making his phonecalls. First, he called Cleveland to confirm that Tommy's mother hadn't undergone any eleventh hour change of heart. Itinerary discussed and agreed, he moved from business to pleasure.

'So when will I see you?' he said.

'Well, Toby has a race a week tonight,' teased Angela, with a sober voice.

'You're joking aren't you?' he moaned, upset by her renewed, patent lack of interest.

'Aye, I'm pulling your leg. I was hoping that I could see you tomorrow night after I finish my shift, then we could discuss some plans for next week. Does that suit you?'

'Aye, but I won't get home till after ten. I have to drop Tom's mommy off at her lodgings on the way.'

'Oh well, if you don't want to,' she baited.

'Oh don't be daft, you know I do,' he returned, convincingly.

'Well, if Tommy's at your house, I can see Toby and wait there with him until you get back, as long as he meets me after work,' she suggested.

'Are you quite sure you feel comfortable with that?'

'I want to see you, don't I? Besides, this week's been so long and lonely, I need a big cuddle. Get Tommy to meet me outside the RVH at 10 p.m. and make sure he brings Toby.'

'I don't really like the idea of you walking on the Falls Road at that hour of night, but I suppose if Tommy's there it should be safe enough, just take care will you,' impressed Paul.

Hearing the pips, he fumbled in his pocket for another ten pence that would buy him the precious time he needed to tell her what he really wanted to say.

'Angela.'

'What?'

'I love you, you know. Are you still there?' he asked upon hearing a long silence.

'Aye, I'm still here. I'll see you tomorrow, take care.'

Tossing and turning in his bunk all night, saturated with the airless humidity, Paul wondered if he'd reached too high, too far, too soon.

Departing Belfast Lough on his penultimate sailing of the week, the heat was stiflingly unbearable. Fidgeting and agitated, he smashed two plates and cut his finger before he was ordered to take a smoke break in case he passed out or had a serious accident. Standing on the blustery deck, Paul perceived the blackest clouds he'd ever seen assemble to swallow up the sun which had dominated the skies for over a week. Although it was a midsummer's afternoon, it looked more like a spooky eclipse from a horror movie in fast-forward mode. He gazed over to the dense forest at the edge of the Lough shore and he could make out, by the arching trees, that a fierce gale was gathering speed with every minute.

Paul had returned to the galley when the ferry was half way across the sea, and this was when the steel vessel commenced to rock and roll and the cutlery began to dance to the good vibrations. Flinching instinctively as he heard a loud rumble accompanied by a grinding groan, he almost jumped from his skin as the public address system crackled into life. An announcement was made over the loudspeaker that adverse weather conditions had forced the ship's navigator to activate the gigantic stabilisers. When the ship anchored in Stranraer at teatime, the heavens cracked open with a brilliant flash of forked lightning and the torrential downpour began in earnest. Watching, spellbound, as the electrical storm sparked to life and the rain lashed on to the countryside, Paul saw steam rising from the parched land to refuel the angry clouds. Within an hour, the moderate winds had soared to force nine on the Beaufort Scale, which signified that the next crossing would have to be postponed if there was no lull in the next half hour.

With no foreseeable end to the storm, a decision founded on safety was announced at 6.30 p.m. to a chorus of sighs from the passengers sheltering in the ferry terminal and the depleted crew onboard. 'Due to the adverse weather conditions and gusts in the excess of seventy-five miles per hour, it is with deep regret that the captain has to inform you that this evening's crossing has been cancelled until further notice.'

Absolutely distraught at having to spend another night away from home and Angela, Paul suddenly remembered that she was going to meet him at his home, and that brought anxiety.

Subsequent to an unsuccessful attempt to call home from the ship, Paul headed onshore to find a working payphone and to meet Tommy's mother, so he could help her locate accommodation for the night, now that it seemed highly improbable the storm would pass to allow a sailing that evening.

When Paul first set eyes upon Mrs O'Brien across the abandoned waiting area of the terminal, he was pleasantly surprised. Although he had had a rough indication as to what she looked like from the old photograph that Tommy had once proudly shown him, he'd expected the years of alcohol abuse to be evident in her overall appearance. Yet this was not the image he now bore witness to. Petite at five feet two inches, she had medium-length blonde hair and her dress sense was one of flawless professionalism. With cosmetics and jewellery worn sparingly for the utmost effect, she portrayed a woman at home in a man's world, but it had been no overnight transition from rags to riches.

For, when she'd arrived in England with resolutions more than aspirations, her first task had been to beat the bottle. At times it had been excruciatingly tempting to revert to the loser's way out as door after door had banged shut in her face but, determined to conquer and succeed, she'd finally secured employment in a bank and within months, thanks to the carrot of promotion, she'd worked the craving from her system. It wasn't until Paul was close up that he could observe the scars of her past life in the fine thread veins etched across her weathered face. As she stood up to greet Paul, she found through her eyes, that he too, was not the type of individual she'd expected to befriend her introverted, anomalous son. For one thing, he appeared normal.

Over in Belfast the weather was no different as a thunderstorm battered the city and threatened to turn the streets into rivers.

As she sat watching television, Paul's mother glanced at the clock on the wall just as the phone rang at 8.30. Looking across to Michael and Bernadette who were enthralled on the settee, she sighed at them before heading to answer the phone.

'Mom,' Paul panicked, 'is Tommy there?'

'I wouldn't have thought so in all this weather. Why?'

'It's looking increasingly unlikely that I'll get home tonight, the winds are too strong,' he said. 'I've organised it with Tommy to meet Angela from work, he's supposed to bring her over to the house so she could spend some time with Toby, then I was going to drive her home. So do you think you can let him know what's happening. Can you tell him to meet her, but to make sure she goes straight home after work. Also, ask him to come back to ours and I'll call him around 10.30, I have someone here I'm sure he'll want to talk to. Will you do that for me, Mom? It's really important.'

'Aye son, I'll see he gets to know,' she replied.

300

Returning to the livingroom, she asked Michael and Bernadette whether they'd seen or knew where Tommy would be.

'Why?' quizzed Michael, 'who was that on the telephone?'

'It was Paul, it looks like he won't get home tonight because of the storm and he was supposed to be giving Angela a lift home when he came back. She's coming here to see the dog after her work, so he wants her to know that she's not to bother now,' his mother said without thinking, more intent on catching up on what she'd missed of the concluding part of the bestseller that had ruled her life for the last month.

'Leave it to me,' assured Michael, 'I'll go find him and explain.'

'Thanks son, you're a gem, oh, and by the way, will you advise Tommy that Paul's gonna phone him at 10.30, he has something important to tell him?' she said, returning to her bag of boiled sweets.

'Will do,' he replied, heading to the kitchen with an evil glint in his eye.

With all the thunder and lightning, Tommy had decided to stay inside the kennel to calm the petrified animal and having spotted him earlier, Michael was aware of this. As Michael stooped to poke his head inside, Tommy almost jumped from his skin.

'Paul's just been on the phone for you, he said he's gonna call you back at half past ten tonight,' Michael betrayed, before turning away to initiate his cold-blooded plan.

'But why will he call then? He's supposed to be home at ten,' shouted Tommy.

'Aye,' said Michael softly, as he racked his brains for a quick-fire solution to suppress Tommy's suspicious mind. 'Oh, he said he's gonna be late, delayed due to the storm, I guess that's why.'

'Okay, thanks,' replied Tommy, convinced by it all.

Making straight for the telephone, Michael called a fair-weather friend whom he knew through his dealings for the Cause. Asking for his assistance, he revealed his sick intention which would bring parity between him and his brother.

Paul returned to the ship after arranging to meet Tommy's mother at ten and headed straight for the bridge to find out exactly when the meteorologists had forecast that it would be safe to sail again. Learning that the ship could not launch until 7.30 the following morning, he was also informed that Martin South had earlier attempted to contact him, leaving a message for him to return his call at the earliest convenience. With the restoration of the onboard telecommunications, Paul got through to Belfast first time.

301

'Ah Paul, thanks for such a swift response, bad news about the weather, never mind I've some good news. Your friend Gerry O'Brien, I've booked him on a survival course at Jordanstown Technical College Wednesday, so will you inform him immediately? If he comes down to the office either tomorrow or Tuesday at the latest, my secretary will have his contract ready for him to sign.'

'So he's got the job?' gasped Paul, thinking that perhaps it was true after all that every cloud did indeed have a silver lining.

'Aye, I said that didn't I? He starts Wednesday, don't let me down.'

'He won't,' returned Paul, 'he won't.'

Having worried all the time over Tommy's ability to perform under the immense pressure of an interview, suddenly, at least one burden had been lifted from Paul's overworked mind. His reference had been more than sufficient to persuade the Onboard Services Manager that Tommy was the man for the position. Heading back to meet Tommy's mother, Paul couldn't wait to hear his friend's response at the other end of the line when he called to play the part of Santa Claus.

Back in Belfast, the wind and thunder had elapsed, but the rain, which had now subsided from torrential to moderate, remained. Meeting Angela, as Paul had earlier instructed him to, Tommy revealed that he was running a little late, due to the terrible change in the weather, yet she knew that was merely a cover to get Tommy's mother to her Bed and Breakfast. Walking the short distance from the hospital to Clonard Street, the severe weather and Tommy's safeguarding presence had calmed her fears about making this perilous journey, as anyone with any sense had taken refuge from the battering electrical monsoon, so the Falls Road was desolate as they joined it. Turning into Clonard Street they proceeded onward chatting merrily, neither minding the cold raindrops nor noticing a bright yellow Ford Escort parked on the corner with two figures in the front. With Toby put to bed for the night, they knocked at the back door and were greeted by Paul's mother.

'Paul said that he would phone me after ten,' said Tommy nervously, 'is it okay if we come in and wait?'

'Aye of course, come away in out of that dreadful rain, I'll make yous both a hot cup of tea.'

Seeing Angela, she could only presume that Michael had failed to find Tommy earlier and had no doubt used the whole thing as an excuse to escape to the greener pastures of the pub, where he'd now be grazing with his father.

At 10.30 p.m. on the dot, Paul rang from a phone box in Stranraer.

'Tom, I mean Gerry, is that you?' he probed, minding his manners in front of Tommy's mother, who was huddled beside him in the confined booth.

'Aye, but why did you call me Gerry?' he asked.

'I have some news, first the bad. We can't get home tonight,' he hinted that he was not alone, 'and the good news is that you start work on Wednesday.'

'Really?' asked Tommy, dumb struck by Paul's revelation.

'Aye, survival course till Friday, then you're out here with me on the high seas, but wait before you go dancing naked in the rain, I've even better news for you.'

'Even better than that?' wheezed Tommy, now that it was all beginning to sink in.

'There's someone here who wants a word with you,' he said, passing the phone to his friend's mother who began to speak timidly, not too sure as to how she'd be received.

'Gerry, it's your mommy.'

'Mommy,' he said, sobbing with exuberance, 'are you coming to visit me?'

'Aye son, I'll be over in the morning. Are you still mad at me?' she asked, gently.

'No, Mom, not at all, I love you.'

'Good,' she said, feeling her own tears welling. 'Listen, son, please don't tell your father I'm coming over to see you, he mustn't know I'm in Belfast. I'll explain everything tomorrow.'

'I promise Mom.'

'So how do you feel?' asked Paul, back on the other end of the line.

'I can't believe all this is happening.'

'Well, you'd better, and you can buy me a pint out of your first week's wages,' Paul bantered, savouring the news as much as his best friend. 'Anyway, did Angela get her bus okay?' he changed the subject, reflecting on his own happiness of late.

'No, she's right here beside me as I speak.'

'But I passed a message on to my mom to tell you I probably wouldn't make it home tonight. Tom, I need you to make sure she gets a taxi home straight away, I'm not happy about her being over there as it is,' he stressed, anxiously.

'Don't worry, I'll make sure. Would you like to speak with her?'

'Aye, but it'll have to be quick, my money's running out fast.'

'Where are you Paul?' she asked, unaware of what was happening.

'I'm stuck in Scotland, Tom will explain everything. I want you to go home immediately and I'll call you tomorrow when I get home, what time's best?'

'Any time before one. I will see you tomorrow night after work, won't I?'

'Of course you will, I'm gonna get cut off now. So please get home safely.'

'Aye, stop getting stressed, I'll be fine. It's deadly quiet on the streets anyhow.'

As his money evaporated and the line went dead, Paul didn't even get the chance to blow her their customary parting kiss. Still holding the receiver, he looked towards the turbulent, swirling current of the Irish Sea and if he'd have thought that those were the last words he'd hear from her honey-sweet lips for a many moons to come, he'd have fought Poseidon there and then, and swam to be by her side.

Obeying his last request, Angela asked Tommy to escort her to the Falls Road, where she could hail a taxi and he duly obliged. As they walked through the incessant rain towards the main drag, Tommy excitedly revealed all his good tidings. Nearing the corner of Clonard Street, as they laughed and chatted freely in the anticipation of what tomorrow would bring, they were brought to an abrupt standstill by the dazzling halogen headlights of a parked vehicle, which almost blinded them into submission on the spot. Heads tilted backwards as they strained their eyes, they saw two men sporting dark ski-masks and one of them was pointing a pistol in their direction from the window of the passenger door.

Chapter 11

Like a Rolling Stone

One of the armed raiders leapt from the car and made his intentions crystal clear through the pitch-dark night.

'You get in the car, and you fuck off,' he spat with venom in his words, attempting to frighten off Angela's chaperone.

Still high on the emotions of his good tidings, Tommy stood his ground reluctant to run for his own life. It was his duty to make a stand for his best friend after all he'd done for him.

'Are you fucking deaf?' panicked the gunman, grabbing Angela around the neck, forcing a loud shriek.

'Let her go,' demanded Tommy, fearlessly.

Backing his captive into the car, the kidnapper kept the gun pointed at Tommy who was inching his way forward awaiting the optimum moment to strike. Bundling her into the car as if she was dirty laundry to a washing machine, the masked man turned to observe that Tommy had pounced to make his move. Seeing the courageous figure flying towards him through the pouring rain, Michael's accomplice lashed out with the pistol catching Tommy across the right temple, sending him crashing on to the concrete unconscious, his shoulder taking most of the impact, as his head missed the kerbstone by a fraction of an inch. Catching sight of her partner collapse on to the ground and not sure whether he had been shot in all the pandemonium, Angela began to scream hysterically for help.

Joining her on the back seat, the gunman began to wrestle with her in an attempt to muffle her cries for assistance, as in the driving seat

305

Michael put his foot to the floor heading deep into the Falls. Managing to restrain her with one hand cupped around her nose and mouth, her assailant pressed the cold-steel gun barrel deep into her left temple, making sure she got the impression that he meant business, then began to catch his breath as hers hyperventilated with the panic of what lay in store. Finding it increasingly difficult to breathe through the heavy hand blocking her airways, her eyes bulged in their sockets as she strained from the back of her throat to draw his attention to her condition of asphyxiation. Quickly realising that her captor was immune to her pleas and that her life would probably end at these men's hands sometime in the very near future, she instinctively retaliated. Sinking her teeth into his sweaty palm, he squealed like the rat he was before cracking the gun across her head. As Angela fell limp to the blow, her tormentor threw her to the side then inspected the teeth marks.

'Fucking bitch bit me,' he roared, to numb the pain.

Looking into the rear view mirror, Michael saw that Angela was unconscious, which allowed him to utilise his vocal chords. Leaning over to the glove compartment, he produced a roll of tape and a tiny polythene bag containing a minute piece of paper.

'Here, do the business,' he urged, passing the goods over his shoulder.

Removing what resembled a miniature postage stamp with a pronounced strawberry usurping the queen's head, his accomplice prised Angela's languid jaws apart, then placed the acid tablet on to her tongue before commencing to handcuff her with the tape. Fifteen minutes later, as the chemicals began to incubate in her system, Michael brought the vehicle to a standstill outside a derelict factory on a stretch of waste ground which was often used by the IRA, serving its purpose as a weapons stash, hideout and, on some occasions, a torture chamber. Swapping places with his colleague in the rear, Michael set about violating the love of his brother's life.

As he tore at the blue nurse's uniform, his heart raced with the thrills and spills of his despicable act of savagery. And when he heard the voluptuous rips as he divested her, they only incited his carnal appetite as he hungered to satisfy his arousal. Using only his mask for protection, Michael entered her with a sordid thrust devoid of finesse or remorse. Feeling the sharp burst of pain, Angela suddenly regained consciousness, yet was unaware of what was occurring as she lay in a pool of her own perspiration, heaving her way into a new dimension whilst hallucinating over the last incident she could remember, which was the conspicuous sight of the pistol pointing at her through the rainy night. With a battalion of shimmering japanned guns trained upon her body, she moaned for salvation as a volley of iridescent flashes shot into her brain.

'By the sound of her, I think she's quite enjoying it,' mocked the lookout, who was abnegating his responsibilities in favour of ogling the live sex show through the rear view mirror, whilst enjoying a cigarette.

With the exception of the occasional spasm of a grunt, Michael maintained his silence throughout, disinclined to chance the potency of the narcotic. After firing his ammunition into her, he climbed off then left the vehicle to cool down in the welcome rain. Removing his mask, he mopped his brow, lit a cigarette and inhaled deeply as he reflected upon the old saying that revenge is always sweeter.

The rain persisted in cascading from the heavens, soaking Tommy to the skin as he lay incapacitated in the gutter, his face growing paler by the minute, whereas the river to the drain flowed red. It was now nearly an hour since the fierce blow to the head had sent him to sleep and not one person had walked the street to precipitate his revival.

Stubbing his cigarette out on the ground, Michael turned to see that Angela was shivering and restless as she fought the haunting images that were bombarding her subconscious.

'Come on,' he whispered, 'let's dump her before they send out a search party. Do you think she'll remember any of this?'

'Not a thing. It'll be another five or six hours before she comes back down to earth,' assured Michael's abettor.

'Good, let's get out of here then. We'll drop her off in Dunville Park, that way they'll think she was raped leaving work.'

Masks discarded, they drove sensibly back towards the Falls Road, so as to avoid being pulled over for something so trivial, such as a failure to indicate or breaching a chevron in the middle of the road, not that that would guarantee them safe passage. The RUC and security forces had a tendency to stop any young men driving late at night within that vicinity. Youths bred their own suspicion, especially when driving with exemplary attention for other road users. Stopping at the entrance gates to the park, they cut the lights and waited until Grosvenor Road was clear of the intermittent taxis and ambulances ferrying patients to and from the RVH. Slinging the delirious Angela over his shoulder, Michael used all his

307

strength to carry her into the deserted grounds. Laying her down gently his eyes darted around the angles of three hundred and sixty degrees, before he casually strolled back to the car satisfied that no one would appear in court at a later date to point the finger at him. Breathing a deep sigh of relief and smiling he turned to his partner in crime.

'Drop me off at home, will ye Sean? I'm literally shagged. I think it's best if we stay out of contact for a while, at least until they convict some poor bastard.'

'Aye, yer not wrong there,' laughed the driver, twisting his neck to check his blind-spot.

Now that a Protestant girl had been raped in the Nationalist vicinity of the Falls, the RUC would do more than everything in their power to bring someone to justice, even if it meant that an innocent took the blame. When the story leaked to the press as it always did, the public outcry would not only spark a reaction of broad condemnation, but also widespread rioting. With the exceptional advantage of having the law on their side, in reality the RUC were to Ireland's Catholic North as the Klu Klux Klan were to America's black South. Founded on bitter prejudice, these were the people who had failed to intervene when a gang of Loyalists set upon, and murdered, a young Catholic as he walked home with his sweetheart. Suffice to say, any left-footer would fit the bill, as in their illiberal minds every Nationalist was a criminal against their denomination. Unwarranted house searches would begin, known sex offenders would be hauled off the streets of shame, grilled and beaten until at least one of them confessed, and someone would, for someone always did, since the RUC were masters of that game. Most likely because they'd had plenty of practice over the years.

Turning into Clonard Street, Sean slowed down the car upon spotting Tommy still lying by the side of the pavement, forming a porous dam between the running water and the drain.

'Do you think he's dead?' he probed, with a mellowing anxiety creeping into his voice.

'I'd better check,' replied Michael.

Kneeling over Tommy's blanched, frozen body, he checked his pulse and felt a flash of inspiration flow through his fingertips. Turning to face the driver, he gave a thumbs up then jogged back over to the vehicle to reveal their alibi.

'I've just had a brainwave. Go home then call the police anonymously. Tell them you witnessed a struggle outside the RVH earlier and that you recognised the male as Gerry O'Brien of 16 Odessa Street. I'll make sure he makes it home in time for his visitors.'

Waiting until the car's red tail lights had vanished into the drizzly, damp darkness, Michael walked over then dragged Tommy on to the pavement. Slapping his face gently and shaking his body to persuade a revival, Tommy stirred to life, his head splitting from the pain of the bang, which had already discoloured his cheekbone deep purple below the abysmal gash over his eyebrow.

'Tom, it's me, Michael. What happened to you?'

Still dazed, he glared into Michael's mendacious eyes before his head slumped again. Raising Tommy's head, Michael patted his cheeks once more, attempting resuscitation. Forcing his eyelids apart, he stared into the vacuum of Michael's face before his brain finally reactivated, as he relived the car's incandescent lights flashing on to dazzle him.

'Angela, where's Angela?' he coughed, spewing out some of the rainwater that had found a bed in his throat.

'What about Angela?' delved Michael, hoping to learn exactly how much of Tommy's amnesia had worn off.

'We were attacked,' he spluttered hysterically. 'I have to find her.'

'Calm down, let's get you home.'

Helping him up, Michael gave him his shoulder to lean on before they began staggering towards Tommy's home. Reclining him on to the sofa in the front room, Michael persuaded him to rest on the promise that he would go and look for Angela. Waiting until Tommy had slipped back into his slumber, Michael smuggled himself home then climbed upstairs to bed.

At 12.45 a.m. the RUC received an anonymous phone call from a male, worried that he may have witnessed a nurse being mugged, or worse, raped by the local simpleton near the entrance to Dunville park.

Angela's father detested working night shifts, and particularly during the marching season which was only a month away from swinging into full flight. The moonlight hours brought apathy, this was the period of the day when your body clock slowed down to deplete the senses, making you vulnerable to attack, especially at the moment when it was least expected. It was also prime time for the nocturnal terrorists to make mischief, as like vampires they'd wait for the sun to go down before coming out to draw blood and put people in coffins. Taking the message of a disturbance in the Falls, a cloud of trepidation penetrated the armour-plated Land Rover in which Bill Hamiton was a passenger. Learning that he and his colleague might have to pick up a twenty-one-year-old Catholic for questioning, they immediately called for army assistance, fearing resistance. A second unit was dispatched to check out the park near the RVH, as no distress call had been made from the victim, that's if there was a victim. The IRA were well renowned for making nameless phone calls, to lure the security forces into their territory where they'd be met by booby traps or violence. It was therefore custom and practice to take no chances in the likelihood of this being the case.

As they entered Clonard Street at 1.15, Bill Hamilton and his driver glanced at each other bemused, for once the streets were spine-chillingly silent. Usually the mere sight of the RUC in this part of town was greeted with the clattering of dustbin lids and an insurgent gang of missile-throwing youths, but not tonight. Pulling up outside Tommy's address, they waited patiently for an incoming report from the second unit less than half a mile away, while their army counterparts positioned themselves at the back entrance to the house.

Cordoning off all the entrances to the park, the security forces cautiously began to search for explosives and perhaps a body. Laid in the swampy grass covered in her own vomit and with her eyes wide open staring at the dark sky, Angela had been trying to find her feet for the past hour, but her brain, full of the delusory narcotic, was paralysed from providing the signal her limbs required to function.

'Over here,' shouted a young soldier in a cockney brogue.

Shining his torch into her eyes, he could see by the way they rolled, that although her lights were on, nobody was home.

'I think you'd better call for an ambulance, she looks to be in a bad state of shock,' the private informed his sergeant, who had just arrived on the scene.

Chivalrously covering her half-naked body with his flak jacket, the appalled soldier was in effect risking his own life to save her from the hypothermic rain and shock. As Michael would have it, Angela's handbag was conveniently situated by her side, the strap wrapped tightly around her wrist just beckoning for attention. Forced to take a back seat, the army presence was upstaged by two RUC officers, whose jurisdiction it was now within to take control of the operation from here on in. Using his investigative training, the younger constable began to search through

310

the contents of her handbag for identification, until he found a kidney donor card which gave them all the information they lacked.

'Her name's Angela Hamilton of 22 Riga Street, wherever the fuck that is.'

'Oh fuck, no,' ululated his elder, 'she must be Bill's daughter, he lives at that address. Christ, he's up at the suspect's house now. What the fuck do I tell him?'

Shaking his head as he stared with pity towards Angela who laid shivering on the wet turf, he clicked on his short-wave radio then gave the green light to the task force suspended on red alert at Odessa Street.

Switching off the crackling radio, he stared into his partner's dismayed eyes then shouted indignantly. 'Well, could you tell your friend his daughter has just been fucking raped? Because if you could, then you're more of a fucking man than I am.'

In a lightning strike reminiscent of the Iranian embassy hostage crisis in 1980, when the SAS shot themselves to instant stardom and the coveted number one position in the popularity charts, the joint RUC and army venture emulated those 'one hit wonders' by completing their daily task and keeping a life intact to boot. Before Tommy had time to say 'taratatatat,' he found himself rights read and under arrest. Bundled into the back of the battleship-grey vehicle, disorientated and bewildered, he was whisked away at high speed towards the RUC headquarters for interrogation, while the army stayed behind to ransack his home for any evidence.

Having earlier radioed in their position and horrendous discovery, the RUC patrol at Dunville Park had followed Angela to the hospital, where they would hold a vigil by her bedside, giving her security while she was diagnosed and treated, as well as being ready to take her full statement when she returned from the immersed trauma she appeared to have sunk into.

Still stupefied and attempting to clear his mind through his quandary, as well as the blinding headache that was tearing his senses apart, Tommy fell forward when the vehicle jolted to a halt. Eyes squinting from the bright halogen floodlights shining in his face as the doors opened, he could make out a huge brick wall supporting coils of razor wire. Suddenly an immense fit of panic brought him back to life when he realised that he was in RUC custody. Focusing to remember the past, he could see Angela being taken hostage at gun point through the pouring rain.

'Why am I here?' he asked, timorously.

'Get out, come on, move it,' roared one of his abductors.

Frog marched across the wet tarmac of the compound, Tommy gulped at the sweet fresh air as if he knew that he was about to be submerged for a long time. Thrown into an ice-cold cell, he buried his head into his knees and began to whimper uncontrollably upon hearing the solid steel door thunder to a close and the key clink to shut out his freedom. What lay ahead was a nightmare without sleep.

At the hospital, indulging in a cup of hot tea and the talent menagerie on offer, as some pretty and some not so pretty nurses paraded back and forth, the RUC officers employed their usual numerical rating system to the opposite sex, as they awaited the medical verdict.

Back at the station, Constable Bill Hamilton and his partner were about to be debriefed, as with coffees in hand they joined their superior. Wishing that he'd taken early retirement, their bald-headed senior pensively collected his composure before delivering the grim news.

'Okay lads, we're still awaiting confirmation from the RVH, though it does look like rape by all accounts, but I hope to God it's not,' he revealed, massaging his eyeballs to relieve the mounting stress.

'Why's that?' the constables chorused.

'I'm truly sorry,' he whispered, looking Bill Hamilton in the eye before returning his attentions to the documents he'd previously been fumbling with for amenity.

For ten discerning seconds a penetrating silence consumed the room then Bill began to quiver with the ignominy of the innuendo. Springing off his chair, he smashed his fist against the wall and began to vociferate ferociously, refusing to believe.

'No, it can't be, for fuck's sake tell me it's not true.'

'Bill, Bill,' his senior's voice ascended to mute his irate subordinate, 'sit down will ye. I know this is difficult, but we don't have confirmation of anything yet. All we have to go on is that the identification found on the girl belonged to your daughter. I know it's bad enough, but there's a good possibility that she's only been mugged.'

'I'll kill the fenian bastard,' he roared, his tempered rage returning with a vengeance.

'Bill, for Christ's sake, will you steady yourself? I think it's best if you go to your daughter's side, there's nothing you can do here,' his boss propounded.

'No, I want to be in on the interrogation with the sick bastard,' he insisted, growling through his teeth, spraying his hatred across the room.

'I don't think that's wise,' returned his superior, glancing at Bill's tacit partner whose face had turned as white as the walls.

'No,' said Bill, 'how would you feel if some bastard raped your daughter? Could you just stand there and politely bribe a confession out of him with the pleasantries of cigarettes and coffee, knowing full well that he'd screwed yer wee girl?'

Although the officer in command gave no verbal reply, biting his lip, he rendered his thoughts with a slow shake of the head and a deep sigh.

As for Tommy, he was still weeping a Dead Sea of tears and shivering like a hydraulic drill, as his thoughts shifted to Paul and to what he would think if he saw him in this immature state of cerebral collapse. Raising his head to see if it was all a dream, he wiped his livid face with the sleeves of his cold damp jersey and found that it was frighteningly tangible. Chilled to the bone in his soggy clothing, with chattering teeth and trembling blue hands, he scanned around the accommodation which was furnished with only a wooden bunk and grey blanket. Stretching his quivering arm out, he pulled the bedding towards him in an attempt to regenerate some warmth into his aching body, then began to study the masses of graffiti which adorned the walls and merged to form a definitive wall of remembrance. With the gradual transition of heat steadying his limbs, he began to think positively. With no idea as to why he was being held and even less of an inkling that he was about to be indicted for rape, Tommy was sure that when the light of morning arrived, Paul and his mother would come and bail him from this shit-creek which he had somehow drifted into.

Over in the RVH, Angela was lying, eyes dilated to childbearing extremes. Head rolling back and forth in spasms of paranoia, her psyche floated elsewhere on a magical supersonic carpet ride, tripping through a kaleidoscope of time where she lived the medley of epochs that her history tutor had fascinated her with as an adolescent. So tired, deranged, distorted and misrepresented, the fear of victimisation, persecution and the alien environment her brain tortured her with sanctioned no sleep. Pinning her startled eyes to the doctor and his assistant as they attempted to clean her up and diagnose her ailment, the squelching of their feet and the clinking of the kidney bowl precipitated visions of a floor covered in bloody organs and the Tinman from The Wizard of Oz, which celeritously led her to the evil face of the Wicked

313

Witch of the North, with her huge, pulsing wart beetling over her face ready to explode a deluge of scalding puss. Squinting her eyes to see a trolley laden with surgical knives, Angela imagined ten-feet long scalpels raining down on her and the doctor laughing at her with a syringe in his hand the height of the leaning tower of Pisa.

Leaving her under observation and in the capable hands of the duty nurse, the consultant left the room to inform the RUC constables of his findings.

'Rape?' inquired one of the officers, rising to greet the specialist.

'Most likely, within the last few hours I'd say. We found traces of fresh semen so there's definitely been sexual activity.'

'When can we interview her?' the other policeman asked.

'Not at present, that's for sure, she's under the influence of drugs, either acid or magic mushrooms so it has to run its course. I'd imagine she'll be coming back down to earth in around four to six hours and then she'll want to rest.'

'Will she remember what happened though?' the constable asked, addressing his notepad.

'Oh aye, eventually the pieces will all fall into place one by one, but that can take up to two days. Whoever did this is very dangerous and knew what they were up to,' concluded the doctor.

'Aye, well luckily we got a tip-off. His feet won't touch the ground, you can be sure of that.'

Leaving his fellow constable to complete his memorandum, the auxiliary policeman updated the station with the worst news possible.

Tommy was startled when he heard the heavy door grind open. Turning his head to greet his jailer, he saw a flash of luminous stars before he felt the pain rush through his nerve-endings.

'Come on get up, you dirty bastard,' yelled one of the two men in green uniforms he could see materialising through his blurred vision.

Feeling a warm but wet trickle down his face, he placed his hand over his right eye and touched the thick blood which was beginning to flow to cloud his sight.

'Get up will ye, for fuck's sake,' pierced the same voice, lashing his foot into Tommy's ribcage.

'Come on Bill, that's enough,' whispered the other policeman, who was no longer visible to the prisoner.

Instinctively curling up into a ball to repel the savage boots, Tommy cowered in intense shock as the severe agony flitted around in his

314

meagre body. Squeezing his eyes tight to shut out the loud dogged barks of the indignant man, he suddenly felt a rugged heat scorch through his knees, as his captors dragged his tense carcass like sandpaper across the floor and out into the corridor. When the voices and footsteps had faded into the early morning, he opened his eyes warily to observe that he'd been transported to another cold, grey and confined room with only a table, two chairs and a lustrous light bulb suspended from the dark intangible ceiling. Raising his nose he could smell the strong pungent odour of undiluted disinfectant which began to nip at his stinging eyes. It was an ironic smell that reminded him of Toby's kennel and the dirty protest the morning after the dog had been imprisoned the night before. Yet not even reflecting on his greatest love could mollify his situation, as he worried whether the animal would come to harm in its attempt to find food, now that he was not going to be there to supply its breakfast. Making out the faint pitter-patter of approaching feet, he scrambled under the table then readopted his hedgehog posture.

'Come on, son, sit in the chair and I'll get you a cup of tea. Would you like that?' offered a calm motherly voice which momentarily allayed Tommy's fears.

Knowing that the suspect was a Catholic, the rule book went out of the window to be replaced by an RUC kangaroo court, where if you didn't ask for legal representation then no one was ever going to enlighten you.

Tommy timidly revealed his head and saw that this man was different. For one he was dressed as a civilian in his white shirt, paisley-patterned tie and shiny black trousers. In shifting his head to the side Tommy could see that the two uniforms, although present, were now silent as they guarded the door and Detective Inspector.

'Bring two cups of tea,' ordered the man in plain clothes, before returning his attentions to the accused. 'Are you gonna come out from under there? I only want to ask you some questions about your whereabouts earlier tonight. The quicker we clear this mess up, the sooner we'll all get home.'

Feeling comfortable with this man, combined with the sight of Bill Hamilton leaving the room, encouraged Tommy to nod his head in agreement and battle the surges of pain to crawl towards the chair.

'Good lad,' commended his inquisitor to be. 'We'll get you that hot drink then we can begin.'

When Bill Hamilton returned with the tea, Tommy's fear was reinstated instantaneously, for this man's unforgettable loathing face had become the Mona Lisa to reopen his gallery of offenders, which the happiness of the last few months had managed to paint over. Cupping his trembling hands desperately around the polystyrene cup to allow himself a much-needed drink, he begged his nerves to bring the cup to his parched mouth, but they would not be denied forcing the red-hot liquid to jump over the sides to burn his lips and scold his fingers. The shock upon shock expeditiously evidenced that on this occasion two wrongs do make a right, as stability was resumed. Swiftly returning the cup to the table he sucked at the instant blisters which had swelled on his bottom lip.

'Okay Gerry, my name's Detective Inspector John Robertson. I'm going to be asking you some questions regarding a serious incident, failure to co-operate will just prolong things. It's up to you. So tell me, what's your name and where do you live?'

Having never told a lie in his life, Tommy wasn't about to start now.

'Do you know Angela Hamilton?' quizzed the detective.

'Aye,' he replied.

Pausing the pen he was using to make notes, the plaintive raised his head and looked into the defendant's eyes. 'You do?'

'Aye, she's my friend.'

'And were you with her tonight and if so between what times?'

'I met her outside the hospital at 10 p.m..'

'Then what happened Gerry?'

'We went to our friend's house.'

'Do you have any witnesses to that?' he stepped up the interrogation, keeping his eyes scanned for prevarication.

'Aye, Paul's mother made us a cup of tea while we waited for him to call us. We thought he was coming home tonight, but he got stuck in Scotland because of the harsh weather. He works on the ferries and I start work next week too,' he beamed with pride.

'So what happened next?' the detective went on smugly, already jumping to his own conclusions.

'Paul phoned and told me to make sure Angela got a taxi home.'

'And I suppose that's the last time you ever saw her?' he declared sarcastically before continuing with the questioning. 'Well, did you put her in a taxi?'

'No. There was a car with bright lights and a man with a gun grabbed Angela, I did try to fight him off but that's the last thing I can remember.'

'Well, you're gonna have to try a lot harder, because a passer-by reported you struggling with a girl meeting Angela's description and now she's lying in hospital drugged up to the eyeballs, and she's been raped. Did you do that Gerry?'

'No, she's my friend,' he pleaded.

'Were you attracted to her?' instigated the detective, changing his tact.

Hesitating for a long hard think, Tommy could find no answer in his search for the answer to that extraneous question.

'You raped her didn't you? Did she tease you into it?'

'No,' shouted Tommy, flustered by the defamatory accusations that were penetrating his exhausted mind.

'But you did rape her, didn't you?'

'No, I told you before, she's my friend. I can't remember what happened, my head's so sore,' revealed Tommy, beginning to rock to and fro on the chair clenching his teeth in his search for an alibi.

'She put up a good fight didn't she? You slipped her some drugs and she still fought hard, that's where the cut over your eye came from. I'm sure our forensics will be able to match your blood to the traces I know we'll find on her handbag,' he continued to bombard him with disparaging theories.

'No, no, no, ask her,' retaliated Tommy, venting some temper under the intense pressure.

'Oh, we intend to as soon as she's fit to talk and then you'll wish you'd never been born. Have you any idea what they do to your kind in prison?'

'But I tell you I've done nothing wrong,' whimpered the suspect.

Glancing at his watch, the detective noticed it was fast approaching 4 a.m. and decided it was time for a break in the proceedings.

'Okay Gerry, we'll take a breather. You have a serious think while I go and find out if Angela's spoken yet. If you want anything that might help you see clearer, like cigarettes, food or drink then the constables will be more than happy to see to your request.'

Walking past the two RUC officers stationed at the door, one of which was Angela's father, he whispered his verdict: 'Guilty.' Turning to take one last look at Tommy, he could see by the way the internee was sobbing head in hands that the cracking process was well underway.

At just after 4 a.m., Angela began to see clearly, the misty paranoia had evaporated and her pores were slowly beginning to close as her mouth opened. At first she smacked her lips together, demanding attention from the nurse who was more interested in monitoring the glossy magazine that she was engrossed in, than her arid patient. Making no significant headway in gaining a response, Angela began to moan for service. Supplying her groggy patient with a cool drink of water the nurse tilted Angela's head to the glass allowing her to quench her burning thirst.

'Where am I and what's happened to me?' she gasped with a weak cough.

'Just take it easy,' instructed the nurse, 'I'll go and get the doctor.'

Making sure the detective had left completely, Bill Hamilton moved forward to apply some of his own brand of interrogation. In his mind, which had twisted on the accumulation of the inspector's cross-examination of the suspect and his wife's impending outcome, there was no possibility of Tommy's innocence.

'Do you know who I am, you fenian bastard?' he growled, swiping away Tommy's hands, which had been supporting his heavy head.

Nerves jangling with the fear of another beating the prisoner just shook his head.

'I'm Angela's father and I want you to take a good look at my face,' he imposed, grabbing Tommy's jaw then moving within a millimetre of his terrorised face. 'Because when you've finished getting fucked off every bent bastard inside, I'll be waiting for you when you get out and then I'm gonna castrate you and that's a promise.'

When the doctor arrived at Angela's side a few minutes after the nurse had left to hunt him down, her eyes had been so heavy from the match sticks of the acid tablet that she had quickly drifted off into a heavy sleep, denying Tommy the crucial alibi he sorely needed. Leaving her to rest the consultant returned to the RUC constables who were themselves experiencing difficulty in combating the soporific tedium of the wait.

'Well, at least the drugs have cleared from her system,' he disclosed.

'So can we have a quick five minute chat with her?'

'No, not at present, she's fallen asleep.'

Passing on the news update to headquarters, the constables were ordered to hold their position at the RVH until the reinforcements of the day shift arrived to sustain the surveillance and receive the answers that only the reinstatement of Angela's consciousness could provide.

Bill Hamilton's partner who had stayed rooted to his guardsman position near the door speaking and seeing no evil, was the first to hear the footsteps of the returning Detective Inspector.

'Bill, the DI's coming back,' he tattled, throwing his voice across the room with an urgent whisper.

Giving Tommy a taste of things to come with a light slap across the face, he imperturbably returned to his wise monkey stance at the door.

'Well, Gerry,' said the DI, holding a fresh cup of tea, 'Angela has regained all of her faculties. So don't you think it's about time you started to come clean and tell me the real story?'

'But I've told you all I know,' replied Tommy dispiritedly, wondering why Angela's revival hadn't resolved this catastrophe with an apology and instant emancipation.

'Are you quite sure?' he impugned.

'I'm telling the truth. You couldn't have asked her,' retorted Tommy, totally confounded by the torment.

'Well, the funny thing is, she made a statement saying that it was you who attacked her,' he lied, paying close attention to the suspect's face for the little tell tale signs that his years in the job could read.

'No,' he began to sob, 'that's impossible. I'm her friend.'

Having noted that Tommy's vocabulary and poise was less than average if not abnormal, the DI began to subject the accused to some serious psychoanalysis and indoctrination, which he hoped would produce the confession he was endeavouring to extract.

'Okay Gerry, here's how I picture last night's events. You've had a soft spot for Angela for quite a while, now haven't you? But you didn't know how to approach the situation, because you're not too wise, are you? You've never had a girlfriend, have you? Then along came Angela and because you shared the same interest in life, stop me if I'm wrong, but you thought in your tiny little mind that she was your girlfriend, so you made a move and she shunned you just like all the girls before and even all the kids at school, 'cause you haven't had many friends, have you?'

Hearing no reply as Tommy's self-esteem was ripped apart at the seams as he relived his schooldays, the speculative psychologist continued with the slanderous onslaught in his bid to succeed.

'Anyway, your dreams of being normal were shattered when she turned you down flat, so you had no option. Nobody likes rejection, that's right Gerry, it wasn't your fault, the little tart deserved it, so you decided to teach her a lesson, didn't you? That was the way you saw it in your mind. She was strong, though, and she put up a damn good fight, hence that bruise you're sporting, the one that stunned your senses. So you see, you were telling the truth about one thing, you really

319

can't remember inflicting the damage, can you? You lost control when everything went blank in your mind and with the force of her resistance against your head, you lost your humanity returning to the basic animal instincts and you raped her, didn't you?'

In the background seething at the analysis, Bill Hamilton clenched his fists and curled up his toes to quell the urge to commit Tommy to the biggest hiding of his insignificant life. Sitting there head pounding from the propagandising allegations, Tommy began to claw at the depths of his mind as he felt himself slipping away. Scratching for the answers, he now pondered as to whether it could actually be true. Here was this man with the fine physique and eloquent tongue versus the underweight, shy failure, that everyone throughout his life had taken great pleasure in making him understand he was.

'You raped her, didn't you, Gerry?' he berated, loudly.

As if a swarm of bees were buzzing in his brain clogging up the honeycomb of his mind to make any train of thought impossible, he collapsed under the crushing strain.

'Fuck, fuck, fuck,' snapped the DI, 'I almost had the bastard there.'

Glancing at his watch, he yawned. It was now 5.30 a.m. and the birds outside as well as those inside Tommy's head were chirping out an incessant chorus. Moving to the door, the senior policeman addressed the constables in a huddle.

'Take him back to his cell, he's physically and mentally drained. Bring him round and make sure he gets a good hot breakfast inside him then let him sleep for a while. I'm gonna head up to the RVH, the girl will be coming around for questioning soon, then he'll have to admit it.'

For the duration of the sickening interrogation, Bill Hamilton's hatred and anger had burgeoned with every minute that he'd watched Tommy play dumb and use his idiocy to his advantage. Like a trapped hair follicle that had turned septic and filled with the poison of his temper, it was just a matter of time before the boil ruptured to release his pain. Tommy was that lance.

With each constable taking an arm to support Tommy's limp body back to his cell, he stirred to life under the crude manhandling. Seeing the petrol-green uniforms which had scarred him so much that evening, fuelled him to make a break for the door without an ounce of thought. It was Bill Hamilton's brain that followed suit, snapping with a flash of insanity, he bolted after Tommy with his truncheon drawn. As he meted out the punishment and the first of many crushing blows rained upon

Tommy's shoulders and skull, Angela's eyes blinked wide open over in the RVH.

'Okay, Bill, for fuck's sake that's enough,' shouted his partner, who had allowed his pent-up work mate just enough time as he saw fit to release his frustrations.

Through the exhilarating madness which had consumed him totally, to such amplitude that he could not see or hear anything, Bill continued to beat the living daylights out of the man suspected of raping his flesh and blood. Racing to Tommy's rescue the second constable brought Bill back down to earth from his almighty high with a fierce right hook, which sent him crashing to the floor.

'I said that was enough,' he panted, shaking as he stood over his coleague.

Turning to inspect the damage, he saw that there was a visible hollow spot in Tommy's cranium a few inches above his forehead, which impelled him to check for a pulse.

'Have I killed him?' inquired Bill, in an ice-cool tone of nonchalance.

Feeling a faint palpitation in Tommy's neck, his colleague turned to answer the question. 'He's still alive. Listen, Bill, if we get him to hospital right away, he may live. I'll bear witness that he attacked you, we have evidence of that,' he said examining the trembling knuckles of his right hand. 'We'll say in the struggle he smacked his head on the wall, no one will make any waves.'

At the break of dawn, as the ambulance screamed towards the RVH, Tommy lay prostrate, clinging tenaciously to life like napalm to a Vietnamese village.

321

Chapter 12

Knowing Me Knowing You Is the Best I Can Do

At 6.15 a.m. on the cold, grey summer's morning of June 13th 1988, Gerry O'Brien was pronounced dead on arrival at the RVH. Only five minutes later Angela Hamilton was making her statement, explaining how Gerry O'Brien had been a hero the night before as he had attempted to protect her honour from a masked gunman. Relieved to be alive as the memories of last night came flooding back, she soon found this being overshadowed by the retention of the rape. Prescribed a light sedation for the scarring trauma, she soon slipped back in time, dreaming of the cherished moments at the lake, innocent of the knowledge that Tommy was dead.

Upon hearing that the number one, and only, suspect had lost his battle for life and had then been awarded with a belated alibi, Bill Hamilton made straight for his daughter's bedside, not so much as to be there for when she needed a comforting shoulder to cry on when the calming sedatives wore off, but to make sure she understood that her statement would have to be retracted. With blood being thicker than water, he was convinced that he could persuade her to have a rethink.

Entering Belfast Lough, Paul sloped off for his traditional cigarette break where he met up with Tommy's mother as earlier scheduled.

'Terrible morning, isn't it?' she remarked, becoming more nervous with every passing nautical mile that was taking her closer to Northern Ireland and her past life.

322

'Aye, but I wouldn't care if it was snowing,' declared Paul, 'I just can't wait to get home to see Gerry's face and Angela.'

'Who's Angela? Is she your girlfriend?'

'Aye,' beamed Paul, 'we're getting there.'

'Does Gerry have a girlfriend?'

'Not at present, but I'm sure someone will come along soon.'

Sitting holding Angela's hand as she slept peacefully, her father looked at her more closely than he'd ever done before. Somewhere along life's highway he'd abandoned her, missed her developing into the pretty young woman she'd become. Smiling at how much she now reminded him of his wife before cancer had come between them, he suddenly remembered that his wife was unaware of the situation. Versed that when Angela left hospital she'd require some sort of counselling, he was also aware the first person she'd look to for comfort was her mother, so any thoughts he might have had of enshrouding last night's obnoxious adversity were soon dispelled. Gently kissing her cool forehead he left her side to find a telephone.

'Liz, it's me.'

'What's happened? Why haven't you been home this morning and where the hell's Angie? She didn't come home last night,' she demanded, needing an explanation for the hours of distress she'd been made to suffer.

'Listen to me Liz, something's happened to Angie.'

'Oh God no. Is she all right? Tell me she's all right,' she screamed at him down the wires, siphoning some of the stress that had been accruing since late last night.

'For heaven's sake, pull yourself together and let me explain,' he rebuked, slapping her across the face with his tongue to numb her hysterics. 'When Angie left work last night, she was attacked near Dunville Park . . . and raped,' he revealed, squeezing his eyes to shut out the pain that the last denigrating word brought.

Although she wanted to shout, scream or cry, nothing would pass from her lips as the shock waves penetrated her fragile body.

'Are you still there Liz?'

'Aye,' she stuttered quietly, still trying to come to terms with the news.

'She's sleeping now, when she wakes, I'll bring her home. She has a nasty bruise to the side of her head where he clubbed her, but thankfully no broken bones. She's gonna need you to help her through this crisis.'

323

'I know,' she acknowledged, staring into space. 'Bill, I want you to promise me that you'll catch this pervert and bring him to justice.'

'There's no need for that,' he began to reveal, 'we pulled him in last night. Someone spotted him attacking her and reported it; he's dead now.'

'For God's sake, you didn't kill him?'

'Of course not, he had an accident. Oh Christ, I warned her about those Catholic friends of hers. How could she betray me and keep on seeing them after all I said?'

'What do you mean?' she probed, puzzled as to what Paul had to do with any of this tragedy.

'That stupid greyhound partnership, it was one of them who attacked her.'

'Paul?' she asked flabbergasted.

'No, the one who didn't look all there. Gerry O'Brien.'

'Surely not, judging by his photograph in the newspaper he looked as if he couldn't hurt a fly. Are you entirely sure? It doesn't add up,' she contended, not convinced that the indisputable culprit had been netted.

'It was him all right,' he asserted. 'Looks can be deceiving. Remember, I come into contact with the scum of the earth every day, so I should know. I want you to change the telephone number immediately. When this leaks to the press they'll be swarming around us likes flies around shit, and that's the last thing Angie's gonna need when she's trying to rehabilitate. Will you do that for me?'

'Aye, you're right,' she sighed, sniffing back the tears.

'Okay honey, I'll see you when I get home.'

Dropping Tommy's mother off at her Bed and Breakfast in Fortwilliam, Paul arranged to bring Tommy and pick her up at midday so they could all go for a spot of lunch. Driving up the shoddy Falls Road, the dreary overcast skies and fine drizzle only added to his escalating contempt for his background and he had a stark sentiment pass through him that he had to make a bolder effort to get out while the tide had turned in his favour. It wasn't the materialistic aspect he yearned for, because he didn't fall into that category, it was love and peace of mind that he longed for above all else. Mind seduced by the endless possibilities that the world offered, he'd always envied the crown-financed explorers from yesteryear, who'd sailed off into the horizon with no preconception of what dangers or pleasures lay ahead on their boundless travels. It was the romance of it all which persuaded him that this was his only way forward, all he had to do now was induce Angela to put aside her benighted fears and join his ship of dreams. Smiling to himself as he parked the car outside his home, he reflected on the days of Columbus and Cook and how much easier it would have been for him living in that epoch, for back then he could have simply press-ganged her aboard.

Heading past the grumbling acoustics of the vacuum cleaner hard at work in the living room, Paul entered the kitchen and looked down the yard for Tommy. Seeing Toby alone parading in impatient orbits, he thought it strange that on a day of such magnitude, the star of the show was nowhere to be seen. Filling the kettle he mused over the situation. It is quite early after all, Tom'll be here any minute, he's probably smartening himself up for his reunion. Agreeing with himself that that had to be the case, his thoughts commuted to Angela. Taking his mother a cup of coffee in an attempt to suspend her noisy cleaning activities so he could make the telephone call in peace, he was about to find out that something was seriously wrong.

'Ah, there you are,' she scorned, letting him know he wasn't flavour of the month.

'Here, I've made you a coffee,' he sighed, handing her the peace-offering. 'What have I done wrong now?'

'Not you, your friend. Tell him I want a word in his ear when he finally materialises.'

'Why, what's he done?'

'That dog of yours has been whining all morning, he's never been anywhere near to feed it.'

'That's strange,' Paul commented, feeling the butterflies of unease begin to flutter their warning of impending catastrophe, worried that the job offer and nerves of meeting his mother had frightened him into sequestration. 'I'm sorry, I'll make sure it doesn't happen again, besides Toby will be moving to Dublin in the very near future.'

'Well, you better,' she reprimanded.

'So you fed Toby then?' he inferred.

'Aye,' she moaned in reply.

'I just have to make a quick phone call, then I'll go find him and get to the bottom of all this.'

If things had got off to a bad start they were about to snowball into disaster. First Paul was met by an engaged tone as he attempted to contact Angela. Replacing the receiver, he swallowed a mouthful of coffee to quench his lassitude and swayed as to whether he should try again in a few minutes, or head out in search of Tommy. With pessimism gathering momentum, Paul ruled that a confidence booster in the form of Angela's voice was what he required to thrust him into action. Picking up the phone, he redialled then heard the ring tone at the other end which began to disperse his nerves instantaneously.

'Is that you Angela?' he asked upon distinguishing a female inflection.

'No, who's this?' demanded the voice.

'It's me, Paul, Paul O'Donnell. Is that you Mrs Hamilton?'

'Aye, it's me,' she confirmed, acrimoniously.

Detecting the hostility in her voice, an air of apprehension swept through him more profound than he'd ever experienced before in his life.

'Can I speak with Angela please?' he asked tamely, almost apologetically.

'She's not here, and even if she was, you'd be the last person she'd want to talk with right now.'

'Why, what's happened?' he panicked, confounded by her attitude, 'I've just returned home this minute from Scotland.'

'Your friend Gerry O'Brien raped my daughter last night.'

'No,' gasped Paul, turning white, 'that's not possible.'

'I want you to stay away from my daughter. I'm sorry that's the way it has to be. This telephone number is getting changed today, so don't bother trying to contact her. If you really feel anything for her you'll leave her alone, find someone else.'

As a tear trickled from the corner of his eye and his lips curled and trembled, he cleared his tight throat to speak. 'So where's Tommy now?'

'He's dead,' she said, with slight remorse emanating from her oration.

Feeling as though a million ravenous piranha fish were stripping him to the bone, he stood paralysed in disbelief at her revelation.

'He couldn't have done something like that,' he defended, unwilling to accept what she was saying, let alone the fact that Tommy was dead. 'This has to be a set-up.'

'Just keep away from my daughter,' Angela's mother stressed, before hanging up on him.

For over an hour Paul just stood, stunned at the cross roads of his kitchen window wishing he could turn back the hands of time twenty-four hours. Every time his thoughts winged to Angela he felt guilty at being able to have them, when she was still alive and Tommy was dead, yet even the monumental onus which would become his crucifix for

326

many a moon to come would not permit him to mourn his deceased friend, as his love for her was too strong. A glance at his watch broke him from his crippling depression. It was nearly 11.30 and he was supposed to be collecting Tommy's mother in half an hour for what should have been a tear-jerking reunion as opposed to a heartbreaking identification.

With his mind frozen in disbelief, Paul drove automatically to fulfil his commitment. Almost asleep at the wheel, suddenly he thundered his foot to the brake as with a flash of cold sweat his brain engaged in the nick of time. With head held in hands he peeked through his fingers to look upon the zebra crossing he'd infringed and observed that he'd missed the pram by a whisker. Gasping for air, he rolled down his window and allowed the head wind to keep him awake and focused, before continuing onward to Fortwilliam, thankful that he had not been the cause of a second death in as many days.

Sensing a gentle tug on his limp hand, Bill Hamilton stirred from the light sleep he'd drifted into. 'How are you sweetheart?' he asked, soothingly.

In need of solace and a supportive family face, Angela let her emotions pour out. Opening his arms to her, she was about to discover that the rape was to have longer lasting consequences than she could have ever imagined. Nuzzling into her father's chest, his rich, overpowering male scent turned her stomach and instigated an immediate barrier between her and the male species. It was an odour that would linger to haunt her for ever, the rancid smell of rape, and it brought with it the disease of misanthropy, an ailment that no course of antibiotics could fend off. There was only one miracle cure for that on the planet and only on her journey through life might she discover the somebody who held the key to that medicine cabinet. Pulling away, repulsed by the nauseous smell, she made her request.

'I want to go home now. I need to be with mommy.'

'I know that, I'll get you out of here as the soon as the doctor gives his authorisation,' he replied, understandingly.

'No, I want to go now,' she said, tyrannically.

'Okay, sweetheart, whatever you want. Angela. . .' he paused, letting her know that something was playing hard on his mind.

'What, Daddy?'

'I realise this isn't a good time, but oh God, I don't know how to say this.'

327

'What's the matter?' she probed anxiously, worried that her mother had passed away in her absence. 'Is mommy okay?'

'Aye, she's fine. You gave a statement this morning saying that this Gerry O'Brien lad didn't attack you. Are you completely sure?'

'I'm positive, he attempted to save me. Where is he anyway? Was he shot in the struggle? He is okay, isn't he?'

Sighing aloud as he looked to the ceiling for assistance, he gave her the brutal truth. 'No, no, he's dead.'

'No, he can't be. He had so much to live for, it can't be true,' she pleaded, bursting into another fit of tears.

Scanning around the room, unable to look her in the eye and wishing too, that he could turn back the clock, he set about explaining the predicament. 'Angie, I know this may sound selfish right now, but you must retract your statement.'

'What?' she quizzed, mortified at her father's ungratefulness towards the boy who'd given the ultimate sacrifice in attempting to save his daughter's life.

'We received an anonymous phone call last night which led us straight to the O'Brien lad. When questioned, he confessed, attacked me then attempted to escape. In the skirmish, he fell into a wall and later died of a brain haemorrhage on his way to hospital. You see, what you've said will only bring prolonged suffering. The courts will insist that you have counselling with a psychiatrist and you'll be dragged through hell with this avowal, they won't leave you in peace. I'm sorry, but the lad's gone, we can't bring him back. If they find out he's innocent, the media will be hunting a head because he died in RUC custody and they'll want me as the scapegoat. Do you realise what effect this will all have on your mother?' he queried, throwing the responsibility on to her.

Staring through him, Angela could decipher the deceit in his eyes. 'You killed him, didn't you? Didn't you?' she screamed, unleashing her pent-up anger through her voice.

'Calm down,' he urged, looking towards the door to see if anyone had been alerted to her frantic broadcasts. 'No, it was an accident.'

'I won't let him take the blame, someone raped me and I want him brought to justice,' she stated.

Accepting that his daughter could not be swayed in this volatile time of distress, he decided to put the situation on hold for the time being.

'Angie, I don't want you ever going near that other boy again. I've had our telephone number changed, I think that perhaps we should all get away from here for a while, take a holiday somewhere nice and warm. I've heard Spain's nice. Just do one thing for me, promise me you won't talk to the media, please.'

'I have no intention whatsoever of entertaining those leeches, they've caused all this,' she revealed, breaking down again, sobbing for herself and Tommy, 'but I won't let him take the blame.'

'Good, at least that's a start,' he said to himself. Realising by the severe tone of her speech that there was no hope of her recanting her earlier account, he decided that he would withdraw it for her. With his membership in the RUC and more so the Orange Lodge, this would be easy, his word would be as good as, if not better, than any written declaration. All he had to do now was make sure that his daughter remained in the dark over his distortion of the truth, and that the media were kept from worming their way into her life through reporters or tabloids. Working on the 'what she didn't know couldn't hurt her' principle, he was convinced that the favourable inquest he anticipated would hammer the final nail into Gerry O'Brien's coffin, as well as letting him off scot free. Leaving his daughter to reflect on Tommy's death, Bill went to find the doctor to inform him that his next of kin was discharging herself.

Stopping the car outside Mrs O'Brien's lodgings, Paul worked his punctuality to his advantage, utilising every minute up until midday in an effort to compose himself for the grimmest assignment of his life. Ringing the bell, the sonorous echoes which reverberated around in his clouded brain alarmed him to run and hide, but he stayed out of duty. Shouldering the blame, as he was in his painful mind, Paul felt that if he'd only left Tommy to his own inconsequential devices then he'd now still be alive to wander around the streets happy, devoid of the worries, stress and responsibility that the real world forces upon us, but no, Paul's concept of life in general where danger and hurt are lurking around every corner was the sophistic dream he'd sold his friend. It was an illusion that he had now paid for with his life, and it hadn't been worth it.

When Mrs O'Brien came to the door, Paul could see that she was anxious by the way she was nibbling at her fingernails and she too saw that something was niggling at him by his inexpressive, bloodless face.

'He's not coming is he?' she said.

'He can't,' replied Paul, morosely, his face etched with lines of misery.

329

For two overlong minutes they just stared nebulously at one and other waiting for the other to lubricate the dehydrated conversation.

'So what . . . I don't,' they uttered in unison, shattering the iceberg which had come between them.

'You go first,' said Paul.

'No, you,' she returned.

Squeezing his eyes shut, he spoke. 'Gerry's dead.'

For a moment there was silence as his penetrating revelation benumbed her senses and sent her into quandary.

'How? Why? What do you mean?' she stammered.

'I don't know what all the circumstances are, we'll have to contact the police,' he explained, lowering his head to the ground, unable to look her in the eye.

'So how the hell did he die?' she shouted, her breath racing with the adrenaline being dispatched to combat the shock. 'Run over? Shot? Heart attack? Murdered? Drowned? What?'

'I don't know,' pleaded Paul, apologetically.

'Then how do you know he's dead?' she demanded.

'Well, I don't,' he replied losing control of his perplexed mind.

'Is this some kind of sick joke?'

'No, Angela's mother told me. In all the shock I didn't think of asking for details, I'm so sorry,' he begged her pardon for his incompetence.

Sitting on the cold step, hypnotised by the rosebushes swaying in the gentle breeze, Paul could hear Tommy's mother on the public telephone in the vestibule of her lodgings, demanding an explanation from the RUC for her son's death, then came a long silence followed by the grievous pandemonium of ratification. As her screams of pain engulfed his body like the beginning of the death of a thousand cuts, Paul found he could take no more. Rising from his trance, he staggered towards his car, fell into the seat then slammed the door to shut out the suffering. Fifteen minutes later, Mrs O'Brien alerted him by knocking on the window. Raising his head from the steering wheel which had left its mark across his forehead, he gazed at her to see that the mascara which had streaked down her face had now dried in dark deposits on her age lines. Throughout his life, Paul had been lucky enough to have avoided the sight of death; his grandparents had long since departed before he was born or could remember, but now death was touching him for the first time and he wasn't prepared for it. Tommy's mother's face – the visage of the weeping clown would

330

remain implanted as a permanent fixture in his mind for ever, this was his haunting image of death.

'Can you drive me to the RVH?' she asked, composedly, as she wiped her angry nose.

Driving towards the Falls, Mrs O'Brien told him what the police had divulged to her.

'They suspected him of raping a girl, they reckon his mind cracked under the questioning so he attacked a policeman and in the ensuing struggle he tripped and fell headfirst into a wall. His father's already made an identification and given his permission for an autopsy, so the coroner's report will validate that there was no foul play involved.'

Paul didn't believe it, not for a minute, but under the lamentable circumstances felt it wise to keep his thoughts to himself in the presence of Mrs O'Brien, the last thing she needed right now was the knowledge of an iniquitous death, for the loss of her son was in itself a travesty of justice.

As Paul entered the doors of the Accident and Emergency department Angela, shepherded by her father, was leaving the main building. Wanting to remember Tommy as the effervescent, animated figure he'd been over the last few months of their association, Paul decided to wait outside in the corridor of the morgue, allowing the mother and child reunion all the unbridled privacy he deemed the final valediction warranted.

Later, after he had dropped Mrs O'Brien off at her guest house, she turned to her chauffeur:

'Thanks for everything this afternoon, I really appreciated it. I've decided to return to England this evening, they reckon by the time the inquest is resolved the funeral could be anything up to a fortnight away. The authorities have promised to contact me, so I'll return for the funeral. I see no point in staying around here, there are too many skeletons waiting to pounce from the cupboard.'

It wasn't until Toby began to whimper for his food at five o'clock that it finally sank in with Paul that Tommy was gone. With all his co-ordination departed, Paul somehow denied his lethargy to prepare the dog's ration before stumbling out into the yard. Watching Toby as he devoured his meal without a care in the wide world, his thoughts again turned to his deceased friend and still there remained a tendency to disbelieve. Taking Toby for his exercise, Paul stopped off at the newsagents to buy the evening edition of the Telegraph and there it was,

331

staring him in the face like an impassable mountain: 'Rape Suspect Dies in RUC Custody.' Reading the whole article he soon discovered that there was no mention of the rape victim or her identity. Walking home lugubriously, he now accepted that Tommy was indeed dead, he would not, however, entertain the notion that his best friend had committed the crime.

Unleashing Toby outside his kennel, Paul felt a cold shiver of solitude run up his spine to reinforce his mournfulness. The dog was all that was left to remind him of the alliance that had waged a war against the evils of Belfast sectarian society and won, now it was all but a memory. Tommy was dead, Angela was out of reach and soon Toby would return to his roots at the foot of the Wicklow Mountains. Having sampled the sweet taste of a friendship second to none and savoured a once-in-a-lifetime love, Paul now found that it was his bitter destiny to go it alone. Maybe it was God above punishing him for his refusal to bow to divine prevarication, no matter what it was in truth, he was back in the land of hell and the only way was up. Entering the kitchen still riddled with the guilt of Tommy's eradication, he found Michael alone. Glancing at the table he saw that there were two glasses guarding the bottle of amber sauce taking centre spot. He was about to walk on to continue his mourning in the isolation of his bedroom when Michael spoke.

'Sit down and have a drink with me.'

'So you can flout Tommy's memory, no thanks,' refused Paul.

'No, I don't want to put him down at all, in fact, I want to drink to his outstanding valour in the face of adversity,' acclaimed his brother, offering his condolences in the form of unexpected kudos.

Pouring Paul a long drink, he handed him the glass, then raising his own, he revealed the toast. 'To another victim of the RUC regime of totalitarianism. You are aware that the bastards murdered him, aren't you?'

For once Paul found that he had to agree with his enemy. Throwing back the truce in one, he blew out the fire with a cough then thundered the glass back on to the table demanding a refill. 'Oh, I know they murdered him all right, but who'll listen to me. I'm a . . . ,' he paused.

'Aye Paul, that's right, why can't you say it? You're a Catholic and again you've hit the nail on the head. Of course there's no way they'll listen to one of us, that's why we must unite to fight these bastards, in the houses, on the beaches, on the streets and in the countryside,' he lectured passionately. 'I want you to join me tonight, a crowd of us are gonna take to the streets in a show of defiance to let them know they can't get away with this, an eye for an eye, isn't that what the Bible says?'

Thinking long and hard, Paul took a third measure of Dutch courage and drank it as if it was tap water then disclosed his determination.

'I can't join you, I'll do it my way.'

'Who do you think you are Paul? Frank Sinatra? So tell me how you plan to take on and beat the biggest mafia in the universe single handed, because I'm dying to hear this,' he rebuked.

Ignoring Michael's riposte, Paul left his incensed brother to top up his hatred.

Paul didn't get much sleep that night as his mind fluctuated between Tommy, Angela and Toby, who pined all night like Greyfriars Bobby for his dead master. At two in the morning, when the petrol bombs had all been thrown and the fire brigade had quenched the fires and drowned the rioters into surrender, Paul joined Toby in his kennel.

'I miss him too boy, that's why we have to keep going for him. He'll be watching us now and I know he'll be with you all the way to Shelbourne Park because that's what he wanted, you to win the Derby.'

Toby rested his tired head onto Paul's leg and they fell asleep together.

Earlier that fateful day, over in the Shankill, Bill Hamilton crept into Angela's bedroom holding a pile of glossy magazines.

'Here, have a look through these,' he said handing her a jungle of holiday brochures, 'I've booked in two weeks' holiday for July 1st, that's a fortnight on Friday. I've spoken to your boss at the hospital and she said you can have as much time off as you need and not to worry, your job will be there for you when you're fit enough in your mind to return. A good holiday is what this family needs, it'll do us all the world of good. I know I've been the main catalyst in the break up of this family and it's led to what happened to you. I'm really sorry for that, Angie. I realise a two-week holiday in the sun won't compensate for that, but it's the start of the way I mean to go on from this day forth.'

'I'll take a look,' she replied.

'Okay, sweetheart, anywhere you want.'

Leaving the room she called him back. 'Daddy, can you fetch me up tonight's Telegraph?'

'I'm sorry but I didn't get one tonight,' he returned, keeping his back to her.

'Why? Was there some mention of me in it?'

333

'No, Angie, rest assured my people have kept a tight lid on your identity, no one knows a thing.'

'Just the rapist,' she scythed, turning her head to the brochures.

Flicking through the sun-drenched enticing pictures where smiling couples frolicked on golden beaches and gazed longingly into each other's eyes over moonlit dinners, she thought of Paul and shed a tear. Perhaps one of these otherworldly, lavish blue-lagoon destinations might have been the paradise where their relationship was heading, as it was she knew in reality their relationship was in ruins and that she had to forget about him for ever.

By Tuesday night Paul was beginning to realise just how instrumental Tommy had been in Toby's success, to such an extent, in fact, that he'd severely underestimated his value and even taken his friend's huge commitment for granted. The first sign that Toby's health was deteriorating through the disappearance of his master was in his appetite. Returning to collect the dog's bowl, Paul found that half the measure remained untouched. Diagnosing that it was Tommy's absence that had precipitated such an effect, Paul headed straight for the telephone.

'Hi, can I speak to Johnny McKenna?'

'I'll just get him,' returned a hospitable southern female voice that engendered celestial visions of log fires and the sweet, warm smell of fresh baking.

'Hi, it's Paul O'Donnell, History Maker's owner. Is the offer still open in regard to training the dog for the Derby?'

'Aye, course it is,' came the enthusiastic male reply.

'When's best to bring him down then?' Paul inquired.

'Now, tomorrow, whenever is convenient, but I suggest the quicker the better, he'll probably need a few weeks settling-in period,' explained Johnny McKenna, allowing his wisdom to counterbalance his eagerness to gain restitution of the dog.

'Maybe more,' revealed Paul with a loud sigh, 'his appetite's gone. He had a real good cohesion with Tommy, you met Tommy didn't you?'

'Aye, he's the Oxo cube genius.'

'Was,' said Paul choking up, 'he passed away yesterday and the dog's missing him badly.'

'I'm sorry,' expressed McKenna before resuming. 'I think, in that case, you should bring him down here sooner rather than later. Perhaps

334

the companionship of my other dogs will bring him around, might even give him a new lease of life.'

Remembering that Toby was booked in for a race on Saturday night, Paul considered cancelling the run, before his thoughts turned to Angela, as they did every second minute of the day. Aware that she knew the dog was racing at the weekend, in his mind he was sure that she would make an appearance at the track.

'I'll bring him on Sunday morning,' Paul decided.

Replacing the receiver, he gazed at the telephone that had once been his ligament to love and he pondered as to whether or not Angela's number had actually been changed. Having no need to pluck up courage, just the burning desire to hear her assuring voice telling him that they could still see each other, he picked up the phone and dialled her number. The long dead tone which greeted him was just another nail in his heart as well as serving to add insult to his injury.

Again the Telegraph made great mention of the rape incident, which had now angered the Nationalist community to such an extent that they had massed on to the streets demanding retribution for another arcane Catholic death at the hands of the RUC. The people wanted the facts, but more so justice, and the IRA was only more than willing to advocate their request to win back declining support. Up and down the length of the Falls Road brand-new black flags were hoisted to drape from the lamp-posts and shop windows, replacing the faded to grey weather-beaten ensigns of the last injustice, to remind everyone that this community had tasted death once again. That night Paul found himself sleeping with Toby again as the animal continued to pine relentlessly for Tommy.

By lunch time on Wednesday, Paul had come to the end of his tether. Watching the unhappy dog from the kitchen window, he cringed as Toby scratched at the concrete slabs attempting to claw himself a path to freedom under the gate. Within an hour, Paul was in the company of Matt Williamson in the box-room sized bar inside Belfast Castle. Joining Paul in the privacy of a small niche in the corner of the medieval, stonewall surroundings, Matt placed two pints of Guinness on to the wobbly round table, then utilised the drip mats to stabilise the warped antediluvian artefact before addressing the situation.

'So what can I do for you?' the journalist asked, when he really meant, 'What can you do for me?'

'Why haven't you printed the victim's name?' quizzed Paul.

'We don't have the information, of course, the RUC gave us a basic statement saying she wanted to remain anonymous, can't say I blame her.'

Not wishing to drag Angela's name through the mud, Paul switched to the real reason for his visit. 'I'm not happy. I know that Gerry O'Brien is innocent, this is nothing more than an RUC fit-up.'

'So what do you want me to do about it?' asked Matt, slightingly.

'I want you to stop printing slanderous shit about Gerry for a kick off, and I want you to demand an inquiry into his death, there's no substantial evidence that he raped the girl,' blasted Paul.

'Aye, and there's no testimony yet to suggest that his death was suspicious, so my hands are well and truly tied until the findings of the inquest are published. I can't help you on this one, that's unless you can give me hard facts. Writing news around here is like walking the wire across the Niagara Falls, do you know what I'm saying? One slip up and you're fucked. I'm sorry, but you'll have to excuse me - I have to get back to work.'

Rising to leave, he remembered the story that had furthered his career. 'Oh, by the way, how's the dog?'

'He's been better. Gerry wanted him to run in the Derby and that's what I'm gonna do, no matter what the cost, I owe him that,' said Paul with mass conviction flowing through his embittered voice.

'Do you think he can win it?'

'Oh, I'm sure he will,' replied Paul arrogantly, through his vexation.

Driving back to his office Matt mulled over Paul's words and reflected on how the antonymous communities had once banded against sectarianism to follow the peace-deriving greyhound, and on how, perhaps, the publicity of a Derby crusade could reinstate that unification. It was a rank outsider, but now that the death threats had diminished he felt it was a gamble worth chancing his career on.

As Paul sat with Toby that night, man and canine helped each other to overcome their heartaches.

Having always presumed that Angela would have attempted to call him, Paul now realised that it wasn't going to happen, so he began to write to her, three letters at a time, which he would post at different intervals during the day, in case any were intercepted. They always ended with the same statement: 'I'm missing you, I love you and I always will, Paul.'

Come Thursday evening and the rape incident and Gerry O'Brien were history, as yet another example of the IRA's heinousness exploded on to the front pages. Earlier that afternoon, six British soldiers participating in a charity fun run in Lisburn had been murdered when a bomb planted underneath their bus had detonated. Someone had summed it up with the understatement of a lifetime: 'Irish Nationalism consists not of the love of one's country, but of hatred of someone else's. Their moving spirit is not love of Ireland, but hatred of Britain. There can be no excuse for savagery.' It was just another mindless attack that would only bring about the same old aftermath, the UVF would hit back, but as ever, harder.

Dreaming of Angela, Paul's eyes suddenly flashed open as his body clock alarmed him that something was out of place. Shifting his sights to the bedside cabinet he perceived that it was 9 a.m. Dressing himself with urgency, he was more worried about facing his mother's scathing tongue than whether Toby had sustained an injury in his attempts to escape, so he could forage for nourishment. Still buttoning his shirt when he entered the kitchen, his mind was still upstairs in bed.

'Mom, I'm sorry it won't happen again,' he apologised to her back, as she sat writing out her shopping list.

'Oh Paul what have you done this time, you haven't wet the bed have you?' she jested.

'Toby, I take it you had to feed him again?'

'No, I haven't heard a whimper out of him,' she said. 'I presumed that you'd gone back to bed after giving him his breakfast.'

Seeing no sign of the dog from the window, Paul strolled down to the kennel, his anxiety growing with every step. Poking his head through the rubber flaps his suspicions were soon confirmed. Just when he'd thought that things couldn't get any more inauspicious, he discovered that he'd misjudged life's obstacle course once again. Turning his head, he noticed that the gate was slightly ajar. With the gate designed to open from the inside only, Paul immediately suspected that there had been foul play, but this supposition was soon dismissed when he walked over to close the gate. Placing his hand on to the round handle, he felt the sticky evidence in the form of dog saliva. The world seemed to be closing in on him from all angles, but he rejected the urge to panic, not through meditated composure, but unmitigated despondency. Returning to the house, he picked up his car keys.

'Are you off out without any breakfast?' asked his mother, noticing that he was pale and drawn, as if he could do with a good feed.

'Aye, Toby's done a runner. Can't say I blame him really, it's something I should've done a long time ago.'

Paul refuelled his car after searching fruitlessly for over an hour and a half; he guesstimated that the dog could be half way to Dublin by now. Heading to the nearest RUC station to report his loss, his thoughts veered to Tommy and how he was sure that his friend had been a victim of his religion, and it provided him with a strong hunch as to Toby's whereabouts. Perhaps Toby was a modern day Greyfriars Bobby, and if this was indeed the case then he wouldn't have run far.

As he drove into Odessa Street to follow up his intuition, he had a strange but ardent feeling pass through him that Tommy was leading him to the missing animal. Walking down the back alley he saw that the rotting gate, which thirsted for a lick of paint, was moaning to and fro in the wind. Observing the head height scratches in the soft wood, Paul knew his quest was over. On the back doorstep, head resting on his long forlegs, there he was waiting at a stop that was no longer part of the route. Lifting his head slowly to distinguish the visitor, Toby simply returned his heavy head to his paws, unmoved by Paul's scent. After unsuccessfully attempting to coax the dog home by rustling an empty crisp packet which had been blowing around the yard, Paul found himself forced into carrying the dead weight of the stubborn animal back to his car.

Once home he tied a long rope to the dog's collar and secured it to the kennel, thus affording Toby sufficient freedom, as well as enough captivity, to thwart him from decamping to Odessa Street.

After posting yet another begging letter early on Saturday morning, Paul looked down the length of the lead at Toby and wondered if man and beast could ever find harmony again. Stopping at the newsagent, Paul bought a newspaper. As he thumbed towards the greyhound card at the rear, Toby relieved himself on mankind's gift to his four-legged friend, a lamppost. Abruptly Paul paused at a small article headed, 'Inquest Findings Put RUC in the Clear'. Shaking his head as he read, he learnt that Tommy had died of a blood clot on the brain emanating from an untoward collision with a wall; verdict, accidental death. Case closed. Reading on, bewildered by the insignificant epitaph, he accepted that the body had now been released for burial and the service would be held at 2 p.m. on Tuesday June 28th. From coroner to constable, each and every remnant of the RUC's close-knit personnel had woven together to sew the case tight shut and at the same time fabricate a carpet big enough to sweep the lie under. Turning to the dog card, he saw that Toby was racing at 9.30 p.m. in a minor sprint open. Reverting back to the 435-yard trip against a field of fast starters would, he hoped, bring an edge to his early running before moving to Dublin. It was a race that on paper Toby should have been able to win pulling a cart, but with all the diabolical events of the week, Paul had his doubts as to whether the animal's lament would allow him to rise to the occasion. The postman again neglected to deliver him word from Angela and his pessimism raged to new limits. Having battled through the week in the hope of seeing Angela at the dog track, he was now convinced that she would fail to appear.

Anticipating another big attendance now that the weather had turned for the better, in conjunction with the reappearance of the track champion, Paul arrived at Dunmore nice and early. If Angela was to break her reclusion then the last thing he needed was to miss her in the congested crowd. Walking towards the kennelling enclosure to enter the dog for his race, he noticed the usual gang of kids touting for business outside the kennels. There, come wind, rain or shine, this assembly of eight to thirteen-year-old youths in bedraggled attire with dirty faces, were the children of the impoverished surrounding neighbourhood. Attracted by the bright lights and glittering romance of rich, cigar-smoking owners with their glamorous fur-coated wives, and the dream of someday trading places to be a part of this high-ranking society, as only they perceived it was, they'd parade your greyhound for the going rate of 50p a circuit. This sum would usually double should the dog come home first. Anent to the snooker-hall hustlers, this was their education for life, some of them would realise their dream while the vast majority would end up scratching to make a living by any means possible, even if this meant turning to crime. These deprived kids were old before their time. Often Paul had overheard them arguing among themselves as to who was the best dog on the track, or who would win a specific race. They were gifted in their analysis and that had to be the reason why the bookmakers permitted these 'under-agers' to place their trivial 50p wagers on their fancies, and pay them out with a little extra when they sailed home. These boys were the cream of the pundits, whereas as a £100 stake from an unknown punter might not result in a shortening of the starting price, a £1 punt from one of these artful dodgers would definitely sway the bookies into slimming the odds. Tonight, Paul felt the time had come to employ their talents.

Scanning the row of youngsters who hadn't dared tender their services in light of the past refusals from this owner, Paul took an instant shine to one in particular, for two reasons. The boy he chose seemed to be distanced from the boisterous huddle yet he was standing alongside them, quiet as a mouse. Wearing faded jeans with black PVC patches sewn over the knees and a scruffy navy parka, he reminded Paul of Tommy. Although Paul had noticed this boy on numerous previous occasions, it suddenly crossed his mind that he'd never actually seen him parade a greyhound around the track. Walking over to him Paul spoke.

'Would you be interested in putting my dog into the starting traps tonight?'

Raising his bowed head his eyes sparkled. 'What me? Really?'

'Aye,' assured Paul, turning to the other boys who had suddenly been stunned into silence.

Staring at them until they had resumed their chatter, he then returned his attention to his new employee.

'So, do you have a name?'

'Aye, mister, my name's Thomas.'

'I guess I should've known that,' smiled Paul, shaking his head at the coincidence, 'so do you think you'll be able to handle him?'

'Aye, mister, no problem. He's History Maker, isn't he? The best dog in all Ireland.'

'Well, that remains to be proven,' Paul replied modestly. 'Tell me Tommy, how much do you charge for your services?'

'Fifty pence,' he returned, blushing.

'Okay, here's the deal,' said Paul, putting his arm around him to whisper into his ear. 'Toby, that's his pet name, has not been feeling too well lately, so I want you to keep a good eye on him. Take him for a stroll every half hour, which means as far as I'm concerned, you're his trainer for the entire evening, that's ten races which by my reckoning is five pounds, what do you think?'

Hearing no reply from the dumbfounded boy, Paul immediately upped his offer. 'Okay, you win, and a five pound bonus if he wins.'

Probably never having held a one pound note in his grubby hands, let alone the brown strip of wallpaper he envisaged a ten pound note to be in dimension, young Tommy grabbed at the chance.

340

'Aye, sir, no problem, I'll make sure he wins.'

Giving another obvious black sheep the care of the white dog, Paul headed round to the grandstand to keep a lookout for Angela. Taking up a vantage point where he could keep one eye on the track and the other on the incoming patrons constantly trickling through the turnstiles, by the time the clock read 9.15 p.m. his neck was stiff and his nerves had abandoned ship. Resigned to the near certainty that she wasn't coming, he found that his interest for the sport, which had brought him into contact with his true soulmate, was fading from his life, as she was but, although he wasn't aware of it, he was not alone in being alone.

Sitting in her mother's company Angela glanced at the clock on the mantelpiece. Toby'll be parading now, she thought. Tempted to call a taxi and leave the house, now that her father had quickly returned to his old ways of drink, drink and more drink since the outcome of the inquest had favoured him, she was frightened as to how Paul would now look at her. Heading to her bedroom, she reached under the mattress and removed the pile of letters that had been arriving with every post for the last few days. Reading every heartfelt line as their song played over and over on her record player in the background, she felt that something was missing, and that was her respect for him. Not once in any of his correspondences had he made any comment on the rape, because of his human nature. In Paul's mind, mention of that affliction could only put distance between them, but as far as she was concerned, the events could never be erased by ignorance for she'd feel defiled for a long time to come, if not perpetually. Ripping up his letters in a wild frenzy of frustration, she then threw them at the walls and began to weep uncontrollably, believing that she would never be able to look him in the eye again and that their fragile relationship, shattered to pieces, was now dead and buried.

As the track came to life, buzzing with anticipation, as it had always done of late when History Maker made an appearance, Paul was convinced that Toby's despondent frame of mind would result in his first defeat after five wins on the bounce. Glancing at young Tommy holding his head high, his eyes then shifted downward to note that Toby's head too had begun to rise for the better, perhaps the youngster also reminded the dog of his master. If this was indeed the case, then

341

maybe Toby would after all end his racing days at Dunmore by bowing out in a blaze of glory.

Sent off at the untouchable odds of 3/1 on, Toby was still asleep when the lids cracked open. Trailing the field by a few lengths when the first bend arrived turned out to be a blessing in disguise. As with so many early-paced dogs converging in the same place at the same time, and only enough racing space for one to swing round unscathed, carnage was inevitable. Losing their footing in the stampede, traps three and four were knocked over, seriously hampering the five dog, who in turn collided into six sending him spinning off the track. Plodding around on three cylinders, Toby found himself meeting the back straight only four lengths adrift of the fortunate trap two runner. The demanding crowd, expecting History Maker to activate his accustomed turbo-charged acceleration down the long straight, were dismayed to see that his heart simply wasn't in it. Going through the motions when he approached the penultimate arc, he was still a length and a half behind the rapidly fading leader. When the line arrived it was not Toby's resilient staying power that had won him the race by a half length but the eventual runner up's lack of the aforementioned trait.

Again the grapevine whispers raged across the stands, but on this occasion the stopwatch would substantiate the rumours that History Maker's reign as king of track was coming to an end. When the winning time of 23.82 was announced, Paul was quick to accept that the ten lengths lost since Tommy's death was just the beginning of a downward slide. Thinking to himself that only his late friend would've been able to recover such a loss of form in time for the opening heats of the Derby, which were now only ten weeks away, Paul was seriously considering withdrawing his charge from the competition. Even though there were over two months to put the matter right, things had to be brought into perspective. It was going to take at least a fortnight for Toby to settle into his new surroundings for starters, and probably another month to master Shelbourne Park, which would only leave a handful of weeks for him to come up to speed. Paul's final decision was founded on many factors. He owed it to Tommy for one, and secondly, he owed it to Toby, for writing him off when he walked into the RUC station that spiteful Sunday afternoon. If anyone that day had told Paul that Toby would've been of the calibre to enter the Derby, he would've been more than happy with that, but with the success of two track records he'd grown greedy, becoming an anomaly to his own principle, suddenly he remembered it's not the winning that counts, it's the taking part.

Picking up the £75 first prize, Paul shook the racing manager's hand for the final time, having revealed his intentions. History Maker's track records would remain intact long after the bulldozers had flattened Dunmore to the ground in the decade to come. Collecting the dog from young Tommy, he handed him the brown envelope containing Toby's earnings.

'I don't want you to open this until I've gone or it'll bring bad luck, do you understand?' impressed Paul.

'Aye, mister,' he replied.

'So, Tommy, what do you want to be when you grow up?'

'A greyhound trainer, mister,' came the expected reply.

'Well, you listen to me, the only way you can achieve that aim is by setting your sights to do well at school first. Get some qualifications, no slacking off and perhaps one day you'll be training a Derby winner. Will you remember what I've said?'

'Aye mister, I promise.'

'Good, and remember, no peeking inside that envelope until I've gone or the leprechauns will come and steal it in the night when you're fast asleep.'

Driving home feeling a little better within himself for his good deed, he wondered if God was watching, and if so would he finally intervene to bring Angela back into his life. At the same time though, he knew that he'd be willing to sell his soul to the devil if it meant things could return to the way they'd once been.

As Paul drove down towards Dublin and further with Toby on Sunday morning, his confused mind fluctuated between the past and the present, but never touched upon the future, as without Angela he just couldn't envisage one. Just over three tiring hours later, a few miles past the village of Rathnew near Wicklow, Paul noticed the signpost for the McKenna kennels overstretching its neck to be seen above the profligate summer vegetation. Pulling off the sinuous country road on to a single lane dirt track, which looked like a target run for the Royal Airforce with its million and one suspension-buckling potholes, he then negotiated a half mile of twists and turns of darkness, as the dense forest canopied to forbid the sun's entrance. Eventually, the winding road ended and the sun's light returned as the road straightened at the

343

clearing, to reveal a lovely little stone cottage with twin chimneypots incessantly coughing out clouds of thick black smoke from the free and abundant fossil fuel of peat; a perk which the house owners were privileged to have an unlimited supply of from their never-ending back garden that reached far beyond the horizon.

Waiting until the chicken's heartbeats had stabilised and the feathers had settled, Paul opened his door to be met by a hundred variant pitches of dog whines, barks and yelps. Keeping Toby on a tight rein to avoid roast chicken for lunch, he walked up to the house then knocked on the wooden door. The woman of the house stood before him, just how he'd imagined she'd look. Small, plump, grey-haired and wearing the flowery apron that one associates with one's grandmother. After being shown around Toby's new home and leaving him to settle in, Paul sat at the kitchen-cum-conference table to thrash out the dog's future. Waiting patiently as Johnny washed his hands in the huge and antiquated square porcelain sink and his wife unloaded an oven full of cakes and biscuits, Paul scanned the unostentatious surroundings of their open-plan home. Although they didn't appear to have much in the way of luxurious decor, or even a solitary rug laid over the cold slate floor, Paul envied them for the way they smiled at each other, warming the home with sparkling eyes that showed their love had stood the test of time to burn eternally. They were a happy couple and, understanding early on in their thirty-three years of marriage that they would never be blessed with offspring, they had devoted themselves to keeping, racing and breeding greyhounds. With over fifty dogs on their farm, they had enough canine children to fill an orphanage.

It was resolved through amicable discussion that Johnny McKenna would train History Maker with one goal in mind, the Derby. After that event had run its course the situation would then be re-addressed. Paying ten weeks' board and lodging in advance for Toby, and promising to return once a fortnight to spend time with the animal, Paul headed home assured that Toby, now reunited with his own species, would soon forget about Tommy and swiftly rediscover his old form.

As he headed through the sliding door at Donegall Quay on Monday morning, Paul recalled how Angela had surprised him a fortnight ago when she'd made an unexpected appearance. He paused for a while in the hope of a repeat performance, stubbed out his cigarette dejectedly then made his way on to the ship. Over the next week in Paul's upside-down world, he sweated when he was cold and shivered when he was warm, as he bungled through his workload, digging deeper by the day to find the energy that he no longer possessed. Each night, whether it be in Scotland or Ireland, he ended the night propped up against the bar glancing at happy couples and reminisced about how he and Angela had once enacted the same ritual.

When he entered his home on Sunday evening, he was dismayed to learn that still there had been no contact through wire or paper from Angela. Mind screaming for the painkiller of alcohol, he found himself in Paddy's Bar at the opposite end of the room from his inimical father. Setting about his fourth pint of Guinness within the hour, he scanned the pub and noticed the aged faces each etched with a thousand hardships, and although he felt as if the world was resting upon his shoulders, he knew that he didn't belong here. He finished his drink off then walked home, leaving the pub behind for good with a fresh attitude. He was relatively healthy, had a decent job and a roof over his head, some had more, but most had less. All he had to do was fool himself that he was over her then he'd be fine.

It was now two weeks since the rape, and having never set a single foot outside the security of her home, Angela was wilting from the lack of daylight she denied to creep into her existence. Rejecting the RUC's offer of rape counselling, she'd thought she'd found treatment in shutting herself away from the outside world, yet now, going stir-crazy in her home made prison, she felt she had to break free if she was ever to experience normality again. Using sunglasses to hide behind she grabbed her worst fears by the scruff of the neck and caught a bus into the city centre. Just walking around and browsing at the shop windows, the crowds and daylight instilled her with renewed confidence as they would do so for her life to come, now she'd fallen prey to agoraphobia and nyctophobia. That evening, when Bill Hamilton came home from work, he threw a wallet of flight tickets on to the dining table to reveal he'd booked a fortnight's holiday on the Spanish island of Mallorca. Picking the tickets off the table, Angela wondered if this was the passport to finally removing the curse of Paul from her mind.

Paul prepared his best and only suit for Tommy's funeral, but couldn't help but think back to his friend parading Toby full of pride and that prompted him to phone Johnny McKenna to find out how Toby was progressing, if at all.

'Things aren't good, Paul. He refused to eat for three days. I had to take him to the vet, but he found nothing untoward. Anyway, he started

345

to eat on Thursday, thank God, but he's lost a lot of weight so I've been pumping him full of the wife's cooking, but here's the bad news. I took him for a trial around Shelbourne this morning. I put him in with a few of my pups so he could pull them around, but they left him for dead, he finished last in a time of 31.65 for the 550 trip. He has no interest whatsoever, just sits there moping all day, if he doesn't buck his ideas up and show some drastic improvement, there's gonna be no Derby. Can you think of anything that might bring him on?'

'Let me sleep on it, and I'll get back to you. I'll be coming down at the weekend so we can put our heads together then,' said Paul.

Collecting Mrs O'Brien from the same Bed and Breakfast in Fortwilliam as she'd intended to stay at before, Paul took a sombre drive through the pouring rain back towards the Falls and the Milltown Cemetery, where Tommy would be laid to rest alongside such Republican martyrs as Bobby Sands and Mairead Farrell. Fortunate enough through life thus far to have never attended a funeral, Paul's luck had now run out on that score and this ground-breaking experience was one which he wasn't particularly cherishing the thought of. As they neared the burial site both turned to each other astounded at the mass turnout for the nobody from the Falls. Over a thousand people had braved the weather in coming to pay their last respects, most were Republican sympathisers who looked upon the unknown soldier as yet another victim of the RUC's autocratic regime, while the odd few had come from Dunmore Stadium to salute off a supreme handler, the remainder were the usual crowd who'd exploited this funeral, as they'd done so many others, to obtain a few paid hours off work.

As he stood at the graveside with a tear in his eye as Tommy was lowered into the ground, Paul scanned the nameless faces with a deep sense of contempt. These were the hypocrites who hadn't gave Tommy the time of day during the living years, even his brother Michael had come to make sure Tommy's face was rubbed in the dirt. As the solemn gathering began to disperse back to the land of the living, the deceased's mother turned to Paul.

'I didn't realise he'd made so many friends.'

Biting his tongue, not wishing to add to her heartache with the bitter truth of the matter, he nodded in agreement.

'I've been meaning to ask you Paul, is there anything of Tommy's you'd like to have?'

'Well, as a matter of fact there is one thing,' he replied, believing the notion, that what he wanted might just hold the key to reopening Toby's fuel tank, 'I'd like his old parka if that's all right? The dog's really missing him and has lost all incentive to eat or run. I've a feeling it may be the answer.'

'Well, I've no objection, but I suppose I'll have to ask his permission,' she said, raising her head across the grave to the man who throughout the service had failed to shed a tear.

Paul left Tommy's mother and father to discuss the past and perhaps the future, and sensing eyes burning into his neck, turned to observe a figure standing alone on the hill a few hundred yards away in the distance. He focused his eyes to see if they were deceiving him, but was convinced that it was Angela. Seeing that he'd spotted her she turned and began to walk away. Desperate to see her again, blinded by the driving rain, he raced the wind and hurdled gravestones to be by her side. But hearing his thundering approach, she quickened her stride and squeezed her eyes tight shut as her heart skipped a beat. He doubled over, panting, in front of her. 'Angie, did you get any of my letters?'

Ignoring him, through her dark sunglasses she redirected her vision to the left, knowing that one glance might reinstate her feelings towards him.

'Talk to me,' he begged her, taking her hands and going down on one knee.

Raising his head, he watched a single tear meander down her ashen face.

'For God's sake say something, I've thought about nothing other than you for the last fortnight,' he continued to wheedle.

'I've thought of you too,' she said softly, 'and I've come to a few conclusions. Too much has happened, I've been attacked, as have you and now Tommy's dead, don't you get it? We all brought this upon ourselves when daring to challenge a code of ethics that numerous generations before us have failed to subvert, and no doubt as many after us will also.'

Listening to her words of pessimism and watching more tears crawl from under her glasses he was sure she was wrong.

'We can make it Angela, I know we can, we've come this far.'

'No, Paul,' she said, 'look, Tommy's dead, who's next?'

347

Looking beyond her into the distance to Tommy's open grave, his thoughts went to his departed friend.

'Tommy didn't lay a finger on you, did he?' he asked, answering the question himself.

'Of course he didn't,' she replied.

'Then you must tell the authorities.'

'Don't you think I've already done that?' she scorned.

'Well, there's been no mention of his innocence in the papers.'

'They do know he was innocent, I swear. I made a statement.'

'Well, make another to the media, somebody's covering something up here.'

'Paul, I'll have to go now.'

Not willing to release his grip on her hand, he hung on for dear life.

'Marry me Angie, be my wife and leave Northern Ireland with me,' he pleaded.

'Stop it Paul, you know I can't.'

'Why can't you?' he demanded an explanation.

'My mother, for starters.'

'Is that the only reason?'

'No, no it's not,' she replied austerely, turning her head away. 'Please Paul, just forget about me and stop sending letters; I won't read them. I'm going to Mallorca on Friday for a fortnight's holiday, then when I come home I'm gonna get on with my life. I don't want to see you again, I'm really sorry if I've messed you about, but this is the way it has to be for both of us.'

'No, Angie, I love you and I know that you love me too,' he sobbed, throwing his arms around her waist and forcing his soaking wet head into her pulsating bosom, as he clung desperately to his love life.

Shaking him loose she began to walk away, leaving him on all fours in the muddy, wet grass.

'Angela,' he shouted to her, 'tell me to my face that you don't love me.'

Stopping dead in her tracks, she turned to face him and removed her sunglasses before taking one long, last look at him.

'I don't love you, Paul,' she stated with sincerity in her voice, before about turning and heading off with his heart.

Totally devastated by her revelation, he remained speechless in a heap. Knowing that her looks never lied, he now had no option but to take it on the chin and face up to the fact that it was over.

Chapter 13

Nothing Compares To You

The next three weeks would prove to be the worst for Paul as he attempted to erase Angela from his battered and bruised, black and blue, mind. It seemed that every way he turned there was always something facing him to keep her memory from fading into his past. And there was just no getting away from it. First it was the romantic ballads on the radio, which belted out all day long. Then from there it evolved into the television set and the exotic, far fetched holiday programme destinations that no ordinary member of the public could afford to visit, where your TV licence scandalously helped to pay for some rich celebrity to enjoy the inequitable perquisite that accompanied the job from heaven.

As Paul drove to Dublin early on the morning of Saturday July 2nd, he solemnly wondered what Angela might be doing and more so, who with. And as his thoughts threatened to capsize his borderline sanity he conceded that he had to find something, or even someone new, to occupy his life. Not only had his love for Angela been dispatched, but his heart was no longer in the greyhound racing, for that too reminded him of the only woman he'd ever truly loved. Glancing at the shabby, torn parka on the passenger seat, he realised that the sole thing which was preventing him from removing Toby from his life was his respect for Tommy. But there was also the guilt that still riddled through him, as he continued to hold himself responsible for his friend's untimely death.

When he'd called Johnny McKenna, the day after Tommy's funeral, with every intention of shelving his weekend visit due to lack of interest,

349

the southern trainer had explained to him that Toby's appetite was slowly returning, although he was still showing nothing like his old self on the gallops. Added to this, McKenna informed the owner that he'd entered History Maker for a minor open, so that they could evaluate Toby's racing status and plan their assault on the Derby. That's if the dog was to remain an entry.

Already the bookmakers were beginning to write off History Maker's chances. His unimpressive last spin around Dunmore, where he failed to set the heather alight, and the emergence of a young new trailblazer by the name of Randy, who'd shot through the candidates' pack with a track-record-breaking first run around Shelbourne Park in a Derby trial to head the ante-post market at 8/1, meant that Toby's burden of favouritism had well and truly been lifted. Although Randy was now the dog on everyone's lips, others too were beginning to sprout wings and take off, barging themselves up the early betting lists. Now friendless in the market, the Greyhound Life's leading authority posed the question, 'Is History Maker Past It?' then proceeded to sum it up in a supporting article that was light years ahead of its time. Using a cosmic comparison, it was measured as follows. 'History Maker; who once rocketed to ante-post favourite has now fizzled out to the enterprising, but damp squib odds of double-carpet, 33/1. Failure to produce a high-octane run tonight, against a field that is not out of this world, would surely see his price soar to 100/1 or greater. Considering the same offerings are available about the discovery of life on Mars, this would highlight the planetary scale of his task.'

Jaded from the journey, Paul arrived at the McKenna stud, then indulged in the pleasantry of a cooked Irish breakfast fit for two. Forcing down the hearty offering so as not to offend the chef, the initial enjoyment of tucking into the greasy platter soon turned into a laborious chore, as the excessive quantities of bacon, eggs, fried bread, tomatoes, sausages and black pudding outweighed the quality. But this was typically characteristic of southern hospitality, because if you could clean your plate then they hadn't given you enough for starters. Fit to explode when the last piece of bacon seemed to come to rest on top of the pile just below his windpipe, Paul felt his heart scream for exercise to burn off the copious cholesterol which had taken a stranglehold on his arteries.

Walking out into the bright morning sunlight, Paul gazed around the stately country surroundings unspoilt by man's exhaustive hands and he found that for him, the grass was greener on this side. This was the picture that had surely been intended, a green sea of tranquillity that stretched as far as the imagination and beyond the reasoning of political minds. Having been confined to the city since birth, Paul now realised that the country life was what he naturally longed for. Marvelling at how splendid it would be to have such phenomenally beautiful scenery on the doorstep, he wished that Angela was by his side to amble over the landscape, but as she was not, Toby would have to do for now. As Paul had lost his sense of direction of late with all the perplexities that life was throwing at him, it was no shock that he allowed Toby to lead the way. During the hour-long round-trip, he looked for signs that would show him the dog was over its grief, but he witnessed none. The lead remained slack throughout and the occasional snapping of a twig in the undergrowth not once alerted the docile animal to erect its floppy antennas. Dragging their feet as they arrived back at the farmhouse they were two of a kind, their passions drained and their morose sentiments running parallel.

For the remainder of the afternoon Paul drifted away on the tedium of Johnny McKenna's highs and lows over his years of involvement with greyhound racing, as he listened without hearing to story after story. Now and again Paul found himself agreeing when he should have been questioning, while at times he was ignorant instead of adulating. Driving up to Dublin that evening, Paul thought of how the dog had become a crutch and how ironically the roles had reversed. Tommy had once been Paul's understudy, yet now through the twist of separation the master had become the servant, yet Paul had made his pledge and he would see it through to the end whether the outcome be futile or fertile.

Refraining at this early stage from introducing the ace he had up his sleeve, whether it would turn out to be a trump card or perhaps a joker, Paul hoped that he wouldn't have to resort to the last resort of Tommy's parka. At 9.05 p.m., following two of the most monotonous hours that Paul could ever remember at a race meeting, History Maker came on parade for the 9.15 contest. Opening at the ridiculously short price of 3/1 on, most of the bookmakers had expediently opted to edit their books offering odds without the favourite, as in their eyes Toby was a stonewall certainty. This method of laying down the odds signified that they had a realistic chance of coaxing the patrons into having a flutter. A price of 3/1 on meant that you had to stake three punts to win one, not an attractive proposition by any means. So taking advantage of

351

having two chances to win as they promoted the offer, you could bet on any of the other five presumed also-rans and still prise money from the miserly bookmakers if your fancy finished runner up to the favourite. Privileged with the inside information that Toby's appetite for the sport had diminished, after having spent the day by his side, Paul's decision, strengthened by the ludicrous betting market, was a refusal to invest a single penny on his out-of-sorts animal.

He had expected the dog to be a little rusty, but was dismayed to discover that the dog had in fact seized up. Left at the start, Toby showed no desire to chase the sport's effigy. Plodding around the first two bends in last position the crowd were hushed in amazement. And with throttle jammed down the back straight, the heartbroken animal showed nothing to suggest he was a leading contender for the Derby. Making no headway as he spluttered off the final arc, History Maker was jeered home by the betrayed public. Shaking his head despondently as Toby ground past the winning line, thrashed a good ten lengths in last place, Paul was certain that he'd just witnessed a pertinacious performance from an animal running on a dry tank, with the only acceptable refill being Tommy's love. After all the speculative theories of high protein diets, jacuzzis, amino acids and the fallacy of miles and miles of walking, Paul was now absolutely convinced that the difference between a hyperactive and an indolent greyhound was down to the fuel of love and affection. Heading to the weigh-in room to bid the dog farewell for another fortnight, Paul walked dejectedly, almost embarrassedly, past the bookmakers who were rubbing their grimy hands together all smiles, now that another favourite had bit the dust. As Paul dragged his shoes, ashamed by Toby's lacklustre attempts, he pulled up lame himself when he overheard one bookmaker in particular essaying to drum up some business.

'Come on now, a hundred to one your punts about the History Maker. I'll ge ye a hundred to one about the rag for the Derby.'

Incensed by the degrading remarks towards Toby, Paul decided it was time to put his money where his mouth was and he had on his person a wad thick enough to choke a pig. Removing the bundle of notes from his pocket to show the bookmaker that he too meant business, the dog's irate owner fanned out his money to reveal just how much was at stake, as he attempted to barter for a little extra. Waiting until he had gained the backing of a small gathering which had formed at the sight of his cash, Paul hoped to use their presence as a lever of provocation to raise the odds.

'Come on give the man on the street punter a realistic price for a change,' Paul whinged, making sure everyone heard. 'You know History Maker can't win the Derby so how's about a hundred and fifty to one?'

Stalling at the alluring sight of the crisp sterling, the short and rotund bookie's face turned bright red and the back of his neck began to sweat from the tension.

'Eh, eh,' he stammered with all the uninvited publicity, 'a hundred to one is a fair price.'

'Oh come on, the way you're shouting your mouth off with conviction you should be confident enough to lay me a hundred and fifty.'

'Aye,' shouted a man from behind Paul before another onlooker joined in the assault on the turf accountant. 'Aye, yer quick enough to take our money any other time.'

Flustered, caught between the devil and the deep blue sea, to keep face, the bookie had no option but to yield to the pressure of public demand.

'Aye, all right I'll take yer money. I'll lay you a hundred and fifty to one.'

Leaving the bookmaker with a few months of sleepless nights, Paul walked away penniless to a loud cheer and many pats on the back.

Meeting up with Johnny McKenna in the car park, he set about lifting the unhappy animal into his trailer. 'I'm heading back to Belfast now. Can you enter him for another race next Saturday?'

'Shouldn't we get clearance from the vet first, he has to be lame after a performance as poor as that,' replied the trainer, challenging the owner's instruction.

'I don't think he's lame,' Paul voiced, 'I'd like you to try something that no vet can prescribe.'

'Well you're the owner,' sighed McKenna, 'what can we lose? Except another week that we can't afford.'

'Trust me on this one,' Paul said, making for his car, detecting that his elder was less than convinced.

Returning with Tommy's old parka, he handed it to McKenna.

McKenna began to scratch his head. 'What's that for?'

'This is Tommy's jacket. Toby's obviously missing him, he idolised him, they were virtually inseparable. It's all that's left and I think it might just work. If he has it beside him it may act as a substitute for what's missing in his life.'

353

'Aye, you never know,' returned McKenna, musing deeply, remembering the story of the Oxo cubes and how far fetched that would have sounded had it been suggested in his presence.

After fastening his seat belt for the journey, Paul rolled down the window to speak. 'I'll give you a call around midnight next Saturday. I hope we'll have turned the corner and be back on the road to the Derby.'

Thanks to the elixir of life emanating from Tommy's spirit in the jacket, Toby's own spirits soon escalated on to a higher plane. By midweek he'd rediscovered his appetite for a plethora of life's delicacies, which ranged from the hours of grooming and massage to the doting Mrs McKenna, who employed Toby as the chief taster in sampling her daily baking exploits in the kitchen. However, it wasn't only the constant pampering and excessive titbits which had brought a renewed spring to his step, Toby was thriving on the company of his own breed. With a show of his sharp incisors, he'd snarled off all comers who'd attempted to relieve him of his prized possession and in doing so, effectively established himself as leader of the pack. Relishing his ranking at the top of the tree in the pecking order, he carried his drive on to the uphill gallops, blazing the trail to stay ahead of the field and so vindicate his position as top dog. But there was one more significant factor that perhaps held par with the introduction of the parka. Toby's new kennel-mate was female, and the magnitude of his love for her was measured by the way he allowed her to share the navy-blue jacket from which he'd made his bed.

When finishing his shift in Scottish waters on Saturday evening, Paul politely passed up the invitation to join his namesake for a drink onshore. As he killed the time up to midnight on deck, with only the crescent moon's reflection for company, his thoughts sailed to the Balearic Islands. Turning up his collar to the cold chill and shrugging his shoulders, he then cringed as he imagined her living it up in some carnival atmosphere, surrounded by bronzed Romeos each flexing their muscles to gain her undivided attention. Little did he know it, but he couldn't have been further from the truth.

The first week of Angela's holiday had been no party whatsoever. Busier than ever caring for her mother, who was not savouring the sultry climate, it was only late at night, when she'd earned the time to relax on the balcony with a glass of wine and to listen to the swish of the incoming tide guided by the moon and stars and the hypnotising crickets, that she was able to analyse what had happened and what she now planned to

354

do with her future. Spending most of her free time thinking of Paul, to some extent it had annoyed her that he hadn't made a bolder effort to see her. Yes, he'd written her a river of ink, but somewhere in the romantic side of her brain that only the red wine could unlock, she'd wanted him to drive into the Shankill and camp out if need be until she'd made an appearance at her window, perhaps even thrown in the odd serenade to keep in the spirit of things. Deeply exhaling at the thought of their last meeting, when she'd pulled no punches in making her intentions crystal clear, leaving his heart torn from his chest in the mud, she realised that she only had herself to blame. Picking up a few postcards she'd bought earlier in the day, she so wanted to send him one, just to let him know that the invitation was still open, but then she flashed back to the rape and understood that a fresh start, where both were chastised from her mind, was her only way forward.

Half way across the Irish Sea, heading homewards on the final trip of the week, Scots Paul returned to the galley from a cigarette break.

'Hey Paul, what are you doing this Friday night?'

'I've nothing planned as far as I know. Why?'

'Well it's Mairead's twenty-first. She's having a night out around town and we're all invited. How do you fancy it?'

'Oh, I don't know,' Paul replied coyly, still feeling somewhat ashamed about the way he'd treated her before.

'Oh come on, it'll be great, besides I need your support. Galley stewards always end up on the receiving end of the craic when the ship's crew gets together. So will you come then?'

Undecided about the offer, Paul reasoned that a night out in new company might just go a long way into forgetting Angela. Perhaps his workmate's proposal was destined to be the beginning of a new chapter in his life, who knew? Maybe his affair with Angela had been a phase of his life that had been put there for a reason, something he could relate to at later date when fate had had enough fun playing around with his heartstrings and moved on to the next unfortunate. Whatever it was, Paul needed to break free from the hostage of the heart situation he was shackled in. Telling himself that as long as he could forget her, then he'd always allow himself to fondly remember her, he gave his reply. 'Aye, okay then, I could do with a night out.'

'Great,' exclaimed the Scot, 'meet me on Friday at 7.30 outside the Botanic Inn.'

Things were definitely on the upturn for Paul. At midnight the night before, when he'd called McKenna, he'd learnt that Toby was well on the mend, indeed the admission of Tommy's parka had induced an overnight transition in his racing form. Improving more than ten lengths on his couldn't-care-less-run the week before, he'd actually won in a time of 30.83, nowhere near fast enough to have a say in the final shake up for the Derby, but it was certainly a giant stride in the right direction. So much so, that his odds for the Grand Prix had been slashed overnight to 33/1.

Leaving the ship and following his habitual routine, Paul raised his head to the skies as he walked to his car, but tonight as he deeply inhaled the Belfast air it was not sweet, yet strong with the distinctive burning smell of charred wood. It was an odour that had characterised the Northern Irish capital every second week in July ever since he could remember, for it was only two days to the twelfth, the climax of the marching season and anniversary of King William III's triumphant victory over the Catholic leader James II at the Battle of the Boyne in 1690. Now, Paul had nothing against the Protestant faith, or any other for that matter, but there were still things he'd been unable to fathom out about this contradictory festival. 'King Billy' as the Orangemen affectionately idolised him, had actually invaded England in 1688 and made himself king, although his ancestry had given him no right whatsoever to claim that throne. No matter how biased or prejudiced an Orangeman in this part of the world can be, surely if they'd had the brains they were born with, then they'd be able to see that this Dutchman was an impostor to their allegiance to the crown, which they worshipped so fervently, and England's sovereignty which they so demanded to be ruled by for ever. Apart from the history involved, Paul had no idea what could possess grown men to dress up in orange sashes and bygone bowler hats, to march through the streets banging drums, behaving like the Third Reich as they invaded the Nationalist areas in a show of childish defiance and inciting misdemeanour, which would inevitably lead to pitch battles when the Republicans returned home from their day jobs.

The Glorious Twelfth, as the Protestants would have their children brainwashed into believing, was not a good time to be a Catholic, as high on the cocktail of alcohol and the emotional remembrance of a conquest won nearly three hundred years ago, the loyalists felt it was their duty to remind the Catholics that any thoughts of an uprising would not be tolerated. This was achieved by gangs foraying into Nationalist territory, where they'd petrol-bomb homes, cars and occasionally execute the odd known sympathiser. It was also a cruel time for the RUC, since the vast majority of them were members of the Orange clan. Ironically, they'd find themselves in the firing line of their own people when they had to protect the communities that they too held in contempt. This year the Orange revelries really annoyed Paul, for it kept Angela on the brink of his mind when all he wanted to do was forget her. If only these people had been able to stop living in the past, then he too might have found it easier to get on with his future.

With no plans outlined for that week apart from a Friday night out with his workmates and a Saturday spent with Toby down South, Paul realised that sitting around bored would only escalate to depression and constant thoughts of Angela.

Climbing from the bath on Monday morning, Paul stood dripping wet and naked in front of the bathroom mirror and he was ashamed by what he saw. With so much change apparent in his life, he could see that the last few weeks of mental torment had taken their toll on his once fine physique. Not even the ripening hot bath could disguise his thin, pale complexion and his broad chest which had shrunk to reveal a ribcage. Looking further down, he perceived that his athletic tree trunk legs of yesteryear were more like branches in the wind, as they trembled with the reintroduction of his blood circulation. Studying his quivering hands, he noticed ingrained blemishes of nicotine, which fortified by his wheezing respiratory system advised him he had to stop smoking. Stepping on to the scales to weigh up exactly how bad the situation had become, he discovered that he'd lost a full stone to now weigh only nine stones seven pounds. The overall picture was an insalubrious image and one that had to be put right before it deteriorated any further. Wrapping a towel around himself, he went into his bedroom in search of some fresh clothing. He sighed as he rummaged through his wardrobe and drawers, and it crossed his mind that he'd been challenging his attire a little too much of late. Uniform to his mood, his clothes were dark and faded and needed to be replaced before he became typecast in an insurmountable rut. Adopting a female peculiarity, Paul began to breathe fresh air into his life by washing away the toxins of melancholy with the aid of a spending spree and a trip to the hairdresser's.

Once reinvigorated with a smart new haircut and stylish, bright new clothes, all that was needed now to renovate his image was to kick his detrimental smoking habit and rebuild his crumbling physique, and they went hand in hand. It would be no easy fight, but one he appreciated had to be won. Every time the desire to light a cigarette crept up on him, Paul gritted his teeth and did twenty press ups. By Tuesday morning that method was no longer an option, as yesterday's over-exertion had torn muscles in his chest and arms which he'd forgotten existed. Reverting to cycling to the shops in town for three Mars bars at a time to beat the craving appeared to be doing the trick, as well as denying his system the demand for nicotine, and soon his fitness and weight began to return to normal, if not better than ever. The public baths were his next port of call, swimming length after length until he felt like jelly he rediscovered his sleeping pattern over the next two nights.

Come Friday evening and with the passing of the riotous commemorations of the Glorious Twelfth three days earlier, Belfast, like Paul, had returned to 'as-good-as-it-gets' sanity. Singing along with the radio in his room as he prepared for his evening on the town, a change of tempo with the next record saw him quickly turn off the appliance before the ballad had time to penetrate his heart. It was the song they had adopted as their own, Never Tear Us Apart, and now that they had been torn apart, he wouldn't allow the melody to affect his new image. Picking up the professionally gift-wrapped perfume with its red silk bow, he left the house endeavouring to discover what life now had in store for him.

After they had gently introduced themselves to the atmosphere of the Belfast night scene over a few quiet pints, the two Pauls then moved up market to a trendy club where Mairead had chosen to celebrate her key-to-the-door birthday. With overpowering music blasting to drown any conversation in the eye-squinting dimness, Paul couldn't see how he was going to enjoy the evening, but knew he had to make the effort. Supporting the bar, nursing their price-inflated drinks which made sure there was no chance of them becoming bloated at the end of play, the boys commenced to talent spot amongst the female contingent, yet not one girl that pervaded Paul's sight was in the same league as Angela, that was until Mairead made her bill-topping arrival. Wearing a black curve-hugging lycra dress with a billion glittering sequins, Paul couldn't help but be dazzled by her presence, especially when the flashing disco lights danced over her inch-perfect figure. Noticing that Paul's eyes were transfixed by Mairead, the Scotsman made comment 'I can't believe that you let something like that slip through your fingers, ever thought of seeing a shrink? If I had someone like her at home I wouldn't come to work.'

358

Paul gave no reply, but just watched, two in a hundred admiring eyes, as every male in the room used her big event to steal a kiss.

Over the next few hours Paul chatted with a whole host of complaisant females, but none of them could conjure up a magic spark to ignite his cold heart. But when, having almost completed the circuit of acknowledgements, the birthday girl finally arrived at the side of the bar where the two Pauls had distanced themselves from the crowded dance floor, all that seemed destined to change.

'Hi Paul, no one told me you were coming tonight. You're looking well,' she complimented.

'You too,' he returned, reaching into his jacket pocket. 'I bought you a present, it's not much, but it's the thought that counts, I'm told.'

'And have you been thinking about me? Or didn't you lose my phone number?' she said, pulling the bow from the box to open her gift.

'Can I get you a drink?' he offered.

'Aye, why not, I'll have a white wine.'

About turning to face her again with her drink, he felt a warm tingle race through him as she planted a kiss on his cheek. 'Thanks, it's my favourite, how did you know?'

'I guess you could say I've a nose for these things,' he jested.

'Very funny. So Paul, tell me, are you still seeing the girl from the Shankill?'

'No,' he revealed with a cough then a sigh. 'No we called it a day a long time ago, the pressure of the media got to us.'

'So, are you seeing anybody new?' she continued to pry.

'No, what about you?'

'I told you I'd wait didn't I,' she said, as she walked off, before half turning to bait him with a teasing smile.

'Well, what are you waiting for?' inquired the Scot who'd been eavesdropping.

'What do you mean?'

'Christ man, are you blind? She wants you, can't you see that? She wants you to follow her, ask her for a dance or something.'

'I'm not sure,' Paul replied timidly, wondering whether it was all a ploy to entice him into a revengeful slap in the face in front of her friends.

Thinking to himself while he watched her stealing glances at him whenever she had free range, he decided that he'd be willing to make a go of a relationship if that's what she wanted. And if so, then surely he would be able to dispel Angela from his mind for once and all. Besides,

359

Mairead was as pretty, if not more so than Angela, and by the way she'd waited around for him to sort out his tangled life, meant she had to be the faithful type. She obviously saw something in him that he thought Angela never had. And therefore maybe it was time to stop flogging dead horses. Turning to the bar to order another drink, Paul began to reflect that Mairead was a good idea after all. He was very nervous, and that had to be a good indication, for only Angela had ever been able to instil such anxiety into him.

Nearing the end of the night and still not having made his move due to the nagging doubts concerning her true intentions, Paul, all alone now that his Scottish namesake had found female companionship, turned away after watching another lad make his manoeuvre on Mairead now that the slow dances had began. Contemplating his lost opportunity through the bottom of the glass, he resolved to call time on yet another barren evening when from nowhere he felt a tap on his shoulder. It was none other than Mairead.

'Would you like to dance with me?' she asked.

Lost for words, he simply led her on to the dance-floor. Dancing cheek to cheek at first, Paul didn't hear the music as he nuzzled into his spitting image replacement for Angela, but then he did. Closing his eyes as he inhaled the Coco Chanel perfume that Mairead, like Angela always wore, the summer number one of Glen Madeiros crooning out 'Nothing's Gonna Change My Love For You' carried his mind to the sticky nights of Majorca thousands of miles away, which aroused him into caressing her neck and running his fingers through her long dark hair, making her feel that the wait had been worth it. When the third and final smoochie played to unite the sexes their lips met spontaneously for a long, slow, expressive embrace. Sharing a taxi they snuggled up together in the back seat, where they kissed with gentle perfection portraying that they had the utmost respect for each other. Breaking for air, Mairead looked deep into his eyes, searching for the truth, worried that when the light of day arrived and the alcohol's spell had worn off, Paul's interest in her would recede to apathy.

'When can I see you again?' she asked apprehensively, fearing a reply of deferment.

'Well, I'm going down to Wicklow tomorrow morning, then up to Dublin to watch Toby in the evening. Would you like to come with me, or have you other plans?'

Although Mairead did have her Saturday mapped out already, she was not willing to spurn the chance and allow Paul to escape from her web again. Arrangements, like rules, are there to be broken and the way she felt about him, she'd have cancelled an audience with the Pope to be by his side.

'No, I have nothing on and aye, I'd love to have a day out in Dublin,' she replied enthusiastically, commandeering the opening.

'Great, I'll pick you up at ten then,' smiled Paul, before they resumed their kissing session.

When morning arrived, Paul sat at the kitchen table head in hands, engaged in battle with another hangover, stomach churning at the thought of the greasy fried breakfast that his mother was preparing for him. Arriving on the scene, Bernadette poured herself a cup of tea from the stewing pot then turned down the offer of a high cholesterol breakfast, determined to keep her lean figure in trim. Placing the steaming hot plate in front of him, his mother then headed to the bathroom.

'Looks like you had a rough night,' remarked Bernadette, 'then again, it must have been a good night judging by the all the lipstick and foundation smudged over your face. So who's the lucky lass this time?'

'Oh God,' thought Paul, as the memories of last night flooded back to remind him that he'd asked Mairead out again and yet he wasn't a hundred per cent certain she was enough to fill the void left in his life by Angela. Realising that he owed it to her to make a commitment before he burnt another bridge through sobriety, Paul reached the same conclusion as he had the previous night and could now only hope that he wouldn't regret it.

'I'm seeing the girl from work again,' he divulged.

'It won't work,' stated Bernadette, sagaciously.

'I beg your pardon?' said Paul, taken aback at the conviction of her criticism.

'It won't, never does,' she continued, smugly.

'What never does?' he said, raising his head, sending a rush of blood to his brain which almost blacked him out.

'Rushing into another relationship on the rebound. I should know. Take Michael and I for the classic example, after you walked out on me. It isn't working.'

Creeping down the stairs upon hearing Paul and Bernadette's voices talking below, Michael stopped half way so he could eavesdrop a little better.

'I don't want to hear all this again. If you don't love Michael then it's up to you to tell him, but don't involve me, it's none of my business,' Paul stressed, his patience wearing thin, tired of covering the same old ground with her.

'Well, that's where you're wrong, Paul. You see, before you came back I was making a new life, but while you're around here I think of nothing except you. It's you and I living under the same roof that upsets my apple-cart.'

'This is my home Bernie,' he laughed, 'and you want me to get out, that's what you're implying isn't it?'

'Aye, but take me with you, just give me one chance and I promise you'll never want to look at another girl again.'

'I don't need all this again. I have to clean up, I've a date,' he concluded, cutting her short.

Hearing Paul's chair screech across the floor as he rose to leave, Michael sneaked back upstairs. Finding the bathroom door locked, he entered Bernadette's room. Standing behind the door not moving a muscle, he heard Paul climb the stairs then slam their bedroom door. About to turn and head back down the stairs, he spotted a diary resting on top of Bernadette's bedside cabinet. Curious to learn what she might be hiding from him, he sat on her bed and began to read her memoirs. As each heartbreaking entry sunk into his stormy mind, he accepted that his fiancé did indeed still love Paul, even although the feeling was not reciprocated. Blinded by his obsession with her, in his eyes she could nevertheless do no wrong and one entry more than any other manipulated his twisted brain. 'While Paul's around here I don't think I can go through with this marriage, not when there remains the slightest chance he may fall back into love with me.' The way Michael interpreted her confession, was that if Paul was to go, then with him he'd take her incertitude and in turn his problems. Suddenly he was not satisfied with the revenge of raping Angela, he wanted to banish his own brother from their lives.

Throughout their away-day together, Paul analysed Mairead more than he'd ever done before. Not lacking in the looks department and with a more extroverted personality than her rival, she did seem to outshine Angela to make her relatively pale by comparison, yet although he couldn't pinpoint the missing factor, it was still the notional nurse that held the upper hand. If there was nothing else initially that he could find off putting, he did sense that there existed from her side, a passive desire to agree to all his wishes without question, or the input as to what she wanted from life. Maybe it was early days as far as their correlation was concerned, but how he saw it developing at this early phase, was that Mairead was nothing other than what Bernadette's promises would have turned out to be if he'd given her the chance.

Desperate to remove the incubus of Angela from the standards he was setting, he tried to shower some love on to Mairead, hoping his feelings would grow. Allowing her to take Toby's lead while they strolled in County Wicklow's abundant greenbelt, he put his arm around her in an attempt to assure her that it was not all one-way traffic. By the time Paul had began to feel at home with her and she felt the same way with Toby and the McKennas, it was time to leave for Shelbourne Park.

'I've really enjoyed today,' she revealed, placing her hand on his thigh as he drove, to once again revive an image of Angela.

'Me too,' he returned. 'I enjoy the solitude of the country life and the safe ambience of Dublin, you know, just being able to walk down any street without the fear of a bomb blasting you to eternity.'

'Perhaps if things go well between us,' she said uneasily, still a little unsure as to how much he really felt for her, 'then maybe we could stop over in Dublin one weekend?'

'Aye, that's sounds like a good idea,' he agreed.

At 9.15 p.m. Toby was loaded into his favourite red berth, raring to go as the hare began another breakneck circumnavigation of the track. Tonight History Maker was easy to back at odds of 5/1 against. Whilst he'd been recovering from his poisoning scare, the death of his master and acclimatising to his new surroundings, the new track-record holder and ante-post Derby favourite, Randy, had been routing all comers, running up a seven-in-a-row winning streak. Although Paul and McKenna comprehended that Toby would still have to improve a mile to have any chance of Derby success, in their minds, both were looking at this race as a dress rehearsal for the final. Sent off at 4/6 favourite, the brindled October 85 dog soon confirmed his standing at the top of the ratings. Exiting the traps in top gear, he quickly blasted clear at the first bend to the delight of his growing legion of followers. Coasting to victory down the back straight unchallenged, Randy maintained his electric pace while it took Toby all his time to shrug off the stragglers. Watching Randy arrive at the penultimate bend with an approximate ten-length lead, Paul could only hope that he was witnessing an animal that was peaking too soon. Finding the throttle in the last half of the race, Toby came with what turned out to be a wet sail as he whittled down the final advantage to five lengths. With Mairead still shouting on Toby way after the line, Paul had to point out to his new girlfriend that the race was actually over. Upon hearing the winner's time of 30.16, Paul was satisfied with History Maker's performance of 30.56. When he met Johnny McKenna for post-race analysis they both agreed that Toby only needed to find half a dozen more lengths to be back to his best. With now only six weeks to the first round of the Irish Greyhound Derby, they had to squeeze one a week to realise their aspiration. A solo trial before racing in two weeks time would indicate whether that length-a-week target was achievable.

Whether it was up on deck, under the moon and stars, or down below in his or her cabin, another week at sea flew by as Mairead kept Paul company night after night and gradually he began to think less and less of Angela. Some nights as he'd wait for Mairead to come knocking, he ached for some space, but after half an hour in her company, he longed for more. At the end of each episode they'd share a long embrace before returning to their respective beds. Keeping it platonic and with no hint on Paul's part of anything otherwise, Mairead, although she respected his gentlemanly conduct, worried that he was only interested in her as a friend. Being a patient girl, she would wait for him as she'd always done, knowing that only time would tell.

On the Monday of that week, Angela had decided that she needed to return to work. The break had done her good, but she really felt that the involvement of work would heal her wounds quicker and fill the vacuum she'd created when blasting Paul from her life. Each day when the bus took her past Clonard Street on the way to the RVH, she'd hope to catch a glimpse of him, but always her heart sank. Over the next month Angela religiously checked the greyhound results, searching in vain for History Maker, whilst on many other occasions she'd stand over the phone contemplating contact, before the fear of rejection and, more so, humiliation, restrained her from burning her fingers on the receiver. What if he has a new girlfriend, she thought time and time again and if indeed that was the case after all she'd been through, then it would've been all too much for her to suffer.

One Saturday night in August, when the open racers came to town for Dunmore's gala night of the year, Angela went in search of him, sure that he would be unable to repudiate such a momentous event as the Dunmore King Stakes. Presuming that if she crossed his path then he would make the first move, she was disappointed when again he failed to materialise. That final insult to her injury had led her to believe that whatever, or whoever he was now involved with, was more important than she'd ever been to him.

During the week leading up to Toby's solo trial, Mairead suggested the venues and Paul was always available. Touring their beautiful country most of the time, the sun followed them around day after day. From Donegal to Dundalk they picnicked alfresco, but still Paul wondered whether this was what he really wanted. Kissing and cuddling for hours on end, he felt insincere most of the time, for when he closed his eyes it was Angela he pretended to be kissing.

On Saturday July 30th, Paul and Mairead watched Toby keep to his side of the bargain in running a 550 yard solo trial in a time of 30.32 which was three lengths faster than his defeat at the hands of the ante-post favourite Randy. The improved time in conjunction with his last competitive effort saw the bookmakers pruning his odds once again to 25/1. Heading back to Belfast that night, Mairead reflected on how Paul's imperceptible shield appeared to be lifted during their jaunts to Eire. For when they were there, he was more kindred towards her, and that made her assume it was the ship, Belfast and her father's position which led him to be so cold and reticent at times. The truth of the matter was that Paul was beginning to see his covenant to Tommy's name unfurl and that was helping to alleviate his guilt.

'You're quiet,' remarked Paul. 'Anything wrong?'

'No, not at all, I was just thinking that perhaps we might stay over in Dublin after Toby's last warm-up trial before the Derby,' she gently proposed. 'You could have a drink for a change, we could have a meal, whatever you fancy?'

'Sounds great,' he agreed, tiring of the five-hour round trips of sustained concentration when his mind was always on other matters.

After another disenchanting fortnight for Paul, where he spent the days with Mairead only to betray her each night when he slept with Angela in his subconscious, he woke intent on giving Mairead the kind of weekend that her loyalty towards him, when he'd been nonplussed with her, merited. Packing her overnight bag, Mairead, too, was determined to show Paul that she was the only woman for him. Smiling to herself as she placed her sexiest lingerie into her tiny travel bag, Mairead felt if she could just fire up Paul's passion and kick start their redundant sex life, then perhaps the consummation of their affair might strengthen their weak relationship.

The day got off to good a start. Picking her up from her house, Paul swept her off her feet and kissed her robustly on the lips to take her breath away. Presenting her with the largest box of chocolates she'd ever seen, Mairead marvelled as to whether Paul had the same idea as the one she'd dreamt of all week. It wasn't until the driving was over and they were all alone walking Toby in the tranquil countryside that Paul felt free to set the record straight. Pulling her in tight to his waist, he kissed the side of her warm head before professing to what had been holding him back all along.

'I'm really sorry if it seems like I've been drifting away lately, but the truth is I have. My friend Tommy died recently, as I'm sure you must've read in the papers, and I truly appreciate the way you've never mentioned it. It's been a stressful time, I blame myself you know. I seemed to delegate his life for him when I should have left him alone. I despise myself for that and that's why it's imperative this dog here produces the goods in the Derby. I know it can't bring him back, but it's all I have to restore some dignity to his name. I realise that my behaviour, if I don't change it, will lead to me losing you and after a great deal of thought I don't think I could handle any more loss, especially you and I know you deserve better, so I'm gonna try my best to be better.'

'I don't mean to pry, but what about the girl?' she probed, needing a little more reassurance.

'What do you mean?' he inquired.

'Well, sometimes I get the distinct feeling you still haven't managed to get over her.'

'I'll admit it, it's taken some time, but I'm sure I'm there now, all yours if you want me?' he declared, questioningly.

'I want nothing else,' she replied sincerely.

For the remainder of the time spent at the McKenna stud farm that afternoon they shared a proper relationship, both finding it easy to express their feelings for one another and Paul had no reservations about giving Mairead his heart. Driving up to Shelbourne Park for

Toby's final trial before the inauguration of the Derby a fortnight on Tuesday, August 29th, Angela couldn't have been further from Paul's thoughts, as he held Mairead's hand at every opportunity the winding road permitted him to.

Toby's final spin kept in line with his owner's melioration, as once again he improved, this time another length on his previous run, to post a warning clock of 30.20, which was no less than anyone could have asked of him.

'Well, that's it,' said McKenna, drying Toby's legs, as he lapped at his bowl of water with the splash of milk in it that he enjoyed so much. 'There's nothing we can do now except pray for the clouds to open and shower us with luck.'

'Aye, you're right there,' agreed Paul.

It was a fact. No matter how fast or blessed with track craft a greyhound was, it would still need a slice of fortune to win such a prestigious event. A bad draw, one mistimed start, a late summer thunderstorm to flood the inside of the track where History Maker always did his running, could mean the difference between delight and dejection. The bottom line, and Paul and Johnny McKenna knew it, was that nothing short of a phenomenon would be good enough to see their charge lift the £30,000 first prize and be crowned the finest and fleetest greyhound in Ireland, Ireland being the world. Paul, though, was starting to believe in miracles, he'd already witnessed the second coming of Toby's form and, to support his faith, Mairead had given him a second bite of the cherry.

'So will you be down in a fortnight?' asked McKenna.

'Aye, I'll have to, seeing as I'm gonna miss the first two rounds thanks to work,' replied Paul.

'Can't you get any holidays?'

'I doubt it, seeing as my job allots me twenty-six weeks' holiday a year as it is,' returned Paul.

'Then won't you miss the final should he make it?' posed the trainer.

'I think we'll just have to have food poisoning that week,' interrupted Mairead with a wink.

'Aye,' smiled Paul in agreement, 'food poisoning it is. Anyway Johnny, we'll not be staying for the racing tonight, we have other plans.'

'Straight back up the road then, is it?'

'No, we're going to have a night out around this fair city,' Paul grinned.

367

Sparing no expense on a night of such magnitude, they booked-in incognito to the plush hundred-and-one year old Central Hotel in the city centre. After sprucing themselves up they hit the town. Opting to eat Chinese, they smiled and laughed at each other across the table as they farcically endeavoured to master the chopsticks, their eyes sparkling in the reflection of the romantic candlelight. Finishing their meal, then following the in crowd, they found themselves in a jam packed to the rafters, paradigmatically Irish tavern, where the stentorian folk music sanctioned no intimacy to enter. Finishing their one and only drink, they decided to head back to the hotel in search of more unobtrusive surroundings where they could enjoy a night cap and each other's company without having to shout to be heard above the discordant din. Swirling his brandy glass and reflecting with a half-inebriated smile upon how he could easily become accustomed to this lifestyle of grandeur, Paul noticed Mairead parting with a fake yawn to indicate that she was ready for bed. Taking the bed closest to the window overlooking the now neon city below, Paul waited while Mairead fashioned the finishing touches to her seductive appearance in the bathroom. Turning to face her, his eyes almost popped from their sockets. Before him, clad in only in the skimpiest matching black bra and knickers with a sumptuous body that begged to be ravished, stood Mairead and he knew exactly what was on her bewitching mind.

'Can I join you?' she purred.

Lost for words at what he'd been denying himself for what seemed like an aeon, he swallowed his Adam's apple and simply nodded. Resting her head on his strong chest, she began to caress his nipples to gauge a reaction. Closing his eyes, soaking up the pleasure as he drew circles of eight around the moles on her goose-pimpled back, his mind deserted to a certain lake near Marino train station. He opened his eyes to shut out the mirage and moved his fingers gently to the base of her neck then began to tickle her into a frenzy. Turning around in a sharp movement to face him, she undid her bra to reveal her breasts as well as her intentions.

'Make love to me, Paul,' she moaned.

He did not dare to argue with his male instincts, but briskly rolled her over, then pinned her to the bed. Enraptured to a sun-drenched calypso beach, they made love in rhythm with the imaginary surf which thundered over their adjoined bodies. Consumed by the passion flowing between them as they neared a simultaneous climax,

Mairead began to shout out Paul's name and Paul could only oblige by returning the call.

'Oh, Angela,' he groaned.

Throwing him off with the shock of his utterance, Mairead jumped from the bed, gathered her clothes then rushed to the bathroom where she locked herself in and began to sob her heart out. Punching the mattress in frustration, Paul realised that he'd just blown another relationship, thanks to his infatuation with the unattainable. Standing by the bathroom door which separated them, he attempted to reconcile the situation.

'I'm really sorry, I. . . I. . . I can't explain what happened,' he dithered like the clown prince to the throne of England.

'Not as sorry as I am, but I can explain it for you. You still love her and don't try to deny it. Just go will ye, I don't want to ever see you again for as long as I live,' she reprimanded him severely, not missing him to hit the wall.

'Can't we discuss this?' he pleaded. 'Surely we can settle this, just give me the chance and I'll show you that it's only you that I'm interested in.'

'No Paul, once bitten, twice shy, if you don't leave this minute then I will.'

Understanding that she could not be swayed in this frame of mind, Paul granted her wishes and left her to weep the anguish from her system.

Sitting at the hotel bar with his head in bits, Paul just couldn't accept that his alliance with Mairead had come to a natural end. With no credit card and a limited cash supply, he was forced to spend the night in his car in the hotel's underground car park. All he could do now was pray that Mairead would change her mind come the light of day.

When, with a brittle neck and an expensive hangover, Paul awoke filled with the shame of last night's slip of the tongue during his moment of wanton zeal, he glanced at his watch hoping there was still sufficient time left to make amends. Noting it was 7.45 a.m. he felt as if he had just enough time to save the day. Dublin is comparable to most British cities on a Sunday morning, the streets were dead with the exception of last night's litter blowing up and down the godforsaken ghost town. Having driven around for thirty unproductive minutes in search of an open shop where he could purchase the peace offering of a bouquet of flowers, Paul aborted his mission when he passed the municipal park at

369

St Stephen's Green for the second time. There he borrowed some of the landscape to meet his requirements, after all, it was there for the public's benefit. He then walked into the Hotel. Looking like he too had just that minute been plucked from a flowerbed, by his dishevelled appearance and hedgehog hairstyle, he headed for the elevator. Fixing his attire and combing his hair with a palm full of saliva, he knocked before placing his key card into the slot. But when he entered the room, he soon discovered that Mairead had already checked out. Quickly gathering his holdall, he instinctively touched the kettle to find it was still relatively warm, which told him that he'd just missed her. With life again kicking him when he was down, he raced along the corridor convinced that he'd passed her coming up in the lift. Handing his key card back to the receptionist who looked at him as if he'd just crawled out from under a stone, he asked for assistance.

'When did the other key holder check out?'

'Eight-thirty,' she replied, perfunctorily.

'Shit,' he exclaimed.

'She ordered a taxi to take her to Connolly train station,' divulged the receptionist.

'Thanks, you're a genius, here, have these,' he said, throwing the soiled flowers on to her paperwork in his excitement.

Whilst driving like a maniac towards the railway station, Paul reckoned that if he could catch Mairead, then he could persuade her to forgive him. After being given the run around by the user-unfriendly departure board, lathered in sweat and with scarlet face, he eventually arrived at the correct platform to view the last carriage of the Enterprise disappearing out of sight. It was a well-esteemed hypothesis that the train to Belfast was a full fifteen minutes quicker than by car, yet Paul felt it was time to put that argument to the test and challenge the statisticians. Motoring unhindered for the first leg of the homeward journey, he reached the border and sensed that he'd drawn level with the train, if not, held a slight edge. But again, as if by God's will, he was delayed from catching Mairead. Still perspiring out last night's alcohol when he slowed at the army checkpoint served only to his disadvantage in automatically drawing him to the attention of the suspicious security forces. It took a full twenty minutes of car and computer search before he was allowed to recommence on his journey. When he skidded the car to a halt at 11.30 a.m., he knew that he'd missed her arrival by only fifteen minutes. Thinking that perhaps she'd had difficulty in hailing a taxi, or might've even called home for a lift, he scoured Central Station and its taxi ranks, but all to no avail. Absolutely devastated, he retired to his vehicle, where he sat and contemplated whether to go straight to her house and beg for her absolution, or head home to offer his pretext by telephone.

Earlier that morning, Matt Williamson had finalised his composition on History Maker's bid for the Derby, having been given the go ahead from his pragmatic editor. Things were bad in the city, both communities had been constantly at each other's throats, condescending to reprisal after reprisal. Amongst the tragedies to rock the island that week were the deaths of two elderly Protestant workmen who had been repairing an RUC station. On their way home from work, they'd been served a lead dinner of 150 bullets for their toils. Matt's sole intention was to initiate another dream, where the people could unite behind something Northern Irish as opposed to Catholic or Protestant. He wanted History Maker to become a conduit for the public to run their sorry lives through, for as long as the dog survived in the competition. The way he'd sold it to his editor was, 'it worked before and it'll work again, this greyhound belongs to the people of Belfast and the owner is convinced it'll win.'

Needing to hear that Paul's faith in his dog hadn't degenerated any, Matt picked up the telephone and dialled only to find the line was busy.

'I'm sorry son, but Mairead's not here you've just missed her. Can I take a message?' offered her mother.

'No, it's okay,' replied Paul morosely, knowing that he was being lied to.

Replacing the receiver in clumsy fashion, seething at how he could do no right in his life for doing wrong, it was inevitable that the next poor individual to cross his path would be in for the backlash of his exasperation. Hearing the phone ring as he ascended the stairs, Paul about turned on his temper hoping that it might be Mairead feeling guilty for snubbing him, but he was to be disappointed.

'Hi, can I speak to Paul O'Donnell?' inquired an articulate voice that he knew only too well

'Speaking,' snapped Paul, 'what do you want?'

'It's Matt Williamson here. Do you remember we had a chat last month about your greyhound. Do you still think it can win the Derby?'

'Of course it'll win the fucking Derby,' he roared, releasing all the rage of the last twelve hours before slamming the phone down.

371

Sprinting back upstairs, still furious at how life was toying with him, Paul could have had no idea that such an inconsequential statement, provoked through sheer frustration, could endanger his life to the brink of death.

With his holdall slung over his shoulder and the largest and most colourful bouquet of flowers that money could buy in hand, Paul joined the ship and immediately made his way to the gift emporium. Arriving at the closed shop, he tapped on the glass door to attract the attention of the girls who were preparing their tills for another day's business. Seeing no sign of Mairead, his mind flashed back to her suggestion of food poisoning.

'Where's Mairead?' he asked when her workmate opened the door, 'food poisoning?'

'No, she got a transfer to another ship. We only found out ten minutes ago when her relief announced her arrival, we didn't even have time to get her a leaving present. It was all so sudden.'

'Oh right, thanks,' he sighed, deflated.

'Were those for her?' the girl asked, looking at the immense nosegay.

'No,' coughed Paul, although he was unable to validate his story with a lie. 'Aye, aye, they were. Perhaps you could find out what ship she's working on now, then I could send them.'

'Okay, I'll try,' comforted the girl, observing that he was perturbed by the anguish and agony of the injunction Mairead had enforced upon him.

That night Paul sat with his injured pride and read Matt Williamson's piece pertaining to the dog, where the reporter urged the public on the owner's wisdom and confidence to invest in their hopes for Northern Ireland's pacifistic future by taking the 25/1 on offer. By Friday night Paul was over Mairead, for in having anatomised his true feelings all week, he realised it had only been his guilt towards her that had goaded him into giving her his best shot. Bernadette had been right on this occasion, since Mairead had been nothing more than the rebound of vulnerability that his ex had forewarned him of. He decided to write his true and only love one last letter and as he rested the notepaper on the evening edition of the Telegraph, he observed that History Maker had raced onto the front page with an unbelievable headline that he realised could only spell trouble for him in the long run: 'Belfast Bookmakers Stand To Lose £100 Million.' As his eyes almost popped out and his heart cowered for safety behind his ribcage, he read enthralled but anxiously, to learn that over £4 million worth of bets had already poured into the city's betting shops and with more overwhelming support anticipated, the turf accountants had been coerced into slashing Toby's odds to 8/1 second favourite, behind Randy at 6/1. Aware that both sides in the war of religion, especially the IRA, depended on extortion funding from the betting shops up and down their United Ireland, Paul worried that once again, he'd just moulded himself into a walking target.

When leaving the ship on Sunday August 21st, Paul reverted to looking under his car for plastic explosives before convincing himself that if any party wanted to prevent Toby from running in the Derby, then they'd simply attack the root of the problem, and that was not him. Not wanting to alarm Johnny McKenna, Paul understood how the IRA system worked. If it was their stipulation that Toby be withdrawn from the event, then Paul would be given the sweet-tempered notice of an amiable threat; they were pretty decent that way, besides intimidation from their reputation did tend to have an excellent success rate. On the way home Paul stopped to post his epistle to Angela. In the letter he'd explained to her that he felt there still existed between them an invisible bond and all she had to do to sever this was to reply once, notifying him that her feelings hadn't varied from those she'd portrayed with such conviction at the funeral.

With no relevant itinerary to follow that week, Paul continued to exhaust his time keeping fit, as he jogged for miles each day and did hundreds of press ups. Burning off his agitation, he trained as if he was a boxer preparing for the biggest fight of his life, and in reality that's how it would turn out.

On Thursday evening Michael's patience with respect to the extradition of his brother from his life was almost rewarded. In the back room of Paddy's Bar he was about to have his education furthered concerning the IRA's embezzlement of the local community to finance their Cause. 'We have another fucking problem,' revealed the cripple, pacing around the room probably unable to sit down from the arse-kicking he'd previously received from his superiors. 'It's your headcase of a brother again and his big mouth. Do you realise that if his fleabitten mongrel wins the fucking Derby it's gonna hit us for millions?'

'What do you mean?' probed Michael.

'We have a large stake in the racing scene. It's an excellent source of revenue for subsidising our fight, just the same way the UVF have their drug money to subsidise their exploits. Now if this dog wins, it stands to hit the bookmakers, and in turn us, for over a hundred million, which is a hell of a lot of guns and semtex.'

'So you want me to kill the dog?' presumed Michael, jumping the gun to show he had initiative.

'No, not at all. Too much public furore and condemnation, they'd never forgive us, Christ there'd be a revolt on the streets. The dog will have to be eliminated from the race fairly, not from the face of God's fucking earth.'

'So what do you want me to do?' quizzed Michael, puzzled.

'Well, we're pretty sure it won't win, but if it should make the final then your brother would be forced to withdraw the mutt. So we want you to make him aware of the consequence were he to deny our request. If this dog wins then someone will have to pay,' he stressed, pausing momentarily as he turned his back to the young volunteer, 'with their life.'

As before, Michael hadn't the slightest intention of forewarning Paul, instead he would closely monitor the Derby heat results, praying that his brother's dog would make the last six, for then the real test would come for him. With an infinite supply of jealousy, his hatred for Paul burned like an eternal flame and it was in the light of this that he felt certain he could commit the cardinal sin without the blink of an eyelid.

When Paul set off for Dublin on Saturday morning, the first round of the Derby was only two days away. Leaving after the postman had failed yet again to bring him any word from Angela, he thought about her all the way to Wicklow and wondered why it was that with so much going on in his life nothing was happening for him.

During her teabreak at the RVH, Angela removed Paul's last correspondence from her handbag where it had taken up permanent residence since its arrival earlier in the week. Although she knew every word off by heart, in just touching his writing, she felt as if it brought them closer together, yet even though she continued to experience a flame burn deep in her heart for him, it wasn't enough for her to write and reply. It simply wouldn't work in Belfast, she told herself, and there was no way she could elope with him while her mother needed constant care and attention. Shaking herself, she'd suddenly realised that she was indirectly wishing her mother's life away.

* * *

374

Paul walked for miles and talked for hours with Toby that day. And similar to the time he'd spent with Tommy, he explained to the dog that he was thinking of moving on soon. Since Angela had favoured him with no response, he was seriously considering relocation in Scotland. Perhaps Glasgow, seeing as there was a sizeable contingent of Irish settlers there and it was within realistic travelling distance for his work at Stranraer. The truth of the matter was that Paul was more confused than ever about where he wanted to go in life. When this occurred the only way out he knew was to run and hide and sadly this was the position he'd been manoeuvred into once again. Saying what he really thought in his farewell to Toby, he spoke from the heart:

'Tobes, I know the next three weeks will be difficult for you and I won't think any less of you if you can't win the Derby, but it's not for me it's for Tommy up there. He had all the faith in you and he was convinced, when I wasn't, that you would run again and win the Derby, so prove me wrong just once more.'

When Toby raised his ears at the mention of his late master's name, Paul smiled knowing that the dog had understood exactly what the docile human had been saying. Leaving Toby to his parka and new wife, Paul made his announcement to the McKennas.

'I've come to a conclusion whereby I think it's only right, that after Toby finishes his Derby duties, win or lose, then I hand him back to you. He's happy here, so why uproot him again?'

'Are you sure?' queried the trainer.

'I'm positive. Anyway, I'll give you a call on Monday then hopefully Saturday night, should he get to the second round. I really have to be making tracks.'

'I take it we'll be seeing you on the seventh and tenth of September for the quarter and semi-finals?' asked McKenna, having heard the doubt filtering from Paul's words.

'If he gets that far, then of course I'll be there to support him, but all I can do in the meantime is keep everything crossed,' replied Paul.

From teatime onwards on Monday August 29th, Paul was trembling with nerves and yet he didn't know why. Toby had received a difficult draw from trap three, though on paper the rest of the field simply couldn't compete with his all-round pace. However, as Paul had always maintained, perhaps at times pessimistically, it wasn't about what the rest did, it was about your own performance. Pacing up and down in his cabin, biting his nails and checking his watch every three seconds for

375

the five minutes leading up to 9.15 p.m. when Toby's Derby crusade well and truly got underway, he ached for a cigarette to steady his concerns.

History Maker made a complete hash of the start as he had forgotten what it was like to race from the middle slot. Switching to the rails immediately, and in doing so forfeiting valuable lengths, the even-money favourite soon found himself relegated to last position as the first bend loomed, to the gasps of the crowd. With things looking bleak as the field turned off the second arc, Toby put his feet to the floor and showed his class with an exhilarating burst of speed. Sweeping from last to first in a matter of ten strides, to the utter delight of his travelling fan club, who'd crawled out from the woodwork to cheer on Northern Ireland's flag bearer, he soon drew clear to win handsomely by five lengths in a time of 30.55. And with that respectable time he had booked his passage into the second round on Saturday evening. But McKenna was worried.

'God, me heart was in me mouth at the first bend.'

'Did he come off sound?' asked Paul.

'Aye, no sign of lameness, but if we don't get the red jacket we can't win this,' stated the trainer, who'd now become the doubting Thomas. 'Randy routed his opposition from the coffin box in a 30.18 and Ardfert Sean did a 30.12 from the orange, we can't avoid this pair for ever.'

'Aye, okay,' acknowledged Paul, 'let's hope he strips fitter come Saturday. If we can sneak into the quarter-finals, I've a method that'll find us another three to four lengths.'

'I'm telling you Paul, I think you'd better divulge that information now, because he's really gonna struggle on tonight's evidence.'

'Okay, Johnny, I'm sorry, but my money's all gone. I'll ring you on Saturday night. Have some good news for me.'

'Wait,' shouted McKenna desperate to learn of the secret, but Paul had already cut him off with the push of a finger.

The most worried of all after History Maker's first-round performance was Michael. Knowing that the dog had won by five lengths, he appeared for his weekly meeting all smiles only to be abased by his lack of wisdom pertaining to greyhound racing.

'I spoke to my brother, but he's adamant to go all the way and I saw that his dog won very easily. Surely it would be better dishing out his punishment now, before he humiliates us any further?'

376

'I could have beaten that field on my one leg, the dog would have to run ten lengths faster to worry us, sources say it can't win unless it starts to grow wings,' educated his adjutant.

By Saturday night the first tremor of doubt rocked the IRA's epicentre. Gaining a solo run from the red-jacket berth, History Maker made amends for his previous run, to coast home unchallenged in a time of 30.32 which turned out to be the second fastest posting of the second-round heats, with only Randy in a win time of 30.20 bettering his effort.

Arriving in the kitchen with his holdall on Monday morning, ready to embark on his voyage to Wicklow where he'd decided to stay on the run-up to Wednesday's quarter-finals and, optimistically, the semi-finals on Saturday evening, Paul found Michael running late for work.

'I've heard Toby's only 5/1 now for the Derby, should I take those odds?' probed his brother.

'Bet what you can afford to lose, that's my motto,' Paul replied distantly, grabbing a slice of toast to eat on his way out.

'So do you really think he can win it?'

'Aye, I think he'll win it,' Paul stated, confidently.

'So where are you off to?'

'County Wicklow, I'll be home late Saturday evening should anyone want me.'

Upon learning that Toby had been sweetly drawn from trap one again for Wednesday's quarter-final, to Johnny McKenna's annoyance and dismay, Paul refused to disclose what he'd banked to gain those extra spots on the stopwatch, opting to bank them for when he alone felt that Toby needed to find them. Meeting Ardfert Sean again in the 9.30 race brought fond memories flooding back for Paul, as he reminisced the last time the dogs had crossed swords and how he'd twirled Angela around in the air under a shower of torn dockets, when Toby had claimed the king of Dublin's crown. Earlier that evening on the card, Paul had witnessed Randy's electric all-round swiftness obliterate a healthy field in a time of 30.18 and he was beginning to worry that the still ante-post favourite would not lapse in his consistency.

When the lids sprang open at 9.32, Toby trailed the white jacket of Ardfert Sean by half a length at the first bend. Roaring him on from the bottom of his new lungs, Paul watched Toby murder him for speed down the far straight and he sensed that he was watching an animal who

377

was finding the best form of his glittering career. Scorching home to win by two and a half lengths and finally put the North and South argument to bed, the announcement of the winning time of 30.02 had the bookmaker's scrubbing his odds from 5/1 to 5/4 favourite, installing him as the new favourite to win the coveted title. As he headed to meet McKenna in the kennelling enclosure, Paul winked as he walked past the slanderous bookmaker who'd accepted his wager at 150/1.

'Not bad for a rag, is he?'

Thursday's edition of the Telegraph infuriated the IRA, as the media congratulated themselves for advising the public to support the Northern Irish Greyhound at 25/1. Plastering the front pages with over twenty stills of last night's action from South of the border and the promise of more to come was all too much for the Republican movement to endure, especially now that they could feel over £100 million beginning to slip through their liquidating fingers. Calling an emergency meeting to re-evaluate the impending crisis, it was decided that a repeat run from History Maker on Saturday night would justify disciplinary procedures.

Waiting at the old wooden table in the operations room of Paddy's Bar, Michael shook his head, fully expecting the powers of wisdom to have postponed his inevitable dark kismet yet again. Entering from the main bar, the cripple bobbed across to the far end of the room keeping his back turned to the young and eager volunteer.

'I've news for you.'

'And?' queried Michael, anticipating the usual derailment of his dual dream of becoming an ASU member and making his brother vanish into thin air in the same subterfuge.

'We're to wait here on Saturday night for a phone call. The way I see it is, if the fucking dog wins then your brother will be the loser. It may be a last-ditch effort, except it has been known in the past for racehorses to be withdrawn in respect of their deceased owners, but then again I see this as more of a punishment because I can't understand why our people just don't kidnap the beast until after the event has run its course.'

'Public outcry?' said Michael, stealing his superior's words with a furtive glance.

'So, if the worst comes to the worst, do you think you'll be able to carry this one out?'

'I'm certain, I have good reasons,' he replied.

'Fair enough, the call's yours. I'll prepare a weapon should it come to this and work out an escape route.'

'No need,' interrupted Michael, 'you won't be able to stalk him this week, he's down South, but he's due home last thing Saturday night. I would appreciate it if you could provide a silencer, though.'

Giving no reply the old man with the uncivil tongue walked to the door then spoke. 'Saturday night then!'

On the eve of the Derby semi-finals, Johnny McKenna sat in front of the crackling open fire plying the owner with drink in an attempt to lubricate his mouth into revealing the information that would make Toby run even faster. Staggering upstairs with his secret still intact, Paul fell sound asleep the instant his head hit the pillow. The following morning, Paul sat at the breakfast table nursing his head, wondering if last night's strange dream that he could remember so vividly would transpire into truth. Standing by the win-line at Shelbourne Park as Toby sailed home first, Angela had appeared from the crowd to reveal her undying love for him.

With it being semi-finals night the stadium was bursting at the seams. Now that the sediment had been filtered from the competition, all that was left were 18 dregs of vintage champagne and a beautiful, short-sleeved late summer's night on which to savour the taste.

Throughout the night leading up to the 9.45 heat, which was the third and final semi-final, Paul wandered around the grandstand from bar to bar, dwelling for long periods with the Northern Irish travelling army, as he scoured for Angela. Postulating that she may have followed all the media hype over the last week and a half, he'd hoped that she'd joined the busloads from Dunmore who'd made the trip southward. As he mingled amongst the upbeat crowd, he wasn't aware of it, but at times he stood within a few feet of the press and the IRA, who'd come to determine his fate. When the light began to fade, Paul had somehow drifted to the finishing line. Relinquishing all belief of seeing Angela, he looked to the race card as Toby walked past on parade.

This was undoubtedly History Maker's toughest assignment to date. Not only was it the semi-final of the Derby, where every runner would be tuned up to give his all, but Randy was berthed from the blue of trap two and an old enemy in O'Dell Schooner, the fastest sprinter on the circuit, had been drawn from the black of trap four, making Toby the meat in the greyhound enthusiast's mouth-watering sandwich. Scrutinising the betting market, Paul observed History Maker and Randy open up at 6/4 against, joint favourites, before a flood of clever money engulfed Randy's odds sinking him to 5/4 on clear favourite whilst Toby drifted out to 2/1. The betting guide was no more than Paul had anticipated, for the prospect of History Maker gaining first-bend clearance was slimmer than the racing room he was expected to receive from two abundantly early paced canines. Just how much the IRA had played their part in the disadvantageously backbreaking draw, which reeked of impending catastrophe, would never be known, but with the stakes so high it was a safe bet to presume that skulduggery was involved. Placing two separate 100 punt wagers, one for himself and the other for McKenna, in his mind, Paul would have been more than happy with the runner-up spot.

As the lids cracked open, the crowd erupted simultaneously upon witnessing the most level of breaks. Flashing past Paul and the win-line for the first time, it was O'Dell Schooner who had taken the initiative to forge a neck clear of Randy and Toby. Sucking in the air through his clamped teeth as the first bend loomed, Paul realised that his Derby dream was about to come off the rails and terminate in a first bend concertina pileup. Sneaking through on the inner at the last possible moment, Randy surged clear of the imminent carnage as O'Dell Schooner cut across to badly impede History Maker, sending him on to the back of the straggling trap one runner who'd arrived on the scene late thanks to the skirmishing. Expecting Toby to end up in a heap with a broken limb into the bargain, Paul gasped in amazement as his undeniable charge rode the bend like a contortionist, somehow weaving in mid-air to come off the second turn, chasing Randy, who had now pilfered a lead of four to five lengths. Knowing from the form book that nothing had ever come from off the pace to collar the leader, although the black and white speed machine had often come from behind to win, with 250 yards still to race, Paul had settled for second best on this occasion and a place in the final, where he could employ his magic hand to defeat Randy, yet Toby had other ideas. Mesmerised in to silence, Paul and a stunned crowd watched in disbelief as Toby went on the rampage down the backstraight to close up the gap at the penultimate arc, where he challenged for pole position before Randy cut him off at the turn forcing him to check. Swinging out wide and probably losing a further two lengths in making his own racing room, History Maker flew off the final bend then put Randy in his place. Paul welled up with emotion, and clenched his fists to warn off the tears of joy, then looked to the heavens; surely nothing now could prevent History

Maker from being crowned world champion in exactly seven days?

Collecting his 600 punts and still shaking from the excitement of Toby's supersonic wonder run, Paul, who hadn't believed his eyes, was now about to be served an announcement that went off in his ears like a sonic boom: 'First History Maker, by a length in a winning time and new track record of 29.99.'

Back in the kennelling enclosure, Johnny McKenna was weeping with joy. Paul hugged him then handed him the scant reward of 300 punts for his endeavours.

'Are we gonna celebrate tonight, or what?' fizzed McKenna.

'I can't, I want to get back up the road tonight, but there's something I want you to do for me midweek. Find a jacuzzi and put Toby in for about ten minutes then rest him, only light walks and no gallops. Oh, and you'll need this,' revealed Paul, removing from his pocket the small bottle of thick liquid which resembled treacle. 'The secret formula; sprinkle a capful over his food the night before and on the morning of the final, then watch him fly.'

'It is legitimate isn't it?' inquired McKenna, worried that disqualification could still ruin the dream.

'Do you think I'd let us get this close, then blow it all now?' stated Paul, shaking his head at how McKenna could have questioned his motives after all they'd achieved via honest teamwork.

'I'm sorry, but I had to ask,' apologised the trainer. 'So you will be here for the final, won't you?'

'Aye, course I will. I'm going to work on Monday, then I foresee myself acquiring a bout of food poisoning when the ship docks in Belfast Lough on Friday night. Nothing will stop me from attending this year's final, nothing.'

Although the trap draw for the 1988 Irish Greyhound Derby would not be made until Monday in Dublin's Jury's Hotel, both the bookmakers and IRA had seen enough to convince them that the final was a foregone conclusion.

Sipping away at a pint of Guinness alone in the clandestine back room of Paddy's Bar, Michael grinned to himself when he heard a loud roar from the main bar penetrate his solitude. All the regulars who had taken the generous ante-post offerings had been watching and waiting by the Teletext for the outcome from Dublin and now Michael knew it was in his favour.

381

Chapter 14

The Dice Was Loaded from the Start

With, perhaps, the only exception being a suicide bombing raid, in the eyes of the IRA what Michael had to commit in passing the final test of initiation was surely the toughest assignment they could ask of any volunteer, yet in his case this was the heaven-sent optimum solution and answer to his immoral supplications.

At 10.15 p.m. the IRA's disabled delegate entered the room to inform the executioner of the court's deliberation and dispense the order to carry out sentence. Tossing a hexagonal-headed key on to the table he revealed the blueprints of the mission.

'You'll find your weapon inside the lamppost at the junction of Clonard and Odessa Street, fitted with a silencer as requested. As before, the gun is loaded with one up the spout, just cock and fire and for fuck's sake don't miss. This is similar to your final exam at school, therefore if you fail all the good efforts that you've put in over the last few years will have counted for nothing, and fundamentally your career prospects with this fraternity will be negligible. If you're clumsy enough to get caught, just remember to denounce the court which is within your right as a prisoner of war. Oh, and last but not least, when you've completed your task, dump the gun over the wall of the Clonard monastery, we'll have a man in position there from midnight onwards.'

Giving no verbal assurances, Michael merely picked up the key then left the room. Heading straight home to prepare for the fratricide, he delved deep into his warped mind for some kind of alibi, aware that he simply could not afford to be related to this crime. It wasn't the fear of a life sentence which bullied him into having second thoughts, it was the trepidation of how his mother would react if she found out that her golden son had been taken from her by his own brother.

Pausing on the doorstep with a million headaches and not an aspirin in sight, he reflected on how his mother had used Paul's model existence as an example to lever him into changing his ways and finding employment. 'You ought to take a leaf out of your brother's book,' she'd constantly harangued. 'He's making something of his life, he has a job, a nice girlfriend and look at you lounging around all day with no aspirations for the future.' It had always been Paul this and Paul that for as long as he could remember. Not once had his mother praised him to his face and never had she given him any support or encouragement, yet entering the house all that was about to change. Walking into the living room to find his mother and fiancé engrossed in their habitual Saturday night pastime of gluing themselves to the television, his face was pale with thoughts of the consequences of the next few hours.

'You're home early,' commented his mother explicitly, glancing at the clock resting on the mantelpiece, 'and sober too. Are you all right? You look awfully pale, you're not coming down with something are you?'

Unable to look her in the eye as the guilt which stole his colour would never allow him to do again, he mumbled a weak reply now that she'd provided him with the ideal cover story.

'No, I'm not feeling too well at all, every bone in my body is aching.'

'Well, there is a flu bug raging at the moment. I think a hot toddy and bed is what you need,' advised his mother.

Bidding the womanfolk goodnight with an Oscar-winning performance, Michael lumbered his way upstairs.

For a change, Paul was savouring the journey homeward, driven by the joyous emotion of Toby's record-breaking victory. Although he wasn't counting his chickens before they'd hatched, the pound signs were beginning to flash before his eyes. Having finally come to terms with the reality that the peace-wall, which separated him from Angela could never be breached, in conjunction with the abstract supposition that Bernadette would never leave him alone for as long as he resided at 6 Clonard Street, Paul had firmly concluded that too much water had passed under the bridge and if Toby could indeed land the £30k first prize, then he was off. There were too many lingering bitter memories impelling him to walk away, now he was only thirty seconds from realising that goal. The prize money, accumulated with the few thousand pounds the bookmaker would grudge paying him out, would hand him sufficient collateral to take the financial sting out of life and to buy his own place, with enough left over to furnish his new abode. All he needed to determine now was the location. Glasgow was favourite at the moment, though realistically anywhere except Belfast would be taken into consideration.

When entering the dependency of Northern Ireland at midnight, Paul resolved that he would empower fate to demarcate his path, for no matter how hard he'd attempted to plan his future in the past, destiny had always appeared to come out on top. It had brought him, Tommy and Angela together and with the same effortless ease forced them apart. Yielding to its supernatural and imponderable forces, he settled for allowing it to carry him again towards wherever it was scheming; though unaware of it, in less than an hour it would reveal what it had in store for him.

Sitting on the edge of his bed in the still darkness with his homemade balaclava in one hand and the key to the lamppost and his future in the other, Michael heard the front door slam then listened carefully as his father crept upstairs drunk, whispering to himself to be quiet so as not to wake the now all-bedded household. He moved his wrist towards the window to utilise the streetlight so he could read his watch, and strained to note that it was now 12.10 a.m. Having estimated that Paul could arrive home no earlier than 12.30 a.m., he inhaled deeply to breathe life into his lethargy, knowing it was high time for him to make a move. Having adorned his darkest clothes for maximum camouflage, he skulked downstairs on tiptoes before leaving the house via the back door. Pausing, he scanned around the backs of the houses for witnesses to his moonlight escapade and, satisfied that there were no ominous signs of nocturnal life, he sneaked into the back alley and soon blended into the night.

Although Saturday night had just turned into Sunday morning, the streets were desolate. Already, the inhabitants of the Falls were respecting the day of worship and rest had arrived. Double-checking that no one was perceiving his manoeuvres, Michael reached the point of no return. He carefully unlocked the metal door on the streetlight, then reached in to locate the answer to all his insecurities. Swiftly concealing the weapon down the front of his jeans, he about turned in search of a decent stalking point where he could lie in wait for his prey's advent. For the last few days leading up to this crucial moment, Michael had endeavoured to do his homework, but still his brain had been unable to fathom out exactly how he could accomplish the perfect murder directly outside his own home, for there was simply insufficient cover. Paul would customarily park his car outside the front door of 6 Clonard Street, then walk around the front of the vehicle before negotiating the approximate forty feet to the safety of his house; this ritual gave Michael precisely 14.6 seconds to attract his attention and fire a clinical shot. With only the neighbour's garden for a shroud, he'd realised the probability of not being spotted or arousing suspicion whilst he waited for his brother was highly improbable. The fact, and he knew it, was Paul could make an appearance at any given time. What if he gets detoured or stopped at the border checkpoints? He might not arrive until 2 a.m. or 4 a.m. or worse, not at all, he'd explained to himself. Having squandered two sleepless nights searching for a position where he could see but not be seen, it was only at present in the heat of the moment that the optimum solution came into view. Scrambling under his nextdoor neighbour's car, all he could do now was wait patiently in the hope that Paul hadn't decided to spend an extra night out of town and if presented with the opportunity, somehow make his 14.6 seconds clinically count.

Tonight while he waited his woollen mask turned out to his advantage. With no fret of his target being armed and faster on the draw than him, he had no reason to perspire. Knowing the capabilities of his mark availed him with all the composure he needed, but it made him shiver just the same, for a kill of this genre and magnitude required an extraordinary effort from his faculties. Squinting to read his watch at 1 a.m., now that cramp was taking hold of his crumpled body due to the tight space restriction under the vehicle, he began to worry that if Paul took much longer in returning home, his limbs might seize up when he needed to propel them into action, but this was not his only anxiety. Michael was starting to sense that a further stay of execution might even expropriate his brain, after all, was any cause worth killing your own flesh and blood for? Then again, this mission was for his own personal ends.

At 1.25 a.m. Paul entered the Falls Road. Flashing his main beam for luck, as many a superstitious motorist did at night, upon the welcoming mural of Our Lady pointing the way through the clouds to heaven, he recognised the end of his journey was only a few minutes away.

Michael, whose hands were numb from the irreverent chill which had set about him with no apparent fear of his stature or reputation, was beginning to suffer a relapse of mistrust relating to the value of his vocation, before his thoughts turned to Bernadette, the love of his life, and that fuelled him with all the warmth and staying power he needed to endure the conditions. She was the most significant thing in his life and nothing else counted now. The last few months had taught him that Paul's theories pertaining to the Republican Cause had been justified. The movement had not lived up to his expectations and the romance had well and truly been ripped from his heart by the IRA's deceit towards their own creed. It had all been an illusion, there was never going to be a United Ireland and he hadn't been fighting for the recrimination of the past atrocities the Catholic denomination had been subjected to. No, he'd been belligerent for the future, to line the pockets of astute, entrepreneurial political minds who saw the enterprise of making a fast buck through the exploitation of history. What he planned to carry out had now become purely a one-off act of brutality. Killing his brother was for his own benefit and thereafter, with staunch resolve, he'd arrived at the conclusion that he would have no more to do with the sycophantic demagogues of the IRA.

Having given up raising his head at the sound of every approaching vehicle a while back, when Paul's car eventually turned off the Falls Road into Clonard Street, Michael was almost caught unawares. Frozen like a jackrabbit by the glare of the headlights, he vied to waken his slumbering legs and stamp out the pins and needles which were crippling his complaining limbs at the most inopportune moment. Noting the number plate of T414 LBA come to a complete standstill within a few feet of his sights, he shuffled backwards in sidewinder fashion, desperate to smooth out the friction which existed between him and his brother once and for all. He then stealthily took cover behind the boot of his neighbour's vehicle.

Still reasonably buoyant on the resolutions he'd made during the drive home, Paul swivelled his legs from the car, stood up then sucked in the sweet cool morning air. Locking the door with an introspective smile, he turned then totally froze in his shoes, for there stood a masked figure pointing an imposing gun in his direction. Swallowing hard and begging his legs to carry him clear of danger, he began to whimper on discovering they would not entertain his request.

386

Behind the mask the first bead of perspiration made its appearance on Michael's forehead as he engaged in combat with his mind, sending shock-waves surging through his arms. Trembling to conquer the twenty-five years of humanity that life had instilled in him, it was again a vision of Bernadette and his brother writhing around naked that initiated a response in his tense index finger to pull the trigger and preserve his sanity.

Realising that the assassin was suffering from nervous hesitation, Paul somehow mustered up the strength and courage to attempt to flee. Half turning to run, he felt the white-hot bullet tear into his back then explode long before he heard the short, dull thud of the gun evicting its deadly payload. Instantaneously hyperventilating, he instinctively clutched his heart as he felt the world slipping away from his grasp. Suddenly the white light fallacy had been blown out of the water, as a luminous swirling of yellow and green stars and flashes clouded his pupils before turning black. Crashing towards the pavement, his skull thundered on to the kerbstone sending him into an instant coma.

Michael boiled up inside with panic and wrenched the mask from his head to tap off his pores which were blinding him with a flash-flood of hot sweat. Licking his parched lips, he glanced at Paul's limp and lifeless body, then quickly scanned around the houses to find that his anonymity was still intact. At first he began to walk calmly towards the monastery up ahead in the distance, then he started to jog, yet after a few seconds he was sprinting from the jail sentence that snapped at his heels, using his jersey to wipe his fingerprints from the gun as he ran. Within twenty yards of the drop-off point, Michael impetuously swerved to the left and backtracked to the alley, abandoning his trust in the IRA now that their love affair had come to a bitter end. Reduced to a tiptoed walk upon entering the dim alley, he stabilised his respiration in preparation for re-entry into his home.

Testing each step gingerly with his weight, Michael slowly zigzagged upstairs and into his bedroom without disturbing the sleeping floorboards once. Somehow he'd made it out and back in unnoticed, now all that remained to complete the perfect crime was to make certain that the offending weapon never saw the light of day again. Slinking into bed, he lay still, eyes wide open for the next half hour, exploring every avenue for a dead certain hiding place, where no young kid playing on his bike might chance upon his incriminating stash. Finally he decided

387

to jettison the gun smack bang in the middle of the River Lagan at the first available opportunity.

Outside, the path leading to 6 Clonard Street, Paul lay on the verge of death with each passing minute and drop of blood that seeped relentlessly from his wound. Face waning from ashen to blue and with no beating mind to detour the impending journey from this world to the next, he could do nothing but await the Grim Reaper's scything arrival.

Having drifted off to sleep, Michael was inconsiderately wakened by the screaming sirens of an ambulance and the security forces. Rising with the remainder of the household and the whole street, who'd appeared on their doorsteps motivated by natural curiosity, he parted the curtains to observe Paul being stretchered into the ambulance. Within a matter of seconds the paramedic team had performed their pitstop and were back on the road again, racing towards the RVH half a mile away.

Fifteen minutes earlier, and quite possibly with the helping hand of fate, a black cab ferrying home a young woman from a city centre nightclub had turned into Clonard Street and the passenger had spotted Paul's body lying by the roadside. Demanding the taxi-driver to stop, the girl had cradled Paul in her arms and unsuccessfully attempted to breathe new life into him while the cabby had radioed for an ambulance. When the medics arrived, they'd discovered a faint pulse and their urgency to get the casualty into the operating theatre meant that no one on Clonard Street had had the time to establish the victim's identity.

Joining the congregation which had assembled in the livingroom, Michael, continuing to feign his illness inquired of what had been ascertained. 'What was all that about?'

'God knows,' replied his mother, 'I think someone's been stabbed outside our front door of all places, beside Paul's car.'

It was like the restoration of power to an entire country when the lightning bolt of deduction hit her. 'Paul's home – where is he? Is he in bed?' she demanded, her voice rising in crescendo with each weighty statement which swung doubt over to panic.

'No,' enlightened Michael, tamely.

'Oh, no,' she groaned, 'it must have been him lying there in a pool of blood. Call the hospital now,' she screamed.

'Calm down,' said Michael impromptu, putting his arm around her for comfort. 'We don't know anything yet. He could be anywhere, let's not jump to any conclusions.'

'Don't patronise me, Michael. If he's not in the house and that's his car outside, then pound to a penny it has to be him who's in the back of that ambulance. Oh God,' she began to sob, looking to the ceiling for an answer.

Casting his eyes over Bernadette, Michael saw in her eyes that he was her main suspect.

For well over an hour the surgeons battled to save Paul's life as he drifted in and out of this world. Arriving at the hospital, Mrs O'Donnell broke down inconsolably when the doctor informed her of the worst possible scenario. It was indeed her son who was under the knife and his condition was 'hypercritical.' At 4.30 a.m. the surgeons, who could do no more, began to scrub their hands of Paul's blood and dress down. Rocking and fumbling with her rosary beads, deep in shock as her salutary son attempted to mollify her, Mrs O'Donnell raised her heavy head when she saw the livid-faced senior surgeon inch towards her with consolation etched across his stale face. The occupation of a surgeon was hard enough as it was, without the added stress of counselling; nevertheless, it was a responsibility they'd taken on board - not through desire but necessity, and they'd become therapeutic experts with their kid-glove handling over the years. Squeezing Michael's hand with such indignation that he winced at her hidden potency, she braced herself for the worst.

'He's dead, isn't he?' she whimpered, staring at the surgeon through her piercing, angry red eyes.

'No, he's alive,' he revealed, 'but he's not out of the woods by any means. We've managed to remove the bullet and he's stable. The shot pierced his lung, though that'll heal with time. However, he's slipped into a deep coma. It appears he's sustained extensive damage to the head when he fell.'

'So what are you saying?' interjected Michael.

'Well,' he sighed, indicating that the bad news had yet to be exposed. 'He has a fractured skull and when we did the cat scan we found some fluid on the brain which we subsequently drained off, however as I said, he's in a coma and the bottom line is, at this moment in time it's too early to determine the extent of his injuries. He . . .' he paused, 'he may never regain consciousness and if he does he could be paralysed, I'm really sorry.'

Holding his mother close, Michael attempted to hold her heart together while Bernadette, who was herself awash with tears, stared him straight in the eye, appalled at his apparent lack of emotion - which had not escaped her attention.

Mrs O'Donnell, in no fit state to answer the RUC's hounding questions, allowed Michael to adopt the role of family spokesman, and in doing so he made certain that no one would even contemplate pointing the finger at him.

By the time the media had got wind of the attempted murder, it had been too late for them to print the story in the morning edition, there was, however, mention of the shooting incident on the radio bulletins throughout the morning, although the security forces would not allow the victim's identity to be divulged at this early stage in their inquiries.

As Angela prepared to leave the house for another afternoon stint she heard last night's news from the Falls, yet thought nothing of it; after all, there was rarely a day went past when a similar incident had failed to occur. If a victim of the conflict lived more than one house either side of you, then as far as you were concerned, it may have as well happened on the moon. Quite simply, no one cared, it was an ongoing feature of everyday life that you couldn't allow to encroach upon your existence, for if you did fall into that humanitarian Venus-fly trap it would take hold to unbalance your cerebral capacities, until finally insanity swallowed you up.

Again the RUC posted two guards outside the restricted hospital room where Paul lay, defenceless, under twenty-four hour surveillance. And they'd remain there as always, until the target had regained consciousness. They kept constant vigil for a few reasons: if the victim had any information pertaining to an early arrest then they wanted to be the first to know and, if indeed this was the issue, the assailant, worried that his sacrifice would disclose his identity in the light of perception, would probably materialise in an effort to rectify his initial incompetence.

Late on that Monday afternoon, Paul's consultant joined his mother at his bedside where she had became a permanent fixture, holding his hand, talking to him and mopping his ghostly, pale brow.

'Mrs O'Donnell you don't look too well. I suggest, no, I have to insist that you go home and get some rest before you endanger your own health. Your son is in the most capable hands in the world, if he comes round we'll inform you immediately. Come back tomorrow, by all means, but please go home for now and recuperate.'

Using the last of her strength, she kissed her son gently on the forehead then walked sombrely from the room on sound medical advice. Walking automatically the half mile from the RVH to her home, the woman felt no pain, merely a total numbness. She stopped on the front path and stared up towards the Clonard monastery and wondered why God was making her suffer again after all the devotion, faith and commitment she'd bestowed upon her invisible deity. Her life was in crumbling ruins, not only had religion destroyed her marriage, but now it deemed to take her flesh and blood from her, with Paul presently laid on the periphery of death and yet she had served no malice, not once in her duration, to any of God's creatures. Half turning to walk the outlying path to her home, the stress and strain which she'd become immersed in suddenly overpowered her, sending her crashing to the pavement. Michael, who had been standing at the front-room window entranced by the scene of his crime, abruptly stirred from his daydream. Startled back to reality by the impact of his mother's crashing fall, he rushed to her assistance. Having carried her upstairs to bed, he paused for a moment before attempting revival. Observing the cruel pain inscribed across her withered face, he realised that when he'd pulled the trigger against Paul, in effect he'd actually fired at his mother as well. Stricken with the guilt of his deed towards her, for an instant, remorse began to creep into his perplexed mind and he found himself wishing for Paul's health to exonerate him from a future of shame. But again it was the sight of Bernadette that stirred him from his interim state of benevolence.

'What's the matter with your mom?' she inquired.

'She fainted in the street,' he replied shakily, still disorientated by his previous reflections.

'Well, don't just stand there, call the doctor while I loosen her blouse and bring her round,' she ordered, taking control of the situation.

After the doctor had administered a substantial sedative and his mother was sleeping her troubles away, Michael sat at the kitchen table while Bernadette set about making a pot of tea.

'I hope to God, for your sake, Paul pulls through,' she scolded with her back to him.

'Why? What do you mean?' he stammered, fearing that his fiancé was centring her speculation upon his involvement in the iniquity.

'The way you've treated him since he came back, all the beatings and abuse of your insecurities. I don't how you'll be able to live with yourself if he dies.'

Panic averted with the realisation that she did not hold him culpable in any way for the attempt on Paul's life, he swiftly turned to more relevant themes.

'So do you still love me and still want to marry me?'

Stalling for a few seconds, she gazed down the back yard to the forsaken kennel before issuing her reply. 'I'll marry you.'

At her evening teabreak, Angela bought a copy of the evening Telegraph to keep her company while she ate. Having lost all her friends at work, initially because of her publicised association with a Catholic of the opposite sex, she had become a reserved figure in the social circle of the canteen and now that everyone had knowledge of her rape, thanks to the hospital's gossip chain, no one had the hypocrisy or audacity to befriend her. Unmoved by the tardy headline of 'Latest Sectarian Victim Fighting For Life In Coma,' she was about to turn the page in search of less disturbing news when the imprinting words of History Maker leapt off the page to clamp her jaws in mid-munch around the apple she was in the process of ingesting. 'The owner of Greyhound Derby finalist and current odds-on favourite History Maker lies in a coma fighting for his life after being gunned down outside his home at 6 Clonard Street. Paul O'Donnell, 22, a ferry steward . . .' Needing to read no further, Angela prised the forbidden fruit from her jaws and rushed from the canteen to be by his side.

Gaining permission from her charge nurse who also pointed her in the right direction, Angela then had to acquire authorisation from the nursing officer. After fabricating that it was her fiancé who lay hanging to life by a thread, she was then allowed to cross the armed guard checkpoint outside the door of Paul's sequestered room. Taking a deep breath before she entered, it wasn't until she saw his unmistakable dimpled chin that it hit her, and it was the heftiest impact she'd ever experienced, even more powerful than the day her mother had explained to her that her illness was terminal. Squeezing her eyes airtight shut to seal off her tears of repentance, she sensed that what lay before her could potentially have been avoided if only she'd succumbed to her sentiments.

'Oh Paul, I'm so sorry. I didn't want to hurt you, I could never hurt you, I love you and I've never stopped loving you.'

Opening her eyes, she walked over to his side, cautiously, then took his limp cold hand into hers. 'Don't die on me Paul, I beg of you. If you can hear me, squeeze my hand.'

Gaining no response, she gazed around the surplus of life-sustaining equipment and watched his heartbeat crawl along the monitor, searching for a murmur from his heart to let her know he could hear her. For ten minutes, Angela just stared at the screen, mesmerised as she reflected on and reminisced their forbidden past, the highs and lows, the pain and pleasure. Breaking from the spell when the nursing officer entered the room, Angela suddenly remembered that Paul was not the only patient in the RVH who needed her attention. Kissing his cheek, she left him with the lifeline of hope.

'I have to go now, but I'll return after my shift so don't go dying on me,' she snivelled then laughed in the same breath. 'Hey, we could spend the night together if you want.'

When Angela finished her shift, she headed straight for the telephone.

'How are you Mom? Is Daddy there?'

'Not yet, why?'

'Nothing, it doesn't matter,' she replied flatly.

'I'll be fine Angie, just do what you have to,' insisted her mother.

'What do you mean?' she inquired, astounded by the prognostication of her mother's statement.

'I've read the newspaper. Go to him, sweetie, like you should've done a long time ago, let me worry about tackling your father when he rolls in.'

'Are you quite sure you'll manage? I only want to help him because we were once partners in the dog,' stressed Angela, attempting unsuccessfully to justify her fidelity.

'Listen, Angela, I'll be fine and when on earth are you gonna stop kidding yourself. You love him and don't dare deny it.'

'I do not,' she chimed in.

'Come on, get a reality check will you, this is your mother you're lying to. I have ears you know.'

'What do you mean by that?' she questioned, biting her lip, wondering whether she talked in her sleep.

'It hasn't escaped my attention the way you play that record over and over. I know he bought you that, I've had records bought for me in my lifetime too, you know.'

Suddenly, Angela was lost for words, not because she'd been discovered, but because her mother had stimulated the turntable inside her head, giving her a notion as to how she might be able to reactivate Paul's consciousness.

'Angela, Angela, are you still there?' demanded her mother.

'Aye, Mom I'll have to go now, take care and I'll see you in the morning.'

Returning to Paul's side, she found that there had been no change in his condition during her absence. Angela had once read in a magazine that on some occasions coma victims had been revived by a visitation from their favourite famous personality, or by having the music of their preferred pop group played incessantly. With Paul having never revealed any infatuation with any female celebrity, Angela was left with only one alternative. With no means of supplying his ears with the sweet music and lyrics of their adopted song, she had no choice but to improvise.

Giving her own rendition of 'Never Tear Us Apart,' for over half an hour, she held his hand and serenaded him relentlessly until her agitation and infuriation stuck her needle. Looking to the ceiling for help, she telepathically summoned her faith. 'Don't do this to me, you bastard. Let him live, I wouldn't be able to live with myself knowing that he went to his grave thinking I meant what I said at our last meeting. Please, you owe me this much, I've already had to sacrifice my mother, surely you can't take from me twice?'

Returning her attentions to Paul, tears of silence streamed down her face to drip on to his cold, morbid flesh, helping her to express her true feelings towards him.

'Paul, if you can hear me than please give me a sign. Squeeze my hand, anything. I'll marry you, Paul. If you come round we can leave Ireland like you wanted just as soon as you're fit enough to travel, I really mean that. I love you, I guess I always have since that day fate brought us together when we both went to claim Toby from the farm. Aye, you were right, we were two worlds colliding and they'll never tear us apart, not ever again.'

Glancing at the cardiac monitor, she was convinced that her pleas were falling on deaf ears, but she was wrong, for although his day was night and his night was everlasting, he could hear every soothing word that she had said and sung. Desperate to give her a signal, his brain worked against the clock to unblock the route to his limbs, but it was going to be a laborious task that would mean working late into the night.

At 2.15 a.m., Angela's eyes could fight the heavy weight of exhaustion no more. Slipping away to join him in the darkness, she dreamt of his smiling face when he'd handed her their record. And how the determination in his eyes had voiced that he would never yield to the ethereal obstacle of sectarianism which threatened to stand between them.

It was over an hour later, when the night's darkness began to pale into a new morning, that Paul's love for Angela had completed rewiring the circuit inside his brain and the lights flickered on to awaken his creaseless eyelids. With the power of life surging through his arteries, it was only a matter of seconds before the anaesthetic of the coma had lost its potency and the pain of a hundred and one childbirths scourged to remind him that he was back in the land of the living. Turning to face his saviour, he felt the explosive pangs detonate under his ribcage and inside his skull. He screamed aloud as the aftershock sent him recoiling on to the bed and panicked for breath, spontaneously squeezing her hand to combat the scorching shock which tore across his nerve endings, in the same way long fingernails scratch down a blackboard.

Alarmed by his excruciating cries of agony, Angela sprang to life and filled up with tears of joy and relief to supersede those of distress and doubt. Releasing his slippery, pyretic hand, she then stormed from the room in search of a doctor. Whimpering at the concept of being all alone, fortified by the insecurity of not knowing at this precise moment whether he was going to live or die, Paul's terror only aggravated the affliction inside his body. Although she was gone no more than two minutes, for Paul it was more terrifying than those infinite two seconds when he'd realised he'd been shot. Whilst Angela held his hand again, as the doctor stabbed him full of morphine to subdue the torture, it was a case of fire to quench fire as the torrid acidic liquid burnt a path to extinguish his searing misery. As the fever melted away, he twisted his neck to see if he'd been duped by a dream all along to find that she was no apparition.

Squeezing her hands to convey his thanks, he found that it involved a supreme effort just to force a sentence through the heavy clouds dulling his mind.

'Ange. . . Angela,' he moaned, licking his lips to loosen them before resuming, 'did, did you . . . mean . . .'

'Rest, Paul,' she intervened, 'you have to rest. We can talk later.'

Wiping the beads of sweat from his humid brow, he half smiled before drifting off to sleep again. Satisfied that she could do no more for him

395

at present, she kissed him on the cheek, having decided it was time for her to go home and leave him in the surrogate hands of the painkiller.

Being sustained by morphine diet, when Bernadette and his mother arrived on Tuesday morning, Paul could only look through them with dark, surly eyes. Acknowledging them with the occasional grunt, he focused on the door all morning, willing Angela to incarnate and fill the shadows of uncertainty in his delirious mind. At 6 p.m. only a thin partition of plasterboard and wooden slats stood between them when Angela was informed by the RUC guards that Mr O'Donnell already had visitors. Leaving him to his family, she toiled through the remaining half of her shift disputing the clock's accuracy as the minutes dragged by, tormenting her with their lacklustre obstinacy.

When 10 p.m. finally clicked into place, Paul's face was wet, as it had been since nine o'clock when his mother had returned home. Paul stared at God demandingly and with intense hatred, as his back broken, he finally succumbed to the invisible force. 'Okay, you've won. I believe in your existence, I'll bow before you and your kingdom, but why can't I have Angela? I don't know what you want from me, but whatever it is just take it, will you. I submit, I swear. Please just give me one moment to speak with her again, that's all I ask. You've torn the spine from me 'cause that's what she was, my backbone. I'm yours now, a cripple to your requests.'

Having made peace with his faith, he closed his eyes and broke down again, wishing he was dead so that all the anguish, both mental and physical would be paralysed for ever. Sobbing so loud that his heartache drowned the click of the door opening, Paul couldn't hear or sense her presence as she stood before the wreckage he'd become. Feeling her unequivocal electric touch as she took his hand his heart skipped a beat and in a flash he'd become a disciple.

'Angela,' he gasped, refusing to open his stinging eyes, 'it's you, isn't it? Tell me it's you.'

'It's me,' she confirmed, morosely, touched by his desperation for her.

Noticing for the first time that his head was shaved behind his right ear, where the surgeons had drained off the fluid, Angela felt a cold shiver pass through her as she remembered her tribulation at the hands of the malicious gang and it made her realise yet again that there could be no future for her and Paul.

'How are you feeling now?' she inquired, involuntarily, her personal feelings restrained by the return to her professional dispensation.

'Alive,' he laughed, 'and delighted to be so. God, am I happy? I love you Angela. I must admit, I was beginning to have my doubts as to whether my angel would return, and yet here you are, large as life.'

'I was worried about you,' she revealed. 'It was the least I could do after the way I treated you at Tommy's funeral, I'm truly sorry for that.'

'Sssh,' he whispered, his adoration for her so great that he felt he merited no apology from her gorgeous lips. 'That was yesterday, tomorrow is ours, a new start.'

'What do you mean?' she asked, her face beginning to blush, coercing her to release her hand from his clinging grip.

Worried that the marriage of the fever and narcotics had been playing tricks on his mind to tell him what he wanted to hear, Paul suffered a panic remission. Hyperventilating to convey his words, he began to choke upon them. 'You. . . you. . . you,' he wheezed.

'Calm down,' Angela urged, gently pinning him on to the pillow, which had been supporting his back.

Taking her advice, he composed himself to rediscover the gift of articulation. 'What you said to me last night, you did mean it, didn't you?'

'What did I say?' she feigned her innocence, 'I think you'd better refresh my memory.'

'You sang to me?' he questioned, pulling a face that expressed to her that he'd been unable to decipher whether it was all a figment of his concussion. 'And you said you'd marry me and leave these wicked shores with me. You promised me, didn't you?'

Sighing aloud, she looked away from his stare, then set about placing a constraint upon his ambitions now that she felt it unfair to delay his misery any longer.

'Now, I really am sorry Paul. I was desperate to revive you, it was the only way I knew to try.'

'So you don't want to marry me and you don't love me, that's the bottom line, right?' he stated dumbfounded, shaking his head in disbelief to deflect her bruising words from penetrating his head and turning them into reality.

'No, Paul, oh God give me strength,' she reprimanded herself. 'I do love you, or at least I think I do, but I can't leave my mother, she's dying. Can't you understand that? If she was fit and healthy then, yes I'd make the break with you, but as she's not, I simply can't, she really needs me.'

397

'I don't want to sound selfish, but I need you too,' stressed Paul. 'I can't live without you either and I can't stay around here, I must leave Belfast. I've no choice, these people are ruthless. They won't fail twice. Why the hell can't we be together?'

'Because of that damn thing you're wearing around your neck,' she lambasted, allowing her frustrations on the gross unfairness of their vexatious situation to show.

'Even if I denounced my Catholicism, which I would for you, they'd still hunt me down. Besides, for a moment back there I was actually starting to believe in the man upstairs. He let me live and I thought he'd blessed me with your love, I was really convinced we'd have a happy ending to tell our children,' he mused with an ironic laugh.

'Don't,' she cut in, 'stop, will ye, this is no easier for me. I have to go home, my mother needs me.'

'Wait,' he called, stopping her at the door. 'I want to kiss you.'

'No, let's not. It'll only make it harder for us when you leave, if that's what you decide to do?' she said, hinting that their future lay solely in his hands.

'I told you, if I stay I die, then again I'm dead already. Will I see you tomorrow?'

'If you want,' she replied.

'Don't ask me what you know is true,' he returned, raising his eyebrows to remind her of how she'd sung him back into this world. 'So what time will I expect you?'

'I'm on afternoons again, so just after ten o'clock; besides, I'm not comfortable when your family's around.'

Although Angela had blown his floating dreams from the water yet again, it was only when she left the room that the agony returned to crucify his body.

On the morning of Wednesday 14 September, Paul issued his statement to the RUC as best he could remember it. Dark and vague as it was, he was unable to shed any light on to his assailant's identity and so he consolidated Michael's alibi, allowing his brother's pores to close with the cold shower of relief.

On a day when Paul yearned for a friends and family boycott so he could recuperate his thoughts and make preparations for the future, Lucozade and grapes bombarded him from all angles, constraining him into making off the cuff decisions that would only save him time

398

but that he would regret in the long run. At lunchtime, Martin South paid a visit which helped to brighten Paul's gloom, when he brought with him all the best wishes from his workmates marooned at sea. Taking the 'get-well-soon' card, he smiled as he perused the signatures and read the witty comments, especially those of his Scottish namesake. 'I knew you'd find an excuse to get off work for the Derby final, but surely this is going overboard. See you soon.' Staring at his colleague's closing words, he bit his lip to numb the hurt that seemed to now dog him perpetually. He'd enjoyed their camaraderie and his work, yet now that could be no more.

'So how are you feeling?' inquired Martin, concerned for his employee.

Shrugging his shoulders, Paul could find no fitting reply which could describe the bitter truth.

'I've just come to tell you not to worry about your job because it's safe. We'll be glad to have you back when you've fully recovered,' assured his employer.

'I won't be coming back,' revealed Paul, with immense regret in his voice.

'But why?'

'I won't be able to. I've a collapsed lung, though that'll get better with time. However, the consultant reckons I'm going to be prone to dizzy spells and the odd blackout if I get up to any strenuous activity. He's advised me to change my career, find a desk job or something. I'm sorry, but this is my resignation.'

Lost for words, Martin South couldn't bring himself to voice what he really wanted to say, which was, 'Why the hell didn't you take my advice? I told you not to mess around with those people.' Instead he replied as best he could under the circumstances. 'I'm really sorry Paul. I can only speak on behalf of all the crew when I say that we'll be sad to see you leave and even sadder that your greyhound won't be running in Saturday's final after all the effort you've put in. We've all backed it, you know.'

'What do you mean?' snapped Paul, confounded.

'Well, I can only presume that this incident will impel you to withdraw the dog. Surely your life's more important,' ventured his boss.

'No way, I'm not prepared to withdraw him,' slammed Paul. 'I haven't been to hell and back to quit now. Toby's gonna run, over my dead body if need be, so you go back and tell them that from me. Oh, just go will ye.'

Blushing from the embarrassment of his supposition, Martin South headed towards the door then stopped abruptly. Reaching into his jacket pocket he produced another envelope then revealed the source as he handed it to Paul, before leaving him alone to fester in his torment.

'It's from Mairead. You know, I once had you down for my future son-in-law. Still!'

Opening her correspondence, he read the confession she'd granted him in her conflicting card of condolence. 'Paul, I'm so sorry, but I wished this upon you and worse, for the way you hurt me in Dublin and now that it's actually happened, I realise it was the last thing I really wanted. I still love you, but appreciate your love lies elsewhere and I sincerely hope that you get what you want, she doesn't know how lucky she is. Love, Mairead.' By the way the ink was smudged where she'd signed her name, Paul could only surmise that she'd shed a tear as she'd written off all hope. Touched by her vindicating communication, he sent her his thoughts, wishing her, too, all the best for the future.

As she took her mother a cup of tea before she had to leave for her final afternoon shift of that week, Angela's hospitality was about to be rewarded with a stern lecture.

'So have you stopped kidding yourself yet?' snarled her mother.

'What?' replied Angela.

'I'm referring to Paul,' continued her mother, not willing to allow her diffident daughter to avoid the subject any longer.

'What about him?' Angela said, pretending to be impassive.

'Well, what are his plans? He's asked you to marry him, hasn't he?'

'What makes you think that?' asked Angela, beginning to wonder whether her mother had psychic abilities.

'I know these things, I was young once too, and in love, besides it's written all over your face. So tell me, what's holding you back? For goodness sake, you can confide in me. I may be bound to this armchair, but my faculties are still intact up top, well, most of the time.'

'Aye,' sighed Angela, conceding some ground. 'He's proposed to me and he wants me to leave Ireland with him, but I can't, I'd never be able to live with myself. You need looking after, whether you like it or not.'

'That's your father's job, not yours. I've hemmed you in for too long. Go with him, make a life, get away from this place and be happy. You'll only look back at this and regret it, should you stay. I know you'd be in safe hands with this lad, he'll treat you right. I don't want to go to my grave knowing that I denied you the love you wanted; you can call or write anytime, be happy and make me happy. If you don't, then I'll feel the guilty one.'

'Stop it, Mom, you know I can't leave you.'

Beating her withered wrist on to the armchair in sheer frustration as her daughter left for work, her mother felt cheated for the second time in her life. If Angela could leave the Shankill then she could rest in peace, knowing that she too had escaped the ghetto of hatred.

Paul's second visitor of the day was his mother, and with her she brought concern now that the initial elation of his survival had been supplanted by anxiety again. On this occasion it was with reference to his impending future.

'Withdraw the dog son, for me, then when you come home these people will leave you alone,' she said militantly.

Pouting as he folded his arms and shook his head horizontally, he gave his reply in silence.

'Have you any idea what you've put me through over the last few days? I couldn't go through that again, I've had enough,' she stuttered, beginning to break down.

'It's okay, Mom, you won't have to worry any longer,' he replied tenderly, endeavouring to comfort her.

'Why's that?' she snivelled.

'I'm leaving Ireland on Saturday for good. You don't understand, I have a commitment to run Toby, not for my gain, but for Tommy. I killed him, you know?' he sniffed, to dam his tears. 'I don't care about me, I can't function on this guilt any more, If I hadn't tried to change him into something he wasn't then he'd still be alive today. I know he's up there hating me.'

'No son, you're terribly wrong, you gave him love through companionship. I watched him that fateful night and I saw a boy who couldn't have been happier within himself. I'm telling you Paul, if someone had given him the choice of a lifetime of loneliness, or the seven months of friendship and hope that you gave him, I know he'd have opted for your kindness any day. What you did for him took courage and I'm proud of you for that, son. He wouldn't want you to die for the sake of a dog race that isn't a means to an end. Please give it up and come home, you can't go anywhere anyhow. Who'd look after you? The doctors say you need to convalesce, you could collapse at any time.'

Having listened carefully to her words of wisdom, Paul felt better about one thing, she was probably right about Tommy, his existence had been on a dead-end street, he hadn't been living before Paul came along to turn him around and set him off in the right direction. Having been held to ransom by the guilt which had racked him, suddenly the ordeal was over now that his mother had paid the demand, yet still he had no intention of diverting Tommy's final dream.

'No Mom, Toby will run in the Derby final come Saturday night, then I'm leaving Ireland for good. It's my destiny, I'm sure of it.'

'Don't be so bloody selfish, you don't know what pain is. I've suffered for twenty-three years. Your father is . . .' she roared, then abruptly put the brakes on her furious tongue before she lost control and off-loaded the burden she'd vowed to carry with her to the grave.

'What about my father?' he probed, intrigued, having always maintained that there was a hidden element in their family's make-up, as well as having never seen her lose her temper before.

'I can't tell you, son,' she replied, looking away, vexed by the truth which hurt so much. 'All I can tell you is I love you and if anything happens to you, I won't be able to hold this family together any longer.'

While he waited for Angela to come as promised, Paul sifted through an array of speculations as to what his mother had been so near to lifting the lid off. At first he wondered if he'd had a twin that had died at birth, but he couldn't fathom out how that aligned with his father's compulsive contempt towards him. When Angela arrived after her shift, he was no further forward in his attempts at trying to solve the riddle of how his birth had rocked his family and led his father to treat him like an outcast.

'I can't stay long,' she announced.

'Why? Scared your real feelings might entice you into fleeing the country with me?' he said sarcastically and yet without realising it, he'd hit the nail on the head.

'Perhaps,' she replied, tantalisingly. 'So how are you feeling today?'

'Piss-poor, pathetic and porous,' he bantered. 'So will you help me? I need to get up and about for a walk so I can build my strength.'

'You're joking aren't you, you've had major surgery. It's not like a shaving cut, you have to rest. You'll not be able to begin to walk for over a week; you won't have the breath or energy to walk the length of yourself.'

'Now it's you who must be joking. I have to be in Dublin on Saturday night at all costs,' he emphasised. 'So will you assist me or not?'

'No, I won't, you'll only do more damage. You could bring on internal bleeding,' she said, snubbing his request.

Throwing off the covers, he revealed his own hard-headed intentions. 'Fair enough, I'll do it myself.'

Gritting his teeth to ward off the shooting pains, just swivelling his legs over the side of the bed to prepare for landing brought a blinding headache, breathlessness and a sledgehammer crashing across his tender ribcage. Rushing around the bed to catch his imminent fall, she rebuked his stubbornness.

'Don't you listen to anything I say? You'll only do more harm.'

'I have to walk, so let me try. If you don't, then I'll just wait until you've gone,' he bribed her professional instincts.

Pressuring his legs to carry his weight, he wavered under the strain, impelling her to grab hold of his shoulders to stabilise him. Gasping, breathless as she'd forecast, he gazed into her flawless, seductive emerald eyes.

'I love it when you hold me,' he breathed.

Closing his eyes, blinded by her beauty, he inched his lips towards hers and she met him half way. Breaking from their embrace, she spoke with a tear curdling in her eye. 'I can't leave with you, God I want to, but I just can't. Don't you understand, I have to stay in Belfast for my mother.'

'And I can't stay here,' he whispered. 'I don't know how to go about trying to persuade you and really I suppose I haven't any right above your mother to do so, but I can't help myself. Don't despise me for being self-centred, but I'm begging you to come with me because I love you so much.'

'Shall we try a few steps?' she suggested, changing the subject before it drove her insane.

After twenty strenuous and tortuous paces, she helped him back into bed.

'I'm on the early shift for the next three days, so I'll come see you after 2 p.m.' she explained, letting him know that visiting time was over for another day.

'Do I get a goodnight kiss?' he asked.

Longing to taste his lips again, she could not repel his charms before heading home to her other private patient. Reflecting long after she'd gone, upon how the night had appeared to turn in his favour, he was quick to realise that now he was going to live, he could no longer compete with her dying mother.

The following day, with Angela's aid, Paul began to acclimatise to the pain and lack of oxygen his perforated lung was unable to accommodate. And once again, he utilised his time with her, treading lightly over the thin-ice matter of attempting to persuade her to leave her mother in her father's matrimonial care.

Standing outside Paddy's Bar in the light drizzle that Thursday evening, Michael inhaled deeply through his nose before barging into the bar, wound up ready to confront his disabled instigator and forward his cutting resignation. Leaving his civil tongue at home as normal, the crippled middleman slammed the door shut to express his anger towards his fallen star pupil.

'What the fuck went wrong and where the fuck's the gun?' he gesticulated, demanding a top-drawer explanation.

'The monastery wasn't on my escape route,' said Michael, audaciously.

'So where the fuck is it then?' he insisted, thundering his fist on the belaboured table.

'It's safe,' returned Michael.

'Where the fuck's safe? Don't fuck me about son.'

'I threw it into the River Lagan,' betrayed Michael.

'Do you have any idea of how much a gun costs?'

'Obviously more than my freedom,' said the misled recruit.

'Don't get wise with me, son, you're in the firing line now thanks to your inefficiency and as far as future advancement within this organisation is concerned, well there won't be any. You'd better start praying that your harebrained brother withdraws his mongrel, or it breaks a fucking leg during the race.'

'Are you threatening me?' said Michael, remaining unflustered, fixing his stare upon the little man with the big mouth.

'Just get out of my fucking sight. Don't call me, I'll call you if I ever need your services again, which is highly improbable.'

Keeping one eye out for any sudden movements from the doormen and one hand close to his back pocket, which housed the flickknife he always carried around with him for insurance purposes, Michael left the bar unchallenged then turned left in the opposite direction of his homeward route. Sneaking into the second alley beyond the public house where he knew the cripple would have to pass on his way home or wherever he went, what Michael planned to do had no modicum of premeditation, although the culmination of his senior's degrading attitude towards him and the dream shattering revelations of how the IRA functioned had long festered in his mind, as it does in a child's discovering that Santa Clause is but a myth. No, this was pure and basic instinct. Michael felt truly intimidated and the only code he understood was to kill, or be killed. It was a deadly systematic conclusion which afforded no time for analysis of consequence, for that anxiety would be born later.

Glimpsing around the corner, he espied the cripple all alone undertaking his final approach. Expeditiously removing his travelling companion from his back pocket and flicking it into action in the same drilled manoeuvre, he then gazed down at the pitted blade, discoloured and ingrained with the porous defects of metal fatigue and he thought to himself that such an ally merited a good sharpening and polishing, if nothing else to remove enough evidence to link him to a string of attempted murders.

It wasn't until Michael's target was half way across the six feet that separated the redbrick gable ends, that he realised there was danger lurking menacingly in the shadows. Activated by the terrified eyes of the man he'd once looked up to for hope and direction, Michael pounced with teeth bared. As, without fear, Michael thrusted the rusty blade into his senior's stomach, his prey buckled under the force of the ardent pain sending the knife deeper. Sustaining the cripple's heavy weight, Michael watched as his eyes expanded and his jaws sagged with the shock. Unable to support him any longer, he retracted his statement then pushed him backwards on to the wall. Watching as his tormentor slipped down the brickwork, the sight of the blood and the reminder of the subtle innuendo reverberating around inside his head inspired Michael to a new high in his brutality. He pulled his compatriot's tongue from his panting mouth and set about slicing it off with the blood-stained knife. Whilst his adjutant screamed from the depths of his throat as the blunt edge made heavy weather of the savage extraction, Michael ruthlessly grabbed his victim's jaw then smashed his head back on to the wall again, providing him with an instantaneous inhumane local anaesthetic before resuming to saw off his immoral tongue. When the final string of lacerated flesh had surrendered to the butcher's persistency, Michael stood filled with euphoria, his hands drenched with thick, tepid blood and he laughed like the schizophrenic he'd become. Placing the blue tongue back into his ex-boss's spewing mouth, he gave reason for his work-to-rule: 'You fucking lied to me all along and I can't abide liars.'

An hour after Michael had made his successful getaway, the cripple had paid the penalty of crossing him with his life. Choking on his own salty blood, he could indoctrinate and enlist the city's blind youth no more. Although no man is infallible, unfortunately neither is any individual irreplaceable, and so the puncture in the IRA's circle of corruption would soon be mended to roll over society again.

When Angela joined Paul on Friday for more physiotherapy and flattery, he knew that this would be his penultimate opportunity to change her mind.

'I'm discharging myself tomorrow, then I'm heading off to wherever my legs carry me after the final. Come with me, Angie,' he pleaded.

'You know I can't,' she replied dejectedly, standing close by him in case he collapsed as he laboriously struggled to walk around the room.

'I won't see you again after today. I'll miss you,' he said, continuing to learn to walk all over again.

'Can't we talk about something else? I know you'll be here tomorrow when I come. You're not fit enough to leave this room, never mind swan off to Dublin and beyond. Where are you gonna go anyway?'

'Anywhere where the wind blows me I guess, and I will be leaving. I must be in Dublin tomorrow night with or without you,' he emphasised. 'I have to see Tommy again, I know he'll be there waiting for me, just say you'll think about it.'

Watching him as he hobbled doggedly, defiant to master his infirmities she saw in her heart that come tomorrow he would be gone for ever, yet still her loyalties remained with her dying mother, but only in her mind.

'Write to me when you get to wherever you're going, will you?' she asked, realising that her mother would not live for ever.

'No,' he replied firmly. 'No, I don't need a penpal, I need a wife and I want you. I'm gonna need all my mental strength to make a go of it out there, so I can't allow myself to dwell on you any longer.'

Walking past him to the door, he watched her leave for the last time. Pausing as she placed her trembling hand upon the handle, she turned and looked into his frightened eyes, then said her definitive farewell. 'I'm sorry Paul, I really am.'

Paul didn't sleep a wink that night, instead he filtered all his emotions into one last missive from the heart that he hoped she'd read then change her mind.

At midnight, Angela was still beside her mother, staring lost into the shimmering glow of the electric fire when her mother stirred again and glanced at the clock doing time on the mantelpiece.

'Shouldn't you be in bed now for a 6 a.m. start?' she remarked.

'Sorry?' replied Angela, breaking from the spell of Paul's impending departure.

'Do you want to talk about it?' offered her mother, detecting her daughter's quandary was as yet unresolved.

Nodding her head gently, she began to sniff before the imminent tears rolled down her pretty face. 'It's Paul, he's leaving in the morning and he's given me an ultimatum. If I don't leave with him, I'll never see or hear from him again.'

'Then go,' her mother stressed. 'What's there to think about if you love him?'

'But I can't leave you, Mom, you need looking after.'

'No sweetie, I'll be fine, I swear, there's nothing you can do for me anyway. I'd rather you were happy, get out there and enjoy life when you have the chance. This house is death, as is this damn city, if you don't break away you'll only live to regret it.'

At 4.30 a.m., Paul, who was tired of not being able to sleep, decided to call it a night and begin his judgement day bright and early. At the same time, Angela had tossed and turned to reach her own decision on her day of reckoning.

It was 5.15 before Paul had finally managed to dress himself ready for the first showdown of his last twenty-four hours on Irish soil. Pressing the call button for assistance, a nurse arrived promptly.

'Is there something I have to sign? I'm discharging myself,' he said.

'I think I'd better call the doctor,' she replied.

Looking out into the morning while he waited, Paul saw the sun beginning to burn off the jealous clouds and he shook his head, feeling that the city below did not deserve such heavenly treatment. Turning to face the doctor, he was prepared for the criticism.

'You can't leave, Mr O'Donnell. I'm strongly advising you for your own good. You need to convalesce under our supervision, besides we still have tests to carry out. You could blackout at any given time and you'll certainly impair the healing process with regard to your lung.'

'I appreciate your professional concern,' thanked Paul, before continuing to emphasise his predicament. 'But I can't stay. I have important business to attend to that cannot be deferred.'

'This is ludicrous, Mr O'Donnell. I can't condone this.'

'Just let me sign out will ye? My signature covers your backside doesn't it? There is, however, one favour you could oblige me with that just might go a long way to improving my health. Come to think of it, she's the only one who can cure me. I want you to make sure Angela Hamilton gets this letter. She'll come to visit me and find I've gone, but she must receive this, can I count on you?'

'Aye,' sighed the doctor, shaking his head at his patient's obstinacy as he took charge of the communication.

Against medical advice, Paul left the RVH. Breathless and aching by the time he'd traversed the short distance from the relative safety of his hospital room back into hazardous, outside world, he paused for respite while his eyes darted to the annals of his sockets, as the bright sunlight attacked them with a scorching vengeance. Stopping to salvage his breath after ten steps, he psyched himself onward, demanding a greater yield after each repose. When he reached the newsagents on the corner of Clonard Street it was now seven o'clock and his thirty-sixth consecutive step without pause. Lumbering into the shop to buy a paper and relieve his ashen neck from the burning sun which was intent on working his supple skin into leather, as well as taking his mind off the pain of the last hundred odd steps to his front door, he filled up with the emotion of the supportive headlines.

THIRTY SECONDS FROM HISTORY

Belfast's very own anti-sectarian greyhound, History Maker, has the world at his four feet tonight. Today will see a mass exodus of Protestants and Catholics, as they converge upon the Southern Irish capital, Dublin, where they'll stand shoulder to shoulder in greyhound racing's indisputable Mecca, Shelbourne Park. At 9.45 p.m. and approximately 30 seconds, television cameras, which will beam their pictures all around the world, could witness unprecedented scenes of rapture to smash down the barricades of religious divide, such is the unanimous backing for History Maker . . .

As he read with pride, it was a vision that he could see before his eyes so vividly, he felt as if he could almost reach out and touch it. No more fighting, no more aching, no more suffering, a dream to die for without hesitation. Matt Williamson had been right all along, it was Paul who had a once-in-a-lifetime opportunity to bring peace, and if only for a fleeting moment then it would be not a moment too soon. Even if the great rivals could unite only for a few hours after the event, then they might get a taste for it, realise that they could live under one almighty roof and so advance to settle their differences. It was a long shot, but so was the dog they'd instilled all their faith into.

Reading on, it was Matt Williamson's concluding sentence that really epitomised the contradiction and confusion of the task in hand and wouldn't allow Paul to forgive the media for Tommy's death: 'So, for the sake of peace, God speed History Maker to victory tonight.'

God, he was the instigator in Paul's eyes, as he'd always been throughout history. Mankind fighting, murdering and exterminating each other since time began and all because of one similar belief under various divergent appellations. Looking to the skies, Paul marvelled as to what would happen if it was proven that the Supreme Being didn't actually exist, then what? Would everybody live in Utopia or not? Would they bow their heads in the shame of their misconception? He doubted it, whatever the reality, Paul was one man in billions, and he alone couldn't change the world, though now, for the first time in his existence, he actually felt that if there was the slightest chance he could, then he would, without hesitation, sacrifice his life for the sake of the human race's future advancement.

As he entered the house, Paul found his mother in her customary environment, preparing the workers' breakfasts. Today being Saturday meant light duties in that respect, since only Bernadette required nourishment to wind her up for the busiest day of her working week.

'You don't know when you're beat, do you son?' she moaned, shaking her head and tightening her face from the pain his appearance induced.

'I have to do this, Mom. This isn't a choice thing, the whole of Belfast is depending on me to follow this through to the end,' he replied.

'And what about me? I'd rather look forward to you being a nobody than back at you as a martyr. You don't even know these people, yet you're willing to jeopardise your life for them. And here I am, only your mother. I felt the pain bringing you into this world. I was the one that suffered in sharing every fall, cut and graze you sustained, worried hours when you played on the streets, sleepless nights when you were in London, wondering if you were being lured into drugs. The list is endless, but no, your allegiance is to outsiders.'

409

'I'm going to pack,' he said, fleeing from her anguish before it forced him to stay.

At nine o'clock, Angela used her entitled teabreak to discover whether Paul had, as he'd threatened, discharged himself. Discovering that he had indeed baled out, she received his letter from the nursing officer. Waiting until she had secured the privacy that his correspondence warranted, she read his final persuasion.

> Angela, I don't know how or where to begin. I've told you I love you till I'm blue in the face and I think you realise that I mean it, so that's not the issue here. I won't beg you to leave with me any more. I guess I was wrong to have ever had the audacity to make such a request in the first place, seeing as your mother obviously needs you more than I. I'm pretty sure if your mother was well, then you would have left with me today, so I suppose that'll have to be enough. It isn't enough though, but I have fond memories to take with me of the wonderful times we spent together at our lake. I love you and I always will, Paul.
>
> PS I want you to leave with me, sorry. I'll be at the Europa bus station from 2.30 p.m. onwards, my bus departs at three.'

Totally confused, Angela felt exactly how he must have done when composing the letter.

Paul packed only two changes of clothing, his passport and slim bankbook, and refrained from carrying the weight of memorabilia that might torture his mind in the days to come. This, as he'd planned it, was a clean break, a fresh start, where he'd deny any past links with Belfast if anyone ever asked. Looking around his room one last time, he left his brother snoring happily then slowly and painfully headed downstairs to say goodbye to his mother. With Bernadette gone, Paul felt confident enough to enter the kitchen with his holdall which was in effect counterbalancing his ailment to assist his walk.

'So you won't be dissuaded then?' quizzed his mother.

'Not even by one of your finest breakfasts.'

Watching him from the opposite end of the table as he ate, she ploughed her mind for a method which would persuade him to stay at home, and she found that there was only one possibility. It was her darkest secret, and although she knew it would hurt her son and herself

410

when she relived the revelation, she felt certain that the time had come. It was her last hope, and had to be worth the pain, perhaps the sacred truth had been designed to enlighten Paul at some stage in his life. For her, that day had dawned.

'Paul, I don't want you to leave, at least unaware of what's scarred this family over the last twenty-three years.'

Placing his cutlery on to the half-eaten breakfast, he pushed the plate towards the middle, saving enough room so he could digest her confession.

'I'm listening,' he replied.

Just about to reveal the clandestine family history, his mother glanced at the door as Michael came bounding into the kitchen to be met by an awkward and embarrassed silence. Seeing Paul sitting there made him so uncomfortable that his eyes never drifted to his brother's in the presence of their mother. Stealing a slice of toast, he made for the door.

'I'm popping into town, is there anything you need?' he addressed his mother.

'No, but thanks anyway, son,' she replied softly.

Hearing the front door slam, she continued the conversation.

'You were saying?' urged Paul, desperately hoping that Michael's untimely intervention had not served to delay the truth for another twenty-three years.

Standing up, she walked over to the kitchen sink keeping her back to him when she spoke. 'I'll forewarn you now, what I have to tell you is gonna hurt you, son. I vowed I'd take this to the grave with me, but I can't hold it back no more, the time is right.' Nodding her head to convince herself, she continued. 'Twenty-three years ago, me and your father shared a perfect marriage, well, as good as it could be. We were in love, had a beautiful baby son in Michael, yet your father was fervent in his beliefs. He was very outspoken in his views towards the unfair treatment of Catholics in the city. Granted, things have got better over the years, but back then we were persecuted to a certain degree. All the good jobs went to the Protestants and the best housing estates too. It was terrible, the army and RUC were empowered with the right to perform house searches at any given time and boy did they revel in the job. They'd rip up the floorboards and break down the thin plasterboard walls and the sickening thing was, you could see it in their eyes, the way they took pleasure.' Pausing for a moment, she used her apron to wipe a tear from her eye.

411

'Anyway, your father would not subscribe to that way of life, but he wasn't involved in the killing machine, no, his forte was the political aspect. He believed human rights' marches were the answer, publicity through peaceful marches and the like. Oh, he held the Orangemen in contempt all right, but not enough to resort to violent tactics.'

As she paused again for what seemed like an eternity, Paul understood that the heartache was imminent.

'It was a sticky spring day in April, as I remember it,' she declared, then exhaled deeply before resuming. 'We had snow only two days prior, anyway, I worked in town in a small book shop, I was a part-time sales assistant,' she reminisced, her eyes glazing over.

'And?' asked Paul timidly, as he attempted to work out his arithmetic.

'I left work at five and began to walk towards the bus stop, there were hundreds of people around, but no one dared stop them, a car just stopped and I was dragged in then . . . then. . .' she stuttered, massaging her eyes to choke the tears.

Affording her all the time in the world, Paul felt sure he knew what was coming next if she had the courage to continue.

'They raped me, son,' she snivelled, 'I could have kept it to myself, but they made sure your father got to find out . . . I fell pregnant and, of course our religion frowns upon and forbids abortion, and I'm glad of that or you wouldn't be here today. Suffice to say mine and your father's marriage died that day. I guess that's why he's never been able to accept you.'

'So my real father is some UVF hoodlum?' stated Paul.

'Aye,' she confirmed sadly. 'But you're my son and you're what God intended.'

Laughing, he spoke, 'Aye you're probably right, maybe that's why this half-breed must go to Dublin to unite the religions. Why haven't you left if your marriage has been defunct for all those years?'

'I still love your father. I made my bed and I'll lie in it until God decides otherwise. There's more though,' she said, turning to face him for the first time. 'When I carried you things were bad, but when I brought you home, your father's hatred turned to violence. He was desperate for revenge, so he joined the IRA to hit back at those people. His first assignment was to assassinate a senior RUC officer, Michael was about five at the time. Your father was perched on a roof with a sniper's rifle when the man collected his young son from school. When he saw the boy around Michael's age, he couldn't squeeze the trigger, that was the last time he ever confided in me, after that day, he turned to drink. The IRA expelled him, he's spent his life thinking he's a failure, yet he's been anything but. I know he's pushed Michael towards the Republican movement and I can see why he's done that. I can only pity your father, but I still love him.'

Benumbed by the overall picture of her revelations, Paul glanced at his watch to note it was fast approaching one o'clock

'I have to be making tracks, Mom, I'll keep in touch, I promise,' he said distantly, through the acute shock.

Forcing himself up, he picked up his holdall then headed towards the door, so bemused that he forgot to kiss her goodbye.

Closing the door on his unhappy childhood and his weeping mother, Paul turned to view Michael approaching; gazing at his tattered, metal-brandishing boots, he felt a recurrence of the pain from that night in late December thunder across his head and it brought with it a flashback to the masked assassin pointing the trembling pistol at him. Suddenly the blackout his consultant had forewarned him of made everything all so very clear.

'Where are you going?' asked Michael.

'Far away,' he replied softly, squinting his eyes from the storm his consciousness was blowing into his face. 'Far away.'

'Well, let me give you some brotherly advice to take with you,' offered Michael, putting his arm around Paul's shoulders. 'By all means get out of Belfast while you still can, but withdraw the dog from tonight's final, or they'll kill you next time.'

Glancing at his car, Paul now realised how it had also been his brother with his diseased mind who'd defaced his property and, all of a sudden, he felt squeamishly vulnerable. Adjusting his breath, which was now racing from the panic brought on by his realisation and the cold touch of his brother's evil hand curdling his flesh, Paul just wanted to run from his fears, but accepted that he was finding it difficult enough to walk, let alone outrun his whippet-framed relative. Battening down the hatches in his mind to ride out the storm, he scratched instinctively for an escape route, convinced that if Michael held the volition to have made an attempt on his life before, then surely his insanity held no barriers, and that not even a sunny Saturday afternoon on his own doorstep could supply enough asylum to deter him from finishing off the job. Focusing his eyes upon his car and wishing he could jump in and drive clear of his worst nightmare, an idea appeared in his

413

desperate mind and all he could do now was pray it was invaluable enough to buy him safe passage.

'Eh, eh,' he bleated like a lamb about to be put to the slaughter. 'I won't be around for your wedding and, as I can't drive with my injuries, I thought that perhaps if you're not offended then you and Bernadette would accept my car as an early wedding present.'

'Are you sure?' asked Michael, turning to look at the bright red vehicle which he had coveted from day one.

'I'm certain,' assured Paul. 'As I said, I can't drive in this state and I've no intention of ever setting foot in Belfast again. Here,' he said, forcing the keys upon Michael. 'And good luck with the wedding, you deserve each other. I really have to go, I have a train to catch.'

Considering what Michael had put his brother through, it seemed such a magnanimous gesture, yet in reality now that Paul had lost all trust in his flesh and blood, he was simply buying enough time to board his bus, unhindered. Michael accepted his proferred hand and shook it firmly farewell. Watching as Paul hobbled towards his destiny, he closed his fist around the keys and thought to himself that maybe his dream of a United Ireland was dead, but at least some promise had come of his IRA dealings, for now he was convinced that he and Bernadette would soon be hearing church bells chime in their honour.

Paul looked back over his shoulder when he reached the crossroads of Clonard Street and the Falls Road, and saw that Michael had vanished and he could only hope that justice might one day catch up with him. Inhaling the ambience of his birthplace one last time as a parting mark of respect, he turned the corner confident he'd made the correct decision. Standing at the bus stop awaiting transport, he watched the silent salt of the earth people go about their weekend business and they filled him with immense pride, for their resilience in the face adversity shone through, even when the dark clouds of life attempted to eclipse their spirits.

'Good luck tonight Paul,' rang in his ears until his bus arrived, as almost every pedestrian commended him on his bravery. Gripping on to the rail of the seat in front, he absorbed the bumps and cracks in the road that the workmen of British politics had turned their backs upon, and it brought home to him the painful injuries he was carrying as part of his luggage. Just as his bus negotiated the curve in the road and the bus stop disappeared from sight, Angela arrived there where he'd stood, missing him by only a dog race. She read his letter again, but it was still to have no bearing on her resolution from her sleepless night. No, that was foregone and she'd now have to live with the agony or ecstasy of her decision for ever.

Paul watched from the window as the Falls Road merged into the city centre, and noticed for the first time in his life that Belfast was a beautiful city which, under any normal circumstances, its citizens would have been proud to boast about, yet for both sides of the war-torn divide it was merely a stigma that brought shame to them whenever they left its boundaries.

He arrived at the Europa with just over half an hour to spare and decided to rest his aching legs. Locating a small café inside the station where he could overlook the city centre and keep a watchful eye out for the twist of fate he felt he deserved, he ordered a cup of coffee then took up a position by the window. Sipping from the stained porcelain cup, he gazed pensively and hopefully out over the busy street, desperate to catch one last glimpse of Angela, now that both his heart and mind had accepted that she wouldn't be embarking with him on the greatest journey of his life. Suddenly, his attention was distracted by a young mother in her early twenties and her two young children, the boy aged perhaps five and his sister younger by a year, who had arrived with a weight of luggage and were sitting at the adjacent table. Returning to his forlorn search, he sensed that the young boy was staring at him curiosly. Paul acknowledged him with a warm smile which frightened the boy towards his mother who was struggling to control her frisky brood. Eavesdropping upon the family as he scanned incessantly, he heard the boy whinge, 'Mommy, I want a Pepsi'.

'You'll get what your given,' she reprimanded, heading to the snack counter to place her order.

'You'll get what you're given,' aped his younger sister, taunting her elder brother over and over.

Face curling up in a half smile, the words bit deep, surging a defeatist attitude through Paul, then in the blink of an eyelid his hopes began to escalate rapidly. Wandering along the main street was his Angela. Swallowing hard, he forced his brain to draw her in his direction, when just then, the young boy's mother returned with a tray supporting two plates of chips and two blue and red paper cups emblazoned with the white trademark of Pepsi-Cola. Glancing at the boy while he kept one eye glued to Angela, Paul watched the youngster's face light up at the sight of the cup, then abruptly pale on discovering the contents were simply orange juice. He wondered to himself if it was a sign of his own impending outcome and gave full attention to Angela.

Suddenly, she began to walk in the right direction for him and Dublin. With heart pounding fit to burst at the exhilaration of her movements, he willed her home. Though when crossing at the traffic lights, to his utter dismay, she turned and headed away for her usual bus stop to the Shankill. Totally deflated and feeling as if he was on his ninety-ninth lash, he returned to the boy and was bewildered to find that his dejection had now turned to a beautiful broad smile as he set about his chips with intent purpose. Holding his head in his hands, Paul could only wonder whether he would be able to vanquish his lament with such nonchalant ease.

Chapter 15

Running For Freedom

As he sat alone on the bus journeying down to Dublin, Paul gazed moodily at the glorious countryside and it confirmed what he'd always envisioned. Slowly autumn was invading 1988 to wither the leaves upon the trees with its beautiful yet deadly aura. And with it, it brought a seasonal affinity, for Paul's relationship with Angela bore a striking resemblance in every aspect to those trees at the mercy of the changing seasons. In the winter of 87 they had been stripped to the branches, weather-beaten, twisted, naked and silently screaming for help, just as he had. Then came the spring and a sweet injection of life, a love resurrection which had sprouted shoots of green. In his case it had been the vernal Angela, budding him with hopes and aspirations. In the high of summer when their relationship had peaked on the shores of their tranquil lake, he'd stood proud and blazing, mellowed by her love like those static wonders of nature ripened by the sun. But now, as autumn dawned and she had gone, the leaves were jaded and bleached, soon they'd curl up crisp, fall from the heavens and die. Paul wasn't much looking forward to this winter because he knew that his love for her would remain evergreen.

Soaking up the fine splendour of his country from his mobile greenhouse for the last time, now that fate had forced him to leave, he reflected upon how he'd miss his origins, yet took some consolation from the knowledge that in exiling himself he wasn't the first to take this route out and he most certainly wouldn't be the last.

417

At just after its scheduled arrival time of 5.30 p.m., Paul's transport pulled into the Busarus bus station in the heart of Dublin's fair city. In no hurry to alight, having plenty of time on his hands, he allowed the stampede to run its course before forcing his sore body from the warm seat. Inching down the penurious aisle, he finally eased off the coach to be met by a lukewarm night, marred only by the sweet stench of diesel fumes.

After meandering through the busy concourse, he arrived at the sole taxi rank. He paused to establish his bearings, then glanced at his watch to note it was 5.45 p.m. and thought it strange that his appetite had yet to call for service, then again he supposed it had good reason. As he contemplated hailing a taxi that minute and heading straight for Shelbourne Park, it was the sight of an Italian restaurant across the street that dissuaded him. Even though he didn't feel like eating, he realised he had to conquer those depressions before they consumed him and made him weak.

And it was at this point that his thoughts went to London when he'd first arrived in the spring of 87. On that occasion it had probably been the excitement that had devoured his hunger, yet tonight it was more like self-pity. He did feel, however, that there was one other reason why he had to put his house in order this time before things got out of hand. In London he'd lived off a menu of take aways paid for by a lean but steady income delivered by his ability to turn his muscle into sterling. Suddenly everything hinged on Toby, for if he failed to come up with the goods tonight, Paul would be poverty-stricken from the first minute he set foot on English shores, but this time with no brawn to toil his way above the bread line. Deciding not to tempt fate, he prepared himself for the worst. He dismissed the upmarket cuisine of the Italian restaurant with its soothing pastel decor and romantic, candlelit ambience and opted to look for something to fit his pessimistic, yet realistic, budget. After locating a small, seedy, back-street café, which was living on borrowed time until it appeared on the health inspector's agenda, he sat staring at a plate of stale bread which the cities hoards of pigeons would have turned their beaks up at, and he couldn't bear the thought of how he was going to manage with his disability. Shaking his head gently when his sausage, egg and chips landed, he part-blamed his newly acquired circumstances for his failure to sell Angela a dream. How could he have expected her to elope with him, when he had no rainy-day nest egg set aside to offer them a start in life and only a fifty-fifty chance of ever salvaging his physique to enable him to find employment so he could provide for them. Totally disillusioned by his predicament, he shook off his cynicism and began force-feeding himself, convincing himself that where there's life there's hope. After all, that was the main reason why he was having to leave Irish shores come what may, reasoning that if he dared to stay around, then surely the IRA would make it third time lucky.

With all his hopes pinned on Toby, Paul decided it was time to head for his date with destiny in the theatre of dreams, Shelbourne Park. Opting for the rich man's transport of a taxi, he perked up, assuring himself that tonight had to be the turning point in his ill-omened life.

When he arrived at the track, he noted that already there was a sizeable crowd gathering. In the car-park, he noticed a fleet of blue and white Ulsterbuses which had ferried the several thousand from Belfast who'd come with the same dream as him, to witness History Maker cross the line first in the final of the 1988 Irish Greyhound Derby. Deciding to put his business behind him early, so he could concentrate on pleasure for the remainder of the evening, if there was to be any, Paul took a steady amble around to the kennelling enclosure where he could forward Toby his encouragement and McKenna his gratitude.

When Paul reached his destination, he found the trainer busy making sure that in the event of defeat there could be no excuses which would haunt him for the rest of his life. Concluding the stretching exercises, McKenna moved on to massage the grateful dog to make certain the animal was supple enough to give his all from the off.

'All right, Johnny?' asked Paul, making his appearance known.

'So you made it then?' he replied, before continuing with relevant oration. 'I'm bloody nervous, that's for sure. I've never been this close. I don't think I'm gonna enjoy tonight.'

'Me neither,' agreed Paul.

As McKenna stepped off the dog, Toby, upon seeing his owner, leapt across the few feet which distanced them then pinned Paul to the wall to display his affection.

'Aaargh,' shrieked Paul, clutching his frail ribcage to shield it from further injury.

Seeing that the owner was in trouble, McKenna rushed to his assistance then pulled the excited greyhound away before uttering his concerns.

'What's up Paul? You don't look too well, and what happened to the side of your head?'

Not wanting to instil any added anxiety into the trainer on a night when he'd no doubt spend most of his time biting his fingernails to the quick upon a toilet seat, Paul spun him a yarn.

'I had an accident at work. I slipped on deck and ironically smashed my head off a safety rail, as well as breaking a few ribs during the fall, pure accident. It was bad at the time, but I'm well on the mend now.'

Having been around a lot longer than Paul, Johnny could smell a lie a mile off and he wondered whether his hope's owner might be mixed up in some kind of debt.

'Do you owe anybody money?' he asked, raising his eyebrows in a fatherly fashion to demand the non-fictional version of Paul's injuries.

'No, why do you ask that?' said Paul.

'Well, the holdall, if I'm not mistaken, appears to suggest that you may be leaving your troubles behind you. Am I right?'

'I don't owe anybody money, but you're right about one thing, I am leaving Ireland after the race. The truth is, my injuries have made me a liability to my employer, so he had to let me go. With no job and no prospects of finding work in Belfast, I've no alternative but to try my hand elsewhere, wherever life takes me. It's the only way I know, besides, I've too many bad love memories back home,' explained Paul, staring solemnly into thin air, attempting to convince McKenna that he was being sincere, when in fact he had only resumed his contortion of the truth.

Taking his story at face value, McKenna, who had accrued immense respect for Paul over the last few months, threw him an umbilical chord.

'Why don't you come and live with us at the stud?' he offered. 'I could give you a job as a kennel hand, you'd be invaluable with your expertise. I wouldn't be able to pay much, but it would be free board and lodge, what do you think?'

If it hadn't been for the fear of the IRA knocking on the door of the elderly couple's sanctuary, Paul might have jumped at the tender.

'No, I can't, but I appreciate the offer. My mind's made up. Anyway, I just want to take this opportunity to thank you and shake your hand for all the effort. If Toby loses, I'll just slip off into the night, besides there's a ferry sailing at 11 p.m. which has my name on the passenger list,' revealed Paul.

Clasping each other's hands firmly, McKenna felt a tear simmering in the corner of his eye.

'You will keep in touch, won't you? This dog here's gonna be a proud father one day. Wouldn't you like one of the pups?'

'Perhaps,' replied Paul, half-heartedly, 'but the way I feel at the moment over Tommy's death, I don't think I'll be pursuing this pastime any longer. Do you mind if I take him for a short walk to say my final farewell?'

'No problem,' replied the trainer.

Walking Toby out into the magnificent arena which was now floodlit to combat the fading light, Paul pointed across the track to the main grandstand now crammed to such extent that it surely must have been in contravention of safety regulations.

'Look, Tobes, they've all come to see you one last time. That's right, no more racing after tonight. Win this race and you can retire. I probably won't see you again after this chat, so I just wanted you to know that I'll always brag about you wherever I go because win or lose you're the best. Anyway, good luck and remember Tommy's here somewhere tonight.'

About turning, Paul half smiled at McKenna who had been stood listening enthralled by his every word.

'I carried out your request concerning the jacuzzi and Falomino.'

'Thanks,' returned Paul, handing him the lead. 'Well, he's all yours now.'

Watching Paul as he hitched away, the trainer sighed in the knowledge that the dog's owner had deeper injuries than were apparent.

It took Paul three races to gain entrance to the grandstand where the Northern Irish coalition had taken up residence. Easing his way through the mayhem and congestion, he'd soon realised the only way to travel through this beehive of madness was when there was a race in progress, for then and only then would the crowd stay still for long enough to authorise unrestrained passage. Scanning through the thick, blue smoke haze and the humid heat of the grandstand bar, a tiny part of him still upheld the belief that Angela would manifest in his time of need, yet that part of him was not his mind. Seeing no sign of her, he began to feel dizzy from the lack of oxygen available in addition to the boisterous atmosphere which rang around his head to stun his senses. Paul swayed as he began to lose the feeling in his legs; then forced his way through the traffic jam making for the terraces before he collapsed and missed the highlight on the race card. Reaching the air supply in the nick of time, he slumped over the wooden handrail, gasping at the cool invisible force and his temper launched to soar, as he began to comprehend that he was going to find it more difficult than he'd initially anticipated to make it alone in the big, bad, outside world.

'Are you all right?' asked a familiar voice, who was once again in the wrong place at the wrong time.

Raising his head, Paul issued his scorching response. 'Have you got fuck all better to do than chasing around after me, screwing up my life. What do you want? Me dead?' he roared.

Grabbing Matt Williamson by the lapels of his suit jacket, Paul's mind fused for a split second with the overload he'd subjected it to. Seizing Paul's hands to prevent his fall, the reporter steadied him from tripping out before showing his concern.

'Are you okay? Shall I escort you to the medical room?'

'No I'll be fine, I've got to be. What do you want from me anyway?' asked Paul, curling his lip and looking beyond the pale journalist.

'I just wanted one last interview before the race,' he revealed tamely.

Laughing out loud and shaking his head in unison, Paul composed himself before turning on the media again.

'You people just don't know when to call it a day, do you? Can't you see you've ruined my life and killed my best friend? Christ, look at me, I won't find employment again, who'd want to hire a useless piece of shit like me? As you've just witnessed, I have a tendency to blackout under stress and I've a collapsed lung into the bargain, and all because of your fucking career. Well, was it worth it? And on the only occasion I asked you for anything, you told me ever so politely to fuck off.'

'You know I couldn't stir up a hornet's nest without evidence,' defended Matt.

'No, my brother was right all along. All you Protestants are alike, well at least in this part of the world, covering each others backs at all costs. Look at you in your fancy designer suit writing shit for a living. Huh,' he laughed, as a whimsical notion crossed his mind. 'I guess that's what I'll have to do, write shit behind a desk, now that I can't do anything fucking strenuous. Did your mommy and daddy put you through university? You see where I come from, the only education we get is off the street and from our own eyes. We're not equal, Matt. I go for an interview, then they find out I'm from the Falls and it's hey, I hope you were deloused before you came in here.'

422

Nodding his head in agreement as he absorbed the criticism, Matt then interrupted. 'Okay point taken, you're right, I'm sorry. I'll leave you in peace. I still can't do anything about clearing your friend's name though. If I only had a written, or even verbal, statement from the rape victim, whoever she may be, then I swear to you, I'd use everything in my power to reinstate Gerry O'Brien's honour and engender an official inquiry to investigate whether there was an RUC cover-up. But until you give me a lead, well, I'm snookered.'

'Just leave me alone,' concluded Paul, beginning to edge his way towards his customary viewpoint at the finishing line.

Reaching the overgrown lollipop of the yardstick just as the lids sprung open for the 9.30 heat, Paul waited until the event had passed and the punters were filtering back to the bars and bookmakers before gaining himself a vantage slot on the rails. Looking to the heavens which had now faded into pitch darkness, he communicated with the Lord. 'I didn't mean what I said back there about the Protestants, hell, I'm in love with one. I accept that this world of yours doesn't owe me a living, but that's not what I'm asking for, just a fair crack of the whip, no more, no less. I've made mistakes like any other and I'll continue to do so, but please let me make them of my own accord, because lately you've been allowing others to do it for me. I don't know what I've done wrong to upset you, but surely I've paid for it twofold. I know you won't let me have Angela and I've come to terms with that, but please let Toby win the Derby, for Tommy; he didn't deserve to die. As you'll be aware, I had the ownership papers transferred solely into his name, so if the dog is empowered to win then his name will be remembered eternally and that's all I ask of you.'

The crackling announcement from the range of loudspeakers around the stadium startled Paul back to actuality and sent a shiver of anticipation running down his spine. 'The greyhounds are now coming on parade for the final of the 1988 Respond Irish Greyhound Derby. There are approximately ten minutes left to finalise your investments for the nine forty-five race.'

The draw made earlier that week in Dublin's premier hotel, Jury's Towers, had been kind to History Maker on this ultimate episode. Clad in his preferred red, the white and fawn greyhound was in effect carrying the colours of the Northern Irish ensign, but in reality, much, much more than that. Adding to his handicap was a tontine basket

423

into which Paul had unceremoniously placed all his eggs, as well as the chance to unite a divided nation, even if only for one night. However, aiding his cause, main rival Randy had been drawn from the difficult middle slot of trap three.

Turning his head to watch the parade as it approached, Paul's eyes widened and his nose tingled as a flood of emotion surged through his entire body, for there heading the march was McKenna adorned with Tommy's old haggard parka. With tears of homage rolling down his face when the trainer walked past and winked, Paul simply smiled and nodded in acknowledgement and appreciation of the befitting gesture.

Now only a minute or so from the off, Paul, who had dreamt of this moment since childhood, couldn't believe that he felt no nervous tension whatsoever, but only the stress of being squashed on to the safety rail, now that the hordes of spectators had deluged from the grandstand, amassing on to the barrier and jostling to gain the best view of the most important thirty seconds on the greyhound racing calendar. Struggling to hold his position, he placed his holdall between his legs before it was swept away in the tidal wave of excitement brewing in the gurgling cauldron. He clamped his hands around the rail to maintain his stance now that the final countdown had begun and glanced left to note that the starting traps were now steadily loading up. All that remained to be seen now was would it be cometh the hour cometh the History Maker?

As the hare began its careering journey, Paul cringed at the immense crescendo of volume being generated by the electric crowd, as they voiced their last-gasp yells of encouragement for their favourites. 'Come on History Maker' and 'come on Randy' was all he could hear. Straightening his head to the finishing post, Paul said his own little prayer in his mind. 'Do your best Tobes, and come home safe and sound, that's all.'

As the traps flashed open, the crowd erupted automatically to turn Paul's head in search of the dog that had hit the sand running. Exploding from the boxes with a fulgural exit, it had been History Maker who'd saved his best opening turn of foot for last. Flashing past his owner at the win-line on the run up to the first arc, Toby had already procured a two-length advantage over arch-rival, Randy. Holding his breath as the first two bends loomed on History Maker's horizon, Paul lost sight of the race thanks to a thousand screaming punters leaning over the rail.

Suddenly in the ambiguity of uncertainty, he had visions of his charge at Dunmore, when his mental injury had inhibited him from negotiating the turns, but it wasn't to be, for that was past form. He exhaled his deep relief when Toby came back into view and began to hurtle down the back straight four clear of the nearest challenger, trap three. His hands jumped from the handrail, as if it were a live circuit, to form two fists with which to fight off the arrival of the nerves he'd always anticipated. Surely now, with only fifteen seconds to travel, Toby was going to live up to his pseudonym . . . but Randy had other ideas. Watching in stark disbelief along with the other ten thousand spectators, Paul saw Randy pick up the pace and begin to devour menacingly away at what at one stage, had looked like an unassailable lead. Snapping at Toby's tired heels, all Randy needed was a clear run on the inside at the third bend and then the rest would be history.

Paul's arms wilted limply to his sides; devastated and distraught, he looked to the skies as a momentary subdued silence engulfed the anxious stadium and he shook his head at God, letting him know that this impending twist of fate was only what he'd come to expect from the almighty.

It was another deafening eruption from the impassioned crowd that shifted Paul's eyes back to the duel at the third turn. For Toby, having used all his stamina and determination, had just, by no more than a neck, held his ground to thwart Randy's gallant challenge, forcing the trap three runner to check. Setting sail again, Toby forged a length and a half clear as he swung off the fourth and final bend. As the red jacket of History Maker straightened up for the energy-sapping run-in, where many a past Derby had been won and lost, Paul himself began to use all his reserve to shout his write-off home and on to the front page of the newspaper and last of the history book.

'Come on Tobes,' he gasped, feeling his head spin from the lack of oxygen. 'Come on Toby, please, just hang on in there, you beauty, come on, come on, come on.'

Flashing past the post to tumultuous applause and alleviation, History Maker had won the 1988 Irish Greyhound Derby. Paul raised his head once more to the dark night sky, as he broke into delirious laughter.

'Thank you,' he acknowledged.

Again, it was the crowd's reaction to the latest drama which prompted his vision to return to the track, as over ten thousand sharp intakes of breath voiced that the lightning bolt he'd divined from above had

425

struck. Struggling to see what had happened, Paul watched as the blue parka raced from the far straight pickup point towards the bend.

Moving his sights quickly to where the hare had terminated its journey, he counted that only five panting greyhounds had pulled into the station, all except the red-jacketed racer. He turned his head back in the direction of the bend below the luminous scoreboard, and now saw McKenna staggering around the running track towards the kennelling enclosure, cradling Toby in his arms.

'What happened?' demanded Paul of anybody who was willing to hear his plea.

'It appeared as if he fell down a pothole or something,' came a voice, 'he was travelling well then he just seemed to jerk and keel over.'

Picking up his holdall, Paul began to wrestle his way through the crowd to be by Toby's side. He escaped the pileup of patrons still hugging the rails whilst they held their own insignificant public inquiries, and hobbled towards the kennels as fast as his punctured lung would allow. In not knowing exactly what had happened to his luminary canine, Paul began to wonder whether an IRA sniper had taken the ultimate revenge.

High up in the grandstand, the Belfast contingent were unaware of their idol's injury, for as soon as History Maker had landed their gambles, both Protestant and Catholic supporters had hugged each other in the kind of jubilation that only success can bring. Their urgency to maraud the bars had been so impetuous that they hadn't even waited for the official result to be announced, instead the festivities had begun with such elation that they'd drowned out the trivial fact of their champion's winning statistics. History Maker, the Northern Irish Greyhound, had won by three-quarters of a length in a time of 30.26 seconds, which although almost four lengths slower than his record-breaking semi-final run, had been more than adequate and was, in fact, the fastest winning Derby time to date, since the competition trip had been hiked from 525 to 550 yards, four years previously.

For a long time to come, many would argue in light of the win-time, that if Randy had not been forced to check at the penultimate bend, then he would surely have taken the spoils, but that was now irrelevant, for tonight belonged to History Maker and the result would stand for ever. Both owner and trainer had been the first to realise they'd need a slice of luck and that was how it had inevitably turned out. And so the riotous celebrations roared on, comparable to how it must have felt for the Allies on D-Day. Perhaps when the final balloon of their party had

426

popped in the late hours of Sunday morning, they'd return to their respective localities then it would be back to the business of sectarianism as usual, but tonight amnesty in a foreign land would reign supreme. The only question left to ask, as Matt Williamson would do in his front page story was, 'If they can embrace each other under the same roof once, when all they require is a common factor to bond their hopes, then why can't they work together to do it all the time? If the dream of peace alone cannot meet the criteria of the aforementioned, then what on God's earth can?'

Arriving inside the kennelling enclosure awash with perspiration, Paul could not see Toby for the gathering of officials who surrounded the wounded animal. As they parted to allow the owner a view, Paul moved in closer to see that Toby was contentedly lapping away at a victory bowl of milk. Turning to Mckenna he spoke. 'What happened?'

'It would appear that he's broken his wrist around that last bend on the way to the pickup. He won't race again that's for sure, but he wasn't going to anyway. It'll heal and he can enjoy his retirement at stud,' revealed McKenna.

'Thank God,' Paul whispered under his breath, straining himself to kneel down before his saviour. 'Do you mind if I have a few minutes alone with him?'

'No, but you'll have to make it quick, he has a legion of impatient fans out there, demanding to witness the crowning of their champion,' said McKenna, reminding him of his statutory duties as an owner.

Paul just smiled in agreement as the trainer began to usher away the inquisitive assembly.

'Well, Tobes, what can I say? You were simply amazing. Tommy would have been so proud of you, as I am,' he commended, before sighing as his mind journeyed to the Shankill, 'and Angela. No doubt she'll read it in tomorrow's papers. Anyway, it's the life of Riley for you now, no more chasing false dreams like me, you're home and hosed in that respect. How's that woman of yours anyway? I'll tell you what, if you can limp around the track one more time with me for your presentation then I'll let you get back home to her. Do you think we could support each other over to the winning line?'

Toby was a true professional and ambassador for his sport and knew what was required. He began to force himself up on to three legs, while Paul had that strange feeling pass through him of eyes burning into his neck, similar to the sensation he'd experienced at the funeral.

427

'Okay we're ready, Johnny,' he said.

Hearing no reply, his heart began to skip a beat and the butterflies began to swarm in his stomach. Taking a deep breath, he raised the question. 'Angela, is that you?'

'Don't ask me what you know is true,' came the soft, sincere reply, which almost knocked him senseless.

Still kneeling with a million fireworks detonating inside his head, he swivelled against the pain to view the apparition he'd dreamt of night after night, but on this night she was no illusion as she stood before him, a billion times more stunning than any memory. At her side he observed a child-sized suitcase. 'So what made you change your mind? You have changed your mind, haven't you?'

'No, I haven't, if I'd changed my mind then I wouldn't be standing here now,' she unveiled with a deep, warm smile which melted his heart.

'But I saw you at the bus station this afternoon and you headed home.'

'Aye, to pack and say goodbye,' she replied.

'So you mean it then, you really do want to be with me?' he said, seeking to hear her confirmation.

'Of course I do.'

Racing over to him she joined him buckled on the floor, where they hugged, kissed and cried, releasing their pent-up love to pour over one another. It was Johnny McKenna's presence that reminded him there still remained a ferry to be caught, if they were to fulfil their dream of running for freedom.

Maybe I don't understand the way things are with you
And I don't know if I could even try
I'd like to help but I'm not sure how or even why
When all the love in the world might not pull you through
Living in a world of hate and confusion
Could it be that love is the solution
I'm here for you and that's a fact
So drop your guard let's make a pact
Let it rest it's for the best
Let the children rule the land
For they can change us take us by the hand
So run with me across the land and sea
We can find a place where we can be what we want to be . . . Free
Running for freedom

428

Nobody asks for anything everybody's looking for something
Some will win and some will lose
A few will stand and fight but most will choose
One day the pain must end
And the wounds of yesterday will someday mend
I've sung my peace that's all I can give
One in a million who wants to live
In a world without fear or segregation
On a beautiful planet where we're all one nation
A crazy dream that I'll probably never see
If it can be for only two then I hope it's for you and me

'Paul, it's five past ten and the crowd are growing restless for an appearance,' reminded McKenna.

'Shall we?' invited Angela.

'Aye,' he smiled, 'but you'll have to help me up. It still hurts when I exert myself.'

'Are you trying to tell me we'll have to put the wedding off?' she inquired, with a tantalising expression.

'What, you want to marry me?'

'Well, I haven't given up everything for nothing,' she beamed.

Helping him up, he denied the pain and hugged her tight, showing that he wasn't ever going to let her go again. All together they walked out into the nippy Dublin Night with a million stars shining over them in the dark sky, perhaps, one of which was Tommy. Smiling into each other's eyes at their success, as they neared the winner's podium by the winning post, where the photographers had amassed to capture the presentation of the resplendent trophy, something flashed into Paul's mind. It was something that he realised might mar their newfound happiness, yet nevertheless, it was something he knew he had to do. Stopping her, he turned and gazed into her eyes.

'Angela, I love you,' he said then paused. 'I'll never mention this again for as long as we're together, I swear, but there's something I need you to do for me.'

'Anything,' she agreed.

'I want you to make a verbal statement to our reporter friend, telling him that you were the victim and that Tommy was innocent. I'm asking you to clear his name.'

429

Turning her stare to Toby who was standing obediently on three good legs, she gently nodded her head. 'Okay,' she whispered softly, 'for Tommy.'

Paul received the trophy to a deafening standing ovation while Angela accepted their starter in life, a cheque for £30,000, then Paul quickly handed the antique silverware to McKenna before shaking his hand as the photographers clicked to their hearts' content.

'I have to be going now,' revealed Paul. 'I just want to thank you for everything. Take good care of Toby, as I know you will, and I'll write as soon as I'm on my feet, oh and yes, I would like one of his first litter.'

Hugging him, McKenna whispered into his ear. 'Good luck son, you'll get your pup all right, that's a promise. I just hope everything works out for you.'

'Oh, it has Johnny, you better believe, it has,' he replied, as he looked into Angela's emerald eyes.

Turning to face the cameras one last time, Paul spotted Matt Williamson applauding with verve, and their eyes met. Glancing his head to the side of the track, he let the reporter know that he wanted to talk. Leaving the running track after patting Toby goodbye for ever, the happy couple were met by a rousing reception, congratulating them with a confetti shower of torn race cards and an inundation of heavy pats on the back, which Paul's adrenaline would not allow him to feel the pain of. Stopping in front of Matt Willamson, Paul glanced at his watch - the time was getting on.

'Angela has something to tell you, but it'll have to be quick, it's up to you how you act upon this information. I just hope that you do what's right, because you know how strongly I feel about the situation,' stressed Paul, before turning to Angela and leaving her with a gentle kiss. 'I have some catching up to do with a certain bookmaker, but I'll be right back, then we'll have to make tracks.'

While Angela kept her vow to her future husband, he wandered off, shaking people's hands as he went.

Paul returned to his beloved in ten minutes. Putting his arm around her, he wiped her tears away and looked at Matt Williamson's face, etched with both remorse and sorrow.

'I'm really sorry,' whispered Matt.

Giving him no reply, Paul simply nodded his head in recognition of his deep regret, before turning again to address his intended. 'Come on, we have to be on a ship in less than half an hour.'

'Wait,' intervened the journalist, returning to his venal ways in the hope of one last scoop. 'Do you have any comments about tonight's events that I can print?'

'I'm sure the owner would be glad to give you a statement, if you can find him,' replied Paul.

'But you are the owner,' replied Williamson, with a puzzled look scribbled all over his face.

'No, you'll find the real owner's identity on the race card,' said Paul, with a wide grin.

Lowering his head to study his programme, Matt located the name of History Maker then shifted his sights directly above to learn, 'Owner Mr G O'Brien (Belfast)'. Raising his head with a smile, he saw that Paul and Angela had slipped through the crowd into the night.

Hailing a taxi outside the stadium, Paul asked the driver whether or not he could reach the port of Dun Laoghaire on the outskirts of Dublin in time for the eleven o'clock sailing. As he put his arm around Angela, he took one last look back at Shelbourne Park, which had after all turned out to be his theatre of dreams and he reminisced back to the first time the four of them had ventured south, and how they'd marvelled at the magnificent stadium resting at the foot of the Wicklow Mountains. Watching with a tinge of sadness as it disappeared from view, he laughed to himself then moved Angela's weary head to rest on his chest.

'Never leave me again,' he said softly.

Gazing up into his sparkling eyes, she replied from her heart. 'Not ever, I swear.'

At 10.55 p.m., just as the doors were beginning to close for sailing, two individuals boarded the ferry with only a holdall, small suitcase and an infinite supply of love to shelter them through any storm that life could throw at them. They headed on deck to bid their sad shores farewell, and stood for a minute's silence as the huge craft pulled away from the mysterious island where they no longer belonged. Turning to each other as the last twinkling light was snuffed out by the darkness, they shared a long embrace before the freezing cold wind forced them apart.

'Will you let me buy you that drink now?' he inquired, reminding her of how she'd turned down his offer on their first, chance encounter.

'Aye,' she smiled.

431

Returning from the bar, he joined her with a bottle of champagne and two glasses. Filling them, he snuggled up to her and called the toast. 'To Tommy and Toby, and us.'

'Can we really afford to be splashing out on champagne like this?' she asked anxiously, now that the reality of their impending struggle to survive had begun to sink in.

'We'll get by,' he assured her. 'Remember, we still have the thirty thousand from Toby's supreme efforts, God bless him.'

'Well, I have seven hundred pounds in my building society and my leaving pay, which brings it up to almost a thousand,' she pitched in.

'Well, there you go then, no worries. Thirty-one grand,' said Paul

'I suppose that much money will give me some breathing space to find a job, speaking of which. Where are we going anyway?' she asked, intrigued.

'I haven't really thought about it,' he admitted. 'I guess we'll just settle where the wind blows us, but first, Scotland. I think we can get married in the morning, that's if you still want to?'

'You mean to tell me, you haven't planned this out,' she said, with an incredulous expression.

Shrugging his shoulders and nodding his head, he took the criticism.

'Oh, you're just incredible,' she moaned sarcastically.

'So will you marry me then, if I'm that good,' he proposed, simmering her rising temper with his quick wit.

'Aye, you know I will,' she sighed, 'but I can't help worry about where we might end up. I thought that you'd have had at least a vague idea. We will make it, won't we?'

Winking at her, again he reminded her of her past treatment towards him. 'Aw, you worry over everything and nothing at the same time. We'll be fine.'

'This is no laughing matter, I wish I had your certainty,' she sulked.

'Oh come on now Angie, can't you leave the nagging out until we're married and you have the licence to do so,' he continued to tease. 'No seriously, joking aside. Tommy, God bless him, well, it was his idea that we buy a greyhound. Anyway, to cut a long story short, I took out a bank loan for two thousand pounds. My car only cost a thousand, so that left the remainder to buy a dog. Well, as you know, Toby was free to a good home.'

'So?' she urged him to continue.

432

'So, I only put the other thousand pounds on Toby to win the Derby,' he paused again, 'at one hundred and fifty to one.'

Speechless as her jaw sagged in disbelief, preparing itself for the drink that she sorely needed to brace the shock, she automatically picked up her glass and sank the whole measure in one long gulp, before beginning to pour them another.

'So,' he said coolly, handing her a slip of paper, 'we're pretty rich.'

Holding the folded cheque in her trembling hands, she opened it and nearly fainted, before her speech stammered it's return.

'Oh my good God, one hundred . . . and . . . fifty . . . one . . . thousand pounds. Oh my God, I think I need a drink.'

Half way across the Irish Sea, when the alcohol had tranquillised Angela to sleep and she lay peacefully with her head cushioned upon his lap, Paul grinned at his achievement as he ran his fingers through her long, silky black hair. Suddenly, his reflections turned to his mother and he prayed to God that somehow her heartache would be alleviated as his had now been; then his thoughts turned to Michael and Bernadette and he hoped that his departure would reunite them and that somehow they could find happiness. At that moment in time, Paul had found it in his heart to forgive his malicious brother, but then again, feeling as high as he did now, he'd have pardoned his father if he'd appeared to give them his blessing.

After a cold two-hour wait in the train station at Holyhead in North Wales, where they'd insulated each other between a few hot coffees and a blanket of conversation, they were on their way again, this time their destination was Gretna Green in the Scottish Borders. Switching from train to bus, they journeyed the last nine miles from Carlisle to the banks of the Solway Firth, where it was their intention to take the plunge. Reaching the Old Blacksmiths Shop at just after 3 p.m., to their utter dismay, they discovered that they'd arrived forty-eight years too late and, because same-day, over the anvil marriages had been outlawed in these parts since 1940, they'd have to wait another twenty one days to say their vows. Now that things had started to turn in his favour, Paul looked to the bright side.

'Never mind,' he consoled her, 'everything we've done so far has been the wrong way round, so why break our tradition? We may as well have our honeymoon first.'

433

Smiling, impressed by his determination to rise above the setbacks, she agreed, besides, after all, they did have a lot of lost time to make up for.

Taking up residence in the quaintly serene village of Gretna Green, they booked into the small but friendly Hazeldene Hotel, which was just a hundred yards from their final objective, the Old Blacksmith's Shop. And that guesthouse would be their first home together, whilst they crossed off the days on the calendar until they could become man and wife.

As they were tired from their marathon journey over the British Isles, they decided an early night was high on the agenda, after a meal and a few quiet drinks. As he lay alone in bed while Angela was in the bathroom preparing herself to join him, Paul yawned, then began to massage his temples to relieve the exhaustion of the last two days. Tensions eased, he glanced at his watch to note it was just shy of ten o'clock. Feeling that if Angela took any longer, he'd nod off to sleep before she came to bed, he picked up the remote control and flicked on the television set to catch the news headlines. As he watched subdued with a divided mind, half on the television and the other on Angela, the newsreader's words seemed to go unheard.

'Tonight, Belfast is yet again in mourning after the latest tragedy to rock the city. Earlier this evening, a young Catholic couple, who were finalising their wedding plans, became the latest victims of sectarianism, when a car bomb detonated as they sat in their vehicle.'

Shaking his head, Paul could only thank his good fortune that he and Angela had managed to escape that world of constant threat and trepidation. He continued to watch the screen, his eyes slowly lowering to the wound in his side, after he'd watched as the on-location television camera had zoomed in on the carnage, for there he'd seen a numberplate amongst the strewn debris. It had read T414 LBA.

434

Epilogue

On the golden autumn afternoon of 10 October 1988 a young couple of newly weds returned the gesture to witness the traditional Gretna Green, over the anvil marriage of Paul O'Donnell to Angela Hamilton. On this occasion it was no improvisation of lost betting slips, but real confetti that fell from the heavens upon them.

Good Friday 1998.
Gazing into each other's eyes as the historic news broke that a peace agreement had been signed which would sanction the inauguration of a unified attempt to bring down the wall of sectarianism, they both simultaneously thought of their country. And they wondered if, at long last, somebody could implement a full stop to the never-ending sentence of tribal contempt, which had been punctuated over the years by only brief stoppages to allow the dead to be laid to rest.

After their wedding, Paul and Angela O'Donnell had followed their noses, so to speak, settling happily in the Klondike of northeast England, which they'd chosen mainly because of the area's abundance of mining villages. For it seemed that wherever there was coal to be found, then accompanying the fossil fuel there was usually always a greyhound track within striking distance. In the January of 1989, Angela found that she was expecting their first child. Unfortunately two weeks after her announcement, her long-suffering mother passed away. Elizabeth O'Donnell entered the world on 2 September and was followed in the winter of 1990 by Thomas O'Donnell. Neither children were christened into any religion, as their parents saw fit. When the children began school, Angela decided she wanted to return to what God had intended, caring for the sick and her understanding husband held no objection. She currently works as a part-time care assistant at an old people's home.

435

Paul, as he'd been advised, was forced to change his career and as fate would have it, he took a desk job to become a writer as he'd threatened. He now writes a twice weekly greyhound column for the local paper.

Matt Williamson kept to his word and began a probe into the RUC's cover-up of Tommy's death, demanding justice for the iniquitous murder. Soon after, his obstinate refusal to drop the story resulted in making him a target of his own creed; yet two attempts on his life and a bullet in the thigh only incited him to follow his obsession to the limit. Making it his crusade, his perseverance paid off in the summer of 1991 when one William Hamilton was convicted for the manslaughter of Gerry O'Brien and subsequently sentenced to five years in jail.

Although Matt's personal efforts did not chastise the RUC's prerogatives on the whole, it did serve to corroborate that they were not above the law and made them wary of their notoriously harsh oppression towards the Catholic persuasion. When Angela's father was released early, for good behaviour, in 1995 there were no pieces left in his life to pick up, only a meagre pension and the glass at the end of the bar. To this day, he remains unaware of his two beautiful grandchildren, a lonely drunkard in the damp darkness of 22 Riga Street, with only memories for company and the clock on the mantelpiece which will never turn back for him.

That same year, Paul's father, who had never really come to terms with the loss of his son and future daughter-in-law, died from a massive heart attack. As the priest read him his last rites, his wife forgave him for the destruction of her family as her faith compelled her to. In the spring of 1996 her suffering was over when, leaving God's sick joke behind, she moved to the north-east of England to be by her son and his new family. She insists on babysitting at every available opportunity which is often, especially as Angela and Paul run their beloved greyhounds at least two nights a week. Although they have their fair share of winners, as of yet, they have failed to discover a greyhound with calibre enough to enter the Derby. To this day, neither Paul nor Angela have ever returned to Ireland and they're not sure they ever will. However, every March 17th they religiously raise a glass to the land that made them refugees. One day soon they will tell their children about their Run For Freedom.